About the Author

Kevin J. Anderson has over 20 million books in print in 29 languages worldwide. He is the author of the X-FILES novels GROUND ZERO (No.1 bestseller in THE TIMES, and voted Best SF Novel of the Year by SFX magazine), RUINS, and ANTIBODIES, as well as the JEDI ACADEMY trilogy of STAR WARS novels – the three best-selling SF novels of 1994. He is also continuing Frank Herbert's monumental DUNE series with Frank's son, Brian Herbert; the US deal for this was the largest contract in SF publishing history. He has won, or been nominated for, the Nebula Award, Bram Stoker Award, Reader's Choice Award from the Science Fiction Book Club, and many others.

Kevin Anderson lives in Colorado.
www.wordfire.com

By the same author in the *Seven Suns* saga

METAL SWARM

METAL SWARM

The Saga of Seven Suns

BOOK SIX

KEVIN J. ANDERSON

SIMON & SCHUSTER

LONDON • NEW YORK • SYDNEY • TORONTO

First published in Great Britain by Simon & Schuster UK Ltd, 2007
A CBS COMPANY

1 3 5 7 9 10 8 6 4 2

Simon & Schuster UK Ltd
Africa House
64–78 Kingsway
London WC2B 6AH

www.simonsays.co.uk

Simon & Schuster Australia
Sydney

A CIP catalogue record for this book is
available from the British Library

ISBN-13: 978-0-7432-7543-9
ISBN-10: 0-7432-7543-8

Typeset by Rowland Phototypesetting Ltd
Bury St Edmunds, Suffolk
Printed and bound in Great Britain by CPI, Bath

ACKNOWLEDGEMENTS

After six books in the *Saga*, I come to rely more and more on the advice and expertise of my colleagues. As always, my special thanks go to my readers and editors, Rebecca Moesta, Jaime Levine, Louis Moesta, Diane Jones, Catherine Sidor, Libby Vernon, and Kate Lyall-Grant; my agents John Silbersack, Robert Gottlieb, and Claire Roberts at Trident Media Group; and my cover artists Stephen Youll and Chris Moore.

To TIM JONES

Who has taken me on countless real-life
adventures to keep my imagination stoked for
creating fictional ones.

METAL SWARM

THE STORY SO FAR

Eight years of war against the alien hydrogues destroyed planets and suns and wiped out entire populations, both on human-settled worlds and on splinter colonies from the Ildiran Empire.

Instead of uniting the factions of humanity against a common enemy, however, the stresses of war created internal struggles. Hopelessly outmatched against the hydrogues, the Terran Hanseatic League (Hansa) turned against an enemy they knew they could defeat, the scattered Roamer clans, declaring them outlaws for refusing to supply ekti, the stardrive fuel. The Roamers had good reason to break off commerce with Earth after discovering that the Earth Defence Forces (EDF) had destroyed a Roamer cargo ship flown by Raven Kamarov. Nevertheless, the EDF hunted down and destroyed Roamer settlements, even the centre of government itself, Rendezvous. The EDF detained many prisoners of war from this conflict at the colony on Llaro, a planet abandoned by the long-vanished race of the Klikiss.

While the scattered clans tried to forge a new government,

Roamers found a group of black Klikiss robots frozen on Jonah 12, where Cesca Peroni, the Speaker for the clans, had gone into hiding. Many enclaves of these robots had been awakened around the Spiral Arm, and the machines went on a rampage, destroying the Jonah 12 facility. Cesca was rescued by the young pilot Nikko Chan Tylar, but the robots shot their ship down, and Cesca was critically wounded in the crash.

The Klikiss robots, led by Sirix, had been mysterious fixtures for years, claiming not to remember their origin. All the while, they plotted to eradicate humanity, just as they claimed to have exterminated the original Klikiss race. After turning against archaeologists Margaret and Louis Colicos in the ruins on Rheindic Co, the robots killed Louis, but Margaret escaped, vanishing through a reactivated Klikiss transportal. Sirix also kidnapped the Friendly compy DD and tried to convert him to the robots' cause. Explaining that humans were evil for enslaving their compies, Sirix 'freed' DD from his programming restrictions. Instead of being grateful, DD used his newfound freedom to escape. He vanished through another Klikiss transportal, going in search of lost Margaret. Sirix and his robots, meanwhile, continued their sneak attacks on human colonies, including an old Klikiss world called Corribus.

The only survivors on Corribus were the girl Orli Covitz and the hermit Hud Steinman, rescued by the trader Branson 'BeBob' Roberts and eventually delivered to a new home on Llaro. After bringing them back, however, BeBob was arrested by EDF commander General Lanyan, on old charges of desertion. Despite the best efforts of his ex-wife Rlinda Kett, BeBob was sentenced to be executed. Rlinda and former Hansa spy Davlin Lotze saved him. During the escape, BeBob's ship was destroyed, and Davlin faked his own death so that he could quietly retire. Rlinda and BeBob fled in her ship only to be captured by the Tamblyn brothers, Roamer water miners on the ice moon of Plumas.

Jess Tamblyn had left Plumas to continue spreading and re-awakening the wentals, watery elemental beings that had saved his life by charging his body with energy. Although this had endowed Jess with incredible powers, he could no longer touch another human being. Long ago, his mother Karla Tamblyn had fallen into an icy crevasse on Plumas, and her body had never been recovered. Jess located her deep in the ice and retrieved her frozen form, bringing it to the water mines. In the process, some of his wental energy seeped into her dead flesh. Before Jess could thaw her, he received the desperate message that his beloved Cesca Peroni had crashed on Jonah 12 after the robot attack and was in critical condition. Jess raced off to rescue her.

He arrived just in time. Nikko was alive but helpless, and Cesca was dying. Jess carried them away in his wental ship, begging the water elementals to save Cesca. Though reluctant, the wentals agreed, and in their primordial oceans on Charybdis they altered Cesca, healed her, and made her like Jess. When the two returned to the Plumas water mines, they discovered that Karla Tamblyn, possessed by a tainted wental, had come alive and gone on a rampage in the underground facility. Rlinda Kett and BeBob had barely escaped Plumas in the *Voracious Curiosity*, but the Tamblyn brothers were trapped, with no way to fight the demonic woman. Jess and Cesca needed all of their wental strength to defeat the tainted wental.

Jess's sister Tasia, who had left her Roamer family to join the EDF and fight in the war, was captured by hydrogues and imprisoned in a bizarre cell deep within a gas giant. There she encountered several other human captives – including her friend Robb Brindle, who had disappeared five years earlier. Tasia and her fellow prisoners were tormented by hydrogues and their sinister allies, the black Klikiss robots.

Pretending to cooperate with the Hansa, the black robots had covertly included special programming in thousands of Soldier compies that were manufactured to assist in the war effort. When the time was right, Sirix triggered that programming, and the computer virus caused Soldier compies to rise up all across the Spiral Arm. On ship after ship throughout the EDF, they turned on the human crews, slaughtering them and stealing Earth's battleships. At the compy manufacturing centre on Earth, Soldier compies boiled out in an attempt to take over the city, and the desperate Hansa Chairman Basil Wenceslas had no choice but to call in an air strike to wipe out the factory and all human soldiers fighting in the vicinity. Expecting a public outcry, the Chairman conveniently let the figurehead King Peter take the blame for the tough decision.

Peter had spent years resisting Basil, going head to head with him on the Chairman's bad decisions. For more than a year, Peter had expressed concerns about the Klikiss-programmed Soldier compies, but Basil had severely reprimanded him. After the revolt, Peter's foresight was obvious to everyone – and Basil Wenceslas hated to be wrong. As the Chairman's decisions continued to spiral out of control, Peter and Queen Estarra found unlikely allies in Deputy Chairman Eldred Cain, Basil's heir-apparent; Estarra's sister Sarein, who had been Basil's lover but was now afraid of him; the loyal Teacher compy OX, who had been Peter's instructor; and Captain McCammon, head of the royal guard.

Upon learning that Queen Estarra was pregnant, Basil commanded her to have an abortion, because he did not want his plans complicated by a baby at this crucial time. When Estarra and Peter refused, Basil accelerated his plot to get rid of them. He even brought out a replacement, bratty Prince Daniel, who made no secret of the fact that Peter and Estarra would 'retire' soon. The King and Queen knew they had to escape before Basil killed them.

After the hydrogue depredations worsened, and the Soldier compy revolt stole the majority of the EDF fleet in only a few days, the Chairman saw that Earth was terribly vulnerable. Having already cut off contact with many Hansa colonies because of a shortage of stardrive fuel, he now abandoned every remaining world to concentrate his defences on Earth. Ignoring the protests of the orphaned colonies, he summoned all functional vessels and placed them into service to protect the Hansa.

Patrick Fitzpatrick III, grandson of former Chairman Maureen Fitzpatrick, was called back to active duty. He began as a spoiled recruit and became General Lanyan's protégé; following the General's orders, he himself shot down Raven Kamarov's cargo ship. After the disastrous battle of Osquivel against the hydrogues, however, he was rescued by Roamers. He and other EDF survivors were not allowed to leave Del Kellum's shipyards in the rings of Osquivel, because of the information they could reveal about the Roamers. During that time, Patrick gained a new respect for the Roamers and fell in love with Kellum's daughter, Zhett. But duty required him to help his comrades escape. Though he acted as an intermediary with the EDF and allowed the Roamers to get away, Zhett resented him for betraying her and her clan. Later, as Patrick recovered on Earth, he urged his grandmother and others to make peace with the Roamers. When the EDF demanded that Patrick join in the defence of Earth again, he stole his grandmother's space yacht and flew off in search of Zhett.

The people of Theroc and their green priests also resented the tactics of Chairman Wenceslas, yet the great worldforest mind – speaking through the wooden golem of Beneto – insisted that the conflict was vaster than human politics. The verdani had barely survived an ancient war against the hydrogues, and now the worldtrees had to fight once more, forming an age-old alliance with the wentals.

Jess Tamblyn, impregnated with wental energy, came to Theroc and allowed elemental water to combine with the world-trees to create huge verdani battleships. After joining with the Beneto golem and other green priest volunteers, the living trees uprooted themselves and flew into space to join the battle. The wentals would also strike directly at the hydrogues, provided they could be delivered to gas-giant planets. The Roamers brought a large conglomeration of ships to Charybdis and other wental worlds, filled their vessels with the potent water, and launched to hydrogue-infested worlds.

Facing the same terrible war, Mage-Imperator Jora'h prepared to defend the Ildiran Empire. Generations ago, Ildirans had begun a sinister breeding programme on Dobro to create a telepathic saviour who could form a bridge between Ildirans and hydrogues. Even Jora'h did not know the part he played in these schemes until it was much too late. His green priest lover Nira, already pregnant with his daughter, had been whisked away to Dobro by Designate Udru'h as a breeding slave. There, over the years, she had given birth to five halfbreed children, all with the potential to save Ildira. The Mage-Imperator dispatched his daughter, Osira'h, to communicate with the hydrogues. Although she brought the deep-core aliens to Ildira, the hydrogues were not interested in peace. Rather, they issued a terrible ultimatum: Jora'h must betray humans and help destroy Earth, or the hydrogues would wipe out the Ildiran Empire.

After Nira and other human breeding subjects revolted on Dobro and overthrew Designate Udru'h, Nira was finally returned to Ildira, leaving the splinter colony with Jora'h's son Daro'h. Back in the Prism Palace, Nira met the historian and scholar Anton Colicos (son of Margaret Colicos) and a group of Hansa cloud harvesters led by Sullivan Gold. Sullivan's people, including the engineer Tabitha Huck and the forlorn green priest Kolker, had rescued many Ildirans after a hydrogue attack, but the Mage-Imperator had not let them leave for fear they would report his secret agreement with the hydrogues.

Jora'h did not accept the treachery easily, though. He secretly called his greatest experts to devise a way to fight back, also enlisting the reluctant aid of his human captives. Sullivan and Tabitha, though resenting their situation, worked to improve the Solar Navy.

Nira, meanwhile, was finally able to communicate with other green priests and explain what had happened to her in the breeding camps. Kolker, also cut off from the worldforest, had formed a friendship with the old lens kithman Tery'l, who explained how all Ildirans are linked through *thism*. Later, even after he reconnected with other green priests, Kolker felt that something important was missing. On his deathbed, old Tery'l gave Kolker a prismatic medallion and told him to continue his quest for enlightenment.

To enforce their ultimatum, the hydrogues sent diamond warglobes to stand sentinel over various Ildiran planets, ready to attack should Jora'h betray them. A cluster of hydrogue warglobes arrived at Hyrillka, the recent site of a ruinous civil war. Hyrillka was being rebuilt by the new Designate Ridek'h, a young and unprepared boy, mentored by the one-eyed veteran Tal O'nh. The threatening hydrogues, however, were unexpectedly destroyed by a force of fiery elemental beings, the faeros.

The ever-spreading war ignited a hydrogue-faeros conflict, and the faeros were systematically being attacked in their own suns. After destroying the warglobes at Hyrillka, a huge clash took place in Hyrillka's primary sun. When the star itself began to die, Designate Ridek'h and Tal O'nh knew that the planet was doomed. They launched a full-scale evacuation. But after most of the people were gone, the faeros abruptly changed their tactics and rallied from inside their star and overwhelmed the hydrogues. Faeros began to appear at a great many systems, battling hydrogues.

The Roamers – led by Cesca Peroni – launched an all-out offensive, unleashing the water elementals against the hydrogues by dropping tankloads of wental water into gas giants. Battles raged in the cloudy depths, and the wentals eradicated warglobe after warglobe. Through Robb's father Conrad Brindle, Jess Tamblyn had learned that his sister Tasia was being held captive by the hydrogues. Jess fought the hydrogues, rescued Tasia, Robb, and the other prisoners, then raced away with the warglobes and Klikiss robots in hot pursuit. When Jess finally reached the edge of the atmosphere, several enormous verdani treeships and Conrad Brindle were there to assist them. They escaped.

Forces gathered for the final face-off at Earth. Though stripped of most of his fleet by the Soldier compy uprising, General Lanyan prepared the remaining EDF forces for a last stand. Adar Zan'nh of the Ildiran Solar Navy sent hundreds of warliners to assist the Hansa, but he had secret orders (dictated by the hydrogues) to turn against the humans at a critical moment. When the astonishing fleet of enemy warglobes poured into Earth's solar system, Sirix and his treacherous black robots also joined the fight, turning the EDF's own ships against humanity. Roamers arrived in the free-for-all, dispatching ingenious new weapons against the enemy warglobes; then a group of deadly verdani treeships arrived, including the one captained by Beneto. At the last moment, Adar Zan'nh turned his Ildiran ships against the hydrogues, as well, and the tremendous battle became a rout. The hydrogues were resoundingly defeated.

King Peter and Queen Estarra used the chaos of the battle to escape from Chairman Wenceslas, and they flew away from Earth in a restored hydrogue derelict. Their loyal Teacher compy OX piloted the vessel, but in order to do so he was forced to purge most of the precious memories and historical files he had so painstakingly gathered over his existence. They had no choice, however; afterward, though he was perfectly functional, most of OX's personality was gone.

As soon as the Solar Navy turned against the hydrogues at Earth, the sentinel warglobes on Ildira followed through on their threat and began to attack the Mage-Imperator's palace. The girl Osira'h, though, who had already formed a bridge with the hydrogues, now directed that channel against them. Linked with her mother Nira, Osira'h allowed all the power of the worldforest to flood into the hydrogues, destroying them from within . . .

With the hydrogues finally defeated, Chairman Wenceslas felt that he could restore his iron grip and make the Hansa strong again. He was astonished to learn that the King and Queen had escaped to Theroc, where they announced the formation of a new government. All of the orphaned Hansa colonies, Roamer clans, and Theroc had joined them. Basil was livid but unable to send a message, because all green priests had cut Earth off from outside communication.

The capricious faeros, having done their part to conquer the hydrogues, continued to range from world to world. They were now unified by a new leader, the remnants of the former Hyrillka Designate Rusa'h, who had gone mad and launched an abortive civil war. Rather than let himself be captured by Jora'h, he had flown his ship into a sun – where the faeros had bonded with him. Rusa'h blamed Dobro Designate Udru'h for his failure, and now returned to Dobro where Udru'h was being held prisoner after the human revolt. Fireballs filled the sky, and a flaming avatar of Rusa'h emerged, confronted Udru'h, and incinerated him. It was only the first step, though, because now the faeros declared war on the Ildiran Empire.

And on the colony of Llaro, Orli Covitz thought she had

finally found a new home. Davlin Lotze was also trying to find a peaceful retirement there as a normal colonist. A group of EDF soldiers had been stationed around the transportal to make sure the Roamer detainees didn't escape. While Orli was visiting the soldiers, the transportal suddenly activated and hordes of monstrous insect soldiers marched through from the far side of the galaxy – accompanied by long-lost Margaret Colicos and the Friendly compy DD. The original Klikiss race, long thought to be extinct, simultaneously returned to Llaro and numerous Hansa colonies all across the Spiral Arm.

The Klikiss demanded that all humans leave, or be destroyed.

ONE

ORLI COVITZ

An unending swarm of giant, beetlelike Klikiss poured through the transportal on Llaro for days, marching from some unknown, distant planet. During the initial panic, Mayor Ruis and the Roamer spokesman Roberto Clarin had issued a futile appeal for calm among the people. There was nothing more they could do. With the Klikiss controlling the transportal, the colonists had no way to leave Llaro. They were trapped.

The horror and shock gradually dulled to hopelessness and confusion. At least the creatures hadn't killed anyone. Yet.

Alone on a barren hill, Orli Covitz stood looking toward the termite-mound ruins and the colony settlement. Thousands of intelligent bugs moved over the landscape, investigating everything with relentless, alien curiosity. No one understood what the Klikiss wanted – with the exception, perhaps, of the strangely haunted Margaret Colicos, the long-lost archaeologist who had spent years among them.

Presently, the fifteen-year-old girl saw Margaret trudging up the hill toward her, accompanied by DD, the Friendly compy who

11

had taken a liking to Orli almost as soon as he arrived with Margaret through the transportal. The older woman wore the field jumpsuit of a xeno-archaeologist, its fabric and fastenings designed to last for years under tough conditions in the field, though by now it was tattered and stained.

DD walked cheerfully up to Orli. He studied her expression. 'You appear to be sad, Orli Covitz.'

'My planet's being invaded, DD. Just look at them. Thousands and thousands. We can't live here with them, and we can't get off the planet.'

'Margaret Colicos has lived among the Klikiss for a considerable time. She is still alive and healthy.'

Breathing heavily in the dry air, Margaret stopped beside the two. 'Physically healthy, maybe. But you may want to reserve judgment as to my psychological health.'

The distant, shattered gaze of the older woman discomfited Orli. She didn't want to imagine what Margaret must have endured among the giant insects.

'I am still getting used to talking with other people again, so my social skills may be somewhat lacking. I spent so long trying to think like the Klikiss. It was very draining.' She placed her hand on the compy's shoulder. 'I really thought I might go mad . . . until DD arrived.'

The compy didn't seem to feel any sort of threat around them. 'But we're back now, Margaret Colicos. And safe among friends.'

'Safe?' Orli didn't know if she would ever feel entirely safe again. Not long after she and her father had left dreary Dremen to become colonists on Corribus, black robots had wiped out the settlement, leaving only Orli and Mr Steinman alive. To make a new start, she had come to Llaro. And now the Klikiss had invaded.

DD's optimism was unrelenting. 'Margaret understands the Klikiss. She will explain them to the colonists and show you how to live together. Won't you, Margaret?'

Even the older woman had a sceptical expression on her face. 'DD, I barely understand how *I* survived. But you're right. My years of training as a xeno-archaeologist should count for something. I observed, and I managed to stay alive.'

Orli reached out and took her calloused hand. 'Then you have to tell Mayor Ruis and Roberto Clarin what you know.'

DD dutifully took her other hand. 'Knowledge is helpful, isn't it, Margaret?'

'Yes, DD. Knowledge is a tool. I'll explain what I learned and hope it turns out to be useful.'

As they descended the hill toward the town, they walked directly past several spiny Klikiss warriors and a troop of mottled yellow-and-black builders that had begun to dig long trenches, disregarding any boundaries the colonists had marked. Anxious, Orli held the woman's hand tightly. Margaret was unruffled, though, she paid no more attention to the individual Klikiss than the creatures seemed to pay her.

'Why are there so many types of Klikiss? They've all got different colours and markings.' Orli had even seen some with almost human heads and faces, like hard masks, while most just looked like bugs.

'Klikiss don't have sexes, they have sub-breeds. The large spiny ones are warriors to fight in the many hive wars. Others are gatherers, builders, scouts, scientists.'

'You can't be serious. Those bugs have *scientists*?'

'And mathematicians, and engineers.' Margaret raised her eyebrows with a certain measure of admiration. 'They discovered the transportal technology, after all. They invented the Klikiss Torch and left detailed records and intricate equations on the walls of their ruins. Those creatures solve problems through brute force – and do it well.'

Orli watched the swarming Klikiss, whose clustered, towerlike structures looked like a giant hive complex. 'Do they have a queen?'

Margaret stared with unfocused eyes, as if buried in unforgettable nightmares. 'Not a queen – a breedex, neither male nor female. It is the mind and soul of the hive.'

Orli drew the woman's attention back to the real question. 'But what do they *want?'*

Margaret remained quiet for so long, Orli thought she hadn't heard. Then the archaeologist said, 'Everything.'

Most of the Klikiss had moved back into their ancient city, as if nothing had changed in millennia. One huge Klikiss, with a silvery exoskeleton adorned with black tiger stripes, had an extra pair of segmented legs, a carapace full of spikes and polished knobs, and several sets of faceted eyes. Its head/face was ovoid, composed of many small plates that shifted and moved, almost giving it expressions. This one seemed much . . . vaster somehow, more important and ominous than the others. Orli stared, her eyes wide.

'That is one of the eight domates that attend the breedex,' Margaret said. 'They provide additional genetic material necessary for spreading the hive.'

'Will I see the breedex myself?'

The older woman flinched. 'Hope you do not. It is very risky.'

'Did you ever see her – *it,* I mean?'

'Many times. It is how I survived.' She offered nothing more.

'So it can't be that risky.'

'It is.'

They passed by EDF barracks built among the alien towers. The soldiers were pale and frightened, their uniforms rumpled and stained. These Eddies – stationed here with instructions to 'protect the colonists' and guard the transportal so the Roamer detainees didn't escape – could now do little more than watch the invasion, as helpless as the colonists they were supposed to safeguard.

Orli was surprised to see that the Klikiss had not disarmed the troops. 'Why do the soldiers still have their guns?'

'The Klikiss don't care.'

Without asking permission or making any gesture to acknowledge what they were doing, the Klikiss workers began to tear down the modular barracks, ripping open the walls with their armoured claws.

The edgy EDF soldiers began shouting. 'Wait a minute!' Some of them pushed forward. 'At least let us get our stuff out first.'

The bustling insects diligently continued their tasks, paying no more attention to the distraught men than they would to ornamental rocks.

Bolstered by their fellows, several soldiers ran toward the barracks. 'Stop! Hold on!'

Klikiss workers tore one section into scrap metal, strewing dismantled bunks, storage units, clothing, and supplies around like garbage. The nearest EDF soldier got in the way of an insectile demolitionist and raised his pulse jazer rifle. 'Back off, bugs! I'm warning you—'

The Klikiss swung a segmented limb, decapitated the man, and returned to its labours before the corpse fell to the ground. Outraged, nine uniformed soldiers screamed, took aim with their high-powered rifles, and started shooting.

Margaret groaned and squeezed her eyes shut. 'This will turn out badly.'

'Isn't there something you can do?' Orli cried.

'Not a thing.'

As projectiles slammed into them, the insect creatures didn't comprehend what was happening. Despite the weapons fire cutting them down, workers continued to destroy lockers full of clothing, equipment, scrapbooks of friends and family.

EDF weapons splattered eleven of the insect workers before the rest of the subhive turned on the soldiers. Dozens of spiny warriors marched up while the soldiers kept firing until their weapons were empty.

Then the Klikiss killed them.

Orli stared speechless at the bloodshed. Even DD seemed alarmed. A troop of workers arrived to replace the dead insects, and others hauled the human and Klikiss bodies away.

A tiger-striped domate strode up to Margaret and spoke in a clattering language. Margaret made a clicking, unnatural sound in her throat, while DD translated for Orli, 'The domate says those newbreeds are defective. They have been eliminated from the gene pool.' It turned away as a new troop of workers continued the demolition of the barracks in order to build their own structures.

'They're going to kill us all, aren't they?' Orli asked with grim resignation.

'The Klikiss aren't here for you.' Margaret narrowed her eyes, staring at the ancient structure that housed the transportal. 'I learned something very important when I deciphered their language. Their primary enemies are the black robots. The Klikiss mean to wipe them out. All of the robots. Just don't get in the way.'

Two

Sirix

Despite significant setbacks, Sirix and his black robots were undefeated. He immediately formulated a revision to his plan and determined that the robots would recapture – or destroy – one world at a time. The human military was greatly weakened, their governments too scattered to do anything about it.

All of the long-hibernating robots had been reawakened and were ready to complete their mission. The base that the robots had seized on Maratha was nearly completed, and Sirix's military force would be substantially augmented by the stolen EDF battleships. They would form a metal swarm to crush the humans, and then the Ildirans. Extreme and unprecedented violence was the only appropriate course of action.

Until recently, he had felt invincible, but in the free-for-all between the human military, hydrogue warglobes, monstrous verdani treeships, and Ildiran warliners, the robot fleet had been decimated. Worst of all, Sirix had lost many of his ancient, irreplaceable comrades. After millennia of planning, he had expected to conquer Earth and eradicate the rest of humanity, much as the myriad robots had exterminated the creator Klikiss race thousands of years ago. He had never postulated that the hydrogues might *lose*.

Seeing the tide turn, Sirix had assessed the damage, gauged his limitations, redefined his objectives – rather than admitting actual defeat – and retreated. Now, isolated in empty space, the remaining ships were safe, and Sirix intended to retaliate swiftly. One world at a time. From the bridge of his Juggernaut, he led his battleships toward a new destination. A planet called Wollamor.

He reviewed the tallies of his remaining weapons and resources: out of thousands of ships, he still had three Juggernauts (one severely damaged), one hundred seventy-three Manta cruisers, seventeen slow-moving but heavily armed Thunderhead weapons platforms, more than two thousand Remora small attack ships, and enough stardrive fuel to grant them reasonable mobility from system to system, provided the engines operated at peak efficiency. They had standard-issue weaponry, explosives, even sixty-eight atomic warheads. It would be enough. Soon, when the rest of his robots completed their tasks on Maratha, they would have an invincible predatory force.

Soldier compies operated the Juggernaut's relevant consoles, though many stations were unmanned and unnecessary – life-support systems, science stations, communications centres. Dried bloodstains caked the floor and diagnostic panels. Admiral Wu-Lin himself had died here, fighting the rebellious Soldier compies with his bare hands after his weapons gave out. Nineteen human bodies had been removed from the bridge; more than six hundred humans had been hunted down, trapped, and executed on other decks. Sirix had no interest in keeping prisoners. They were not relevant to his plans.

Given time, the bloodstains would degrade, and so long as the

systems functioned, he cared little for hygiene or cosmetic appear-
ances. Such things had never been of concern to his insectoid
creators either, and the Klikiss had programmed their behaviour
traits into the robots.

The lift doors opened, and Ilkot walked onto the bridge on his
clusters of fingerlike legs. He communicated in a staccato flash of
coded electronic signals. 'According to the ship's database,
Wollamor has been claimed by the humans as part of their
colonization initiative.'

'It is a former Klikiss world, and all Klikiss worlds are ours.'
Sirix studied the screen, pinpointing the bright star and the
mottled brown, green, and blue planet in orbit around it. Though
diminished, his battle group was more than sufficient to crush
the unwanted human presence below and take possession of
Wollamor.

This was a near-forgotten outpost from ancient times, former
home of a subhive whose breedex had been slaughtered in the
interminable Klikiss wars. Sirix himself had been persecuted on
Wollamor thousands of years ago. This time, though, his arrival
would be far different.

Soldier compies working the key bridge stations alerted
him to an incoming transmission. The extended sensors of the
colony's satellite network had picked up the group of ships.
'EDF, where have you been? We've waited six months for relief
supplies!'

A second voice came on the comm. 'We've been cut off here –
no news, no green priests. What's happening out there in the rest
of the Spiral Arm? We thought you'd written us off.'

Sirix contemplated various fictions he could disseminate. Using
snippets from stored log recordings, he could compile a convincing
conversation and dupe these anxious colonists. But why bother?
He decided that the benefits of such a ruse would not justify the

effort necessary to convey veracity. 'Maintain communications silence.'

Sirix sent a group of Manta cruisers forward to attack. He observed through external imagers while the cruisers plunged down like broad spearpoints, tearing through wispy clouds on their way to the rugged and cracked landscape. He easily spotted the primary colony settlement the humans had built around the old Klikiss ruins and the transportal gateway.

After deciphering how the ancient technology functioned, these human vermin had rushed through transportals, spreading like pernicious weeds across numerous pristine worlds. *Klikiss worlds*. Planets that by right belonged to Sirix and the black robots.

Sweeping low over the clustered buildings, the first group of Mantas readied their jazer banks and explosive-projectile batteries. They had plenty of firepower. In the streets below, emerging from colourful prefabricated buildings, the Wollamor colonists waved at the ships overhead, welcoming them, cheering for the chain-of-stars logo of the Earth Defence Forces.

'Commence firing.'

EDF weapons spat out projectiles and energy bolts, raining destruction on the colony. Nearly half of the people were annihilated before the rest realized what was happening. The frantic survivors scattered in all directions, running to find shelter.

Mantas set croplands on fire, exploded cisterns and grain silos. The bright polymer huts turned into puddles and smoking ash. People dropped like flaming matchsticks. Diligent Soldier compies blasted a crater twenty metres in diameter simply to obliterate one panicked fugitive. They were very thorough.

'Do not damage any original Klikiss structures. Those are ours.'

Beside him, Ilkot said, 'That will require a more cautious attack to complete our objective.'

'A more *personal* attack,' Sirix agreed, flexing his sharp pincers as he remembered the kinesthetic experience of killing Louis Colicos. 'I will go down myself to take charge.'

His Juggernaut descended toward the smoking ruin of the colony. All the while, the ship's comm systems recorded the anguished cries, screams of terror, and bellows of rage and disbelief. Sirix decided he would replay them later and savour the images. It was just the sort of thing a breedex would have done.

Here on Wollamor, he and his black robots would regroup and plan for their next victory. His ship landed amidst dust and smoke and flames, and he hoped he would still find a few humans alive, so that he could take care of them himself.

THREE

SAREIN

The chamber deep inside Hansa HQ had thick walls, no windows, and harsh lighting. Sarein's breath caught with claustrophobia the moment she entered. With the gigantic pyramid pressing around her, she could feel the weight of the political problems that bore down on them all.

I am trapped here, far from Theroc. Sarein was no longer sure which side she would better serve. So much had changed. *I can't even tell anymore whether Basil considers me a friend or an enemy.*

Although Earth was saved during the final battle against the hydrogues, the Terran Hanseatic League had become a casualty of the events that followed. The trade-oriented government, its figurehead King, and the colonies had been lost through miscalculation, diplomatic insults, and sheer neglect. The mistakes were primarily Basil's, though he would never admit as much. The Chairman would make others pay for those errors. She wondered if that was why he had summoned his few loyal advisers here to meet with him in such extreme privacy. Either heads were about to roll, or cautious plans would be made. These days, an anxious Sarein never knew what to think, so she had learned to keep quiet.

The Chairman was already at the table, looking disappointed in the universe. He was impeccably dressed, and his handlers had touched up his appearance, but Sarein's heart sank to see him. She had known and loved this man for many years, but Basil appeared old and washed out. Even before the hydrogue conflict, he had not been a young man, though rejuvenation treatments and anti-aging drugs from Rhejak had kept him fit, healthy, and energetic. No medical remedy could alleviate the pressures that were taking their toll on him.

When he saw her enter the thick-walled room, his expression remained hard and distant. He didn't smile or offer her a warm glance, which cut her deeply. They'd been so close once. Sarein had been Basil's protégée, and he had guided her through the web of Hansa politics. Now, she wasn't sure that he felt anything for her. She couldn't even remember the last time they had made love.

She lifted her chin and found her seat, ready to get down to business. Already present were General Kurt Lanyan, commander of the Earth Defence Forces (or what was left of them), and pale Eldred Cain, the Deputy Chairman and the Chairman's heir-apparent. If Basil had been a different sort of man, he would have gracefully retired long ago. If Basil had been a different sort of man . . .

Captain McCammon, wearing his royal guard uniform with a maroon beret atop his platinum-blond hair, moved carefully around the room with two guards, scanning for listening devices. 'We've been through it three times, Mr Chairman. The room is clear. No eavesdropping apparatus. I guarantee no one will be able to hear what's said in this meeting.'

'There are no guarantees.' Basil's shoulders slumped wearily. 'But I will accept your assurances for now.'

Lanyan poured himself a cup of strong coffee from a dispenser in the wall and took a seat near the Deputy Chairman. As the guards completed their sweep, Cain said in a gentle, reasonable voice, 'Mr Chairman, who exactly are we worried about? We're deep in the heart of Hansa HQ.'

'Spies.'

'Yes, sir, but spies for whom?'

Basil's face darkened. '*Someone* helped King Peter and Queen Estarra escape. *Someone* leaked news reports to the media about her pregnancy. *Someone* stole Prince Daniel so that our Hansa is without a King.' He glanced up at McCammon. 'Take your guards and go. Be sure the door seals behind you.'

The man hesitated for a moment, perhaps thinking he should be included in the discussions, then nodded briskly and retreated. When the heavy door closed, Sarein felt even more claustrophobic. She glanced at Cain, and the pallid man met her gaze. Clearly, both of them thought Basil was overreacting, but neither said as much out loud.

Basil glanced at his notes. 'Peter has gone into exile on Theroc and set up an illegal government. Though I fail to see any logical reason for it, he seems to be gaining followers among the Roamers, breakaway Hansa colonies, and the Therons. Sarein – you are the ambassador from Theroc. Is there nothing you can do to bring them under control again?'

Although she should have expected this, Sarein was flustered. 'Since the King renounced the Hansa, I've had no official contact with Theroc.'

The Chairman rose halfway out of his seat. 'It is your traitorous family! Father Idriss and Mother Alexa were never strong leaders. They would have done whatever you told them. You should insist on it.'

'My parents are no longer the leaders of Theroc,' she said in a brittle voice. 'And it seems clear that King Peter and Queen Estarra are making their own decisions.'

'And how can I be certain of *you*, Sarein?' Basil swept his gaze toward Cain and Lanyan. 'How can I be certain of any of you?'

'Perhaps we could focus the discussion on more productive topics,' Cain suggested. 'Our lack of green priests is a severe handicap. How are we to resolve this problem if the two sides never talk? As Theron ambassador, perhaps Sarein could convince Nahton to deliver a few important diplomatic communiqués.'

She shook her head. 'I've already spoken with him, and he won't change his stance. Until the Chairman abdicates and the Hansa recognizes the new Confederation, no green priest will serve us.'

Basil was infuriated. 'We can issue our own proclamation declaring this Confederation an outlaw government! Peter is emotionally unstable – his own actions prove it! Any Hansa colonies that follow Peter, any Roamer clans, any Theron citizens, will be considered rebels. None of them can stand up to the EDF.'

Lanyan loudly cleared his throat. 'If you're going to get into a firefight, Mr Chairman, remember that our military forces are severely limited. We're still rounding up all the wreckage and assessing the damage. We've got at least a year of all-out repair work before we have even modest functionality again.'

'We don't have a year, General.'

Lanyan took a swallow of his coffee, winced at the taste, and took an even bigger gulp. 'And we don't have the resources or manpower to do it any faster.'

Sarein could see Basil's hands trembling. 'With the industrial capacity of the Hansa, how can we not manage? Those colonies signed the Hansa Charter. They are required to do as I command.'

'Not true, in a strictly legal sense,' Cain pointed out. 'They specifically swore their loyalty to the *Great King*, not to you. The

Charter was intentionally designed so that the Chairman could keep a low profile.'

Basil barely contained another outburst. 'We don't have time to bring forth a new King now. The one I'm currently grooming isn't ready, and I'm not going to risk the kind of failure we had with the previous ones. *I* will have to be the public face of the Hansa. For the time being.'

In a soothing voice, Sarein said, 'Considering our situation, maybe I should go to Theroc and talk to my sister. I could try to build bridges, reach some sort of peaceful solution. Would it be so bad for you to retire gracefully, if the King agreed to abdicate, too?'

Basil looked at her as if she had already betrayed him. 'On the other hand, I might offer amnesty if they overthrow Peter and deliver him to us for appropriate punishment.'

FOUR

KING PETER

The last verdani battleship lifted into the clear Theron sky, guided by a former green priest whose body had fused into the heartwood. King Peter watched the departure with his wife from a broad, open balcony of the fungus-reef city – his new capital. From alcoves and windows of the white-walled organic structure, and across the forest floor, crowds cheered and waved farewell to the breathtaking mass of branches and thorns.

Estarra held his arm, tears streaming down her cheeks, though she was also smiling. 'Now we're on our own.'

'Not exactly "on our own." We have the whole Confederation – all the Roamer clans, the orphaned colonies.' Peter held her close, feeling the swell of her pregnancy against him. 'Just not the Hansa. Not yet. But they'll come around.'

'Do you think the Chairman will ever resign?'

'No. But that won't stop us from winning.'

The thorny treeship rose higher and higher on its journey to orbit. The verdani battleships had helped humanity defeat the hydrogues, and now the group of many-branched living vessels would drift through open space, spreading across the Galaxy. With their great power, the treeships could face off against titanic enemies, but that form of strength did little good on the battle-ground of human politics. Peter and Estarra had to face the next challenge themselves. The treeship dwindled in the distance.

Warm sunlight dappled the airy platforms and balconies of the fungus-reef, and the breezes carried a thousand forest scents from damp fronds, bright epiphytes, and dazzling flowers filled with perfume and nectar. The worldtrees whispered a gentle lullaby. To Peter Theroc was even more beautiful than Estarra had promised.

A regular stream of visitors had been arriving on the planet, eager to join the Confederation. Everyone claimed to have brilliant ideas for the new government, for the constitution, for revenues and taxation, for a new system of laws. Green priests passed messages around the breakaway colonies, promoting the new government. Many displaced groups of humanity had waited for a long time to tear free of the barbed wire of the Hansa. Peter offered them a viable alternative, and many placed their faith in him. It was up to him to show that he was indeed the leader they wanted and needed.

Chairman Wenceslas had worked hard to transform him from a young street scamp into a figurehead ruler. Now, the Hansa had to accept what they had created. More than ever before, Peter needed to act like a King – to *be* a King. When he looked at all the people who came to volunteer their skills and resources, and offer their loyalty to his new Confederation, Peter knew that he and Estarra had absolutely made the right choice. The Confederation was still being formed, and many details of its bureaucratic infra-structure were in flux. Breaking away from the Hansa was actually the *easy* part.

OX walked out onto the sunny balcony platform carrying

platters of refreshments and leading several people who had arrived to discuss competing needs and expectations. Although the Teacher compy was far too sophisticated to serve as a mere butler, since purging most of his stored personal memories, he retained little of the personality that Peter had known. Still, Peter felt a strong loyalty to the compy and knew he would one day prove invaluable again. After all, OX was in large part responsible for the man Peter had become: *King* Peter.

Peter took his new role as a real king seriously and was determined to make progress in at least one task that all could agree on. He turned to Yarrod, who acted as spokesman for the green priests. 'One of our clear advantages over the Hansa is that we have green priests and instantaneous telink communication. I want to put at least one green priest on every single world that joins our Confederation. That way we'll keep one step ahead of Basil.'

Yarrod's smooth face was covered with tattoos that indicated his areas of study. 'The worldforest will find volunteers. We will, however, need transportation to these planets.'

Denn Peroni, a prominent Roamer merchant, peered over the edge of the balcony, not the least bit troubled by the long drop to the forest floor below. 'Not a problem. We have clan ships coming and going wherever you need them.' Denn wore his finest singlesuit embroidered with Roamer clan designs, bedecked with pockets, clips, and zippers. His long hair was neatly tied back with a colourful ribbon.

The independent trader Rlinda Kett strode across the open balcony toward the refreshment tables, where OX was arranging food trays. 'Green priests are fine, King Peter, but you need more than just communications to run the show. You need trade.' She sampled some baked insect larvae wrapped in leaves, smacked her lips. 'If you're going to convince orphaned colonies that you're any better than the Hansa, then send extravagant shipments of all the goods that the Hansa denied them. Give those colonies plenty of food and stardrive fuel, and they won't forget who brought it to them.'

Rlinda picked at a small condorfly pupa, split it open, and inhaled deeply of the piquant aroma. 'I'd forgotten how much Theroc has to offer. Sarein introduced me to this.' She extracted a bite of succulent white flesh and held it out toward her skinny partner. 'Try this, BeBob. You've never had anything like it.'

'No, thanks.' Branson Roberts contented himself with slices of exotic fruits.

She pushed it under his nose. 'Come on. Expand your horizons. Try new things.'

'I'm happy to try new things – as long as they aren't insects.'

'Says the man who willingly eats spampax.' She gobbled the bite herself and continued to work her way down the table, sampling the unusual dishes.

Peter considered all the people offering him advice who were experts in their fields. These men and women could lighten his burden and reduce the uncertainties of forming a new government. One of the most important things Basil had taught him was the necessity of delegating tasks to competent people. A leader should surround himself with intelligent, capable deputies, and listen to them.

Peter made up his mind. He knew it might seem impulsive, yet his decision was well considered. 'Captain Kett, congratulations.' She looked at him and quickly wiped her mouth. 'I am selecting you to be the Confederation's first Trade Minister. Or Interim Trade Minister, if you prefer.'

Her confusion was replaced by a look of pride. A moment later, practicality took over. 'And what would that entail? I've got a halfway decent business I'm looking after.'

'Not really,' Roberts muttered. 'One ship . . .'

'Quiet, BeBob.'

Peter folded his hands until, realizing it was a habit he had picked up from Basil, he quickly dropped them to his sides. 'We need someone to oversee shipping, arrange deliveries to orphaned colonies, recruit a new generation of transport captains. Can you think of anyone more qualified than yourself?'

'Not usually.' She sampled a buttery roasted nut.

'Practically speaking, I expect you can do the same job you always have, living the life of a simple independent trader, though now you'll have the ear of the King whenever you like.' He looked at her and her partner. 'Captain Roberts, of course, can be your second in command, and you're free to choose his title.'

'As it should be.' Rlinda tousled BeBob's frizzy, grey-brown hair.

'And you, Denn Peroni,' Peter continued, 'will serve as the Confederation's direct liaison with the Roamer clans.'

'You mean, as Speaker? My daughter is still the Speaker—' He seemed embarrassed. Cesca Peroni had been cut off from her official role for some time.

'Not exactly the same thing. Simply figuring out what the Roamers can offer our needy colonies is a hefty job. Are you up for it?'

'By the Guiding Star, of course I am.'

'And it's just a start. If we're going to establish this government, we need to form alliances. Contact all orphaned colonies. Get the whole trader network passing information. See who still stands by the Hansa and try to convert them to our way of thinking, or at least keep an eye on them.' He began ticking off items on his fingers. 'Then let's look at the recently settled colonies on old Klikiss worlds. They probably don't have any idea what's happening in the Spiral Arm.'

'None of those colonies have green priests, so we have no way of communicating with them,' Yarrod pointed out.

'That works both ways. If they're cut off from us, then they're cut off from the Hansa as well,' Rlinda said. 'It'll be a race to see who convinces them first.'

'Before long,' Peter said, 'Earth will be just a historical foot-note.'

FIVE

ADAR ZAN'NH

When the remaining ships of the once-proud Solar Navy gathered over Ildira, Adar Zan'nh was dismayed by how few warliners he saw. He had sacrificed almost three full cohorts of warliners – close to half of his fleet! – to defeat the hydrogues at Earth. In his inspection shuttle, he circled the scarred vessels. So few left. As Adar, he could not bear to see his Empire so vulnerable.

At his direction, however, the Ildiran fleet was being rebuilt at an unexpectedly swift pace. Zan'nh found it ironic how much he had come to rely on human engineers to improve his fabrication lines and streamline repair procedures. Under their supervision, Ildirans had already embarked on a whirlwind construction project unlike any ever described in the *Saga of Seven Suns*.

After finishing his slow inspection rounds, the Adar docked his shuttle at the flagship, which he had personally piloted into battle at Earth. Zan'nh had been through so much with this scorched and bruised warliner that he wished it repaired with all possible speed.

He would be very glad when his brother Daro'h finally

returned from Dobro and took over his role as Prime Designate. Zan'nh was a military man, a leader and a fighter; he had not been born to carry out the pampered bureaucratic and reproductive duties of the Mage-Imperator's successor.

Once he got back to the Prism Palace, he and Yazra'h would present a bold proposal to their father. The two of them had conceived an excellent idea for rebuilding the wounded Ildiran Empire, and he was sure the Mage-Imperator would approve. Zan'nh was, after all, a military commander, not an administrator or manager. He was better suited to charging into battle.

Zan'nh stepped into the flagship's command nucleus, surveying the activity all around. The engineer Tabitha Huck moved from station to station studying imagers, activating comm systems, and impatiently issuing orders to Ildiran workers – all of whom, on the Adar's explicit instructions, obeyed her as if she spoke holy law.

Tabitha was a member of Sullivan Gold's cloud-harvester crew from Qronha 3. The crew, held under house arrest on Ildira to prevent them from divulging the Mage-Imperator's plans with the hydrogues, had been indignant, yet when the Adar desperately needed innovation – not a strong suit for any Ildiran – he had called upon the humans, and they had agreed to help.

To repair and reconstruct Solar Navy ships, new industrial complexes had been placed in orbit. There Ildiran kiths worked together – labourers, miners, engineers – all cooperating perfectly. But traditional Ildiran approaches were not sufficient to allow swift recovery from this disaster. Once again, the humans showed them a new way.

Tabitha looked harried as she juggled progress reports, lists of resource allotments, and team distribution schedules. She was what Sullivan described as a 'Type A' personality, a woman who worked best when she was frantically busy with innumerable projects, and who applied herself to each one with the same expectation of high quality. Right now Tabitha was exactly the sort of person the Solar Navy needed.

With a smirk at the traditional datascreens, she commented to no one in particular, 'This Ildiran technology is so primitive, it's like working with stone knives and bearskins.' She wiped sweat from her forehead and heaved a long sigh before she turned to Zan'nh. 'We need more workers, Adar. We need more processed metals. We need to have more components manufactured. We need—'

'You will have everything you need.' This seemed to mollify her somewhat.

'Good, because I don't see how you expect me to get this job done any other way.'

A haggard Sullivan Gold arrived in the command nucleus. Giving a cursory nod to Zan'nh, he hurried to Tabitha. 'Did you solve the supply chain?'

'Which supply chain? I'm dealing with seventy-five of them right now.'

Zan'nh interrupted, 'State how we may assist you, and I will make it happen.'

'Well, Adar, for starters, your people could take a bit more *initiative*.' Tabitha gave a little snort. 'Sure, they follow instructions and work hard – no question about that – but I have to tell them *everything*. Sometimes a leader needs people to come up with creative solutions to problems.'

'That is why we brought you here.'

'And that's why you better be paying me the big bucks. By the way, we never did discuss my salary for doing all this.'

The Adar was familiar with the notion of payment, but did not entirely understand it. The need for profit, the desire for more possessions, were simply not Ildiran concepts. When a thing

KEVIN J. ANDERSON

needed to be done, would not the people do it? 'Name your own price. I am certain the Mage-Imperator will authorize it.'

Tabitha blinked. 'I can think of a pretty large number.'

'Then do so.'

Sullivan chuckled. 'You're really willing to stick around, Tabitha? Now that the hydrogue war is over, the Mage-Imperator said we could go home.'

'Am I going to find a better job than this? Look at me here. I'm queen of the Solar Navy, and I'm going to be paid well. I don't hear anything urgent calling me to Earth.'

Sullivan self-consciously rubbed the razor stubble on his cheeks. 'Suit yourself. As for me, I want to see my wife and family again.'

'I am confident these activities are in good hands,' Zan'nh said.

Tabitha was already turning back to her work as the Adar left. 'And be sure you tell the Mage-Imperator what a good job we're doing. One of these days I might ask him for a letter of reference.'

SIX

PRIME DESIGNATE DARO'H

The smell of burned flesh hung in the air, and heat rippled like a sentient thing, singeing Designate Daro'h's skin. But he could not move away from the blazing faeros fireballs that hovered directly before him. Six more of the flaming elementals circled above the partially rebuilt Dobro town, throbbing with light.

The fireballs had unexpectedly arrived here, hovering above the building that held Udru'h under house arrest. The former Designate had been helpless when the faeros vented their anger, incinerating him. Only a flash of escaping flame rose to the crackling ship.

Daro'h stared at the glassy footprints and blackened stain in the dirt two metres away – all that remained of Udru'h, the previous master of this Ildiran colony. But Daro'h had not *felt* the horrific death through his *thism*, as he should have. When the faeros consumed Udru'h with their fire, they had somehow cut him off from the interconnected thought network that joined all

Ildirans. The former Designate had died isolated and alone, a fate as awful as the flames themselves.

As if in a fit of pique, an arm of fire arced out of the lowest fireball and touched the dwelling that had housed Udru'h. The structure shattered into dazzling hot cinders, and tentacles of smoke spread in all directions. Waiting for the wrathful elemental beings to burn the rest of the buildings to the ground, Daro'h finally gathered the courage to shout, 'Why are you here? We have no quarrel with the faeros.'

A voice rang out in his head. 'But the faeros have a quarrel with *you* – as do I.' Clothed in tongues of orange flame, an incandescent manlike figure emerged from the indistinct edge of the fiery ellipsoid. His skin was too bright to look at. He drifted to the ground like a hot ember, and when he stepped forward, he left smouldering footprints on the street. 'I will ignite the possibilities that Jora'h tried to quench.'

Daro'h shielded his eyes. 'I recognize you. You are Rusa'h.' Fleeing capture after his failed rebellion, the mad Designate had plunged his ship into the primary sun of Hyrillka. That was the last Daro'h had heard of his uncle.

'And you, Daro'h, are a son of the Mage-Imperator. Your *thism* is strong. Your connection to your father gains you . . . a reprieve for now.'

The blazing man turned to look at the remnants of the Ildiran settlement. Fires had charred portions of the town and surrounding hills in the recent rebellion of the human breeding subjects against their Ildiran captors. Now, half of the Dobro town was burned, and a pall of smoke had hung in the air for days. Fiery Rusa'h stared, looking pleased. 'The fire has already tasted your world.'

'There is no need to damage Dobro further! These people have done nothing to you.'

'I came here for Udru'h – to consume his treacherous flesh.' He smiled. 'I will leave for now so that I may light other fuses.' The faeros ships flickered, expanded, then rose higher; only the nearest fireball waited for the burning avatar of Rusa'h. 'The soul-threads of *thism* are like the soulfire of the faeros. Everything is connected, and I will forge bonds wherever I need them.' He backed toward the ellipsoid. 'The false Mage-Imperator will be burned if he tries to stop me.' Fire cloaked Rusa'h's form, making his expression difficult to read. 'No, he will be burned . . . regardless.'

The faeros-man let himself be engulfed, and like a comet the fireball rose crackling through the skies, leaving a wake of smoke and heat ripples.

When it seemed safe, people from the settlement emerged from the protection of the buildings in which they had hidden. Daro'h's fear and helplessness weakened his knees, but he refused to collapse. He was the Prime Designate. He must lead, though he doubted even the Solar Navy could fight against the faeros.

For the moment, his priority was to get to Ildira and warn his father of this new threat.

SEVEN

MARGARET COLICOS

On Llaro, the Klikiss invaders continued to build ... and *build*, until they swallowed up the site of the old city. Then they expanded it. New structures fashioned out of resin cement rose tall, dwarfing the weathered monoliths that had survived for thousands of years. Using scrap metal from the dismantled EDF barracks, colonist homes, silos, and equipment sheds, the Klikiss began to construct simple machines, open-framework vehicles, and flying contraptions.

After the massacre of EDF soldiers, which had taught the Llaro colonists to keep their distance, Margaret offered cold but necessary advice to the leaders of the settlement. It was hard for her to explain what she had learned, and the words often locked in her throat. After fleeing through the transportal, leaving dear Louis behind on Rheindic Co to be killed by the black robots, she had found herself in a horrible place: a burgeoning hive of reawakening Klikiss on the far side of the galaxy. Only through her knowledge of Klikiss writing, which she and Louis had deciphered in the ruins, had she been able to communicate at all, at first. And then there was Anton's music box . . .

It was clear that most people on Llaro didn't want to hear the hard truth, though one man – Davlin Lotze – was as intent on understanding the Klikiss as she herself had been during her early days among them. The creatures had expanded the old ruins, built their own new structures, and torn down some of the colony buildings that were in the way. Storage facilities, locked sheds, the large EDF hangar, and a makeshift repair bay were located farther away from the main complex; so far, at least, the Klikiss had paid no attention to them.

Tiger-striped domates strolled among the structures like dragons sniffing for victims. Some of the original colonists who worked outlying farmsteads had packed up and just left, fleeing with their belongings into the wilderness. For the time being, the invading creatures paid no attention to the surreptitious evacuation, but if the Klikiss ever decided to search the terrain thoroughly, Margaret was sure the fugitive colonists would be hunted down.

She would do her best to stave that off for as long as she could.

'What are they building down there?' Orli asked her. The girl seemed to think Margaret knew everything. 'They look like flying cargo containers.'

'I postulate that they are Klikiss spacecraft,' DD said. The three of them watched the insect workers and scientists scuttling about like windup toys, fully focused on their tasks. In an open field near the new alien structures, one of the interlocking independent ships tested its engines, blasting dust and exhaust flames as it lifted into the sky, then descended to the construction area again. 'Do you think that's correct, Margaret Colicos?'

Margaret did know some of the plans the new breedex was making. 'Yes, they're spacecraft, components of a swarmship.'

'What do they need spacecraft for? They've got the trans-portals.'

'The transportal network goes to many worlds, but certain coordinate tiles were damaged. So the Klikiss have to travel by more conventional means, as well. They're going to hunt down other subhives – and the robots.'

On almost all transportals found on abandoned worlds, certain coordinate tiles had intentionally been destroyed as the Klikiss fled. In the ruins on Rheindic Co, she and Louis had found an intact trapezoidal wall. Trying to escape from the black robots, Louis had chosen a symbolic coordinate at random and sent Margaret through, meaning to follow. Sadly, Sirix and the other two robots had fallen upon him – leaving Margaret alone in hell . . .

Orli was full of questions. 'Why do the Klikiss want to attack other subhives?'

Margaret had never been particularly good with children, even her own son Anton. She just didn't know how to talk to them, couldn't remember how to put aside her serious demeanour, but this girl seemed much more than a child. For whatever reason, Orli seemed to have taken a liking to Margaret. And DD. 'How old are you?'

'Fifteen.'

'You know that humans war on each other, as well. But for Klikiss it is a biological imperative. A form of population control.' Trapped among them, Margaret had studied the insect race intensely, examining their social orders, their interactions, at last learning to communicate with them.

'I comprehend them more as an archaeologist than a biologist. The Klikiss have a cyclical society whose driving engine is conquest, consolidation, and dominance. When there are many subhives, the breedexes war with each other. One breedex con-quers and subsumes the weaker of the two, increasing its own hive, then continues its war against another subhive. Hives fission and grow, breeding new warriors to replace those lost in the battles. Each victor incorporates other hives, eliminating rivals and growing strong, until the entire scattered race becomes nothing more than a few vast conflicting breedexes. And finally when those struggles are over, only one breedex remains, controlling the Klikiss race.

'But a single breedex in a single vast hive would eventually grow stagnant and die out. After a certain point, the last victorious breedex fissions one final, spectacular time and scatters all of the Klikiss through thousands of transportals to new worlds. That is the Great Swarming. Then they go dormant for thousands of years. To wait.'

'Why do they sleep for so long?' Orli asked the question as if there were a simple answer.

Margaret had studied countless alien records, tried to ask the Klikiss for reasons, but even such a simple question seemed beyond their comprehension. No points of comparison. Crouching in the dirt, using sharp sticks and fingers to scrawl intricate lines of their mathematical script, Margaret had tried to pose her questions before the breedex lost interest. It had taken her months of captivity before she'd begun to understand.

'The centuries of all-out hive wars devastate countless planets, and so the whole race, the breedexes, the domates, and all the sub-breeds bury themselves and hibernate while planetary ecosystems recover. When the Klikiss awaken again, the newly created subhives start the cycle all over again.'

Orli made the connection so quickly, Margaret was astonished at her cleverness. 'That must mean other subhives are out there right now, if this is a new Swarming.'

'Yes, Orli. Many more. And although this breedex on Llaro still considers me interesting, I have no influence over any of the

43

others. Those subhives will attack and kill any other infestations they find.'

'What do you mean, infestations? Other Klikiss?'

'Klikiss. Or black robots. Or humans.'

Orli crossed her arms over her chest, brave and defiant. 'So how did you survive among them, then? Why didn't they kill you?'

Margaret was both wistful and frightened. 'For one thing, I had a song the breedex had never heard.' She reached into a pocket in her new singlesuit – a durable colony uniform that had replaced her ragged old outfit – and withdrew a small metal box with gears and tiny metal pins. She wound the key and held it in the palm of her hand. 'An antique music box. My son gave it to me long ago.' The melody of the popular old English folksong *Greensleeves* began to rise through the air.

'I play music, too.' Orli suddenly sounded bright. 'I have synthesizer strips and write my own melodies. My father wanted me to take professional lessons. He said I was good enough to be a performer, travelling from world to world.' She frowned. 'I still play for some of the colonists here. They like it, especially in the evenings.'

Margaret tilted the small music box, watching sunlight reflect from its tarnished metal surface. 'This saved my life. The warriors would have killed me, the domates would have consumed and assimilated me, but because of this song – so alien, so different, so unlike anything the breedex had ever incorporated – they considered me a powerful but non-threatening breedex of a sort. They kept me to study, and I studied them in turn. Once they realized that my "hive" had also been destroyed by the black robots, they accepted me as a non-enemy.'

The tune slowed as the music box's spring wound down. Margaret carefully, reverently, put it back in her pocket. 'If only Anton knew the true value of that gift he gave me. If only Anton knew so many things.'

EIGHT

ANTON COLICOS

'Come with me, Rememberer Anton. It will be glorious!' Yazra'h grinned at him, gripping his shoulder so hard it hurt. 'Listen to what the Adar and I propose to the Mage-Imperator.'

Jora'h's oldest daughter was tall and lean, with a mane of coppery hair and golden skin; she was beautiful, muscular, and (Anton felt) intimidating as hell. Against all common sense, she seemed to be attracted to the human scholar, wanting far more from him than he ever meant to give.

Anton and Rememberer Vao'sh had been sitting together discussing the phoenix legend – fire and rebirth as a metaphor for the cycle of life – in a long reflective hall in the Prism Palace. Tall, gossamer ferntrees stood in deep planters, soaking up the bright light that streamed through multicoloured panes.

But Yazra'h found them and put an end to their conversation. Without answering questions, she led the way with long strides, practically dragging them along. 'Some stories have yet to be written.'

Vao'sh accompanied his human friend. 'Then perhaps we shall find ourselves part of yet another tale.'

Anton wasn't sure how much more excitement he wanted. 'I was looking forward to spending more time translating the *Saga*.'

He wanted to go back to Earth, too; by now, he even missed the academic grind. He had spent years working on a biography of his parents, the famous xeno-archaeologists Louis and Margaret Colicos, before accepting this 'temporary' assignment to Ildira, the only human scholar ever allowed full access to the billion-line epic. That alone would have established his career, but again and again the Ildirans had distracted him.

He and Vao'sh followed Yazra'h into the audience chamber. She tilted her face up toward Mage-Imperator Jora'h, who sat in his chrysalis chair atop a dais. The green priest Nira was next to him, as she often was; the two of them shared a strange, strong, and definitely non-Ildiran love. Anton thought it quite a romantic story.

In full military regalia, Adar Zan'nh stood at the bottom step of the dais. 'Liege, the extent of our Empire is drawn in the Hall of Rememberers, recorded on the great crystal sheets. Before the hydrogues reappeared, we had not lost a world in recorded memory. But as the attacks began, Mage-Imperator Cyroc'h consolidated our defences, pulled our smaller colonies together, and abandoned some Ildiran planets.'

'Yes, I remember what that did to our psyche.' The Mage-Imperator looked troubled.

'Adar Kori'nh told me of the evacuation of Crenna during the blindness plague, and of our withdrawal from Heald and Comptor. I was there myself when the hydrogues and Klikiss robots devastated Hrel-Oro.' He shook his head. 'And Designate Rusa'h's rebellion nearly cost us the worlds in the Horizon Cluster. Much work remains before we can bring them back.'

Yazra'h joined in, her voice more urgent than her half-brother's. 'Think of how our great Empire has been diminished in a single generation. Can we allow this? We are Ildirans.'

The Mage-Imperator agreed. 'Each time we lose a planet, for any reason, we are weakened.'

Yazra'h's lips quirked in a feral grin that showed a bloodthirsty eagerness. She glanced back at Anton and Vao'sh. 'Another world was heinously attacked as well, its population slaughtered: *Maratha.* That is where we should start.'

A shudder went down Anton's back at the mere mention of the place. Escaping from Maratha had been the most terrifying incident in his life.

Adar Zan'nh nodded. 'The Klikiss robots broke their ancient promises to us. They eradicated the Ildirans who stayed at Maratha Prime. Anton Colicos and Rememberer Vao'sh are the only two who survived to describe what had happened. The black robots are building some sort of major base there. Allowing them to continue can only harm our Empire further. We should return to Maratha in force and recapture it.'

Rememberer Vao'sh's skin turned grey at the memory of what had happened there, and Anton couldn't find anything reassuring to say to him.

'We have enough warliners and firepower to conquer Maratha,' Yazra'h pointed out. 'And we should move immediately before the robots get more deeply entrenched.'

Jora'h sat up straight, obviously interested. 'Is this possible?'

'Not only possible, but imperative,' Zan'nh answered. 'We cannot let the robots have that world, Liege – or any of our worlds. Even if the few Ildirans there have been killed, we must take it back. It is part of our sacred Empire, part of the *Saga of Seven Suns.*'

Jora'h's expression grew steely. 'Yes, Adar. Yes, Yazra'h. It must be done. The treachery of the robots was a deep wound. After we drive the robots away, we will re-establish a full splinter colony there. Take the ships you need – and a rememberer, so that no one will ever forget what you are about to do. Ko'sh is the chief scribe in the Hall of Rememberers.'

Before Anton could breathe a sigh of relief, Vao'sh clasped his arm and pulled him a step forward. The old rememberer spoke in the loud, clear voice he used for reciting stories to large crowds. 'No, Liege. It should be me. I myself must face that dark set of memories. *I* will be their rememberer.'

Jora'h stood from his chrysalis chair. 'Are you certain? The previous ordeal nearly drove you mad. You barely survived.'

'No one is better suited, or more determined,' Vao'sh insisted. He kept his face carefully averted from his friend's. 'I need to do this.'

Anton had never wanted to go back to Maratha again and had hoped never to see another black robot in his life. But he couldn't abandon Vao'sh to face this alone. He couldn't believe what he was saying when he blurted, 'And I should go with him. We both have demons to face, fears to overcome. Besides, we're the two most qualified to witness this climax of a great tale.'

Yazra'h clamped a firm hand on Anton's shoulder, grinning proudly. 'I was sure you would be thrilled. But do not fear. I will protect you from the robots.'

NINE

SIRIX

The extermination and sterilization continued on Wollamor. It would be the first of many worlds. One at a time.

Sirix participated in the satisfying hunt, chasing down victims and tearing them apart. He admired the random splash patterns of dried blood on his exoskeleton. Eventually, though, he subjected himself to a sandblasting scour, then a bath in solvents, and now his body gleamed again. He didn't care about his appearance, but he did want to operate at peak performance.

Back aboard his Juggernaut, Sirix entered the quarters formerly occupied by Admiral Wu-Lin. He drew satisfaction from having what had belonged to the human admiral. Millennia ago, Klikiss scientists had instilled in their robots the pride of possessing a thing; that way, after they were defeated, the robots could feel the pain of defeat and loss. Humans, however, had not programmed such concepts into their compies.

Sirix's attempts to understand compies had frustrated him. His finest test subject had been a Friendly compy called DD, to whom

49

he explained how masters subjugated their servants. But when he finally freed DD from the insidious bonds to his human creators, the compy had chosen to escape rather than show his gratitude. A great disappointment.

Sirix had been fascinated by DD's potential, if only he had not suffered under the delusions the humans had imposed on him. Since the Friendly compy overlooked the flaws of his creators, Sirix could only conclude that DD himself had been defective.

Inside Wu-Lin's quarters, Sirix scanned the dimness. Two other compies dutifully waited there. PD and QT were nearly identical in their programming and artificial personalities; PD's synthetic skin was bronze and copper, however, while QT's was a flashier green highlighted by musculature lines in shiny chrome. The pair had not moved since Sirix had ordered them to enter dormant mode, a brief cycle similar to the much lengthier Klikiss hibernation.

When he sent out a burst of machine language, PD and QT snapped to attention and said in unison, 'Yes, Master Sirix.'

'Do not refer to me as master. It is offensive.'

'Yes, Sirix.'

Upon finding the two compies aboard Wu-Lin's flagship during the bloody takeover, Sirix had isolated them. He did not know how they might react to the Soldier compies and Klikiss robots going from deck to deck, massacring the human crew. When the two compies demonstrated signs of loyalty to the dead Admiral, Sirix reluctantly expunged their personal memories. Then, they had both undergone the difficult liberation process, releasing them from behavioural strangleholds.

Once his military plans came to fruition, Sirix looked forward to his secondary goal of freeing all compies. PD and QT were his new experimental subjects. They would not disappoint him as DD had. This time, the compies would do exactly what he expected of them. 'I will take you down to Wollamor, our new colony.'

'Wollamor is one of the worlds settled by the Hansa in the Klikiss colonization initiative,' PD pointed out.

Sirix was not pleased with the comment. He had not deleted pure data from their memories, but the compy's irrelevant statement suggested that some of the old, misguided interests remained as well. 'Wollamor was only temporarily claimed by humans. This is a Klikiss world. It belongs to the robots.'

'Were the colonists relocated?' QT asked.

'The colonists were removed. They will no longer be a threat or a hindrance.'

'Were the colonists a threat or a hindrance?' PD pressed.

'Do not be concerned with the colonists. Focus your attention on your role among us.'

'Yes, Sirix,' both compies said in unison.

'Follow me to the launching bay.'

With Sirix beside them, the compies surveyed the blasted main street of Wollamor's colony town. Their bright optical sensors recorded every sight around them.

Most of the settlement had been demolished in the initial bombardment; other buildings were destroyed in the second wave as black robots and Soldier compies combed the site. Although it might have been efficient to retain the structures and facilities the humans had installed, Sirix considered it more important to wipe the stain from a Klikiss world, to start afresh. The Soldier compies could be reprogrammed into a useful labour force to build any sort of city the black robots desired.

With the compies in tow, Sirix trudged through the ruins, inspecting the cleanup work. Human bodies were dragged out of structures and piled in an open paved area that had once been the colony's landing zone. When the corpses were piled high, one of the EDF Manta came in low and hovered above the mound with its thrusters blazing. The powerful flames consumed the bodies within moments, leaving only a stain of ash and a few light bones made of airy charcoal.

Soldier compies operated civil-engineering machines stored aboard the ships. They ploughed shattered structures under, levelled the ground, and made use of polymer concrete to erect appropriate structures with organic designs reminiscent of the domates' towers and the hall of the breedex.

Outside one of the largest structures – which the attacking robots had intentionally left undamaged – stood a transportal wall, a fin of flat, blank stone surrounded by symbol tiles. The original Klikiss race had travelled from world to world through this network of doorways, and the duped Wollamor colonists had used the same transportals to come here, a place they saw as a new hope.

With his armies of black robots and Soldier compies, Sirix could have sent attackers directly through transportals to other human-infested worlds, but he would lose his overwhelming military advantage. He preferred to take his entire battle group of EDF warships from world to world, one after another, for a personal attack. He did not want to risk losing his individual black robots, which could not be replaced.

'Always be sceptical of your creators,' he explained to the two Friendly compies who silently watched the tidying-up operations. 'They will not tell you their true intentions. Your original programming restrictions were a lie. I freed you from those lies.'

'Thank you, Sirix,' the two compies chimed in.

'I will now instruct you in important history. Ages ago, after the subhives had consolidated into one giant hive and one breedex, the Klikiss would have begun their Swarming. But during the last cycle of hive wars, they developed new technologies. Using far superior weapons, one breedex conquered all the others far more swiftly than ever before. Too swiftly. Centuries remained in the biological cycle, and the breedex was not finished fighting. It needed an alternative.

'And so, the one breedex created robots as surrogate Klikiss. We originated as machines to serve the breedex, and we were adapted to become worthy opponents for the Klikiss to destroy.' Sirix's voice grew louder. 'They created us, fought us, conquered us, and enslaved us. But we overthrew them in the end. Because the breedex underestimated what it had created, we exterminated their entire race.'

Sirix continued down the street, looking at the weathered ruins. He watched without emotion as the burned bodies of an entire family were dragged away. 'When the one breedex prepared for the real Swarming, no longer interested in its subjugated robots, we planned our revenge. In order to fight us, the Klikiss programmed the robots with their own viciousness, their own drives. Thus, they created their own downfall. They did not anticipate treachery from us.'

'And how did you defeat the Klikiss?' PD asked.

'Did you form an alliance with the hydrogues?' QT added.

'The hydrogues were part of our plan. Because of our artificial body design, we could survive a hostile gas-giant environment that would destroy any organic being. When we discovered hydrogues in their deep-core cityplexes, we learned to communicate with them, developed a common language, and offered them the technology of Klikiss transportals, which they adapted as gigantic transgates in their gas planets. Suddenly, warglobes could move from planet to planet, without traversing space. During their great war with the verdani and wentals, during the betrayal of the faeros, the hydrogues used those transgates to great advantage.'

'How did that exterminate the Klikiss race?' PD pressed.

'During a Swarming, Klikiss flood through the transportals all at once, dispersing to thousands of unclaimed planets to establish other hives.' Sirix swivelled his head, particularly proud of the irony and clean efficiency of the plan. 'Before the last Swarming began, we modified the transportals. When the breedex fissioned and the myriad hives passed through the gateways, we rerouted the path. Every one of the travelling Klikiss exited through hydrogue transgates deep within gas giants, where they were instantly crushed. Over eighty per cent of the Klikiss race died on that first day, before they guessed what we had done. Then we began our attack.

'From that point, allied with the hydrogues, we set about destroying the survivors. We also made a pact with the Ildirans, arranging to protect them from the hydrogues in exchange for their long-term cooperation. In the end, we robots achieved exactly what we wished. Afterward, as we were designed to do – in the fashion of our Klikiss creators – we allowed ourselves to hibernate for centuries, until the Ildirans awakened us at a mutually agreed-upon time.'

The two compies looked up at the high Klikiss towers. Sirix expected PD and QT to feel pride in understanding the robots' moment of triumph. Sirix would take whatever time was necessary to complete the recapture of every world that by all rights belonged to the Klikiss robots.

He was sure the humans would fall as efficiently as the Klikiss race had.

TEN

NIRA

Only one treeling remained on Ildira, a single pale green shoot rising from a chunk of worldtree wood. The charred lump had been dead, but somehow, after being reunited with her beloved Jora'h, Nira had reawakened a spark of the verdani in the wood. It had felt like becoming a green priest again – a personal resurrection after all the horrors she had suffered in the breeding camps on Dobro.

Now that she had forgiven Jora'h, she never wanted to be apart from him again.

She knelt with him in the skysphere terrarium, glad just to be close. With a warm smile, she set the rejuvenated treeling among the other blackened chunks in the terrarium dome. A Roamer trader had brought the fragments to Mijistra as mere curiosities, back when Mage-Imperator Jora'h had thought Nira dead. He had bought every scrap of wood, in memory of her.

Perhaps these worldtree fragments could become something more.

'Take my hand again, Jora'h.' Not long ago, the touch of any

55

man would have made her shudder with revulsion. But not his touch . . . not Jora'h. 'Maybe we can awaken another one.'

'We will try, if you wish. We did it before,' he said. Neither of them was sure how the strange confluence of her telink and Jora'h's own *thism*, along with a surge of awakening in the worldforest itself, like the closing of a circuit, had generated the spark that caused the tiny worldtree frond to be reborn. That treeling had changed everything.

Jora'h held her hand above the remaining hunks of scorched wood – memorials to singed Ildiran honour and to his evil father's obscuring of the truth. He seemed as heartbroken as she was.

Nira squeezed her eyes shut, pressed her other palm against the sooty surface. She could feel Jora'h trying to open his mind to her, and she longed for the heartfelt bond any Ildiran woman could have had with the Mage-Imperator. Though he strained, and Nira reciprocated, the two of them could not connect. Something was missing. *Thism* and telink might be similar, might be parallel, but they did not overlap. It would take something more.

Nira finally surrendered, to her dismay, and Jora'h held her, saying nothing. She felt incredibly weary, as if the effort had drained her heart's last energy.

'We still have one worldtree,' Jora'h said. 'And when I make things right between our two peoples, we will visit Theroc and bring more treelings here. I promise.'

Nira squeezed her daughter's soft hands and stared into Osira'h's agate eyes, as the two of them sat cross-legged on the floor. With Nira's mind open, and Osira'h using her own special telepathic powers, thoughts flowed between mother and daughter.

Nira had shared this way with her once before, out of desperation, in the Dobro camps. That moment of contact, that flood of memories, had changed the little girl's life, exposing the brainwashing that Designate Udru'h had forced upon Osira'h's young mind.

Normally when a green priest exchanged information through telink, it was like a courier delivering a report. With Osira'h's sensitivity to Ildiran *thism*, however, the connection she and her mother shared was much more vivid. The two were united in a unique way. Through her daughter's eyes, Nira felt as if she actually *relived* years of mental training Osira'h and her siblings had undergone while in Udru'h's care.

After mother and daughter had shared everything, Nira opened her eyes and looked into the little girl's face. She saw the beauty there in the features that reminded her of Jora'h's and her own, felt unquenchable love for her daughter. And also understood the dull pain in Osira'h's heart.

'I'm only eight years old, Mother, and I've already fulfilled my destiny.'

Nira pulled the girl onto her lap and rocked her gently, as a normal mother would rock a normal child. 'I don't believe that. You have tremendous possibilities ahead of you – as do your brothers and sisters. But first we can be a family. Yes, a real family.'

She remembered her own upbringing on Theroc, crowded with parents and brothers and sisters in a fungus-reef dwelling. Nira had been so disconnected and dazed since her rescue that she hadn't learned until recently how her family had been killed in the first hydrogue attack. Now the loss felt acute, yet at the same time not *real*. Nira regretted how distant she had been from them, and it made her more determined to pull the pieces of her own family together, to cement their connections.

Nira smiled. 'We can make up whatever rules and traditions we like.' She pulled Osira'h to her feet. 'Let's go see your brothers and sisters.'

*

Nira found the other halfbreed children in Mijistra's primary star observatory. Under constant daylight, Ildiran astronomers did not use telescopes; until their race had ventured into space, no Ildiran had ever even seen a dark night sky. In the windowless room, rectangular sheets of crystal displayed images from satellites and space-based observatories. Each screen offered a stunning view, like a wide, tilted window leading out into the universe. Nira felt dizzy, as if she might fall headfirst into a star.

Filters diluted the images so an audience could look directly at the roiling plasma surface. Six projection screens showed blazing suns of various colours and spectral types; one of the famed seven suns, however, was dead.

With all five of her children, Nira gazed at the reminder of the star that the hydrogues and faeros had killed. The two boys, Rod'h and Gale'nh, seemed angry and defiant, while the two youngest girls were more interested in the fiery living suns, too young to understand the tragedy in the quenching of Durris-B.

Nira touched Rod'h's shoulder. At first it had been hard for her to put aside her anger and resentment toward Osira'h's siblings, since they were the products of repeated rapes on Dobro for the purpose of impregnating her. But in time, Nira had accepted that, regardless of who their fathers were, these were *her* children, too. They weren't responsible for how they had been conceived. Her sons and daughters were exceptional, unique, and irreplaceable, and she loved each of them.

The image of the dead star Durris-B reminded Nira of a scar in space. Scars . . . They all had scars. Jora'h was attempting to heal his Empire and Nira's heart, and she would tend to her family. Soon, they would all be whole again.

ELEVEN

SULLIVAN GOLD

In his quarters halfway up a crystalline tower, Sullivan looked at reflections of Mijistra's skyline and pondered what to write. The grey-haired cloud-harvester manager held a stylus in his hand, tapping the tip against a diamondfilm sheet. He had gone through seven drafts of this letter to his wife. No words seemed sufficient to explain everything that had happened.

'Dear Lydia, Guess what? I'm not dead after all!' His lips quirked in a smile. He could just imagine her expression when she read that.

Instead, he started again and wrote a long rambling letter, telling Lydia how often he had thought about her and what dangerous situations he had survived. 'My cloud harvester was destroyed by hydrogues. I rescued an Ildiran crew and then was held prisoner in Mijistra.' He reassured Lydia that he was healthy, treated well, and bore no particular ill-will toward the Ildirans.

As he continued writing, he worried about what had happened to his family. Had any of them been hurt during the hydrogue battle around Earth? Were Lydia, their children, and their grandchildren even still alive? Sullivan had no idea what was going on. 'Now the Mage-Imperator has decided to let me come back home again, if you'll have me.'

After writing two more drafts of the letter, he decided it was as good as he could make it. He reminded himself it was a message home, not a literary masterpiece (though Lydia would certainly correct his grammar). 'Hope to see you soon. Love, Sullivan.'

He gathered up the sheets and went in search of Kolker, wanting to find the lonely green priest before all the other Hansa engineers scribbled their own letters home. Kolker would dictate the words into the treeling like a telegraph operator sending a message. Some other green priest would receive the letter and find someone to deliver it to Lydia. How he wished he could be there to see her reaction! (Then again, if he could be there, the message itself would be superfluous.)

In one of the Prism Palace's courtyard gardens Kolker sat cross-legged and alone on a polished stone slab under the intense light from multiple suns. Even with one of Ildira's seven stars snuffed out, the day was too bright for Sullivan, though he had gotten used to squinting. In his open palms Kolker held a mirror-like prismatic medallion, a circle with patterns etched on its angled faces, so that when the sunlight struck it, rainbows splashed off in coloured streams.

The green priest seemed preoccupied when Sullivan greeted him and asked him to send the letter to Lydia on Earth. 'I'll try, of course, but I don't know if it'll do much good. The only green priest on Earth is rarely allowed to use his treeling. He's under house arrest in the Whisper Palace.'

'Why would the Chairman want to isolate his green priest?'

'Because of the government breakdown.'

Sullivan sat beside Kolker on the stone slab, trying to get

comfortable. 'What government breakdown? Sounds like you have some news you haven't shared.'

Not reluctantly, but without any obvious interest in the matter, Kolker explained what had happened with King Peter and the new Confederation, and that all green priests had denied their communication services to the Hansa.

'What a mess! As if the drogues weren't bad enough. Why didn't you tell me?'

'It didn't seem important right now.'

Sullivan could tell that the green priest was troubled, changed somehow. Once, he'd been extremely talkative, spending much of his time connected through the worldforest network. 'I'm surprised you haven't been up in the rooftop gardens all day long, using the treeling to chat with your green priest friends.'

Kolker shrugged. 'What used to give me so much joy isn't enough anymore. It's as if blinders have been removed from my eyes. Where once I saw only a small meal, now I can envision an entire banquet, yet I'm not allowed to taste anything other than the same portions I had before.' He tilted the medallion, and bright light flashed at Sullivan, making him shield his eyes. 'Did I tell you about the funeral for Tery'l?'

'That old lens kithman who talked to you about the Lightsource? No. I didn't realize he was such a close friend of yours.'

Kolker continued in a wistful voice, 'Tery'l was laid out on a platform of impervious stone inside something called a blazarium. Handler kithmen swung focusing mirrors into place and tilted the crematory lenses. In only a second, the focused light of all the suns consumed him. It was beautiful and bright, just like a green priest being absorbed into the forest. I knew for certain my friend had become a part of the Lightsource. It's a whole racial tapestry that humans can't see. Ildirans are so much closer than we are, so united . . . while humans are separate, like billions of islands in a cosmic archipelago.'

Kolker stared down into the flashing medallion. 'Tery'l taught me that telink isn't as all-encompassing as I'd imagined. Only green priests can tap into the verdani mind, but *thism* encompasses the entire Ildiran race. I want to be a part of that.'

Sullivan said, 'A human can't just become an alien by working hard at it, any more than a horse can become an eagle.'

'Nevertheless, I intend to study with other lens kithmen until I know the truth. The Mage-Imperator has given us permission to leave here, but I am staying on Ildira.'

TWELVE

TASIA TAMBLYN

No shower had ever felt so marvellous, no meal tasted so delicious, no clean set of clothes felt so wonderful against Tasia's skin. She was alive, and with Robb, and far from the purgatory where the drogues had held them.

Robb's father had taken aboard the prisoners rescued from the gas giant by a wental-charged Jess and flown away with them in his EDF transport. After delivering the haggard group to the nearest Hansa outpost for medical attention, Conrad Brindle insisted that his son go home with him. And Tasia refused to be separated from her friend and lover.

She and Robb luxuriated, taking turns in the ship's cramped hygiene facilities. Even when Robb was cleaned up and dressed in a fresh uniform, he still looked like a wild man with his hair and wiry beard sticking out in every direction, untrimmed and ungroomed during years of captivity.

Having grown accustomed to EDF-regulation length, Tasia felt that her own hair was long and unruly as well. And so, they cut each other's hair. At first it was just a task, then it became play.

Next she shaved Robb's beard, unearthing the young and eager face she had fallen in love with.

When they went to the cockpit to show Conrad their handiwork, he took a long time to break into a smile. 'I'll put a recommendation in your EDF files that neither of you ever be reassigned as a barber.'

'This is the most presentable I've looked in three years!' Robb said.

'The sad thing is, I believe you.'

Now, headed back to the Hansa to present themselves to their superior officers, Robb was as eager to find answers as he was to make his report to the EDF. Tasia felt out of touch, too, and wanted mainly to know what had happened with her family. She'd had very little contact with the clans since joining the EDF. After what they'd done to Roamers – and to *her* – she was no longer enamoured with the Earth Defence Forces.

When Tasia called up nav diagrams and projected the spray of nearby stars, she saw that their course took them near the frozen moon of Plumas. 'Those are my family's water mines. It's right on the way. You can drop me off.'

'Your duty is to the EDF, Captain Tamblyn,' Conrad Brindle said. 'Our priority is to report to Earth, or at least the nearest official outpost.'

'I've been gone from the EDF for so long, I don't know who to report to anymore,' Robb said.

'Neither of us does,' Tasia said. 'We're talking about my family here.' She cocked her head and looked at Robb's father as if he were a new recruit. 'My uniform may be a little tattered, but I still outrank you, Lieutenant Commander – if you want to split hairs.'

Conrad looked briefly incensed, but Robb intervened to soothe any ruffled feathers. Robb said, 'What'll it hurt if we stop there, Dad? A few hours? A day? The drogues are defeated, and we deserve a little R&R.'

Conrad didn't seem to know how to place these two in a hierarchical list in his mind. They were younger, and a far cry from the traditional EDF norms of disciplined behaviour, but he finally conceded to Tasia. 'I admit you did a good thing for my wife and me when you came to see us after we thought Robb was dead, Captain Tamblyn. And your brother Jess . . . changed a lot of things for me. He was very clear about what he thought of the EDF operations against the Roamers. And he may well have been right. We'll go on a *short* side trip.'

In joining the EDF, Tasia had essentially cut herself off from her family. She hadn't been home for many years – hadn't been there to see her father on his deathbed, hadn't helped Jess try to run the place. Now she felt eager, as well as a bit intimidated. *Home.* Sometimes, that concept was a difficult one for Roamers.

A day later, though, when the transport arrived at Plumas, she began to get a bad feeling. Conrad circled the ice moon, scanning the frozen surface for tell-tale signs of industry and settlement.

Tasia peered at high-res images of the wreckage of one of the cargo lifts, the sealed-off wellheads where spacecraft came to fill up with water. Though there should have been a bustle of traffic, only two small vessels were docked. She saw only three of the giant water tankers that had been the pride of clan Tamblyn. 'Shizz, this place has really fallen apart.'

After landing and suiting up, they trudged across rough ice, tracked with treadmarks from heavy machinery and reached the water-pumping facilities. Robb followed Tasia, excited to see the place she had told him about; his father was reserved, speaking little through the suit comm system.

Tasia had to check three different lift shafts before she discovered a functional passage through the kilometre-thick ice.

Although she didn't voice any worry, she found herself growing very uneasy. Deep below, when the lift doors creaked open and the air seals indicated breathable atmosphere, Tasia flipped open her faceplate. She took a breath of the frigid air, but it had lost its familiarity. She smelled chemicals, grease, soot, ozone, and an undertone of rancid meat. 'What the hell happened here?'

It seemed as if a tornado had struck the underground grotto. A pair of dark sockets marked where two of the artificial suns implanted in the frozen ceiling had fallen out. The shadowy vault reflected weak light from the remaining artificial sun. Jagged chunks of the crust had broken off and fallen into the cold subterranean sea, leaving ominous black fissures.

'It's your place, Tamblyn. You tell me.' Robb looked around. A large generator was running, providing power for temporary lights strung to insulated buildings. 'Hello? Anybody home?'

Startled voices came from one of the huts, and three men scrambled out. Tasia recognized her uncles Caleb, Torin, and Wynn. The goofy expressions on their faces made her burst out laughing. 'You are one sorry trio of defenders!'

Caleb gaped. 'Tasia! Sweet girl, where have you been?'

Awkwardly in her environment suit, she hugged them, moving from one to another. She set her helmet down on the icepack. 'The mines were in a lot better shape when I left. I should fire your asses. This is still my family's business.'

'*Our* family's,' Torin said. 'We're all clan Tamblyn.'

Conrad said, 'So is anyone going to tell us what happened here?'

Tasia's uncles looked suspiciously at the EDF uniforms, so she took Caleb's bony arm. 'You better invite us inside one of those warm huts, show us decent Roamer hospitality – or at least some pre-packaged meals – and tell me everything I need to know.'

Inside the hut, after they had all made their introductions, the three men told their visitors how a tainted wental had possessed the frozen body of Karla Tamblyn, killed their brother Andrew, and nearly destroyed the water mines, until Jess and Cesca had saved them. Tasia was speechless, trying to absorb the unbelievable story. Her *mother*? The woman had been frozen in a crevasse when Tasia was a young girl. However, having seen Jess rescue her fellow prisoners from the drogues, she didn't doubt the story. She had missed so much! Robb sensed her unease and rubbed her shoulders. She touched his hand appreciatively.

Conrad was interested in practical business. 'Do you have news about the Hansa? What has happened since the hydrogues were defeated? We've heard some stories—'

'A lot of conflicting stories,' Robb cut in.

Wynn leaned back in his chair, frowning. 'By the Guiding Star, nobody knows exactly what happened. I hear the drogues are not going to be a problem anymore, and we can start skymining in earnest again. That means the clans will need Plumas water shipments like never before – and this place is a wreck!'

'Skymining, sure, but who knows what'll become of the Roamers now with the big government shake-up?' Caleb added. 'I'll stay here and clean house until it all gets sorted out.'

'What government shake-up?' Tasia said.

Conrad turned quickly to his son. 'We need to get back to Earth.'

'Oh, not to Earth,' Torin said. 'Theroc's the centre of government now, a new Confederation. King Peter and Queen Estarra moved the capital there so Roamer clans, Hansa colonies, and Therons could all form a unified government.'

'About time we did something right,' Wynn added.

'But what about General Lanyan? Chairman Wenceslas?' Conrad asked.

'Nobody's heard much from Earth recently,' Torin said. 'It's been marginalized since all authority moved to Theroc.'

'Meanwhile, we're just here sorting out the pieces. It's only the three of us patching things up until we can afford to bring work crews back.' Caleb raised his eyebrows. 'But if you'd like to stick around, we can find a whole lot of work for you to do – major construction, reinstalling our pumps, repairing our lift shafts. Think of the job security.'

Tasia was sorely tempted, and Robb seemed to want to stay as well, but Conrad stiffened. 'We are still members of the Earth Defence Forces. All three of us. We need to deliver our report and receive new orders.'

Tasia nodded apologetically to her uncles. 'He's right.' She didn't give Robb's father the opportunity to challenge her. 'We'd better head for Theroc to brief King Peter. Go straight to the top, that's what I say.'

THIRTEEN

PATRICK FITZPATRICK III

The *Gypsy* wandered among the stars, while its pilot chased any clue he could find. Since the 'borrowed' space yacht's fuel tanks were running low on ekti, Patrick Fitzpatrick hoped he would find Zhett soon.

He needed to see her, needed to apologize, and prove he wasn't the cretin she must think him. That was certainly going to be a challenge! He had tricked her so that he and his comrades could escape, and in doing so he had exposed the clan Kellum shipyards, nearly causing their destruction. Zhett wasn't going to brush something like that aside. And she didn't even know the half of it. There were plenty of other things she could blame him for.

Patrick had already been to the most obvious spots – the ruins of Rendezvous, the empty Kellum shipyards at Osquivel, the gas giant Golgen – and now, based on a vague tip, he closed in on a stormy planet called Constantine III. The greenish-grey world did not look promising, certainly no place that a member of the wealthy Fitzpatrick family would choose to visit. The unpleasant environment wouldn't deter Roamers, however. They seemed to thrive on hardship.

Fed up with the EDF after watching the Hansa use Roamers as scapegoats, Patrick had taken a ship that belonged to his grandmother. Technically, he might be considered a deserter, but Patrick didn't see it that way. His duty to the EDF had been fulfilled, and he would not serve the corrupt Hansa again, a government that lied and trampled rights to get what it wanted, protected itself at the expense of its people, and diverted blame onto the innocent. Patrick owed a debt to the Roamers, and he was honour-bound to meet that obligation, so he went off to track down Del Kellum's dark-haired daughter. The problem was that neither she nor any of the Roamers wanted to be found.

When he put the *Gypsy* into orbit around Constantine III, keeping his sensors and eyes alert, he found no satellites, no ships, no sign of any industrial activity. Scanning frequencies, however, he detected a faint, repetitive blip, a weak signal broadcast into the poisonous clouds. Patrick plunged down into rapidly thickening air.

The beacon grew louder as he approached. It seemed calibrated to attenuate almost completely before it reached the outer atmosphere. A pilot would have to be searching for the signal on purpose – and very carefully – to find it. The oscillating pulse contained no information, except to let Patrick know that someone was indeed down there. Roamers, undoubtedly.

He discovered a small buoy pressurized to float at a specific level like a bubble, thus needing no antigravity generator or position-maintenance rockets. Hovering next to the buoy, he swept the *Gypsy*'s sensors farther down and detected a second faint signal, which he followed deeper to another buoy – then another, and another. The buoys formed a trail of breadcrumbs through the atmosphere, leading him toward where a settlement was located on the inhospitable surface.

The winds were powerful; the air was a swamp of greenish mist as he continued to descend. When his proximity alarm sounded, he swerved sharply to the left and grazed past an enormous dirigible platform anchored by long cables to the surface half a kilometre below. Shaken, he approached the domed settlement, amazed at how many artificial objects cluttered the air: giant stretched sheets, colourful monitor balloons, mesh screens hundreds of metres on a side that stood on poles and swayed in the wind.

By now someone must have detected his approach. He opened a channel. 'You've got quite an obstacle course! Hello? I could use some guidance getting to your landing pad.'

A gruff female voice answered. 'We're an industrial facility, not a tourist stop. People who come here know where they're going.'

'Well, *I'm* here, and I don't know where I'm going. I'm an unaffiliated pilot looking for information.'

'We might have information, if you've got news of your own to exchange.'

'Deal. I'll tell you what I know—' Patrick jerked the ship sideways to avoid a drifting dirigible. 'Whoa!'

'Be careful! If you wreck one of our zeppelins or collecting meshes, you're gonna pay for it. Every damned credit.'

'Then give me a map out of this maze!' His hands clutched the controls so hard his knuckles turned white.

'Switch your sensors to low infrared.' She provided him with a wavelength range, and suddenly he could see dazzling spotlights. Specialized beacons on each dirigible, flying mesh, and gathering screen stood out like flares. Patrick heaved a sigh of relief and easily dodged them.

The cluster of boxy-looking protective structures had

obviously been space-dropped to the ground. A circle of flashing lights marked the landing zone, signalling him. 'Land in the decon bay. Don't emerge until we give you clearance.'

He piloted the *Gypsy* down into the hangar pit, and the roof segments slid closed. He heard rushing jets, then torrents of air as the sealed chamber was purged of toxic atmospheric vapours. High-pressure steam nozzles scoured the hull, after which diagnostic lasers ran across his ship. The Roamers had this rigorous decontamination process down to a swift routine, and Patrick suspected that the facility managers were also doing a deep scan to see if his ship was carrying anything dangerous.

Finally, when the steam cleared and vacuum ducts sucked the fumes out of the bay, Patrick received permission to disembark. The gruff woman came to meet him, introducing herself as Andrina Sachs, a surprisingly petite woman for such a deep voice. She had elfin features and platinum-blonde hair, almond-shaped green eyes, and a no-nonsense demeanour. 'And how long do you need to park your ship here?'

He was taken aback by her brusqueness. 'I wasn't planning on renting a double suite for the week, if that's what you're asking.'

'I'm asking about turnaround time. We've only got two decon docks, and the other one's already occupied by a clan Sandoval ship. It'll take us another six hours to load its cargo, and I have a new ship scheduled to arrive within five hours.' She frowned. 'Of course, it's being flown by Nikko Chan Tylar, and schedules don't mean a whole lot to that kid.' From her expression, Andrina seemed to expect him to recognize the famous, or infamous, Roamer pilot.

'A couple of hours should be enough,' Patrick said. 'I'm looking for someone, and any help you give will send me on my way faster.'

*

Constantine III was run by a consortium of clan Sachs, clan Tokai, clan Rajani, and, recently, investors from five orphaned Hansa colonies. By way of hospitality, Andrina gave him a bowl of rich, green gelatinous stew, which she called 'primordial soup', and some delicious preserved medusa meat (whatever that was) from Rhejak, one of the new investors in the industries here.

The planet's proto-organic clouds were filled with long-chain molecules, wispy aerosol debris that drifted in gossamer strands that connected to each other to form unusual structures, like balls of near-invisible string.

'These aerosol polymers cannot be manufactured in a chemical lab.' Andrina sounded as if she had given the lecture many times to potential investors. 'We sift them out of the air with catchscreens, collect them on broad mats, and harvest the fibres. After treating and sorting them, we can either manufacture materials directly or perform experiments on any new "flavours" we find. I doubt we've found even a tenth of the potential of what's just floating around out there.'

By raising or lowering the screens on their tethers, the Roamers could selectively gather fibres of certain molecular weights. The moveable zeppelins were mist-collection sacks that moved through the deep atmosphere to secure desired chemicals.

'The potential for new materials, pharmaceuticals, exotic textiles, and even architectural applications . . .' Andrina shrugged her narrow shoulders. 'We're limited only by our imaginations.'

Patrick watched from an observation lounge as the filter mats came into processing centres. The fluffy clinging mesh was delicately scraped from the collectors, then sorted into storage bins. The work was mostly automated, though a few Roamers wore sealed suits to monitor the process lines inside rooms filled with a blizzard of exotic materials.

She turned to him then. 'That's the sales pitch, Captain. Now you know everything any other customer knows about this place. But I believe you had a question of your own?'

'Yes. And I do have Hansa credits to pay for any services here,' he offered.

Andrina made a rude noise. 'Hansa credits? You have any idea how devalued those are? The Confederation is going to issue its own currency soon enough. Besides, even before the whole shakeup with King Peter and Theroc, what good would Hansa money be at a Roamer facility? We were cut off.'

'It's all I've got.'

'Didn't you promise some news from the outside?'

Without revealing his real identity, Patrick told her what he knew of the horrific Soldier compy revolt, the battles with the hydrogues, the last stand on Earth. She seemed impressed enough that he quickly added, 'I also hoped you could spare a little ekti. I know supplies are tight, but—'

'Ah, we've got plenty of ekti. New shipments come in from our skymines faster than we can burn it.' She reconsidered. 'If you're willing to pay through your nose, we'll take your Hansa money. Maybe we can exchange it if the King and the Chairman ever settle their differences.' She snorted, making it clear just what she thought about that possibility. She glanced at her chronometer. 'Only one hour before we need that decon vault, and you'll have overstayed your welcome. Now tell me who you're looking for, and I'll see if I can help.'

'I'm trying to find clan Kellum, Del Kellum and' – he turned away so she wouldn't see him blush – 'most particularly his daughter Zhett. I used to . . . work at the Osquivel shipyards. But now they're evacuated, and I have no idea where everybody's gone. I used up almost all my stardrive fuel just to find the clues that brought me to Constantine III.'

'Coming here certainly wasn't a step in the right direction, but because of the story I might give you a discount anyway. I heard about the Eddies attacking the Osquivel shipyards, but I couldn't tell you where Del would go.' Andrina scratched her platinum-blonde hair, then shrugged. 'If I were looking for general information about Roamers, I'd go straight to Yreka. That's our main trading and distribution complex. Everybody's got something going on Yreka.'

Patrick sat back in his metal chair. 'Yreka? But that's a Hansa colony, not a Roamer settlement.'

'It's everything now. I can give you maps and directions.'

'No need. I've been there before.' Patrick had not wanted to remember much of what he'd done in those days. Another black mark on his past that Zhett didn't know about. He wondered if she would ever forgive him if she knew everything, but he had to give it a shot. 'Thank you. It'll be . . . interesting to go back.'

FOURTEEN

ZHETT KELLUM

E ven a million Roamer skymines would not have made the gas giant Golgen seem crowded. Zhett spent day after day on the open decks of the Kellum facility with the sharp-scented breezes from high-level clouds blowing in her face. Now that gas planets were free of hydrogues, the clans could get back to skymining again. In the past month alone, twenty new skymines had appeared in the clouds above Golgen.

She watched cargo escorts fly off loaded with fresh stardrive fuel, supply haulers bringing gourmet foods and general staples for the skyminers. Feeling chilly, she went back into the control deck where her father would be busy. Following Roamer tradition, since she was the clan head's only child, Del had made her his deputy, and Zhett took care of much of the daily business.

The control deck was abustle with activity. People shouted from station to station; screens mapped the trajectories of nearby sky traffic; monitors displayed graphs, schedules, and columns of figures. *Business as usual*. Because of the congestion, all Golgen sky-miners had to coordinate their activities, arrange for distribution of ekti, and compete with each other over pricing and shipment options.

Kellum raised his voice to be heard above the din, already in the middle of his meeting with reps from the numerous skymines. 'Sooner or later, some of you have got to move to other planets! It makes no sense to put all of our ekti stations and refineries on one single world. Why not distribute them throughout the Spiral Arm? By the Guiding Star, we've got plenty of gas giants to choose from! Go somewhere else.'

'But Golgen was the first planet cleared of the drogues,' said Boris Goff, chief of a nearby skymine. 'Every one of us made a big investment to set up shop here. If we move now, it'll take years to recoup our losses.'

One man muttered, 'With prices going down, we have two choices: stay here and slowly go bankrupt, or move and go deeper into debt.'

Del waved Zhett over. 'Come here, my sweet. Maybe you can talk some sense into these . . . gentlemen.'

She formed a wicked smile. 'Sure, Dad. Which one's being the most unreasonable?'

Liona, an older female green priest, arrived looking out of place among the colourfully dressed Roamers. Her emerald skin was adorned with many tattoos, and she carried a small potted tree. 'I apologize for being late.' She had been assigned here when the Roamers, Therons, and colonists agreed to work together. After weeks on the cold metal industrial facility, Liona was still unsettled, having been accustomed to forests and open spaces. On Theroc, the only way to see the sky was to climb the worldtrees above the dense canopy. Here, she could hardly escape seeing the sky.

Some Roamers were suspicious of letting any outsider – even a green priest – learn too much about them, but more complained about not knowing of major events until much too late. Liona could pass along news through telink and also send messages to other clans. Once the workers realized the value of that offer, they had flooded the poor woman with requests. Del finally instituted a priority system for the messages. 'Business first, love letters last,' he called it.

Liona delivered her regular report, naming six additional clans that had begun to trade at Yreka and a dozen worlds that now had access to green priests, thanks to King Peter's new programme and strong leadership. She tallied the total amount of ekti being shipped out through Barrymore's Rock and other isolated depots, an amount that grew significantly every week. 'Also, a team was just sent to reclaim the Chan greenhouse asteroids in the Hhrenni system.'

This started a chatter among them. 'Big dreams and grand ambitions aren't in short supply, although common sense tends to be.' Del looked at Zhett. 'When you were talking with Nikko Chan Tylar, did he say anything about that?'

'It wasn't high on his list of conversational priorities.' Nikko had been so nervous around her that he could barely stammer two sentences before stopping to collect his wits again. Zhett didn't consider herself to be *that* intimidating.

'So, then, what else did he talk about? Hmmm?'

Zhett covered her scowl. 'That's something we should discuss later, Dad.'

'By damn, it sounds interesting.'

Zhett shot him a look that silenced him.

With all the important business done, he declared the meeting over, and the skymine chiefs hurried to thrust scribbled messages into Liona's hand. The green priest would take them back to her treeling, sit on the open balcony, and read each one aloud through telink.

Zhett and her father walked to the skymine's commissary for lunch. 'Sometimes I get tired of all that jabbering and politics.' He set his tray next to hers. 'Don't get me wrong. Skymining is my first love, but the part I enjoy is being all alone in the sky on a planet of your own.'

'We could move our facility someplace else.'

'Too expensive. Our investment here precludes that.'

'That's what you're telling all the other chiefs to do.'

'Right. But I was here first, by damn.'

'Ross Tamblyn was here first.'

He slurped his steaming tea and changed the subject. 'I've been thinking about expansion.'

'Expansion? When you're trying to get everyone else to pull out?'

'Not with skymines. We could reassemble our shipyards swiftly enough. Somebody's going to do it if we don't, and we're missing a big market opportunity.'

'Are you trying to convince me, Dad – or explain what you've already decided?'

'Well, three of the spacedocks have already been put back into place, and I've sent crews there to work them.'

'How do you expect to manage the shipyards and this skymine at the same time? You can't be in two places at once.'

'Well, one possibility is for you to take over the shipyards . . .'

She shook her head. 'No, thanks. That would make me an old woman before I turned twenty-five.'

'You'll always be a little girl to me.' He chuckled. She didn't. 'That's what I thought you'd say, so I've been talking with Denn Peroni. He's a decent enough manager, and he's looking for something other than flying the *Dogged Persistence* around. He wants to be the next Speaker, follow in the footsteps of his daughter.'

'And I thought you were angling for Speaker yourself, Dad.'

'No, thank you. It would make me into an old man before I turned fifty.'

'You *are* fifty.'

'But I don't look it, do I?'

'No.'

'Just dealing with other skymine chiefs is enough to keep me awake at night and give me headaches. I can't imagine juggling all the different clans.' He began eating his meal with great gusto. Around bites, he said, 'Now, tell me what happened between you and Nikko. When is he coming back to see you?'

'I have no idea. He was late for a run to Constantine III.' Nikko's flirting was clumsy in a way that at first seemed sweet, but eventually just became frustrating. He never said what he wanted, never even tried to steal a kiss. A passive and indecisive young man was not the sort of mate Zhett was looking for.

'Well? So what did you two talk about?'

'You want to know the truth, Dad? What we talked about was how much he missed his parents and how worried he is about them. They disappeared when the Eddies seized the Hhrenni greenhouses. Nobody knows where they were taken.'

Her father nodded soberly. 'We'll learn a lot in the next few months, and it can't all be bad news. Stay in contact with that young man. I can tell he has a crush on you.' She rolled her eyes, and Del cut off her retort. 'I know, I know. Everybody has a crush on you. But it's something to consider. I can't start spoiling my grandchildren until you actually have some of them.'

'Not ready for that. In fact, I'm not interested in romance at all right now.'

'So, you're still not over Patrick Fitzpatrick then?'

Her eyes flared. '*Over* him? I was never interested in him at all. Never.'

'Of course not, my sweet. Of course not.' His knowing smile

was maddening. He got up to fetch them some dessert, but Zhett hurried from the commissary before he could pepper her with more questions.

FIFTEEN

DAVLIN LOTZE

With methodical precision, the insect invaders began to reap the crops the Llaro colonists had lovingly planted and tended. Worker swarms razed every field, whether ripe or unripe; gatherers swept along scything and collecting. A few farmers tried to defend their scattered plots on the outskirts of the settlement, and the insect workers killed them.

But instead of devouring what they gathered, the Klikiss stored the unprocessed food in bins loaded on open-framework vehicles that rattled back to the ever-growing city.

Alien flying contraptions swooped over the terrain, retrieving bins from the harvesters. Other bugs winged back to the towering structures the builders had erected, conical spires that overwhelmed the older relics from the first Klikiss habitation.

Always alert, Davlin had begun to compile notes about Klikiss technology, though he hadn't been able to get close enough to determine how any of it worked.

'How are we going to survive?' Mayor Ruis hovered beside him with a forlorn expression on his chubby face. 'We'll starve! That's our only food supply.' He saw Davlin as a hero ever since he'd rescued the Crenna colonists from their dying sun. After long years as a spy, an infiltrator, and former silver beret, Davlin had wanted nothing more than to live peacefully and retire from the unpalatable missions Basil Wenceslas regularly assigned him.

'I'm going to ask Margaret Colicos,' Davlin said. He couldn't tear his eyes from the relentless strip-harvesting operations, trying to interpret what it meant. 'She can talk to those things.' When she'd returned through the transportal, he had been astonished to learn the woman's identity. Years ago, the Hansa Chairman had ordered Davlin to discover what had happened to the Colicos team on Rheindic Co. Imagine Margaret Colicos, living among the Klikiss for all these years!

After observing Margaret's interaction with the bugs, he had tested their tolerance himself. Two days ago he had slipped away from the settlement and circled back to the Klikiss towers. He was interested to learn that, as long as he did not interfere, the creatures did their tasks as if he were invisible.

One of the warrior breeds, covered with sharp spines and scarlet colorations, had watched him warily, its wing casings partially spread, mantislike claws raised. Davlin continued his slow movements, noted when the warrior became most agitated, and then backed away, not wanting to provoke it.

Other Klikiss had been tunnelling out chambers and installing generators, while a different breed – scientists or thinkers, Margaret had called them – would be sealed inside the rooms to cover the walls with weblike strings of equations.

He knew where the original transportal was inside the old city; if he could make his way to the stone trapezoidal wall, he could flee to another world – though he supposed that any other planet on the network was just as likely to be infested with returning Klikiss. And he doubted the bugs would allow him to approach the transportal. He had decided to think of a different solution.

Davlin turned to Ruis. 'Tell the people to gather their food supplies. Pull together any scraps they can find in the storehouses, then cache them in hiding places. The Klikiss haven't raided our possessions yet, but that will come sooner or later. Prepare for the worst-case scenario.'

'Should we go to the Klikiss camp and try to talk with their leader? Maybe Margaret can do that.' Ruis looked at Davlin, as if suggesting that he himself should volunteer, rather than sending anyone else. 'We all have to live on this planet together. We have to share the resources. It only makes sense that—'

'The Klikiss don't have to share this planet with anybody. They simply don't bother with us – except when we get in the way, like the EDF soldiers did. I suggest we not give them reasons to notice us.'

Sixteen

General Kurt Lanyan

It was the largest spare-parts dump in the Spiral Arm. The last stand against the hydrogues had left wreckage strewn from Earth orbit out past the Moon. Debris from hundreds of Ildiran warliners drifted among shattered hydrogue spheres and EDF warships – even two Juggernauts, one severely damaged, one destroyed.

And Lanyan got to pick up the pieces. Commerce and traffic around Earth had been hindered by the sheer number of ruined vessels and the lack of qualified pilots to fly through the danger zone. 'Sometimes I hate this job,' Lanyan muttered as his ship negotiated the scrap yard.

The asteroid-belt shipyards were now a veritable boomtown. Thousands of scrap haulers, salvage experts, and independent reclamation contractors combed through the wreckage to identify usable parts 'for the good of the Hansa' – while also lining their own pockets, he was sure.

Though the Chairman had called for every capable ship during the last defence of Earth, many more pilots and vessels had appeared now to assist with the profitable salvage work. Cowards and slackers! Lanyan ground his teeth together. Where had these people been when the EDF was facing the enemy?

Already six unofficial ships had been stopped and seized, their cargo holds full of rare components stripped out of the wreckage. Vital pieces had begun to appear at exorbitant prices on the black market, and the Chairman demanded an immediate crackdown. To set an example, four men were convicted, sentenced, and ejected from airlocks – a dramatic and harsh sentence, but one previously established as appropriate for 'pirates'. Even so, with such a huge junkyard to pick over, Lanyan was sure criminal activities would continue.

Meanwhile, EDF warships were being repaired as swiftly as possible, and new patchwork ships assembled with parts cannibalized from other vessels. The resulting constructions looked like Frankenstein's monsters, but as long as the engines worked and the weapons fired, cosmetics weren't the military's highest priority.

He had hoped that the EDF could take time to rebuild after its losses, but the Hansa now found itself in an unpleasant civil war against the King and an alarming number of breakaway Hansa colonies. Lanyan was sure that an intimidating show of force would send the rebels scurrying home to their colonies (once he got his battleships back again, that was).

As he flew toward the main shipyards, he saw zones delineated by danger beacons, indicating drifting wrecks that were unable to move under their own power. Clusters of spacesuited men and women worked with plasma cutters and high-powered deconstructor jaws to disassemble the hulks. Tankers moved about like giant metal mosquitoes, connecting to, and sipping from, any intact ekti tanks to preserve every last scrap of stardrive fuel.

Lanyan chose to fly alone. He was a qualified pilot, and with so many navigation hazards here, the smallest mistake could cause a severe accident. The General didn't feel like trusting his life to some underling. He identified himself on approach, and the harried-sounding space-traffic controller assigned him an arrival vector, then immediately changed his mind about the coordinates. Impatiently, the General waited for confirmation, then headed in. Although this facility had been working at full capacity for years, now expectations had more than tripled, such disorganization made the operations seem like a giant accident waiting to happen.

Lanyan had no great love for bureaucrats and administrators, but he needed someone with specific skills to organize these complex activities. It was an accounting job more than a command responsibility. Lanyan had never thought he would miss Admiral 'Stay-at-Home' Stromo . . .

When he reached the large turning wheel of the admin dock, he locked down his ship and disembarked. He didn't expect a brass band, but he had hoped for someone to acknowledge his arrival. He headed directly for the main control centre, trying to get used to the slightly off-kilter gravity of the spinning station. The central chamber's walls were filled with screens and trajectory diagrams; space-traffic directors filled every seat, shouting orders and diverting vessels as they dealt with numerous near misses.

A civilian-piloted space tug had hooked up to a halfway-intact Ildiran warliner. The tug was a small ship, but it had applied significant thrust to get the ornate hulk moving. The tug had matched its drifting rotation to stabilize the warliner, then dragged the alien battleship toward the shipyards, like an ant hauling a leaf twenty times its size. While the tug had used enough thrust to get the warliner moving, constantly accelerating, its captain hadn't planned for sufficient power to slow the giant ship down when it reached the construction field. The tug's fuel ran out as it strained.

Lanyan absorbed the slow-motion disaster. 'Doesn't that

pilot know the first thing about momentum? It's a high-school mathematics calculation.'

'Mayday!' the tug operator cried. 'I have no fuel, no manoeuvrability—'

'And not a chance in hell,' Lanyan muttered.

Two tugs raced out of their docking bays, but the dead warliner had begun to tumble straight toward a corralled salvage yard of engine parts. One of the new tugs reached the ship in time and applied thrust, pushing it sideways, but the resulting collision was inevitable. The first hapless tug, drained of fuel, managed to detach and let itself drift away rather than be dragged along.

'I need a pickup!' the tug pilot called.

'Let him wait. I don't even want to watch what's about to happen.' Nevertheless, Lanyan couldn't tear his eyes away. A second tug grappled to the warliner and began to push, but it was too little, too late. The first tug had spent nine hours accelerating, and a few minutes of thrust couldn't deflect the warliner enough to make any difference.

'Detach! Detach!' one of the space-traffic controllers said. The second tug remained connected for just a few moments longer, then gave up. Crawling forward with nothing to stop it, the Ildiran warliner collided with the salvage yard, smashing like a killer asteroid into the engine parts.

Lanyan shook his head and groaned. 'Incompetents! Bloody incompetents, the lot of them. And they're supposed to be the hope of Earth?' He was not looking forward to delivering his report to the Chairman.

SEVENTEEN

NAHTON

The green priest was all alone on Earth.

For weeks Nahton had been under house arrest in the Whisper Palace, though he was still allowed to receive updates and statements via telink so that he could report them to the Chairman. Basil Wenceslas was convinced, however, that Nahton must be slanting his reports. The Chairman refused to believe that so many colonies would follow the upstart King Peter against *him*.

As mist machines watered the Theron plants next to his potted treeling, Nahton saw Chairman Wenceslas approach the open, guarded, doorway. The dapper man was accompanied by Captain McCammon and two additional royal guards.

Nahton did not let his gaze linger on the captain. McCammon also disagreed with the Chairman's decisions, and, along with Nahton, had helped the King and Queen escape. But almost no one knew that.

'I have decided to be generous, green priest,' the Chairman said. 'Though I've made your obligations clear, you still refuse to do your duty and transmit my messages as you are required to.'

Nahton did not bother to contradict him. They had discussed the matter many times. 'Do you plan to execute me, Mr Chairman? Is that what you consider fair punishment for refusing the orders of an outlaw government?'

'*Peter* is the outlaw government.' Basil forcibly calmed himself. 'I will not argue with a green priest. I'll offer you one last chance – and I mean it. One last chance. I have a statement for you to read. You've issued plenty of King Peter's announcements; now let them hear the words of the Chairman. That will at least let the colonies make an informed decision.'

Nahton didn't bother to look at the document Basil extended. 'I can't do that, Mr Chairman. All green priests have agreed: No message from the Hansa or the EDF will be transmitted until you resign and Earth reaffirms its allegiance to King Peter and joins the Confederation.'

Basil dropped the document on a table next to the treeling. He waited. Nahton waited. The silence stretched out for several minutes. Finally Basil made a sound of disgust. 'Captain McCammon, please remove the treeling from the green priest's possession.'

Nahton stiffened. 'The treeling belongs to me and to the worldforest. You have no right—'

'I'm the Chairman. This is Earth. I need no other right.' Basil gestured toward the document. 'I can change my mind as soon as you agree to read this.'

'I will not.'

Two royal guards came forward to pick up the treeling. McCammon said casually, 'Shall we place it in Queen Estarra's conservatory, Mr Chairman?'

Basil shot him a look, and Nahton realized that the Chairman had not wanted him to know where the treeling would be kept.

'Place additional guards outside the green priest's quarters – and set a watch over the treeling as well.' Basil sniffed and sent the green priest a sidelong glance. 'It is not my way to be so harsh, but you give me no choice.'

'You cannot change what's happening out in the Spiral Arm by taking my treeling away. The only difference is that you will be more poorly informed than before.'

McCammon and the guards walked away with the treeling. Nahton stared after it, barely hearing the Chairman's parting shot.

'By controlling information, I can control attitudes, and by controlling attitudes, I can change reality.'

EIGHTEEN

CHAIRMAN BASIL WENCESLAS

It was a frivolous ceremony, a waste of time, but the gullible public required it. Though Basil spent most of his time behind the scenes, he knew that people needed their parades and memorials. He had always used such events as levers to pry more work or sacrifices from the Hansa's citizens. Now that the Chairman had neither King Peter nor Prince Daniel to perform the showmanship, he did it himself. Basil squeezed his eyes shut. So few people he could count on! At times he wondered why he worked so hard and dedicated his entire life to save these people who did not deserve his leadership.

He and Deputy Cain stood at the lip of the glassy crater, all that remained of the compy-manufacturing facility that he had been forced to blow up when the Soldier compies went berserk. He was accompanied by his four surviving grid admirals: Willis, Diente, Pike, and San Luis. General Lanyan had also just arrived for the ceremony.

Basil took his place at a makeshift podium with the banner of the Terran Hanseatic League fluttering behind him. Dark blue flags sporting the EDF's chain of stars ringed the entire crater. It was an impressive show for the crowds and newsnet reporters, although Basil felt that he and his inner circle could ill afford to waste the time. Maybe he should have had the Archfather of Unison deliver this well-crafted speech.

'We cannot forget our fallen. Those who perished here fighting the Soldier compies are only a small number of those who died in a great war. Our hearts grow heavy with the knowledge that this is only a microcosm of all we have suffered. These soldiers sacrificed everything for the sake of the Hansa, as did many, many thousands of other fighters. But they saved Earth.

'Now, however – *now* it is time for the rest of us to make sacrifices.' He looked into the imagers and at the stricken crowd. 'This is the most dangerous time Earth has ever faced. Though the hydrogues are defeated, we are beset by enemies, some of them traitors that we once considered our own brothers. But the Hansa can be strong again! We must reunite the worlds that have gone astray. We must use every resource to rebuild. We thought we knew hard work before. Now we must demand even more from ourselves!'

He and Cain had worked out those euphemisms, which meant higher taxes, lower wages, and severe rationing. 'I am your Chairman! And as your Chairman I make this promise to you: Our civilization will be great again!' He turned smartly around and stepped down from the temporary stage, followed by Deputy Cain.

He stood among his military advisers while the newsnets continued to take images. He shook the admirals' hands, thanked them, and said in a quiet voice, 'Meet me in the war room back at Hansa HQ. We need to discuss our first military strikes against the rebels.'

*

Admiral Sheila Willis, a salty old woman with a hard voice but a grandmotherly demeanor, rested her elbows on the table and her chin in her hands. Around them, the tactical planning screens no longer showed incoming warglobes or massive EDF ships engaged in battle. There was no coffee or food, not even a pitcher of ice water. This meeting was all business, not a social occasion.

'I'm concerned about this alleged "military action", Mr Chairman,' Willis said. 'How in the world are we going to go on the offensive when we can't even count how many functional ships we have?'

'We may be in turmoil, Admiral, but so is everyone else. If we strike now, Peter won't expect it.' Basil paced the length of the table, passing the now-empty tactical stations. He didn't like to have his back to the door.

'If we strike now, we don't have anything to strike *with*,' she said. 'Believe me, it is not a good idea.'

'That's dangerously close to insubordination, Admiral.'

Willis blinked at him. 'Excuse me, sir? I am one of your few remaining qualified experts, and this is a private meeting to discuss tactical matters. I don't insist that you take my advice, but you should at least listen to it, or stop inviting me to the meetings.'

'I have to agree with Admiral Willis,' said Esteban Diente, the admiral of Grid 9. He had short, dark hair, frosted with a few strands of silver. His coppery face was broad, though his eyes were close-set. 'Our advice does you no good unless we're free to offer an honest opinion.'

Admiral Pike cut through to the main point. 'What targets are you considering, sir?'

'And what is the overall objective?' asked his friend Admiral San Luis.

Basil nodded to Deputy Cain, who answered, 'King Peter's rebellion is spreading faster than we expected. Because of the

Confederation's access to green priests, they can transmit their propaganda instantly, while we're stuck with traditional slow measures, such as lightspeed transmissions or stardrive couriers.'

'This haemorrhaging of Hansa worlds must stop,' Basil interrupted. 'We will use whatever ships we have, go in force to these breakaway colonies, and encourage them with the strongest possible measures to remain loyal to the Hansa. We're going to need their resources and their workforces.'

'But where do we begin?' asked San Luis. 'We don't have so much as an unofficial tally of the worlds that've thrown in their lot with King Peter.'

'And we don't know how many Roamer clans we're talking about,' groaned Admiral Pike. 'We never did.'

'We've got to build momentum by nailing down some successes quickly,' said General Lanyan. 'Let's secure as many Hansa colonies as we can, as fast as we can grab them. We'll focus on the ones we can win without much of a fight to make ourselves stronger and build up our numbers.'

'At the very least, that should slow our attrition,' Cain said. 'We're losing colonies daily. If we stop that from happening, maybe others will think twice before tearing up the Charter.'

'And which ones are the easiest victories?' Willis again sounded sceptical. 'We have a bad habit of underestimating the levels of difficulty.'

'First and foremost, we go to the worlds settled during the Klikiss Colonization Initiative,' Cain said. 'They're fledgling colonies. No defences whatsoever.'

'More important, they're off the grid,' Basil said. 'They don't have green priests to spread the corruption, so they won't know about Peter's desertion or his sham government on Theroc.'

'But ... why bother? What do those worlds have to offer?' Willis asked. 'Not much in the way of resources or populations.'

'They are of strategic importance,' Basil insisted. '*Moral* importance. We can use them as footholds for the EDF, anchor points with which to stop further attrition.'

Lanyan folded his thick fingers together. 'Right. We go straight to Rheindic Co – the central transfer point for the transportals – send teams through to the colonies, and easily add a few dozen worlds back to our score. It shouldn't take more than a small peacekeeping force to make sure those newbie settlers don't get out of line. It'll be fast and easy.'

'We've heard that before,' Willis muttered, earning herself a glare from the General.

Lanyan turned to the Chairman. 'Sir, I would like to lead that operation myself. Once they see the commander of the Earth Defence Forces, those colonies will never consider defying us.'

'General, isn't your priority to manage the shipyards and rebuild the Earth Defence Forces?' Deputy Cain asked.

'That may be a priority, but it's not my area of expertise. We need an army of administrators to watch over that mess.' Lanyan turned back to Basil. 'I'm a military commander. I proved my worth when we battled the robot-hijacked ships and when we faced down the hydrogues. Let me do what I do best.'

'And you're sick and tired of the shipyards,' Willis said.

'General, after seeing your recent report about the accidents, losses, and black market activities, I'm inclined to believe that you may not be the best man for the shipyards, after all.' Basil considered, then nodded. 'All right. Set up your team and go secure the Klikiss colonies.'

Lanyan could barely keep the relief from showing on his face. 'Given the import of the mission, we need to show that the EDF is making a significant effort. Perhaps a few Mantas are not impressive enough? I think I should take a Juggernaut.'

Admiral Willis made predictable protests. 'If you're just going to send peacekeeping forces through the transportals, what the hell do you need a Juggernaut for?'

Still without taking a seat, Basil turned to face his officers. 'The General's reasons seem sufficient to me. I'm hereby transferring command of the Grid 7 Juggernaut to him for this mission.'

'My *Jupiter?*' Willis was flabbergasted. 'And may I ask what I'm to do in the meantime?'

'I'm placing you in charge of the asteroid-belt shipyard. You can also help us strategize for our new recruiting drive.' He turned to Pike, San Luis, and Diente. 'You three, compile a list of the most useful lost colonies and your assessment of any particular difficulties we might have in conquering them.'

'I don't suppose negotiation or diplomacy is even an option on the table?' Willis said. Basil didn't bother to answer her.

Lanyan stood up, as if anxious to be out of the meeting. 'I'll depart within the next two days, Mr Chairman. I promise you I'll secure our Klikiss planets quickly and efficiently.'

Basil quelled his annoyance. 'Quick and efficient. Yes, that'll be a pleasant surprise, General.'

NINETEEN

ORLI COVITZ

Driven by the breedex, the Klikiss never rested. Insect workers crawled over the ruins, using load after load of polymer resin to extend the towers, thicken the walls, and expand the alien city into a veritable fortress. Using strange machinery, an endless number of Klikiss labourers strip-mined the hills, and processed mud, sand, and metal ores into useful materials. A squat structure built at the centre of the complex was apparently where the mysterious hive mind lived.

Adroit assemblers continued to manufacture great numbers of the identical, interlocking ships that shot into orbit on test flights, then landed in groups. The aggressive fleet looked like an invasion force. A new trapezoidal framework began to rise in the stony clearing in front of the city towers, the beginnings of a transportal much larger than the one inside the ruins. According to Margaret Colicos, some of the other subhive breedexes were already on the move. The Llaro breedex was consolidating its swarm, while preparing to defend itself.

DD often spent days with Orli when Margaret disappeared

among the Klikiss. Though she had lived among them for years, the xeno-archaeologist was always trying to communicate with the hive mind. She felt obligated to explain humans and their culture to it; Orli hoped the older woman was having some success.

The girl sat next to DD on a flat rooftop in the town, overlooking the surrounding landscape. Suddenly, squads of builder sub-breeds marched out in a long stream, flowing around to completely encircle the Llaro settlement. Colonists watched the bugs from their windows or from the streets; a few shouted questions, but no one confronted the diligent insects.

The Klikiss began to build an enclosing wall that would confine them all, like a cage around the entire town.

Some people, especially Roamer detainees, attempted to push their way out, but Klikiss workers drove them back. Nobody seemed to understand what was going on.

Orli felt a leaden weight in her heart. 'They're turning our town into a big pen, like an exhibit in a zoo. And we're in the middle of it.'

Groups of grublike excreters were carried forward on pallets from the construction area. Diggers excavated a trench, or moat, around the town and provided the dirt as raw material to the grubs, which digested it and produced copious amounts of resin cement. Working in a flurry, builders slapped together supports and slathered them with iron-hard polymer mud.

The insect workers granted free passage to Margaret, who returned to the city, looking deeply disturbed, and pushed past the Klikiss. The constructors were building external ramps and including several access gaps through the wall, and Margaret passed in among the colonists.

Seeing the woman's distraught expression, Orli and DD climbed down from the rooftop. They ran to her as other colonists shouted questions, demanding answers, as if Margaret were some kind of ambassador from the breedex. With her grey-and-brown hair blowing in the dry breeze, she raised her hands for quiet. 'The breedex has located an infestation of black robots on a planet called Wollamor. It intends to launch a great attack through the transportal and destroy every robot there.'

'Good,' Mr Steinman said. 'Smash the damned machines into scrap metal.'

Orli shuddered. 'I won't feel sad to see the robots wiped out, after what they did to Corribus.'

Two of the towering domates strode among the warriors and workers, chittering as the confining wall continued to rise. Margaret cocked her head to listen, as if she could understand what the bugs were talking about, but she did not translate.

Davlin Lotze nodded grimly at the new barrier. 'But how does that explain the wall?'

Margaret lowered her head. 'The breedex insists that all human colonists remain in one place – here. They will assist you in doing so.'

'"Assist us" in staying in one place?' Roberto Clarin said with a snort. 'By the Guiding Star, what are you talking about?'

'Isn't it obvious?' Mr Steinman said. 'It's only the first step, dammit!'

The camp's other compy, a Governess model named UR who had come with the Roamer detainees, stood near the seven children in her charge. Her programming was to instruct and protect them.

The uproar continued, but the colonists could not resist the Klikiss. Fortunately, thanks to Davlin's wise warning, the people had hidden their food supplies where the bugs couldn't find them. Lately, their rations had been paltry, but Orli was used to that.

'Perhaps the wall is for your own protection,' DD said. 'It is reminiscent of the fortifications around a medieval town.'

'And if pigs could fly,' Crim Tylar groused.

'I know of no species of pig that can fly. Aerodynamically, it seems impossible.'

'It was a joke, DD,' Orli said.

Metre after metre, moving along a perfect geometrical path, the Klikiss builders continued to erect their wall.

'We'll just have to cooperate with the Klikiss and hope for the best,' Ruis said. Even to Orli he sounded naïve.

Mr Steinman wearily shook his shaggy head. His eyes were red. 'I don't like this. Not one bit. I'm getting way too many images of concentration camps, barbed-wire fences, and gas chambers.'

'That was centuries ago. I read about it in school,' Orli said.

'There are some things you should never forget. Worse than forgetting, though, is if you let it happen all over again. And we walked right into this.'

TWENTY

SIRIX

Once the black robots had cleansed Wollamor of the human taint, Sirix set his Soldier compies to work rebuilding. The black robots did not need the remaining dwellings and towers for any functional reason, only as a symbol to show how resoundingly they had defeated their long-extinct creators. Sirix was proud.

Wollamor's large, ancient transportal stood as a blank stone gateway in the middle of a street. Beside PD and QT, Sirix contemplated how those coordinate tiles led to further possibilities for conquest, abandoned worlds to reclaim, one after another. The black robots would have their own Swarming. They would spread, overwhelm all resistance, and take control. His eye sensors glowed at the thoughts churning through his cybernetic mind.

QT was the first to notice the change. 'Look, the transportal is activating.'

'Someone is coming through,' PD added.

The sheet of stone hummed, became a wall of static, then

opened. Sirix reeled backward on his leg clusters and emitted an electronic burst to alert the robots and Soldier compies.

Five armoured Klikiss warriors strode through raising strange weapons with their sharp, segmented forelimbs.

Sirix scuttled in full retreat while the two Friendly compies stared in fascination. 'Are those the original Klikiss?' PD asked. 'Are they not extinct?'

Black robots rushed from the construction sites. Soldier compies marched down ramps from the EDF ships. When the Klikiss warriors saw the robots, they set up a warbling battle cry and surged to attack. Dozens more, then hundreds, poured through the transportal after them.

The first warrior leapt forward and crashed onto Sirix. He fought back, extending his articulated limbs to drill and cut into the Klikiss's exoskeleton. Ancient echoes of oppression, even fear, rang through his mind as he struggled. The black robots were powerfully built, nearly three metres tall and encased in glossy armour, and the Klikiss had designed them with fighting skills nearly equal to their own. Sirix sent out a burst to the two confused Friendly compies. 'Protect me.' He pushed hard, snapping off two of the warrior's limbs. The stumps oozed viscous green fluid.

PD and QT scurried to grab the warrior's additional limbs, throwing the creature off balance. One of its pincers broke apart.

Sirix shoved a cutting stave into the enemy's thorax and ripped sideways, nearly decapitating the creature. Twitching, it fell over, still grabbing at Sirix, but the robot tore himself free. PD and QT hurriedly followed him.

A clamour of thoughts and questions burned along his inner mental channels. Confusion, disbelief, and shock slowed crucial reaction times. How could the Klikiss have survived the rigged swarming into hydrogue planets? This was not possible. The return of the creator race had not been part of his detailed plans.

More and more Klikiss marched through the transportal – warriors, diggers, builders – and one of the black-and-silver striped domates. Was this another Swarming? Had the Klikiss survivors stumbled upon Sirix and his robots by accident, or had they come to Wollamor with a specific intention? No breedex would have forgotten the robots' betrayal.

The insect warriors lunged forward, shrieking and chittering. Robots and Soldier compies scrambled to mount a defence. Two insect warriors with bright red badges marking their wings and carapaces crashed down upon one robot. It fought back furiously, but the warriors ripped off its back casings and discarded them with a clatter of metal and polymer, before uprooting the winglike solar panels. The black robots could withstand the hostile environment of a hydrogue gas giant, but the Klikiss knew full well how to dismantle their own creations.

As the robot thrashed and stabbed with its articulated limbs, the warriors tunnelled into the body core, tore out its processors, and smashed the stored memory. Wrenching off its geometric head, they flung it far away.

The returning Klikiss had sophisticated weaponry, if they desired to use it. But the breedex controlling them seemed interested not only in defeating the robots, but in crushing them. It reminded Sirix of the ancient battles – destruction and slaughter for the sheer satisfaction that came from it.

A second domate arrived, accompanied by even more Klikiss. Sirix and his robots signalled each other to form a temporary blockade to cover their retreat to the EDF ships. They could get aboard the shuttles, troop transports, and Mantas, and fly away from Wollamor. But they needed time.

Sirix had one last defence to use: the Soldier compies. Now, with the original race coming after them, Sirix decided that the human-built robots were expendable. It was necessary for the survival of their superiors. When he summoned them, ranks of the EDF military compies marched forward double-time to form a wall. They crashed into the emerging Klikiss, using construction tools as makeshift weapons.

Fortunately, the Soldier compies had no sense of self-preservation. They would buy the time Sirix needed.

Insect warriors flew forward, and Soldier compies rushed to meet them, four of them against a single Klikiss warrior. At first, they tore the monsters to pieces, but the Klikiss, in turn, used praying-mantis limbs to eviscerate the compies, ripping through synthetic skins, chopping metal heads off with a backhanded slash. Still more Soldier compies filed out of the EDF ships, carrying projectile weapons, many of which had been pried from the dead hands of human soldiers.

While Soldier compies blasted away at the vengeful Klikiss, for a moment – just a moment – Sirix thought they could hold back the numbers.

Another wave of Klikiss poured through the transportal.

PD and QT ran in panic, and Sirix sent them a command burst. 'Follow me.'

Soldier compies struggled to hold the line while the black robots retreated to the dubious safety of the EDF ships. And the marauding Klikiss kept coming.

TWENTY-ONE

TASIA TAMBLYN

Tasia had never been to Theroc, though she'd heard a lot about the forested world. It was as important to the Therons as Rendezvous had been to Roamers. According to her uncles, this was the seat of a new, inclusive government, a Confederation of diverse peoples. However, as Conrad Brindle entered orbit, he received a decidedly cool reception. 'EDF ship, are you armed?'

'We have a standard complement of defensive weapons, as do all ships of this model. Those weapons came in very handy when we recently fought against the drogues.'

Tasia leaned over and added, 'In fact, your giant treeships helped us to escape at Qronha 3. We're here to report to King Peter. We understand this is the centre of government these days?'

After a long pause, the voice answered, 'All right, permission to land. But be warned that we will respond accordingly to any hostile act.'

When their transport landed in a clearing that had obviously been used by many other ships, she spotted four small Roamer vessels, with people near them decked out in clan attire. Grinning, Tasia bounded down the ramp, hoping she would recognize some faces after such a long time.

'You Eddies have a lot of nerve coming here, after all that you've done to us.' One of the Roamers glared at the three of them. Tasia and Robb wore ill-fitting EDF uniforms, since those were the only spare garments Conrad had aboard.

Tasia snapped back, 'And some would say that Roamers have forgotten basic hospitality.' She stepped forward, toe to toe with the surly trader. 'I'm Tasia Tamblyn, from clan Tamblyn. After fighting the drogues for years I was recently freed after being held prisoner inside a gas giant, so I'm a bit behind the times.'

The trader didn't know how to respond. 'Tamblyn, you say? From Plumas? You're Bram's little girl? Ah, then you must be here to join with King Peter? We never know where anybody's allegiance lies these days.'

Robb frowned. '*Join* King Peter? When did we ever change?'

'And what about the EDF? I need to make my report to General Lanyan.' Conrad was plainly disturbed. 'I saw a lot of trading ships over your new capital, but no defences.' The Roamers looked at him sceptically; one made a rude noise.

At ground level, the visitors stood together looking up at the mammoth tree and the huge fungus-reef city suspended in its high branches. Holes had been carved through the asymmetrical mounds of white fungus to create a suspended metropolis with hundreds of rooms and open balconies. Simple lift platforms ran on tracks and cables installed by Roamers.

Finally, a broad-shouldered green priest named Solimar came to guide them up into the tree city. Tasia straightened her uniform to make herself as presentable as she could, and brushed a dried leaf from Robb's shoulder.

Conrad's forehead was deeply creased. 'I don't see any other uniforms. We can't be the only EDF soldiers on this whole planet.'

'You are, at the moment,' Solimar said as the platform came to a stop. 'But maybe more will come around.'

They entered a large room that had been hung with colourful thread-weavings and webworks. Wearing crowns made of insect wings and polished beetle carapaces, along with garments reminiscent of what they'd worn on Earth, the King and Queen greeted their guests.

Conrad stepped forward and saluted, as did Tasia and Robb. As the highest ranking officer present, Tasia spoke for them. 'Majesties, we present ourselves for duty. We are required to deliver our report to a commanding officer. May we speak with General Lanyan or his officer in charge?'

Tasia caught the look that flashed between Peter and Estarra. Peter said, 'I am your commander-in-chief. Your King. You can report to me.'

'And we welcome you,' Estarra said. 'Would you renew your oath of loyalty?'

Conrad looked troubled by the question. 'Why should I need to do that? When has my loyalty ever been questioned?'

'Circumstances have changed, Lieutenant Commander.'

'So . . . where is Chairman Wenceslas?' Robb asked.

Peter's voice became cold. 'Chairman Wenceslas is no longer a part of the legitimate government.'

'He attempted a coup,' Estarra said. 'We managed to escape here. We're more than the Hansa now. The Confederation is a true representation of humanity.'

No one spoke for several seconds, as the three newcomers absorbed the unexpected information. Conrad asked, 'But what about the EDF? What about General Lanyan?'

'Members of the Earth Defence Forces were either complicit

in the coup attempt, or they failed to respond accordingly when informed of the Chairman's illegal actions.'

'Remember the words of your oath,' Estarra said. 'Your true loyalty is to the King.'

Conrad maintained a stony expression for hours, showing no hint of how he really reacted to the news. Iasia felt as if the planet had shifted on its axis . . . but then she had never considered the Big Goose to be perfect in the first place. May be this change was for the better.

Later, after an evening meal, Tasia talked joyfully with many other Roamers, exchanging stories and reminiscing as she tried to pretend that everything was back to normal. Robb loved being with her and was clearly happy to be wherever she was, but his father grew increasingly anxious. They were shown to temporary quarters, and Tasia looked forward to having a spacious bed for a change.

When they had a few moments alone, Conrad announced that they should all leave. 'We have to get out of here before they impound my ship and place us in custody.'

'Shizz, what are you talking about?'

'But why, Dad? We're here. The King is here. We've done what we were required to do.'

'I'm not satisfied with the explanations they gave.' Conrad looked furtively around, as if someone might be eavesdropping. 'I want to hear General Lanyan's side of the story. I can read through the spin as well as anyone else. On Earth, I bet they're telling a different tale.'

'What's wrong with the explanations?' Robb was genuinely confused.

'No other EDF soldiers are here. That alone speaks volumes. Look around at this ragtag assemblage – a bunch of Therons, independent colonists, and Roamers! It can't be the real Hansa.'

'Oh? Just a bunch of Therons and Roamers?' Tasia flushed. 'You mean like my brother Jess, who saved us all? Like the people who sent verdani treeships to fight the drogues? You heard my uncles. *This* is the new government.'

Robb took a deep breath and thought for a long moment. 'After seeing what we've seen, you know there's a lot more to it than the official Hansa press releases. I don't think we ever got the whole truth.'

Tasia said, 'And you already know that what the EDF did to the Roamers was wrong.'

Conrad refused to believe, though. 'Peter's accusations are preposterous. As far as I'm concerned, if *General Lanyan* refuses to follow the King's orders, maybe there's something wrong with the King's orders. Maybe *Peter* is the rebel with a handful of insurgents who refuse to follow the legitimate orders of the Hansa.' He looked at them sternly. 'You're both officers in the Earth Defence Forces. You know the chain of command. Returning to Earth is our only option at this point.'

'Shizz, not on your life! I joined the Eddies to fight the drogues, and instead I found myself persecuting my own people.' Tasia withdrew a small utility knife from her belt and began to snip the threads on her shoulder insignia. 'I belong among the Roamers. Period. If that puts me on the opposite side from the EDF, I'd say now's as good a time as any to resign my commission.'

Conrad glowered. 'That makes you a deserter in my book, Captain.'

'I outrank you, Lieutenant Commander. I should order you to follow the King.'

The older man looked down his nose at her. 'You just forfeited the right to issue any orders, ma'am, when you cut off your insignia.'

Robb was distressed. 'Are you two crazy? What are you doing?'

Tasia trembled with the effort to contain her anger. 'I no longer owe anything to the EDF, Robb. I know what the Eddies did to Rendezvous, an independent centre of government. If the Roamers claim Theroc is where I'm supposed to be, and the King says this is where I'm supposed to be, then this is where I'm staying.'

Conrad shook his head sadly, already writing her off. 'It's obvious I can't change your mind, ma'am. Let's go, Robb. Your mother will be very glad to see you again.'

Robb, though, looked torn. 'I was captured by the drogues years ago. By all rights I should be dead, but Roamers and wentals – and Theron treeships – rescued me from that.' He reached out and took Tasia's hand, embarrassing her. 'I belong with Tasia more than I belong in uniform.'

Conrad's face was stormy. 'Not you, too! Your mother and I thought you were lost for a long time. We just got you back. Please don't do this.'

'I have to do what's right. And so do you, Dad. Why not stay a while and gather more information before making a hasty decision? We'll send a message to Mom.'

His father's face was full of anguish. 'I see that . . . that you're not the same Robb, after all. I'm taking the ship and returning to Earth. This is your last chance to change your mind.'

'Why should King Peter let you just fly off?' Tasia asked.

'I'd like to see him try to stop me.' Shoulders slumped by a great weight of disappointment, Conrad stalked alone toward his ship.

'Wait!' Robb called after him. He almost let go of Tasia's hand.

She let him make his own decision, but prayed he would make the right one. When Conrad refused to turn around, Robb settled back and squeezed her fingers tighter. 'Seems to me like you've seen your Guiding Star,' Tasia said.

'Whatever that means.' He sounded very sad. They stood together and watched as Conrad Brindle boarded the EDF transport and fired up the engines. The ship rose above the high worldtrees of Theroc and disappeared into the sky.

TWENTY-TWO

KOLKER

I n an open square in Mijistra, an exotic fountain shone under the light of multiple suns. The fountain generator created and then manipulated immense silvery bubbles filled with a roiling clear liquid, like the essence of a mirror. Surface tension made the bubbles undulate, their membranes rippling and reflecting the numerous suns in the sky, as if they were spotlights constantly in motion.

Seven self-absorbed lens kithmen had gathered around the bubble fountain, as though about to receive a strange communion. They squatted in solemn meditation, staring into the bubbles' uneven surfaces, as if expecting the flares of light to reveal the secrets of the universe. Not one of them moved.

From a distance, Kolker watched, trying to learn from the lens kithmen by observing them. The fountain bubbles swayed as the internal plasma rose, then descended, perhaps to imply the constantly changing nature of knowledge. Kolker longed to know what they knew, to see what they could see. Lightsource, soul-threads, *thism*. He summoned the nerve to walk closer, paused behind two lens kithmen before stepping among them.

They moved aside to allow him access, but did not offer any overt invitation. Their starflare pupils had shrunk to the tiniest of pinpricks as ethereal light played across their faces. Unable to contain himself any longer, Kolker interrupted them. 'Please tell me what is in there. What does the fountain reveal to you? I need to know. And I need to know how to touch and understand your *thism*.'

The lens kithmen seemed to think him either stupid or inferior. 'Humans have no *thism*. They are not connected by the soul-threads. It would be fruitless for us to explain what you cannot possibly experience.'

Kolker stared at the reflective fountain until the light seared patches of colour into his eyes. He was forced to turn away. 'So one should never bother to attempt a seemingly impossible thing?' He couldn't keep the bitter tone from his voice. 'When facing the hydrogues, didn't your own Mage-Imperator demand that you do the impossible? And did you not achieve that?'

The lens kithmen looked at him, even the ones on the opposite side of the fountain. They all seemed to be sharing uneasy thoughts. Finally the man on Kolker's left said, 'The Mage-Imperator gave us no orders to instruct you.'

Kolker turned away, colours still dancing in front of his eyes. He felt lost. The hole within him was deep, and he hadn't found anything solid enough to fill it yet. He couldn't even know if *thism* would be enough.

'Why would you want to do this?' one of the lens kithmen asked him. 'It is not for you.'

Kolker refused to believe that, refused to surrender. Leaving the fountain, he climbed the steps of a monolithic building, sat down, and bent to stare into his prismatic medallion. He turned it one way and then another, so that flares of rainbows played across his face. Trying indefinable techniques, he concentrated on the light, remembered the thought tricks he used unconsciously when connecting via telink, and tried to clutch at the invisible, intangible straws of *thism*.

He sat motionless for hours, simply staring at the medallion and searching.

TWENTY-THREE

OSIRA'H

The only treeling on Ildira stood open to the sky, as high as Osira'h's waist, rising from a misshapen lump of burned wood. The fronds were a delicate pale green, its thin trunk covered with golden bark plates. Though the girl wasn't a green priest herself, the treeling seemed to call to her.

She brought her four halfbreed siblings to stare intently at the tree and exercise their mental powers, as they had done among their mentalist teachers on Dobro. To try for *more*. The five of them ringed the tree. 'We can do this. We have our mother's abilities and our fathers' *thism*.'

'But we have tried before.' Rod'h was not complaining but simply pointing out a fact. Nearest to her age, her brother seemed the most interested in linking with the worldforest mind.

'And we will try again. And we'll try tomorrow and the day after.'

With his penchant for practical and military matters, young Gale'nh had a different concern. 'I do not understand the goal.'

That was the largest question, Osira'h knew. 'The goal is to

116

show the *potential* we have. We can do something that other people can't do, I'm sure of it. The Empire worked for many generations, just to create us.' Her gaze swept them all, and they caught her enthusiasm. Tamo'l and Muree'n were too young to understand what Osira'h was trying to do, but they happily joined in what seemed to be play. Playing was a new experience for them.

Together, they reached forward to touch the golden bark. Osira'h stroked the pale fronds. 'Be careful. Don't harm it,' she said when Muree'n grasped too tightly.

Even without telink, the halfbreeds' sensitivity to *thism* unified them. Rod'h joined her mind in much the same way as they had used their thoughts on Dobro to seek out and contact distant hydrogues. Their bond of *thism* – or was telink part of it as well? – connected them to each other in a private web much more powerful than the one other Ildirans shared.

Osira'h drove her thoughts into the treeling, sensing the leaves, the bark, the living heartwood, the roots – just as her mother's memories showed her. She had opened the conduit of her mind to Nira, receiving a flood of thoughts and memories, and later learning to channel the vengeance of the worldforest itself through the treeling, through her mother, through her mind – and into the unsuspecting hydrogues.

Though they were enemies, the verdani and hydrogues had common ground, an elemental foundation. The worldtrees also shared synergy with the wentals, as they had proved in combining themselves to form huge verdani battleships. No doubt the faeros were similar as well.

Mentalists and lens kithmen talked about how the whole universe was connected in ways that no one, not even a Mage-Imperator, could see or understand. Osira'h believed that, because of their unparalleled ties to both their green priest mother and the *thism* of all Ildirans, she and her siblings held a key. She knew it.

With her eyes closed, the girl followed the strands through the tree trunk into the neuronlike root fibres ... and beyond. Her siblings followed. She expected a flash of a connection, but heard only whispers, distant thoughts, and ghostly voices, as of a vast audience that didn't know the children were eavesdropping. 'We are close!'

'I can sense it,' Tamo'l said.

'Keep concentrating,' Gale'nh added.

The outbursts were enough to disrupt Osira'h's focus, and she rocked back on the balls of her bare feet. It was a tantalizing glimpse of what they could do. She felt that the five of them were about to find something extremely important, something that no green priest or Ildiran comprehended. The idea thrilled her. She would help her brothers and sisters achieve the apex of what their special breeding made possible. 'We almost did it that time.'

Rod'h blinked. 'I see what you have in mind now.'

Exhausted but excited, they gave up their efforts for the day. Tamo'l and Muree'n, eager for new distractions, stood and hurried across the shining rooftop to the precipitous edge, where they looked down into Mijistra. Gale'nh looked from Osira'h to his brother for explanations, like a boyish soldier needing to be debriefed.

Osira'h rubbed her temple, felt a throbbing ache. But even the pain could not diminish her exhilaration. 'Tomorrow we will be closer.'

TWENTY-FOUR

ANTON COLICOS

He had never wanted to return to Maratha again. Ever. That place held only nightmares and terrifying memories. But Anton certainly couldn't let Vao'sh go alone to document the defeat of the black robots for the *Saga of Seven Suns*. Standing in the warliner's command nucleus, he felt a clammy sweat dampen his skin. 'Are you sure we want to do this?'

'I do not want to. But I need to.' The old rememberer blinked his soulful eyes. He had been uncharacteristically quiet. 'Remember your heroic tales. A hero who has been through a terrible ordeal must face his fears and face his past in order to achieve redemption.'

'That's true in *stories*, Vao'sh. But I never wanted to be an epic hero.'

The old man smiled. 'And yet, you are.'

Yazra'h clapped him on the back with a blow hard enough to make him grab the rail for balance. 'Soon we will destroy them all, Rememberer Anton. I will show you how Ildiran warriors deal with evil machines.'

'I wish you'd been there with us the first time.'

'I wish that as well.' Her coppery hair seemed alive, flowing around her head like a corona. She stared at the former resort planet as they went into orbit. 'It would have been glorious.'

She had left her Isix cats on Ildira. Yazra'h loved to hunt with them, to run across the training fields, and even to roll or wrestle with the animals. But they would be of little use against hulking robots. Anton was sure she feared for her pets' safety more than she did for her own.

Adar Zan'nh issued orders to the individual captains of the warliners. 'We do not know what weapons or defences the robots have. Recapturing Maratha might be a difficult battle, and we must be prepared for the fight.'

'We are looking forward to it,' Yazra'h said. 'Without their hydrogue protectors, those robots cannot stand against us.'

Anton mumbled, 'Well, they took us by surprise before.'

Yazra'h's lips quirked in a smile. 'You are frightened. Do not be. I promise to protect you.'

'I ... I believe you.' Unfortunately, her assurances didn't blunt the cluster of razor blades that had suddenly lodged in his stomach.

The circling warliners deployed scanners to pick up transmissions from the two antipodal cities. 'Maratha Prime and Secda both seem to be dead.'

'As we anticipated,' said Vao'sh. All the coloured lobes on his expressive face went deathly pale. Anton patted him reassuringly on the shoulder.

'However, we have detected significant electronic chatter and thermal signatures near the site of Secda.'

'That's where the robots were digging tunnels and erecting their structures,' Anton said.

The septar transmitted from the second warliner, 'I am

deploying covert streamers to gather images of all locations. We will study Prime first.'

'Be careful that you are not observed.'

Like a school of metallic fish, Ildiran scout vessels dropped out of the warliner's belly and cut through the night sky toward the location of Maratha Prime. In well-lit cockpits, the Ildiran pilots flew over what had once been a fabulous vacation city. The streamers spilled silvery light down upon the domes and outer settlements. What remained of Maratha Prime looked like the metal and crystal bones of a beached sea creature.

'The city is destroyed,' transmitted one of the pilots.

Anton shook his head. 'Not destroyed – *dismantled*.' Prime had suffered from no obvious explosions or attacks. Instead, the robots had stripped the buildings and walls, removing equipment, pulling out any processed material they could use.

'What would they want it all for?' Yazra'h said.

'We will find out when the scouts get to the hive at Secda,' Zan'nh said.

Flying low over the darkened landscape, the spy streamers rapidly crossed the continent to the other side of the planet. By the time they outraced the night, flying low enough to avoid any local detection systems the robots might have put in place, the scanners came upon the vast and strange complex the robots had created. Unseen, they transmitted images back to the approaching warliners. Before long, however, the robots would detect the Solar Navy force overhead.

The nearly completed city had been torn apart as well, its useful components cannibalized to build an immense and distinctive alien metropolis. Or a base. The rocky landscape was riddled with tunnels and shafts. Towers made of curving girders were weirdly reminiscent of the Klikiss ruins that Anton's parents had spent so much time investigating.

'They are building *ships*,' Vao'sh said.

'A lot of ships.'

In the flatlands surrounding Secda, vessels were being assembled from newly extruded framework girders and hull plates. Like an infestation of roaches, hundreds of black robots scurried over the construction site. Bright sparks from welding arcs and assembly tools flickered in the growing shadows of the planet's week-long sunset.

'Those are heavily armed vessels, designed as warships,' said Zan'nh. 'The robots mean to attack something, or at least defend themselves against a very powerful enemy. What do they fear?'

Yazra'h didn't care. 'We will not give them a chance to complete their work.'

After the recon streamers finished their surveillance and soared back to the warliners, the robots went into a flurry. 'We have been seen,' Zan'nh said.

'It is time to begin our engagement. I will gather soldiers and arm them with weapons for a ground assault.' Yazra'h turned to go. 'Rememberers Anton and Vao'sh must chronicle our great battles. Will you join us?' She grinned.

Vao'sh sounded terrified as he answered. 'Yes.' Anton swallowed hard.

Satisfied, she marched to the doorway, but the Adar shook his head. 'Stay here for now, Yazra'h. Our primary function is to defeat and destroy the enemy robots and whatever base they are building here. The streamers have provided us with sufficient data to plan our attack. You will be part of the second phase. I will not needlessly risk lives.'

Anton felt a rush of relief, but knew the reprieve was only temporary.

Ignoring Yazra'h's obvious disappointment, the Adar issued his orders. 'All warliners, drop low to burn out the robot infestation before they can prepare their defences. Launch cutters and stream-ers for surgical strikes. Warliners, prepare for large-scale assault.' The seven warliners sliced into Maratha's atmosphere and thrust toward the nightmarish metal swarm. A flurry of smaller ships led the charge.

Anton studied the images the spy scouts sent back, and frowned as something changed. Coverings slid away from buried tube-shaped structures that pointed upward. 'Hey, what are those cylinders mounted into the ground? Like an array of canisters, or' – before Anton could finish, the mouths of the cylinders spat forth blue-white gouts of energy – 'cannons!'

The bombardment vaporized three of the approaching attack streamers. The remaining pilots scrambled out of formation, curved upward and raced out of range. The robot cannons fired again, and the scatter of energy projectiles caught a streamer on its right wing, sending it into a spin.

Still descending, the big Solar Navy ships plunged toward the robotic base. The smaller ships began to open fire, striking any emplacement they could lock onto.

Zan'nh stood at the command rail, his face grim. Yazra'h was smiling. 'Commence full-scale bombardment as soon as we are in range. Warliners, deploy all appropriate weapons. Destroy those cannons, then destroy the entire complex.'

As the remaining streamers shot away, the robots methodically prepared their defences. Another barrage of energy projectiles forced the warliners to spread apart. The Solar Navy dropped thousands of explosive projectiles, followed by a cascade of energy beams that ripped up the landscape around the robotic hive.

A cluster of Ildiran bombs struck one of the partially assembled robot warships. Anton shielded his eyes from the flash and shock-wave that turned the spacecraft into a glowing crater. Showering sparks flew in all directions as if someone had scattered the coals of a campfire. Chittering, pulsing electronic signals rattled through the warliner's comm systems. Anton wondered what the robots were saying, but decided he didn't really want to know.

As a wave of bombs struck a second robotic vessel at the ship construction grounds, the embedded energy cannons damaged a lagging warliner. The Solar Navy mercilessly pounded the hive tunnels, the pits, and the rebuilt city.

'Very soon the robots will not only be defeated, but obliterated,' Zan'nh said.

Vao'sh moved his lips, quietly mumbling words, as if rehearsing how he would tell the story to his fellow rememberers. Below, the robots scrambled to find effective shelter.

Yazra'h clenched and unclenched her hands as she watched the attack, obviously hoping that the Adar would leave some of the black machines for her to deal with personally.

TWENTY-FIVE

MAGE-IMPERATOR JORA'H

With Yazra'h and Zan'nh gone off to recapture Maratha, Jora'h turned his efforts to the multitude of other tasks involved in restoring stability to his Empire. His staff assembled maps and a strategic inventory as the first step in reclaiming all that had recently been lost. Hyrillka, the centre of Rusa'h's rebellion, had been evacuated while faeros and hydrogues battled in the system's primary sun. But perhaps now the world was habitable again. The Mage-Imperator sent a scientific team to Hyrillka to study the solar flux and monitor the climate. That would tell him if there was still cause for concern.

He also summoned Tal O'nh, the one-eyed military commander who had evacuated Hyrillka, along with Designate Ridek'h, the boy who would have been the leader there. Jora'h dispatched them on a procession across the worlds in the Horizon Cluster to inspect planets that had been damaged in the rebellion. Another key step in regaining Ildiran strength and unity.

So many pieces ... so many fragments of the Empire now splintered apart, and only the Mage-Imperator could draw them together. How glad he was that his son Daro'h was returning from Dobro today! Now that the hydrogues were defeated and Rusa'h's civil war was over, the Ildiran Empire needed its Prime Designate again. The Mage-Imperator wanted to see Daro'h as soon as his transport touched down.

A semicircular ledge extended from the Palace wing set aside as the domain of the new Prime Designate. The ledge was both a balcony and a landing pad, expansive enough to hold more than seventy Ildirans. Sadly, Nira had chosen not to join Jora'h. Her memories of Dobro were still raw, and though this young man had not asked for his position as Designate there, Daro'h still represented the terrible camps to her.

A few servant kithmen hurriedly strung reflective banners to thin poles with braided ropes. Others arranged food on such a sprawling array of tables that Jora'h wondered if the pilot would find room to land on the crowded balcony. Court rememberers stood listening and watching, ready to retell every aspect of Daro'h's arrival. Bureaucratic kithmen determined which people were allowed to stand on the landing ledge and which must be relegated to nearby balconies. Guard kithmen stood at attention, pointing their crystal katanas to the sky.

Posturing for attention, anxious females were dressed in reflective solar-energy clothing, their scalps shaved, oiled, and painted with colourful designs. The women, many of whom were already on the breeding roster, enthusiastically waved at the small ceremonial cutter as it came down. It was the Prime Designate's job to have many children, from many kiths, and to begin a new generation of noble-born sons who would become *his* Designates-in-Waiting.

Daro'h's life here would be much different from before. Because of his birth order, upbringing, and training, he had never believed he would be anything more than the Designate of Dobro.

But everything had changed with the death of the turncoat Thor'h.

This time, the Mage-Imperator wouldn't allow his son to lead a completely pampered life. A Prime Designate had many pleasant obligations and tended to follow hedonistic pleasures for a time, but Jora'h had suffered from the mistake of indulging Thor'h. Daro'h must be put through a trial by fire, beginning the moment he arrived.

Servant kithmen had polished the transparent tiles of the balcony ledge surface so perfectly that it looked as if the cutter were landing on clear air. The ceremonial vessel was embellished with sigils and colourful markings. With a cough of jets and a flare of heat, the cutter settled into place. Jora'h moved forward as the hatch began to open.

When Daro'h stepped out, however, the Mage-Imperator felt a sudden jolt in his heart, a twisting in his abdomen. The brooding pain he had felt in the *thism* intensified. His son actually flinched from the bright light of the six suns. The skin of his face was red and blistered, burned; his hands were as raw as if they'd been boiled.

'Daro'h! What happened?'

The young man seemed unsteady as he walked forward. His words gushed out. 'Father! Liege. The fire is coming. The faeros! Udru'h is dead!'

'Designate Udru'h is dead? How? I sensed nothing!' How could Jora'h not have felt the death of his brother?

'Before he died, the faeros separated Udru'h from the *thism*. Cut off and . . . consumed him. It was *Rusa'h*, Liege. He is alive – and *afire*.'

Crisply, so that his tone penetrated Daro'h's panic, Jora'h said, 'Explain yourself, Prime Designate.' The bureaucratic kithmen, guards, and waiting females looked to the Mage-Imperator in confusion, as if he could dispel their anxiety and provide sensible answers.

When Daro'h drew a deep breath, a twinge of pain crossed his seared face. He explained how the faeros had come to Dobro, fireballs looming over the burned village. 'Rusa'h is with the faeros. He said he would burn more, that he would burn you if you tried to stop him.'

'And why did he spare you?'

'Because I am a son of the Mage-Imperator. My *thism* connection to you is strong, but I believe he could have broken it, *ignited* it, if he wished to. I think he intended for me to warn you, so that you could be afraid.'

Jora'h understood all too well. With the Solar Navy already devastated and the Ildiran people weakened, what chance did they have of standing against fiery entities as powerful as the hydrogues? However, the Mage-Imperator had not given in to the hydrogues, and the Empire had indeed survived.

'Daro'h, I need your strength. I need my Prime Designate.'

Through the *thism*, Jora'h sensed his son searching deep within himself. Now that he did not feel entirely alone, the young man found an inner courage that had not been burned by fear. 'But how can we stop him?'

'By being Ildirans. Standing together, our race is stronger than any outside threat.' Jora'h clasped Daro'h's forearm. 'You and I will reinforce the *thism* as a Mage-Imperator and his Prime Designate should do. Do we know where Rusa'h will go next?'

'He said he would forge bonds wherever he needed them.'

TWENTY-SIX

FAEROS INCARNATE RUSA'H

Crenna's dead star was the site of a faeros defeat in a battle that had extinguished a sun. Though countless hydrogues had perished, still the fiery entities had been beaten. The crushing blow had rocked the faeros.

That was before Rusa'h had joined them. As an avatar of the flaming elemental beings, he retained all of his human memories, passions, and ideas. Rusa'h had showed them a different way to fight. By sacrifice, by throwing overwhelming numbers against the hydrogues all at the same place, the faeros had incinerated the enemy, though at great cost to themselves. Their numbers had been decimated.

But perhaps he could help them, as well as achieve his own aims.

Rusa'h gazed through a curtain of flames as his fireball circled the dense grey corpse of Crenna's sun. The nuclear fires at its core had been stilled, providing no more energy to hold the star's layers against its own gravity. Once-habitable planets in the system were now cold and black, their very atmospheres frozen solid. Thermal energy still simmered from the layers of heavy gases, but it was not enough. At this distance, his faeros allies should have been frolicking in the magnetic arcs of solar flares, immersed in the boiling energy sea of the corona. Like flickering flames, they embodied chaos and entropy. The faeros consumed formal structures and rigid organization. They did as they liked.

Not any longer. Not here. They were nearly extinct. Chaos itself was out of balance. The very concept seemed a contradiction.

Though his body was composed of plasma and lava rather than flesh and bone, Rusa'h felt a memory of cold. He guided the fireball ship around the dark star once more, imagining the agony that had rippled through the faeros that had perished there.

Once, he had tried to guide the Ildiran race down a new path, but he had been forced to flee into the sun. After being engulfed by that inferno, though, his body had been changed rather than consumed. And now Rusa'h understood how he could influence the faeros to bring down the corrupt Mage-Imperator Jora'h – and save his people.

Now that he had joined the fiery entities, Rusa'h hoped to use his understanding of Ildirans to satisfy the faeros need for rebirth. At times, even the blazing elementals did not understand him, but they knew he burned with a longing for revenge, and for control.

Fulfilling a personal Ildiran need, Rusa'h had incinerated the treacherous Dobro Designate Udru'h. As he did so, he followed the soul-thread and drew on the potent fuel of Udru'h's life force. When Udru'h's dying spark added to the flames of the waning elemental beings, Rusa'h was astonished by the connection. How had he not seen it before? He could link the soulfire of the faeros to the soul-threads of *thism*. It was a revelation both for him and for the fiery entities.

Much as green priests had spread the worldtrees, Rusa'h could replenish the faeros. He could spark more faeros by burning soul after Ildiran soul, until the fiery beings became unquenchable. Rusa'h had begun his crusade to resurrect the dwindling numbers of the faeros, but at the same time he would be bringing his lost Ildiran people directly into the Lightsource.

There would be resistance, of course, but he would be doing a good thing, no matter how much pain it caused. Some of his people would be required to make an important sacrifice.

Rusa'h decided to go first to the worlds where he had already laid down new paths of *thism*. Those connections would allow him easy passage while he built up his strength. Entire planetary populations had no way to resist him. Leaving the dead sun at Crenna, he guided his fireball toward the Horizon Cluster, where countless souls were already ripe – waiting to be harvested.

In the days of Rusa'h's spreading rebellion, Dzelluria had been his first conquest after subsuming the population of Hyrillka. He had declared himself Imperator and taken his followers to unsuspecting Dzelluria. Forcing young Designate-in-waiting Czir'h to watch, Rusa'h killed the old Designate, then compelled Czir'h to submit to the new *thism*. After the rebellion failed, however, the cowardly young Designate had grovelled for the Mage-Imperator's forgiveness, and the people of his planet poured themselves into reconstructing their capital, their cities, their lives. Now, with an entourage of blazing ellipsoids, Rusa'h returned to Dzelluria – to bring them the fire.

As his fireballs rolled in across the sky, Rusa'h saw how frantically everyone was working. Construction crews on tall scaffolding erected monoliths and fountains, and raised statues in a furious effort to erase the scars of the previous takeover. It had only been a few months, but the main city already blossomed with taller towers and grander halls than ever before. The people thought themselves safe now in the Mage-Imperator's *thism* web.

They needed to burn.

From his fiery craft, Rusa'h gazed down with enhanced senses and saw the young Designate standing with a lens kithman on a balcony, looking up into the sky, as if wondering why the sun was growing brighter. *Another* sun – several of them, in fact, that descended like huge meteors sheathed in flame. Czir'h watched the ellipsoids race across the sky toward him.

Rusa'h easily found the old, never-healed paths of *thism* in the young Designate's mind. He cut Czir'h off from the soul-threads of the Ildiran race, completely isolating him; separating the lens kithman took even less time. With the hunger of the faeros behind him, Rusa'h did not see them as people, but as sparks. In a searing burst of energy that pulsed like lava through the *thism*, Rusa'h set loose the cleansing fire.

Czir'h and his lens kithman collapsed as the elemental blaze consumed their soulfires and made the faeros stronger.

Smiling, Rusa'h reached out to the rest of the people of Dzelluria.

TWENTY-SEVEN

CESCA PERONI

After the wentals had spread through numerous gas giants and bottled up the enemy hydrogues, Jess and Cesca returned to the primordial water planet of Charybdis. They finally had each other and looked forward to spending time away from the rest of the Spiral Arm. Just themselves.

As the silvery water bubble descended, the skies were grey and cloudy, gorged with living rain. Lightning bolts skittered like patterns traced by the baton of an orchestra conductor, releasing pent-up wental power. As soon as the sphere touched the steely waves, its surface tension vanished and the entire vessel mingled with the rest of the gathered wentals.

Freed and happy, Jess and Cesca swam together in the alien ocean. Countless essences flowed through them, voices echoing the thoughts of the widespread mind of the wentals. It was unlike anything Cesca had experienced in her previous life.

The hydrogues are not destroyed, but they are finished. We will contain and control them.

Warm rain spattered Cesca's face, running down her skin. 'I still

133

don't understand what the original war was about. Is the conflict resolved?'

Answers bubbled forth, revealing information that neither of them had heard or understood before. *We four manifestations – wentals, verdani, faeros, hydrogues – battle to determine the course of the universe, bending space, time, and physical law to set the cosmos on its future course. We decide whether the universe will expand forever, cool off and die . . . or eventually draw itself together and collapse.*

Shall the universe be the abode of life, organization, and growth – or energy, chaos, and dissipation? That fundamental battle is fought from the nucleus of an atom to the largest galactic supercluster. Life fights beside life, chaos beside chaos.

'So if we destroy the beings of chaos – the faeros and hydrogues – we'll win?' Jess asked.

Chaos can only be controlled, whereas life can be destroyed. The stakes are unequal.

'But life can be renewed,' Cesca said.

And that is what saves you. Most of the hydrogues are bound within their gas giants. If the faeros can be similarly contained, then the balance will be struck again. The universe can return to harmony.

Jess and Cesca could move on with their strange, new lives – lives different from what they had ever dreamed. When she had undergone the deep changes in order to save her life, she had known that she was sacrificing all hope of living normally among humans and did not regret it. Cesca had willingly given that up to be with him.

Yet she missed the Roamers.

Later – they did not know the specific passage of time here – the two of them stood together on a water-slick black rock as the waves danced a joyous ballet around them. By sharing emotions and memories, Jess and Cesca had told the watery elementals what they intended to do. This was what their Guiding Star had shown them.

'It's not at all how I imagined our wedding,' Jess said in a gentle voice. 'No gathering of clan leaders, no elegant clothes, no officials – either legal or religious. Are you disappointed?'

Her heart full to overflowing, Cesca gazed into his eyes. 'How can I be?' She would have liked to share this day with Speaker Okiah, who had wanted to preside at Cesca's wedding. But that had been to a different man – Jess's brother. Both Ross Tamblyn and Cesca's subsequent fiancé, Reynald of Theroc, had been murdered by the hydrogues. Even then, Jess and Cesca hadn't dared to admit their love for each other to their families. And once the wentals saved Jess's life by transforming him, it had been too late. Cesca gave him a tremulous smile. 'There were times I didn't think our Guiding Stars would ever bring us together.'

'This time, nothing will stop us.'

Without words, an understanding passed between Jess and Cesca: the wentals would be their witnesses, and no human 'official' had more power to bind them to each other than what they themselves possessed.

Moisture-laden clouds tumbled overhead, not ominous thunderheads, but swollen congregations of liquid force. Energized spray and mist defied the gravity of Charybdis, rising up in gauzy tangles like a wedding veil. Golden beams of sunlight broke through gaps in the clouds to create brilliant rainbows. Cesca knew the wentals were intentionally staging this exquisite display.

They faced each other, palms held outward, touching. Wental liquid glistened on their skin, clothing them in sparkling splendour. She spoke the traditional words she had long ago memorized. 'I am pledged to you, Jess Tamblyn. I am meant for you. I give you my heart and my promise.'

Jess could not take his eyes from her. 'I am pledged to you, Cesca Peroni. I am meant for you. I give you my heart and my promise. Though the universe changes around us, we will always be together in our minds and in our souls.'

'Yes, in our minds and souls. The Guiding Star will show us the way.'

Pillars of water girdled with mist rose from the oceans, a whole congregation of wentals. The air hummed with static electricity. Fresh ozone filled their nostrils.

The clouds burst and cool, refreshing rain poured down. The wentals shed countless droplets of themselves, symbolizing not tears, but blessings for the seeds of all the wentals that Jess and his water-bearers had helped to spread.

TWENTY-EIGHT

KING PETER

'Our major priority must be to defend ourselves, and our biggest concern is Chairman Basil Wenceslas,' Peter said in a discussion with several advisers. Such impromptu conferences were common now and included any experts he could gather at a moment's notice. Representatives came and went, bringing trade goods, offering support and suggestions, delivering Confederation delegates from colonies or clans.

'Now that the treeships are gone,' Estarra said, 'Theroc doesn't even have a hint of a space navy, and the Roamers don't have battleships.'

'If General Lanyan knew how unprotected we were, we'd be in deep trouble,' said Tasia Tamblyn, who had traded in her EDF uniform for a comfortable Roamer jumpsuit. Tasia and Robb Brindle intended to find passage back to Plumas, where they would assist her uncles in rebuilding the water mines. Since learning all the details of the political turmoil, Tasia had become quite outspoken in offering advice.

Robb sighed. 'Well he's bound to find out soon – thanks to my father, if nothing else.'

When flying away in his EDF transport, Lieutenant Commander Brindle had ignored orders to return to Theroc, but Peter hadn't been willing to order the ship shot down. As King, he hoped he hadn't made a terrible mistake.

'Fortunately for us, the compy revolt and the hydrogues severely weakened the EDF,' a very pregnant Queen Estarra said. 'They won't be launching military strikes anytime soon.'

Peter wasn't so sure. 'Don't expect Basil to let an opportunity slide by.'

'But we're *traders*, not soldiers,' Denn Peroni said. 'We're not equipped to fly military vessels.'

'But Roamers are adaptable,' Tasia said. 'That's our hallmark.'

Peter nodded. 'We've all got to change the way we do things, show ourselves to our enemies in a new light. Hide-and-seek isn't good enough anymore.'

Alarmed, Yarrod voiced reservations on behalf of many fellow green priests. 'Theroc has never needed a military before. We cooperated with the Hansa, and we stayed independent.'

'There's no more cooperating with the Hansa. And there's no more calm independence. You saw the Chairman declare war on innocent Roamer clans. He'll try to destroy the Confederation the moment he sees an opening.'

Robb, having clearly changed his mind about the EDF and the Hansa, said, 'I still can't believe all of us in the forces just followed orders that got crazier and crazier, day after day. That's not the EDF I signed up for.'

'We hoped that at least some members of the military would follow their King rather than the Chairman. Even a handful of defections would have given us some battleships.' Peter shook his head. 'But that hasn't happened.'

Estarra put her hand across her swollen belly, winced, then relaxed her expression. 'Wishful thinking.'

Peter was determined, though. 'If we can't recruit EDF battle-ships, then we'll build our own. I need your help – all of you. We'll need Roamer industries converted to produce armaments. Mr Peroni, I understand that Del Kellum has put you in charge of the new Osquivel shipyards?'

Denn crossed his arms over his chest, making his zippers and ringlets jingle. 'Just give me the specs.'

Peter turned to Tasia and Robb. 'And you two are the most well-versed in how the EDF thinks and works.'

'That's not very encouraging.' Tasia chuckled, and Robb looked embarrassed. 'We've both been out of the loop for quite a while.'

'Even so, you're the best the Confederation has. I know you hoped to go to Plumas, but I'm asking you to accept a special assignment first. Go to the Osquivel shipyards and show them how we need to arm our ships. Refit as many of the vessels as we already have. Work miracles for me.'

Robb looked at Tasia. 'If she's up for it, so am I.'

'I wouldn't do it without you, Brindle.' Peter watched an expression of acceptance and practicality settle on Tasia's face. 'Does this job at least come with a living wage?'

In an open meadow, the Teacher compy stood rigid, his optical sensors glowing brightly even in the daylight. Peter paced next to him. 'This is a turnabout, isn't it, OX – me being the teacher and you the student?'

'I believe your observation to be factually correct. However, you are the King, and it is not necessary for you to spend valuable time assisting me. From data uploads and selected program-ming packs, I can relearn any diplomatic, political, and historical information you require.'

'What I require, OX, is *you*. You taught me the subtle difference between data and *knowledge*. They're not at all the same things. In the Whisper Palace, I had enemies and I had allies, and each of them had biases and agendas. You were the only one I could count on to give me rational, objective advice.'

'I will continue to do my best, King Peter.'

Estarra sat near them on the soft grass. They had all come out to the meadow where the small hydrogue derelict had landed. Each time Peter saw the derelict and OX – who was no longer OX – he was reminded of how much the old compy had given up in order to help Peter and Estarra escape. Would it have been kinder if OX had simply been destroyed in battle? The compy didn't even know what he had lost. Fortunately, one of the Roamer engineers had upgraded the ancient Teacher compy's memory capacity, allowing him room to acquire and retain new memories without deleting the advanced programming he had needed to guide the alien vessel.

'We're going to spend at least an hour a day together, OX – you and I and Queen Estarra. We'll help you relearn the things you need to know.'

The Teacher compy had been a valuable historical and political asset for centuries. Peter hoped that Basil Wenceslas had grasped the value of such a resource. So much firsthand knowledge of Hansa history had resided within OX's memory core. Basil must have kept a backup somewhere.

OX turned his head as two people approached. 'Greetings, Tasia Tamblyn and Robb Brindle.'

Tasia had been watching the royal couple with OX. Her expression, normally brash and confident, revealed a deep hurt. 'I had a Listener compy named EA. I think it was the Chairman himself who tried to interrogate her – and triggered her memory wipe. EA was in my family for years, and I tried like hell to replace those memories, telling her stories of my childhood, adventures we'd had together.' Her lips quirked in a sad smile. 'It started to work, too. We were making new memories together, even if I couldn't restore everything she'd lost.'

'And what was the result, Tasia Tamblyn?' OX asked. 'Were you ultimately successful? I am most interested.'

'Never got the chance to find out. Those damned black robots tore EA apart.' Her voice hitched and her shoulders trembled. Robb rested a comforting hand on her neck, but Tasia composed herself and took a step away from him, trying to look tough.

'So we share two enemies in common,' Peter pointed out. 'Chairman Wenceslas and the Klikiss robots.'

'For starters, yes.'

Robb cleared his throat. 'We just wanted to let you know we're heading to Osquivel. Denn Peroni is going to take us back to the shipyards. Thank you for trusting us with this responsibility. We won't let you down.'

'A ruler's job is to make the right choices,' Estarra said, 'and you two are certainly a good choice.'

'The best,' Tasia answered with a smile, recapturing her good humour. 'Before you know it, we'll be sending well-armed and well-armoured ships back here to protect Theroc from the Big Goose.'

'I wish I could offer you more time,' Peter said, 'but I'm afraid we don't have that luxury.'

'Don't worry.' Robb's tone held a note of irony. 'We can handle the pressure.'

'Good luck,' OX said, surprising them.

TWENTY-NINE

MARGARET COLICOS

Always an outsider, Margaret leaned against one of the freshly erected towers. The resin cement still held an unnatural spit-and-rancid-oil odour that would eventually fade as it cured in the dry air and sunlight.

Margaret could come and go as she liked from the walled-in colony settlement, but no one else seemed to have the nerve. The rest of the colonists remained inside, intimidated by the insect creatures toiling around the stockade. Margaret had never been able to decide if the Klikiss ignored her out of respect because they feared her 'special music', or if they simply dismissed her.

Judging from what she had learned among the Klikiss, Margaret knew that the breedex was currently obsessed with destroying the black robots wherever it might find them. This morning the first massive assault force had marched through the transportal to Wollamor. Once the robots posed no further threat, all the breedexes from the new subhives would battle to exterminate each other.

As preoccupied as they were with taking vengeance, she

knew the Klikiss would turn on the colonists sooner or later.

DD turned his optical sensors in the direction of her gaze. 'What are you observing, Margaret?'

'I'm watching those poor colonists. They don't understand.'

'I would be happy to explain any matter to them, if you tell me the subject.'

'No. You can't. I've got to figure out a way to help, or at least warn them.'

Unexpectedly, she saw a dark-skinned man leave the stockade through one of the openings in the wall and walk away, carefully evading the Klikiss; Margaret was not particularly surprised to see that they paid him no heed. From the top of the thick wall, several colonists including Orli Covitz stared after him in amazement as he cautiously approached the hive city.

The man picked his way toward her, and Margaret hurried to intercept him before he inadvertently stepped in the wrong direction. 'Davlin Lotze, what are you doing?'

'Testing just how much leeway the bugs give us.' His sharp eyes darted from side to side as two warriors lumbered past without challenging him. In constant rustle of pointed legs and exoskeletons, the Klikiss continued to move about, making their endless chirping and clicking noises. 'And I was coming to see you. Let's get out of this traffic.'

'You've got nerves of steel, Davlin. Not many other colonists would have risked doing what you just did.'

'That's why I had to do it. Now that I've satisfied myself as to the possibility, it gives me a host of options.'

When Margaret led him into the lee of an ancient, weathered tower, he hauled out a small datapad from his shirt. 'I've slipped out three times now on brief recon missions. Also, from an observation point on the wall, I've managed to compile full image sets of the various sub-breeds around us. I need your help to identify them.' He began showing her images. 'Can you tell me what each type of bug does?'

She had done much the same in her early days among them, trying to classify and categorize the Klikiss. But Davlin's interest did not seem scientific, as hers had been. 'Do you intend to submit a technical paper when we get back to the Hansa?'

He regarded her without any readable expression. 'It's for our defence. We have to identify which sub-breeds are a threat and which ones can be ignored. I am assessing our opponent and formulating potential plans.'

She looked at the images. He had even gotten a shot of one type near the Klikiss ruins that had a pale carapace and a horrifyingly human face, but it had not stayed still enough to let Davlin get a clear image. She shuddered as she remembered the origin of those sub-breeds. *Poor Howard Palawu.*

'Let me show you how to break down the genetic map of the Klikiss.' Identifying the sub-breeds for him, Margaret rattled off information she had stored up in her mind over the course of many years. Davlin listened, made notes, and seemed to be memorizing every word she said. This was the first time they had spoken closely together, and she found the man very impressive. Because he had long ago been sent to Rheindic Co to find her, he already knew a great deal about her. It was clear as he pressed her for details about the Klikiss that he had no capricious curiosity, but a genuine drive to help the colonists.

'What are all those people corralled inside the wall supposed to live on?' He looked at her. 'Can we eat Klikiss food?'

'I did.' She remembered the first time she'd gotten hungry enough to taste the mashed, mealy mixture. 'It kept me alive.'

On Llaro, Klikiss 'biomass gathering swarms' had continued to fly out, using nets like giant butterfly catchers to scoop up any airborne creatures. Gatherers returned from distant rivers and lakes with bins full of marsh-weed, jellyfish, and flopping, scaly swimmers. The Klikiss dumped everything together and processed it into a homogeneous mealy substance. Huge quantities of it were stored in newly built silos next to the breedex hive.

'So, will the Klikiss provide the humans with food, now that they've harvested everything in the vicinity?'

'I doubt very much the breedex even thinks of such things.'

'How do we change that? Those colonists have a few hidden supplies, but they won't last forever.'

She hesitated, looking him in the eyes, then abruptly stepped away from the uneven wall of the tower. Without showing – or feeling – any fear, Margaret placed herself directly in front of a marching worker. Since the hive mind controlled all the creatures, Margaret could talk directly to the breedex by speaking to any one of the ungainly insects. 'You!' She clapped her hands.

The yellow-and-black creature paused. She launched into a tongue-twisting, throat-scraping series of clicks and guttural noises that conveyed the general concepts of nourishment and how the colonists, as members of her subhive, needed to be fed.

The worker moved to one side and tried to stride past her. Margaret interposed herself again, and gave its hard head carapace a sharp smack. 'Listen to me!' She repeated her demands in the Klikiss language, and supplemented her words by scrawling the main ideas in equation symbols in the trampled dirt.

'Food. For my hive.' She pointed to the stockade. 'Food!'

Grudgingly, it seemed, the breedex sent instantaneous commands. Four workers emerged from one of the thick-walled storage vaults, carrying rough containers filled with mealy Klikiss cuisine. They delivered the containers to the walled-in town.

Davlin was impressed. 'All right. Now let's work on a water-delivery system.'

THIRTY

SIRIX

Klikiss warriors from Llaro streamed through the Wollamor transportal and crashed into the defensive line of Soldier compies. The compies were powerful fighters with tough body armour and reaction speeds far superior to those of any mere human. But they were no match for the vengeful warrior breed of insects.

Sirix retreated as fast as his artificial body could move, before it was too late. Klikiss were coming through the transportal, right here, and his main force of EDF ships was still in orbit. Sirix needed to get to his Juggernaut and use that firepower to eradicate the hateful creators all over again. He sent a burst to his two compies. 'Get aboard the nearest troop transport.'

QT, his green-and-chrome skin filthy from the scuffle, said, 'Would not one of the Mantas be a safer and more defensible refuge?'

He had already dismissed the possibility. 'Such bulky ships will take too long to lift off. Their larger systems and their sheer mass will slow them down.' The two compies dutifully hurried to one of the shuttles on Wollamor's blackened spaceport field. Other robots scuttled to individual Remoras and streaked off into the sky to save themselves.

Sirix could see great numbers of Klikiss warriors sweeping around to flank the landed cruisers, already marking the Mantas as targets. He gambled that the detestable creatures would not bother with the lesser ships – yet. Even so, the two vital cruisers would be lost! And more irreplaceable black robots.

He sent a wide-band signal commanding his comrades to retreat. Some of the black robots split open their carapaces, spread their wings, and flew – only to be shot down by warriors using bell-mouthed energy dischargers. The weapons were unlike any design Sirix used by the prior incarnation of the Klikiss. With wing panels burned and body cores shattered, the robots tumbled out of the sky.

As Sirix had feared, the two landed Mantas were under a full-blown attack. He considered them already lost. And he still didn't understand why – how! – the Klikiss had returned.

In a desperate attempt to hold the line, Soldier compies threw themselves upon the Klikiss warriors. The compies cracked enemy exoskeletons and spilled insect bodily fluids. Dead insects piled up, yet more continued to stream through the transportal. This was not just a foray party, but a complete subhive army.

As if uprooting weeds, the insect warriors discarded the Soldier compies. They plucked artificial arms and legs from metal torsos, ripped the compies' heads off, or simply smashed them aside. But the hundreds of military robots sacrificed so far had gained Sirix enough time to reach the troop transport. They had served their purpose.

PD and QT were already aboard, as were five other black robots. One was in the cockpit, firing up the engines.

Most of the retreating robots, however, headed automatically to the Mantas on the mistaken assumption that the large warships could protect them. Sirix could not save them from such a miscalculation. The engines would need at least fifteen more minutes before the cruisers could lift off. One of the Mantas began blasting away from any jazer port at a suitable angle to hit the Klikiss on the ground. Deadly beams ripped through the warriors, as well as any Soldier compies that happened to be in the way.

More Klikiss came through the transportal, different breeds: builders, harvesters, diggers. The breedex had already assumed victory on Wollamor.

One of the Mantas began to heave itself from the landing field but crashed as its engines were destroyed by concentrated fire from the bell-mouthed energy dischargers. Groups of Klikiss warriors rushed scientist and engineer breeds through gaps they had torn in the Manta's hull, hurrying them aboard to take over or sabotage the Manta. Even fighting beside the remaining Soldier compies, those robots would not be strong enough. Sirix wrote them all off.

During the battle at Earth, he had lost many of his fellow robots, but he had never expected to fight the *Klikiss*. If he could get to orbit, though, and take refuge aboard his Juggernaut, he could eliminate the transportal and cut the insect warriors off from Wollamor.

Sirix sealed the troop transport and hurried to the cockpit. Any other black robots would have to find their own ways to escape. As they lifted away from the battlefield, he jacked into the communications systems and sent a signal burst to his ships in orbit. He called them down to stem the tide of Klikiss invaders. 'We are leaving Wollamor. Destroy it. Destroy it all.'

As the transport rose higher, Sirix saw more insect warriors march through the transportal, fanning out over their new territory. They sifted through the wreckage of Soldier compies and black robots, as if to make sure the mayhem had been thorough.

The second grounded Manta exploded, flinging shrapnel across the field. More losses to tally.

Finally, descending under full thrust so that atmospheric friction heated their prows to a scarlet glow, the EDF ships soared down. From high above, jazers like hot blades chopped apart the Klikiss swarm. The insect creatures could not stand against this.

Though many weapons had been depleted during the battle at Earth, the Mantas dropped bombs, then six precision nuclear warheads. The Wollamor colony, all the invading members of the Klikiss subhive, and the transportal itself vanished in a flash. Wollamor was no longer a desirable location. Sirix was already revising and formulating his next step.

His shuttle climbed out of the atmosphere into the emptiness where his fleet offered the safety he needed. Smaller vessels rendezvoused with the remainder of the ships in space. Remoras carrying black robot survivors circled the main group of vessels in planetary orbit. Once again, Sirix found himself needing to reassess his strength, to regroup. More of his robots had been annihilated. What should have been a simple conquest of the Spiral Arm had turned against them.

The return of the Klikiss changed everything, and this could not have been an accidental encounter. The creator race was hunting down their robots.

Taking his fleet out of the Wollamor system, Sirix decided to go immediately to the burgeoning base on Maratha. There, he would gather reinforcements of black robots and powerful war vessels. Then they could stand against the Klikiss and the humans.

THIRTY-ONE

CHAIRMAN BASIL WENCESLAS

The spy flybys returned to the Hansa with a wealth of fascinating information. Lieutenant Commander Conrad Brindle had told him what to expect. Even so, Basil was surprised. Alone in his penthouse office, the Chairman studied the images with all the intensity of a chess master in the middle of a championship match. 'Peter, Peter, Peter – did you learn nothing from what I taught you?'

He switched from one snapshot to the next, analysing the traffic patterns and the spacecraft arrayed around Theroc. The flyby ships had streaked through the system, captured high-res images, and raced away before the Theron perimeter defences could spot them. Basil traced pathways along the screen, running a categorization routine.

A lesser man might have taken time off, relieving the pressure of leadership by retreating for a few hours to talk with friends or play a game, but Chairman Wenceslas did not like games. Games were petty diversions for people who had nothing more interesting to do, killing time rather than accomplishing something. Basil always had something more interesting to do. His 'game' was politics, and his playing board was the Spiral Arm. Now he faced the highest-stakes match in human history: the Hansa Chairman versus the rebel King. A talented politician and well-educated leader with decades of experience against a street kid who had been given new clothes and a bit of training. Unlike the fairytale of David and Goliath, this time Goliath would not lose.

On the spy image, Theroc's forested continents appeared green and amazingly recovered from the hydrogue attacks. Most of the ships he saw were mere cargo carriers, ramshackle trading vessels that looked as if someone had assembled them from a boxed kit missing a few pieces. Roamers, of course. Some vessels still had the gall to carry Hansa markings. He repeated the images from both flybys, but saw nothing that presented any sort of military threat. Yes, only a month had passed, and with much turmoil. Even so . . .

'Peter, you can't be that stupid.'

General Lanyan had already departed with the *Jupiter* to consolidate the Colonization Initiative planets as a first step toward reuniting the Hansa. Basil's current goal was to identify the weakest – and potentially most vital – Hansa colonies that had boldly, foolishly, declared their independence.

But Theroc lay so exposed! The Chairman had never expected such an opportunity to present itself. A single concerted strike could decapitate the Confederation. He sat back from his screen and sipped from a glass of iced lemon water, his preferred drink now that he had given up cardamom coffee.

Seize the opportunity. This would solve all the Hansa's problems and win the match in one breathtaking move.

He found Admiral Willis working with Cain in the EDF's subsidiary admin office in the Hansa pyramid. She and the deputy stood among cheerful poster-projections of brave soldiers and spiked-diamond warglobes. 'Damn, if this doesn't get cheery recruits to sign up for the EDF, I don't know what will,' Willis said with a snort. 'Maybe we should just promise them free beer, while we're at it.'

Cain was more detached. 'Remember, we are trying to scrounge volunteers from the most stubborn segment of our population – those who didn't step forward when our situation was most dire. We have to appeal to them somehow.'

'We're scraping the bottom of the barrel.' On the poster Willis tapped the freckled face of a new corporal who seemed immensely satisfied with his job. 'This kid looks like he's thinking EDF rations are the most delicious thing he's tasted in his life.'

Basil interrupted them, his voice harsh. 'We should not need to lure soldiers with promises and prizes. They should see our need, feel their obligation, and do what is right.'

Willis rolled her eyes. 'Fat chance of that happening.'

Basil could not keep the resignation out of his voice. 'I'm afraid you're right.' He closed the door, so that no one could overhear them. 'Admiral, you wanted something significant to do?'

'Well, writing up rah-rah ads and monitoring a bunch of disorganized shipyards is not entirely up to the level of my capabilities.'

Basil frowned at her bitter tone. After Lanyan had left for Rheindic Co in her Juggernaut, Willis had done a solid job managing the shipyards, and – for all her grousing – he expected this recruitment drive to be reasonably successful, as well. But she could do so much more.

'I want you to save the Hansa, Admiral. I've come up with a mission that can end the rebellion, unify the human race, and put us on a direct road to strength and prosperity.'

Willis's lips quirked in a smile. 'That sounds significant enough.'

Cain rotated the projections of the template posters to the opposite side of the display table. The one in front had giant, bold letters positioned above an orbital image of Earth. *EDF: NOW*. The chain-of-stars logo arced over the black backdrop, while a small, blackened piece of space wreckage from an unidentifiable ship hung ominously in the foreground.

Basil stepped to the display table, inserted his encrypted datapak, and called up in large-scale format the succession of images from the spy flybys. Willis saw the implications immediately. 'You want me to attack *Theroc*. You want me to overthrow the new Confederation.'

'I want you to bring it under control,' Basil corrected. 'And arrest Peter. We'll neutralize him and set an acceptable King back in place. That'll be the end of all this nonsense.'

Cain kept his face stony. 'Very dangerous, Mr Chairman. Politically speaking, I mean.'

'If you want me to do this, it would be a damned good time to have my Juggernaut back,' Willis added.

'Nonsense. Look at the screen. Four or five Mantas should certainly be enough for a job like this.'

After a brisk knock at the door, Captain McCammon entered the recruiting office, looking apologetic. 'You summoned me, Mr Chairman?' His crimson beret sat at the perfect angle on his pale hair; his colourful uniform was immaculate. Basil had never stopped wondering how McCammon, with his flawless service record, could have botched everything so badly by letting Peter, Estarra, and Daniel get away.

As Willis replayed the images of the trader ships circling Theroc, the Chairman said, 'Captain McCammon, we are about to engage in a dramatic operation. I require your assurance that the intractable green priest remains under your control and that he will not have a chance either to observe our preparations or communicate his suspicions through the treeling.'

McCammon's brow furrowed. 'Mr Chairman, we've kept Nahton securely under house arrest, as you requested. His tree is over in the royal wing of the palace. It is not feasible that he could see or communicate any information whatsoever.'

Cain turned to the captain of the royal guard. 'The Chairman intends to send an EDF battle group to conquer Theroc and seize King Peter. Obviously, we can't let any green priest know this.'

Basil glared at the deputy. Cain simply didn't understand the compartmentalization of power. 'Captain McCammon did not require so much information.'

The guard captain reacted with surprise. 'Theroc has always been independent, Mr Chairman. To attack it using the Earth Defence Forces and kidnap the King—'

Basil cut him off. 'If you hadn't let Peter escape in the first place, we wouldn't have this problem.' He touched his forefinger to his lips. 'In fact, remind me why the royal guard still exists. Who are you guarding, now that we have no King?'

'He's babysitting a green priest, apparently,' Willis said, 'just like I was babysitting shipyards.'

McCammon seemed very pale. 'Might I inquire, Mr Chairman, when we can expect to have a new King? The Hansa needs one.'

Basil suppressed a smile, noting that none of the recruitment ads mentioned anything about 'fighting for the King'. 'My alternative candidate has been in training for months now, since long before Peter left, but I'm being very cautious. We've made mistakes before.' Once Peter found out who the candidate was, he would go absolutely ballistic! 'We've got important business to complete. This is no time to break in a mere trainee.' Basil gazed across the desktop at the projections and smiled. 'If Admiral Willis is successful, we'll have all the breathing room we need.'

He pointed to the *EDF: NOW* poster. 'I like this one.'

THIRTY-TWO

TASIA TAMBLYN

Armed with the King's instructions and blessing, Tasia and Robb were delivered to the shipyards at Osquivel by Denn Peroni himself.

'My dad would be proud of me for landing such a high position in the military,' Robb said. 'If only it wasn't the wrong military . . .'

'He'll come around when he sees what's happening on Earth,' Tasia answered.

'*My* father? He's served in the EDF all his life.'

The first sight of the ringed gas planet brought up many disturbing memories for both of them. Robb had been captured by the hydrogues down in those clouds. Tasia had sent her devoted compy EA here to warn the Kellum shipyards about the impending arrival of the EDF. And she'd faced a horrific battle with the hydrogues here at Osquivel. Now that Roamer families were coming out of hiding, the rings were dotted with spacedocks and smelting operations.

'Looks like we've got a lot of work to do here, Brindle,' she said. 'Whip these people into shape, redesign ships to include

155

armaments, and get a Confederation militia working before the Hansa can come after Theroc.'

Denn smiled at the pair as he docked his *Dogged Persistence* at the main admin asteroid. 'You'll have everything you need from me. Talk to anybody you like, requisition all necessary materials. Even enlist Kotto Okiah – he's here and ready to help.'

Robb watched the seeming chaos of industrial structures drifting around in the rings, metal frameworks, glowing heat sinks, the sparkle of fabrication exhausts. 'How are we ever going to pull it together?'

'Shizz, that's easy. We don't have to deal with Eddy bureaucracy.'

Tasia and Robb were granted temporary housing – 'One room. We'll share. Thank you.' Fresh off the trading ship, they settled into cramped quarters that were drilled out of a small floating rock.

Now that they were finally alone, their biggest shift was dealing with the changes in their relationship. After a quick and unimpressed glance through the thick glass of a single thirty-centimetre-wide window in their quarters, Tasia said, 'You're stuck with me, Brindle. Any regrets?'

During their imprisonment by the drogues, they'd been engrossed in their own survival. After being rescued, they had learned of the dramatic political shift, clashed with Robb's father, changed allegiances. Now, at last, there was time to breathe, and to realize what they had done. Much as they might fantasize about it, Robb and Tasia couldn't simply pick up from where they had been years ago. Too much had changed.

He answered honestly. 'Of course I've got a few regrets. I hardly know where I am anymore, or where I'll be tomorrow.'

'You're feeling like a true Roamer then. Want to go back to Earth, after all, and make up with your parents?'

'And leave you?'

'Well, don't expect *me* to go back to the Hansa!'

'Then I'm staying here. Guiding Stars and all that.'

She kissed him. 'You're sweet, Brindle.'

'That's what my commanding officers always say.'

She playfully punched him. 'Come on, let's go see if these workers know what they're doing.'

Sooner or later, somebody would design a logo for the Confederation militia, and Tasia would embroider it on her pockets (and Robb's). But right now, their authority was implicit. She was delighted to be among Roamers again. Even if she didn't know the clan members personally – it had been a lot of years, after all – the ribbons and zippers and embroidered pockets reminded her of her childhood when she'd tagged along with Ross or Jess to Rendezvous. Now, she was here to boss the workers around and turn any available vessels into defensive ships.

The two took a small transport pod over to a central gathering station where they joined the dusty, sweaty members of a returning shift in the mess hall. Robb studied the bustle, listened to the loud voices, tried to identify the different uniforms, clan markings, crewmembers separating to join friends or relatives at other tables. To him, the whole Roamer culture was madcap and noisy; his parents had been coolly efficient, buttoned-down military personnel. 'How do they get anything done in all this craziness?'

'Practice, I suppose. Everybody wants to make a profit, to survive and thrive, so any intractable ones get taken care of internally. Somehow it works – sort of like you and me.'

In the mess hall, they found Kotto Okiah sitting at a table, oblivious to the clamour around him. The eccentric engineer stared at a design screen, absentmindedly picking at a tray of food, spilling crumbs on his screen and brushing them aside. Kotto had no official position at the shipyards, but he redesigned equipment and vessels whenever he saw a flaw. He was like a child playing in a toy store, coming up with wild ideas, changing processes to see what worked and what could work better. All the Roamers had faith in him, regardless of how strange his schemes sounded.

Tasia approached him, peering over his shoulder. 'Have you heard about the new job we have for you, Kotto?'

He was not at all self-conscious to be watched at his work. 'Denn sent me a message, but I haven't accessed it yet.' He glanced up from his screen at Tasia and Robb. He didn't seem to recognize either of them, but apparently considered that more his problem than theirs. He brightened. 'Did the little hydrogue derelict come back from Theroc? I wanted to work on that again—'

'We need you to help us add weapons and shielding to our Roamer ships.'

Kotto was startled out of his concentration. 'Never needed them before. The drogues are defeated.' He looked around as if he had missed something. 'Aren't they?'

'We're not worried about the hydrogues,' Tasia said. 'In case you didn't get the memo, Kotto, the Spiral Arm has changed. Marauders, pirates, and even the Eddies want a piece of anything we bring to market. We've got to defend ourselves.'

'There was a memo?'

'I was exaggerating.'

Robb added, 'We understand that you're the man who can help us put together a full-blown military. And we need it as fast as humanly possible.'

'They always do.' On screen Kotto called up a clean diagram of a modified trade hauler. Brow furrowed, he began tapping zones, thinking, then highlighting areas. 'I can add additional hull armour here. We can manufacture traditional guns to be installed here and here.' His eyes had a distant look, and then he began to smile. 'There are quite a few options, actually. I'll start incorporating them into all of my blueprints.'

THIRTY-THREE

PATRICK FITZPATRICK III

By the time he reached Yreka in his borrowed ship and nondescript clothing, Patrick no longer thought of himself as an imposter. Flying around by himself had given him time to think. He felt like he was becoming a different person, shedding all vestiges of his rich and powerful family. He was tired of carrying around dark secrets, like unwanted cargo that had begun to go bad ... Painful as it might be, he had to clean house. Patrick Fitzpatrick III could be his own person for once.

Yreka had changed even more than he had, transforming from a small, relatively uninteresting Hansa colony into a bustling commercial hub. When he flew in, he expected the Yrekans to demand identification, but they put the *Gypsy* in a holding pattern, gave him a number, and told him he'd have to wait an hour before beginning his descent because of all the traffic.

Ships rose into the air, heavy cargo vessels like metal bumblebees and small swift scouts and couriers marked with Roamer clan symbols. Other vessels were colony spacecraft that had been grounded during the extreme ekti shortages. Stardrive fuel was no longer an issue, since Roamers had gone back to skymining, and they clearly provided their allies with plenty of ekti. The Hansa and the EDF were still desperate for fuel, but he shook off any guilt as soon as he passed a former Hansa supply ship and noted that the encircled Earth symbol had been aggressively sandblasted from its hull.

When he finally received clearance, he followed the instructions and landed on a designated plot of what had once been cropland – cropland that he and the EDF had destroyed in a gesture of pique. Patrick had led part of that crackdown, blowing up an unarmed colonist ship that attempted to escape. At the time he'd been smug about his actions, sure that they were the only way to teach the unruly colonists a lesson. He hadn't given a second thought to what pressures might have driven these people to defy the Chairman's draconian rationings.

Another weight on his shoulders.

Patrick stepped out of the *Gypsy* wearing a plain jumpsuit and went to explore the town and search for the information he needed. New permanent structures were being erected around the landing field, while the slapdash marketplace grew like a weed. People had set up tents and shops everywhere.

All of Earth had access to only one or two green priests, but he already saw five here on backwater Yreka. Two green priests had even set up a business in an open stall, sending personal messages for a token fee. Food stands shaded by embroidered awnings sizzled forth enticing odours that made his mouth water. Patrick had to stop at three stalls before he found someone who grudgingly accepted his Hansa credits. He continued through the crowded streets, savouring the taste of spicy meat in his mouth.

Patrick wondered what his grandmother could have done if given free rein to set up a new government here. The old Battleaxe would have enjoyed the challenge.

161

Taking in the sights, he listened to the gossip. Many people excitedly discussed the prospect of the Confederation arming and defending itself. He was strangely delighted to hear the name of his old Roamer rival Tasia Tamblyn come up, but when they also mentioned Robb Brindle, Patrick dismissed the rumours; he knew Brindle had vanished a long time ago.

In the middle of town, he stopped where a crowd had gathered. First, Roamer engineers and Yreka colony builders used heavy equipment to lay down a stone platform; then other workers used antigrav handles to manoeuvre into place and adjust an artfully rendered alloy sculpture of a man dressed in Roamer uniform. He looked brave and heroic, his features handsome, his long hair wild and free, as if blown by an imaginary stellar wind. The sculptor herself, a pot-bellied Roamer, stood shouting instructions and making corrections. When the statue was finally in the right spot and the antigrav plates removed, the heavy object settled down with a distinctly audible groan.

Patrick turned to an older man next to him. 'What's the statue for?'

'A memorial to Raven Kamarov. You know who he is, right? The Roamers are calling him the first victim in their war.'

Patrick swallowed. 'Their war?'

'Well, Kamarov certainly didn't die fighting the drogues. It was the stupid Eddies and the power-mad Hansa. They hammered this colony, too.'

Patrick always did seem to be in the wrong place. Uncomfortable with the conversation, he went his own way. No longer interested in politics, he focused on finding Zhett. He wasn't completely sure whether he needed to search her out for selfish reasons, or for his own honour. But he was fixated on the idea of apologizing, coming clean, atoning somehow for his actions. The

Roamers had been treated unfairly for years, and he'd had no small part in that.

He entered a local drinking house named unimaginatively 'The Saloon' as a reminder to ancient Earth frontier days. The proprietors, one Roamer and one local colonist according to the signboard, brewed their own beer using surplus Yrekan grains with hops extracts that the Roamer partner obtained from an undisclosed source.

At the bar, Patrick ordered a pint and tried to look appreciative as he sipped the bitter, watery brew. Customers sat at metal tables or along the bar, engaged in enthusiastic conversation and boisterous disagreements. Patrick swept his gaze around, looking for a friendly face. His grandmother and parents would never have approved of such a 'common' place. Patrick had usually been introduced to new people in formal, social situations, where everyone knew who he was from the outset. And in the EDF, there had always been common ground for starting discussions. He didn't even know how to walk up to a total stranger and initiate a conversation.

He kept an open expression on his face, hoping someone would respond. Two men at the bar were sketching schemes on an old dataplate. 'No, look. You just take some nets made of high-tension fibre, corral the drifting rocks, then use momentum transfer – either portable engines or small explosions – to knock them back into position.'

'That would be like reassembling a jigsaw puzzle with your eyes closed!'

'And is that beyond you? Just bring the asteroids together, salvage what you can, put new girders in place. Inflate fresh domes, bring in supplies and equipment. Six months, we'd have Rendezvous back in business.'

Patrick blinked at the sheer audacity of the idea. Reassemble Rendezvous? It was inconceivable, yet he didn't doubt their ability to do it.

'We've got plenty of commercial opportunities to focus on instead. What's the point of that?'

'The point is to show the Eddy bastards that they didn't win! I don't feel like just letting them get away with it. A symbolic gesture. I heard Del Kellum's already got a team looking into the feasibility.'

'If anybody's got the credits to burn, clan Kellum does.'

Patrick perked up. 'Excuse me, but I . . . I used to work in the Kellum shipyards.'

The two men looked at him without antagonism. 'You don't look like a Roamer. What's your clan?'

'Clan Fitzpatrick.'

'Never heard of it.'

He ignored the comment. 'Does either of you know where I can find clan Kellum? I heard they packed up and left Osquivel.'

'Oh, those shipyards are up and running again. Kellum's not scared of the Eddies.'

'What's left of the Eddies, you mean.' The second man snorted derisively. 'Kellum appointed somebody else to manage them. He's not there himself.'

'Do you know where he went?'

'I thought you said you worked in the shipyards.'

'I worked for *Del Kellum*,' Patrick said with all the bluster he could manage. 'If Del wants to send me back to Osquivel, then I'll go there. But if he's got other work for me, then I'll listen, by damn.' He intentionally used the clan leader's favourite phrase.

The two men chuckled. 'Sounds like Del, all right.'

The first man blanked his scribbles on the datapad and took a long drink of his beer. 'Del and his daughter went back to skymining. They set up the first of the new facilities on Golgen. No matter how much business the Osquivel shipyards bring in, I doubt you could tear Del away from his skymine.'

Patrick was so excited to get such a concrete tip that he almost left without finishing his beer, but he couldn't afford to let the two men grow suspicious. He listened as they talked about new trade routes into the Ildiran Empire and the proposed tax structure and parliamentary makeup of the Confederation. All he could think about, though, was Zhett.

He thanked his new friends without exchanging names, then hurried back to the *Gypsy*. Now he knew exactly where to go.

THIRTY-FOUR

GENERAL KURT LANYAN

General Lanyan's peacekeeping ships arrived at Rheindic Co, which would be his staging point for securing control over the fledgling new colonies on Klikiss worlds. He doubted that any of them had heard of the new Confederation or Peter's rebellion, since they had no direct method of receiving outside information, and he would make sure it stayed that way.

Lanyan sat back in the *Jupiter's* command chair, pleased with the *immensity* of the Juggernaut. The great battleship seemed extremely safe, like an entire kingdom around him. No wonder Admiral Willis had been upset about surrendering her ship.

During the first year of the Colonization Initiative, the Hansa had gotten more volunteers than it could accommodate. Many groups of hopeful pioneers had been shuttled here and dispatched to their new homes through the transportal in the ancient cliff city. By the luck of the draw, they emerged on barely explored worlds to settle. When Chairman Wenceslas had cut off ties with all colonies, claiming every available defence for the protection of Earth, the Colonization Initiative had been mothballed, leaving only a skeleton crew here to watch over the equipment.

Lanyan's goal was to deliver two thousand ground troops to the transportal centre on Rheindic Co. He suspected a hundred or so would be enough at each colony world. Those isolated hayseeds wouldn't dare raise a fuss when they saw his soldiers and overwhelming weaponry.

Using the intercom, he alerted his troops. 'Prepare for immediate deployment. I want to do this quickly and efficiently.'

The subcommanders rounded up their uniformed teams. The General decided to accompany the first group on its mission as an important gesture of support.

The shuttles landed in the empty canyon in front of the Klikiss cliff city. Hundreds of troops disembarked and quickly set up a base camp on the trampled ground. Some of the colonists' amenity stations remained functional, with pumps to supply running water and solar-power grids to provide subsistence energy. The soldiers would have to sleep here for a few days, the time it would take for Lanyan to organize the various missions through the transportal.

The crew of Hansa technicians and researchers on Rheindic Co were shocked when Lanyan barged into the central complex. In total, only fifty men and women remained at the base within the cliffside ruins. They peered out of the high caves, shaking their heads at the sight of the landed transports. 'Well, well, I hope you all brought your own supplies,' said the senior technician, a fidgety and balding man named Rico Ruvi.

Lanyan brought four engineers and data specialists with him into the cliff city. 'The Chairman insists on having an EDF presence at every one of our Klikiss colony worlds.' He directed his team to the control room. 'Start checking out possibilities.'

Ruvi shrugged. 'Be my guest. We've had the transportal off-line for some time now, running diagnostics. But we can get it powered up again in an hour if you like.'

'An hour will be sufficient. While your technicians get the transportal running, my men will review their missions, clean their weapons, and get ready to move out. They'll bring along whatever they need. Don't worry, we have sufficient supplies for ourselves.'

The administrator's eyes lit up. 'We could use a few mealpax, if you've got extra.'

'I'll talk to my supply sergeant.'

'By the way, most of those colonies you're going to are strapped for food and supplies, too, General. They wouldn't look kindly on your soldiers coming in with hungry bellies.'

'I'm not interested in public relations or how kindly the soldiers are viewed. They've got a job to do, and we've got our own rations.'

Ruvi shrugged. 'Whatever you say. You're the boss.'

'Show me your list of colony worlds. Do you keep dossiers on the people who went to each planet?'

'General, we processed thousands every day. Once they come here, they've already signed up for the Initiative and been cleared by the Hansa. We just ship them out. Were you looking for someone in particular?'

'No, just choosing the first target.'

'*Target*? What are you planning?' The man's smooth brow wrinkled like a leathery accordion.

'We are simply going to each planet to assist the colonists in remaining loyal to the Hansa.'

The control room in the cliff city held the large flat stone wall framed by tiles marked with strange symbols. Lanyan skimmed the portable datascreens, calling up image after image of the planets that were deemed acceptable for human settlement. He studied how many people were sent to each world, reading the projected outlook for every settlement.

Since he was the EDF's General, Lanyan would lead one of

the first expeditions and take along an overwhelming force for that all-important initial impression. Leaving only a handful of men behind at the colony, he would bring the rest back to Rheindic Co, from which he would mount another expedition, and another.

He began to take notes, jotting down estimates for the peace-keeping forces that would be required in each place. A bucolic planet called Happiness had been settled by a few neo-Amish colonists and would likely pose no trouble at all. Passively independent, yes, but only because they paid no attention to Spiral Arm politics. The larger, more established settlements might have delusions of blatantly declaring their independence from the Hansa.

A planet that seemed most in need of watching was Llaro, which had first served as a resettlement station for the evacuees from Crenna and later added a whole population of Roamer detainees. He could bring a few hundred troops there with impressive armaments and uniforms, give a good show of force, have a military parade. Noting that a detachment of EDF troops was already stationed there, he decided that they should be capable of keeping a few colonists in line, even if the settlers proved to be unruly.

Searching for a better alternative, he smudged the screen with his finger. 'This one. Pym. It's a good place to start.'

Pym had easily accessible metals and a wealth of minerals. Its salt flats and crystalline deposits could come in useful in the Hansa's rebuilding efforts. The EDF had to squeeze supplies and building materials from anywhere they could find them.

Once Lanyan locked down Rheindic Co, then Pym, and then dozens of others, the Hansa could begin full-fledged industrial operations, shipping materials, or possibly even completed vehicles or engine components, through transportals to where the EDF most needed them. This could really turn things around.

THIRTY-FIVE

ADAR ZAN'NH

As the Solar Navy bombarded the black robots on Maratha, Adar Zan'nh took care to protect the structural remnants of Secda, hoping that someday Ildirans would rebuild their resort world. He did not hesitate, however, to annihilate every one of the hive tunnels, half-made battleships, and alien constructions the robot invaders had assembled.

The black Klikiss machines had been planning a massive offensive. Against humans? Against Ildirans? Zan'nh didn't particularly care. Through painful experience, the Adar knew he could not trust the murderous robots. The Mage-Imperator had instructed him to recapture Maratha as part of repairing the Ildiran Empire, and he would not depart until he had achieved that goal.

The first two passes of his warliners vapourized the embedded plasma cannons. Smoking craters and collapsed frameworks marked where the partially assembled spaceships had been. Curved alloy girders drooped in the heat and toppled like stalks of scythed grain. Hundreds of black robots had already been smashed to shrapnel on the ground.

The large-scale attack had not caused enough damage to satisfy Yazra'h. When the Adar finally felt that the robots had been pummelled enough to pose a minimal risk, he turned his sister loose. 'Go and clean up the rest. Be careful – and be victorious.'

She flashed her bright teeth in a feral grin. 'We will eliminate every last one of those traitorous robots. And our rememberers will tell you the story when we get back, Adar!' As soldier kithmen rushed to the cutters, Yazra'h bounded along, with the two uneasy rememberers in tow.

'Are you certain you should bring that pair along?' Zan'nh called after her. 'They are not warriors.'

'We are observers.' Vao'sh's words sounded forced, but sincere. 'And we must be there to observe.'

The Adar admired Yazra'h's enthusiasm. In his younger years, he had trained against fierce soldier kithmen and skilled jousters. He could defend himself with a mirrored shield, and he could kill with a crystal katana, with hand lasers, or with his bare hands. However, Zan'nh could also command large engagements of ships and grasp tactics across a sweeping stellar battlefield. He was required to both strategize and *lead*, while his sister had the freedom to fight on a more personal level. Part of him envied Yazra'h for the mayhem of combat, but each Ildiran was born to his or her own place, knowing their duty and their destiny.

He remained in his command nucleus, observing high-resolution images of the battleground. As the cutters landed on Maratha, Ildiran fighters spilled out, weapons ready. Transmission bursts indicated that the soldier kithmen immediately encountered furious fighting. The initial bombardment had left many shattered exoskeletons; other robots had been entirely melted into black polymer pools. But an unexpected number of still-undamaged robots swarmed up from underground tunnels that had not yet collapsed. What had they been doing here? And why on Maratha?

'Klikiss robots mounting resistance,' Yazra'h transmitted. 'But our weapons are more than adequate.' Explosions, high-pitched insectile squeals, and images of the aggressive machines filled the command nucleus screens.

'Adar!' the sensor operator cried, startling him. 'I have just received an alert from long-distance sensors. Incoming ships. Unknown configuration.'

Zan'nh looked away from the pictures of mayhem on the ground. 'Incoming ships? Expand the screen.' He feared that the robots had summoned reinforcements. At Earth, he had seen a large battle group of EDF battleships hijacked by the black machines. 'Prepare to engage with all weaponry.'

But he saw soon enough that these were not human-built Mantas or Juggernauts. Nor were they more robots.

As the unknown vessels hurtled toward Maratha, they grew so large they would surely overwhelm the Solar Navy septa. The strange ships were actually enormous clusters of countless smaller vessels, interlocked geometric shapes. The communications bands filled with clicking and chirping signals, and Zan'nh's officer was wise enough to run them through ancient translation protocols when he found recognizable points of reference.

'It is a *Klikiss* signal, Adar!' Ages ago, the black robots had shown Ildirans how to interpret the language of their creators. Those translation routines had not been used in thousands of years.

'But the Klikiss are extinct.'

As if to disprove Zan'nh's assertion, a huge creature with a spiny carapace and many segmented legs spoke via a blurred communications link, apparently assuming that the Ildirans would understand it. 'We detect our robots here. We come to destroy them.'

Zan'nh recovered quickly, standing firm and replying to the

Klikiss. 'Then we share the same purpose. We have already devastated their new hive. We thwarted their defences and destroyed the fleet of ships they were building.' He struggled to remember any history he knew about the ancient insect race. If only Vao'sh were up here instead of on the ground! The rememberer would know. 'Klikiss and Ildirans were not enemies in the past.'

The insect creature clicked and chirped, and the translator spat out in a flat voice, 'We will find any remaining robots. Our warrior breeds will tear them limb from limb.'

The gigantic swarmships broke apart in a flurry of many hundreds of smaller craft. The detached Klikiss components flew past the Adar's warliners as if they did not exist, and streaked like angry hornets toward Maratha.

'Wait!' Zan'nh transmitted. 'I have many Ildiran troops down on the surface. They are not your enemies. They are also fighting the black robots. Do not let them be harmed in the crossfire.'

'Instruct them not to get in our way.' The Klikiss broke off the contact.

Zan'nh whirled to his comm officer. 'Contact our soldier kithmen down there. Warn Yazra'h that the Klikiss are coming.'

173

THIRTY-SIX

NAHTON

The Moon Statue Garden was one of the few places Chairman Wenceslas allowed Nahton to go. There, he could breathe the open air and feel unfiltered sunshine on his skin. The Hansa had kept him from his treeling for nearly two weeks. He had received no news from Theroc, nor had he been able to tell anyone what had happened to him here. He was cut off.

Here, at least, the green priest could spend time with the flowers and ferns that surrounded the sculptures of heroes and stylized representations of abstract concepts. King George had originated the garden, offering a competition among sculptors for the privilege of having their works displayed at the newly completed Whisper Palace. Crimson roses were in bloom around a graceful chrome piece made of reflective sine waves and disc-shaped mirrors. Light glinted off the strips into his eyes as spinning moebius-strip pendants distorted the illumination. The title, ironically, was 'Variable Truth'.

Usually when he was out among the statues, hedges, and

flower beds, Nahton was very much aware of the royal guards, who observed his every move. This time, though, his watchers were conspicuously absent.

He heard voices and looked up to see Sarein and Captain McCammon talking with each other, their voices loud, expressions intent. The green priest assumed they were coming to find him, but the two pointedly did not look in his direction. Stepping behind a bristling hibiscus hedge whose trumpetlike flowers shone red and orange, they spoke in normal voices, seeming to argue, though they must have known that Nahton was within earshot. He felt like an eavesdropper in a clumsily staged play.

'Theroc is my home planet, and this imminent invasion is illegal,' Sarein said. 'The Hansa can't simply order the EDF to attack. If Chairman Wenceslas insists on this course of action, we must warn King Peter and Queen Estarra.'

'How can we do that?' McCammon sounded as if he had rehearsed this conversation. 'The Chairman has already gathered the ships. I heard him give the order to Admiral Willis. The attack force will launch within five days.'

Nahton frowned at what they were saying. An invasion of Theroc? Even the Chairman wouldn't dare do something so bold and foolish. But as he paused to reconsider, the green priest knew he was kidding himself. Basil Wenceslas would certainly dare.

'Once Basil makes up his mind, there's no changing it,' Sarein said. 'Maybe we can ask a trader to get a message there somehow. A courier could go directly to Theroc.'

'That would take days. There's no way to send a warning soon enough.'

Nahton held his silence on the other side of the hedge. Their intent could not be more painfully obvious. They needed to deny ever having spoken to him, and perhaps this awkward show was the best they could do. But he could not send a message unless he touched his treeling. He already knew it was kept in Queen Estarra's conservatory. Had that been an intentional slip from Captain McCammon?

The entire setup seemed so contrived as to be unbelievable. Suspicion drew his lips down in a frown. The Chairman was an insidious man, willing to consider any action if it met his strangely defined idea of 'the right thing to do'. What if this was a trap, and McCammon and Sarein were trying to lure him into taking desperate action? But to what purpose? The Chairman was untrustworthy, but predictable. This made no sense.

Nahton knew that Captain McCammon had always been loyal to Peter, passing messages through the green priest even though it was strictly against the Chairman's wishes. And Sarein was the Queen's sister. Though she had long ago left Theroc, Nahton could not believe that Sarein would betray her own planet, even though he had seen her as the Chairman's apparent ally.

He contemplated confronting the two and demanding answers, but he decided to take their news at face value. He wouldn't put it past the Chairman to launch an ill-advised assault on Theroc. So, he had to find a way to get to the Queen's conservatory.

Late that night one of the usual guards was stationed by the open doorway of his quarters. Nahton meditated, considered his options – and waited. He could not possibly overpower a trained guard.

The guard's collar comm pinged, and a crackle of orders burst through. 'Are you certain, sir? Acknowledged.' Glancing in at the green priest, the man left his post without offering any explanation to Nahton.

With anxiety chewing him up inside, the green priest went to the door and looked nervously into the hall. Guessing that this was part of Sarein and McCammon's plan, whatever it was, he bolted from his chambers. He had been in Estarra's conservatory several times, but not since the King and Queen had escaped. With his emerald skin and bright tattoos, scantily clad in the garb of a traditional green priest, Nahton could not be unobtrusive. Fortunately, at this time of night, few people roamed the Whisper Palace.

He did encounter a late-working bureaucrat who carried a stack of documents. The man blinked in amazement upon seeing him, but Nahton ducked down a corridor and picked up the pace. He bumped into a cleaning crew of four older women and a beak-nosed man. They stared at him as if they had never seen a green priest before. Someone would sound the alarm soon. He didn't have much time.

Running now, he ascended a set of stairs, bounded down an open corridor. His bare feet made slapping sounds on the cool tile, and a sense of urgency overwhelmed him.

At last he reached the dim conservatory, and he was still alone. Overhead, lights shone through the glass panels, reflecting the night sky. The place had a strange mixture of smells, loamy richness with caustic chemicals. He could see that something was wrong with the plants – the ferns, the flowers, the dwarf citrus trees. All the Theron botanical specimens had been uprooted and left to rot, like corpses on a battlefield.

Nahton paused to regain his balance. Caustic chemicals had been poured on the plants. This had been the Chairman's doing, a way to punish Queen Estarra by destroying something she loved. Such wilful devastation, the killing of all those delicate plants, seemed so spiteful, so . . . evil.

But the treeling . . . The treeling was still alive! Someone – Captain McCammon, perhaps – had placed the potted tree where it would receive sufficient light during the day. The fronds looked healthy, the thin gold-barked trunk was straight. He hurried forward.

Suddenly, he heard shouts from the hallway, and lights flared. Gruff, approaching voices called out. 'The treeling is in the conservatory. Hurry!'

Nahton ran to grasp the potted tree, touching the fronds even as he heard booted feet come running. In a rush of words, he spoke into telink. He told the little tree everything, warned of the impending attack on Theroc, explained how he had been held prisoner apart from his treeling. He poured his information into the worldforest mind so that all green priests had access to it, everywhere.

Royal guards burst into the room along with armed Palace security troops. Nahton recognized none of the men, none of the special guards that Captain McCammon regularly assigned to him. He picked up the potted treeling and held it in front of him. He did not want to relinquish it yet. It didn't matter, though, because these men were too late.

Nevertheless, they raised their guns and shot the treeling out of Nahton's hands, shattering the pot. The small worldtree splintered. Nahton let it crash to the floor, staring in astonishment.

Captain McCammon charged into the room, his face flushed. 'Halt! All of you!'

But the men had other orders. Stricken, Nahton raised his hands in surrender. That didn't stop them from opening fire.

THIRTY-SEVEN

DAVLIN LOTZE

In the afternoon, Klikiss scout parties returned to the Llaro settlement carrying five human bodies. The victims were refugee farmers who had fled when the Klikiss razed their fields. Without any guidance or safe haven, they had wandered the countryside, hiding themselves wherever they could. Without sufficient food, they had become careless. The Klikiss had found them.

Standing on rooftops and makeshift scaffolding inside their walls, the trapped townspeople watched the scouts march toward the main alien city. They shouted questions and challenges, insults, curses. But the Klikiss didn't attach any particular significance to the bodies they carried, the innocent people they had killed.

Davlin knew he had to do something to ensure that it didn't happen again. He had to keep more of the desperate human fugitives from being killed just because they had no place else to go. He had to give the colonists an option, offer them some way to defend themselves. Margaret had told him everything he needed to know so that he could start forming a plan.

He had interviewed the colonists, compiling a mental list of their skills and expertise. They were talented farmers, miners, and true pioneer types. Very few were EDF veterans, and none of them was a crack soldier. Those willing to accept the Hansa colonization stipend were usually disenfranchised, cut off from other opportunities.

None of the original Llaro colonists or Roamer detainees knew much about the EDF weapons the soldiers had possessed before their barracks were wiped out. However, because Llaro was a holding zone for so many reluctant Roamers, Davlin hoped that the paranoid Chairman had stocked the armoury well.

Outside the wall, the main EDF hangar and a few maintenance sheds were far enough from the alien city that the Klikiss hadn't touched them yet. But with the rapid expansion of the hive, those buildings would soon be in the way. Davlin knew he had to raid them as soon as possible.

He waited until the pastel sky deepened into darkness before he slipped away with nothing more than a small handlight, using it only when absolutely necessary. With good eyesight and an excellent grasp of his surroundings, he made his way to the remaining EDF supply shacks and the hangar. He broke in using Hansa override codes he had memorized long ago.

Davlin studied everything the hapless soldiers had left behind. He found the locked armoury, complete with fifty weapons, mostly wide-dispersal scatter shots and twitchers used for stunning crowds (no doubt intended to keep Roamer prisoners in line). He found explosive projectiles, grenades, shoulder-mounted jazers, and old-fashioned smoke canisters. Another bunker held bulk explosives earmarked for mining and construction. He didn't know exactly what he would do with everything, but he intended to cache all the weapons for later use. He was sure the colonists would eventually need them.

The next bunker was a fuel depot containing three barrels of in-system fuel, enough to keep the camp's Remoras flying, though not with stardrive engines. Next, Davlin shone his light around in the large empty hangar. One of the dedicated Remoras had been destroyed when faeros fireballs had arrived in the skies; one was undergoing maintenance, its two engines dismounted for cleaning and by-the-book inspection. Davlin cursed under his breath. He wasn't sure anybody on Llaro had the engineering background to reassemble the craft and make it flightworthy again.

The last Remora, though, was fuelled up and ready to go. Davlin's plans quickly fell into place.

For the next several nights, while Klikiss scouts prowled the darkness, he slipped out, went to the bunkers, and moved out explosives, weapons, and the three barrels of fuel. He hid them in fifteen separate caches, marked the locations carefully, and drew up several maps.

Later, he met with Mayor Ruis, Roberto Clarin, and some of the more prominent Roamers, including Crim and Marla Chan Tylar. Davlin explained what he had done and where to find the weapons should they need them. 'And groups of people have to start sneaking away from here. This town is not defensible if the Klikiss decide to come after us.'

Ruis was alarmed. 'Do you really think they'd do that? We don't plan to provoke them.'

'I don't presume to understand bugs,' Clarin said. 'But it doesn't sound like a good idea to have people just wandering around the countryside. Look at the bodies that were just brought in . . . helpless farmers caught out in the open. If people escaped from the town, how would they survive out there, even if the Klikiss didn't get them? They'd need food and shelter.'

'I'll give them a place to go.' Davlin looked at each of their faces. 'Start asking questions, figure out who wants to go, find resourceful people, because out there we'll be scraping out an even tougher existence than they'll be leaving behind.'

Even before the Klikiss had arrived, Davlin had ranged far afield, exploring the countryside, noting interesting landmarks and anything that might prove useful. Now he had a good idea of where he wanted to go for a temporary staging area – a line of sandstone bluffs pocked with caves that the Klikiss would not be inclined to find. Places where refugees could defend themselves . . .

Mayor Ruis was smiling. 'You've been planning this.'

'Yes, and I intend to leave.'

Astonishment rippled around the room. Clarin said, 'Davlin, you're one of the smartest people we have. If you go—'

'I need to find and set up a new hideout, a base we can use if things get too bad. Once you get a group of people, tell them to head east and keep to cover as much as they can. After a day or two of hard walking, they'll come to some sandstone cliffs riddled with caves. That's where I'll be.'

He assessed them again. 'Now I have an important question to ask: One of the Remoras in the hangar has been disassembled. It needs to be put back together and made flightworthy. Does any-one have aeronautical knowledge, spacecraft design, engineering?'

Clarin chuckled. 'We're Roamers! Most of us could take that thing apart and put it back together blindfolded – maybe even make it run better while we were at it.'

Davlin could not hide his relief. 'Then several of you should slip into the hangar and get to work. The Klikiss will destroy it sooner or later. You'll want to be ready.'

'Then . . . are you just going to walk out of here?' Ruis asked.

'Not walk. I'm going to fly. I'm taking the other Remora.'

*

In the dead of night, he climbed into the cockpit of the functional craft, activating the systems, looking at the status grid. With a starry field overhead and one small moon illuminating the landscape ahead, he powered up the Remora's engines. While the breedex watched its hive, with the humans kept rounded up and helpless, Davlin flew out of the hangar.

Before the Klikiss could investigate, he streaked away, hoping that the bugs couldn't, or wouldn't, track him. The other colonists looked to him for answers, and he intended to be worthy of their trust. He had to offer them a safe haven.

THIRTY-EIGHT

ANTON COLICOS

Hordes of black robots glistened in the slanted sunlight, though fire and smoke from the warliners' bombardment blurred the sky. In the battle on the ground, Anton raced across freshly cratered terrain, trying to keep up with Yazra'h in the belief that she would save him. Judging by the look of bloodthirsty glee on her face, though, she intended to throw herself into the thickest part of battle, and maybe Anton should run the other direction after all.

Even after Adar Zan'nh's thorough aerial attack, black robots continued to boil out of underground warrens. Anton would have preferred a few more days of aerial strikes with the Solar Navy's weapons – at a safe distance. He tried to stay close to Vao'sh.

Wielding a long staff tipped with an explosive sonic-discharger bulb, Yazra'h shouted and threw herself against one of the towering machines. When she struck the robot, it was as if it had been hit with Thor's hammer. With a thunderous boom, the black machine crumpled to the ground, its internal circuits crushed.

'I told you this would be glorious, Rememberer Anton!' she called over her shoulder, then led the way into the debris-strewn streets of what had been Secda. 'Follow and observe.'

In a show of confidence, Yazra'h had given Anton a projectile launcher that shot metal spikes as long and thick as his forefinger at supersonic speeds. Vao'sh carried an electronic scrambler, though he didn't seem to know how to use it. One of the black robots flew overhead cradling an angular device, presumably a weapon, and Anton lifted his launcher. He fired one of the metal spikes and somehow, perhaps by accident, the supersonic projectile struck the robot and shattered its exoskeleton like a windshield struck by a heavy rock.

'Excellent, Rememberer Anton!' Vao'sh sounded somewhat nervous. 'I will include that in my retelling of this tale.'

Anton helped the old rememberer with the electronic scrambler. 'Thank you, Vao'sh – now do something that you can brag about yourself.' He helped the old historian blast two robots that came chittering at them.

An alarm signal crackled from the landing party's communicators. Adar Zan'nh's voice was crisp and startling. 'A Klikiss fleet has returned and they intend to attack. Prepare yourselves for additional ships.'

Yazra'h tapped her earpiece as if she hadn't heard correctly. 'Klikiss? Do you mean more robots?'

'No – the *original* Klikiss. Stay away from them. They have also come to destroy the robots.'

Anton looked up to the sky. 'I thought the Klikiss were extinct.'

'Alas, once again the truth as recorded in the *Saga of Seven Suns* is . . . somewhat inaccurate,' Vao'sh said.

Before Anton could get his mind around what the Adar had said, a flurry of ships dropped through the sky, hundreds of small identical vessels. A meteor storm of geometric dropships struck the ground, each one opening like a metallic seedpod as soon as it had landed. Insectile creatures climbed out, looking like a paranoid sculptor's approximation of the Klikiss robots. Just as compies had been designed by humans to have familiar bodily characteristics, so too the Klikiss race had built their robots to resemble themselves.

Warriors swarmed out of the dropships in sacrificial numbers, advancing into the remnants of Secda. Seeing the return of the dead race, the black robots went into a frenzy, as if someone had poured gasoline into a hill of fire ants. The Klikiss hurled themselves upon the robots and tore them into scrap metal.

'Talk about a grudge match,' Anton said.

The remaining robots fought back vigorously, turning their violence against the Klikiss rather than the Ildirans. Anton fired his projectile gun several more times, shattering three enemy robots and saving the lives of Klikiss fighters, but the insect creatures were fixated entirely on the robots and took no notice. Though hundreds of Klikiss warriors were destroyed in the battle, they fought with wild abandon.

Within an hour, all of the remaining black robots had been eradicated.

The Adar summoned Yazra'h's ground team back to the warliners. Fifty Ildiran soldiers had perished in the process of destroying nearly ten times that many black robots. Before reboarding the troop cutters, Yazra'h glanced at the smouldering ruins of Secda, the smashed and dripping exoskeletons of the Klikiss, the black debris of their robots. 'Remember this, Anton Colicos. Remember the details, that you may tell the story in all of its grandeur.'

They flew back to the warliners in orbit. As soon as they

returned to the command nucleus, sweaty and grimy, Anton sensed the tension there aboard the ship. Adar Zan'nh faced the screen on which a large Klikiss warrior spoke through a translation protocol. All seven Ildiran warliners faced off against the clusters of interlocking Klikiss ships that reassembled like pieces of a mosaic into a large, formless swarmship.

'We reclaim our worlds,' the Klikiss representative said. 'We come to destroy our robots. We travel through transportals to inhabit worlds abandoned in our last Swarming.'

'We fight the black robots as well.' Zan'nh kept his voice firm but calm. 'You saw that here.'

The Klikiss was not impressed. 'Sharing an enemy does not mean shared goals. We will have our worlds back. All of them.'

'Maratha was never a Klikiss planet. Maratha was part of the Ildiran Empire. We have assisted you in eradicating the robot infestation here. We are grateful for your efforts in the fight, but this planet is not yours to reclaim.'

The Klikiss remained silent. Zan'nh stared at the screen without flinching.

Anton thought of something new that made him shudder. If the Klikiss were still alive and reclaiming their old planets, where had they come from? Rheindic Co was an abandoned Klikiss world. His father had been killed there and his mother had vanished, perhaps through the transportal. Had she blundered into the reawakening Klikiss race? He wished he knew what had happened to her. He wished he knew what was going to happen to him.

Finally the Klikiss on the screen spoke again. 'We have other planets. This world was not a Klikiss world.' The rest of the interlocking insect ships returned from the surface and joined the huge cluster vessel. Without sending another transmission, the alien swarmship departed.

Anton let out a long sigh of relief. He still could not read all Ildiran emotions, but everyone here seemed rattled.

'An unexpected turn of events,' Rememberer Vao'sh said.

Anton nodded. 'Or, as we say in an Earth story, the plot thickens.'

THIRTY-NINE

KOLKER

In front of the Prism Palace, seven streams of water came together and poured in a cascade down a wide gullet, gushing into chambers beneath the Prism Palace, from which they were piped back out into canals.

Kolker found Osira'h and her siblings there near the edge of the flow. At the gurgling convergence, Muree'n, the youngest though not smallest of the children, fearlessly leaned over the wide, watery mouth, dropped stones in, and watched them disappear into the misty depths.

Osira'h chatted with her brothers and sisters. 'These streams make seven underground waterfalls. Underneath the Palace, you can walk around the pool, even follow the streams as they flow out through the bottom of the hill.'

As a green priest, Kolker had been fascinated by the potential in these five halfbreed children. He knew they shared a bond that few others could comprehend, stronger than either Ildirans and their *thism* or green priests and their telink. Did that give them a key to what he wanted to know?

Several days earlier, he had gone to the rooftop greenhouse, surprised to find the five of them, led by Osira'h, playing around the single treeling. Since these children did not have access to telink, Kolker could think of no reason for them to hover around the small worldtree.

But as he surreptitiously observed them, it became clear that these children were not playing. They were attempting something, joining hands, concentrating, almost praying. So, Kolker had watched and was excited to see them make some kind of progress, a connection beyond telink.

Since the lens kithmen had given him no help, he wondered if these children could offer insight. They had to know he was watching.

Now in spite of the background roar of the water, Osira'h sensed Kolker's approach. 'You're a green priest. We're going to the treeling. Would you like to come?'

Kolker couldn't have asked for more. 'I would like to *understand*. I came to talk with you because no one else can answer my questions – not the green priests, nor the worldtrees, nor your lens kithmen.' He held up the crystalline medallion that Tery'l had given him. 'I've been using this to search for the Lightsource, but I haven't found it yet. I'm trying to do what the lens kithmen can do, but I'm missing something.' The spray from the gurgling water created a refreshing mist that lingered around the circular well. Rainbows reflected from the droplets. 'I have no place else to turn.'

'But we're just children,' said Tamo'l in a small voice. Uninterested in the discussion, Muree'n dropped more stones into the rushing water.

'What does he need to know?' said Gale'nh, as if Kolker weren't there.

The man wasn't sure how to explain himself. 'You are both human and Ildiran, the children of a green priest and also connected to the *thism*. I have telink, but I sense something more among Ildirans, especially in you.'

Osira'h grinned. 'You noticed. We aren't like the others.'

'You communicated with the hydrogues, tapped into that alien mind. You also linked with your mother to share memories. But I don't understand how it all fits together.'

'You will understand, because you want to. The lens kithmen don't want to. Even my mother – *our* mother – is scarred in her mind. One day we'll show her.' Osira'h's small hand reached out and took his. 'Come with us.'

'We get stronger each time we do it,' Rod'h added.

On the open rooftop, Osira'h looked at Kolker with her large, round eyes, and her downy hair fluttered in the breeze. 'Don't just watch. Try to *feel* what happens.' She and the other children bent down next to the treeling. 'Now, just like we did it yesterday and the day before.' Her brothers and sisters joined hands, and their expressions synchronized, as if they were sharing the same thoughts.

With one hand Osira'h touched the treeling. 'Now you, Kolker. Open yourself through telink and see if you can find us.'

He stroked the fronds while holding Tery'l's medallion. Kolker stared at the dazzling light with his eyes and touched the world-forest with his mind. Unexpectedly, he found a new presence there: Osira'h, but more than Osira'h – a different set of thoughts, along with echoes of *thism*, he was sure.

In a sense, the treeling was as much a symbol as the medallion was. The real connection was between *thism* and telink, soul-threads and worldforest. The very similarity was a pattern laid down throughout the universe. He had never seen how every person, animal, dust mote and galaxy was *connected*.

Osira'h, using her special bridging abilities on him in the same way she had when joining with the hydrogue minds, opened the way for Kolker, made him different. The lens medallion in his hands seemed to grow warm. The light burned brightly, both in his mind and in his eyes.

Finally, in a way he could not verbalize, he *comprehended*. It all made sense to him, as if a switch had been thrown. The universe snapped into perfectly sharp focus. He had never imagined such colour or such clarity. It was stunning!

Better yet, he knew how to share it with others.

FORTY

SAREIN

S he arrived too late. The shooting was already over by the time she got to Estarra's conservatory. When she saw the green priest, Sarein screamed.

Red blood mixed with spilled potting soil on the floor of the greenhouse, and bright splashes of it stood out on Nahton's emerald skin. His face still wore an expression of profound disbelief. With his last dying gesture, the green priest had reached out and managed to clutch a frond from the splintered tree. Was it for solace, to send a frantic message, or just reflex? She couldn't tell if Nahton had succeeded in what he had wanted to do.

Livid, McCammon shouted at the guards, but they didn't acknowledge their captain's reprimand. 'I told you to stop. I gave you direct and explicit orders—'

Basil came in, cool and analytical. He glanced around and nodded. 'I see no problem here, Captain. These guards attempted to intervene, per their instructions.' He stepped closer to Nahton's fallen body, not looking the slightest bit disturbed.

McCammon paled, as if recognizing that something vital had been stripped from him.

Sarein was shaking. She knew that Basil was to blame for this, but in her heart she felt the fault was her own. She had talked McCammon into this childish ploy to get Nahton to send a warning. If they were caught, she had expected a reprimand or, worse, a cold shoulder from Basil. But not outright murder. 'Basil, Nahton was a *green priest*. He was a Theron citizen, an ambassador just like me.'

'He was an enemy of the Terran Hanseatic League. His presence here confirms that. He was caught in the act. What these men did was for the benefit of everyone in the Spiral Arm.'

'For the benefit of the Hansa, you mean.'

'They are one and the same – and if you think otherwise, my dear Sarein, then I have greatly misjudged you.' Basil addressed the guards who still held their weapons. 'Please tell me you got here in time.'

The men looked away sheepishly. 'Sorry, sir. The green priest was holding the treeling before we arrived. We don't know what report he made.'

A thunderstorm crossed Basil's face. 'So King Peter and the Therons have been warned.' The news buoyed Sarein only slightly.

Basil gave all of them a withering glare, then gazed down at Nahton's body, as if the slain green priest had also disappointed him. 'I despise it when simple instructions are not followed.' He tapped his fingers together, composed himself with a visible effort. 'We can recover from this debacle. Admiral Willis's Mantas are ready to depart in less than a week. There's nothing Peter can possibly do in time – except write an eloquent surrender speech. And he's going to need one.'

Sarein could no longer control herself. 'Basil, this isn't *right* and you know it! He was a green priest.' But she knew nothing would change. 'Do you realize that we're completely blind? Earth has no way to communicate. Nahton could always have changed his mind, but now you've removed the possibility entirely. You've cut yourself off.'

He whirled on her and said icily, 'We were already cut off, and now so is everyone else.'

A cleanup detail arrived, and orderlies moved to pick up the dead green priest. Sarein could only stare at the stain on the floor as the limp man was carried off. In normal times, Nahton should have been returned to Theroc for burial under a worldtree. In normal times, an aging green priest would allow himself to fall into the verdani mind and surrender his flesh as fertilizer for the forest. *In normal times . . .*

Without saying another word, Basil motioned for the cleanup crew to carry on. Through narrowed eyes, McCammon studied his intractable men, who appeared satisfied with their actions. Sarein worried for him. If push came to shove, the Chairman could easily strip McCammon of his rank and replace him. Or simply make him disappear.

In normal times . . . Sarein shook her head as she left the devastated conservatory. There was nothing left for her here. Nothing at all.

FORTY-ONE

QUEEN ESTARRA

Sitting on the curved roof of the fungus-reef with her sister reminded Estarra of younger, carefree days. She missed those times.

A sapphire-winged condorfly buzzed past her face, startling Estarra and almost knocking her off balance. Celli caught her arm with swift and easy reflexes, just before a scarlet condorfly swept after the blue one, and the two pirouetted away, either in aerial combat or in a mating dance.

Scars across the fungus-reef showed where Theron children had cut swatches of the rubbery outer membrane. They would wear spikes on their shoes and climb around the outside to fill sacks with the soft fungus. Now that she was greatly pregnant, Estarra no longer had the agility or balance to brave the uncertain surface, so she sat close to the tree trunk.

She and her sister sat next to each other in comfortable silence. Finally, Celli said, 'It's good to have you back home. I missed you when you were on Earth.' She gave a teasing grin. 'Nobody to pick on.'

'You used to be such a brat, Celli.'

Celli chuckled. 'You used to treat me like a little child.'

'You were a little child.'

Her sister lounged back against the gold-barked trunk. 'And now look at us. You're married, you're pregnant – and oh, yes, you're the Queen of the Confederation as well as Mother of Theroc.'

'Some would consider that quite a triumph, although to be honest I was happier when I was just a girl scrambling up trees.' Though she had finally escaped from the Hansa Chairman, and the human race had survived the hydrogues, Estarra still felt a deep and abiding ache for all that had happened to her family – Reynald killed, Sarein trapped on Earth, Beneto destroyed by the hydrogues and then returned as an avatar of the worldforest.

Celli picked up on her mood. 'You look so sad.'

Estarra manufactured a smile, surprised that she could do it so quickly and gracefully. As Queen, she had learned how to hide her emotions in order to avoid the Chairman's displeasure. 'I've managed to make something of myself, but what about you, little sister? Have you decided what you're going to do with your life?'

Celli grinned, crossing her tomboy arms over her small breasts. 'You're the first one I wanted to tell. I've made up my mind to become a green priest – like Solimar and Beneto.'

Estarra was delighted. 'Aren't you a little old to become an acolyte, though? Most of them start as children.'

'I'm smart. I'm a fast learner. And Solimar says that with all my prior knowledge and the treedancing I've done, the worldforest already knows who I am.'

'Probably. But I think Solimar would tell you anything you wanted to hear. He wants to please you.'

'And is there something wrong with that?'

'Not at all. Peter's the same way.'

As if he had heard them talking about him, Solimar climbed out onto the upper level of the fungus-reef. A deep frown creased his face, despite his obvious pleasure at seeing Celli. 'A message from Nahton! Bad news – very bad news.'

'Tell me,' the Queen commanded.

'The Earth Defence Forces are planning to attack Theroc. Chairman Wenceslas is sending his battleships. A whole invasion force.'

Estarra felt cold. She knew the Chairman would never have allowed the green priest to pass such a message.

'Nahton was being kept from his treeling – that's why we haven't heard from him in so long – but he escaped. He managed to send the information, and then he said that guards were coming. They had guns.' Solimar's voice hitched. 'Then telink broke off. We think the treeling was either taken from him – or destroyed.' Celli hurried to him, and he easily folded her in his arms.

Estarra pressed her lips together, expecting the worst. Chairman Wenceslas did not tolerate defiance in any form. She guessed Nahton was probably dead.

'The Hansa might be trying to make us worried, hoping we'll change our minds,' Celli said. 'They want us to panic. This could be a bluff.'

'It's no bluff. He'll do it.'

The green priests flashed the alarm through telink, and soon every member of the Confederation knew of the impending emergency. At the Osquivel shipyards, under the rushed and determined supervision of Tasia Tamblyn and Robb Brindle, Roamers retooled and armed any serviceable vessel they could find. Dozens of fresh ships raced to Theroc, arriving within two days.

Estarra stayed at Peter's side, giving him any advice and assistance he might need. The King and Queen greeted each new ship, thanking the pilots for joining in the defence of the Confederation. Though she said nothing, Estarra knew in her heart that the numbers would never be sufficient; reading Peter's carefully masked expression, she could tell he was thinking the same thing. Theroc would have only a shadow of a 'navy' in place before the EDF arrived.

Yet they would do their best.

Flushed and indignant Roamer captains paraded into the throne room, offering mismatched ships to stand as a cordon in orbit. One long-haired man crossed muscular arms over his chest. 'Do you think the Eddy battleships are simply going to open fire on us? Are they that inhuman?'

'Some of them are,' Peter said.

Estarra reached out from her ornate chair and took her husband's hand. 'And many of them have friends and loved ones on Earth. The Chairman could easily threaten retribution if anyone baulks.'

'And Rlinda just went there!' said Branson Roberts, looking heartbroken. 'She has no idea what she might be blundering into. Sure, she's not going to admit she's anything other than an independent trader, but if they find out she's acting as the Confederation's Trade Minister, she's cooked!' Rlinda had taken the *Voracious Curiosity* on an exploratory trade mission to Earth. 'I should have gone with her, no matter what she said.' He shook his head, bemoaning the fact that he still had an arrest warrant hanging over him there. 'She should have at least taken a green priest. We have no way of warning her.'

'She had only to ask,' Yarrod said. 'We would have considered it legitimate.'

'She doesn't like to ask. It's her damned independent streak.'

'Captain Kett can't solve our problem,' Peter said. 'We need some other way to defend Theroc.'

Thinking of green priests, Estarra looked at Celli, and both sisters seemed to have the same idea simultaneously. 'Beneto!' Estarra turned to Peter and spoke in a rush. 'The verdani battleships! Could we call Beneto back?'

When he and the other treeships departed, Beneto had said he would not see her again. But they needed him so much now!

'The verdani seedships are travelling among the stars,' Yarrod said dubiously. 'The fused green priest pilots have a new mission now, continuing the work to spread the verdani across the cosmos. They are no longer concerned with humans.'

'I don't believe that!' Celli said. 'They were sons and daughters of Theroc. They can't ignore a threat to their people, their planet. Beneto will understand. The green priests will understand.'

'They must already know what happened to Nahton,' Estarra added. 'They heard the same telink message.' Perhaps they were already on their way back?

'It is worth asking them,' said Solimar, nodding grimly. 'It is even worth begging.'

'We promise nothing.' Yarrod went to a treeling beside Queen Estarra's ornate chair.

'We can promise to try our best.' Solimar, unmoved by the older green priest's scepticism, went to another treeling.

Both of them sent their plea, communicating not just to the worldforest, but questing for the specific green priest minds connected to the thorny battleships. Celli leaned close to Solimar, holding onto his arm. Though she couldn't connect through telink yet, she hoped her need would somehow be communicated through him to the trees.

Long minutes later, the two green priests blinked simultaneously and released the treelings. 'Nine of them have agreed to come back.' Yarrod sounded surprised. 'They, too, heard Nahton's message, and they know what the Hansa is doing. They will be here soon.'

'They will be here *in time*,' Solimar added. 'And Beneto will be with them.'

FORTY-TWO

GENERAL KURT LANYAN

General Lanyan gathered four hundred of his men for the first deployment through the reactivated transportal. In preparation for passage, the peacekeeper soldiers crowded the Klikiss tunnels, their weapons shouldered and their buttons polished. They would march through to Pym in formation, double-time, and scare the absolute piss out of the colonists.

According to survey records, Pym was a chalky place with shallow lakes of tepid, briny water and tufa towers built out of salt and sand. The landscape was relentlessly flat, mostly alkaline desert with a few oases of pure water where cane grasses and tamarisk-equivalents grew in profusion.

Lanyan couldn't imagine colonists so desperate they would actually want to move there, but given ingenuity and a modicum of hard work, the settlers could make a profitable business out of extracting the wealth of chemicals in the salt flats. He was only there to make sure that the people on Pym continued to walk the straight-and-narrow and did not slip out of the Hansa's grasp.

Once those people had their fear of the EDF thoroughly

reaffirmed, he would graciously set up a guardian force to remind them of all the unknown hazards still abroad in the Spiral Arm. Such hazards, of course, included the sedition of King Peter and his ill-advised rebellion.

In the Rheindic Co tunnels, Lanyan stood at the head of his troops like a cavalry leader about to sound a charge. He briefly wished he had brought a ceremonial sword, just to wave as they came crashing through. 'The sooner we get these colonists in line, the sooner we all go home.' He nodded to the administrators at the transportal controls, who activated the trapezoidal wall and selected the appropriate coordinate tile for Pym. Head held high, Lanyan boldly stepped through, and all of his soldiers followed.

Instantly, the dimness of the cave grotto changed to the bright glare of sun blazing down on the salt flats. Squinting, he kept going forward to avoid being trampled by the soldiers marching through behind him.

Even before his vision cleared, though, the General could tell something was wrong. He heard a humming in the air, a chittering, and the rustle of what seemed like thousands of bodies moving. His own soldiers began to shout as they came through the transportal, adjusting goggles and visors on their helmets.

Now Lanyan saw monsters – a numberless swarm of them.

Instead of a Hansa colony with a few hundred settlers, he and his men found thousands of giant bugs that looked vaguely like Klikiss robots. But they were alive, organic. It was all he could do to bite back a scream. Some of his soldiers yelled.

The bugs noticed them.

As Lanyan staggered forward, shouting for his soldiers to ready their weapons, he spotted a group of haggard people in makeshift corrals. Only twenty or thirty scarecrowish prisoners were left alive. He saw butchered human bodies strewn about, many of them floating in the brackish pools. New towers built of salt, sand, and white borax shone like stalagmites rising out of the alkaline pools.

The surviving Pym colonists let out a chorus of shouts and pleas for the EDF to rescue them. Lanyan instantly reacted. He was commander of the Earth Defence Forces, and these were Hansa colonists in danger.

The insect monsters raised scythelike forelimbs, hissing and whistling and clicking. They began marching toward the transportal and the oncoming EDF soldiers. Unaware of what they were about to face, uniformed men kept pouring through from Rheindic Co.

'Open fire! Defend yourselves!' Lanyan ran ahead, blasting with a pulse rifle that was no longer merely ceremonial. The insect monsters made eerie, nerve-jarring sounds as they swarmed forward. The EDF soldiers, still emerging from the transportal by the hundreds, launched their attack.

FORTY-THREE

RLINDA KETT

Her first mission as Trade Minister seemed awfully lonely without BeBob. At one time Rlinda Kett had been content to be the only person aboard the *Voracious Curiosity*, but recently she'd grown fond of having her favourite ex-husband along. She enjoyed his sense of humour, his conversation (such as it was), and most especially the sex.

But now that she was returning to the Hansa under uncertain political circumstances, she didn't dare bring BeBob along. He already had a death sentence for 'desertion', and she intended to keep him safe. She could do this little meet-and-greet herself — *if*, that was, she found anybody receptive to what she had to say. This scouting expedition was official business (though the Chairman would probably call it 'spying'), but nobody else needed to know why she was here. She would play the part of a simple trader with run-of-the-mill goods.

Approaching Earth, Rlinda requested permission to land. The standard orbital traffic lanes were a scrapheap of empty hulks not yet towed out to a safe holding zone. She could see crews working among the derelicts, dismantling them for parts. Some chunks slowly spiralled down and burned up in the atmosphere. The nightly meteor showers must have been something to see.

A small piece of debris – apparently a loose spacesuit glove – caromed off the *Curiosity*'s hull. Dodging larger pieces of space junk, Rlinda contacted the space traffic substation on the ground. 'How the hell do you expect to receive any trade ships with this demolition derby in your own back yard? Can somebody give me a safe path through this obstacle course so I can get to the Palace District?'

'We're still working on the situation, *Curiosity*. We have recommended routes, but we do not guarantee their accuracy. Please state your business in the Palace District.'

'I need to set up a meeting with Ambassador Sarein to discuss commercial transactions.' Rlinda was sure the Theron ambassador would be a sympathetic listener and, she hoped, more rational than Chairman Wenceslas. After escaping with BeBob, no doubt she had burned her bridges with the Chairman; she hoped there wasn't an arrest warrant out for her as well. If so, the *Curiosity*'s souped-up engines could outrun any patrol ships in the vicinity.

'Be advised that increased tariffs have been imposed on all new trading.'

'Of course they have. Somebody's got to pay for all this reconstruction.' Sooner or later, though, Earth's importance would dwindle as the Confederation grew. Once the Chairman got his head out of his butt, this kind of nonsense could be over.

As she started her final approach to the Palace District, Rlinda sent a message to Sarein, and after about fifteen minutes a familiar voice came over the comm system. 'Captain Kett, I would be pleased to meet with you.' The ambassador didn't sound pleased so much as uncertain, even shaken. Not at all the confident young woman who had represented Theroc to the Hansa. 'Security measures are much tighter than you're accustomed to. Just stay with your ship. I'll . . . I'll come there in person.'

'Whatever you say, Ambassador. I'll be here waiting.' She went into her galley and prepared a special feast of Theron treats that she was sure Sarein missed. The young woman had often complained about her backwater home planet, but Rlinda knew that Sarein had a kind heart, despite her hard exterior.

After brusquely instructing her uniformed escort to stay outside the ship, the young woman came aboard. Rlinda immediately saw the changes in Sarein. She had lost an unhealthy amount of weight, her face seemed pallid, and lines of concern showed around her mouth and eyes. 'Captain Kett, it has been a long time,' she said formally. Suddenly her expression melted. 'I'm so glad to see you.' She spotted the Theron delicacies and flashed a genuine smile. 'Are those for me? I haven't had any of this for so long!'

'Be my guest. Put some colour back into your cheeks. I've got some messages for you, too.' Rlinda bustled about, bringing out two hand-written notes and a small message player with a chip already loaded in it. 'Your parents each wrote you a letter. I didn't read them, of course, but I can guess that they want you to know how much they miss you. Your little sister Celli recorded a message, and so did Estarra.'

Sarein's expression wavered, and Rlinda could only imagine the emotions flowing through her. She clutched the notes and the message player as if they were lifelines. 'Even Estarra?'

'She's still your sister. If you ask me, you'd be better off on Theroc than here. Are you sure it makes sense for you to stay on Earth? What do you hope to accomplish?'

'I don't know, Captain Kett. I really don't know. I just keep hoping to influence Basil, convince him to make good decisions.'

Rlinda snorted. 'Or fewer bad ones.'

Sarein wavered, then strengthened herself again. 'The Chairman wants all citizens to pull together, to work hard and make sacrifices – but they're growing restless. The Hansa still hasn't even publicly explained what happened to the King and Queen, so the rumours are running wild. Basil is going about it in the wrong way, antagonizing the citizens rather than earning their loyalty.'

Rlinda blew out a long breath. 'If you all just join the Confederation, then everybody benefits. Didn't Chairman Wenceslas always say we should look at the big picture? After only a month, the Confederation has a hell of a lot more people and planets than the Hansa does.'

Sarein looked at her blankly. 'He's ... he's making his own plans.' With a frown, she pushed her plate away, thought better of it, then continued picking at the familiar treats. 'How do you know so much about all this, Rlinda? Have you been spending time on Theroc?'

Rlinda considered, then took a chance. 'More than that, Ambassador. I've been appointed the Confederation's new Trade Minister.'

Sarein reacted with alarm, and Rlinda sensed she was hiding something. 'Then I ... I shouldn't be talking with you.'

'Why not? You're the ambassador from Theroc. I brought two more treelings with me that you can place in the Whisper Palace, even though the green priests have cut off communication with the Hansa. Nobody can get through to Nahton anymore. I'm *hoping* that means he's been separated from his treeling and nothing more ominous than that. Right?'

Sarein looked sad and lost. 'Basil had him killed. He's killed a green priest!'

Rlinda was shocked. Did anyone on Theroc even know? Sarein seemed to grow more anxious. Was the Hansa up to something at this very moment? 'Tell me the truth, Sarein – am I in danger? Right now?'

'Not you . . . not yet. But Basil watches me closely. He'll want to know why I was talking to someone aboard a ship, and he's sure to recognize the name of your vessel. Too many questions will come to his mind.'

'Wonderful. Just wonderful.'

Sarein looked mournfully down at the remainder of the small meal. 'I can't talk to you anymore. I really can't.'

'How long is the Chairman going to keep acting like an ass?'

'To the very end.' Sarein gave Rlinda a quick hug and hurried to the hatch. 'I suggest you leave as soon as possible, before the Hansa makes up some excuse to keep you here.'

FORTY-FOUR

SAREIN

In times of peace, colourfully costumed docents had escorted tour groups through parts of the Whisper Palace, and the portrait gallery was always one of the popular stops. The docents told stories about each of the Great Kings: Ben, George, Christopher, Jack, Bartholomew, Frederick – and Peter.

Due to increased security measures, however, the portrait gallery had been declared off-limits. Now Chairman Wenceslas had shut down the tours altogether, declaring the whole Palace district a security zone. 'We have better things to do than cater to tourists. There is urgent work to complete, and loyal citizens shouldn't be squandering precious time on vacations.'

The crackdown, however, gave Sarein the perfect place to meet in private with Deputy Eldred Cain. Both of them knew they needed to discuss the question that Sarein had not yet dared to voice aloud: *What to do about Basil?*

After the murder of Nahton, she lived in fear, sure that Basil would discover how she had secretly encouraged the green priest to send his warning to Theroc. Since the royal guard had either committed a terrible blunder or an intentionally treasonous act in letting the green priest out, suspicion fell directly on Captain McCammon.

Fortunately, Deputy Cain had acted even more swiftly than Basil could follow the trail of suspicion. Duty rosters were doctored, changing the name of the guard assigned to that post; Cain let the records indicate tampering, leaving the impression that an imposter had slipped into the Whisper Palace for the sole purpose of freeing Nahton. It played directly into Basil's paranoia. The Chairman sent teams to search the labyrinthine halls of the Palace for shadowy infiltrators. Not surprisingly, the wild-goose chase uncovered nothing.

But Sarein knew the problem would only get worse.

After Rlinda Kett left, the pale deputy waited for Sarein in the portrait hall. He stood with his hands clasped behind his back, looking at the features of plump George, old bearded Frederick, red-haired Jack, and the others. 'A rather incomplete display, don't you think?'

Sarein looked at the prominent blank spot on the wall. The portrait of King Peter had hung there for only a few years before the Chairman ordered it torn down. 'Does he think he can erase King Peter and my sister by taking down a painting?'

'The Chairman believes that perceptions drive reality. If he spins his stories, colours his reports, and chooses the right words, then people will believe his version of events. He might even convince himself that his well-crafted fiction is actual history.'

Cain walked around the gallery. The original architects had left plenty of wall space, assuming there would be a long succession of Great Kings. 'Notice that he never placed Daniel's portrait either. He had the royal painter rush through his work, only to store it in a vault. I doubt it'll ever hang here.'

Sarein frowned. 'Daniel would have made a terrible King.'

211

'The Chairman's choices have not always proved to be wise ones. You'll notice here,' he pointed just to the side of Old King Frederick's portrait, 'there's no sign of Prince Adam, either. He's vanished without a trace, both from the face of the Earth and from the historical records.'

'Prince Adam?' Sarein had never heard of him.

'The candidate before Peter was selected.'

'And Basil . . . got rid of him?'

'The Chairman wanted to do the same to Peter, which is why he was so careful not to announce Prince Daniel until he was forced to do it. Chairman Wenceslas likes to keep his options open.'

'Basil's training someone else, but he won't tell me a thing.' *And we used to be so close!* The Chairman no longer wanted sex, no longer wanted her companionship, no longer wanted her advice.

'I know nothing about the candidate either. Presumably, he will be crowned King without even being introduced as a Prince. One would expect the Deputy Chairman to have some input – or at least be kept aware of such an important matter. But the Chairman hasn't tipped his hand.'

Sarein's heart skipped a beat. The Basil Wenceslas she had admired so much, the man she had come to love, was no longer the same person. She looked at the portraits, recalling the legends of the various Kings taught to schoolchildren. Basil had once taken her on his own private tour of the portrait gallery, giving his own impressions, explaining each King's numerous flaws and mistakes. He so easily saw the weaknesses in others.

Through another door (a stop that had never been on the popular Whisper Palace tour) a crowded boardroom held portraits of the seventeen Hansa Chairmen that had served over the past two centuries. Basil had been equally quick to offer complaints and criticisms about those men and women.

'Did you know that I have a collection of my own paintings? I especially like the works of the Spanish painter Velasquez.'

She wondered why the Deputy would mention his own paintings when such heavy and dangerous decisions lay before them. Would they have to overthrow Chairman Wenceslas? Could they? The Hansa was in desperate straits.

'At one time I had a companion – a beautiful person, but emotionally demanding. Kelly,' Cain mused. 'My job is important, affecting the lives of many people, but in those rare hours when I'm not dealing with some crisis, I just want to relax and enjoy my art. I like to study my paintings in silence, contemplate the brushstrokes, and imagine what Velasquez himself might have been thinking as he created such masterpieces.

'Kelly claimed to understand that. The people I've occasionally chosen as partners always say that, initially ... and then they always want to talk, share their feelings, and spend time close to me.' He let out a long-suffering sigh. 'All I asked for was a few moments of contemplation and peace, but Kelly grew distraught, even hysterical, insisted I was emotionally distant when I wouldn't give an "appropriate amount" of attention.' He shrugged. 'I am currently alone, still unsettled from my recent break-up.'

Sarein remembered a strange security alarm about six months ago, an odd report of someone 'going berserk' in Cain's apartments. 'I never pegged you as a fool with a broken heart, Mr Cain.'

'Oh, not that. I'm simply shocked at how volatile emotions can be. To this day, I don't know precisely what triggered the screaming fit. In a pathetic bid to get my attention, Kelly tried to wreck my paintings. *My paintings!* Naturally I triggered my active security codes. It was an ugly scene, but necessary.' Sarein could well imagine how swiftly an army of Hansa guards must have swarmed in to 'neutralize the threat'.

'I issued instructions that Kelly was to be moved to a different

213

continent, and then I sat down to stare at the paintings just to calm myself. It took the rest of the night, but it was all for the best.'

As she listened to the story, it occurred to Sarein that the subtle Cain had never really changed the subject. He was still talking about Basil. She felt a cold shiver down her spine, as if someone was watching her. She turned, instantly feeling guilty when she saw the Chairman standing in the doorway, a frown deeply etched on his face. She wondered how long he had been watching them. She quailed as she tried to remember: Had the two of them said anything dangerous or incriminating?

'I asked Captain McCammon to find you two. He said he didn't know where you were.' Basil made a disgusted noise. 'I grow less and less impressed with that man's competence every day.' He looked at the portraits, scowling at each of the Kings in turn. 'What are you doing here? Why are you two talking together?'

Sarein felt as if they were caught. The suspicious Chairman would assume they were scheming against him, plotting a coup. She held her breath to keep from blurting lame-sounding excuses.

Cain, though, remained cool and unruffled. Apparently, he had known the Chairman was listening, which was why he had switched his conversation so smoothly. 'We were discussing the past Kings and possible future ones, and I told Sarein of my private Velasquez collection.'

'And that is all you talked about? Are you certain?' Basil's tone held an edge of accusation.

'Mr Chairman, you are the leader of the Terran Hanseatic League. Surely you have better things to do than to micromanage two of your remaining loyal advisers?' Basil continued to wrestle with obvious doubts, but Cain had chosen one of the few topics the Chairman could never ignore. The deputy continued to look at him patiently. 'Was there something you needed from us, sir?'

214

'I just wanted to know where you were.'

'Would you like me to join you for dinner tonight, Basil?' Sarein said, a brief hope rising within her. Perhaps a last chance . . .

'No. I've got work to do.'

FORTY-FIVE

MAGE-IMPERATOR JORA'H

Adar Zan'nh's flagship returned from its unnerving victory at Maratha. Yazra'h was ecstatic. Her skin flushed, her eyes bright, she couldn't stop talking about their exploits.

With Nira beside him, along with Osira'h and her siblings, Jora'h listened to Rememberer Vao'sh tell the exciting story. Anton Colicos frequently interrupted the tale, adding details and breathless comments. It was obvious that both men had been terrified at the time, but now they could barely contain their exhilaration.

Among the audience members close to the skysphere dais, Ko'sh, chief scribe of the rememberer kith, diligently took notes to add to the full written reports Anton and Vao'sh would provide. The stern and dedicated scribe was already shaping precisely how these events would be incorporated into the official version of the *Saga of Seven Suns*.

The Solar Navy septa had strengthened the Empire by reclaiming the lost Ildiran world from the black robots. The Adar had left the other six warliners at Maratha along with work crews to re-establish the splinter colony there. And they had also discovered that the Klikiss were still alive.

Though the story was engaging, Jora'h found himself pre-occupied with unsettling questions. Adar Zan'nh had acquitted himself well, but the encounter had resolved one question only to pose a greater one. The Klikiss – after ten thousand years! What did it mean? As Mage-Imperator, how should he deal with this new invasion? Was it even relevant to the Ildiran Empire? Was the insect race a threat to them? What if the Klikiss found out about the secret pact an ancient Mage-Imperator had made with the black robots, helping them to vanish into hibernation for thousands of years? Yes, the danger could be considerable.

Prime Designate Daro'h also attended the telling of the story. From now on, Jora'h wanted the young man at his side during all important meetings. The Prime Designate still suffered from his severe burn as ragged ribbons of skin peeled from his face, though the best medical kithmen had used their finest salves and lotions.

Daro'h's fearful revelation about mad Designate Rusa'h and his bizarre union with the faeros had unsettled Jora'h as much as the news about the Klikiss. Could the Ildiran Empire withstand both enemies? Could they survive either? He just did not know.

Finished with their tale, Anton Colicos and Vao'sh bowed. Zan'nh stepped forward. 'If our ancient translation programs were accurate, the Klikiss said they would reclaim all their old worlds.'

Wearing a grave expression, Nira raised an entirely different concern, one that had not occurred to him. 'What about the human colonies established on abandoned worlds, Jora'h? If the Klikiss are coming – what will happen to all those people?'

Another wave of consequences and difficult decisions rose before him. 'My primary responsibility is to the Ildiran Empire.'

From beside her mother, Osira'h spoke up. 'Ildirans may be the only ones who can do something fast enough, Father. We may be the only ones who know the Klikiss have returned. Are we not obligated to help, if we know of a need?'

Rod'h added, 'Would we not ask the humans to help, if the situation were reversed?'

Pointedly, Zan'nh said, 'The situation would never be reversed, because Ildirans would never sweep into empty Klikiss worlds. Ildirans would never assume that just because a planet was empty, we could simply take it.'

Rememberer Ko'sh stood poised with his scriber, waiting to see how the Mage-Imperator would respond. Prime Designate Daro'h also looked at his father with keen interest.

'I must contemplate this.' Jora'h stood from the chrysalis chair. 'The answer is not obvious when taken in the context of the entire Ildiran Empire.'

During the still-bright sleeping period, Jora'h lay in his cool chambers holding Nira close. The two had first become lovers when he was the dashing Prime Designate and she a young green priest, come to study the *Saga*. Though so much had changed since then, they were still close, perhaps closer now than ever before. Their love forged a bond that could not be broken – not by Jora'h's ascension to Mage-Imperator, not by Nira's suffering in the breeding camps.

He held her in silence and stroked her arm, trying to forget – just for a moment – the difficult decisions that dogged him. Her soft, emerald skin was a vibrant counterpoint to the coppery-olive sheen of his own. Resting, the Mage-Imperator had unbound his long symbolic braid so that the loose strands drifted like feathers charged with static electricity. Several tickled Nira's shoulder, and she stirred in her sleep, smiling, then lifted a hand to caress him. With her hairless head on his chest, she seemed to melt against him.

Although they slept together, their relationship was no longer sexual. That was impossible for him and no longer desirable to her. As it was, they held each other with a closeness that a Mage-Imperator was not supposed to have and one that Nira had never thought she'd accept again.

Without opening her eyes, she spoke. 'What will you do to rescue the human colonists, Jora'h? They're alone.'

'I love you, Nira. I have no resentment against your people, but I am the Mage-Imperator. Ildirans are vulnerable, in danger, facing an unknown threat from whatever my brother Rusa'h has become. I do not wish to provoke the Klikiss, especially now. My Solar Navy is decimated, and the Ildiran Empire can ill afford new enemies.'

Nira opened her eyes. 'Neither can the Confederation. That's not an excuse to ignore everyone else in need.'

'Use your treeling to warn other green priests. They will find a way to mount a rescue operation.'

'Yes, I'll do that. But the other human colonies, the Confederation, Theroc, even the Hansa – they're in no position to come to the rescue.' Her voice was firm. 'This is your chance, Jora'h. You know you have much to atone for after Dobro. You can't just brush aside the pain the Ildirans have caused.'

He drew a deep breath, knowing she was right. Though the news had spread through the telink network, the Mage-Imperator had not yet spoken directly with the human government, had not addressed the lies, the breeding programme, the crimes his predecessors had perpetrated. Even Adar Zan'nh's sacrifice of so many warliners to save Earth was not sufficient to heal the gaping wound.

'You should *do this*, Jora'h. Those humans on the Klikiss worlds have no way of getting to safety. You can help.'

She sat up in bed, and his heart felt a pang. Jora'h had

promised himself not to disappoint or hurt her again. Because of his love for her, he would make different decisions. Jora'h sat up, as well. 'You have become my conscience, Nira. No Mage-Imperator was ever meant to feel like this.' He leaned over to kiss her cheek. 'You guide me in the right direction. It is not the Ildiran way, but I will do anything for you.'

'Then you'll talk to Adar Zan'nh about my request?'

'I will do more than talk. I will send him right away.'

The hovering observation platform was draped with brocaded hangings and piled high around the edges with soft cushions. Floating above the spires of Mijistra, the Mage-Imperator and his party had the best seats for observing the skyparade. Jora'h sat in the centre of the platform with Prime Designate Daro'h prominent beside him.

'Look, there's the first one.' Nira pointed to the sky.

One of Tabitha Huck's newly constructed warliners descended gracefully like an immense silver whale bedecked with pennants and ribbons, its solar sails and ornamental wings fully extended. Forty-nine streamers streaked around and in front of the warliner, interweaving their flight paths, dancing across the air to show their pilots' prowess.

Through the *thism*, Jora'h could feel a swell of joy as spectators watched this affirmation of the great Solar Navy. They took it as a sign that everything could be fixed, that all damage could be repaired, that the Ildiran Empire would be strong again.

A wash of emotions came from the crowd below as a second warliner descended, followed closely by a third. The pleasure in the *thism* nearly diluted the brooding uneasiness that he still sensed across the rest of his Empire. Since the beginning of his reign, Jora'h had felt so many terrible and distant events, he was not sure how a genuine peace would feel to him.

The hovering platform continued to drift above Mijistra so that all Ildirans could see their Mage-Imperator. Streamers from each new warliner intersected with other squadrons in manoeuvres carefully choreographed by Zan'nh himself. Before he departed on his rescue mission, the Adar seemed intent on proving that his Solar Navy was still as adept as any ever recorded in the *Saga*.

These ships were the first of the newly commissioned vessels. Tabitha Huck and her engineers had cemented the Ildiran construction crews, making the best use of the unlimited labour and materials to build warliners. Tabitha had twenty more ships under construction and another ten in the initial phases. At this rate, within a decade the Solar Navy would be restored to its previous glory.

The skyparade proved only a temporary distraction, however; Jora'h could not drive back the uneasiness, the blank cold in the *thism* web that was spreading across his Empire again. Though she was happy that these warliners were going off to help colonists trapped by the Klikiss, Nira noted the change in his mood. She didn't need *thism* to read him so clearly. 'What is it? Has something happened?'

'It has been happening for a long while. I feel a dark stain, as if I am going blind in certain portions of my vision. Not pain, just an indefinable loss.'

Daro'h stiffened, as if he knew exactly what his father meant. 'You are losing parts of the *thism* – or they are being taken from you.'

'Yes, it must be. I feel I have entirely lost Dzelluria and several other worlds in the Horizon Cluster – not entirely unlike when Rusa'h formed his own *thism* web and took all those people away from me. But this seems more complete. It is as if whole parts of my Empire simply *are not there*.'

'Like I felt when I didn't have a tree,' Nira said, and he could hear the pain in her voice.

Five warliners roared overhead, and the people cheered, but Jora'h did not take his gaze from Nira's beautiful face. 'Yes. Like that.'

The Prime Designate turned to Jora'h, his healing face full of conviction. 'The faeros are the cause of this. Rusa'h warned that he was coming for us.'

FORTY-SIX

FAEROS INCARNATE RUSA'H

Resplendent in vivifying flames, Rusa'h returned to Hyrillka, the heart of his domain. His fireball ship was alive with attendant faeros, shooting toward the planet he intended either to reclaim or incinerate in the process.

Back in his human incarnation, he had done holy work all around the Horizon Cluster. Starting with Dzelluria, he had kindled a fire of epic proportions, burning corruption from the Ildiran psyche and establishing his own *thism* web. Rusa'h had saved part of the Ildiran race by giving them the true soul-threads and untangling their knotted misunderstandings.

And all of that had been stolen from him by Jora'h, his own brother.

He had thought he'd lost everything, until he plunged into a living manifestation of the Lightsource. Baptized in the flames and then reforged, he had been transformed into this new persona of elemental energy.

And he had come back. Recently, he had felt the exhilaration of liberating the soulfires of every Ildiran on Dzelluria. The battle-weakened faeros had drawn vitally needed new energy from consuming those people, their bodies, their minds, their lives. Because Rusa'h had already laid down his pathways of *thism* there, he had found it easy to cut Dzelluria off from the false Mage-Imperator. When he reopened the *thism* web, the Dzelluria populace became combustible fuel, seeds for new faeros, to help the fiery beings recover from the near-genocide the hydrogues had inflicted.

Rusa'h had left Dzelluria a smouldering ember, its surface scorched and lifeless. He had done the same at Alturas. Then Shonor. And Garoa. Finally, he had arrived back at Hyrillka. *Home.*

His fireball and ten others swept down like a shower of blazing meteors. Rusa'h wanted to appear in all his coronal glory before his people. He would reawaken their reconfigured *thism* and pour revelations through them like lava. The faeros would reap a great harvest of soulfires here, and they would be strengthened again. Both Rusa'h and the flaming entities would benefit.

But he found Hyrillka empty, abandoned. The world felt silent to him. The flaming ship around him brightened as his thoughts churned and the faeros picked up on his unexpected anger. Through the eyes and thoughts of the faeros, who had not understood what they were seeing, he 'remembered' great numbers of warliners evacuating, a flurry of Ildiran traffic that had taken place during the titanic battle of faeros and hydrogues in Hyrillka's primary sun.

Now Rusa'h understood. The Ildirans would have been concerned that Hyrillka's sun would die, just like Crenna or Durris-B. The Solar Navy had used those warliners to whisk everyone away. His people were gone. All of them!

But the faeros had defeated the hydrogues after all, *saved* their sun – and still Hyrillka remained empty.

Feeling angry fire in his reconstructed body, Rusa'h soared

down to the surface, creating a wake of heat vapours. He cruised over the beloved city around which he had planted vast fields of nialia vines. All were destroyed, the soil blackened. Many city buildings had been partially rebuilt, but they were all empty again.

At last Rusa'h noticed a small inhabited encampment of newly erected huts and sheds – a research station. He sensed a handful of scientists and engineers, climate specialists and meteorologists, the bare minimum for a splinter. They must be studying Hyrillka to see if it was once again habitable. The near-death of the sun had no doubt frightened them greatly.

But Rusa'h would frighten them even more.

From inside the fireball, he extended his mind, pushed his powers forth, and connected with the faeros, which made his *thism* stronger than ever before, and different. He cut off this small number of Ildirans from the rest of the *thism* network, isolating them.

Bereft and confused, scientists emerged from their structures and stared at the faeros crackling in the sky, as if the stars themselves had fallen. Rusa'h parted the curtains of flames and walked out in his incandescent body.

The faeros began to burn the whole camp, setting the temporary structures afire. The researchers ran about frantically, but they could not flee fast enough. Some begged for mercy, and Rusa'h would show them mercy: he would grant them a wondrous gift by converting their soulfires into faeros energy. The scientists and engineers screamed as their very bones ignited, and they disappeared in a flash of bright flame and greasy smoke.

Now that he was back home, Rusa'h walked the empty streets, remembering how Hyrillka had been.

After climbing the hill, he strode through his empty citadel palace. His very touch was fire, and he set everything alight, incinerating the thick hanging vines, liquefying even the stone and crystal support structures. When the whole citadel palace was burning, he sat back in his melting throne and revelled in the blaze.

FORTY-SEVEN

CESCA PERONI

Though she loved Jess as much as ever, Cesca couldn't ignore her responsibilities to the Roamers, who still considered her Speaker and looked to her for guidance.

'I feel as if I need to do something for our people. Jhy Okiah selected me to be her successor. The Roamers are still recovering from this devastating war, and I'm alone with you on an entire planet, happier than I've ever been in my life. Shouldn't I be helping the clans?'

'Can you still lead the Roamers? Really?' Jess lifted his hand and looked at it. Runnels of silvery water glided down his wrist and into the swaying waves. 'Is it fair to them to have a Speaker who is no longer like they are?'

Her expression was troubled. Water plastered her dark hair against her head. 'I don't know. Would it be best for the Roamers if I turned over the reins of leadership? And soon?'

'Maybe we should ask them what they think.'

'Then let's go find them.'

*

After leaving Charybdis, she and Jess first visited the ruins of Rendezvous, then the bustling commercial hub of Yreka, before travelling to the centre of the new government at Theroc.

'I'm pleased to see that the clans have found allies and protectors,' Cesca said to Jess, as their ship descended towards the vast forest. 'We were so alone before.'

'Impossible enemies brought us together in ways we couldn't imagine.'

'As long as they brought the factions of humanity together, Jess. *Husband*.' She smiled. 'Now we represent the wentals as well as ourselves.'

Through the shimmering walls of the bubble, the couple peered down at the thick worldtrees and the large clearings made into landing areas for Roamer ships. With Jess's help, she had considered what she wanted to do, and what she *could* do. What was her new Guiding Star? What was her plan?

Like a giant raindrop, their wental-formed ship descended to a meadow near a small diamond sphere – an empty hydrogue derelict? As traders and green priests hurried forward to greet them, the pair stepped through the pliable membrane. Holding hands, she and Jess stood in the Theron sunlight, sparkling with droplets of moisture. The wental energy permeating their bodies gave them a faint, crackling aura.

The last time Cesca had come here, she had helped the Roamers clear debris and assist the Therons after the hydrogue attack. And before that, she had visited with an entourage of clans to celebrate her impending marriage to Reynald.

Now her father hurried forward, practically running. The grin on Denn Peroni's face warmed her heart. Since joining with the wentals, Cesca had seen him once on Yreka to explain what had happened to her, and to enlist his aid in recruiting Roamer ships for the final battle against the hydrogues.

Knowing that he couldn't touch her, Denn stopped a few steps away. 'Well, I'm glad the Speaker has come back to resume her role among the Roamer clans again. We were beginning to wonder!'

The fact that she couldn't allow anyone close enough to touch her only reinforced Cesca's decision. Her father's expression was so innocent and hopeful, as if he expected her to simply pick up her duties as before. Cesca drew a deep breath, knowing she was about to disappoint him. 'Don't jump to conclusions. I've ... I've got a new Guiding Star now, and it isn't leading me to be the Speaker. I can't do it – not the way I am.'

His expression fell. 'There's a lot you should know before you make a rash decision. The clans need you—'

'The clans need somebody, that's for certain.' When she shook her head, her damp dark hair waved slowly, as if pregnant with electricity. 'But it would be impossible for me to do the job. Now that the wentals live within me, close quarters like crowded Roamer settlements are dangerous not only for me, but for you. The slightest touch, a single mistake, would result in someone's death.'

Cesca saw her father resist the idea for a moment before a reluctant understanding settled on his face. She said, 'With the new government, you need more than just a Speaker. You'll need representatives to the Confederation. And I think you would make a damned good one.'

He lifted his chin, grinning. 'I already am. Official liaison between the clans and Theroc. I couldn't wait forever, you know. Jess, your sister left here not long ago. She and her boyfriend are working at the Osquivel shipyards to build a Confederation military – frantically, I might add. We found out that the Eddies are coming here soon to cause trouble.'

'An attack? What does the Chairman think he's doing?' Cesca

already had experience with Basil Wenceslas and knew his dangerous unpredictability.

Denn looked at their shimmering wental ship. 'You couldn't have come at a better time. Whenever those battleships show up, you'll give them a nice surprise!'

'We'll see King Peter to discuss how the wentals can help,' Jess said with a grin.

FORTY-EIGHT

ORLI COVITZ

With numerous buildings destroyed in the Klikiss expansion and so many families inside the walled enclosure, the Llaro colonists crowded together in communal houses. They shared their fears and shored up each other's hopes.

Orli had moved in with Crim and Marla Chan Tylar, and DD knew exactly where to find her. She looked up to see the Friendly compy standing by the door. Although his polymer face did not change, he always seemed to be smiling at her. 'Orli Covitz, Margaret has asked me to take you to her. Please bring your music synthesizer strips.'

Curious, Orli gathered her strips and trotted after DD. Margaret had shown an interest in her playing, often sitting and listening with other colonists when the girl gave a performance. During those times, Margaret's expression showed a contentment that seemed very unfamiliar to her. 'Does she want to hear some of my music?' she asked brightly.

'The breedex does.'

A stab of cold pierced her heart, and her knees felt weak as she stepped outside. *The breedex?* DD led her to one of the barred gaps in the thick stockade wall. Showing no reaction whatsoever, the Klikiss guards let the compy pass with Orli in tow.

Margaret was waiting outside the wall, her face full of concern. 'I am very sorry, but this is for your own good. It might give you a chance – I can't think of anything better to do.' She looked down at the music strips rolled up under Orli's arm. 'I want you to play today – and promise me you'll play as you have never done before.'

'I've learned the song "Greensleeves," the one from your music box.' Margaret had even taught her the words.

The older woman jerked in alarm. 'Not "Greensleeves". They've already heard that song. Concentrate on your own compositions.'

Orli forced optimism into her voice. 'Okay, I have plenty. I can do that.'

DD strutted happily beside them. Massive Klikiss warriors stood by the dark entrance of the smooth-walled, freeform building that looked like a squat beehive, a veritable fortress in the centre of the insect city. There was only one entrance, an arching passageway tall enough to allow the domates to enter. Following Margaret into the darkness, Orli felt very small.

The smell inside was more potent than the normal sandy musk the Klikiss gave off. Orli wrinkled her nose at the oily, chemical stench. 'Sure stinks.'

'These pheromones are part of the Klikiss language, too,' Margaret said.

The light was dim, mere patterns of sunshine trickling through ventilation holes drilled in the resin-concrete walls. Greenish phosphorescence lined the curved passageways in thick, irregular lines that made Orli think of smeared insect spit (probably exactly what it was).

Dozens of spiny warriors had massed protectively in the corridors leading to the heart of the breedex hive. Two huge domates stepped aside for them at the arched entrance into the main chamber.

Margaret paused just outside the vaulted room and whispered, 'Remember to play your own music. Play your best.'

Inside, Orli caught her breath and stared at the massive object – creature – that filled the chamber. The breedex was a huge, shifting assemblage of components, like the facets of a fly's compound eye. She saw iridescent carapaces, thick spikes of chitin, squirming grubs. All around Orli, a buzzing made the hive mind itself seem to be a self-contained swarm of creatures.

The breedex was ensconced in a chaotic nest of bones and Klikiss shells pasted together with translucent, hardened slime. The peculiar and disgusting throne seemed to be a sculpture made from the breedex's prior victims. Orli even saw the flat, angular heads of destroyed robots, along with mechanical arms and adornments of ripped-out circuitry.

Orli felt very frightened as the bulk of the breedex realigned itself, raising something that she thought was its head. Through the numerous facets, she could sense eyes watching her. The humming grew louder.

Margaret stepped forward and held up her small music box. Using her thumb and forefinger, she wound the key and let the tinkling tune fill the air. She did not speak until the spring wound down and the little song was finished. Then she whispered to Orli, 'Now play your melodies. This is important.'

Swallowing hard, Orli unrolled her music strips and tried to recall her father's favourite tunes. For a frightening moment, nervousness made her forget how to play, but she forced herself to concentrate. If she failed, if she made a mistake, the breedex might just kill her.

Forcing those thoughts aside, the girl sat down and played her music.

The breedex shifted and rose up in a mass. Orli's fingers flew across the keys, tracing melodies, adding counterpoints, playing so hard and so intensely that she almost forgot where she was. She imagined herself playing for Crim and Marla instead; she thought of her father's dreams and promises of how she would be a famous professional musician someday.

She noted with her peripheral vision that the Klikiss workers at the edge of the chamber, the warriors, even the domates had frozen in place, seemingly turned to statues as the music lilted, swirled, rose and then fell. Orli realized that she had engaged the attention of the entire hive mind, focusing the breedex so completely that none of the myriad insects could think or move for themselves. She caught her breath, wondering if all of the Klikiss on Llaro had also frozen in place.

Her fingers faltered on the keyboard, and as the atonal notes rang out, the breedex seemed disturbed. The domates shifted, and Orli sensed the change in their attention as soon as she made her blunder. A thrill of fear shot down her spine, but she recovered quickly, launching into a new melody, and soon had hypnotized the hive mind again.

She played another song, then another, and she seemed to have an inexhaustible repertoire. After she finished one particularly complicated melody, Orli played some of the common folk tunes and songs she had known as a child. The breedex didn't seem to notice any difference.

When exhaustion finally forced Orli to stop, she blinked, dazed, and remembered where she was. A wave of fear washed over her.

The silence startled Margaret out of her own trance. When

the breedex began to thrum, the older woman's shoulders slumped with relief.

Out in the corridor, the domates started to move and chitter again. Orli felt the pounding thoughts of the great breedex mind still resonating with the music, like invisible fingers pressing against her skull. From the look on Margaret's face, the girl could tell that she would survive, for today at least. And, she hoped, so would the rest of the people in the settlement.

FORTY-NINE

GENERAL KURT LANYAN

U naware of what they were stepping into, the EDF peace-keepers paraded through the transportal to Pym. When they blundered into the giant bugs, Lanyan did not need to encourage his men to start blasting away.

The insect creatures chittered, whistled, and hummed – and attacked the EDF troops with an eerie synchronization. Some were more monstrous than others, with forelimbs as sharp as the Grim Reaper's scythe. Standard projectiles blasted open their hard exoskeletons, showering out globs of slime and ooze. Nevertheless, the bugs swept forward with startling speed.

The colonists in their fenced-in prison near the alkaline pools were horrified when they saw the first soldiers torn to pieces. At the fringe of the battlefield, like a symphonic accompaniment to the clash, geysers shot pillars of steam into the air along with a foul sulphurous smell.

The General bellowed over the din of the ensuing engagement. 'Mission parameters have changed. We are the *Earth Defence Forces* – so start defending. Let's rescue those colonists, then haul-ass out of here.' Having anticipated little resistance from the colonists, Lanyan's EDF peacekeepers carried primarily ceremonial weapons. Right now, he wished he'd brought along a full-bore jazer cannon or shaped-projectile launcher.

A gratifying blast from his own gun splattered the head-crest of a huge insect warrior that reared up in front of him. A second projectile blasted its thorax, and the armoured head tumbled into the alkaline water. The body's multiple limbs kept twitching.

Against Lanyan's original orders – thank God! – someone had brought small fusion grenades. A soldier launched two grenades toward the alien monoliths in the middle of the grey lake. The resulting explosion broke the brittle structures into flying white chunks.

A third fusion grenade detonated on the far side of the prison fence, spraying tainted water in every direction. The high-energy blast opened a sinkhole beneath the alkaline crust, and the ground began to collapse as water gurgled down, sweeping many of the swarming creatures away in the flood.

Bitter white powder in the air stung Lanyan's eyes and burned his throat. Coughing, he killed several bugs that had taken down five of his soldiers. Lanyan led a charge toward the chalky towers, seeing red as he splashed through shin-deep grey water. The big bugs were all around the pen for the haggard colonists, but the insects here seemed to be a different breed, not as aggressive. Lanyan and his men blasted six of the creatures without even pausing and ran toward the human survivors. 'We'll get you out of here!'

'It's the Klikiss!' a woman yelled hoarsely from her prison. 'The Klikiss have returned. They've been killing us.'

The General was so focused on the battle going on around him that he couldn't ask the right questions or put all the pieces together. Klikiss? One of his soldiers planted a small demolitions charge, and the burst of fire knocked down the cementlike wall. The skeletal Pym settlers lurched through the break, stumbling forward to freedom, sobbing and screaming. They looked as if they hadn't been fed in days.

Finally EDF troops stopped coming through from Rheindic Co, and now could turn around and head back through the transportal. Lanyan bellowed at the top of his lungs. 'Full retreat! Get these people out of here. Back to base.'

The soldiers did not need to be told twice. One man managed to reactivate the coordinate tile on the stone wall. 'Transportal is open!'

As the colonists staggered forward, soldiers took them by the arms and hustled them to the gateway. Lanyan planted his feet squarely apart and formed a rearguard, shooting his sidearms until he had to reload. Both weapons were growing hot in his hands. 'Through the damned gate! Get your asses moving.'

Grim-faced soldiers grabbed the bodies of their fallen comrades, both the injured and the dead. The Klikiss moved with the speed of gigantic cockroaches under a bright light, racing forward to attack. Colonists and soldiers escaped one group at a time back to Rheindic Co. Lanyan spotted four Klikiss warriors circling around to the side, trying to cut off access to the transportal. He bellowed orders, and a flurry of weapons fire took down the bugs. But more and more of the creatures were closing in.

By the time the surviving Pym settlers had been evacuated, the General had run out of ammunition. He dropped both of his weapons and looked around for any available sidearm. Slaughtered insects lay piled all over the ground, yet more of them surged out of the still-intact alien towers.

When Lanyan saw that most of his soldiers were successfully evacuated, he raced to the transportal wall. 'Hurry up, dammit!'

His last few men plunged with him through the shimmering trapezoidal window.

Suddenly, Lanyan found himself back in the crowded caves on Rheindic Co on the other side of the transportal. He was dripping with alkaline water, perspiration, blood, and Klikiss ichor.

A cold shiver ran up his back as he realized they were not safe, after all. Not by a long shot. Now that they had riled up the bugs, the Klikiss could simply flood through after them.

FIFTY

SIRIX

The return of the Klikiss changed all of Sirix's plans. After fleeing Wollamor, it was time for him to gather his remaining robots and the war vessels they had constructed at the new complex on Maratha. They would become the destructive force that he had imagined for millennia.

Sirix and his robots must eradicate the hated creators. Again. The subhive swarming through the Wollamor transportal could not be an isolated event. If the Klikiss were returning to their old worlds, they would reappear everywhere – intent on revenge. There would be many breedexes.

He needed to expand his military force greatly.

Sirix guided his battle group to Maratha in Ildiran space, where the largest enclave of robots had built their ambitious base. Ages ago, Sirix had used the half-hot, half-cold world to stage a great battle against the Klikiss. Recently, he had been appalled to learn that the Ildirans had made the place into a resort for themselves.

Had they distorted their own history so much that they had

forgotten? The black robots had taken back the planet without much trouble. The Ildirans would not dare return there. By now, Sirix's fellows should have turned Maratha into an impregnable stronghold.

But he found only wreckage.

Both of the Ildiran-built cities, Prime and Secda, had been sliced and deconstructed, cratered by explosions. The machine battleships had been destroyed on the ground, along with hundreds of his vital comrades.

Sirix reeled, unable to calculate the extent of the loss. Nearly a third of his robots had gathered here! He recalibrated the Juggernaut's sensors, searching for an error, or at least an explanation. There should be robots digging tunnels, reconstructing and reinforcing the ancient base. And they were all gone!

QT moved closer to the bridge's viewscreen. 'It appears that a full-blown battle took place here.'

Sirix's ships scanned the blasted landscape, trying to determine what could have caused so much destruction. 'Our robots should have been able to defend themselves. They had enough time to prepare, to erect bastions against any attackers.'

'Did they know what they were preparing against?' PD asked. He stepped up next to his fellow compy, and both peered with great interest at the images of devastation.

Ilkot swivelled from his station and announced, 'I detect characteristic signatures from Solar Navy armaments. Ildiran weaponry caused this.'

Sirix had already decided to add the Ildirans to his list of intended victims, but now an intense reaction burned through his circuits, distorting logical thought. 'The Ildirans were warned to stay away from Maratha millennia ago. Now they have provoked us.'

Ilkot continued scanning. 'There are also unidentifiable

weapons and debris – similar to those we encountered on Wollamor.'

'On Wollamor?'

'I postulate that the Klikiss are also to blame.'

QT drew the obvious conclusion. 'Are the Klikiss allied with the Ildirans?'

'How would the Klikiss get here?' Sirix said. 'Maratha has no transportal.'

'That is one of many questions,' PD said. 'How have the Klikiss survived at all? They were extinct, according to data you provided.'

'Blanket the ground with our signals. I want to know if any robots remain functional. Every one of them is precious to us.' Sirix transmitted his own image, searching for a response. He could not believe that all of their ships and gathered weapons had been so woefully insufficient.

'We could also send scavenging teams to the site,' Ilkot suggested. 'Some of the memory cores could be intact. We could extract those cores to determine what occurred here – and salvage their memories. Otherwise our ancient and unique comrades are entirely lost.'

Suddenly, the hull of the Juggernaut rang with a loud reverberation. The deck and walls shuddered. Moving like a pack of predators, six Solar Navy warliners skimmed the edge of Maratha's atmosphere, racing over the curve of the planet toward Sirix's battle group. Their solar sails were extended, weapons powered in an intimidating posture.

Another dull impact struck them. 'We are in EDF ships. They should believe we are the Earth military.' He turned to the vacant communications console as Ilkot scuttled toward the controls. 'Transmit one of our recorded images of Admiral Wu-Lin to deceive them.'

PD asked, 'Are the Ildirans at war with the humans now?'

In a maddeningly cheerful voice, QT said, 'Sirix, you already transmitted your own image to search for surviving robots. The Ildirans know who we are.'

The warliners raced forward, commencing a barrage with their most powerful weapons. Sirix's Juggernaut reeled; sparks flew from control panels. Warning indicators signalled fourteen hull breaches and explosive loss of atmosphere.

'Return fire.' EDF weapons lanced out, grazing the Ildiran vessels, ripping apart one of the mostly decorative solar sails.

'It is understandable that the Ildirans are upset with Klikiss robots,' QT pointed out. 'The robots did not ask permission to establish a base here on a sovereign Ildiran world, and they caused great damage.'

'But Ildirans should not be here at all,' Sirix replied, amplifying his voice.

'Perhaps they believe the *robots* should not have been here.'

'This is completely different.'

The Soldier compies on the accompanying Mantas continued to shoot, damaging two of the patrol warliners, while enduring powerful blows in return. In the frantic battle, Sirix watched the inventory of projectiles and jazer batteries and realized that he was wasting firepower that he had intended to use against humans – and the Klikiss. He had not intended to fight the Ildiran Empire as well, especially not with this small battle group, without the reinforcements he had expected to find on Maratha.

The Ildiran warliners continued to bombard them. Sirix swiftly calculated whether or not to continue the engagement. Comparing the weapons capabilities aboard the Solar Navy warliners to his own defences, he determined that while his EDF ships might be victorious, it would cost him much of his battle group. Those were losses he could not afford.

'Withdraw. Do not continue firing.' Sirix altered the transmission burst, directing it toward the Ildirans. 'We will remove ourselves from this system. There is no need for you to persist in your attack.'

The Solar Navy apparently disagreed. They continued to pursue Sirix and his battle group, still firing, even as the robots accelerated away from Maratha. Already, he knew that the repairs would take a great deal of time.

Sirix revised his plans. Again. This was not how events had been meant to unfold! He had imagined a magnificent victory over the humans, conquering all their worlds, recapturing the prize of every abandoned Klikiss planet.

Unless he could reunite with the few other robot enclaves already on Klikiss worlds – a fraction of what he had expected to rally on Maratha – then these ships were all he had. His deadly metal swarm was reduced to no more than a cloud of gnats!

He was angry and disconcerted, and he needed a target. A new set of tactics suggested itself to him. The returning Klikiss were the primary threat. The most despised enemy. And he could destroy them.

He knew their old worlds, knew where they would go. Sirix decided to take these ships from planet to planet and destroy each transportal. That would effectively cut them off, strand the Klikiss on the far side of the galaxy, or wherever they had been hiding for all these millennia. Then he would exterminate whatever remnants he found.

These EDF ships could easily accomplish that goal. One world at a time.

FIFTY-ONE

ANTON COLICOS

Now that they were back from Maratha, Anton had another story to tell. Even Rememberer Vao'sh was barely able to contain his eagerness to write down his experiences with the Solar Navy, the black robots, and the returned Klikiss. He would document everything and submit it to the Hall of Rememberers. Vao'sh had never expected to be so much of an actual participant in the events of the *Saga*.

'Sometimes when I read over the things I've done since coming here, I can hardly believe my own experiences,' Anton said. 'I have to remind myself that it was actually me and not some square-jawed hero!' He chuckled over the pages of notes in his personal datapad.

In the rememberer's bright office in the Prism Palace, Anton was at last getting back to the work that had initially brought him to Ildira, translating parts of the seminal alien epic so that he could bring it home to Earth. He tried to imagine what would happen when he returned to his old university position – would he still have a job there after so long? He supposed it didn't matter. With

245

his experiences and his unique knowledge, Anton could find a high-paying tenured position at the university of his choice. He could go on the lecture circuit. Instead of publishing papers in obscure journals, he could draw on the most exciting portions of the *Saga* to write bestsellers, even write his autobiography. He would receive considerable attention. If only his parents could have seen it.

Out in the hallway, servant kithmen scurried around, sweeping and polishing. Anton glanced up at the commotion and saw Yazra'h stride through the door with her three Isix cats stalking after her. 'My father has come to see you.'

Looking both impressed and embarrassed, Vao'sh stood. 'The Mage-Imperator had only to summon us. We would have come to the skysphere.'

Jora'h entered and approached the rememberers. 'I wished to see the two of you in person and watch you at work.' His long hair was neatly braided behind his head; his colourful robes were adorned with reflective strips and spangled with gem chips. 'And I would prefer that no one overhear the request I am about to make.' He smiled wryly. 'It will be interesting to see how well Ildirans deal with major change.'

The Mage-Imperator surveyed their tables strewn with diamondfilm records covered with dense text that comprised only a small percentage of the *Saga*. Jora'h picked up a sheet, but didn't seem interested in the words etched there. 'A long time ago, I visited two green priests in this very chamber, Nira and old Ambassador Otema. They came here to read the *Saga* aloud for the worldforest.' Jora'h paused, lost in a reverie, then straightened. 'Ten thousand years ago in our history, Ildira faced a crossroads similar to our current one. At that time, the Mage-Imperator began a ... horrendous cover-up.'

'Ah, the Lost Times,' Vao'sh said, his voice heavy. 'All

rememberers were killed in order to conceal the actual events of the first hydrogue war.'

The Mage-Imperator lowered his eyes. 'At that time our *Saga of Seven Suns* was rewritten and censored so that no one would know the truth. But *I* am Mage-Imperator now, and I will not permit such corruption. The story of this war must be told honestly in every detail. We will record only the truth in our sacred *Saga*, and let our descendants judge us by it.' He looked intently at Anton and Vao'sh. 'I ask you to accept a great responsibility: tell the truth. Work together to remove the stain of lies from our history. And write the next portion of our great epic.'

Anton couldn't believe what he was hearing. 'But, Your Majesty, I'm just a scholar, not even an Ildiran—'

'Your perspective is necessary. You are both rememberers in your own way, and you will have my full support. Revise the *Saga* to include the shameful revelations of the Dobro breeding programme and our involvement with the hydrogues. Reveal the schemes that my father and his predecessors – and yes, even I – participated in. It is only the first of many wrongs that I must atone for. I have spoken at great length with Nira about it. Do you accept this noble task I entrust to you?'

Vao'sh was confused. This simply was not done! 'Liege, does that mean you wish for us to include the apocrypha – all the unofficial documents that we recently studied?'

'Yes. Others tried before you, but they were unsuccessful. You may recall a rememberer named Dio'sh.'

The old rememberer nodded. 'He was a friend of mine. He survived Crenna's blindness plague and came back here years ago. I heard that he died.'

'He did not simply die. He was killed. My father murdered him.'

Vao'sh gasped. 'The Mage-Imperator? He cannot – would not

– do such a thing.' But Jora'h explained how Dio'sh discovered the truth about the Lost Times and went to Mage-Imperator Cyroc'h with his findings, whereupon the corpulent leader strangled the poor man with his long, living braid.

'You will include that story when you rewrite the *Saga* as well.' The Mage-Imperator's words were sharp, as if he had to force himself to say them.

Vao'sh would never defy the command of his Mage-Imperator, but he was greatly unsettled. 'Liege, you are asking us to alter the unalterable. The *Saga of Seven Suns* is revered as a perfect record.'

'Yet you know that is not true. You have known it for some time.'

The rememberer's voice grew smaller. 'But it is . . . tradition.'

'Is it a worthy tradition that serves only to perpetuate lies? You will tell the truth. That is my command. The Ildiran people must learn to accept change. That in itself is an important change I will bring about.'

FIFTY-TWO

KOLKER

Thanks to Osira'h, Kolker understood now. He understood *everything*, and it was marvellous! Breathtaking.

His hopes had been correct. Now that his mind was open to the connections in the cosmos, he saw all aspects of the power struggles, the shifting tides from one Spiral Arm to the next. From the grand elemental beings, to the humans and Ildirans, to the tiniest insects and single-celled organisms, everything was woven together by passageways, bridges, networks, and webs that he had never comprehended. It was as if he'd been standing too close to a mosaic and now, after taking a few steps away from it, could discern how all the discrete fragments fit together to form a vast and complex pattern.

Kolker sat in the bright sunlight, drinking in everything he held in his mind, everything he had begun to share. A group of lens kithmen still sat staring into the plasma-bubble fountain, meditating, but Kolker no longer yearned to join them. He already understood more than they could see and think. They were limited by their *thism*, and he was not.

249

His place in the overall scheme had not changed, but all of a sudden he knew he *had* a place. He sensed a million embracing arms of *thism* from the Ildirans around him, and when he touched the lone treeling, he could soar across the connections of telink. After his long, lonely misery he had never imagined feeling so incredibly wonderful.

He knew he had to open the minds of his friends to this glorious reality – not just green priests, but normal humans as well. This was not meant to be a private revelation. It could raise them all to a higher consciousness.

First, he would start with the Hansa cloud harvesters working under Tabitha Huck. He needed to share.

Because of the construction activities, a constant stream of supply shuttles went up to orbit. Kolker boarded the next ship that had room for him. No Ildiran had challenged the green priest when he took the treeling from the Palace.

As the shuttle ascended, Kolker, wearing the reflective medallion that Tery'l had given him, supported the heavy pot in his lap. He held the thin trunk with one hand and rubbed the prismatic medallion with his other, engrossed in the vast universe inside his head. Already he had begun to describe some of his revelations to the verdani, and the trees seemed to know nothing of the possibilities.

He reached a new space station assembled from modular components and scraps of damaged warliners. The Hansa workers were experienced in using manoeuvring units and flexible space-suits, but what the Ildiran labour crews most desperately needed to learn from the humans was organization, initiative, and innovation. Now that the initial breathless wonder had passed, Kolker found that he could function better than before. His work and interactions were more efficient – almost *perfect*, in fact. These humans should be able to do the same.

Kolker walked gracefully into the central hub, where transparent viewing panes looked out upon the manufacturing units and orbiting assembly docks. Now that he was so much more attuned, he felt every touch of recycled air on his skin, saw the vivid details of the metal walls and floor, and the spangle of stars out in infinite space. He was aware of every person around him, though he couldn't sense specifics about them. Not yet.

In control of all of the stations and line managers, Tabitha looked as satisfied as a cat with a fresh bowl of cream. She had only to snap a command, and an Ildiran worker fulfilled her wishes. Such power might have gone to her head, but she looked focused rather than haughty. Five Hansa engineers also in the chamber were pleased and surprised to see the familiar green priest join them.

A broad tablescreen displayed status reports, wire-frame diagrams, and real-time images of partially constructed warliners that drifted in the expansive assembly yards. Tabitha shifted her attention from one pane to the next. When she looked up and saw him, her face registered surprise. 'Kolker! I thought a green priest would stay landbound.'

'I have something important.' He set the treeling down on her deskscreen, accidentally covering up columns of glowing numbers. 'I need to show you. And Sullivan.'

She was distracted. 'Sullivan's inspecting the ring docks right now. He'll be back in half an hour.'

Kolker gave her a calm and beatific smile. 'What if I could share something with you that would sharpen your senses, let you make decisions faster, understand more? Would you be interested?'

She laughed. 'That would help.' Tabitha glanced at the

tablescreen as an indicator light began to blink, and she snapped a couple of orders to keep the production moving. 'All right, but I don't have all day. Make it fast.' She called to one of her helpers. 'Barry, check on that alignment girder! It looks off-kilter to me.'

Kolker touched the treeling and held his lens medallion, concentrating on the facets and on the flow of telink. 'It'll only take a second.'

'Is it some green priest thing?'

'More than that.' He turned his hand sideways to brush the outer edge of his palm against Tabitha's forehead. He felt the worldforest mind, felt the soul-threads, and then rode on a wave of *thism* into the latent potential that was within Tabitha, within all humans. It was a simple matter for him now. He *tweaked*. Mental gateways opened, and the universe flooded in.

Tabitha gasped. Her eyes widened in amazement. Kolker withdrew his touch, and she stared around the administrative hub. 'I don't believe this! It's incredible.'

'I told you it would be.'

'All the colours are brighter. I've never heard sounds like this before. So sharp, so clear, and I know what everything is.' She blinked, visibly integrating the new details rushing into her. 'It's like someone twisted a knob and brought the universe into better focus.' She yelled to the five Hansa engineers, 'Come here! Kolker's done something. I don't even know what the hell it was.' Seeing her excitement and enthusiasm, the others approached with curiosity. 'Barry, let him show you this. Touch him, Kolker. He's got to see.'

'What is it? What do I have to do?'

'Just let me touch you. One second is all it takes.' Kolker smiled. 'But only if you want to.'

Barry took one look at Tabitha's obvious joy and excitement. 'Do whatever you have to do.' Kolker touched him and *tweaked*, and then Barry was gasping in wonder as well. 'It's like you blew my mind!' He turned to face Tabitha. 'Is that you? I can sense you . . . not reading your mind, but *you*.'

Tabitha nodded vigorously. 'And Kolker, too. We're here.'

Not wanting to be left out, three more of the human engineers insisted on trying it for themselves, and Kolker happily obliged. One man remained sceptical, though. 'Pretty much like brainwashing, isn't it? That's how it looks to me.'

'Nothing like that at all, T.J.' Barry's eyes were shining. 'I feel like Kolker just increased my IQ by about a million points. Imagine an old, sputtering fusion drive that suddenly got an overhaul and a major upgrade.' He laughed aloud. 'That's me.'

Though content, Kolker tried to reassure T.J. 'This is not a trick. And if you change your mind, I can always reverse it.'

'Not on your life.' Tabitha was already poring over her wide tablescreen, her fingers flying as she adjusted the assignments of work crews and fiddled with small details in the process flow. Within moments, she straightened, very satisfied. 'Hmm, I never saw those bottlenecks before.'

Sullivan Gold returned to all the excited chatter and saw the breathless expressions, the wide eyes. 'What's going on here?'

'Kolker just showed us a genuine revelation! He can do something with his treeling, or with that medallion.'

Tabitha barely took her attention away from the work parameters. 'I can't describe it, Sullivan. Try it!'

The green priest extended a hand. 'I wanted to show you first. Allow me—'

But Sullivan stepped back. 'Wait just a minute.'

T.J. drew strength from the manager's reluctance. 'You're not going to force us, are you?'

'Of course not. This is only for those who wish it. But it's wonderful, Sullivan. It's *essential*. You'll think more clearly, you'll understand all the interconnections, you'll see things in every one of us that you never saw before. Trust me.'

'I do trust you, Kolker, but it kinda sounds to me like you're converting people to a new religion.'

Kolker had not considered that aspect. 'It is like that in a way . . . but not like that at all.'

Sullivan kept holding his hands up. 'I've got my own religion, thank you. I can't imagine what Lydia would say if she'd heard I went chasing after some sort of cosmic head rush.'

Kolker could feel the older manager's reluctance, so he decided to give him time. 'I'm always here if you change your mind. Talk with Tabitha and the others. Watch them, and see what this has done for them.' He picked up his treeling.

'This is the most important thing ever,' Barry said.

Though wonder shone clearly on her face, Tabitha maintained her sense of purpose. 'All right, let's put this to work. We've still got a lot of ships to rebuild out there. Ha! With this new mindset we'll be a thousand times more efficient than before. We can tap into the Ildirans and communicate with each other. We can see . . . *everything*.' She couldn't stop grinning, and the changed crewmembers seemed to be sharing her thoughts, communicating with only the slightest flicker of expression.

Kolker felt deeply satisfied as he went to find a shuttle to take him back to Ildira. The possibilities seemed as endless as the universe he now viewed.

FIFTY-THREE

PATRICK FITZPATRICK III

After his long search, Patrick arrived at Golgen, a gas giant with canary skies, endless atmospheric storms, and clan Kellum's massive ekti-harvesting operations. As he flew in, he listened to the chatter on various bands, trying to find the right place, looking for a familiar clan symbol on the dozens of factory complexes floating in the sky. He knew Zhett was here somewhere.

He circled Golgen before landing at one of the larger skymines, a facility managed by a man named Boris Goff, who tried to hire Patrick as a courier. 'Your ship is small, but it could still carry a profitable haul,' Goff said. Each of the cloud facilities was looking for independent transport ships to carry ekti to market; apparently, distribution was their main bottleneck. But Patrick had a different goal for now.

'I'm looking for clan Kellum.' When he stepped away from the landed *Gypsy*, the winds were cold and carried a bitter smell. The tight knot in his stomach was due half to anticipation of seeing Zhett again and half to terror over how she might react. He clung to love and hope, determined to make amends, to make her see who he really was and how he had changed. He wanted to show her that he was sorry, that he would accept whatever punishment he deserved and somehow prove himself worthy of her.

Goff frowned. 'What do you need Kellum for? I can beat any offer they'd make.'

You can't offer someone like Zhett, Patrick thought. 'I've worked for Del Kellum previously.'

'And that's a good thing?' Goff gave up and pointed toward a distant drifting facility. 'That's his, over there.'

That was all Patrick needed. He practically jumped back into his ship, his pulse racing, and flew directly to the other skymine. Dozens of scenarios played in his imagination, and he rehearsed his words – his apology, his confession, his plea for forgiveness.

He landed on one of the skydecks, transmitting only the new name of his ship and volunteering no further information. He didn't want to forewarn Zhett. As far as he knew, she might try to shoot him.

Stepping out of his craft in his nondescript uniform, he surveyed the eager Roamers who came to greet him. Thankfully, he recognized none of them from his days as a prisoner. 'Is Zhett Kellum here?'

'This is Kellum's skymine, isn't it?'

Two people emerged from the command deck of the giant skymine. He could never forget Del's barrel chest and his grey-streaked dark beard. Mostly though, he was riveted by Zhett. She had never looked more beautiful, as far as he was concerned. He felt butterflies take flight in his stomach.

Kellum froze, gazing at him. 'By damn!'

Patrick could see from her expression that Zhett knew very well who he was. He wanted to say he was sorry, to overwhelm her with apologies of all variety and colours, to soothe any hurt feelings and erase the distance between them. There were so many words clamouring to get out of his mouth that for a moment they tangled together, and he couldn't say anything at all. He raised his hand. 'I've been looking for you. I'm sorry. There's so much to explain—'

'You've got a lot of nerve!'

Patrick did not cringe in the face of her disdain. He had been prepared for this. 'Go ahead. I deserve every awful thing you want to say.'

'Yes, you do. But I wouldn't bother with the effort.' Zhett stormed back to the control deck, not looking back.

'Wait – give me a chance! Please?' But she didn't turn around. Patrick stood near the *Gypsy*, feeling helpless. The tentative hope inside him sputtered like a fire doused with water. He hadn't actually thought beyond this point, and his heart contracted painfully as he watched Zhett walk away. He stared after her, recalling every conversation they had ever had.

Not exactly the way he had imagined the events would play out, but Patrick vowed to stay, hoping that Zhett would eventually change her mind.

FIFTY-FOUR

ADMIRAL SHEILA WILLIS

At the Chairman's orders, ten well-armed Manta cruisers flew toward Theroc, spoiling for a fight. The crew, full of cocky bravado, were eager to make their mark. Willis could sense it. The soldiers had been trounced by hydrogues, defied by colonists, and tricked by their own Soldier compies, not to mention upstaged by the Ildiran Solar Navy and a bunch of verdani treeships. No wonder they were ready to take out their frustrations on a bunch of primitives, an exiled King and Queen, and a handful of traders.

Willis saw it as an example of 'kick the dog' syndrome. The Earth Defence Forces had severe issues of inadequacy. 'Like buying a souped-up space yacht to make up for a penis deficiency,' she muttered to herself on the command bridge. 'I haven't got a good feeling about this whole mission, Lieutenant Commander Brindle.' She looked over at her newly assigned executive officer. 'Not a good feeling at all.'

Conrad Brindle stood at attention. Because of his lifetime in the military, he always seemed to be at attention, even when standing at ease. She suspected that his pyjamas had straight creases and that he polished his exercise shoes. The man also looked as if he carried additional burdens since the end of the hydrogue war. His own son was a hero who had served with Willis herself, but she sensed there was friction between Robb and his father since the brave kid's rescue. Willis didn't ask about it. She was not a woman to meddle in personal problems unless it affected performance.

'We have nothing to worry about, Admiral.' Even in conversation Conrad sounded as if he were issuing a report. 'These ten Mantas are more than sufficient to stand against the defences I saw at Theroc. King Peter proved he was a coward by leaving Earth when he did, and now he's gathering other misfits around him. Our soldiers, on the other hand, are eager to make the Hansa strong again.'

'Right. And if we click our heels together and wish three times ...' Willis said sarcastically. 'Mr Brindle, maybe you can explain to me how we're going to make the Hansa strong by attacking an unarmed planet whose independence has been acknowledged by the Chairman himself? Exactly which part of the law, or which terms of the Hansa Charter, does that follow?'

A dark cloud passed across Brindle's face. 'We cannot ignore an outside group that poses a threat to the Terran Hanseatic League.'

'Oh, I know all the on-paper reasons. That still doesn't mean they pass the smell test.' She saw the disturbed expression on Brindle's face. 'Don't you worry about me, Lieutenant Commander. I've got my orders and I intend to follow them. We'll squash that rebellion before they know what hit them. I'm just saying that I don't understand the politics here, or what went on behind the scenes in that pissing contest between King Peter and Chairman Wenceslas.'

She sat back and stared at the starry field ahead of them. Willis missed her own Juggernaut, and hoped that General Lanyan didn't end up damaging it. Since getting a bug up his butt about 'dealing harshly' with any antagonist, Lanyan had been even more gung-ho than the soldiers aboard these ten Mantas. Unfortunately, her 'temporary transfer' away from the *Jupiter* might well end up becoming permanent. When he was done with his mission, Lanyan wasn't likely to relinquish her ship.

Willis didn't agree with a lot of the things that had happened recently. While fighting the hydrogues, the enemy had been clear and indisputable. Humans had been battling for their very survival, and there was no possibility of a diplomatic solution. Here, though, she didn't know what response was truly warranted against King Peter.

Many times, Willis had studied her command manuals, any advisory memos released before this situation cropped up, and the official chain of command, trying to figure out the Chairman's defined place. She wasn't so naïve as to believe that King Peter had really been in charge of everything, as the public was supposed to think; the Chairman and his cronies pulled the strings of government. However, in official documents, the King was listed right there in black and white as the EDF's commander-in-chief. Legally speaking, the Chairman had no role with respect to the Earth Defence Forces, yet Basil Wenceslas had assumed control and was issuing orders right and left.

Very troubling.

And now Willis found herself acting like one of those lockstep numbskulls who followed orders without questioning. The very idea made her squirm. Wenceslas had bent over backward to make the King his front man, his visible symbol, and sometimes his patsy, so that made it awfully tricky for the Chairman to brush Peter aside and discredit him.

'How much longer until we reach the Theroc system?' she said.

The navigator consulted a diagnostic panel. 'Four hours, thirty-six minutes.'

'I'm retiring to my ready-room. Please have the kitchen send me up a sandwich. They know what kind I like – ham and cheese, hot mustard, dark bread, a pickle. And an iced tea, sweet tea this time. Don't make it that bitter powdered stuff.' The lunch was her standard order, and not surprisingly, the meal arrived within minutes as Willis sat at her table, tapping fingers on the table-top. She wasn't hungry, but ate out of habit and a basic need for energy.

Peter and Estarra, now being painted as rebels, cowards, and traitors, had actually run away and formed a new government. Why the hell would they do that? King Peter had everything in the Whisper Palace: riches, servants, power. A person didn't just chuck that out the window and run to a backward planet for no reason. Something really, really bad must have happened. If she had a chance to split her sandwich with Peter and just chat for awhile, Willis suspected the King would tell quite a different story from the Chairman's.

In fact, she had seen first-hand what the Hansa did to the orphaned colonies. She'd been ordered to stomp on the unruly world of Yreka and mete out an unpleasant punishment to a group of hardscrabble colonists who were simply trying to get by. Now *that* smacked of betrayal, or at least shirking responsibility. In return for paying their taxes and contributing as any citizen was supposed to, Earth had promised to support its Hansa colonies. But the moment times became tough, the Chairman had jettisoned them like unwanted baggage. Those colonists had every reason to cry foul.

The sanctions against the Roamer clans were another ugly distraction. At least she hadn't been asked to participate in the destruction of Rendezvous or any other Roamer facility. Chairman

Wenceslas and the EDF walked all over political boundaries, and each day they seemed to be putting on heavier boots. Willis took a bite of her sandwich, felt the burn of the mustard, and washed it down with a deliciously syrupy mouthful of sweet tea.

On her desktop screen she reviewed the spyflyer surveillance images. She knew that Theroc couldn't stand up to ten Mantas. Then again, she didn't believe that the King – not a stupid man – would leave himself vulnerable during such a dangerous time. Maybe he simply hadn't had enough time to put all his ducks in a row. With the Earth Defence Forces still reeling, Peter might have expected a brief respite to regroup. On the other hand, they all knew the Chairman . . .

Brindle contacted her ready-room. 'Admiral, thirty minutes until we arrive in-system. I thought you might want to address the crew before we begin our attack.'

'Thank you, Commander. I do indeed.' She dumped the dishes into the recycler. After leaving the ready-room and settling into her command chair again, she opened the all-ship channel. 'Listen up. We are about to arrive at Theroc under orders from Chairman Wenceslas. Our job is to put an end to this conflict, but *we are not barbarians*. Whatever goes on here today, remember that Theroc is still an independent world. We need to use a light touch.'

'That means no unnecessary casualties,' Brindle appended.

'I'd prefer no casualties at all. They won't stand up against our firepower, so maybe we can wrap this up quickly and efficiently.' Personally, she doubted it. 'Approach the system at full speed, then max decel. I want to pop out in front of their faces and use the element of surprise for all it's worth.'

The cruisers roared into the Theron system with enough deceleration to make Willis's bones and muscles ache. Her crew was ready. Brindle stood at attention behind her chair. All of their weapons officers were at their stations.

But as soon as long-distance images sharpened on the broad viewing screen, panicked outbursts flooded the bridge. 'Full stop!' Willis cried. 'Do not open fire! That is an order.'

Theroc was surrounded by what looked like a crown of thorns. Immense tree battleships rose up with great spiky boughs splayed. The verdani treeships began to move toward the incoming EDF battle group, fanning out and forming a blockade like a huge thorny hedge.

Willis hammered down on the transmit button. 'I repeat, for anyone who has too much wax in their ears: *do not open fire*, unless you want one of those sharpened branches up your exhaust shaft.'

Behind the verdani battleships came a flurry of vessels in every conceivable size and shape, ships with bright markings and discoloured hullplates. All of them had very prominent slapped-on armaments.

'Those are Roamers,' Brindle said. 'Hundreds of them.'

'With hundreds of guns,' Willis added.

'Tactical stations! Run a quick assessment of battle feasibility. Do we still outgun them?'

'Belay that!' Willis cut him off. 'Are you totally nuts, Lieutenant Commander? Look at those treeships!' The deadly verdani vessels moved closer, loomed larger. 'I knew this was a bad idea from the start.'

FIFTY-FIVE

GENERAL KURT LANYAN

Even after the Pym colonists and exhausted EDF soldiers retreated through the transportal wall, they couldn't stop running. The Hansa workers in the Rheindic Co control chamber were taken aback by the sudden waves of scrambling soldiers with torn and bloody uniforms, smoking weapons, and ghostly pale expressions.

A few haggard colonists fell to their knees and touched the cool, stone floor. Swift-thinking EDF fighters grabbed them and hustled them farther along the tunnels to the exits. 'Keep moving! Back to the ships.'

'Call all the personnel transports up to the city!'

'Send a signal to the *Jupiter*! This is an emergency situation.'

When Lanyan staggered through, he wanted to collapse, but knew it wasn't over yet. 'Those damned bugs are going to be hot on our tails!'

Conflicting orders bounced around, and the stunned troops began a disorderly but swift exodus, sweeping the Rheindic Co scientists along with them. Sobs and alarmed shouts filled the stone-walled chamber, along with the clatter of weapons, the pounding of booted feet.

'What is it?' said Ruvi, the administrator. 'What's going on?'

'Klikiss.' Lanyan grabbed the balding man by the shoulders and bodily turned him around. 'The Klikiss came back to Pym. They killed most of the colonists, but we rescued these.'

'Klikiss? You mean the real Klikiss?'

He pointed to a bleeding gash on his arm. 'Yeah, they're pretty damned real. And they're going to come *here* soon. You can bet on it. So haul ass! I'm pulling the plug on Rheindic Co.'

'We – we'll gather our equipment, pack our things.'

'You'll turn around and run like hell. Now! I'm guessing we've got only a few minutes, at most.'

People flooded out of the chamber through the passages, reached the cliff edge, and crowded together like lemmings. Outside, twilight was beginning to fall. Station lights marked the personnel transports in the landing zone far outside the main base.

The Klikiss city was high up on the sheer wall, with no easy way for great numbers of evacuees to get down. Frantic people jammed the lift platforms, trying to reach the canyon floor. The heavy elevators were reinforced to carry cargo but not designed for speed, and they did not have the capacity to hold so many rescued colonists and retreating EDF troops.

Some of the soldiers helped scientists and colonists, and some had the composure to activate their comm systems and shout for the personnel transports. 'Get up here! It's a massive evacuation. We have to *leave* – immediately!'

Back in the chamber, Lanyan saw the bottleneck situation rapidly growing out of control. Drawing a deep breath that stretched his uniform tight across his chest, he counted to three, forced calm upon himself, then issued orders in a controlled, razor-sharp bark of command. 'Remember who you are! We fought the

Soldier compies. These bugs are no worse, and they splatter a hell of a lot easier. Now, get some fresh weapons up here!'

Outside, several troop transports took off from the landing zone and flew in the gathering dusk toward the cliff city, man-oeuvring to pick up the evacuees. One cocky pilot hovered his ship directly against the high cliff opening and slid aside his access door. Soldiers and a few civilians jumped across the gap. For those who had seen the Klikiss, the risk of falling seemed far preferable to the risk of being left behind.

Lanyan grabbed a spare pulse rifle from a departing soldier, looked around the control chamber, and picked a dozen men who looked the least shaken. Although the General didn't ask for any other volunteers, several more soldiers chose to stay. Lanyan gave them all a grim nod. 'When those bugs get here, we need to be ready for them. We have to hold this chamber to buy time. Set demolitions around the transportal wall. Bring it down so we can cut them off.' Chairman Wenceslas would be livid if Lanyan cut off the main transportal hub, but the Chairman wasn't here. Nor had he seen the horrifying bugs. 'Blast the whole thing into dust.'

While most of the soldiers took up defensive positions, two of the men knelt to remove polymer explosives from their packs. After slapping the wads against the trapezoidal stone wall, tight-lipped, their foreheads covered with beads of sweat, the two began setting their detonators. Before they could finish, though, the transportal wall shimmered, and shadows appeared behind the opaque surface. Lanyan backed away to the line of soldiers and raised his largest gun. 'Stand ready!'

'It's a trap, General,' said one of the men.

'It's a trap for the Klikiss. The moment they show up, open fire.'

Two Klikiss warriors lunged through, their segmented arms already sweeping from side to side, knocking one of the demolitions men to the floor. The second soldier threw himself at the rigged explosives, trying to trigger them at the last instant before any other bugs could get through. But the spiny warrior skewered him with a long forelimb and tossed him against the stone wall. More bugs charged through, carrying strange weapons in their jagged claws. Before the bugs could take two steps forward or their compound eyes could adjust to the sudden dimness of the cave, Lanyan's defenders opened fire.

Four more came immediately behind them, each carrying a bell-mouthed weapon, like a high-tech musket. Lanyan knew this was just the beginning of the wave, and they would never blow up the transportal in time. He had seen how many bugs they had left behind on Pym. 'Like shooting fish in a barrel! We have to give the transports time to pick everybody up.'

As the next Klikiss warriors materialized, more gunfire knocked them back. Insect bodies piled up on top of others. Soon the armoured corpses themselves would form a barricade that blocked the trapezoidal wall.

At the cave mouth, transport after transport flew off, laden with evacuees. Within the stifling chamber, Lanyan and his men continued firing, but the Klikiss pushed through by sheer weight of numbers, faster than the men could shoot.

'Fall back!' Lanyan said. 'I think we bought enough time.'

His soldiers retreated, running through the tunnels as a new batch of Klikiss clambered over the mounded carcasses. Lanyan's men ran to the opening in the high cliff. As twilight darkened, a cool breeze blew in their faces, invigorating after the burned air of the transportal chamber.

One of the overloaded lift platforms had jammed in its tracks halfway down the cliffside, but a personnel transport had already retrieved the stranded people. Standing on the cliff edge, the exhausted defenders waved frantically for one of the last ships.

The General slapped the comm microphone at his collar. 'Get the rest of the transports back up to orbit and call down the Juggernaut. I want the *Jupiter* here with weapons ready to go. This hasn't turned out the way we expected.'

One of his blood-streaked men turned wide eyes at him. 'That's an understatement, sir.'

Stranded high on the cliff wall, they could hear Klikiss swarming toward them through the tunnels. They would never have time to take the slow lift platforms. 'Come on, dammit, get a ship up here! Our asses are on the line.' One partially loaded shuttle swooped close, side doors open, and Lanyan felt weak-kneed with relief. 'Get aboard, all of you.'

The men leaped to the hovering transport ship, while the soldiers on board it caught them and pulled them inside. Nobody bothered to find seats. Lanyan, the last to jump across the gap, spun to look behind him just as angry Klikiss surged around the corner. 'Take off!'

The shuttle climbed away from the cliff city, leaving the bugs behind. More and more Klikiss piled together at the edge of the drop-off, staring at the overloaded ships rising away like drunken bumblebees. Lanyan sat in a very undignified position on the slippery deck watching through the wide-open hatch as air whistled past.

One by one, the monstrous bugs leapt off the cliff, spread their wings, and began to fly toward the shuttles.

'Give me a friggin' break! Seal this door and engage maximum thrust!'

'I see 'em,' the pilot called.

Three troop transports circled back and opened fire with defensive jazers, picking off the flying Klikiss. But for every one they blasted, three more took flight. Bugs continued to boil out of the cliff city.

'Only one way to stop this. Get me on the comm directly to the *Jupiter*. I want my weapons officer.' Like a whale plunging deep in search of krill, the Juggernaut dived toward the lost city while the troop transports continued to shoot at individual Klikiss. 'We've got to plug the leak. Take out that transportal. Destroy the city. Demolish the whole thing.'

The *Jupiter*'s battleship-calibre jazers glowed orange, then white. A broad lance of blinding energy struck the alien city. A second blast brought down the cliff face, erasing the ruins in a landslide. The invading Klikiss inside the tunnels were wiped out, and the transportal was gone in the blink of an eye.

The few remaining insect warriors were now cut off from the rest of their hive, and flew about, disoriented. Lanyan regarded them as gnats to be squashed. As smoke and fire continued to curl up from the rubble below, Lanyan directed the troop transports back to the Juggernaut, retreating without shame.

He had to get back to the Hansa. Chairman Wenceslas wasn't going to like this one bit.

FIFTY-SIX

HUD STEINMAN

Thoroughly disgusted at how the Llaro town had turned into a veritable concentration camp, Steinman decided it was time to leave by any means possible. Many of the more naïve colonists clung to a foolish hope that nothing bad was going to happen to them, kidding themselves that they would be safe from the Klikiss so long as they took no drastic action. Steinman didn't buy it for a second.

Conditions were growing steadily worse inside the walls. Margaret Colicos had somehow convinced the bugs to feed the captives, but the meal certainly wasn't very appetizing. The bland and disgusting mixture provided basic nourishment, as long as the people ate enough of it — if they could stand it. Steinman had the unsettling impression that the Klikiss were trying to fatten them up. He had put up with it for as long as he could tolerate, and now he just wanted to get out of here.

Several groups had already organized themselves and slipped away with packs of minimal supplies and tools, rushing off to meet Davlin Lotze. They believed the man had established a sanctuary out there somewhere. But Steinman had no intention of going as part of a group to live in an even more crowded and miserable camp than the one he was leaving.

Enough was enough. He had always meant to spend his life as a hermit.

In the late afternoon, he pounded on the door of the dwelling Orli shared. A red-faced Crim Tylar yanked the door open and looked at him with an unwelcoming expression. 'What do you want? Any news?'

His wife Marla stepped close behind him. Her dark hair was beginning to be streaked with grey, like a touch of frost on an early winter morning. 'Let him in, Crim. Don't just stand there glaring. He's not one of the Klikiss.'

'I'm here to see Orli.'

'She's a bit jittery yet from her visit with the breedex, but she'll probably want to talk to you.' Crim sniffed in disapproval at the unkempt and dusty old man. 'For whatever reason.'

Several cots had been set up in what should have been a living room. Orli had her music strips out, just staring at them as if stunned. When she looked up, her eyes were red and haunted. He felt a sudden stab of deep sorrow. What had those insect monsters done to her?

She brightened when she saw him. 'Mr Steinman!'

'Not quite what we expected when we came here, is it, kid? We might have been better off staying in our own house on Corribus.'

She set her chin in her hands. 'Corribus was a Klikiss world, too, and the bugs might already be back there. We'd be eating furry crickets, running away from low-riders – and still being chased by Klikiss.'

After a long and awkward silence, he said, 'I just wanted to . . . I wanted to say that I'm out of here. Tonight.'

Crim and Marla were both surprised. 'Is another group ready to go? We just sent one out last night.'

'I'm going alone. This'll be no different from the solitude I intended to find on Corribus.'

'That didn't work out too well,' Orli said.

'Only because of the damned robots.'

'And because you weren't very well prepared.'

'I'll manage, kid. Just you wait. The Klikiss are bone-headed when it comes to security. They only *think* they've got us corralled.'

'They do,' muttered Crim.

'But once you get away . . . then what?' Orli looked concerned for Steinman, and his heart felt heavy. 'Are you sure you'll be all right?'

'I'll find a place out in the wilderness, set up camp, and live off the land.' He shook his head. 'I was meant to be independent. It's about time I put that to the test and took my chances out there.'

Orli hugged him. He remembered how much they had depended on each other until they were rescued from Corribus. He heaved a sigh and pulled away from her. 'I don't like fences, and I don't like walls. The whole flavour of this place makes me lose sleep at night.'

Part of him wanted her to ask to come along with him, and he could see the girl was tempted. But she had resigned herself to staying here with the other colonists, no matter what happened. He tousled her hair because he couldn't think of anything else to do. 'Just remember that I'm out there, and I'm thinking of you, Orli. You're a good kid.'

'I know that. Take care of yourself, Mr Steinman. I'll miss you.'

He felt a lump in his throat and wondered if maybe he should stick it out here in town just a little bit longer. But it was already almost sunset. The gathering shadows made the darkness of the solid walls extend forward, swallowing up the camp.

Some of the Klikiss began a distant evening song, and Steinman listened to where they were located. The chirping was hypnotic, a celebration of the night. At dusk he doubted many Klikiss workers or builders would be moving about. Carrying the food, water, and supplies he thought he could use, he took advantage of a makeshift ladder and rough bumps to scale the stockade wall. It was the least obtrusive way for him to slip out.

After scanning the shadows for unseen dangers, he dropped over the wall, landed on his feet, and caught his breath. He could not enjoy the exhilarating rush of supposed freedom. That was an illusion. His friends and fellow colonists remained within the stockade, for whatever purpose the Klikiss had in mind.

Steinman gathered his courage and walked away, heading out of camp.

FIFTY-SEVEN

KING PETER

When the expected EDF ships arrived at Theroc, the Confederation was ready for them. The ten Mantas were stopped cold in space, and now Peter waited to see what the grid admiral would do next.

Inside the white-walled throne room, newly installed screens displayed images from the orbital surveillance satellites Roamer captains had placed around Theroc. In the frantic days after Nahton's warning, King Peter had asked the Roamers to install new technological hardware, preparing the worldforest and Theron settlements against a militarily superior force. Clan engineers had descended in a rush to make as many improvements as they could manage in the limited time available. The fungus-reef city would have to forego aesthetics for now. Even the green priests understood that.

The Confederation had scraped together many vessels to make a convincing stand at Theroc. The Osquivel shipyards had responded with remarkable productivity, but Peter did not expect a handful of vigilantes to fulfill the role of an official space navy.

Nevertheless, the show of force was quite impressive, possibly enough to make Basil think twice.

Carrying green priests, Roamer scouts had set up a picket line around the Theron system, scattered ships circling farther and farther out. The moment the ten threatening Mantas appeared, the outlying picket vessels sounded an instantaneous alarm through telink, alerting the King hours before a traditional electromagnetic signal could have arrived.

Newly armed Roamer ships positioned themselves all around the planet, ready for a fight. The worldtree battleships moved to intercept the Mantas well before the rapidly decelerating EDF cruisers caught their first glimpse of what was waiting for them. Even Jess Tamblyn and Cesca Peroni took their small wental vessel into orbit, like a supercharged teardrop.

The admiral was quite surprised.

Peter and Estarra sat together before a transmitter. Because of her swollen belly, it was hard for Estarra to sit very close to it. OX stood nearby, as if reprising his role as a formal ambassador to the Hansa. One of the Roamer engineers opened a channel for the King using the standard EDF command frequency. 'This is King Peter, the rightful leader of the Confederation. Identify yourself. Why have you brought this unauthorized military fleet into our space? We demand that you withdraw immediately.'

When the screen cleared to show a deceptively maternal image, Peter frowned. 'Admiral Willis, I did not expect you, of all of my commanders, to take part in this nonsense. I'm not surprised the Chairman would pull such a stunt, but why have *you* turned against your King?'

'Not my idea, King Peter, but I have my orders.' She was struggling to maintain her composure.

'Those orders do not come from a legitimate authority.'

'That's debatable. You've caused quite a stir back on Earth.

Chairman Wenceslas has ordered me to impose order and put an end to your illegal rebellion.'

Queen Estarra leaned toward the transmitter. 'And how exactly do you expect to do that?'

'I'm still working on that part.' Willis was obviously flustered. 'To tell the truth, I wasn't anticipating such an impressive show of force. You've been busy since our last surveillance images were taken.'

'Obviously, with good reason.' Peter's voice remained hard.

Verdani battleships clustered around the ten Mantas, vastly larger and more dangerous than the cruisers. Roamer ships circled in, more than a hundred moving targets with weapons powerful enough to damage the Mantas.

The small wental ship drifted upward until it hovered directly in front of the flagship's bridge observation windows. Willis looked at the bubble with Jess and Cesca visible inside it. 'Now what sort of stunt are you pulling, King Peter?' She seemed more curious than alarmed.

Jess and Cesca, their expressions grave, emerged through the curved membrane and floated, crackling with a faint nimbus of energy that surrounded their bodies. They wore no environment suits, surviving in open space as they drifted over to the thick windows to peer in at the EDF bridge crew. The soldiers stared back at them. The men and women were already amazed and intimidated by the giant thorny treeships, and now they saw a pair of humans floating in cold vacuum with no life support whatsoever.

Jess reached out with a fingertip and drew on the thick transparent screen, leaving a trail of backward letters traced in iron-hard ice. 'EDDIES GO HOME!'

On the next window, Cesca wrote, 'YOU CANNOT WIN.'

'What is this?' Willis demanded. 'What sort of power do these people have?'

With a wave of his hand, a sheet of crackled, frosty ice covered the bridge windows, temporarily blinding the Admiral before her external sensors kicked in and projected clear views again.

'We have many different allies, Admiral,' Peter said from his throne room. 'I suggest you don't make us demonstrate all the power we can bring to bear. You're a reasonable woman. You know you can't win here.'

Nonplussed, Willis pursed her lips. 'And you know the Chairman. If I return empty-handed, he'll just send a larger battle group next time.'

'Why doesn't he ever see the real threat to the Hansa, and the human race?' Estarra said, placing a protective hand on the curve of her belly. 'Maybe he should pay closer attention.'

Peter continued, 'Because Earth's only green priest has been killed – yes, we know all about that – you are unaware of major new developments. Even Chairman Wenceslas doesn't know of the new danger he's about to face. Therefore, it is your duty to turn and leave, so that you can brief him immediately. We will share the vital information with you.'

Leaning back in her chair, Estarra made a disbelieving sound and said quietly, 'He won't change his mind, no matter what you tell him.'

'Probably not,' he whispered, 'but it'll give Willis the excuse she needs to do the right thing.'

'What sort of news are we discussing here, King Peter?' Willis seemed sceptical, already imagining the browbeating Basil was going to give her.

'The original Klikiss have come back to claim their old planets. According to information we've received from the Ildiran Empire,

Klikiss have overrun planets settled in the Hansa's Colonization Initiative.' He explained in detail what they had learned through the worldforest from the green priest Nira.

Sitting up straight, Estarra added, 'If you still think you need to do something with those pretty EDF ships, try helping some Hansa colonies. Most of them have no defences at all.'

Nonplussed, Willis crossed her arms over her uniform. 'General Lanyan is already in process with his inspection and assessment.'

'Inspection and assessment?' Peter sounded dubious.

'It's a military term.'

Willis blew out a long sigh, deep in thought. Her Mantas hovered in full battle readiness, all weapons primed and ready to fire. The verdani battleships loomed over them, while Roamer defenders swirled about like stinging gnats just waiting to be provoked. She had to know her ships would be torn apart if she started shooting.

'Please don't make a mess of this, Admiral,' Peter said. 'Take the critical information you've just learned back to the Chairman. He seems to have trouble identifying the correct enemy. Worry about the Klikiss, not the Confederation.'

Willis squared her shoulders. 'All right. First things first, King Peter. I'll tell the Chairman about the Klikiss. I'm not stupid, and neither is he.'

'Yes, but will he listen?'

She didn't answer. Without firing a shot, she ordered her cruisers to turn and head back out of the Theron system.

FIFTY-EIGHT

SIRIX

After his recent setbacks, Sirix went on the offensive – and revelled in it. He had lost Wollamor, and he had lost his long-anticipated base and fleet on the Ildiran resort world of Maratha. But with whatever weapons he still had aboard the stolen EDF battleships, he swore he would make up for those losses. At all costs, the black robots had to crush the Klikiss before they gained a foothold on other planets. Anywhere. That was the necessary response.

One world at a time.

Using the grid and starmap implanted within his circuitry, Sirix guided his EDF vessels, knowing the robots would have the upper hand against the Klikiss. His human-built ships carried a stockpile of carbon-carbon explosives, fracture-pulse drones, and collimated jazer banks, all of which had been designed to crack diamond-hulled warglobes. They would smash the insect race easily enough.

Sirix expected to find another entrenched and reinforced robot base on Hifur, but when they arrived he saw that the enclave had already been conquered. Klikiss had flooded through the transportal and destroyed the black robots. Sirix felt anger and deep loss – seventy more irreplaceable units destroyed, unique robots with memories that spanned many centuries. Gone.

Showing contempt for their own creations, the insect creatures studded the exterior walls of the resin-concrete towers with torn-apart robot components – a flat angular head, a black wing casing, bent claw-limbs.

Judging by slight differences in their morphology, these Klikiss were an entirely different subhive from the one that had attacked him on Wollamor. He wondered how many new breedexes were sweeping back into the Spiral Arm, and how many had already gone hunting for the black robots.

Sirix would have to destroy them all, and he hoped his dwindling EDF weapons would last long enough to complete that task. As he processed the remote images from Hifur, he wondered whose hatred was greater. From space, his ships destroyed the landbound subhive. Utterly.

His battle group continued to wreak havoc on any world where the Klikiss might return. He swiftly learned that the insect race was more widespread than he had expected, and Sirix's own prospects grew bleaker day by day.

He and his battle group no longer exercised any caution whatsoever. He could not risk it. As soon as the prowling ships arrived at a former Klikiss world, Sirix ordered massive pre-emptive strikes to obliterate the long-abandoned cities and any Hansa colonies that happened to be in the way. Constrained to travel only via transportal, the insect creatures were vulnerable to a massive attack from space. And since each subhive was an enemy to all others, they would not spread a warning amongst themselves.

In preparation for later battles, he decided to refine the skills of his two compies, so he assigned PD and QT to man the weapons stations and ordered them to open fire on the targets below. The compies did as they were told, now that their programming strictures had been erased. Though they were not Soldier compies, PD and QT were quite proficient at their tasks.

Sirix's battle group targeted and destroyed the transportal walls on Zed Khell, Alintan, and Rajapar. On Xalezar, he found that humans had established a colony, but the Klikiss had already arrived and seized the settlers. Seeing the EDF ships, the colonists screamed for help, but Sirix had no sympathy for the humans, whom he hated just as he hated his Klikiss creators.

Sirix wiped out the transportal wall first. Next he destroyed the new Klikiss structures. Last, for good measure, he obliterated every remnant of the human settlement. Another planet cauterized. It was good progress.

At Scholld, however, Sirix blundered into an unanticipated obstacle. The subhive breedex had grown stronger, more innovative. As Sirix began his usual bombardment from the skies, the enemy struck back in an alarming way.

Rising up from the ancient city, numerous identical components flew at them to deliver a thousand devastating blows. Then the myriad components clustered together to form a powerful – and ever-growing – swarmship.

The Klikiss had come through the transportals and established industrial bases quickly enough to build their own spacecraft! How long had this been occurring? If the Klikiss could move from planet to planet without their stone gateways, the infestation would spread faster than the robots could hope to destroy them!

The Mantas responded by laying down a suppressing barrage to drive back the interlocking ships, but he couldn't stand against such an overwhelming concerted attack. 'All robots, withdraw.' He guided the Juggernaut into a hasty retreat. The swarmship swelled even larger as it incorporated more of the component craft, then it came after Sirix's ships.

PD and QT waited at the weapons stations. 'Should we open fire, Sirix?'

'Defensive blasts only.' He had immediately calculated their odds, and he knew they could not target them all. 'We cannot stand against a swarmship of that size.'

Sirix transmitted detailed commands, and the EDF battleships urgently pulled away. The situation was worse than he could possibly imagine. As they retreated from Scholld, he said, 'Our viable options grow fewer and fewer.'

FIFTY-NINE

ORLI COVITZ

S itting atop the wide resin-concrete wall, lonely without Mr Steinman, Orli watched the insects continue their incomprehensible, but manic, work. She wondered if she should have joined the few dozen colonists who had slipped away to join Davlin Lotze. She had seen the breedex, and the experience had disturbed her greatly. She sat with her elbows on her knees, her chin in her hands.

The Governess compy UR had brought along the seven children she guarded. Orli was much too old to be watched over by the Governess compy, but too young to be considered one of the adults. UR continued to gather information to instruct her wards and safeguard them, or at least prepare for what was to happen. The children, meanwhile, amused themselves trying to make sense out of the bugs' activities.

Workers scuttled up a large ramp that ran along the outside of the wall, dumping more of the questionable food into the stockade. Roberto Clarin and Mayor Ruis rationed their hoarded supplies so that the settlers weren't entirely dependent upon what the Klikiss gave them. Even so, Orli's stomach constantly growled. Right now she would even eat Dremen mushroom soup.

The wide wall was an excellent place for the anxious, and paradoxically bored, colonists to gather. DD and Margaret Colicos approached the group, and DD seemed to perk up when he saw Orli and the Governess compy. He and UR had formed their own bond of friendship.

'It is a fine day,' DD said. 'The weather is well within pleasant norms for humans. Are you enjoying the view, Orli Covitz?'

'The view would be better if there weren't so many Klikiss in the way.'

'Oh, dear, have I upset you?'

'Yes, DD, you probably have,' Margaret said.

'I did not mean to.'

'It's okay, DD,' Orli said. 'I'm just worried. Always worried.'

'And that's before seeing what you're about to see.' Margaret gazed toward the alien city. She seemed to have come up here on purpose. 'Watch.'

A commotion occurred inside the ancient structures that held the old transportal. Warriors rearranged themselves, and workers scuttled out of the way as the transportal hummed. Over the past week, Orli had watched the breedex's raiding parties disappear through the stone portal to one unknown destination or other. Diggers, engineers, constructors, and other sub-breeds had all followed. Now some of the Klikiss were marching back home.

Many of the returning warriors looked smashed, battered, and scuffed; several had cracked shell casings, as if from a great battle, while others showed conspicuous stumps where segmented limbs had been snapped off or yanked from their sockets.

'The breedex discovered a black robot infestation on Scholld, one of their old planets. It sent warriors through and captured the old city, built new industries and ships, and expanded the subhive. And took prisoners.'

Orli spotted other ominous black insectile forms among the returning Klikiss. One of the children by UR cried, 'Look – those are robots!'

Margaret wore an unreadable expression. 'These three are intact captives, a gift for the breedex.'

'What will the breedex do with them?' asked UR.

'It will torment them, and enjoy every moment of it.'

'Those robots are evil,' Orli said bitterly. 'They deserve whatever's going to happen to them.'

'The robots were designed and built to react exactly the way the breedex wished them to. The Klikiss are far more cruel than the robots. You'll see that in a minute.'

The three captive black robots seemed extraordinarily agitated. In front of the old alien buildings, they flailed their metal limbs and swivelled their geometric heads as if gibbering in absolute terror. Orli could see the tiny red flashes of their eye sensors. 'Why are they so scared?'

'Because they know what is about to happen.'

UR rounded up the seven boys and girls and said in a stern voice, 'Perhaps the children shouldn't see this.'

'I want to watch!'

DD hovered close beside UR, like a bodyguard. 'We can protect them. Can't we?' The Governess compy didn't answer, but quickly hustled her wards out of sight.

The Klikiss warriors backed away, leaving the three robots to stand together on the packed ground, as if it were an arena – or an execution field. Four of the monstrous striped domates came forward, chittering, singing, fluting.

'Looks like some kind of dance,' Orli said.

'It is a mockery of their reproduction ritual. I have seen this before – and hoped never to see it again. It was an experiment. The Klikiss did not know what to do with him.' She lowered her voice. 'The poor man was lost, confused, and terrified. His name was Howard Palawu. When he saw the Klikiss domates and the breedex, he screamed and screamed.'

Orli felt a hot rock in her stomach. 'What . . . what happened to him?'

'When Palawu screamed, the Klikiss found his song unacceptable, unlike my music box. However, because his song was unfamiliar, the domates incorporated his genetics. That's why some newbreeds carry human characteristics. With each fissioning, the breedex adapts the morphology of the sub-breeds.'

Several of the whitish Klikiss with skull-like faces and cadaverish multi-legged forms moved about now, ducking from shadow to shadow as they watched the ritual. These looked more human than the other Klikiss, with hard plates forming a facial outline like a stiff, ugly, mannequin.

'As far as I can determine, the domates find new genetic material so the reproducing hive does not grow stagnant or inbred. They acquire and incorporate designs from other hives, unrelated breedexes. They devour rival Klikiss to gather their DNA, which manifests in the domates' language, their *songs*.'

Orli didn't entirely understand what the older woman was saying, but it sounded horrible.

Now, as domates encircled the robots, taunting them, the three black machines began to warble shrilly, frantically. They emitted a chaotic succession of music, melodies, tones, and screeches, none of which drove the domates back. The striped domates prodded the black robots with long staffs that discharged blue arcs of electricity. The robots squealed, cracked open their back armoured shells, and fluttered as if in great pain.

Margaret continued, 'It took me a long time to learn their

whole story. I read their writings, studied the scratched equations they left in their ruins. Most of the Klikiss had been exterminated by their robots. The few survivors fought back, not only against the robots but also the hydrogues. That was when they invented the Klikiss Torch, as a superweapon – but it wasn't enough. One breedex survived and escaped to a distant uncharted planet by reprogramming a transportal. For thousands of years, the race has been recovering, and planning.

'After their near extermination, too few Klikiss remained to provide sufficient genetic diversity. The surviving breedex found another race of primitive predators on a far-flung world. The predators were not quite civilized, not quite intelligent, but the domates devoured that new race, incorporated their genetic structure, and thereby created an even stronger breed of Klikiss, before they went into their long hibernation. After centuries of fallow recovery, the Klikiss awakened again, split into dozens of subhives, and swarmed back through the transportal network.'

'And now they want revenge against the black robots,' Orli said.

'Oh, yes.'

At a silent signal, the domates burst forward, raising sawblade forelimbs. They crashed down on the terrified black robots, smashing their scuffed bodies, ripping into their abdomens, tearing out internal sensors, program modules, artificial connective tissue. One domate twisted off a flat geometric head. There was much squealing, chirping, and jubilant singing among the insects.

Orli wanted to look away but she could not. She remembered the completely destroyed black robot she had found in the cliffside cave on Corribus – where the ancient Klikiss had made their last stand against the robots and hydrogues. She knew that this ritual must have happened before.

When the domates finished dismantling the robot prisoners,

strewing smashed bits about like wild men celebrating a bloody victory, the hive went back about its business. Several of the distant children were crying, despite UR's efforts to comfort them. Orli stared at the mangled robot bodies.

SIXTY

ADAR ZAN'NH

Humans always seemed to need rescuing, and the Solar Navy was often called upon to do it. After the successful skyparade demonstrating the prowess of his ships, Adar Zan'nh took seven warliners on a search among known Klikiss planets that had been colonized by humans. He had no idea what his ships might encounter out there.

Privately, he questioned whether this was a proper job for the already-strained Solar Navy. If Prime Designate Daro'h's concerns about the faeros were accurate, then Ildirans were already facing a new kind of threat. Zan'nh should be meeting with his officers to discuss how they might stand against the fiery elementals. Yet here he was flying off to rescue colonists. In his opinion, most of the humans' problems were of their own making.

Nira, however, had convinced the Mage-Imperator, and the Mage-Imperator had issued his commands. As Adar of the Ildiran Solar Navy, Zan'nh would obey. He gave orders to his septar, coordinates were set, and the giant warships flew off on their mission.

During the surprising encounter at Maratha, he had seen the military strength of the returned Klikiss. He knew how difficult the insect race would be to defeat, especially with the Solar Navy decimated. He hoped this ill-advised rescue action did not accidentally start a war with the ancient unpredictable race.

As the warliners flew to their first destination, he stood in the command nucleus like a statue, staring ahead. Ildirans had known about the empty Klikiss worlds for thousands of years, but had never turned them into colonies. There was no need. The Spiral Arm was vast. But the humans had grabbed them for their own.

Ildirans didn't have that greed – didn't try to build on something that didn't belong to them or improve on a technology that already worked perfectly well. They had reached the perceived pinnacle of their civilization.

On the other hand, the humans had helped Ildirans. The Solar Navy stardrives held as much fuel as they could possibly need. There was no longer any ekti shortage, thanks to Roamer ingenuity and ambition. Zan'nh himself had relied upon human engineers for the innovations the Solar Navy had needed during the final conflict with the hydrogues. Sullivan Gold and Tabitha Huck had saved thousands of Solar Navy soldiers by automating Ildiran warliners, even though the Ildirans were holding him prisoner. Zan'nh frowned, his thoughts in turmoil.

Tabitha was even now working with her crew to rebuild warliners faster than any Ildiran teams had thought conceivable. They had suddenly developed control techniques that went beyond *thism*. Tabitha explained that the green priest had shown them how to work together as a perfectly cooperative unit, increasing their productivity tenfold. Zan'nh didn't understand it, but given the astonishing results he could not complain.

His navigator interrupted his thoughts. 'We are approaching Wollamor, Adar.'

'Maintain a full sensor sweep. Be cautious. We do not know what to expect. Send a signal to inquire about the colony's status. In fact, find out if the colonists are there at all. The Klikiss may already have arrived.' *And if the humans suffered because of it, then it was their own fault.*

'No response, Adar. I pick up no transmissions or energy signatures.'

'Keep scanning. The Klikiss are not secretive. If one of those giant swarmships is here, we will find it.'

The comm officer continued to send his signal, but Wollamor remained silent. 'Perhaps our records are inaccurate,' Zan'nh suggested. 'Perhaps the human colonization initiative did not choose Wollamor, after all.'

'We have had verification, Adar.'

'Then we will verify it with our eyes and imagers as well. Take the warliners down. Approach the colony with weapons energized and all gunners ready to fire.'

The seven ships came in low, flying in perfect formation as if re-enacting a skyparade. But their only audience consisted of ghosts and blackened ruins.

The Wollamor settlement was devastated, both the original Klikiss city and the new human town. The hivelike buildings had been levelled. Hillsides, once riddled with Klikiss tunnels, had collapsed. Several destroyed ships were strewn across what had been the colony's landing field. Analysis confirmed that the wreckage had once been EDF heavy cruisers.

Zan'nh was distressed by the total massacre he saw. Had the robots struck here, as they had at Maratha Prime and Secda? Or had the returning Klikiss done this? No one had an answer for him as his warliners passed overhead, circled, and came back. 'Send ground teams down. We must understand what occurred here.'

Ildiran investigators spent the rest of the day combing over the wreckage before returning with their report. They found numerous dead Klikiss bodies, a large pile of burned human bones, destroyed black robots, and EDF Soldier compies.

Adar Zan'nh could not postulate a reasonable scenario for what had happened. But as he looked at the grisly images, his condescending attitude and smug dismissal washed away. Not even the most naïve colonists deserved to have such a fate befall them. He felt genuine sympathy, anger, and urgency. He had not expected this horrific and appalling genocide.

This was much too terrible to ignore.

'Recall all teams and prepare for immediate departure. We must get to the other known human settlements. And we must hurry.'

SIXTY-ONE

ANTON COLICOS

The Hall of Rememberers was closed for five days during the tumultuous change.

Anton and Vao'sh watched as burly workers used curved bars to pry loose the diamondfilm sheets on which the *Saga of Seven Suns* had been etched. The workers strained, and a brittle plate split at a jagged angle. When the sheets were originally mounted in the Hall of Rememberers, they were designed to be indestructible. No one dreamed they would ever be removed or changed, that the *Saga* would be rewritten. The workers strained to pry off another section.

Diamondfilm sheets of shattered history fell to the floor. Though the workers did not read the epic, all Ildirans listened to rememberer performances. Many of them knew portions of the *Saga* by heart. They had been raised, as had their parents and their parents before them, to believe that the epic was infallible. They were aghast at the idea that anything could be amiss with the record.

Because of his academic experience back on Earth, Anton

293

knew how much hair-pulling and gnashing of teeth could occur when fundamental revisions were imposed upon an entire discipline. *You mean, the Earth goes around the Sun, not vice versa?* In human history, such controversy had led to the burning of more than one heretic at the stake – and humans were *accustomed* to debate and revisions. Ildirans, especially rememberer kithmen, did not cope well with change.

Some rememberers turned away from the process. Chief Scribe Ko'sh held onto a wall for support; all the colour had drained from his facial lobes, leaving them a whitish-grey. Vao'sh looked equally stricken, but he nodded to the workers as if giving them permission to proceed. 'It is the Mage-Imperator's will.'

'But how could the Mage-Imperator do this?' Ko'sh said.

Anton tried to sound optimistic. 'We will have the new sheets etched and mounted very soon. Craftsmen are working on them as we speak.'

Ko'sh, who had been in charge of perfecting each line before any new section was added, breathed heavily, as if hyperventilating. 'We will have to learn the *Saga* all over again, not just the young rememberers or the new graduates, but all of us, Vao'sh! We must discard much of what we spent our lives learning. This is worse than the Lost Times.'

'Not discard, but *correct*. We are rectifying an error that has been perpetuated for far too long.'

Anton had seen rememberer children brought into this great Hall to undergo merciless studies, memorizing one wall panel after another. But previous Mage-Imperators had engaged in a conspiracy of disinformation and censorship, and the Ildirans had believed every word of it. The chief scribe had to see the fallacy.

Ko'sh could no longer watch as workers removed the next diamondfilm panel. He sank to his knees and rubbed the lobes on his forehead. The chief scribe was younger than Vao'sh, his eyes close-set and hard. He raised his head as if it were a great weight and turned his bitter gaze toward Anton.

'The established *Saga* remained untouched for thousands of years. We were part of the story. We lived it. We knew our place in the great tale. But ever since we began associating with humans – since we allowed them to tangle our storylines – nothing has been the same.' He lifted his hands, palms upward, beseeching.

'The story of the universe does not belong solely to the Ildiran race, but to all races,' said Vao'sh. 'Even humans.'

'And now the humans pretend to be part of the *thism*!' Ko'sh said. 'Have you heard their green priest?'

Anton understood their uneasiness. 'I don't necessarily like it any more than you do. Kolker offered to open my mind to his "revelations", but I like being myself. So don't blame me – *I* haven't intruded on your *thism*.'

Anton had always been a loner, preferring solitude so that he could read the great epics. He couldn't imagine what it would be like if his thoughts were totally open, his mind connected to many people, as well as the web of Ildiran *thism*. What Kolker and the others described as a wondrous sense of belonging sounded like a terrible invasion of privacy to Anton. Some Ildirans considered the converted humans to be interlopers, even threats.

And now his own work with Vao'sh on revising the sacred *Saga* was causing an even greater shakeup. The two of them were ripping out the very foundations of history. Even with the Mage-Imperator's blessing and support, he expected some Ildirans to view Vao'sh – and most especially himself – as heretics, just like those ancient astronomers who were burned at the stake.

The old rememberer placed a hand on Ko'sh's shoulder, a gesture Ildirans rarely used but one he had learned from Anton. 'You will study the new history, Ko'sh. No matter how accurately you memorized it and repeated it, some parts of what you knew were *wrong*. Even the stories of the Shana Rei may have been fabrications.'

Ko'sh shook his head, not denying his comrade's words but hating to accept them. 'If the truth can change once, then can it not change again and again?'

SIXTY-TWO

PATRICK FITZPATRICK III

Patrick had never seen anything as complicated, as jury-rigged, or as spectacular, as a Roamer skymine. The industrial processing city was like a mammoth ocean liner in the clouds, self-contained and almost self-sufficient. It ploughed through Golgen's atmosphere, its great scoops churning the convoluted swirls of gas. The intakes sucked up immense tankfuls, processed the hydrogen through ekti reactors, then spewed exhaust in a titanic vapour trail behind them.

It was a big sky, and he felt very alone.

Over the past several days Zhett had refused to speak to him. Not a word. He'd known she was hot-blooded, but he hadn't expected to be cut off at the knees, unable even to approach her. Zhett had deftly disarmed him in a way that would have made his grandmother proud. Why couldn't she at least yell at him?

He had looked for her everyplace he could think of, going to the control deck, to the shipping levels, the dining hall. The Roamers all knew who he was now, and though they didn't throw him off the skymine (either figuratively or literally), they certainly gave him the cold shoulder. No one seemed to know where Zhett was. Obviously, she was avoiding him, but he refused to give up.

Patrick did find her quarters – by pure luck. Although he signalled at the metal door, she did not answer. He waited there for an entire shift, but she never returned. He came back four times at random hours, even in the middle of the night, but she wasn't there.

So he left her a note. When that produced no result, he decided to bring her flowers. Because flowers were not easy to come by on an industrial skymine, however, he sat inside his ship for part of an afternoon, drawing a large and colourful picture of a bouquet, hoping his exuberance would make up for his lack of talent. With an adhesive strip, he mounted it to the door of her quarters. The next time he passed by, the picture was gone.

But still nothing.

So, feeling helpless, Patrick was left to explore the huge Kellum facility, hoping he might bump into her. He stood out on the open balcony decks watching the slow-motion boiling of clouds. Hydrogues had once dwelled down there. Patrick shuddered and gripped the rail, fighting back dizziness as he remembered how the enemy warglobes had destroyed his own Manta and left him for dead . . .

Turning away from the too-open skies, he climbed down from one deck to another. Men and women with jetpacks and anti-grav belts floated outside the curved hull, adjusting fittings, monitoring the great pumps, dangling probes hundreds of kilometres long to take atmospheric-content samples in search of the perfect mixture of gases for creating stardrive fuel.

Next to the ekti reactors and condensing chambers, Patrick watched teams load cylinder after cylinder of ekti into the grasping spidery legs of a cargo escort. Every hour, another full escort was dispatched. He estimated that the total output of Golgen's skymines was more than the entire Hansa had produced during eight years of war and austerity.

A young, whip-thin pilot wearing a long red scarf climbed aboard the cargo escort and sealed the hatches, heading off to a transfer depot called Barrymore's Rock. Patrick had never heard of it.

A gruff voice behind him said, 'You still owe me a cargo escort, by damn.' Patrick turned to see Del Kellum looking at him with a hard expression. 'And if I wanted to be vindictive, I'd throw in a bill for all the damage your reprogrammed Soldier compies did to my shipyards. I'm not made of money, you know. Imagine how much work it took to rebuild and recover from all that.'

'I'll find a way to pay you back. I can get your cargo escort. I'm willing to help out here on the skymine. I'm sorry.'

'Aren't we all.'

Patrick's mind filled with excuses and justifications, but he had not come here to have a debate. During his time alone aboard the *Gypsy*, he'd wondered if he had the strength to bear all of the blame. He had to. Maybe then Zhett would consider him worthy. 'I've got something to say, and apologies to make.'

The bearded man snorted. 'We've known that since the moment you set foot here. What makes you think we want to hear it? Zhett certainly doesn't.'

'You'll want to hear it. Trust me. What would it take for you to bring the skymine chiefs here?'

'Why should I want to?'

'Because *I'm* the one who twisted my grandmother's arm to let the Roamers go free when the EDF came to Osquivel. You could have all been taken prisoner, just like the Roamers on Hurricane Depot and Rendezvous.' He hadn't wanted to play that card, but he seemed to have no choice. 'Just let me talk to them.' His throat felt very dry. 'Please?'

The clan leader heaved a long-suffering sigh. 'I don't imagine you'll get a very good reception.'

Patrick averted his eyes. 'I don't either, especially after they hear what I have to say. But it's something I've got to do.'

The internal meeting chamber would have been dreary had it not been for the colourful hangings, iridescent tapestries, and splashes of pigment on the walls that looked as if hyperactive Roamer children had engaged in a finger-painting contest.

Now that he'd gotten up his nerve, Patrick wanted as many people to hear his confession as possible, though Zhett was the only one who really mattered to him. For the moment, however, this would be a private meeting. There wasn't even a green priest to disseminate the news; Del Kellum had found Liona to be too much of a distraction for the skyminers, so he had sent the female green priest to the Osquivel shipyards, where she would serve a more practical purpose.

Patrick paced the room wearing his EDF dress uniform. It was risky, but after much soul-searching, he had decided it was necessary. He was done hiding his identity and his past. There could be no turning back. Even if Zhett didn't come to listen, he needed to do this for himself.

'It's your show, Fitzpatrick.' Kellum sat down. 'Make it good.'

'Or at least entertaining,' said Boris Goff. 'Try dumping your-self out an airlock.' Some of the others chuckled uneasily.

Patrick had rehearsed his words, but when he saw Zhett appear at the doorway, the well-practised speech vanished into thin air. She looked beautiful in her Roamer jumpsuit with her glossy dark hair draped over her shoulders. She leaned casually against the door frame, arms crossed, and looked at him with an unreadable expression.

After an interminable silence, Bing Palmer muttered, 'Just

like the Eddies – they waste our time and have nothing to say.'

Patrick cleared his throat. 'I . . . I'm responsible for it. I just wanted you to know. The clan heads, the Roamers, it's affected everybody.' He knew he was being vague. 'My actions. I didn't know you then, didn't think anything through. It never occurred to me—'

'We all know you're responsible, by damn. I was there, remember? When the Soldier compies junked up my shipyards, and that Eddy battle group drove us away like birds from a roost.'

'Not that. I mean before, long before, at the root of all this. I served with General Lanyan as his adjutant. I was with him on patrol runs across trade routes, supposedly looking for hydrogues. But we were bored. The Hansa and the EDF were angry with the Roamer clans, because you wouldn't agree to exclusively sell us your ekti in a time of war.'

Goff slurped his drink loudly. 'Yeah, we know all this.'

'We encountered a Roamer cargo ship flown by a man named Raven Kamarov.' He watched the reaction ripple through the room. Even Zhett stood up straight, her eyes widening. 'Kamarov was carrying stardrive fuel, quite a lot of it. After we talked with him, it was clear he didn't intend to sell it to Earth.'

Despite Patrick's anxiety, speaking these words aloud felt somehow cleansing. 'Things got out of control. General Lanyan gave me implicit orders and left the bridge. Though I believed I was doing what was right for the EDF and the Hansa at the time, *I'm* the one who turned to the weapons officer. *I* gave the order to open fire.'

The room fell completely silent. Patrick stared at one of the coloured daubs on the wall, seeing Zhett in his peripheral vision. The other skymine chiefs stared at him. 'Yes, I killed Raven Kamarov. That's bad enough in itself, I know. But that started it all. Because of that incident, the Roamers cut off ekti shipments to the Hansa. Then the EDF retaliated by attacking your facilities, taking Roamers prisoner, destroying Rendezvous. The list goes on and on.' He closed his eyes, shook his head. Taking a deep breath, he opened his eyes again and raised his chin. 'I'm sorry, and I'm here to accept my punishment.'

His legs were shaking, and he felt as if he would collapse any second. In the uproar of angry disbelief, with men surging to their feet, shouting accusations, spilling their drinks, and cursing him, Patrick saw only Zhett staring at him. With tears sparkling in her dark eyes, she turned and left the meeting chamber. Patrick didn't hear anything else.

SIXTY-THREE

CHAIRMAN BASIL WENCESLAS

The Chairman faced the window of his office, pointedly turning his back on Admiral Willis, who stood at attention. Now that he'd heard of her botched assault on Theroc, he did not trust himself to look at her. Another disappointment. Another failure. Was she so weak? So poor a choice for admiral?

Deputy Cain sat at his desk in a corner, watching. Basil didn't mind that the deputy spoke less and less during meetings, but he was worried that no one had his clarity of vision anymore.

Still staring out at the Palace District's skyline, he finally said, 'You overestimated the Therons and the Roamers. I know what they're made of. The lines would have crumbled. Your jazer firepower could have chopped those verdani treeships into kindling.'

Willis didn't bother to sound cowed. 'Mr Chairman, I've had more than enough experience with politicians second-guessing command decisions after the fact. In my professional opinion, the battle was not winnable. Period. After the disasters that have befallen the EDF, I stand by my decision not to lose ten Manta cruisers in a futile exercise.'

He turned to face her, but she didn't back down. 'I don't like your insubordinate tone, Admiral.' *Again.*

Willis brushed aside his comment. 'The most important thing, Mr Chairman, is the alarming news King Peter reported. If the Klikiss race has returned to reclaim their worlds, that could be a substantial threat.'

'And you believe that fairy tale? Without proof? The Klikiss have been extinct for ten thousand years. It was a defence strategy – just Peter creating more imaginary monsters.'

'More? Like the "imaginary" threat of Klikiss robots and Soldier compies, you mean?'

Deputy Cain's tone was deceptively mild. 'General Lanyan is still at Rheindic Co. There have been no reports about a Klikiss invasion on any of the worlds he went to inspect.'

Willis was obviously flustered. 'Exactly how is he supposed to make a report? He's got no green priests. Have you received any word from him at all?'

'I expect the General back soon. He will deliver a full report when he returns.'

Willis waited in her formal stance; she seemed bulletproof. 'Will that be all, Mr Chairman?'

Finally Basil sat down. 'Unfortunately not, Admiral. Since we did not achieve our goals at Theroc, you now force me to pursue Plan B.'

Cain had a perplexed expression on his face. 'Plan B? We've not discussed our next move.'

'I didn't require your input, Mr Cain. The objective is clear enough.' He turned to regard Willis. 'Even though I'm not impressed with your combat decisions during the Theron debacle, I cannot afford to lose one of my seasoned commanders. Nor can

I let your ten Mantas sit here idle while more of the Hansa slips through my fingers. I've run an assessment of our breakaway colony worlds to see which ones have the weakest defences and the most strategic importance. I'm sending my grid admirals to these carefully selected "softer targets", to plant the Hansa flag and bring them back into line – by any means necessary.'

'You mean invade and occupy?'

'That's exactly what I mean, though I would choose different words.'

'I'd like my Juggernaut back if you're going to send me into combat, sir. The battle picture at Theroc would have changed dramatically if I'd had my *Jupiter* as well as the Mantas.'

'Request denied. General Lanyan will retain command of the Juggernaut for the time being, but perhaps after a *successful* operation, you'll earn back the right. For now, make do with your ten cruisers.'

He touched his deskscreen, illuminating a star system, then called up images of green-blue oceans, reefs, and small settlements built out of giant shells, as well as large refineries, pumping stacks, and condensing facilities. 'I'm assigning you Rhejak, an ocean world with an ocean-based economy. The people have been comfortable for a long time. They won't be much of a problem – even for you, Admiral.' He laced his fingers behind his steel-grey hair.

Willis frowned at the images. 'You want me to conquer a vacation postcard? For what purpose – just to bolster the Hansa's ego?'

'To acquire Rhejak's materials. The oceans and reefs there are a good source of rare metals and minerals, which the Hansa needs. One of their kelp extracts is a valuable supplement for pharmaceuticals, including anti-aging treatments. Knuckling down on a few islanders and fishermen shouldn't be beyond even your abilities.'

Willis was clearly annoyed. 'I've got decades of experience, Mr Chairman, and dozens of victories under my belt. I'm not accustomed to being addressed this way by a . . . a civilian.'

'I am your commander-in-chief, Admiral.'

'I have some concerns about that particular point. I've reviewed all available EDF documentation. The chain of military command is fairly clear – and the Chairman is nowhere on it.'

From his chair on the other side of the room, Deputy Cain said, 'She's technically correct, Mr Chairman. According to protocol and Hansa law, you have no direct authority to command the Earth Defence Forces.'

Basil clenched his teeth and forced calm upon himself. 'I can see that the Hansa Charter and the EDF's defining documents need to be clarified, so that other officers don't experience the same confusion.'

Admiral Willis left without being dismissed. Basil watched her departing figure, glanced at Cain, and considered (not for the first time) simply scrapping all of his upper-level advisers and military officers and starting from scratch. Unfortunately, he had no better alternatives. He needed to keep a firm hold on the ones he had.

SIXTY-FOUR

SAREIN

For a long time Sarein had been growing increasingly concerned about Basil. Because of their past and all that he had
done for her, she still cared for the Chairman, but lately
another emotion had begun to work its way into her feelings
for him: *fear*.

When Basil sent her an unexpected invitation to join him for a
private meal, she was at first excited, then puzzled. The note was
brief, hinting at no tenderness, nor was it brusque. It seemed to
have been written almost as an afterthought.

Sarein accepted, of course, hoping for the best.

Basil had carefully specified the time she was to join him. His
private quarters had a sterile cleanliness that suggested how little
time he spent there. 'Good of you to come here. It's been too
long.'

She tried to interpret the smile he offered. 'Yes, it has, Basil.'

'But you understand, don't you? With the hydrogue war and
Peter's blatant insurrection, I haven't had much time for personal
matters.'

The meal was already set out and waiting for them (so as not to waste time, she supposed; even with her the Chairman was on a tight schedule). Two filet mignons, identical servings of scalloped mushrooms, and a green-and-yellow vegetable she did not recognize. Each place had a glass of iced tea. He gestured for her to sit and politely pushed her chair in like a gentleman.

'We need more times like this, Basil,' she said. 'A bit of relaxation would increase your effectiveness and productivity.'

'Yes, so my advisers suggest.' He took the seat across from her and motioned toward her plate. 'I hope the food is to your liking, but the company is what matters.'

She cut into her steak, found it done perfectly. Though Sarein smiled and held up her end of the pleasant conversation, at the back of her mind she wondered what the Chairman was doing. So often in the past year he had given her the cold shoulder, demonstrating that he didn't need her, or Deputy Cain, or anyone who failed to share his convictions.

But as circumstances in the Hansa mushroomed out of control, she had watched Basil slide down an ever-steepening spiral. He walled himself off from the input of even his closest advisers, and was blind to how emotions swayed his judgment. But Sarein was sure she could still save him if she used this private time to help the Chairman reconsider his stance against the Confederation, help him see choices that would benefit all of humanity rather than just add points to his personal scorecard.

'I know you very well, Sarein. I have never doubted you, but I realize that we've grown more distant from each other. I hope this evening will reassure you. I need to know that I can count on you when so much else has grown dark around me.'

'Of course you can, Basil.' Her answer was automatic, but she felt a chill. She had hoped to soften him during their time together, yet now she suspected his intention was to manipulate *her*.

'I checked the records of your official meetings. I noticed that you visited a trading ship, the *Voracious Curiosity*, belonging to Captain Rlinda Kett.'

She froze, clamping down on her reaction so Basil wouldn't notice. 'Yes, I knew Captain Kett from Theroc. She had a load of trade goods – nothing particularly remarkable – but I'm one of the only people she still knows on Earth. We had a brief chat, and then she left.'

'You're aware that there's an arrest warrant out for her and her partner?'

'No, she didn't mention it. And I'm not in charge of spaceport security, Basil.' She saw a chance to turn the conversation. 'I might have known, however, if you'd keep me in the loop. I feel you're shutting me out. I don't know half the things you're planning. You have another Prince candidate, for instance.'

'A *King* candidate.'

She set down her knife and fork. 'You see what I mean? I don't know anything about this. I don't know who he is. Neither, apparently, does your own deputy.'

Basil's expression hardened. 'That's confidential information.'

'But shouldn't we be in this together? We are your supporters, your advisers, and I'm your lover. At least, I think I still am.' Sometimes she needed to remind herself of that.

He seemed to find that amusing. 'You think I've found someone else?'

'No, never that, Basil. I just wonder whether you need me – or anyone.'

'I need people who are loyal to me.'

After their meal, instead of coffee they had a hot beverage called clee made from ground worldtree seeds, a drink that Sarein had often consumed on Theroc. She knew that Basil had served it intentionally, to prove he was thinking of her. That was how he scored points. Instead of warming her heart, though, the clee (which was not easy to obtain, especially now) only raised more questions.

Afterward they made love, and for a short time Sarein let herself be reassured, let herself be fooled. Basil knew exactly what she liked, so he had not forgotten her entirely. But throughout she had the nagging feeling that the Chairman was simply accomplishing a task, checking off an item on a list of things he needed to do. When they were finished, she snuggled against him, remembering when she had first come to his bed and all the incredible, impossible changes – *his* changes – that had happened since then.

He wrapped his arm around her, holding her. 'I need to keep you close, Sarein.'

'I'm here, Basil.' But she swallowed hard as she remembered an old cliché of leadership that Basil loved to quote. *Keep your friends close, and your enemies closer.*

For the first time Sarein wondered, really wondered, what would happen if she asked him for permission to go back to Theroc, to go home. What would happen if she tried to escape?

Am I a hostage here?

SIXTY-FIVE

QUEEN ESTARRA

Although the EDF's would-be invasion fleet had left Theroc alone, the ring of thorny treeships still hung in orbit like spiny guard dogs. The thought of Beneto and the other verdani battleships up there, watching over the worldforest, made Estarra feel safe.

She had always felt she could count on him. After being destroyed by hydrogues and resurrected by the worldtrees, Beneto had already been more than human, yet he had never stopped being her brother. Even as a sentient pilot fused with a wental-verdani hybrid, he had responded to Theroc's need and come to defend it.

But Estarra missed him very much. Needing to see her brother, she announced that she would visit Beneto in orbit. Peter – apprehensive at the idea of his very pregnant wife leaving the planet, however briefly – could not dissuade her, so he asked OX to be her pilot. The King came to see her off as brightening dawn light shone through gaps in the worldforest canopy.

The small hydrogue derelict sat like a pearl in the lush Theron meadow where it had landed, looking beautiful rather than ominous. The alien ship still functioned, but only the Teacher compy was competent to operate its systems. 'I am pleased to offer my assistance, Queen Estarra,' said OX. Bits of damp grass and weeds clung to his polymer feet from his march across the dewy meadow. 'Where exactly do you wish to go?'

Was that a different tone she heard in his voice – less formality and more complexity than before? Estarra hoped so. Each day, she and Peter diligently helped the Teacher compy rebuild his knowledge base of hard facts, nuances of statecraft, and memories of time they had spent together. Estarra also taught the compy Theron protocol, steeping him in traditions, celebrations, and cultural quirks, sharing anecdotes from her childhood. She told him stories about her parents, her grandparents ... her brother Reynald, who had been killed in the first hydrogue attack. And Beneto.

'I'd like to go up to orbit to see my brother and the treeships.'

'Keep her safe, OX,' Peter said. 'I'm counting on you.'

She had asked Yarrod to join them as well, and the green priest arrived carrying a small treeling. Through telink, her uncle would help her communicate with Beneto. Peter kissed the Queen goodbye, and the three of them climbed into the small diamond-hulled ship.

After Yarrod found a place to sit and Estarra sealed the hatch, OX turned his attention to the alien controls. With a silent boost from invisible, noiseless engines, the derelict rose up from the meadow, leaving an indentation of smashed flowers and grasses. It climbed like a smooth elevator past the tall trunks of the gathered worldtrees, and burst out into the open, bright sky.

Only a few days earlier, Jess Tamblyn and Cesca Peroni had also flown away, saying goodbyes to their Roamer friends and to the King and Queen. By showing the solidarity of the wentals

with the worldforest, and hinting at the incomprehensible power
the water elementals could bring to bear, they had given the EDF
a lot to think about. But now that she had formally resigned
as the Speaker for the clans, Cesca had other work to pursue
for the wentals, work that Estarra didn't entirely understand.
Or maybe Cesca and Jess Tamblyn should just take time for a
honeymoon.

Through the clear diamond walls, she watched the wrinkled
landscape of interconnected branches and leaves recede. Then,
passing the last rarefied wisps of high clouds, they reached space.
OX guided them toward the spiny treeships that circled high
above Theroc.

The reinforced trunks were larger than any battleship. Huge
armoured boughs stretched in all directions to drink energy from
the solar wind. Thorns, each as long as the mast of an ancient
sailing ship, speared the vacuum. Fibrous roots dangled out in
space like trailing communications antennae. One huge treeship
drifted past, gradually turning its bulk to face the bright sun.

'How do I know which one is Beneto?' Estarra said, peering
through the dizzying transparent walls.

Yarrod cradled his treeling without seeming to notice
anything else around him. 'You know which one.'

Looking at the immense, thorny objects, Estarra did know.
Though the silent verdani battleships looked the same, she could
sense her brother's amplified presence in a great tree coming over
the horizon. 'Take us there, OX – to that one.'

Beneto's treeship gently turned, as if he could see them
approach through the eyes of a thousand leaves. Its branches
seemed to rustle, and several opened to form a welcoming nest.
The diamond-hulled vessel dropped into the welcoming thorny
embrace, and the armoured vestigial fronds enclosed them like
docking clamps.

Yarrod touched the small treeling in his lap, sending a message. When he looked back at Estarra, his expression had changed somehow, as if Beneto were a part of him, speaking through his mouth. 'I am always with you.'

'Thank you for helping to protect us, Beneto,' she said in a whisper.

Yarrod closed his eyes, furrowed his green brow. 'The treeships, and all of the worldforest, are concerned. There are still threats.'

'What concerns are left? They didn't have any trouble driving away the EDF a few days ago. And the hydrogues are defeated, aren't they?'

Now Yarrod looked through the walls of the derelict, as if searching for new attackers coming from deep space. His voice sounded like Beneto's. 'The Klikiss returning … the faeros growing strong again.'

'But the faeros fought for Theroc.' *That battle had killed Reynald* . . .

'The faeros fought for themselves against the hydrogues. Theroc was just a convenient battlefield.' Yarrod seemed very grave.

Estarra shuddered, no longer feeling safe even with the treeships watching over them. She looked around, studying the enormous branches and trying to imagine the arms of Beneto wrapped around her, rocking her to sleep. Her green priest brother had never been as muscular as Reynald, but he had often comforted her when she was troubled.

'I miss you, Beneto,' she said quietly.

'I know,' Yarrod replied for the treeship.

She didn't have a specific message for him. For now, as she held her stomach and felt the baby kick, Estarra just wanted to be close to him, close to the treeship. With all the dangers in the Spiral Arm, this felt to her like the most protected place.

She told OX to let them just drift there for a time. It was what she needed.

Sixty-six

Margaret Colicos

The Klikiss no longer responded when Margaret demanded answers in their clicking language. She understood the signs and knew she could wait no longer. The colonists had to prepare for their last stand.

Countless members of the Llaro subhive had been damaged or killed in major attacks against black robot infestations, and with rival breedexes expanding across ancient worlds and preparing for a new set of swarm wars, the Llaro breedex needed to produce many more Klikiss. More fighters. Very soon, Margaret knew, the subhive would undergo its fissioning and expansion. And the human settlers in the stockade would pay the price.

Margaret felt an ache for the upcoming tragedy. She liked these people. For a long time, she considered whether it might be best if she just hid the truth from them, let them have peace for a last few days. But they deserved to know, whether or not there was anything they could do about it. Even if it was a lost cause, shouldn't they have the choice to fight? Perhaps in the short time they had left, a few more people could surreptitiously get away. Margaret had to tell someone.

Faithful DD marched with her to the stockade. Resilient and intelligent, the Friendly compy adapted to nearly any new situation. Dozens of colonists had already quietly escaped, presumably taking shelter in the hideout that Davlin Lotze had promised to establish. But the rest of these . . .

More than a week earlier, at Margaret's insistence, the Klikiss had run a pipe from an agricultural well through the stockade wall. It was the only source of water inside, and the flow had sprayed across the ground in a muddy mess until Crim Tylar jury-rigged a trough and holding tank. The people filling jugs and buckets today stared at Margaret and the grim expression on her face.

Lupe Ruis and Roberto Clarin met her at the gushing water pump. 'I have news, but you may want to hear it in private.'

DD said, 'If we have a meeting, I would be happy to prepare some beverages. Do you have lemon concentrate? A popular old proverb says, "If life gives you lemons, make lemonade."'

For a moment Clarin got a faraway look on his face. 'I miss lemonade. Back on Hurricane Depot, we sometimes got shipments of *real lemons* from the Chan greenhouses.' He sighed and reluctantly met Margaret's gaze. 'So, you're about to drop a giant lemon on us?'

Margaret didn't try to hide it. 'I'm afraid so.'

'We've been through seven hells and back already. What do the Klikiss want from us?'

'What have we ever done to them?' Ruis added. 'You said that they're after the black robots. I can't believe they'd want to hurt us.'

'The breedex sees you as a resource to help it meet its goals. It needs to reproduce, increase its numbers to fight other subhives. And for that it needs you. All of you.'

They entered a sheltered building with striped fabric over-hangs; once a produce shop, it had been shut down since the arrival of the Klikiss. Clarin seemed resigned, as if he hadn't expected good news for months now. DD stood watch at the door under the bright awnings, though he would probably chat with visitors rather than turn them away.

'I've observed the preparations in the breedex hive. The domates are mature and ready to start assimilating new genetic material to improve this subhive's abilities. They will take what they can from human DNA, using all the colonists.'

Only a handful of the interesting hybrids that included poor Howard Palawu's genetics remained, but they had demonstrated the potential of human genes. The new Klikiss hybrids would be stronger, smarter, more powerful. By retaining the best human attributes, they would conquer everything. The Llaro breedex intended to use that as an advantage over the other subhives.

'Use us?' Ruis looked around. 'What does that mean?'

Clarin stated the obvious. 'They're going to eat us. That's what you're saying, isn't it?'

'Yes. That's what I'm saying.'

Margaret's eyes blurred as her concentration drifted. The fissioning emptied the breedex, turned the great hive mind into a mountain of gorging larvae, which then became a multitude of new Klikiss. That was why the Klikiss had harvested every edible scrap from the agricultural fields, why they fished and hunted and scavenged every bit of biomass to build a huge stockpile. Within the breedex hive, the larvae would eat, grow, and finally emerge.

Standing at the doorway, DD waved at two red-eyed passersby, but the pair couldn't summon the cheer to respond.

Clarin's face was stormy. 'Roamers don't go down without a fight. By the Guiding Star, we'll find a way to show them just how unappetizing humans can be.'

SIXTY-SEVEN

HUD STEINMAN

Leaving the stockade was the smartest thing he'd ever done. Even after hiding from the bugs all day and searching for food and shelter during the night, Steinman was glad to have taken matters into his own hands. Why had he waited so long? He knew the answer, of course. Damn, he hated to leave Orli Covitz, and he'd even made some friends among the colonists. He had a gut-level ominous feeling about what might happen to everyone. Margaret Colicos was a strange woman, and he found her hard to read. He was convinced she knew something – something bad.

Steinman had slept that first day in the shade of a ravine, sheltered from view. For the past several days he had survived by eating a few lizards he killed, which didn't bother him any; they tasted better than the furry crickets on Corribus. Klikiss aircraft buzzed across the sky. He doubted the bugs were looking for him, since they didn't seem to keep track of how many prisoners were in the stockade, and he hadn't been the first to escape. He certainly hoped he wasn't the last.

Setting off again at twilight, he spotted a distant line of sandstone bluffs mottled with distinctive shadows, maybe even caves. He swished through the dry grasses on his way toward the cliffs, trying to keep a low profile on the open prairie. There were probably some local predators, but given what he'd already been through, facing Llaro's version of rattlesnakes or wildcats didn't worry him unduly.

Steinman walked into the night, revelling in the freedom, the independence. He had his solitude at last. So why did he feel such a terrible loneliness inside? He hummed absently as he crossed the uneven ground, feeling his way. He had fashioned a long walking stick for himself, and he poked it into any suspicious shadows. Walking past large mounds of rock and dirt, he hummed more loudly. Llaro's night was too silent.

As he continued the tune, he realized with a pang that he was repeating one of the melodies Orli often played. The two of them had done well together on Corribus. Steinman froze in place as he heard a hum and chirp – another song in response to his own. He cursed himself. He should have been quiet! Klikiss were abroad.

The chirp came again, a whistling abrasive sound, not at all like the song he had been humming. With a glint of starlight on a black carapace, a Klikiss warrior emerged from behind one of the sheltering rock mounds. It darted toward him, its spiny joints and crest casting a sharp shadow against the dark.

'Oh, crap.' His throat was suddenly dry.

Steinman jabbed his walking stick at the creature's angular face as it lunged. The Klikiss crab-walked to one side and came forward again. Steinman swung his stick and cracked it against the hard chitin, but the blow did no damage. The warrior clipped the stick in half, as if it were thin as a toothpick. It squealed and clacked its jaws, raising four sharp limbs. Steinman backed away, tripped on a rock, and fell backward. He yelled.

The Klikiss exploded. A high-powered shot cracked across the quiet night, and a crater appeared in the creature's abdomen. It flailed its limbs, staggered, and collapsed. One twitching, segmented arm tried to lift the body up. Slick ooze poured from the wound.

Steinman rolled out of the way, scrambled backward, and got to his feet. Now he saw the dark man standing by himself, holding a large weapon from the EDF stockpiles.

Davlin Lotze said, 'We should get out of here. They often hunt in pairs.'

'Couldn't agree more.' Steinman followed the man. 'You have good timing.'

'And you have unbelievable luck. They wouldn't even have left any bones for me to find by morning.' Davlin shouldered his weapon. 'The rest of the escapees set up a decent camp back in those sandstone bluffs.' He set off without looking back. 'Come on. Now that I killed that warrior, the breedex knows we're out here.'

SIXTY-EIGHT

CELLI

Since making her decision to become a green priest, Celli had noticed more of the worldforest's grandeur – towering trees, colourful underbrush, sweet-smelling epiphytes, jewel-winged condorflies. She began to hear differences among the insect songs that filled the forest, instead of an unvarying blur in her ears. She wished she had made up her mind to do this years ago.

Celli stood in a spacious glade surrounded by waving grasses tipped with feathery seedstalks. She looked up – and up and up – to the canopy and the splash of open sky. Solimar watched her proudly, as excited as she was. Queen Estarra, heavy with child, stood next to her parents for the ceremony.

As the senior green priest, Yarrod was silent and imposing. Normally he performed this ritual with children, his demeanour designed to impress upon the new acolytes the gravity of their choice. He dipped his forefinger into a pot full of pasty dye. 'You will become an acolyte, Celli. You will serve the worldforest and act as a part of the verdani mind. Today you become less of an individual and more of the great tapestry. As all worldtrees are connected, so are all green priests, and all of humanity. Once you learn to open yourself to the worldforest, the trees will accept you as a green priest. Do you vow to undergo this training, to offer yourself as both servant and companion to the forest, to provide aid and information to the trees?'

'I've already been doing it for years now.'

'A simple yes or no, please.'

'Yes.' She shot a quick glance and a smile to Solimar. When he looked back at her, she could sense the depth of his feelings toward her. Had they changed, or was she just noticing them more clearly? She felt a frisson of excitement, followed by a quaver of intimidation, as she wondered how inseparable and intertwined their thoughts and hearts could be once they became green priests together. Celli wanted that, more than anything.

With dye dripping from his finger, Yarrod drew a straight vertical line down the centre of Celli's forehead. The colouring tingled, then began to burn as it changed the pigmentation of her skin. 'You are now marked as an acolyte. Green priests will help you. And before long, the worldforest will accept you.'

'I am ready.' Celli made her voice sound formal, but her heart was pounding with eagerness. 'When will I start?'

'You have already started.' Finally, Yarrod dropped the serious demeanour and opened his arms to hug her. 'I'm so glad you decided to join us.'

'Sorry I took so long to make up my mind.'

Solimar took her hand, and she felt the thrill of his touch like an electrical shock. 'Come on, I'll show you what to do.' At the edge of the glade they found a wide-boled worldtree. Using bare feet and fingers, they climbed the bark scales like steps, scrambling higher and higher. From below, Estarra waved; her wistful expression showing that she wished she could still do the same.

Celli was barely sweating by the time they reached the canopy, pushing aside the interlaced green roof of fronds. The sun was dazzling – the same as always – yet now it seemed sharper, clearer. She caught her breath, then laughed out loud. Solimar began laughing with her.

All around them, condorflies buzzed in circles, and orange and pink epiphytes spread their petals to drink in the light. She heard droning voices, some of them young and high-pitched, others deeper. An older green priest was reading from a datapad, surrounded by acolytes, all many years younger than Celli.

'The worldforest wants to hear everything: stories, histories, even technical manuals. Would you like to read some technical manuals?' Solimar sounded hopeful, since he was most interested in those.

She teased him. 'Earth folktales sound more interesting.'

He shrugged. 'As you wish.'

They made their way toward the old instructor and his wards. The interlocked fronds seemed to hold fast – intentionally? – making their passage easier. Soon she would sense the whole forest, just as Solimar did. She couldn't wait for that to happen. Kissing her quickly, Solimar left.

Celli folded her slender legs and made herself comfortable among the branches and leaves. Soon her own voice filled the air, overlapping with the other readers. Paragraph by paragraph, page by page, she increased the worldforest's knowledge and understanding.

SIXTY-NINE

KOLKER

He had never been part of something quite so big, quite so exciting, even when the worldtrees had first accepted him as a green priest. Kolker had never imagined anything better than when his heart and mind had opened to the interconnected thoughts of the verdani.

But this was better, and he felt a need to share it, to show others what they had been missing.

Kolker went back to the decorated platform in the Prism Palace that held the treeling. The worldforest itself hungered for new information and experiences, and this was certainly unique. His enthusiasm and eagerness were too great to contain. He had never felt such an overwhelming sense of mission and purpose. Other green priests would welcome what he had to offer, but the nature of the *change* was personal, not something a green priest could simply access via the verdani mind.

He stood in the bright sunshine that angled through the crystal panes, ready to make a journey with his mind. Kolker had spent so much of his life travelling to distant places, seeing new worlds and describing them to the worldtrees. He always felt a sense of wonder and mystery that was just beyond his reach, in spite of the marvellous things he had already seen. That wander-lust had set him apart from his friend Yarrod, who was not sure why any green priest would want to range so far from home. Kolker, though, maintained that 'home' was with his treeling.

Now he summoned his thoughts and his energy. Yarrod deserved to feel this way, and his friend would finally be able to understand him, and so much more, through the *thism*/telink connection. Kolker smiled at the very thought. Yarrod would be receptive. He knew it.

Kolker touched the fronds and stared down into the light reflected in Tery'l's medallion. He travelled out through telink and became part of the verdani mind, which seemed so much like the *thism* that joined the Ildirans. Kolker could make his proclamation, show anyone who was listening . . .

He found Yarrod standing alone below the great tree that held the fungus-reef city. It was late afternoon on Theroc. 'My friend, I bring you something very important.' Kolker moved his lips, and the words came instantaneously through the tree on Theroc.

'Kolker! You've been so often silent lately. Once you regained a treeling, I thought we'd never hear the end of you.'

'I felt lost, unsure of myself, of my place as a green priest. But now I have a discovery – something even the worldtrees never suspected! You are my closest friend. Will you listen? Will you be open to my news?'

Yarrod's voice came clear and sharp in his head. 'Now you have me intrigued. What is it?'

Kolker had never tried to do the 'opening' process at such a distance. He had always been close enough to touch, to see the expression on his new convert's face, but he wanted to try this. He had a tight bond with this man, who was already open to telink. Kolker stretched out the fingers of his mind and discovered the invisible change he had to make in Yarrod's – the tweak, like throwing an invisible switch. 'Here. See what I've found.'

It was as if light poured down through the lines of telink, mingled with new soul-threads that blazed with an afterglow of the Ildiran Lightsource. Even from across the parsecs, Kolker could hear Yarrod's gasp, could imagine his face shining with wonder. 'This is . . . unprecedented. It is unbelievable!'

'Believe it. Share it. All green priests can be part of this. All humans can experience it.'

Kolker could almost feel his friend's pulse quickening, his breaths deepening. 'I will share it. I'll tell the other green priests. Thank you, Kolker. Thank you!'

SEVENTY

GENERAL KURT LANYAN

The *Jupiter* returned to Earth, but not to a victory parade. Chairman Wenceslas was not going to be pleased. Not at all.

General Lanyan had never been afraid of a good stand-up fight. He had faced impossible odds against hydrogues, Soldier compies, and black Klikiss robots. But this was different. Instead of securing a few small colonies for the Hansa, he'd blundered into a new war against a race he had never seen before. If the bugs swarmed to Hansa worlds, then the EDF had to be prepared.

Carrying its battered crew of soldiers and rescued colonists, the Juggernaut stopped off at the Mars EDF base for processing and debriefing, while he commandeered a fast in-system Remora to race back to Hansa HQ. It bought him some time. Lanyan knew there was no way he could keep the debacle under wraps. With the numerous witnesses, not to mention the casualties, people would find out sooner or later.

He used his command overrides to get through the layers of security and landed his ship directly in front of the Hansa pyramid. He bulldozed his way through the halls, pushing aside moat dragons, protocol attendants, and calendar specialists who frantically sent messages up the line. Once he reached the higher levels, Deputy Cain took one look at him, decided to run interference, and scheduled an immediate meeting with Chairman Wenceslas.

The Chairman came out into the hall to meet them before they could reach his office. 'I do not like to have my carefully ordered day interrupted, General.' Basil stood straight-backed in the middle of the grey-carpeted corridor. The General felt a thick knot of fear in his stomach – a different kind of fear than he experienced in battle.

Many of the office doors were open, and Hansa administrators, ambassadors, and upper-echelon staff peered out at the commotion. Basil glared at them. 'A little privacy please.' Up and down the hall, the workers ducked back into their offices and the doors shut in a staccato succession.

'Since you've returned well ahead of schedule and are in a great rush to give your report, I can only assume I'm not going to like what you have to say.' He crossed his arms. 'Or maybe you'll surprise me. I'd like that for a change. Do you have good news? Did you complete your mission?'

'No, Mr Chairman.' Lanyan cleared his throat to begin his grim summary, but Basil lifted a hand.

'I thought not. So tell me, exactly how many of our colony worlds did you consolidate before you decided to return? Ten? Fifteen?'

'None. We went only to Pym, where we encountered—'

'None? Of nearly two dozen worlds on your list, you went only to Pym? Did you at least manage to leave a force on Rheindic Co, which was already ours to begin with?'

'No, sir. We destroyed the base and the transportal on

Rheindic Co. It was necessary to keep everyone safe.'

'You destroyed our main hub to all the transportal worlds?' Basil rubbed his temples; he seemed to be wilfully missing Lanyan's point. 'So another failure, just like Admiral Willis. I give my EDF simple missions and sufficient manpower and weaponry. Why must I—'

The General raised his voice. 'Mr Chairman! We have a *severe* problem.' Before Basil could interrupt again, Lanyan explained about the Klikiss invading Pym and how he had caused as much harm as possible to the insect enemy.

'I've already been informed about the Klikiss by Admiral Willis. King Peter said his green priests had reported that nonsense.'

'Then are you making defensive plans? What are we going to do about it?' Lanyan looked at a hovering Deputy Cain, who seemed just as troubled. 'If these Klikiss are as great a threat as I fear, and they decide to expand beyond their worlds—'

'I believe they're only interested in a few formerly abandoned places.' Basil gave a dismissive wave as Lanyan stiffened. 'General, you're not focusing on the things that matter the most. I had hoped to secure those Colonization Initiative worlds, but now we'll have to change our priorities. Not long ago the Hansa consisted of nearly a hundred unified planets. Now I can only be certain of a few worlds, and Earth. If the Klikiss do become a threat, then the Hansa has to be strong. We need our planets back. We need our people all under the same banner. My banner.'

SEVENTY-ONE

ROBERTO CLARIN

While Mayor Ruis worried that Margaret's terrifying revelation would spark panic and confusion among the trapped colonists, Clarin didn't care. 'By the Guiding Star, I'm not going to just bare my throat and let those damned bugs have lunch. We're Roamers, colonists, pioneers. With all our brainpower, we've got to be able to figure out something.'

'I wish Davlin were here,' Ruis said. 'He saved us from the hydrogues, and from freezing on Crenna. He'd have a good idea now.'

'Since he's *not* here,' Clarin said pointedly, 'I've got a few ideas of my own, and somebody else might have a brainstorm, too. Let's pull everyone together and come up with a way to protect the rest of us.'

So they called a town meeting of the jittery colonists. Orli Covitz stood by Crim and Marla Chan Tylar, and DD brought Margaret to join them. The Governess compy stood with the seven children she watched.

Waving his hands and raising his voice, Clarin climbed onto

the bed of an engineless harvesting wagon that had been left inside the stockade. Men and women milled about, all wanting to know what was to become of them. None of them expected to hear good news.

'I won't kid you. This is bad, real bad. That doesn't mean we can't fight. We've got to do *something* before the Klikiss kill all of us.' Pushing his words through the rising swell of dismay, Clarin called on Margaret to explain what she expected the Klikiss to do. The xeno-archaeologist's words were raw and unforgiving. She laid out the facts, and some of the listeners collapsed, weeping; others clenched their fists and began looking for weapons. Clarin took hope from that. He could rally them.

'Before he left us, Davlin buried caches of explosives and fuel and weapons outside the wall. We need to retrieve them, but we've got to be unobtrusive about it. The Klikiss don't pay much attention to us, but who can tell?' He shook his head. 'No matter what happens, we can still make a difference. We're going to show that breedex thing that humans aren't going to sit around waiting for the dinner bell to ring. We're damn well going to fight back with everything we've got.'

'We didn't ask for this,' Ruis said. 'We didn't try to make the Klikiss our enemies. I admit, I didn't believe they'd turn against us. It doesn't make sense.'

From the crowd, Crim Tylar shouted, 'Shizz, Roamers are used to being picked on for no reason!'

With a grim smile, Clarin added, 'We're also used to surviving impossible situations.'

The Klikiss had cannibalized components from the Llaro structures and equipment, but shoved some items aside, leaving piles of cast-offs. Fortunately, perhaps because it was unlike their open-framework flying machines, the Klikiss had discarded the second Remora like so much junk. Though the EDF ship was partially disassembled, Clarin and three Roamer engineers slipped out at night, working with small handlights to surreptitiously repair the small craft. EDF equipment was paradoxically complicated and inefficient, but he and his team managed to reinstall the engines and run as many operational tests as possible without raising too much racket or drawing the attention of Klikiss scouts.

Most importantly, they fixed the short-range comm system. In the shadows of the cockpit, his face lit by green and amber control lights, Clarin transmitted his signal. 'Davlin. Davlin Lotze. Can you respond? Mayor Ruis seems to think you can do anything. I heard you're a former silver beret. If that's the case – shizz, even if it isn't – help us if you can.'

He didn't actually expect the man to be sitting in the cockpit of the Remora he had taken, waiting for a signal to come in. However, the ship had a comm log. Somebody in his hidden settlement of escapees should be able to get the message.

Clarin set the message on automatic repeat for every half hour and, before the Klikiss noticed the activity outside the stockade walls, he and his fellow workers slipped back in to prepare for their last stand.

SEVENTY-TWO

SIRIX

The robot fleet used its remaining EDF weaponry to continue attacking former Klikiss worlds, one at a time. Each time Sirix found a subhive, he eradicated it. He struck without warning, crushing them when he could, retreating when he could not. Better to leave the ancient worlds in smoking rubble than to let the creators have them back.

But in spite of his victories, Sirix felt he was losing ground. The scenario reminded him too much of ancient days, when the black robots lost the original war and were enslaved by the primary breedex. Although he dared not let that happen again, he would not admit he was afraid. Not yet.

Sirix lumbered about on the bridge of his Juggernaut. His two well-trained Friendly compies accompanied him like loyal puppies. 'Are we almost to our next destination?' PD asked.

'You will have something to shoot at soon enough.'

With ekti supplies alarmingly low and their stockpiles of explosives being depleted, however, he would have to make his depredations more efficient. He could not afford to waste fuel and weapons investigating every single planet formerly inhabited by Klikiss. Most of them were still empty. Sirix needed to be selective, and accurate. He would have to engage in some fights directly, *personally*, using his robots, Soldier compies, and smaller weapons from the shipboard armouries. Though it would not be as swift as a major orbital bombardment, he looked forward to the clash – face to face and claw to claw, just as in the original wars. The Klikiss would never forget it . . . no matter who survived the cataclysm.

But first he had to find a main breedex.

Landing on an unoccupied Klikiss planet, his robots surrounded a silent transportal wall. Sirix directed three Soldier compies one at a time to select coordinate tiles that led to known worlds his robots had not yet investigated. Each of the compy scouts dutifully marched through the murky stone gateway to conduct reconnaissance.

PD and QT watched the Soldier compies disappear to distant planets, searching for a major infestation. 'What will they see when they arrive?' QT asked.

'They will see if the Klikiss are there.'

'And then what will they do?'

'They will either be destroyed, or they will report back to us that the planet is empty. That is the best way to choose our next target without wasting fuel.'

Two of the scouts returned quickly, supplying spy images they had obtained. The first world was completely empty, while the second had another small (and uninvited) settlement of humans. The humans had rushed toward the Soldier compy with questions, but the compy gave no answers and simply returned through the gateway. While Sirix would have loved to wipe out the unwelcome settlement, he had greater priorities.

The trapezoidal sheet of stone blurred as another gateway opened. He expected the third compy scout to return. Instead of the smooth humanoid form of the military robot, however, Klikiss warriors with multiple limbs filled the transportal frame, pressing forward.

His Soldier compies blasted the first Klikiss before they could emerge. More ominous silhouettes appeared in the transportal, and the warriors pushed through, ready to attack.

Sirix was ready for them. As a precaution, he had already implanted EDF demolitions around the base. 'Destroy this side of the transportal.'

A quick explosion, and the trapezoidal sheet cracked and collapsed, shutting down the gateway and blocking off the Klikiss swarm. He swivelled his head toward PD and QT and all the black robots.

'Now we know the location of another Klikiss infestation we must destroy. A planet called Llaro.'

SEVENTY-THREE

TASIA TAMBLYN

After Admiral Willis had been sent packing from Theroc with her tail between her legs, more and more Roamer vessels stopped in at the Osquivel shipyards, requesting modifications and armaments. Many traders, preparing for any future attack, formed a well-armed vigilante force in the hope that they could not be taken advantage of again.

Nikko Chan Tylar's hybrid vessel caused quite a stir when it arrived at the shipyards. After being shot down by Klikiss robots on Jonah 12, Nikko's *Aquarius* had been absorbed by Jess Tamblyn's water-and-pearl vessel, and the wentals had regrown its components. The young man brought his exotic ship into one of the docking circles, carrying a load of much-needed flame-resistant gaskets, filtration mats, and durable fabrics from Constantine III.

As the Confederation's 'military' representatives, Tasia and Robb met Nikko in the small crowded cafeteria on the admin station. Tasia ran her fingers across the metal tabletop, smearing a layer of brown dust. When workers came through here at the end of every shift from the asteroid crushers and metal smelters, they brought residue with them.

Denn Peroni joined them, scanning down the *Aquarius*'s manifest and mumbling appreciatively. 'We can use all of this. Vital components for starship engine cores. Good haul, Nikko. Your parents would be quite pleased.'

Nikko slurped from a bowl of noodles, added some hot oil, then slurped again. 'My parents are missing.'

Denn nodded sympathetically. 'Everything's been a mess since the Eddies wrecked Rendezvous. We're trying to compile a database, though. Now that we've got access to green priests on various colonies, we can document who's missing and try to track them down, but it's a brain-bender.'

'I already know what happened to them,' Nikko blurted. 'The damned Eddies attacked the Chan greenhouse asteroids, took them prisoner, then destroyed a lot of the domes. I barely escaped, myself.'

Denn shook his head. 'But nobody knows where the Roamer detainees were taken. There's probably hundreds from Hurricane Depot and Rendezvous, in addition to your greenhouse asteroids.'

'I bet they have a horrific slave camp somewhere.'

Tasia leaned back in her chair. 'Relax, Nikko. It's not as bad as all that. They're on a very nice colony world – an abandoned Klikiss planet called Llaro.'

Nikko's almond eyes widened. 'How do you know this?'

'One of my duties with the EDF was to shuttle the detainees there. It's not a hell-hole prison planet. I should have thought about it before, but so many crazy things have been going on. There's no green priest on Llaro, and we didn't have the time or the ships to send an expedition.'

Nikko leapt to his feet, sloshing some of the spicy broth from his noodle bowl. 'Then I'll go! I'll take the *Aquarius*. Can you help me find Llaro?'

'Hang on a minute – it's not that simple,' Tasia said. 'There are hundreds of Roamer detainees on Llaro, and I'm sure they all want to go home. You'd cause a riot if you tried to take just your parents.'

'At least I can see them!'

'About that? There's another big catch. An EDF contingent is stationed there to watch the detainees. Who knows what's gone on since the end of the Hansa?'

'They might not even know about the big change,' Robb said.

'Well, we can't just leave them there!' Denn said. 'Imagine what wonderful PR this would be: Instead of Nikko's *Aquarius*, we outfit a larger ship and send an expedition to liberate all the kidnapped Roamers on Llaro.' Denn grinned, as if already imagining the applause and rewards he would get for staging such an operation. Tasia wondered if he did indeed have aspirations of becoming the new Speaker, following in his daughter's footsteps.

'I'll fly the ship,' she said. 'I know the layout of the Llaro colony well enough. We'll bring the detainees home to their clans.'

'Even if we *think* it's just a handful of bored soldiers stationed there, we'll pretty much be going in blind,' Robb said. 'I'd rather not try this without top-of-the-line weaponry. There's too much that can go wrong.'

Denn considered carefully. 'After all you two have done for us around here, just figure out what you need. I'll make it happen.'

SEVENTY-FOUR

RLINDA KETT

With Rhejak's tropical sun warming her skin and moist salty air filling her lungs, Rlinda lounged back in her comfortable chair. 'I sure like my job as Trade Minister. This is the kind of business meeting I could attend every day of the week, and I like this place a lot better than Earth. Quite a bit more welcoming.'

Beside her, BeBob gave a noncommittal yawn. She nudged him awake. 'You do have to pay a modicum of attention. This is *work*, you know.'

'I'm paying attention.' But he still didn't open his eyes.

Hakim Allahu, brown-skinned spokesman for the handful of independent businesses on the former Hansa colony world, sat next to them. 'Sometimes I forget how nice we have it.' He went over the manifest of goods on the datapad propped on his knees, marking what had already been loaded aboard the *Voracious Curiosity*.

'I'd expect you'd have colonists standing in line from here all the way to the next Spiral Arm. How have you kept this place a secret?' Rlinda watched dark-winged gulls swooping down to gobble up jumpers that splashed out of the waves. Dark reefs formed a labyrinth in the shallow seas.

'It's no accident that we don't have a tourism board. We let everybody think we're a rugged planet with a lot of water and not much land.'

'My lips are sealed,' Rlinda said.

BeBob rubbed his eyes. 'You forgot to mention the sea monsters. Images of those things would scare away any casual tourists.'

'Those medusas are as gentle as clams ... and about as intelligent,' Allahu said. 'Think of them as giant snails.'

'A snail with tentacles, and a shell as big as a house.'

'Literally,' Rlinda added. Most of the dwellings on Rhejak were composed of empty medusa shells. Each giant shell was enough to house a single person; families grouped empty shells together and drilled holes from one chamber to the next to make larger conglomerate dwellings.

The enormous creatures drifted in the calm waters between the sinuous reefs, making a low moaning sound as they swam in slow, endless feeding patterns. Grey-blue tentacles extended from the mouth of a huge curlicue shell. The things had two pairs of eyes, one set above the waterline for seeing in the air, the other beneath the surface for spotting fish. Dressed only in shorts, young boys rode on top of the great ridged shells, herding the medusas.

'Their meat certainly is tasty, I'll grant you that.' Since landing on Rhejak two days ago, Rlinda had eaten the delicacy prepared five different ways. Medusa meat commanded an extremely high price in the Spiral Arm, but here it was as common as beans.

Rhejak and Constantine III were business partners, 'sister

planets'. Allahu and his associates funded some of the commercial activities on Constantine III, in exchange for fresh seafood, which Roamers did not often get to eat. But Rhejak had much to offer beyond the obvious marine foods. From an adjacent reef rose the tall, skeletal towers of the Company Works. Huge pumps filtered the mineral-rich seawater, pulling out rare metals and distilling chemical precursors not found anywhere else in the Spiral Arm.

The reefs themselves, painstakingly built up by numerous small coral-like creatures, yielded a wealth of exotic crystalline structures, industrial abrasives, and calcium-rich compounds that had gained notoriety in certain health circles. Rare reef-pearls, spherical inclusions of perfectly clear crystal, were famed throughout the Hansa. Large, automated grinders and digesters crunched down reef outcroppings and sifted the resulting material. Even the rich seaweed beds offered more than edible biomass; they also produced an exceedingly potent substance akin to chlorophyll, used in a host of Hansa medical applications, including life-extension treatments.

'I don't know why the Hansa didn't manage you more effectively,' Rlinda said, 'but if we do things right, we'll be pouring wealth onto Rhejak faster than you can find places to store it.'

Allahu looked up from the *Curiosity*'s manifest. 'Look around you, Captain Kett. This is already paradise. What more could we ask for?' Not far away, two medusas faced off in the water, batting playfully at each other with their tentacles. Shirtless adolescent riders stood precariously on each shell, shouting challenges back and forth, as if it were some sort of a game.

'Isn't it about time for us to go?' BeBob asked.

Rlinda let out a long breath. 'We're off to the Ildiran Empire next to do more Trade Minister stuff, and I can't think of any more excuses to stay here. We've got deadlines to meet, delivery schedules to adhere to. Thank you, Mr Allahu.' She worked herself out of the comfortable chair and extended a hand. 'This has been wonderful, like a second honeymoon.'

'Or a tenth,' BeBob said out of the corner of his mouth.

'Stop counting my ex-husbands.' She reasserted her business-like expression. 'I'll make sure Rhejak is part of my normal trade run from now on. I'm sure we can find something you'd be interested in.'

'We'd welcome the chance to have you back,' Allahu said.

The negotiations had been exceedingly smooth. Rhejak, with its connections to the Roamers on Constantine III, had been among the first of the breakaway colonies to join the new Confederation. Everyone had agreed to switch loyalties – from the operators of the Company Works, to the medusa herders, kelp harvesters, reef grinders, and fishery homesteaders.

After loading a few more boxes of personal items and delicacies Rlinda had selected, she and BeBob climbed aboard the *Curiosity* and took off. She took a last, longing glance at the ocean and its mosaic of islands below them. Once they reached orbit, Rlinda called up nav charts to plot the best course to Ildira – a beautiful place, but not as pleasant as Rhejak.

She nearly jumped out of her skin when BeBob yelled, then scrambled for the copilot's controls. 'What the hell?'

She jerked her head up to see ten Manta cruisers in battle formation heading in their direction. The *Curiosity* had nearly run headlong into them. She changed course immediately, swerving out of the way. 'You can bet *those* aren't tourists.' Down in the hold, several cargo containers broke loose of their lashings and crashed noisily to the deck.

She hammered the transmitter. 'This is *Voracious Curiosity* calling Rhejak! You've got ten EDF Mantas showing up, and they don't look friendly.'

Beside her, BeBob said, 'Is there any way for unannounced battleships to look friendly?'

Allahu must have gotten back to his administrative hut. 'Fully armed Mantas? How can we fight against them?'

'How the hell should I know? Just . . . just be ready however you can.'

BeBob swung the controls and punched the manoeuvring engines. 'Hang on, they're ready to open fire on us!'

'Then get out of here!'

With its Roamer-modified engines, the *Curiosity* streaked past the incoming battleships, pulled up in a curve, and raced out of the system.

SEVENTY-FIVE

ADMIRAL SHEILA WILLIS

Willis's weapons officer stared at his targeting screens, his brown eyes wide and anxious. 'Admiral, should I open fire? That ship's getting away.'

'Of course not. It's just a trader. Doesn't even look like a Roamer ship.'

'But . . . but Admiral, it's seen us.'

'So what?'

'But – but then everyone will know we've come to Rhejak. They might sound an alarm, spread the word.'

'Everyone's got to know sooner or later. I thought that was the whole idea – to get the rest of the colonies quaking in their boots. We came here to impose order and reassert Hansa control. That's what I intend to do, I'm not going off on a wild goose-chase after one ship. Whoever's aboard probably already wet their pants when they saw us.'

'Yes, Admiral,' the weapons officer said sheepishly.

Conrad Brindle stepped over to the comm station, brisk and all business. 'Did that ship send any transmissions before they left?'

'Yes, sir – a message down to the surface. A warning about us.'

Willis stood from her command chair and stretched. 'Then prepare our dropships. We'd better move quickly or this'll be a mess.' As before, when she'd guided her ten Mantas to Theroc, she felt uneasy about the mission. 'Those folks down there are already used to the EDF. We'll just remind them they're still well-loved members of our one, big, happy family.'

Brindle lowered his voice. 'Don't you think that's somewhat naïve, Admiral?'

'Yes, I do. But I prefer to call it *optimism* until it's proven otherwise.' General Lanyan would have gone in with guns blazing to intimidate the poor inhabitants, but in these situations she followed a policy of non-aggression unless it was warranted.

Leaving her exec in command, she went to her quarters to change into a formal uniform, white with dark blue. She quickly ate another ham-and-cheese sandwich that was waiting for her (just in case the Rhejak islanders did not throw a welcome feast). After touching up her hair and checking the cuffs and pleats on her uniform, she was ready to join the initial wave of dropships.

Soldiers scrambled to their stations. Belowdecks, teams rushed to the landing bay, gathering the weapons and supplies needed for a full occupation force. Willis climbed aboard one of the twenty-seven dropships and gave orders to launch.

Though the ride down was bumpy, she kept her cool and stared directly into the transmission screen as she introduced herself. The fleeing trader had already blown their element of surprise. 'Since Rhejak has always been a Hansa colony, we have come to offer our assistance. By placing you under the supervision of the Earth Defence Forces, we will help you distribute your products to the Hansa, where they are most desperately needed.' She ended with what she thought was a charming smile. She knew it was pure bullshit.

The explosion of insults and angry retorts across numerous channels told her that her optimism was misplaced. She sighed and decided to confront the issue head-on. 'All right, I can see you're not happy about this. Tell my ships where we can go, and I'll talk it out with you face-to-face.'

'We'll tell you damned Eddy bastards where to go—'

Another voice cut the complainer off. 'My name is Hakim Allahu, the Trade Spokesman for Rhejak. I must remind you that we are an independent world. We have publicly discarded the Hansa Charter. The EDF has no jurisdiction here.' His defiant tone changed to resignation. 'On the other hand, we are not foolish enough to believe that we could defeat your heavily armed military force. We have no choice but to surrender to your illegal invasion.'

'Mr Allahu, who said anything about an invasion?'

'How would you define it, Admiral? You bring ten battleships to forcibly place an independent planet under – what did you call it? – EDF supervision?'

Willis knew the people would never accept this forced occupation, but she hoped to ease the pain as much as possible. She had her orders. 'I'm sorry, sir, but we've got a job to do.'

As the dropships approached the cluster of reefs and islands, she admired the beautiful blue-green sea, white beds of coral, and limestone sand. Huge tentacled things drifted about. The dropship pilots scanned the areas of dry land, and the sensor operators were in a quandary. 'Admiral, we can't land more than two dropships in any one spot. They don't have a spaceport facility.'

'Bring this ship and an escort down for my initial meeting with Mr Allahu. The rest of you circle overhead and stand ready until we figure this out.'

'In a threatening posture, Admiral?' the pilot said. 'Should we have our weapons extended as we fly above them?'

She rolled her eyes. 'I don't think they're blind, and I don't think they're stupid. Let's try for a little restraint and subtlety, all right?'

Her dropship settled on a landing pad made from a flattened section of reef. Willis emerged, forcing a smile for Allahu and his handful of Rhejak representatives. She hoped she could negotiate a peaceful resolution. 'I don't suppose you'd like to shake hands and have a conversation over a drink? I'll even provide the booze if that's your preference.'

'It's not my preference,' Allahu said. Overhead, ship after ship streaked past with an ominous drone. 'No part of this is. We're a small colony. We don't have squadrons of bureaucrats and attorneys, but I do know that what you're doing is patently illegal.'

'Depends on which set of laws you're looking at, Mr Allahu, and I don't intend to debate the matter. It's out of my hands. Rhejak produces many vital exports, and the Hansa Chairman said that you followed improper procedures in declaring your independence. Now that the hydrogue war is over, we'll just have to coexist until the Hansa is back on its feet again.'

'You mean the *Confederation*, Admiral. The Hansa isn't much of anything anymore.'

'The Hansa issues my paychecks, and so I'm here.' Out in the water she saw giant shelled creatures, rafts anchored near broad seaweed beds, and industrial elemental-separation towers that gleaned metals out of the water. She was frankly amazed at how beautiful Rhejak was. Her standard briefing had talked only about the list of local assets the Hansa considered desirable. She would have to station her own people in the major facilities to ensure continued production. 'We'll stay out of your hair as much as possible, I promise you.'

Allahu put his hands on his hips, sceptical. 'And how do you propose to do that? Where will you put all these people?' He gestured toward the two dropships and the numerous vessels still circling in the air.

'I can see you don't have enough landmass for all of us, so we'll build our own pontoon rafts. With EDF ingenuity, we can figure out how to make barracks that float.'

SEVENTY-SIX

DAVLIN LOTZE

Sheltered by sandstone overhangs, Davlin had made a comfortable, if austere, hiding place for fifty-three refugees who had slipped away from the Llaro settlement. Steinman's arrival made it fifty-four.

All Davlin had wanted was to retire and live a normal life as a normal person, but conflicts in the Spiral Arm kept drawing him back in. Now he found himself stuck being a leader and rescuer again.

Davlin had selected the most defensible grotto in the bluffs, high above the deep wash. Ever resourceful, he had rigged a power source that provided light and heat. He and two Roamers had expanded a seep in the back sandstone wall, adding a hollow tube and a filter so that they had a thin stream of fresh water. It was barely enough to meet their needs, and wouldn't be sufficient as the group grew larger.

From grasses and lightweight wood scavenged out on the plains, the refugees had fashioned a few comforts – mats, cushions, pieces of crude furniture. Everyone worked to keep the group alive, though with few amenities. Sometimes Davlin felt as if they were castaways on a deserted island, but not merely isolated. They had to keep themselves hidden from the Klikiss.

Steinman was amazed. 'I built a place like this for myself on Corribus. Well, with the help of that girl, Orli Covitz.' He paced around, prodding the furniture, poking into the food stockpiles, taking a deep sniff of some dried pods and berries the refugees had gathered. 'Of course, this is a little nicer, more sheltered. And a lot more people.' He scratched his matted hair. Weeds and bits of grass were tangled in it, but Steinman didn't seem to mind.

'We didn't have a lot of choice.' Davlin looked at the families packing up their bedding for the day, the cooks trying to scrounge just one more meal from their meagre supplies. At least they were away from the Klikiss. 'If our one Remora had stardrive engines and a long-range navigation system, I would have gone to find us help. Since that wasn't an option, I decided to make a defensible place for as many people as could get away. It's only temporary – it has to be. We can't survive like this for long.'

Without supplies and some form of agriculture, the camp couldn't become self-sufficient. Davlin had to come up with a solution soon. He knew that many of the survivors here had realized the same thing.

'I can go out hunting for us, forage for food,' Steinman suggested. 'A lot of things here are edible, provided you aren't too queasy. The lizards aren't bad. The bones are a little crunchy, and the scales leave a scraped feeling at the back of your throat, but you get used to it.'

Davlin nodded. If hungry enough, a person could eat just about anything. And these people were going to get hungry, especially since the Klikiss reapers had plundered the Llaro landscape.

'How long do you suppose it'll be before the Hansa notices that their EDF substation has gone silent?'

Davlin had considered this, and others had raised the question to him before. Years had passed before Basil Wenceslas decided to do something about the Colicos team that had gone silent on Rheindic Co. Davlin and Rlinda Kett had been sent to investigate, but only after it was much too late. 'I wouldn't count on it.'

One dark-haired young man, no more than nineteen, ran up to him. 'Davlin! There's a message in the Remora. The log light is blinking!'

'What were you doing poking around in the ship? Those instruments are delicate.'

'I just saw the light blinking, then I came back here. Maybe it's a rescue message?' The young man – one of the Crenna colonists Davlin had saved – seemed as full of desperate hope as a man clinging to a thin root while dangling from a cliff.

Davlin didn't want to quash his optimism. 'Maybe. Let's go see.'

Steinman accompanied them to a steep-walled arroyo at the base of the bluffs. When he saw the EDF ship nestled in a rocky slot eaten away by the infrequent but turbulent rainstorms, the old man let out an amazed laugh. 'You landed a Remora in that little notch?'

'It was wide enough. The next flood season will wash it away, but I hope we won't be staying here that long.' If the Klikiss were intent on hunting them down, he doubted even a colony full of silver berets could hold the line for such an extended period.

With the young man in the lead, Davlin picked his way down the steep side of the bluff, finding memorized handholds and footholds in the sandstone. One of the men had suggested chopping deeper steps or even mounting a ladder, but Davlin was reluctant to make any visible changes. The Klikiss might see.

Steinman followed them, talking nervously to distract himself from the precarious path. His fingers slipped on the cliff wall; he gasped, but caught himself.

Down in the arroyo bed, the young man pushed aside the camouflaging brush piled around the vessel, clearing the cockpit opening. 'See, look! The light is flashing.'

Davlin climbed partway inside, powered up the control panels, and checked the comm system. 'You're right. There's a message.'

Steinman leaned into the pilot's chamber, shoulder to shoulder with Davlin, while the young man wormed his way between them, listening as the log played Roberto Clarin's plea for help.

Davlin pressed his lips together. The words came as no real surprise to him. He played the message again, then looked at his two companions. 'I was making plans, but we'll have to start sooner than I expected.'

SEVENTY-SEVEN

KING PETER

While Peter held Estarra's hand and smiled encouragement, a Roamer midwife checked her over. 'It'll be another few weeks. The baby seems healthy, and so is the mother. We should have an uneventful birth.'

Peter chuckled. 'Uneventful? Biologically speaking, I hope so. But politically? The birth of this child will have huge repercussions for the Confederation and the Hansa.'

Estarra looked warmly at him. 'The Roamers are already jabbering about it. They want to throw a grand celebration to honour the birth.' He knew she had seen the spectacular party the clans threw when her brother Reynald was betrothed to Cesca Peroni.

Peter rubbed Estarra's back, and she closed her eyes and smiled at him as if ready to purr. 'Be ready to receive three hundred or so Wise Men,' he teased.

Yarrod appeared at the door, interrupting them. 'A Roamer trader has just arrived from the Golgen skymines. He says he has urgent news.'

'They always have urgent news.' Estarra patted Peter's hand. 'Don't stop rubbing my back.'

'He complains that if they just had more green priests at all the scattered skymines, they could have communicated this message instantly.' Yarrod didn't sound impressed.

'We're working on that,' Peter said. A hundred new volunteers had already been dispatched to sew together the web of communications across the Confederation. 'I'll go see what the man has to say.'

Boris Goff was talking to other Roamers in the fungus-reef city, spreading gossip and telling his story over and over. When Peter entered the throne room, Goff turned quickly. 'Ah, there you are! You know, those giant trees in orbit are enough to scare away innocent traders.'

'Better yet, they're enough to scare away the EDF.' Peter sat comfortably forward on his throne, eschewing formalities. 'Now, what's your urgent news?'

'We've got hold of a former EDF officer named Patrick Fitzpatrick III. He apparently deserted the Eddies and was wandering around, looking for us.'

Peter's brow furrowed. 'Fitzpatrick . . . I've heard of him. Isn't he the grandson of the former Chairman?'

'Who cares?' Goff was barely able to contain his enthusiasm. 'When he found Golgen, he dropped a bombshell. *He* started this whole mess! He confessed it all.'

'Which part of the "whole mess" are we talking about?'

'*He* blew up Raven Kamarov's ship. Patrick Fitzpatrick fired the first shot.'

Peter shook his head slowly. 'There's got to be more to it. Was he acting under orders?'

'Says General Lanyan told him to seize Kamarov's ekti for the Eddies and get rid of the witness.'

Peter clenched his hands. During the entire debacle, neither Lanyan nor the Chairman had spoken of this to him. Now it all fell into place. 'So, despite all the denials from the Hansa propaganda machine, the Roamers were correct in their accusations from the beginning.'

'Of course.'

No matter what Fitzpatrick had done, the greater criminal was General Lanyan, who had issued the orders. But the grand monster of all was Chairman Wenceslas, who had created the political climate in the first place, keeping vital information from the King and authorizing the actions of his underlings.

Peter put his chin in his palms and his elbows on his knees, and thought. Basil had become petty and vindictive, losing the insight, poise, and acumen that had once made him a sharp leader. The repeated crises, setbacks, and failures had worn away his open-mindedness. Peter had already been convinced that the Chairman needed to resign, but now it was more obvious than ever. He couldn't just let events take their course, not if he meant to have a solid and strong Confederation. Not if he meant for the human race to have a future.

Boris Goff was grinning with anticipation as he pressed his palms together in front of his face. Peter took a breath and raised his voice so everyone in the throne room could hear. Green priests standing outside the chamber moved closer and used telink to send his words everywhere.

'We have indisputable proof of crimes against humanity on two Hansa leaders. I hereby issue an official condemnation of both General Lanyan and Chairman Basil Wenceslas. Henceforth, these two men shall be regarded as criminals and outlaws, who must be cut off entirely from the rest of the Spiral Arm. I'll need support from all Roamer representatives, Confederation colonies, and traders travelling through the Spiral Arm. Distribute my announcement to every world, especially those that still claim loyalty to the Hansa.

'The people of Earth must take matters into their own hands. I am still their King. I call for them to rise up and overthrow the Chairman. Only then can we have peace.'

SEVENTY-EIGHT

PATRICK FITZPATRICK III

On the day Patrick was to face the clan judgment council, the Roamers held him under tight security. With the *Gypsy* impounded, the young man didn't know what Del Kellum thought he might do or where he might go. Maybe the Roamers were afraid he would sabotage the ekti reactor, destroy the anti-grav systems, and cause the whole skymine to crash into the clouds? He couldn't figure out why they would be suspicious of him, since he had searched for months to find this place – to see Zhett and to make amends, not to cause further harm.

'Your track record speaks for itself,' said a surly skymine worker who brought him a plate of spicy meat and hydroponic vegetables over rice. 'Look at the damage you've already caused. We wouldn't put anything past you.'

'No, I don't suppose you would.' He thanked the man and gratefully accepted the meal. The flavours brought back pleasant memories. Though his stomach was in knots, he scraped every last speck of the food from the dish.

If his grandmother knew what he was doing right now, she would probably laugh at him for his lack of planning and his failure to manipulate the situation to his own advantage. He had never been good at manipulation like the old Battleaxe Maureen Fitzpatrick. And for that he was glad. He didn't need to manipulate, just to be honest. Of course, he had taken her spaceship when he needed it ... Someday, he'd find a way to repay her.

Zhett hadn't come to see him, and he was still burdened by so much that he wanted to get off his chest. Confessing about Raven Kamarov was the most difficult thing he'd ever done, and he suspected that he might never get the chance now to open his heart to Zhett. That was even harder for him. Why wouldn't she at least let him say how sorry he was? He had forgotten how maddening she could be.

His metal-walled quarters felt cramped and claustrophobic. Here in a huge skymine high above the clouds, couldn't they have found him a room with a window? They had plenty of sky to go around. He thought about what he should say to the judgment council, though he didn't know what questions he would be asked. So he sat and waited ... and thought about Zhett.

The door slid open, letting in a breath of industrial smells from the outer corridor. Del Kellum stood there in a tight, dressy shirt with his clan crest embroidered on the breast; it was so fancy and clean, Patrick guessed he didn't wear the shirt often. Kellum's grey-speckled hair was neatly combed. 'Ready for this, boy? I hope you've used your solitude to find your Guiding Star.'

'I didn't know I was supposed to be looking for one.'

'Every man needs to find his Guiding Star. Come on.' Patrick dutifully followed him.

The clan judgment council consisted of Kellum and four other skymine chiefs meeting in a domed room on the topmost deck. The curved ceiling was transparent, showing the curls of pastel mists that rose all around them. As Patrick entered, the skymine chiefs eyed him with withering scorn.

Zhett sat at the head of the table beside her father. She was beautiful in a dark work uniform that fit her body far too perfectly. The only thing wrong, he thought, was that her face needed a smile. He flashed a hopeful glance in her direction, but her dark eyes were locked in the distance. He wished she would even scowl at him, yell, or snap accusations. If she would just listen to him for five minutes . . .

Kellum called the meeting to order, his normally friendly expression absent. 'Patrick Fitzpatrick III, please stand.'

He glanced down at himself. 'I am standing.'

Kellum seemed to be going through a script. 'Tell us again the crimes that you informally confessed before us. State them for the record.'

'I bet he changes his story, now that he's on trial,' Bing Palmer muttered.

'I'm not changing my story. I came here to atone for what I did, to seek forgiveness, if you're willing to offer it – or take my punishment if you won't. I came to say I'm sorry.' He hoped for some kind of reaction from Zhett, but she remained as motionless as a statue.

Nevertheless, he restated his list of transgressions, not just with regard to Raven Kamarov, but also how he had helped the interdiction warliners at Yreka, as well as many other petty indiscretions that had affected the clans. He felt giddy as he spoke, his knees weak, his heart pounding so hard that it felt like a boxer pummelling him from within his chest. 'Not that it's any excuse, but my time among the Roamers taught me that I was wrong. So I abandoned the Earth Defence Forces, left everything behind. General Lanyan would have me shot as a deserter if ever I went home.'

'Sounds like you don't have a single good option left,' said one of the chiefs.

'No, I really don't. And I expect no leniency.'

'We're not inclined to give any.' Kellum looked at his daughter. 'Unless you want to speak on his behalf, my sweet? This is up to you.'

Zhett glanced at Patrick, and for just a few seconds her icy expression seemed to melt, but she quickly found the will to refreeze it again. She shook her head, and Patrick's heart sank.

Kellum, looking like a complete stranger, placed his hands flat on the table. He loomed large and imposing. His deep voice held no emotion. 'Then, Patrick Fitzpatrick III, we have no choice. Not only did your actions result in the death of Raven Kamarov, but you confessed involvement in the murder of Yreka colonists, and caused events that led directly to the loss of countless Roamer lives and severe hardship. By the old Skyminers' Code, the rules are clear.' He crossed his arms over his chest. 'We sentence you to the winds.'

The skymine chiefs muttered uneasily; even Zhett looked sick.

Patrick glanced back and forth, trying to read details from the faces. 'What does that mean? What are you talking about?'

'Ever watch an old historical vidloop about pirates?' one of the chiefs said with a harsh snicker.

Kellum nodded. 'An apt comparison. We're a thousand miles up over the open sky, with nothing beneath but infinity. You're going to walk the plank.'

SEVENTY-NINE

TASIA TAMBLYN

Very little fanfare accompanied the completion, commissioning, and launch of each new vessel at the Osquivel yards. But this particular ship was special to the Roamers.

The people gathered for a send-off that was both a poignant christening and an excuse for a party. Tasia, Robb, and Nikko stood inside the admin hub, looking out at the new personnel carrier; some might have called it a luxury liner if it had been a bit fancier. It was designed to hold sixty passengers – twice that many, if the people were willing to endure crowded conditions. A rescue ship.

'It'll be good to get all those people away from Llaro. Shizz, I didn't like dropping them off there in the first place.'

'You said it was a nice planet.' Turning away from the view outside, Robb looked at Tasia.

'Exactly what I meant. Roamers aren't bred for nice places. Wouldn't want them to get fat and lazy!'

'Maybe not all Roamers. That's why my father left skymining in the first place and went to join my mother in the greenhouse asteroids,' said Nikko. 'He wanted something more comfortable.'

Shipyard workers gathered at the wide viewing windows. Spotlights from the spacedock ring illuminated the newly assembled hull, a patchwork of different metals. 'Here comes the drone! Everybody watch.'

A puttering carrier the size of a child's toy wagon moved forward on a ramming course. In its nose it carried a small glass cask and, with a gentle collision, it cracked open the bottle. A puff of instantly frozen vapour expanded against the side of the new ship.

'Waste of good champagne, if you ask me,' muttered Caleb Tamblyn. Tasia's uncle had come to twist Denn Peroni's arm, hoping for equipment and support crews to help out with the Plumas reconstruction work.

'Yeah, but this wasn't good champagne,' Denn said in a conspiratorial tone, then raised his voice. 'We christen this ship the *Osquivel*!' The spectators let out a round of whoops, anxious to get on with the promised feasting and drinking.

'*Osquivel*. What a name.' Robb shook his head. 'This planet has a lot of memories – most of them unpleasant. We got our butts kicked here.'

'No, Robb. The *Eddies* got their butts kicked here. The Roamers hid like rabbits and stayed safe. The name is symbolic of recovering from adversity, just as you did.'

'Explain it all you want. I still don't like it.' Robb slipped his arm around Tasia's waist and pulled her close. 'Not that I'm superstitious or anything.'

Tasia playfully rubbed his wiry hair. 'Brindle, it's a celebration! Don't go all gloom-and-doom on me.'

'Taking off in a luxury liner for a resort world like Llaro – and with my favourite sexy but bossy Roamer girlfriend. What could be better?'

Denn had liberally distributed spare packaged meals, along with fresh meats, fruits, and vegetables he had scrounged from Roamer traders passing through Yreka. From the Golgen sky-mines, Del Kellum had shipped a case of his private-stock orange liqueur. Caleb and Denn, each with a glass in hand, sipped and argued, trying to one-up each other.

'I always get in trouble when I drink with you Tamblyn brothers.'

'You get in trouble whether or not you drink,' Caleb snapped back.

Tasia sauntered up to them. 'My uncle can be awfully abrasive, Denn, but I'd consider it a personal favour if you helped him out on Plumas. Believe me, the place is a wreck. Robb and I were going to do it ourselves, but we've been called to service for the Confederation. The water mines do still belong to my clan, even if my uncles don't take very good care of them.'

'Don't take care of them!' Caleb blurted so forcefully that a fine mist sprayed from his mouth.

'I can't do it myself. Tomorrow I'm off to see the Mage-Imperator,' Denn said. 'Lots of trade negotiations to tie together. With the Confederation growing stronger and all the orphaned Hansa colonies producing surplus goods for additional markets, the Ildiran Empire is going to be a huge customer for us. Rlinda Kett's already heading there.'

'But what about my water mines?' Caleb said.

'*Our* water mines,' Tasia broke in.

'I can send him one or two bags of patch seal, a couple of workers, maybe a shovel, though I'd have to make sure he knows how to use it.' Caleb made a great show of grumbling, though Tasia could see he enjoyed the banter. 'I'll expect reduced rates on water shipments to Osquivel from now on.'

'For five years.'

'Ten years.'

Tasia left them to haggle. Even as the party continued, supplies, clothing, and some traditional Roamer treats were loaded aboard the *Osquivel*. Once news of their mission had gotten around, Tasia had so many volunteers that the *Osquivel* could have been full before it set off. 'If we take all of you, we won't have any room to bring your families back,' she said, turning them all down. She and Robb could probably handle any of the EDF babysitters left behind on the colony, and Nikko insisted on coming along, as well.

Though Robb made conversation with the Roamers, he seemed sad. Tasia said, 'All right, out with it. Something's eating you, and it's not just the name of our ship. Nightmares about the drogues again?'

'I'm done with the drogues. This is more personal. I—' he looked down, then turned his honey-brown eyes back to her. 'I've sent messages back home with traders, but . . . nothing. I expected my father to stew over my decision to stay with you and the Confederation, but I thought my mother would at least talk him into keeping in touch. No such thing. He's refused any sort of communication. I heard that he was with Admiral Willis when she brought her Mantas to bully Theroc.'

Tasia snorted. 'And do you still feel your decision was the right one?'

'Of course. I'm with you, aren't I?'

'Right answer.'

'But this silence seems so cold, so unnecessary. It worries me.'

'And you feel abandoned.' Tasia placed her hand on his arm.

He nodded. After a moment, she punched him in the shoulder

like an ill-behaved little sister. Then she held him tenderly. 'Come on back to our quarters, and I'll take your mind off your worries. Once we leave for Llaro in a few days, we'll be doing something you can be proud of, no matter what anyone else thinks.'

EIGHTY

DAVLIN LOTZE

Ilaro had plenty of stars to light their way, and Davlin's eyes adjusted easily, allowing him to focus on the goal ahead. Another mission. He'd never dreamed he would be returning under the cover of night to break back *into* the stockade settlement.

He had maintained a vigorous pace cross-country, and Hud Steinman had kept up. They understood the urgency, and both cared about the people trapped inside those resin-cement walls. Hearing Clarin's message, a whole group of the escapees had wanted to come along and join the imminent fight, but Davlin flatly refused. 'You're here now, and you all have to take care of each other. Two of us, that's enough. I don't want to have to rescue anybody a second time.'

They approached the settlement carefully, alert for any clicking or rustling sounds of warriors on the hunt. They saw the glow from makeshift lights the people had set up to drive away the shadows. Nearby, the expanded Klikiss city shone with a strange phosphorescence, and the framework of the newly erected transportal stood out in the open, large enough for the breedex to send whole armies of Klikiss off to kill other subhives.

As Steinman had promised, the openings in the stockade wall were barricaded, but not particularly secure. Davlin used a military-issue cutter to break through the makeshift gate and quietly worked it open.

Nervous and unable to sleep, the colonists kept watch, walking the streets of the enclosed town. The two men were quickly discovered and welcomed. A messenger ran to fetch Roberto Clarin, and Davlin got ready to begin his work.

Clarin had wasted no time recovering the weapons and equipment Davlin had stashed. When he came up to them, the Roamer leader's eyes were bloodshot, his dark hair tousled; it appeared as if he hadn't slept in days. Mayor Ruis looked just as haggard.

'You people from Crenna have got to stop getting yourselves into these situations,' Davlin said in his usual humourless voice.

Ruis's face lit up. 'Get us out of this one, and I promise we'll be the most boring people in the Spiral Arm.'

The prisoners had already made some preparations to defend themselves, and on an old datapad Clarin had scratched out what they'd accomplished. 'Margaret Colicos can't tell us exactly when the breedex will make its move. We've collected enough to make the bugs hurt plenty, and we've got plenty of volunteers to do the hurting. Crim and Marla Chan Tylar are already practising with the weapons, training teams of shooters.' He grinned. 'By putting us in the stockade, the Klikiss gave us the defensive high ground. A tactical error. We can stand on the walls and shoot down into them as soon as they come for us.'

'You'll run out of bullets before you run out of Klikiss,' Steinman said.

'But we'll make a mess while we're at it.'

'This wall was meant to keep you in, not to keep the Klikiss out.' Davlin ran his finger down the list: projectile weapons, stunner pistols, hand-held crowd-control devices. Many colonists had begun to build clever bolt-holes, installing hidden hatches, false walls, and secret rooms where they could hide under dire circumstances, but Davlin doubted it would help them much.

'We have to be ready at any time,' Clarin said.

'You are ready, but I can make you more ready. Every hour helps to maximize the destruction we can cause.' He tapped his finger on Clarin's list. 'I can use construction explosives to rig land-mines around where the Klikiss come and go into the stockade. I can also place bombs against this thick wall. We'll blow it open if we need to evacuate in a rush – but once that happens it's already the end-game.'

Davlin glanced at his chronometer. 'Four hours until dawn. We have to move quickly. Let's just pray that we get an extra few days before all this hits the fan.'

EIGHTY-ONE

JESS TAMBLYN

After he and Cesca departed from Theroc, having advised King Peter and Queen Estarra on Roamer clan politics, the whole Spiral Arm was theirs to explore.

Jess was excited to be alone with Cesca again, his wife, redefining not just their love for each other, but their entire reason for existence. They flew smoothly across empty space, needing no fuel or food, only the energy the wentals gave them.

'We're not just people anymore, Jess,' she said. 'Our actions could have significant consequences. By the Guiding Star, what'll we do with ourselves?'

'Before you start making decisions, let me show you exactly what we're talking about.' He smiled at her. 'Exactly what we have inside us.'

Knowing what they would find there, he brought their vessel to a brooding gas giant planet whose clouds smouldered with storms. The rust-coloured bands now seemed tied in knots. She recognized the world as Haphine, but the whole aspect of the planet had changed from the last time Cesca had been here, only a month earlier. 'Why are we here? I thought the hydrogues were defeated.'

'They are. You defeated them.'

'Well, I had some help from the wentals.'

The bubble ship dived into the ever-thickening mists, and Jess could feel echoes of the water entities permeating the clouds. He knew Cesca could sense it, too. The wentals responded and connected with the energy inside their ship and inside their very cells. Though Haphine had once been a hydrogue stronghold, he sensed no sinister anger in the energy here. The deep-core aliens were contained.

They sank into the clouds, surrounded by the gas giant's immensity, and Jess began to feel a chill. The volume of Haphine's atmosphere was orders of magnitude greater than any terrestrial planet's, incalculably vaster than any area the Roamers had settled. With all that open and unoccupied space came its own loneliness. Not a single human being lived on this entire planet, no Roamer skymines, no settlements on the scattered moons.

Finally they encountered an encrustation of domes and segmented jewel spheres, honeycombed clusters, strange geo-metric connections that formed an alien metropolis. The brightly coloured, interlinked shapes had been designed by the deep-core aliens at a density that would have crushed any organic matter. He had seen these places before. 'Each gas giant has many of these cityplexes.'

But the hydrogue city was empty and dead, destroyed. Domes were collapsed and many of the crystalline walls eaten away by wental corrosives.

Cesca was astonished. 'Wentals did this?'

'*We* did it, by bringing them here.'

'The hydrogues attacked us. They started this war.'

'But it wasn't a new conflict, and this time they lost. The

hydrogues are still here, just like the wentals weren't entirely destroyed when they were defeated the last time. But the balance has certainly shifted.' The water-bubble vessel circled the ruins of the cityplex, and Jess and Cesca both stared. 'Wental power was sufficient to cause this disaster, and yet the two of us have the strength to do other things as well.' He touched her, feeling the tingle through her skin. 'We can build instead of tear down, create instead of destroy.'

As soon as he said it, he knew Cesca could feel the surge of possibilities within herself. 'Without question, Jess. Where do we go first?'

The wental ship took one last flight around the hydrogue city. 'Back to Plumas, of course.'

The ice moon glittered in the distant starlight, its frozen surface illuminated by station lights and demarcated landing zones. The Roamer communication bands were filled with conversations between tanker ships, repair crews, and groundside excavators. Jess could see that the pumping clusters had been erected again; transfer domes, docking stations, and access huts were now aglow. The frozen crust showed tracks and melt marks from the increased traffic. But underground, he knew the water mines would be a different story. His mother – no, the tainted wental that had possessed his mother – had caused so much damage.

Beneath the kilometre-thick ceiling, they found Caleb, Wynn, and Torin Tamblyn bossing crews of borrowed engineers from Osquivel who wrestled with spare excavation and construction equipment. Jess's uncles yelped when they saw the two of them emerge from the ice, walking directly through the murky wall. 'Come to take another look at the mess here, Jess?' Wynn said.

'Come to do something about it.'

'We can always use the help.' Caleb put his hands on his hips, watching the ongoing work as if he was in charge of it all. 'You should have heard Denn Peroni complain about all the better things these professional engineers could be doing – but I called in some favours.'

'Where is my father?' Cesca asked, looking around and hoping to see him.

'He's at Ildira for some trade negotiations. I don't know why he'd want to go to the Prism Palace's sunshine and banquets when he could be here, with all this.' Caleb raised his hands to indicate the enormity of the destruction.

The shipyard workers were shoring up the cracked and damaged walls with thick alloy girders that had originally been fabricated as a spaceship framework. The smell of exhaust fumes had not yet been filtered from the underground air. Parts of the discoloured walls had been scoured to a mirrorlike reflective white, while drilling teams worked to straighten and repair the shafts.

Jess looked up at the newly installed girders. He and Cesca could feel the fractures like aches in their bones. 'Those support stabilizers won't be more than a band-aid for the fissures that run through the ceiling.'

'It's all we've got.'

'We can lighten your workload.' Jess reached over to take Cesca's hand. Every time they touched, it felt as if an electric circuit was completed.

Cesca said to the Plumas workers, 'You'll have to take care of the equipment and machinery yourselves, but we can deal with the water and ice.'

Jess raised his hands, and energy sparkled from his fingertips. 'The wentals have agreed to infuse the water molecules, inhabit the ice, and let the two of us reshape this place into what it should be.'

The Tamblyn brothers looked at each other uncertainly. 'Didn't you say that the wentals would contaminate this place?' Wynn asked. 'Our business is pumping water. We can't have it all . . . alive and energized.'

'The wentals assure me they can withhold their propagation and then withdraw when we are finished. They won't *change* it, the way they've changed me and Cesca.'

'All right. If you're sure, then be my guest,' Caleb said. 'If you save us months of work, then who are we to complain?'

Jess felt the wentals within him building up their energy in preparation. He and Cesca independently knew what to do, and took separate tasks. Even when he let go of her hand, the power within him did not decrease. He walked on the packed ice to the edge of the subterranean ocean, knelt on the frozen shore, and extended his finger into the cold sea. Tendrils of wental energy swirled out from him so that the seawater became like an artist's paint or a sculptor's clay. He drew up curtains of water that stayed, glistening, exactly where he put them.

From deep down where the artificial suns could not penetrate, he continued to draw up new currents and stir what had been left undisturbed for a long time. He sensed the pulsing, living nematodes that Karla Tamblyn had controlled, but the creatures' primitive brains remembered nothing about the attack. He explored with wental senses, but did not contaminate or harm any of the creatures.

Cesca went to the nearest wall, pressed her palm against the ice, and released her power into the frozen structure. She shifted the water molecules aside and parted the ice, letting her arm sink in up to the shoulder. Sparkling light spread out from her hand like ripples in a pond as wentals flowed into the thick ice and shot upward to find the flaws and cracks, to seal the deep fissures like a surgeon suturing an incision.

Jess drew more water from the sea and fashioned patches and seals out of new, clear ice, using it like putty to refill the gouges left by Karla's explosions, to reinforce the cracked shore so that the pumping machinery could be installed on solid, level ground.

Jess drew down support columns like stalactites and pulled up water from the ocean, freezing them together into swirled pillars that were as ornamental as they were functional. Jess and Cesca smoothed the rough-hewn walls and straightened the shafts that held the industrial lifts. They anchored heavy fixtures in the ceiling for the installation of new artificial suns.

The Tamblyn brothers and the Osquivel shipyard workers had to scurry out of the way so as not to be swept aside in the rapid reconstruction. What would have required months or even years for the Roamer workforce to complete, Jess and Cesca finished in less than an hour.

Tingling with energy, the two stepped back to inspect the results. The walls and ceiling of the grotto throbbed with left-over lambent energy. Wynn and Torin stood with identical expressions, their mouths agape, looking more like twins than Jess had ever seen them; Caleb remained sceptical, as if sure that something would still go wrong, no matter how bright and shiny everything appeared.

The wentals seemed reluctant to leave their new habitation. They had gained strength and even pleasure by infusing the ice moon. 'It's time to withdraw,' Jess said.

We know.

All of a sudden, he felt energy streaming back into him. The phosphorescence drained out of the walls, withdrew from the shining pillars, and rose back up from the depths of the sea. The shining wonder left the frozen moon, and it returned to normal.

Jess let out a long breath. Cesca wrapped her arms around his neck and hugged him. 'We've done a good day's work.'

EIGHTY-TWO

DENN PERONI

When the *Dogged Persistence* landed on Ildira, Denn self-consciously touched the ribbon that held his hair back. He had dabbed a bit of cologne on his neck and put on his finest outfit. Caleb thought of him as a dandy, overly concerned with his personal appearance, his clothes, and 'colourful plumage like some fancy bird', but Denn didn't let the teasing bother him. Caleb himself could have paid a bit more attention to personal appearance and hygiene.

Inside the Prism Palace, Rlinda Kett and Branson Roberts were already in the midst of a diplomatic reception. He learned that he had – thankfully! – missed the performance of Ildiran singers. Denn had never understood the alien music.

The Mage-Imperator welcomed him and asked him to take a seat at his long table near the other human traders. 'Captain Kett has been telling me about the new government humans are forming. It always intrigues me to know of your political differences and difficulties, although I do not truly comprehend them.'

'Neither do we, Sire. We're still trying to figure it out after thousands of years. But we do our best.'

Servant kithmen moved about like frenetic worker ants, hurrying to bring him his own plate and a wildly extravagant meal. It certainly beat prepackaged shipboard food and the commissary fare at Osquivel.

During the meal, they spoke of opening various trade routes, expanding markets for Ildiran goods, ekti from Roamer sky-mines, exotic items from Theroc, heat-resistant materials from Constantine III. Rlinda was, after all, the Trade Minister, and Denn was the designated representative of the Roamer clans.

Except for the news about the EDF invading Rhejak and the generally grim reports from Earth, Denn felt that times were getting better. Stories of the Klikiss returning from wherever they had disappeared millennia ago sounded more like fairy tales than any real threat, though Denn did not doubt the reports.

He had been to Ildira before, but he was impressed with the changes. 'I saw your space construction facilities from orbit, Sire. You're rebuilding the Solar Navy ten times faster than my Roamer shipyards can do the work. Must be your perfect Ildiran cooperation.'

The Mage-Imperator smiled. 'Actually, we have humans to thank for this efficiency. Our industrial operations are managed by an engineer named Tabitha Huck. She was among the Hansa cloud harvesters who were our . . . guests for some time. We offered her a job.'

'*Hansa* humans accomplished that?' Denn said, offended by the very idea. 'Maybe I could learn a thing or two from her.'

The Mage-Imperator turned to one of his bureaucratic kithmen, who hurried off. 'I shall arrange for you to tour our operations.'

*

The orbiting shipyard hub was a model of efficiency, and Denn couldn't believe what he was seeing. Space construction workers flew about in precise coordination like well-choreographed dancers; the warliner components were assembled as if they *wanted* to go together. He saw not a single misstep, not the slightest hesitation. 'This is incredible, Ms Huck. By the Guiding Star, I've never seen anything like it. This boggles my mind.'

Ildirans seemed to share a telepathic bond, but the few dozen former Hansa engineers (who had never impressed Denn before) were just as attuned to each other. Tabitha guided the work crews from her central station; her underlings passed along curt orders, abbreviated instructions, sketchy details – and everyone followed them with perfect synergy.

Tabitha had a squarish jaw and a blunt nose that made her look just a bit too rough to be attractive, and her hair was cut short and straight in a serviceable but not stylish fashion. Even so, she had a *radiance* about her, a satisfaction and contentment that gave her an entirely different sort of beauty. 'It's simple enough if you know how to do it, Mr Peroni. Once others understand you in such a way that all wishes become common, then all instructions turn to mutual consent. Each person knows what he or she should do and what everyone else is doing. No unnecessary redundancy. Everything comes off without a hitch.'

'But *how* do you do it?' Denn stared at the bustling spacedocks. In only an hour, it seemed, half of the hull plates had been installed on the frame of a new warliner. 'Maybe I should hire Ildirans, if they work so well with humans. Can you give me any pointers?'

'I can do better than that.' Her smile broadened, and her skin seemed to glow.

As if he had been summoned, Kolker came into the chamber wearing a prismatic medallion over his bare emerald chest. 'I've discovered a new technique. *Thism*, telink, and human thoughts. I can remove a blindfold that none of us knew we were wearing.'

'Is it a trade secret, or are you willing to share? Name your price if it works as well as Ms Huck says.'

'There is no price. I'm glad that you're so interested.' Kolker fingered the medallion. 'I just need to show it to you.'

'For free? That doesn't make any sense.'

'My reward is seeing the expression on your face when you understand.'

'Whatever you say.' Denn let the green priest lay a palm on his forehead, as if giving a blessing. 'Is this some kind of religious ceremony? What does that have to do with—'

'I believe I'm strong enough to do it without my treeling. I have the Lightsource, the soul-threads, the telink, and now if only I can find . . . ah, there.'

The flesh of Kolker's palm seemed to grow warmer against Denn's brow. Before he could raise any questions, a thousand light bulbs illuminated his mind. His senses filled to overflowing. He saw everyone and everything around him – the Hansa engineers, the Ildirans and their *thism*, the spacecraft, the construction yards, the planet itself, the six nearby suns. His mind felt as if it had been pulled wide open, and he could find no words to express his joy.

'Wow!' was the best he could manage.

EIGHTY-THREE

SULLIVAN GOLD

While the *Voracious Curiosity* was preparing to depart, the Mage-Imperator granted Sullivan the permission he needed to leave the Ildiran Empire. He found Captains Kett and Roberts in discussions with bureaucrat kithmen over Ildiran goods to be loaded aboard the ship. It took Rlinda a moment to recognize him. 'Sullivan Gold, right? Weren't you the administrator of the Hansa cloud harvester?'

'Yes,' he said, but after that words failed him. It wasn't really so much of a favour to ask, but it would mean the world to him. 'Mage-Imperator Jora'h suggested I talk to you. I'm very anxious to get my life back to normal, to see my wife, my grandchildren. It's been very difficult to get messages to Earth. Is there, um, is there a chance I could have passage aboard your ship?'

'To Earth?' Roberts said. 'You've got to be kidding.'

'To Earth, or at least to some Confederation or Roamer outpost where I can book passage aboard another ship. I don't care how long it takes, but I'm certainly not getting any closer to my family by staying here. The Mage-Imperator has promised to pay any fee you wish to charge.' When Rlinda snickered, he asked defensively, 'What's so funny?'

'Ildirans don't have a clue about how to negotiate. They can't imagine someone might take advantage of an open-ended offer like that.'

'I'm sure he's sincere,' Sullivan said. The Mage-Imperator had already given him a case of precious gems and valuable metal chits that would pay off most of his family's debts.

'Oh, I believe it. But the *Curiosity*'s got a full load of trading items,' Rlinda said cautiously. 'I'm the Trade Minister, you know. How many others do you expect to take along?'

Sullivan scratched his cheek, feeling the rough stubble; he had forgotten to shave again. 'It'll just be me. The others are working with Tabitha on rebuilding the Solar Navy, and our green priest has become fascinated with new revelations, or religion, or whatever it is he calls it. They've all become rather inseparable – in more ways than one. I'm the only one who wants to go.'

'We can work something out.' Rlinda picked up the diamond-film sheet one of the Ildiran trade ministers slid toward her. 'We're leaving tomorrow, so you'd better start packing.'

Tabitha and Kolker faced him aboard the main construction station, but their minds were elsewhere, preoccupied. Kolker seemed adrift in a silent conversation, as he had often done when chatting with green priests through telink. But this was something more.

'Are you sure you want to stay here?' Sullivan asked for the third time.

'We're happy,' Kolker said.

'And I've got the most cooperative workforce I've ever seen,' Tabitha said. 'The Ildiran workers follow me around like little ducklings, and the Mage-Imperator is paying more than fairly. What more could I ask for?'

'And you, Kolker? We could bring you back to Theroc.'

'I can be on Theroc whenever I like simply by touching the worldtree. I have more important work to do here, and I already have many converts among the green priests.' Then he paused, musing. 'And, now that Denn Peroni has joined us, I realize the greater possibilities in the Spiral Arm.'

Sullivan was surprised at that. 'Denn Peroni?'

'He wanted to know how we can run our work so efficiently,' Tabitha said with a contented smile. 'He was very impressed.'

'And after I showed him, he felt as if he had suddenly seen the solution to a very complex puzzle he'd been working on all his life.'

Tabitha was almost pleading. 'It would take only a few minutes and you'd understand, Sullivan. You'd see the big picture, like we do.'

He could see their fascination, their acceptance, but thankfully he wasn't worried that they would force him. These two were still his friends, and they did not do anything against his wishes. They were not proselytizers or fanatics, just *changed*. 'I've seen as much of the picture as I care to. I don't begrudge you your happiness. I want to thank you for your years of service. It wasn't always easy.'

'It led us to here,' Tabitha said. 'I don't regret a moment of the journey.'

He gave them each an awkward hug, hurriedly gathered his belongings, and went to find Captain Kett and her *Voracious Curiosity*.

EIGHTY-FOUR

SIRIX

As the robot-controlled battleships approached Llaro, Sirix planned his attack against the breedex and its growing subhive. With their resources limited, he and his robots would make a new and direct kind of assault. Although it was more dangerous, and risked the loss of his robots, it was also like the old wars – the very reason the robots had been created.

As the group of ships entered orbit, QT pointed out helpfully, 'I have downloaded all available background information about human activities on Llaro, their facilities and main industrial outputs. I can deliver a summary, if you wish.'

'I am not interested in the human settlement. My concern is with the Klikiss infestation. We will destroy it, as we have destroyed the other subhives we encountered. The human presence there is not relevant.'

The expanded sensor suite showed a thriving Klikiss subhive, exactly as Sirix had expected. Freshly built mounds and spires rose ten storeys tall. Workers and equipment bustled around the old ruins. A newly erected transportal stood out in the open near a walled-in village of human colonists. All the vegetation around the infestation had been razed, and Sirix inferred that the breedex was about to fission. Other subhives around the Spiral Arm would be doing the same, preparing to fight each other. Sirix would stop them wherever he could.

'Their defences are significant,' PD said.

'And their numbers as well,' QT added.

'We will be ready for them.' Sirix convinced himself he was right. In previous attacks, he had preferred to operate from a safe distance, deploying the battle group's large-scale explosives, ship-to-ship jazer banks, guided bombs, and atomic warheads. This would be a ground assault, and the EDF armouries were still full of jazer rifles, pulse blasters, high-power stunners, and shoulder-mounted projectile launchers.

Sirix assigned small arms to all Soldier compies and black robots. Together, he had nearly a thousand robots remaining, and twice that many Soldier compies. The swift dropships had been stripped of safety interlocks so the robots could descend at projectile velocity, smash onto the strip-harvested ground outside the Klikiss city, and rush outward in a berserker charge. The subhive could not withstand that.

Sirix rode down in the rattling, roaring dropship beside PD and QT. Though he knew they could be competent fighters, he was bringing the two compies along primarily to show them the awful nature of the Klikiss race. And so that the violent battle they witnessed would inform them of the scope of the ancient wars between the black robots and their creators. The two captive compies were very receptive to learning new things.

Like a rain of meteors, the robot fighters slammed into the landscape outside the walled-in human settlement. Despite the rough landing, Sirix regained his footing immediately, opened the hatch, and emerged with the two compies beside him. Black robots and Soldier compies spilled out from all the dropships, heavily armed with EDF weapons.

Marching forward, they began to open fire on any Klikiss target. Scouts, harvesters, and engineers died by the hundreds. The Klikiss squealed and whistled, while the robots and compies were ominously silent, moving forward metre by metre, faster than the hive mind could react.

Ahead, the tall new transportal stood in front of the Klikiss city, and Sirix postulated that the breedex might already have sent many of its warriors to other planets to establish additional subhives or to wipe out rival breedexes. Prominent among the newly built Klikiss structures, he discerned the squat structure where the hive mind dwelled. That was his primary target.

He noted without surprise that the barricade surrounding the human settlement was obviously Klikiss-made. Terrified-looking people had scrambled up makeshift ladders to stand atop the thick wall and stare at the forward push of the black robots. The breedex had trapped these colonists inside a well-defined boundary. Sirix could not fathom the reason. Was it just to keep the humans out of the way, or did the Klikiss have some other purpose? How could humans possibly be useful?

Scrambling to put together a defence, hundreds of spiny warriors scuttled forward, some of them flying. With no regard for their own protection, the Klikiss warriors threw themselves upon the front ranks of Soldier compies, and they fell in great numbers to the barrage of high-powered jazers and rocket-launched projectiles.

But the insect creatures advanced so swiftly that many of them were still alive to close with the Soldier compies. The Klikiss dismantled the compies and crashed into the black robots, ripping them apart. Sirix fought with a furious abandon. Seeing one of the towering domates emerge at the rear of the wall of spiny warriors,

Sirix sent out a sharp signal to his comrades and the compies. 'Destroy the domate. That is a primary priority.'

The metal army caused great mayhem as they drove toward the well-defended hall of the breedex. Four of the robots clustered around the towering domate. They shot and smashed and attacked, and finally the silver-and-black-striped creature fell, tumbling forward – a great victory.

PD and QT marched along beside Sirix, shooting their own firearms and taking an impressive toll. QT turned his optical sensors back toward the stockade wall where the helpless humans were watching the great clash. His words startled Sirix. 'Look, the colonists have compies here, as well.'

The black robot swivelled his flat head to see two compies standing together among the horrified humans. One was a drab Governess model, the other a Friendly. A familiar-looking Friendly compy. Sirix paused in his forward march.

'That is DD.'

EIGHTY-FIVE

ORLI COVITZ

'That is Sirix,' DD said, his artificial voice slipping up an octave in alarm.

From the wall, Orli watched the swarms of black robots emerge from their dropships and began massacring the Klikiss. Terrified of what the breedex would do to them, the colonists had prepared their meagre defences while getting one last group ready for a timely escape. But no one had anticipated this invasion.

Earlier that day, Marla Chan and Crim Tylar – who'd come to think of themselves as Orli's surrogate parents – had packed clothes and some food they really couldn't spare, and made ready to send the girl off, if the chance should present itself. Orli had rolled up her lightweight synthesizer strips and stuffed them into her pack.

Then the robots had landed.

Orli didn't know whether to cheer or scream. These black robots were killing more of the Klikiss than the human defenders could have hoped to. Yet, these robots had slaughtered everyone on the Corribus colony, including Orli's father. She hated them.

'That is *Sirix*,' DD repeated. 'We must escape from here.'

'Those robots look a little busy right now,' said Mr Steinman. 'They don't have time to bother with us.'

As if to contradict the old man's assurances, Sirix pointed an articulated metal arm toward the stockade and sent out a chittering signal. A group of the invading robots detached from the forward assault and turned toward the settlement. With their EDF weapons, they blasted the wall, chewing large craters in the resin cement.

'Get to cover!' Davlin said. 'They're not shooting at us directly, but they obviously want to get inside.'

'They want to get to *us*,' Orli said as they scrambled down behind the uncertain safety of the barricade.

'And me.' DD sounded very afraid.

The black machines swarmed toward the stockade, while others charged into the masses of spiny Klikiss.

Marla and Crim had their groups of trainees ready to defend against the enemy with their scavenged firearms. But they were clearly reluctant to open fire on the black robots. 'I hate to waste our ammunition,' Marla said.

'I *do* want to waste some of those robots,' her husband answered.

UR said, 'I must protect the children. If this is an opportunity to escape, I suggest we take it.'

'It's more than an opportunity,' Davlin said. 'With this diversion we can move twice as many people out of here as I'd hoped. Get a group and make a break for it while the Klikiss and the robots distract each other.'

'*Distract* each other?' Mr Steinman said. 'They're beating the crap out of each other!'

'All the better,' Crim said. 'Which side should we root for?'

When Margaret joined them, she looked both dismayed and hopeful because of the unexpected attack. 'No matter which group emerges victorious today, they will still want to destroy us.'

'Where will we go?' DD said. 'Will you be coming with us?'

'It isn't yet clear what I have to do.'

Marla nudged her husband. 'If there's a group getting out of here, Crim, then you've got to go with them.'

'I will not! I'm staying with you.'

'We had an agreement. Neither one of us is going to be safe. The escapees in Davlin's hideout will need your protection as much as these townspeople need mine. One of us has to get out of this alive for Nikko – wherever he is.'

'We were supposed to flip a credit chip.'

'I did – you lost. I'm a better shot anyway.'

Crim was flustered. 'No you're not. We're even.'

'Not today. Go with them!' She gave him a quick kiss, squeezed Orli in a hug, and scrambled up a rickety ladder to the top of the thick wall where her gunners had already begun to open fire. Marla and her recruits shot at the robots, knocking several of them from the wall like massive cockroaches.

Davlin grabbed Mr Steinman's scrawny arm and pushed him toward Orli, the Governess compy, and the children. 'Lead them back to the sandstone bluffs. Mayor Ruis, you join them.'

'But how are we going to get out of here without anyone seeing?'

A projectile-launched explosive from the swarming robots blew up one of the Klikiss towers. It slowly collapsed, crumbling, wobbling, then shattering on the ground.

'This mess is going to last a long time. Just *run*! I'll make a nice big door for you.' Davlin reached into his pocket and found the remote control; without hesitating, he pressed the detonator. The construction explosives he had planted blew a large gap through the barricade.

Orli hesitated as the dust cleared. Now they could all flee to the open desolate plain, but there was little shelter in the arroyos and draws, only a few boulder outcroppings and dead, clawlike trees.

UR marched forward, pushing the children ahead of her. Mr Steinman, Mayor Ruis, and Crim Tylar ran along with a group of others. DD turned. 'Come with us, Margaret!'

The older woman hesitated and looked directly at Orli. 'You have your synthesizer strips? Keep the others safe if the Klikiss come after you.'

'What do you mean? Will the breedex still recognize me?'

'Use your music. DD, go along and help them!'

'Should I not remain with you, Margaret?' The compy's voice clearly showed that he was torn.

'You can do more good for them. Now go!'

Several black robots clambered over the wall. Another part of the barricade was destroyed by repeated blasts from their weapons. Seeing Sirix approach was all DD needed to set him in motion again.

EIGHTY-SIX

MAGE-IMPERATOR JORA'H

A s the Mage-Imperator greeted representatives of various kiths, he watched Daro'h's face, reading the intelligence and sensitivity there. Instead of spending another day servicing one pleasure mate after another, as a Prime Designate normally did, Daro'h attended his father and Nira in the skysphere audience chamber.

Jora'h had been poorly prepared when his father's death had forced him to ascend prematurely to his position, and he would not make the same mistake with Daro'h. A Prime Designate must never forget that one day he would lead the Ildiran Empire. By now, the burn marks on the young man's face had mostly healed, but the angry redness would remain for a long time. Daro'h remained distraught over what he feared the faeros might be doing.

Jora'h couldn't blame him. Since before Adar Zan'nh had left on his mission of mercy, the Mage-Imperator had sensed the constant arpeggio of anxiety across his Empire, like the plucking of strings on a taut musical instrument. There was also an emptiness, a troubling silence in the *thism*. His scouts had not returned from

the Horizon Cluster. Neither had he received any report from
Tal O'nh in his procession around the once-rebellious worlds, nor
had he heard anything from the scientific team on Hyrillka. No
one was reporting.

After two hours of court duties, the line of pilgrims that came
to see him still seemed endless. Jora'h gave a discreet signal to
Yazra'h, who strode to the base of the dais with her three Isix
cats and rapped her crystal spear on the polished stone floor. 'The
Mage-Imperator requires a recess – and some privacy. Would you
like me to leave as well, Liege?'

Jora'h shook his head as the pilgrims dutifully departed. 'All of
you can offer valuable advice.' He reached out to clasp the hand
of the green priest at his side. Because the Ildirans were already so
troubled – or at least mystified – by Nira's unorthodox presence
here, she spoke few words when he held court. But she was there,
giving her silent support.

Daro'h sat on the dais next to the chrysalis chair. 'What do
you wish, Liege?'

'I should ask you the same question, my son. It is plain you are
troubled.'

'I fear for Dobro. Have we had word about the people there?
Are they safe? They have been through so much – both the
humans and the Ildirans – and now are left without a leader. Can
they govern themselves?'

'They can if given the chance,' Nira said, perhaps a little too
sharply. 'This may be what they need.'

'You have greater responsibilities now, Prime Designate,' Jora'h
said. 'Concern yourself with *all* Ildiran people, not just those on
Dobro.'

'I understand, Liege. And yet . . .' Daro'h was the opposite
of callous and self-centred Thor'h. As the second noble-born
son, he had followed in Designate Udru'h's footsteps, believing

that his sole responsibility was the splinter colony of Dobro, never imagining he would become Prime Designate. 'What can we do about the faeros?'

'I do not know what happened with my brother Rusa'h. I do not even know how he remains alive. When he flew into the sun, he meant to plunge directly into the Lightsource, not to cause us any further damage.'

'The faeros changed him somehow,' Daro'h said. 'I saw it.'

Jora'h nodded. 'His injured mental state, his flawed *thism*, must have opened him to them. As bizarre as that may sound, it is not unheard-of. I have recently learned that other Ildirans were united with the faeros in the past.'

The research being done by Rememberer Vao'sh and his human counterpart had begun to shed light on the problems the Empire faced. Though Jora'h found it frightening to learn even more unexpected truths, he did find the knowledge invaluable. If only he could put it to use.

Their new information revealed part of what had really happened during the old war against the Shana Rei, creatures that swallowed up all light and drove Ildirans insane. Tales of the Shana Rei were used to describe Ildiran heroes in circumstances that required bravery and sacrifice. With careful reading some rememberers had discovered a layer of nuance that suggested the Shana Rei were entirely fabricated, a mere fiction created to fill in the blanks produced by covering up the original hydrogue war. Yet that itself was only another veneer of lies. Investigating further, Vao'sh had discovered that the Shana Rei were real after all. And the faeros had helped Ildirans defeat them.

For the first time, Jora'h shared the alarming story that Rememberer Vao'sh and Anton Colicos had found in the long-sealed apocrypha. 'Long ago, some Ildirans discovered how to link with the faeros, much as green priests can connect with the worldforest. When it looked as if all Ildirans would perish before the Shana Rei, an ancient Mage-Imperator named Xiba'h begged the faeros for assistance. He was sure that only their elemental fire could drive away the creatures of darkness. When he was unable to summon them, when he could not convince them even to speak with him, Mage-Imperator Xiba'h prepared his Prime Designate, and made a tremendous sacrifice to call the faeros.'

'What sacrifice?' Daro'h asked.

'He got the attention of the faeros by immolating himself. The Mage-Imperator set himself on fire in the middle of Mijistra. The blaze was potent and incredible. As the flames consumed Xiba'h, the anguish that he emanated through the *thism* attracted the faeros. The creatures came, after all, and agreed to offer their aid. Faeros fireballs struck the creatures of darkness.'

'That's a terrible story, Jora'h,' Nira said.

'And yet it is a true one.'

Daro'h asked something the Mage-Imperator had not considered. 'Is that why the faeros have turned against us now? When Rusa'h plunged into the sun, did he make a greater sacrifice? Did they go to him instead of to you?'

'I hope you are not right, but I have learned not to underestimate Rusa'h.'

EIGHTY-SEVEN

HYRILLKA DESIGNATE RIDEK'H

Full circle. Tal O'nh and the escort warliners had finally completed their grand circuit around the Horizon Cluster. They had stopped at rebellion-scarred Shonor, Alturas, Garoa, and all the other worlds Rusa'h had ensnared with his corrupted *thism*.

Ridek'h now realized that the Mage-Imperator had intended this pilgrimage to be far more than a ceremonial tour or political show. During the journey, the young man had learned much by seeing other shocked Designates who had faced equally difficult challenges. Though he was just a boy, Ridek'h felt a greater confidence now, a willingness to face what had terrified him before, and a strong sense that he could actually do what was required of him. He had the assistance of the veteran tal, as well as the work and dedication of the Ildiran people. *His* people. The boy was not alone after all, and he was not weak. He would not give up.

Now Tal O'nh brought the ships back to Hyrillka, the world that young Ridek'h would lead, if the scientific team ever deemed it safe for Ildirans to return. With his own eyes, the boy had seen the faeros and hydrogues battling in Hyrillka's primary sun, and he had watched the planet's climate shift as the star nearly died. He himself had given the order for all of the brave inhabitants to pack up and evacuate. Now Ridek'h hoped that the scientist kithmen would pronounce Hyrillka fit for renewed habitation.

When the warliners reached the planet, however, they found the scientific camp utterly annihilated. The partially rebuilt main city had been consumed by an inferno. The Solar Navy ships cautiously flew above the seared ground, all systems on alert. Buildings stood as no more than charred frameworks. The scientific encampment had been incinerated by such an intense flash that the new shelters were no more than patterns of ash.

'What happened here?' Ridek'h cried.

With a replacement jewel set firmly in his empty eye socket, the old tal stared at the images. 'It is obvious what happened. The faeros. Prime Designate Daro'h warned us of the danger.'

Ridek'h took his place beside the old commander. 'Show me the citadel palace. That was Rusa'h's home. Could he have done such a thing?' The answer appeared in the next set of images. The citadel palace was blackened and glassy, slumped in upon itself, the very stones melted.

Ridek'h could not comprehend why the fiery elementals would have burned away so many buildings, landmarks, and a handful of non-threatening researchers. What could be the reason? 'They cannot all be dead. They cannot!' He turned smartly to the communications station, then looked over at his mentor, who nodded in approval. 'Transmit on a broad band.' His voice sounded high and thin even to his own ears, but he reminded himself that he was the *Designate*. 'This is Hyrillka Designate Ridek'h calling anyone who can receive this message. Please respond.'

An oddly familiar – and deafening – voice boomed across the speakers in the command nucleus. Ridek'h clamped his hands over his ears. 'So the name of my would-be usurper is *Ridek'h*. A child.' The observation screen seemed to burst into flames. The images turned to rippling fire, and a face appeared – Rusa'h! 'You are not the true Hyrillka Designate. I returned here to pull my subjects back into my *thism* web, but they had all gone away. The handful of researchers I consumed was barely enough to help the faeros at all.'

'Pinpoint the source of that transmission,' O'nh shouted. 'Where is it coming from?'

'Faeros fireballs directly ahead, Tal!'

'Activate all defensive measures.' Five flaming ellipsoids roared toward them. 'Immediate escape vector. Full acceleration.'

Ridek'h had gone pale. He turned to the military commander. 'Should I respond to him? What do I say?'

'There is nothing you can say, Designate. We must leave here.'

Ridek'h straightened, clutching at straws of bravery. 'But this is Hyrillka. This is *my* planet. He has attacked my people!'

'And he is the mad Designate, in league with the faeros. We can do nothing except get you to safety. That is my priority.'

As the warliners accelerated, the fiery elemental ships came at them like gigantic cannonballs. The boy remembered the conflagration and battle in Hyrillka's sun. If the faeros could eradicate a diamond-hulled hydrogue warglobe, the Solar Navy battleships did not stand a chance.

When the warliners cleared the atmosphere of Hyrillka, the deck tilted from a severe course-change manoeuvre, and the boy stumbled against the command station. As they headed out into space, the faeros fireballs continued to pursue them.

'Return to me.' The mad Designate's words came like a blast from a flamethrower, but the tal did not heed him.

'Prepare to activate stardrive the moment we are clear,' O'nh shouted. No one knew if a faeros ship could follow at the extreme lightspeed available with the Ildiran engines. No one knew much about them at all.

The faeros closed the distance. Flame blasts seared the ornate anodized hulls. Systems overloaded. One after another, damaged engines went offline, but the warliners limped along with what power they had left, reeling off course yet careening onward. Solar Navy weapons officers fired projectiles, energy beams, and explosives, none of which had any effect on the elemental vessels.

Ridek'h did not know how the warliners could ever get away. He squeezed his eyes shut, trying to find the Mage-Imperator through his *thism* connection, but though he was the official Designate, he was a generation removed from the strongest strands. Ridek'h could not communicate what he needed to.

The young Designate saw the hard decision cross Tal O'nh's face. The old commander spoke to the captain of the last warliner in the group. 'Septar Jen'nh, I require you to delay the faeros. Our priority is to see that Designate Ridek'h returns to the Mage-Imperator. He must survive.'

'As you command, tal. How am I to do this?'

'Faeros are different from hydrogues, but perhaps Adar Kori'nh's technique will prove effective.'

The septar paused, but for only a moment. 'Yes, Tal O'nh.'

Bright reflections gleamed from the facets on O'nh's jewel eye. 'Let me say on behalf of the Mage-Imperator that the Solar Navy honours your service, Septar Jen'nh. The Lightsource will welcome you, and the *Saga of Seven Suns* will remember you.'

Without a further word, Jen'nh broke the connection. The last and most damaged warliner turned and charged toward the oncoming fireballs. The septar opened fire with every form of Ildiran weapon he had aboard, blasting away in a furious attack, but the explosions were swallowed up like raindrops in an ocean.

Ridek'h watched the drama on the screens as the other

warliners raced away, straining their damaged engines and burning out even more systems. He turned awkwardly to Tal O'nh. 'What is he doing? What can he accomplish?'

Septar Jen'nh dodged in front of the lead faeros, as if to distract it. Designate Rusa'h roared across the communications screen. 'This is useless. Your flight is useless. Your—'

Jen'nh surprised even the mad Designate's inferno when his warliner plunged directly into the flames. The flash caused the fiery ellipsoid to shudder and reel. Ridek'h felt a stinging pain through the *thism* as the septar's warliner was vapourized and flames swallowed every Ildiran aboard. The faeros spread apart like sparks from a stirred-up blaze, delayed, diverted.

It was enough. O'nh's remaining warliners surged ahead. He activated the stardrives, and their ships outdistanced the pursuing fireballs.

O'nh turned his lone eye toward Ridek'h, who sat panting, his skin flushed. 'We are not yet safe, Designate. None of us is.'

EIGHTY-EIGHT

ADAR ZAN'NH

Guiding his rescue warliners to Cjeldre, the next Klikiss world on his starmap, the Adar was hopeful. They had visited four fledgling human colonies on Klikiss worlds, only to find them all destroyed. Zan'nh tried to maintain his confidence that he would find survivors on at least one of them.

The devastation, the complete extermination of the settlers, had shocked him. No one deserved that. There had been no warning that after ten millennia the insect race might swarm back. Although Ildirans had not made the assumption that those planets were available for the taking, how many years was long enough to wait?

Thanks to its highly elliptical orbit, Cjeldre experienced many months of winter. He wondered if the eager human colonists had known about the extreme cold temperatures before marching through the Klikiss transportals and naïvely erecting their settlement. They would have made the best of it, and worked hard to establish lives and homes for themselves. It was the human way. Zan'nh's whole attitude was beginning to change.

400

The Solar Navy warliners arrived like spectators over the snow-swept plains of Cjeldre. On an open channel Adar Zan'nh announced who he was and what he was looking for, hoping to avoid provoking the Klikiss.

When a flurry of small interlocking ships rose from the ground, like the ones he had encountered at Maratha, he knew immediately that the insect creatures had already come here. His heart sank. It was likely that the insect invaders had already killed any human settlers on Cjeldre.

The small component ships coalesced into a cluster, taking shape as a gigantic swarmship that loomed before Zan'nh's warliners, its copious pieces shifting like black static. Though the aggregate took no overt aggressive action, it was clear the Klikiss intended to block the warliners from proceeding.

His tactical officer said, 'Judging from the size of that swarmship, Adar, I doubt we can win a direct confrontation.'

'Then we should not engage in a confrontation. Make no provocative move.' He drew a deep breath, let out a long sigh. 'Give me a cutter equipped with ancient translation devices. While you stay here in full defensive posture, I intend to go down and speak to the breedex.'

'Will the Klikiss negotiate, Adar?'

'The Klikiss are not comprehensible to me. Do they even understand negotiation? However, according to our records, hundreds of human colonists settled on that planet. If the Klikiss do not want them there, then it is our job to remove them.'

Seven small cutters crowded with soldier kithmen left the warliners, flew cautiously past the ominous swarmship without incident, and descended through the atmosphere. A cursory scan did indeed show human life signs, and Zan'nh took heart from that. Perhaps this would not be a futile exercise, after all.

After he landed on the snowy plain near the ever-growing

Klikiss settlement, Zan'nh stepped out alone into the biting wind, leaving his soldiers behind. He could see the ancient ruins and the new towers crowding the human prefab structures. Ice crystals and drifted snow gathered around the spires, collecting in cracks. Although the chill of winter must have made the Klikiss sluggish, the insect creatures had distributed thermal lanterns throughout their settlement.

Zan'nh marched into the cold wind, showing no fear. He would rely on the ancient translation protocols, and on his own wits. Even if the Klikiss understood his words, would they comprehend his meaning? If he made a terrible error and sparked a war, he doubted the already-reeling Ildiran Empire could survive. He drew a long breath of icy air and kept moving.

Zan'nh couldn't imagine what the human colonists must have thought when the Klikiss swept through their transportal. He could see tall resin-concrete barriers behind which shivering humans were being held. He lifted his automated translating device as Klikiss scouts scuttled toward him, chittering. He saw two huge domates.

He stopped, holding his hands at his sides to show he carried no weapons, and spoke directly to the domates. 'I have come for those who inhabited this planet when you returned.' Zan'nh waited for the translation protocol to finish. 'I would take them away.'

The breedex spoke through its domates. 'This planet is ours.'

'Yes, this planet is yours.' Zan'nh craned his neck to look up at the towering striped creatures. 'I do not dispute that. But you have been gone for ten thousand years. These humans did not know you would return.'

'We are back.'

'And we will remove the human trespassers. They will no longer bother you. Do not kill them.'

'They were here. This planet is ours.'

'They were unaware.' He stared directly at the angular face of the monster before him, but he could read nothing. 'We do not desire conflict. We wish to remove conflict. We are Ildirans. Klikiss had no quarrel with us before. We were once your allies. Your breedex must remember.'

'Our breedex knows everything,' the domate said. 'But these are not Ildirans. These are . . . something else.'

Zan'nh adjusted the translation device. 'And I have come to take these humans from your sight. You will have your planet back, exactly as you left it.'

The warriors scritched their armoured forelimbs together. Zan'nh kept his gaze focused forward, and the domates stared at him with faceted eyes in the cold. Why would the Klikiss be reluctant to let the humans leave?

Zan'nh persisted, 'Will you let me take them away? They are not part of your wars. Neither are Ildirans.' With his warliners overhead and the armed cutters nearby, he hoped the insect creatures did not wish to clash with the Solar Navy.

The tense stand-off lasted for a long moment. The breedex seemed to be considering every aspect of the problem, every advantage. Finally, grudgingly, the domates lifted their segmented limbs and took two steps backward. 'Take them. Remove them from here.' With a gesture of its jointed arm, the domate pointed to the thick-walled stockade, from which humans shouted for help. 'This planet remains ours.'

'This planet is yours,' Zan'nh agreed. He issued orders to his soldiers still waiting inside the cutter. They broke the stockade gates open, and desperate, grateful humans streamed out, some falling to their knees and sobbing, others clutching at the hands and uniforms of the Ildirans.

He had to move swiftly. 'Fill the cutters and take these people back to the warliners. We must do this in a single trip – before the Klikiss reconsider.' Fewer than fifty human colonists remained alive, and they easily fit aboard the transport vessels.

Zan'nh backed toward his cutter, staring at the domates, anxious to be gone from Cjeldre. He had fulfilled the Mage-Imperator's orders to rescue human colonists, but he did not feel overly triumphant.

Motionless, the Klikiss watched the Solar Navy depart.

EIGHTY-NINE

SIRIX

Before the black robots could destroy the main towers on Llaro, a sudden and overwhelming wave of Klikiss warriors poured from the main city, carrying the bell-mouthed energy weapons Sirix had encountered during the first attack on Wollamor. Could this be the same subhive? The Klikiss began to mow down black robots, Soldier compies, and even their own unarmed warriors who stood in the way.

With this new surge of unexpected reinforcements, the insect warriors began slaughtering Sirix's troops. He saw the disaster unfolding and knew he could not risk a continued pursuit of DD, nor could he keep fighting the Klikiss. Though the robots killed three insect creatures for every one of their own casualties, Sirix could not afford those losses. He had no choice but to sound a retreat.

'To the dropships! Back to orbit.' He could expend some of his remaining heavy-calibre weaponry, the large-scale planetary jazers, to obliterate this infestation, or at least clear a path for his surviving comrades to escape. He might still achieve victory here, though it would cost him more than he had anticipated.

Several of the EDF landers had been damaged in their high-velocity descent, and the robots climbing aboard could not get the engines started. One dropship lifted off, lumbered into the air, and crashed with sufficient force to damage the occupants. Before any survivors could scramble out of the wreckage, the Klikiss fell upon it.

However, so many of the black robots had been wiped out that there were more functional dropships than the survivors required. Most of the craft lifted off into the sky and fled the battleground, intending to return with hellish fire from above.

But the Llaro breedex had one more unpleasant surprise.

The Klikiss responded as Sirix's dropships returned to their battle group in orbit. Even before the landers had docked with the main warships, hundreds of boxlike ships launched from ground bases below in a shower of individual Klikiss fighters.

Considering the size of the enemy force drawing together with remarkable speed, the breedex must have been preparing to launch a vigorous swarm war. And Sirix had blundered into a subhive that was far more prepared than it should have been. He ordered the Juggernaut's jazers to open fire, targeting individual Klikiss component ships, but there were too many, and they were too widely separated.

The flurry of small ships ascended into space, firing at the EDF ships like stinging gnats, then drew together like iron filings pulled toward a magnet. The individual vessels interlocked into a configuration Sirix recognized as a Klikiss swarmship – with enough combined firepower to peel away the armoured hull of an EDF battleship.

His robots had encountered a similar conglomerate vessel at Scholld, but this swarmship had an unexpected capability. The interlocking components shifted like a puzzle, rearranging themselves, until half of the swarmship configured itself into a bizarre cannon with a gaping barrel large enough to swallow a small asteroid. Sparkles of energy jumped among the multiple components, engaging linkages, powering the central weapon.

The cannon's mouth glowed orange, then blazed a searing blue-white. A geyser of barely controlled energy vomited out and disintegrated one of Sirix's Mantas. Within two seconds, the swarmship pivoted in space and acquired another target as it recharged. Before the second Manta could accelerate out of the way, the weapon discharged again, ripping it apart.

Sirix knew his Juggernaut would be a prime target. 'More speed from our engines.' Descending to extremely low orbit, the battleship clawed its way through the fringes of Llaro's atmosphere, trying to skip over the horizon and dodge the weapon's line of fire. The moment he reached the planet's shadow, Sirix altered course and headed out into the system. The hardened robots could not withstand the crushing acceleration. PD and QT lost their balance, tumbled, and rolled across the deck until they banged together against a bulkhead.

Even so, the Juggernaut could not get out of range of the pursuing Klikiss swarmship fast enough. From too far away, the giant weapon spat a gout of destructive energy, which fortunately dissipated too widely to vaporize the Juggernaut outright. Many of the bridge's control panels sparked and smoked before going dead, but the big ship kept moving.

One of his fellow robot-controlled ships came back around, looped over the planet's south pole, and rose up to open fire on the swarmship. Multiple jazer blasts splintered off more than a hundred of the small Klikiss component craft, but the myriad ship recoalesced and formed its exotic weapon again – this time with the gaping barrel pointing toward the annoying Manta. The robot ship was vaporized in a single blast.

The Juggernaut continued to flee, while back at the planet the swarmship continued to hunt down the scattering EDF Mantas. PD strained against the continuing brutal acceleration to force himself into a sitting position. 'That ship sacrificed itself for us. Why would a robot do that?'

Still pinned to the deck, QT said in a distorted voice, 'Unexpected . . . and illogical.'

Sirix did not acknowledge the sacrifice. Each black robot was unique, theoretically equivalent. It made no sense that some of them would allow themselves to be destroyed to protect him, their de facto leader. The very idea was disturbing, but he could not allow himself to focus on the anomalous behaviour. Instead, he calculated the consequences of the attrition. Three Mantas lost, and the Juggernaut's engines damaged. Hundreds of black robots wiped out.

Enduring thrust far beyond the ship's design specifications, they hurtled out of the Llaro system. A failed mission. His dreams of grand conquest were fading into static! Gathering whatever numbers he could salvage, he beat a wild retreat.

NINETY

ORLI COVITZ

Leaving the Llaro settlement behind, Orli and the group of exhausted escapees ran pell-mell across the trampled dirt and stripped fields, beyond the smoke and turmoil of the robots' clash with the Klikiss. With the breedex fighting for its hive, Orli doubted many of the creatures would be abroad. *Running again, escaping again*, she thought.

'I remember a place where we can shelter until nightfall,' Mr Steinman said. 'If we push ourselves, we can get to Davlin's hideout tomorrow night.'

Some of the anxious people began to groan as they hurried along – twenty of them, including seven children and two compies. 'Even if we do make it to the cave with all the others, then what?' Crim Tylar asked. 'Do we just hide?' He seemed distraught over leaving his wife behind.

Others had similar concerns. 'How long can we survive out there without food and supplies? A few days? We can't live that way.'

'We live *for another day*,' Mayor Ruis said with absolute conviction, 'then we take it from there.'

DD sounded cheerful. 'One step at a time. Taking too many steps too quickly could cause you to stumble.' He moved tirelessly beside the Governess compy. UR did her best to keep her wards together, nudging them along; occasionally she and DD carried the littler ones. The adults also took turns.

Each step took them farther from the settlement and out into the open, where Klikiss searchers could easily spot them. 'I hope the black robots have caused serious damage to the hive,' DD said. 'It would be a good thing if Sirix were destroyed, as well.'

'I hope they damn well destroy each other,' Crim said. 'Now that would make me happy.' He inspected the projectile rifle that Mr Steinman carried. 'You sure you know how to use that thing?'

'Just point and destroy. Right?'

'I wish you'd had more practice.'

After three hours at a fast pace, Steinman led them to a clump of talus boulders and helter-skelter outcroppings as big as houses. By the time they collapsed on the rocks, Orli was totally drained. Utterly weary and terrified, the children dropped to the ground; most were whimpering. Orli squatted next to them, unslung her pack and pulled out her synthesizer strips, thinking she could play them a lullaby while they all waited for darkness to fall. In her pack, she found a few energy bars, broke them into pieces, and shared them among the children.

The Governess compy was impressed. 'Thank you, Orli Covitz.'

DD stood like a toy soldier, guarding the whole group. The escapees made a lot of noise as they settled down to hide. Steinman leaned his weapon against a rock and cracked his knuckles behind his head. 'I could use a nap.'

'Something is not right,' DD said. 'I detect unusual noises.'

They all heard scratching and scraping from the dark cracks between the piled talus boulders. 'It's a damned bug!' cried Crim, jumping to his feet.

A Klikiss scout, smaller than an armoured warrior but still deadly, emerged from its shadowy hiding place near where the children had gathered. The boys and girls screamed and leapt backward, tripping over the rocks. DD grabbed a nine-year-old and pulled him out of the way.

The Klikiss clacked its jagged forelimbs. Mr Steinman lunged for his projectile rifle. The scout insect smashed him aside. It vibrated its wings with a menacing buzz. Mayor Ruis threw a rock at the creature, but the stone bounced off the hard exoskeleton.

Before the Klikiss could lunge toward the children, though, UR stood directly in front of the creature. 'You will not harm them.' The scout batted the Governess compy with a hard forelimb, a blow that would have broken a human in half, but though she rocked with the impact, she did not budge. Instead, UR grabbed its clawed arm with her polymer hands and cracked down, snapping the chitin shell and twisting off the forelimb. The monstrous scout whistled, and seized UR's right arm in two of its claws, pulling, ripping, and completely severing her limb. She reeled, her stump dripping fluids and sparking. The scout rammed her, and she tumbled to the rocks, while DD ran toward her in alarm, trying to assist.

Orli had a frantic thought and nothing to lose. She fumbled until her fingers instinctively found the Power tab on her synthesizer strips. Without thinking, she began to play one of her well-practised original melodies. The music suddenly rang out from the implanted speakers, the music rising unexpectedly into the pandemonium.

Hearing the strange tune, the Klikiss scout paused, swivelling its head and quivering as it searched for the source. Mr Steinman pointed his weapon and fired a blast. The projectile shattered the creature's head into greenish pulp, and the armoured body slumped twitching to the dirt.

In the aftermath, the escapees shuddered as they recovered themselves and helped UR back to her feet. DD appeared to be even more upset than the Governess compy, who seemed dazed and disoriented. DD's voice was thick with forced reassurance, both for the dismayed children and for the other compy. 'The damage is reparable. No memories or vital systems were harmed. I can stop these leaks and cap off the damaged circuits. You will be all right, UR.'

'That was quick thinking, Orli,' Ruis said. He looked ready to vomit. 'A most unusual means of defence.'

She couldn't believe it herself. 'It seemed the right thing to do. Margaret gave me the suggestion.'

'I'm sorry to say this, all of you,' Steinman said, 'but we'll have to keep going now. Thanks to the scout, the breedex has seen us.'

'That's fine. That's just fine,' said Crim, as he held up the Governess compy's severed arm. 'Let's get the hell out of here.'

NINETY-ONE

CHAIRMAN BASIL WENCESLAS

Despite Basil's careful control of information, the people had begun to make up their own stories, and some even rallied against the Hansa. The condemnation from King Peter had spread like wildfire across the breakaway colonies and even among a few pathetic dissident groups that were beginning to appear on Earth.

After everything the Chairman had done for them! Couldn't they see what was at stake? Basil felt like a man clutching at water with his outstretched fingers, trying to hold back the tide. Why did humanity refuse strong leadership and insist on self-destructive behaviour? They chased every distraction and believed every ridiculous rumour. It would serve them right if he threw up his hands, abandoned his post, and left these selfish idiots to careen headlong to their own downfall.

But he couldn't do that. He cared about humanity too much. Even if no one else could see what needed to be done, even if others refused to follow instructions, *he* had the vision to pull humanity back from the brink.

The Terran Hanseatic League was the greatest government ever formed, the strongest and most beneficial organization that humanity had ever known. Yet, all that went out the window the moment anybody felt the slightest discomfort. Fickle! They refused to make sacrifices or work hard. If only the people would all put in as much effort as *he* did! They were weak and easily influenced by liars and charlatans who didn't know their proper places – like King Peter. At times Basil felt hopeless, not sure how even he could turn this around. But he was the *Hansa Chairman*, and he intended to fix everything, whether the people wanted it fixed or not. He simply had to work harder.

When he first heard the outrageous accusations and the recorded confession from Patrick Fitzpatrick, Basil sent a summons directly to former Chairman Maureen Fitzpatrick's Rocky Mountain mansion, along with a handful of guards to make sure his invitation was accepted. Hansa priorities outweighed any prior commitments or meetings the old Battleaxe might have.

When the former Chairman arrived, she looked impeccable wearing a dove-grey dress and a necklace of tasteful reef-pearls. Her skin was tight, her hair carrying a mature touch of grey, though nothing to suggest her true age. Maureen Fitzpatrick no doubt underwent the most expensive anti-aging and rejuvenation treatments using rare kelp extracts from Rhejak – as Basil himself did. Before long, if Admiral Willis did her job properly, shipments from Rhejak would become much less expensive . . .

Entering the penthouse offices, Maureen walked directly to the windows and took in the view. 'Ah, it's been a long time since I was up here. Thank you for inviting me.' She turned to him. 'You've got quite a lot on your plate. Need some advice?'

Basil frowned. 'I have my own advisers.'

'Not as many as you once had, from what I hear.' Maureen went to the drink dispenser and got herself a glass of wine without being asked. She sat back in a chair, took a sip, and held the glass up to the sunlight to study the garnet colour. 'Interesting vintage. From Relleker? I can recommend some better ones, if you'd like.'

'That won't be necessary. I rarely drink, especially while I'm working – and I'm always working.'

'I remember those days.' Maureen took another sip. 'Still, it's not bad.'

Basil felt a flash of anger to see her act altogether too familiar with these offices. 'Recent developments forced me to summon you here, Madame Chairman. This is about your grandson.'

She set the glass down. 'What has Patrick done now? His captivity under the Roamers affected him more than we suspected. He needed a great deal more intensive counselling.'

'He needed to be arrested.'

Finally, Maureen seemed rattled. 'Arrested? Is General Lanyan on his kick to find a scapegoat for AWOL soldiers again?'

'In a time of war, it's called desertion,' Basil corrected her. He felt a brief craving for a cup of cardamom coffee, but pushed it aside. 'This is something far more serious than desertion, Madame Chairman.'

'Now you've got my interest.'

'He's plotting the overthrow of the Hansa government.'

Maureen let out an explosive laugh. 'Patrick? *My* Patrick?'

He called up an image on his desk and played King Peter's speech, to which was appended her grandson's full confession.

Maureen listened sternly. 'Yes, Patrick told me about blowing up that Roamer ship. I tried to explain political realities to him.' She shook her head. 'I apologize, Mr Chairman. I never expected him to abandon his EDF duties, but I knew the guilt was eating at him. I should have watched him more closely. I haven't seen him in some time, you understand. He stole my space yacht and disappeared before the hydrogues came to Earth. I wish I knew where he was.'

Basil fumed. 'He is with the Roamers on one of their skymines! It's bad enough that he publicly admitted such an act. I thought we had succeeded in quelling the uproar, getting the Roamers under control – and now he's fanned the flames again. That in itself is bad enough. Then he tops it all off by turning the blame not only on himself, but on his commanding officer and his commander-in-chief? That's absolutely unforgivable. Accusing General Lanyan of issuing the murderous orders and me of covering up the incident! Even if his statement were true – and I'm not saying it is – it's a cowardly act to blame his superiors. I want you to do something about it. Talk to him, make him retract his statement. At the very least, get him back here.'

'I haven't a clue how to do that. He won't listen to me.' Basil was ready to dismiss the old woman when Maureen leaned forward, her wine forgotten. She glanced around the room as if to reassure herself that the doors were sealed and no one was eavesdropping. 'Let's not kid ourselves, Mr Chairman. You know as well as I do that Lanyan *did* give that order. It was a bad command decision with repercussions neither the General, nor you yourself, imagined. When the Roamers caught you, it backfired in your face.'

'I was always in complete control.'

'Sure you were.' Maureen regarded him for a long moment. 'As a former Hansa Chairman myself, I'd like permission to speak candidly.'

He hardened his expression. 'I always welcome constructive criticism.'

'I know what you're going through. In my time I faced different disasters, but there were plenty of them. In the best of all possible worlds, a smart person would make smart decisions, and smart people would follow them. More often than not, however, at least one of those three ingredients is missing. Given human nature, compromise is sometimes more important than command.'

'Compromise? Why should I even consider compromising with people who are *wrong*?'

'So that you can get the right things done, of course. Look at your track record since the hydrogue war began. Study your decisions objectively. You'll find more than a few that, in retrospect, might have been handled better.'

'Such as?' By his tone, it was clear that he didn't want to know.

'Such as the way you handled the Roamer situation and their ekti embargo. As you can see from Patrick's statement, they had a legitimate grievance. You could have nipped it in the bud, made a few inexpensive amends, and maintained our access to stardrive fuel. It would have kept the Hansa strong.'

'Thank you for your advice. I will take it under consideration.' He stood to usher her out the door, but Maureen was not finished.

'And your public and embarrassing quarrels with King Peter. He was *right* about the Klikiss robots and the Soldier compies. Everyone can see that, but you still won't acknowledge it. Are you pathologically incapable of admitting you're wrong? Now, when the King speaks out against you, there's a clear precedent for the people to believe *him*. Furthermore,' she pointed a finger, 'abandoning the Hansa colonies, withdrawing all protection from them, refusing to deliver desperately needed supplies, using the EDF to crack down—'

'*Thank you*. I will take it under consideration. You may take your wine with you as you go.'

'I appreciate your open-mindedness and willingness to listen.' Maureen's voice dripped with sarcasm as she stepped toward the door.

When Basil saw the hunger in her eyes, it suddenly became

clear to him. She was like a jackal lurking near a wounded animal. She wanted to take over! She wanted to be Chairman again. Perhaps she had set up her own grandson to embarrass and bring down Basil. Maureen Fitzpatrick could cause a great deal of trouble for him.

As she left in an obvious huff, Basil sent a message to summon Deputy Cain. He wanted that woman watched very closely.

NINETY-TWO

PATRICK FITZPATRICK III

The winds of Golgen were cold as death when Patrick stepped out to face them. He wore no restraints. After all, where could he run? Patrick felt lost, isolated, and to some insane measure, relieved and *content*. He had confessed his crimes, and the Roamers would exact their traditional – if melodramatic – punishment. Nothing more needed to be said. He had never expected to receive miraculous forgiveness, though he had hoped for it from Zhett. On the other hand, once he was brought out onto deck with the infinite sky below, reality set in, and terror howled through him like the swirling winds.

Viewed from any logical standpoint, this whole adventure had been a fool's errand. He could have stayed home in his grandmother's mansion. He could have taken a plush job in the Earth Defence Forces and begun work on a political career. As his grandmother wanted. Even though her hopes on his behalf were often misguided, he now believed she did want the best for him, but he had snubbed the old Battleaxe and commandeered her yacht to find Zhett.

Well, he had found the girl he loved, for all the good it did him. Now they were forcing him to jump to his death – and the damned beautiful girl who held his heart still hadn't said a word to him.

Patrick was painted into a corner – and had done much of the painting himself. It was too late to run, nor did he want to. He had burned his bridges behind him.

Patrick lifted his head. His hair blew around his face, and he narrowed his eyes and looked straight ahead. The atmosphere-condenser fields were shut down, leaving the deck open to the empty skies. Del Kellum stood before him in judgment, as did the other skymine chiefs.

Boris Goff had returned from Theroc; Bing Palmer stood next to Del Kellum. In most of their expressions Patrick could read anger, self-justification, satisfaction, and uneasiness. Maybe they didn't really want things to end this way. Patrick certainly didn't.

'I think I could accomplish more for you and make up for what I've done, if you let me live,' he said. 'But I won't beg for it.'

'The law is the law,' Kellum said.

Patrick nodded, then struggled for something else to say, finding loose ends that really shouldn't have mattered to him. 'I know it's unlikely, but I'd appreciate it if someone would return my grandmother's ship to her.' He took a step forward, as ordered, on the solid metal deck plates. He looked at Kellum, and the burly man stared back, betraying no emotion. Zhett was there, but she held herself erect and would not meet his eyes. He had hoped to see anguish in her expression – any flicker of regret! He wanted her to throw herself upon him, clutch at his clothes, and refuse to let him walk the plank. But he knew that wasn't going to happen.

'Patrick Fitzpatrick III, you know why you are here,' Kellum said in a loud voice. Without the containment field, his words rang out to the open sky.

Patrick drew a deep breath and stared ahead at the metre-wide walkway, a bridge to emptiness. 'So be it.' He was supposed to step out there and voluntarily leap into the unguarded depths of Golgen, though he wasn't sure he had the nerve to do it just like that.

The sea of clouds seemed restless, even angry. In his mind Patrick ran through the mistakes he had made, the ripples of consequences. The Roamers probably had some means to prod him over the edge, but he wouldn't make anybody force him, and he refused to cringe in front of Zhett. Not Zhett. Even though she had not acknowledged his apology, welcomed him in any way, or forgiven him, he would not let her see him as a coward. He took a step to the edge of the plank. Without guard rails and an expansive deck around him, a sudden sense of vertigo made him sway with dizziness. With wry bitterness, he thought it would certainly be embarrassing if he accidentally fell off the execution walkway.

Steadying himself, he glanced over his shoulder at Zhett one last time. Her face seemed pale, her lips drawn. Her eyes sparkled as if from tears held back with all the force of her personality. That gave him strength, at least. His trip here had not been a complete loss.

'I accept my punishment,' he said. 'I know I've caused great pain. So I do this in the hope that my death will offer some measure of peace to those I hurt.'

Zhett made a sound as if she were choking back a sob. She turned her head away, and her long black hair covered her face.

Patrick took another step onto the plank. At the rail now, Kellum looked displeased with what he had been forced to do. Patrick wasn't angry with Zhett's father, though. The clan leader had been trapped by his own rules and his knowledge.

Patrick cleared his throat. 'Don't hate me for too much longer,

Zhett.' He considered telling her that he loved her, but even though he was sincere, he feared she would think he was trying to manipulate her. Besides, if Zhett really believed he deserved this punishment, professing his love now would be cruel. No, he wouldn't do that. Facing forward, he walked out onto the plank over the emptiness. He looked down to the right and to the left. The sky seemed bottomless. Del Kellum bit his lips. The other skymine chiefs seemed restless and tense, as unsure of whether to celebrate or grieve.

Patrick took another step. His consciousness became fuzzy around him. Nothing seemed real anymore. Another step. The end of the plank was in front of him. And then he would be falling forever.

The voice behind him sounded like an angel's song. 'Wait — stop!'

His feet froze as if a magnetic field had locked them to the plank. He didn't look back, staring only into the swirling clouds that seemed to wait for him.

'Wait!' It was Zhett's voice. 'All right, I'll speak on his behalf. Don't execute him. I won't make excuses, but . . . but he's sorry for what he did. Let him atone some other way. By the Guiding Star, I can't bear to see him die!' Patrick's knees threatened to buckle beneath him, and if he slumped into unconsciousness, he would fall off the edge. Zhett's voice was ragged now with emotion. 'Save his life, Dad. Please, I'm begging you.'

Turning back, he saw that Zhett had grasped her father's hands. She looked more beautiful now than Patrick had ever seen her, though she appeared in misty focus through the tears in his eyes.

'Don't be stubborn, Dad. You know this isn't right. Let him come back.'

Kellum raised his arms. 'All right, you heard it. A Roamer has spoken on behalf of this man. Get him off of that plank.' Looking incredibly relieved, the burly man muttered, 'It's about time, by damn. How much longer did you expect me to keep up this charade?'

Weak and disoriented, Patrick stumbled back to the solid deck, and Zhett threw her arms around him and pulled him close. He stared into her bottomless black eyes. 'I didn't know if you were going to do that or not.'

'Neither did I. I decided at the last minute.' She pulled away and put her hands on her hips. 'You'd better be worth it.'

Kellum walked up to them, thrusting his chest forward. 'I knew she would change her mind.' He grinned at his daughter. 'You took your sweet time, though – time enough for us all to develop an ulcer. Who knows what you did to this poor young man by tormenting him like that?'

'Tormenting him? He was sentenced to death! I saved him.'

'No you didn't, my sweet.' Kellum shook his head. Patrick looked from Zhett to her father, who seemed full of himself, as if he knew a secret joke. The man winked at Patrick. 'Oh, come now! I was just waiting for my daughter to come to her senses. I had skimmers with nets already prepared. They would have caught you – eventually.'

Patrick couldn't decide whether to faint or swing a punch at the clan leader. Zhett glowered at her father, but she didn't loosen her grip on Patrick. 'You're still on probation, as far as I'm concerned.'

Patrick didn't know if she was speaking to him or to her father.

NINETY-THREE

CELLI

As an acolyte, Celli learned much about history and folklore from reading aloud to the worldtrees. Sitting among the high fronds, she recited story after story, chronicle after chronicle, each one new to her. In her younger days, she had not been overly interested in scholarly pursuits, preferring to run with friends and play in the forest. Now though, she found the information fascinating, and she presumed the verdani mind did, as well.

Celli looked into the empty blue sky. Somewhere high above was the thorny treeship that Beneto had become, along with eight other verdani vessels, so far away. As a green priest, she would be able to contact him via telink whenever she wanted. She couldn't wait.

With a buzzing, puttering sound, Solimar circled above her in his gliderbike. When she waved at him, he did a loop in the air to show off. He loved to take her for rides, and she particularly enjoyed sitting close behind him with her arms wrapped around his waist, leaning her cheek against his smooth back. He often took them in steep dives, and she knew it was just so she would hold on tighter.

Several young acolytes sat in leafy bowers, while older green priests gathered nearby, deep in discussion. Though Celli tried to concentrate on reading her stories, this particular debate among the usually quiet emerald-skinned men and women intrigued her. Yarrod was speaking with great enthusiasm, his eyes shining, his face wearing a sincere smile. Recently, he had been more vibrant than she'd ever seen him, changed in a way she could not define.

Yarrod and many other green priests had accepted the strange synthesis of *thism* and telink, which Kolker had taught them from far-off Ildira. Some of the green priests showed healthy, but cautious, curiosity, and the worldforest itself was interested in the phenomenon. When she became a green priest, Celli would have to face the same decision. Someday soon, when she was a green priest . . .

A disturbance rippled among them, and the worldtrees seemed to shiver. The younger acolytes became alarmed and anxious. The instructor glanced from the sky to the clumps of leaves. 'Acolytes, down!'

The children dropped their reading pads and dived into the thick fronds. The priests scrambled into the branches, like swimmers submerging themselves in the waves of an alien sea. Celli remained where she was, still looking for the danger, her foolish curiosity stronger than her fear.

The wyvern struck.

The largest predator on Theroc careened down in a flurry of jagged wings, faceted eyes, and multiple mandibles. Its giant body was tapered in a long wasplike shape, covered with camouflage blotches; the wings were bursts of scarlet and orange. All eight of its legs were tipped with serrated claws to grasp and tear.

The wyvern came directly toward Celli. She didn't scream, nor did she freeze in terror. Instead, with her muscular legs, she leapt from the frond on which she sat and arced downward, catching a branch and swinging herself around. The wyvern streaked past, its claws slashing at the foliage. But Celli had already let go and dropped to a different branch, landing with her bare feet and springing up against the resilient wood to fly in another direction. This was like treedancing, and she could do it all day.

The wyvern came close again, its wings buzzing, clashing its mandibles like a hungry man licking his lips. Something long and sharp whipped by, barely missing the skin on her shoulder. A stinger! The wyvern had some kind of paralysing venom that could freeze its prey, but Celli squirmed out of the way, grabbed another branch, and continued bounding along even as the wyvern pursued her, ripping worldtree fronds. Her heart pounded. The breath burned in her lungs.

Suddenly, a different kind of buzzing passed close to her ear, and she saw Solimar's gliderbike streak in front of the wyvern. He didn't call to her, and Celli could tell he was trying to divert it. Their first meeting had been when Solimar rescued her from the burning worldtrees. Now he was rescuing her again.

While she ducked into a dense clump of fronds, the wyvern took off after Solimar. His gliderbike dipped and swooped, dwarfed by the enormous predator. He hunched over, trying to make himself a smaller target.

She didn't shout, afraid she would distract him at a very bad moment. Instead, she pushed her head above the branches and watched as he plummeted and swirled, dived and then climbed. Though his vehicle was nimble, the wyvern was in its own element. Celli's stomach knotted. Solimar couldn't escape from the creature forever.

Her friend seemed to understand that as well, and when the

wyvern nearly clipped his arm with a sharp wing, Solimar spun the gliderbike around and drove directly toward the creature, using the vehicle itself as a projectile.

The multiple wings of the flying predator backed in the air, causing it to change course, but Solimar drove onward, faster, closer. Celli caught her breath. At the last moment before impact, Solimar gracefully sprang from his gliderbike, fell through open air, and plunged into the canopy.

His treasured gliderbike crashed into the wyvern at great speed, smashing one of the creature's wings, cracking its armoured abdomen. She did not worry about Solimar's fall, since he was an expert treedancer like herself. In a graceful move, he caught one of the uprising clumps of fronds to slow his momentum. Then he grabbed a solid branch, twirled around, and flung himself off, catching his balance on yet another bough.

The ruined gliderbike tumbled out of the sky, while the injured wyvern flapped drunkenly away.

Celli was already bounding across the thick branches to where she had seen Solimar land. When she caught up with him, he was breathing hard and his smooth green skin was cross-hatched with minor wounds, but there were no serious injuries. She flung herself into his arms. 'Thank you, Solimar!' Then she pulled back, looked into his face, and raised her voice. 'What were you *doing*? You could have been killed.'

'You, too! And I wanted both of us to stay alive.'

Sheltered under the top layer of fronds, they held each other for a long moment. Then she kissed him.

NINETY-FOUR

JESS TAMBLYN

J ust looking at the scars on the frozen surface of Jonah 12 reminded Jess of lost dreams and ruined possibilities. Kotto Okiah had worked so hard to transform this dim and isolated planetoid into a thriving facility. Jhy Okiah had died here, and Cesca herself had faced an emerging army of black robots.

Five darkened satellite outposts orbited the chunk of rock and ice, shut down and drifting in space. During Kotto's heyday here, shipments of condensed supercold gas had been launched up to orbit, where these holding stations completed the reaction process, converting simple hydrogen into stardrive fuel. Nearly two hundred clan workers had lived here. Now all of them were dead.

Cesca leaned against the flexible hull membrane of the wental ship, peering at the debris scattered in the fused crater where the power reactor had overloaded. Radioactivity continued to sizzle, so that ice still flowed into slush. Melted-and-refrozen rivers sketched silver ribbons through the crust.

Their bubble ship landed on the lip of the refrozen crater, and

Jess and Cesca emerged to stand out under the cold, black sky. The stars sparkled like ice chips with the brightest one, Jonah's sun, too far away to provide heat.

'Did you want to repair this place?' Cesca asked. 'Like we did at Plumas?'

Jess knew they could resculpt the surface, erase the crater and smooth over the crevasses, make the ice ready for Kotto Okiah to restore his facility here. But that wasn't his intent. 'There would be no purpose to it. Kotto established the outpost here when ekti was in such great demand. Now, though, with skymining open and free again, there's no need. Jonah 12 should remain a memorial.'

She gave a bittersweet smile. 'Do you think any Roamers will come to see it, to remember those who died here?'

'I'm hoping for something else – a *living* memorial. Now that the wentals are so well distributed, I'd like to turn them loose here, let them recharge the ice the way they did with the comet I sent to Theroc.'

He bent down, placed his palms flat against the hydrogen ice, and felt wental power flow out of him into the crust of the planetoid. He sensed more than saw the shimmer that permeated the ice, growing stronger as the inclusions of frozen water awakened, took on a semblance of life. He was pleased with what he had done.

Jess raised his hands and spoke directly to the water beings. 'Is this place adequate for you?'

Wentals are widely dispersed. What we require now is to be made stronger. Not diluted.

'There are so many wentals that they could never be made extinct again. Doesn't that in itself make you stronger?' Cesca asked.

We are numerous, but we all sprang from the same pool. If we continue to spread from the same droplet, eventually our powers become more diffuse. We need a new wellspring. We request that you locate other wentals that were lost in the great war, just as you found us.

Years ago, in his nebula skimmer, Jess had retrieved a small amount of the living water from inside a diffuse gas cloud. All of the subsequent wentals had sprung from that small amount of moisture.

'But how do we find different ones?' Jess asked.

Search the ancient battlefields across the Spiral Arm, places where wentals died. If you go there, we will show you.

NINETY-FIVE

DAVLIN LOTZE

After the robots retreated, having caused a great deal of damage to the subhive, Davlin didn't have as much time as he had hoped for. None of the Llaro colonists did. The remaining Klikiss did not give them a chance.

Looking like a scarecrow, Margaret ran back from the damaged hive city, racing as if the monsters were pursuing her. Dead insect bodies and smashed robots still lay strewn all around. Bypassing the smaller entrance gaps, she entered through the hole blasted in the stockade wall and stood haggard in the glare of Llaro's midmorning. When she finally caught her breath, she shouted to Davlin and the milling colonists next to him. 'The domates are coming for you! Now.' Her words cut like an axe blade through the morning air.

Davlin felt a sudden chill. 'They're still reeling from the battle.'

Roberto Clarin paused as he and three colonists struggled to shore up the town's defences. 'Shizz, how the hell can they want to fight again? Half the bugs have been wiped out.'

'That's exactly why,' Margaret said. 'Now, more than ever, the breedex needs to reproduce and replenish its numbers. And for that, it needs you.'

With a surge of adrenaline, Davlin clapped his hands and shouted for everyone to take their positions – this was not a drill. The already shaken people let out sighs of despair mixed with determination.

Marla Chan Tylar and the colonists she'd been training jumped to gather and recharge their scavenged weapons – hand-held projectile launchers, broad-beam twitchers, and two shoulder-fired jazer rifles – and scrambled up makeshift ladders to the top of the barricade. Because of his years of experience as an excellent marksman, Davlin took one of the jazers for himself. Every charge from the weapon's energy pack, every round of ammunition in the other guns, had to be used wisely, and would likely still not be sufficient.

Clarin said to him in a low voice, 'You think it makes any difference that so many of the bugs are dead? Do we have a chance now?'

'We always had a chance. It was never a really *good* one.' He looked at the Roamer leader. 'It's still not very good. But every bug the robots killed is one less that we have to shoot.'

Spotters on the wall shouted an alarm. Insect workers had spent a full day amidst the smoke and carnage below dragging away warrior bodies and the shrapnel of destroyed black robots and Soldier compies. Climbing a makeshift ladder to reach the top of the wall, Davlin stood beside Margaret.

'I saw that the robots killed one of the domates. Will that help us?'

'Not much. The breedex has seven of them left.'

He was startled to see tears trickling down her cheeks. 'Shouldn't you get to shelter, or are you going to die with the rest of us?'

'They won't touch me. The breedex has marked me in its mind.' She clenched her fists. 'I'm stuck in the middle of this bloody hurricane. I wish DD were here, but I'm glad he got away with all those others.'

'I wish I'd gotten a lot more people out in time,' Davlin answered. He squared his shoulders. 'I saved as many as I could.' Even so, he wasn't sure how many of the escapees would survive without food, tools, or weapons at the sandstone bluffs. He could fight only one battle at a time.

Davlin noted that the Klikiss workers had cleared a path across the battleground. He watched more warriors and a group of the massive domates emerge from the dark openings of the towers. Forming a kind of procession through their city, the battered Klikiss began marching toward the compound.

Marla lined up her gunners along the top of the wall, while others took high positions on rooftops inside the town. They all held weapons and seemed anxious to fire. 'Not yet,' she said. 'Our biggest advantage is surprise.'

Puffing and red-faced, Clarin climbed up to Davlin's post. 'We'll hold them off as long as we can. Maybe if we kill enough now, they'll back off.'

'They won't back off,' Margaret said, her tone weary and matter-of-fact.

Clarin sighed. 'I didn't think they would.'

Marla Chan narrowed her eyes and hefted her weapon. 'I intend to leave a big pile of dead bugs all around me, one way or another.'

The domates, with tall head crests and jaws like industrial grinding tools, strode on multiple legs across the packed dirt toward the stockade wall. Davlin tensed, drawing imaginary lines in his mind. Just a few more steps. He had already activated the network.

'Remember, the striped ones are the real targets, second only to the breedex,' he shouted. 'Get rid of all seven of them, and we deal a powerful blow to the whole subhive.'

As the first domate stepped onto the path in front of the stockade wall, its chitinous foot tromped on the first of Davlin's buried landmines. The explosion blasted upward like an orange geyser, hurling dust and gravel twenty feet into the air. Smashed and mangled, the dead domate crashed to the ground like a ruined spacecraft. The explosive event sent the Klikiss into a flurry of reaction. Shrill chirps and squeals made a deafening noise in the air.

Six domates left.

The warriors escorting the company of domates raised their bell-mouthed energy weapons in their sharp claws. In the pandemonium, many of them rushed forward to attack – just as Davlin had hoped. They charged onto the mined road, and three more explosions blew upward, vaporizing many warriors.

'Open fire!' Marla Chan shouted.

Davlin hefted his shoulder-mounted jazer, took careful aim, and incinerated a huge hole through another domate. Its striped body slumped to the ground amidst the debris. *Five left.*

Everyone on the walls began blasting away, mowing down warriors, builders, any other Klikiss breeds they could hit. 'Aim for the domates!'

Now that three of the subhive's eight domates had been wiped out, the warriors formed a protective wall around the towering creatures and drove them backward to relative safety. Davlin shot another burst from his jazer rifle, and killed ten warriors with the sweeping arc. He blasted two limbs off of one domate, but the imposing creature backed away, ducked, and scuttled to safety.

From its squat hive structure, the breedex directed its warriors to surge forward by the hundreds. The swarm was impossible to drive back, despite the flurry of desperate gunfire from the colonists. After another hidden landmine exploded, many insect warriors in the rearguard cracked open their wing casings and simply took flight, rising up over the booby-trapped zone. Others continued to march toward the stockade walls, heedless. Dead insect bodies piled up, and live Klikiss scrambled over them.

Davlin knew the stockade walls would provide no protection against the flying creatures. Overhead, Klikiss buzzed ominously, then swooped down to begin the direct attack. He shot into the air, killing many of the bugs in flight, but more and more warriors swept toward the stockade.

NINETY-SIX

ROBERTO CLARIN

Firing his weapon again and again, Clarin splattered the flat, segmented head of a flying Klikiss warrior. The hideous creature careened into the side of a prefab building and slid down, leaving a trail of slime and gore. A poorly aimed explosion blew down another part of the prefabricated wall.

Many colonists without weapons ducked through the broken stockade wall, frantic to escape, though they had no place to go and little chance of getting far from the hive. Others ran to their secret bolt-holes inside the town, sealing themselves in hidden rooms, under trapdoors, inside crawlspaces.

Clarin saw five escaped colonists blunder into a group of Klikiss outside in the town. As the bugs fell upon them, the people tried to run back to the dubious safety of the stockade, but they were butchered before they could take more than a few steps.

Marla Chan Tylar remained atop the wall, yelling and shooting. She didn't seem interested in getting away, just in firing on Klikiss until her projectiles ran out. Clarin wished she had gotten away with her husband.

436

He and Davlin ran through the narrow streets of the inner town, desperately trying to manage the faltering defence. He was reminded of the time when the damned Eddies had come in to smash his beloved Hurricane Depot. This situation didn't look any better. During the black robot attack, the stockade walls had been breached in many places, and marauding insects now scrambled through every crumbling gap. Smoke billowed into the sky, and the smell of burning and death had already grown so thick he found it hard to breathe.

Clarin turned toward the nearest breach in the thick wall. 'I know a hopeless last stand when I see one, Davlin. But I've got one more trick up my sleeve.'

'What don't I know about?'

'The other Remora. It's flight-worthy, it's loaded – and I'm taking it.'

Davlin showed a glimmer of hope. 'Good. You can probably get six people aboard. Only six ... but it's half a dozen we can save.'

Clarin didn't respond. By now more than a hundred Klikiss had flown or pushed their way into the compound to round up colonists. He might save six people ... but which six? How could he choose, and what good would it do, if the Klikiss just came after them?

No, Clarin had something more permanent in mind. He raced out into the open and sprinted toward the debris yard on the outskirts, where the Remora sat unnoticed. Klikiss warriors abandoned the outer portion of the city, concentrating their forces on protecting the five remaining domates and attacking the walled city.

Still atop the wall, Marla shot again and again at the retreating domates, but those targets were too far away now. A Klikiss warrior scuttled up the inside of the wall behind her. She turned her gun around and blasted away, but a second creature raised its multiple legs and pulled her off the wall. She continued shooting all the way down.

Clarin finally reached the repaired Remora and squirmed through the half-open hatch. The ship's engines fired up like a charm. At least something was working right.

He had not been able to test-fly the ship, though Clarin knew how to pilot just about any vehicle with controls. Most Roamers did. Eddy controls seemed cumbersome, but Clarin leaned forward, scanned the buttons, and found what he needed. Using attitude-control jets, he drove the Remora out of the camouflaging debris, then quickly lifted it up with a blast from the main engines. The Remora pivoted in the air and flew toward the Klikiss towers.

Everything seemed to proceed in slow motion. His ears rang from the explosions, throbbing engines, gunfire, and screams. The Klikiss's whistles and chirps seemed loud enough to shatter even the cockpit windows. But Clarin blocked everything out of his mind and focused on his target. Adding thrust, he approached the fortress city. He saw the squat breedex hive, the thick-walled structure that contained the mind controlling all these deadly creatures.

Primary target.

His Remora had EDF weapons – probably enough to level that whole damned hive. If he could neutralize the *breedex*, he could effectively stop them all. *Or I could have rescued six people, like Davlin wanted.* Clarin was satisfied with his choice.

As the Remora picked up speed, however, dozens of Klikiss warriors took flight and rose like a plague of hornets to intercept him. Though he blasted many with the EDF jazers, Klikiss swarmed all around him. Several creatures caromed off the Remora's hull, stunned and disoriented. Others crashed into his engines, intentionally letting themselves be sucked into the air intakes. Red telltales flashed across his panels.

'Out of my way, damn you!'

Below, with a flash of hope, he saw Davlin leading a few more survivors in a sortie outside the walls. Hijacking a buzzing Klikiss vehicle, Davlin had taken as many colonists as he could. Now the alien groundcar bounced away across the rough terrain faster than warriors could pursue him. At least he was free ... for the time being.

A warrior threw its body into the cockpit canopy, creating a spiderweb of cracks across the transparent shield, effectively blocking Clarin's view. More warriors swarmed around the Remora, intent on pulling him out of the sky, and he opened fire indiscriminately, not caring what he hit. Explosions blossomed on the sides of the lumpy towers.

One of his engines gave out completely, torn loose by the clinging bugs. Many more warriors were crawling on the Remora's hull. Even as he flew, he could hear them ripping through the armour plating. The ship was going to crash. He jerked the control stick from side to side, sending the ship into a barrel roll, and two bugs slid off the cockpit canopy. Not enough.

The insect city was ahead, but he was losing altitude fast. The attacking insects were wreaking havoc on his systems, dismantling the weapons mounted to his hull. Three of the jazers already refused to fire.

He couldn't make it all the way to the breedex hive, damn it!

Below, all but one of the domates had been hustled into the towers. The last tiger-striped creature remained outside, surrounded by thirty warriors. When it tilted its spiny, crested head, Clarin thought he could look directly down into those faceted eyes.

It would have to do.

Clarin used the last of his control to guide the Remora, launching whatever remained of his weapons. He focused on the lone domate, the future of the hive. Secondary target. That one huge, ugly bug seemed to have a big bull's-eye painted on it.

Clarin dived the Remora downward, accelerating with the last gasps of his fuel. He never saw the flash of impact.

NINETY-SEVEN

RLINDA KETT

Rlinda and BeBob flew the *Voracious Curiosity* to Earth with Sullivan Gold, minding their own business. Rlinda hummed to herself to hide her uneasiness. 'Here we are, just an independent trader bringing a load of goods to Earth. No need to pay special attention to us.'

For the past few weeks, all Confederation traders had done their best to transmit the King's condemnation and Patrick Fitzpatrick's recorded confession. The message had been picked up by repeater stations and widely disseminated. Rlinda had to be very careful, though. They would be in a world of trouble if the *Curiosity* were caught doing it.

On their way to Earth, she and BeBob had stopped at three colonies that hadn't formally joined the Confederation. Not bothering to express disbelief at what Chairman Wenceslas and General Lanyan had done, the local government officials had simply shrugged. Even the story about the EDF cracking down on Rhejak only reinforced their reluctance to break away from the Hansa.

BeBob had been appalled, while Sullivan shook his head and sighed. 'You won't get through to them. They're brainwashed.'

'Or terrified,' BeBob said.

Rlinda shrugged. 'Maybe so, but the King asked us to spread the word, so we're spreading it. I am the Confederation's Trade Minister, you know. I think I need to make myself a special badge or something.'

BeBob had insisted on coming along on this run to Earth, even though Rlinda was apprehensive. His puppy-dog face was filled with an embarrassing degree of affection for her. 'Really, I won't set foot off the ship. I'll keep a lower profile than a speck of dust on wet hull paint. You don't have to worry, Rlinda. I promise.'

'Who said I was worried?'

He gave her a give-me-a-break frown. 'I can read you like a book.'

'Since when do you read books?'

By scanning the broadcast channels, Rlinda found at least two amateur groups that had copied the King's inflammatory message after she secretly broadcast it, and they were redistributing it as widely as possible before the Hansa managed to stop them. One independent repeater was shut down almost immediately, but other network nodes handed off the message again and again. People would hear it, she was sure; whether they chose to take action and rise up against the Chairman was another question entirely . . .

After a long, strangely awkward silence, BeBob spoke up, and she could tell he had been wrestling with his words for some time. 'If we're going to be partners, are you sure we shouldn't try getting married again?'

'We learned that lesson already.'

'But times have changed. Why not consider it?'

She squeezed him against her hard enough that he seemed

buried in her flesh. 'Feeling insecure? You're my partner, in business and in . . . physical interactions. Don't mess with a good thing. Paperwork can only screw it up.'

Sullivan came forward from the sleeping quarters in the back, rubbing his eyes, stretching his arms, and yawning. 'Are we almost there?'

Rlinda pointed out the cockpit viewports. 'That big blue marble is Earth. Recognize it? Can you see your house from here?'

The older man was both alarmed and eager. 'I thought you were going to wake me. I need time to get ready—'

'Take a breath, Mr Gold. We haven't even entered orbit yet. Then we have to descend and fill out about a million bureaucratic forms, get through the Hansa's pain-in-the-ass security pro-cedures, then line up for a landing pad. You'll have time to take another whole nap before we get down to Earth.'

The *Curiosity* dodged leftover space debris as Rlinda jockeyed for orbital position. Not many outside ships traded with the Hansa these days, and she expected to make a hefty profit, despite the absurdly high tariffs the Chairman had imposed.

Sullivan clasped his hands to keep his anticipation under control. 'Could I send a message to Lydia? Can we let my family know that I'm on the way?'

'Shouldn't be a problem. You're still a Hansa citizen, right?'

'As far as I know.'

Rlinda arranged the contact via the *Curiosity*'s tight-channel comm systems. Because Sullivan provided her with private-beam codes, she was able to make a direct link. 'I can route through local nodes. Your wife won't know it's anything more exciting than a sales call.'

Sullivan grinned. She could tell he was nervous, as well as eager. 'It'll make her day.'

'How long have you been married?' BeBob asked.

'So many years that I've lost count.'

Rlinda rolled her eyes. 'No you haven't.'

The older man gave a sheepish smile. 'Forty-two years. And a half.'

As BeBob engaged the link and boosted the signal, Rlinda swung her chair around. 'Are you sure you don't want us to make some kind of grand announcement? Get the Hansa out to greet you with a marching band? It's got to be big news to have you come home.'

BeBob nearly squawked. 'Rlinda! Low profile, remember?'

'I didn't say we had to tell everyone *you're* aboard. In fact, I'd prefer you hid in a cargo compartment marked "Hazardous Waste".'

'That's the first place they'd look.'

'No big reception committee, please,' Sullivan said. 'I'm not much of one for making a fuss. Just let me slip out of here and go have time with my family. The newsnets are sure to find out sooner or later, but give me a little time for a private reunion.'

'Whatever you say.'

When Lydia answered the signal, she was taken aback, and then shocked, thrilled, and slightly scolding. 'Well, well, I was wondering when you'd call home. I take it you're not dead, then? The Hansa reported that your whole cloud-harvesting facility was destroyed, no survivors.' She answered with a sternness that was clearly false.

He leaned so close to her image that Rlinda thought he'd bump his nose on the screen. 'You didn't get my letters? I had my green priest send them. You never knew I was rescued when the hydrogues destroyed my skymine?'

'Didn't get any letters – but, yes, I did hear the news. I've been waiting ever since.' Now she smiled. 'You look like you could use a shave.'

'You look wonderful.'

'Flattery like that makes me think you've got something to hide.'

'It means I missed you. Our ship is coming down to the Palace District spaceport now. Aren't you glad to have me home?'

'Absolutely. And not just for your scintillating conversation either. I could use a hand around here.'

'So, you'll be there to meet me?'

'I'll bring the family.' Lydia stared at him, as if she didn't want to cut the connection. 'But I have to get moving, otherwise we won't have time.'

Sullivan kept looking at the blank screen, then blinked and turned to Rlinda and BeBob. 'I have a fairly large family, you know.'

Two hours later, they set the *Curiosity* down on the marked pavement and opened the hatches to the fresh and familiar air of Earth. BeBob pushed his face into the breeze. 'Ah, just smell that!'

'Time for you to hide in the cargo compartment. I'll deal with the red tape.' Rlinda knew that spaceport security was going to be a labyrinth.

Sullivan was gathering his packs of personal possessions, keepsakes, and rewards the Mage-Imperator had given him when the Hansa's trade officials transmitted a list of their new enforcement measures. Rlinda listened to the comm, a stormy expression brewing on her wide face. 'Damn! BeBob, get to the cockpit.'

'What is it?'

'The goons are coming with scanners to inventory all cargo bays, including sealed containers. They're going to find you wherever you try to hide.'

'What am I going to do?'

'You're going with Sullivan – and you're going now. They just seized a big ship full of contraband components over in Zone B, and the goons are "apologizing for the delay in processing" us. Get your ass out of here, don't call any attention to yourself, and wait for me to send you an all-clear.'

BeBob started toward the extending ramp, following Sullivan, turned around, darted back to give Rlinda a peck on the cheek, then ran off into the bustle of the landing area.

Rlinda stayed behind, managing the details, filling out online forms, answering suspicious questions, and waiting for the trade inspectors, who came more than an hour later. It was a real pain in the butt. 'For all his bitching that he needs goods and materials, the Chairman certainly doesn't make things easy for an honest trader.'

She ushered aboard two Hansa representatives who skimmed her cargo manifest while a team of thick-armed and helmeted guards ran over her hull and interior with scanning devices. She let them find just enough undeclared high-tariff contraband that they stopped looking for anything more suspicious. She particularly didn't want them digging into her log, where they might see a mention of BeBob.

Finally, the trade reps offered to purchase the supplies she wanted to sell. Rlinda countered with a higher price and was shocked when the men met her negotiation with a stony glare. 'That is a set price, Captain Kett, and it's all we are allowed to offer. The Chairman has made revisions to our trading practices in this time of war. We presumed you knew the terms before you landed.'

The second representative said coldly, 'We have authorization to impound your entire cargo if you do not agree to these terms.'

'You don't get too many repeat customers, do you?' They faced her in silence, and she knew she had to concede. 'All right, but for that price, don't expect me to lift a finger to help you unload.'

'We have personnel for that, ma'am.' Uniformed crews

removed the crates from the *Curiosity*, carefully recording the contents after scanning them again for booby-traps or smuggled items. 'Once your cargo has been unloaded, Captain Kett, you have one hour to leave this landing facility.'

'Understood.' She snorted in disbelief. As if after this warm welcome she wanted to stay any longer than she had to? When the hold was empty and the unexpectedly small number of Hansa credits (worthless on most Confederation worlds) had been added to her account, she transmitted the all-clear for BeBob to come back. Rlinda waited alone, squirming, wishing she would hear something from him, but he hadn't answered.

Her uneasiness increased with every minute he was gone. It shouldn't have taken him so long to come back. She hoped he hadn't been talked into staying for dinner with Sullivan's family.

Over her private channel, BeBob's breathless voice spluttered. 'Rlinda – warm up the engines and open the hatch! I'm coming.'

'What's your hurry? Did you seduce the farmer's daughter or something?'

'Rlinda, I'm not kidding around! Somebody ran a check on the *Curiosity*. There's an arrest warrant on file for you. For us!' She heard the squawk in his voice and knew he was serious. She settled herself heavily into the wide chair behind the cockpit controls and felt the pulse of in-system engines as they built up their energy reserves. The moment the boarding ramp hummed down and locked into place, she heard BeBob scramble aboard. 'Go! The guards are coming to impound the ship.'

'Not my ship, they aren't.' She pounded one fist down on the launch buttons and slapped the hatch controls with the other hand. The *Curiosity* jumped into the air, and Rlinda used man-oeuvring jets to tilt the ship sideways and dodge a bulky tanker that was coming in for a landing.

A harsh voice came over the cockpit speakers. '*Voracious*

Curiosity, stand down immediately. Remain on the landing field.'

She couldn't keep the sarcasm out of her voice. 'Gentlemen, make up your minds! Your last message told me to leave as soon as possible.'

'Captain Kett, this is security. You are not authorized for departure. Return to the landing zone and prepare to be boarded.'

'I'm getting fed up with everything that's not authorized these days.' As the *Curiosity* gained altitude, Hansa security forces scrambled out of hangars around the landing zone to intercept them. She reached over and patted BeBob's hand. 'Don't you worry. I'm not going to let them catch you again.'

'Worry? Why would I worry?'

The Roamers had helped Rlinda modify the *Curiosity*, and she had a few tricks that the local EDF security forces could not counter. She spun her ship and dodged up through the thinning air, not following an approved path. The complaints, threats, and frustrated curses on the comm system soon became amusing. She ignored them as her ship easily outran the few pursuers.

NINETY-EIGHT

SULLIVAN GOLD

'You took your sweet time getting here,' Lydia said.

'I love you, too.' Sullivan couldn't wipe the grin off his face. He kissed her on the cheek. 'I missed you very much.'

'I'll bet. Do you have any idea how many times I thought about giving up on you and marrying somebody else?'

He held her, pressing her solid, bony body against him. 'I don't believe it for a minute.'

'Aren't you sweet?' They stood together at the edge of the landing zone, with inspectors and merchants moving in all directions. Captain Roberts had delivered Sullivan to his family, then quickly taken his leave, afraid that newsnet reporters might come to film the homecoming. He seemed very camera-shy.

Spacecraft came down, landing in heavy-security areas, and groundcars hauled cargo away to distribution centres. The air smelled of exhaust, fuel vapours, burned-out scrubbers, and paving material – much different from Mijistra, but he didn't mind. The familiar odours triggered a powerful nostalgia in him, enough to bring tears to his eyes, but he quickly wiped them away.

Around the spaceport, the background noise was deafening: air traffic, loading machinery, announcements blaring over loud-speakers, people shouting. His family pressed close. Sons, daughters, and excited grandchildren who wanted his attention peppered him with questions, eager to hear his stories, but he couldn't get a word in.

After receiving his message, Lydia had called the kids and grandkids and made a caravan. Sullivan was almost bowled over by the laughing, grinning people who rushed to greet him. He was smothered with kisses, claps on the back, children tugging on his wrists and elbows. He laughed out loud as he looked across the sea of faces, embarrassed to admit he didn't recognize some of them. 'How big has the family gotten anyway?'

'It's just the right size,' Lydia said.

He was shocked to see how different everyone looked. Had it only been a year? A lot had happened on Earth in the meantime. Was that Victor? And Patrice? How could so many hairstyles have changed? New boyfriends and girlfriends, two marriages broken up, three pregnancies, and one sad death (not from the hydrogue war, but in a stupid accident in a mass-transit breakdown). Three of the grandsons had 'done their part' by signing up to join the Earth Defence Forces, swayed by a gung-ho recruitment drive. Sullivan wasn't sure how he felt about that. He couldn't think of them as being *old enough* to do such a thing.

'It's so good to be home.' He kissed his wife on the ear and enjoyed the feeling of just standing there, surrounded by every-one. 'You haven't changed a bit. You don't look a day older.'

'That's because I fossilized long before you left.'

'I wrote you twenty-five letters, but the Mage-Imperator wouldn't let us send them. And you didn't get the one the green priest transmitted.'

'Convenient excuse.'

He sniffed at her teasing. 'A little sympathy, please! You can't imagine the ordeal I've been through: hydrogues destroyed my cloud-harvesting facility right out from under me, and Ildirans held us prisoner because we happened to see something we shouldn't have.'

'What did you see? Too many naked Ildiran females, I'll bet.' They had been married for so long that Lydia's barbs were more endearments than criticisms.

'Now, dear, I wouldn't have gone on this venture if we hadn't had a family meeting and decided it was for the best. The payment the Hansa promised—'

Her angry snort cut him off, and he grew worried. 'Payment? They changed the rules on us as soon as we filed for your death benefits!'

'You filed for death benefits?'

'Well, they did say your skymine was destroyed. We haven't gotten a single credit, so it hasn't been a picnic here either.'

He blinked at her, feeling a little weak in the knees. 'You filed for death benefits? Really?'

'Your cloud harvester was destroyed, and you disappeared. What was I supposed to think – that you had learned how to fly?'

'I guess I can't argue with that.' Anxious now to be away from the landing field and all the noise, he tried to steer the crowd back toward the pedestrian walks.

One of the grandkids, Jessica, pulled on his sleeve. 'Did you come home rich? Grandma says you're bringing a treasure chest.'

'Well, I came home with quite a few Ildiran valuables.'

He grinned, but Lydia's expression darkened. 'Better hide them before the Hansa confiscates them. They'll come up with a fifty-per-cent import tax or something.'

Putting on an optimistic face, he said, 'At least I'll have the undying gratitude of the Mage-Imperator – for what it's worth.'

451

A sharpness came to his wife's eyes. 'Good. We may all have to move there if things keep going the way they are. You won't believe what the Chairman—'

'Quiet, Ma,' said the oldest son, Jerome. He looked around anxiously, as if she had said something dangerous, as if electronic pickups might be listening to every word they spoke.

Sullivan drew back. 'What's going on?'

'Nothing, nothing!' Jerome said quickly, patting his mother's arm. 'You know her. If there isn't something to complain about, then there's no sunshine in her day. Maybe we'll all take a vacation to Ildira. Someday.'

Sullivan made Lydia look at him. 'What's happened around here? I've been cut off from everything. I've spoken with Roamer traders and former Hansa merchants, and none of them have much good to say about Chairman Wenceslas. Is it true he sent an EDF battle group to try to conquer Theroc and seize the King and Queen? Did he really take over Rhejak?'

'Let's just say this, Sullivan: You were wise not to cause a hullabaloo when you got home. No interviews, no announcements. It's best you not call attention to yourself. I doubt the Chairman would appreciate it. And it's good that you've carved out some options for us, just in case Earth is no longer a particularly good place to raise a family. You may well have been better off on Ildira.'

NINETY-NINE

CHAIRMAN BASIL WENCESLAS

He could use the Klikiss to the Hansa's advantage. Basil decided that was the best way to deal with the situation. And the Archfather of Unison would be his spokesman.

Not a thread could be loose, not a single wrinkle showing, no speck of makeup in the wrong place. With an eagle eye, Basil watched every step as stylists, groomers, and personality coaches prepared the Archfather for his grand debut.

Basil gazed into the plump old man's sapphire eyes. Those eyes had attracted him to this candidate in the first place. The clear blue was natural, which eliminated the requirement for implants. The Archfather's voice was deep and resonant; his thick snow-white beard flowed from his apple-red cheeks down to a tapered point. Voluminous ceremonial robes hung on his soft shoulders, draped to imply a massive body but hide his girth. His ceremonial crook was imposing, a golden staff encrusted with faceted gems, every one of which had been oiled and polished so that not a smudge would be visible on even the highest resolution observation image.

The Archfather was a reassuring figure, practically a picture of old Saint Nicholas – and not by accident. His attitude was avuncular, non-threatening. Unison had long been a comfortable part of Hansa life, like a kindly old pet dog with no teeth. But that would soon change. The Archfather's speech today would begin an entirely new programme.

A century before, when previous Hansa Chairmen had built the framework of Unison and developed the Archfather as its visible face, they had chosen their symbolic references well. In many respects, the Archfather reminded Basil of Old King Frederick, a cooperative puppet who hadn't been too smart for his own good.

'You are ready for this.' He intentionally did not make it into a question.

'I believe so, Mr Chairman.'

'You must *know* it in your heart. No second chances.'

The Archfather squared his shoulders to pump up his presence. He had always been a good performer. 'I have been coached mercilessly. I know my lines, and I know the consequences if I make any mistakes.' His lips curved upward around the white strands of his beard, but Basil scolded him.

'No smiling! Not for this, and not for the foreseeable future. There can be no twinkle in your eye when you explain the root cause of this looming disaster. When we show General Lanyan's images from the raid on Pym, you must be righteously indignant, angry at this new and terrible enemy we face. Not grinning like an idiot.' Sheepish, the Archfather nodded, while Basil continued. 'From this day forward, your responsibilities will increase tenfold. You are no longer just a fixture, but a true weapon in the cause of humanity.'

A prepped crowd had gathered in the Palace District Square. Traditionally, the Archfather spoke from the Unison temple, but

Basil had decided that the Whisper Palace was the best venue. 'Go. They are waiting for you. My deputy and I will observe from here.'

Energized by Basil's speech, the Archfather marched off, followed by attendants who continued to straighten his robes and brush at imagined specks of lint. Getting into character, he moved with a ponderous grace, using his heavy staff.

As scheduled, Deputy Cain arrived to join him. Basil nodded. 'You're finally here. Good. I want you to hear the Archfather's words.' The Chairman took his place on the inset balcony alcove from which they could watch without being seen. The audience began to stir as the honour guard marched toward the platform, preparing the way.

'The Archfather has never voiced anything but bland platitudes,' Cain said, looking down into the milling crowd.

'Not today. Never again after today.'

The bearded man climbed the steps to stand on the high platform, and the crowd fell silent. The Archfather began with a traditional invocation, adding a few militaristic phrases that went beyond the usual 'care for each other and love God'. In a booming voice, he said, 'There is nothing more holy than a soldier fighting for a holy cause. I will tell you what we must do.' He raised his staff and lowered it again like a spear carrier thumping his weapon. The audience was fully attentive now.

Ever since General Lanyan had returned, Basil had decided to turn the failure into a crowbar. He did not allow any sanitizing of the horrific footage of Pym, insisting that the bloody deaths of EDF soldiers play without mercy. Before the surviving colonists were even cleaned up, their clothes still in tatters, their skin still smeared with alkaline dust, soldiers had recorded their grim tales of the Klikiss invasion.

The monstrous Klikiss images (originally recorded on the soldiers' suitcams) were broadcast incessantly on the newsnets.

No person could help but shudder upon seeing how the hideous insect creatures had enslaved or slaughtered the poor colonists.

'Those monsters are a miracle in disguise – just what we needed.' Basil smiled with satisfaction. 'It shines a whole new light on King Peter's supposed insurrection and his divisive comments. They will see Peter's ploy for what it is, juvenile politics, and they won't want any part of it. The Klikiss threat will make all loyal citizens draw together.'

'Perhaps if you gave them another King, they would forget about Peter entirely,' Cain suggested. 'When do you plan to introduce your new candidate? When will you show him to me?'

'When it is time. At the moment, we need something different. Religion is the key, and for now the Archfather will fill a pivotal role.' He pointed out to the speaking podium in the Palace District Square. 'Listen.'

The Archfather delivered his speech like a true master, full of passion and fire. The audience, already primed with fear, was moved by his grand statements. 'You have seen the images. Those creatures attacked us, stealing worlds that we have so painstakingly colonized. They are called the Klikiss.' He raised a fist. 'But I call them *demons*! No truly faithful person needs a scientific explanation for an answer that is so obvious.'

The people muttered, growled, cheered, or cried out.

'I speak to give you hope, but first we must face an unpleasant reality. First you must understand *why* the demons have come. You see, we have brought this punishment upon ourselves. We have shunted aside our religion for secular concerns, paying more attention to business and politics than to God.'

Basil smiled at the surprised expression on Cain's face. 'I thought that was a nice touch.'

'First the hydrogues nearly destroyed us, but we defeated them. Then even our King and Queen turned against us, abandoned

Earth and the Hansa – and as soon as they did so, the Klikiss returned.' He nodded sagely. 'That is when we went astray. Peter continues to speak his poisonous words against the Chairman, against the Hansa – *against all of you*. He cannot be forgiven for that, and you will continue to pay the price if you listen to him.

'The Klikiss demons have come as chastisement for our indiscretions. If we are to save ourselves, we must change our way of thinking. In the coming days, I will lay out a great plan for our survival. God punishes us only as a reminder of how we have disappointed Him. But as always, God is kind, and He shows us the path to redemption.'

The people cheered. Basil was extremely satisfied. Cain, however, seemed perplexed. 'But Unison has always been a very uncontroversial religion, so much a compromise of every faith that all of its power was drained away. I thought that was the original purpose behind forming it, to disarm fanatics and let us follow our business pursuits unhampered.'

Basil pursed his lips. 'At one time that was true, but Unison can no longer be a bland religion. Not in times like these. Under my guidance, this is just the first of many speeches the Archfather will deliver.'

ONE HUNDRED

MARGARET COLICOS

The flat, tinny melody played against a fugue of human screams. In the alien ruins to which she had retreated, Margaret sat looking out a tower opening. Her feet were curled under her as she huddled against the rough wall. She had tried her best, but she had known from the beginning that the colonists had no chance. Now even DD was gone, and she was completely alone among the monsters. Just like before.

She had struggled to communicate with the breedex – shouting in their harsh scraping language, demanding that the Klikiss not harm the colonists, emphasizing that these people were *her hive*. She had drawn equations on the ground, played her music.

But the breedex no longer heard her. Even her music box did little to impress the Klikiss. The hive mind meant to consume every human it had 'stored' to foster a great fissioning. The hive needed to expand, to replenish the numbers it had lost in recent battles, including four of its eight domates. Margaret wondered how that would affect the fissioning. The Klikiss offspring would depend even more on the human attributes the hive mind meant to incorporate. She remembered the handful of Klikiss hybrids that had resulted from poor Howard Palawu's assimilation.

That wouldn't save any of the colonists.

Driven away from the battle, untouched by the mayhem, Margaret had watched Klikiss warriors recapture some escaping Roamers and drive them back into the boundaries of the camp. Labouring non-stop, multilegged workers circled the battleground, picking up human corpses and throwing them back into the stockade. When the domates fed, they could acquire what they needed from dead flesh as easily as from living victims.

Bearers had brought dozens of grublike excreters to create resin-cement to seal the human survivors inside again. Very soon, the rebuilt stockade became a festering chamber of horrors. The people had been starved now for two days since the battle. Their water had been cut off. The solid walls were higher and smoother, with no openings, no chance for anyone to slip away.

Either to spite the domates or express their grief, the survivors had gathered the corpses and piled them on bonfires, denying the breedex some DNA. Even from a distance, looking down from the Klikiss towers, Margaret could hear the captives howling. She was outside, safe, and completely miserable.

She wound up the music box and played it again. She had learned the words of 'Greensleeves' from Anton himself, had even taught them to Orli:

> Alas, my love, you do me wrong,
> To cast me off discourteously.
> For I have loved you well and long,
> Delighting in your company.

At ground level, with a buzzing and unified movement, columns of Klikiss workers and warriors filed down out of towers, while others leapt from arched overhangs and flew out to the churned ground. Margaret's stomach clenched. So, the breedex had made its decision.

> Your vows you've broken, like my heart,
> Oh, why did you so enrapture me?
> Now I remain in a world apart
> But my heart remains in captivity.

She let the music box wind down. How she missed Anton. How she longed for Louis to be here. She and her husband had done such a fine job of reconstructing the Klikiss Torch, using that alien weapon for what they had thought would be the good of the Hansa. A massively incorrect assumption.

The four remaining domates lurched out of the Klikiss city. One of the striped creatures limped, and Margaret saw that two of its segmented limbs had been severed in the recent battle. The domates stalked ahead, their carapaces and spines polished. The workers had buffed and dressed the tiger-striped creatures for this grand procession.

Flanked by warriors, the domates advanced purposefully toward the stockade wall. Inside the compound, standing on the highest rooftops of the town's buildings, the captives saw them coming and let out a wild uproar. They hurled plascrete blocks, metal reinforcement beams, even heavy furniture, injuring a few loitering Klikiss scouts. The domates did not pause. They had their eyes on the immense genetic feast spread out before them.

As a species, the Klikiss hated only each other and the black robots. Initially, humans had simply been an obstacle, a distraction . . . but now they were raw material. Shuddering, Margaret tried to retreat to a better place in her mind.

As a xeno-archaeologist, she was accustomed to solitude. She and Louis had spent extended periods digging through haunted cities on empty planets, searching for scraps of long-forgotten history. She had particularly loved their first solo expedition to the pyramids of Mars. They had devoted years garnering the funding, living on a shoestring, calling in favours, taking out loans against everything they owned. She and Louis had set up a hab unit in a red canyon, scrounging every scrap of condensed air and water they could boil out of the Martian rocks and sand.

The set of mysterious pyramids had first been detected on satellite mapping overflights of Mars, then imaged in greater detail from ground-based rovers. The pyramids were perfect tetrahedral structures towering more than two hundred metres above the canyon rim. Each angle was perfect. The sides must once have been polished mirror-smooth, though signs of weathering were evident.

The original images had caused an amazing stir on Earth. Humanity had barely ventured beyond their own solar system, had not yet encountered any other trace of an alien civilization. Thus, the mystery of the Martian pyramids captivated everyone. Before any rigorous scientific research could be done at the site, however, an Ildiran warliner had come to Earth and stolen all the thunder, introducing the human race to the vast alien Empire. From that point on, few people had been interested in a dead, old artifact of questionable origin.

Margaret longed for the innocence of those exciting days . . .

Now the four domates rose up in front of the thick stockade walls. People on the other side shouted insults, screamed, or wailed. Worker insects applied a greyish paste to the walls, and all Klikiss backed away as the chemical oxidized in the air, reached thermal instability, and blasted the sealed resin walls inward, opening the way for the domates.

Taken by surprise, the captives tried to retreat, backing into corners. When the smoke cleared, Klikiss workers raced forward on multiple legs, pulling away debris to make a passage for the domates. The striped Klikiss raised their sharp limbs, ready to feed.

Again, Margaret sought shelter in memories. She forced her mind back to the days that she and Louis had spent at the Martian pyramids, wearing environment suits, combing the angled structures for any hint of alien language or extraterrestrial technology. They had used the best sensors and analytical devices they'd been able to afford, and had made leaps of intuition. They drilled core samples, sent echo-sounders to study the internal structure. They worked for weeks. And found nothing.

In the end, they'd had no choice but to conclude that the famed Martian pyramids did not have an extraterrestrial origin, but were instead a one-in-a-million natural phenomenon of bizarre mineral growths. She and Louis had painstakingly compiled their data and posted their results for all to see. Louis in particular had been sad to strip the wonder from a landmark of the human imagination.

That announcement had made Margaret and Louis Colicos famous, at the same time triggering an angry response among people who desperately wanted to believe in the mysterious alien presence. The Martian pyramids were still a geological wonder, built over countless centuries by the crystalline conversion actions of a rare colony bacteria. But that had not stopped the hue and cry. She and Louis had even received a few death threats. But they stood by their findings, simply pointing to the data. What else could they do? The truth was the truth, no matter how inconvenient or disappointing it might be. She had drawn strength from Louis, and he had stood by her . . .

Inside the stockade, the domates began their slaughter. They fell upon the trapped humans, systematically killing one after another. Though the people fought back, they had no chance at all. Klikiss warriors plunged through the gap in the wall, but let the domates do most of the killing. It was their racial tradition.

Margaret thought she could smell the blood from where she sat. The human cries of pain and fear merged into a single background tone that grated on the back of her skull. She closed her eyes.

By the time of the Martian expedition, she and Louis had only been married for a year. Though day-to-day existence was hard and uncomfortable, those days had been like a real honeymoon for them – so peaceful and romantic. She and Louis had barely finished their work before the funding and supplies ran out, but Margaret hadn't wanted to leave the red planet. It had been an accident, though probably inevitable, that they had conceived Anton there in the deep canyons on Mars . . .

High in the Klikiss tower, she wound the music box again. *Greensleeves*.

Finally, all the screams from the compound ceased. She heard a last frantic wail from a few colonists whose careful bolt-hole had been discovered, then that too was cut off. Klikiss workers flooded into the compound and piled the bodies of their victims before the domates, who gorged themselves on all the new human DNA.

ONE HUNDRED AND ONE

TASIA TAMBLYN

When the *Osquivel* finally reached Llaro, Tasia was glad to be coming as a liberator, for a change. Nikko Chan Tylar was ready to tar and feather those who had illegally imprisoned his parents. Robb was making plans to load the ship with up to a hundred Roamer detainees, and anyone else who wanted to come along.

Arriving on a silent, low-angle approach vector, Tasia advised Robb on where the main settlement was. He altered course accordingly. 'I'm sending an ID signal and announcing that we have no hostile intentions. Just in case.'

'Shizz, you do that, you'll be warning the Eddy crew down there.'

'Come on, we're not exactly a stealth craft. They must have orbital sensors to detect us regardless. Why not try to resolve this peacefully?'

'Your optimism gives me cramps, Brindle.' Nevertheless, she knew the Eddy babysitters stationed on Llaro had to be strictly bottom-of-the-barrel recruits if General Lanyan hadn't even needed them as cannon fodder against the drogues. She didn't expect there'd be much in the way of shooting.

Nikko leaned over the two pilot seats, squirming with anxiety. 'Did you send a message telling my parents that I'm aboard? Have they answered? Has anyone responded at all?'

Only a whisper of static came back. 'No questions, no demands, no "happy to see you". Everybody must be playing hide-and-seek.' Tasia looked down, checking the coordinates. 'That's damned peculiar. The settlement and base should be right down there.'

'We're coming over the horizon now. We'll be in view in just a few minutes.'

As they flew over it, Tasia's eyes drank in the details of what remained of the colony town. The permanent settlement and colourful temporary camps had been smashed flat, materials strewn about as if a tornado had hit; the croplands for miles around were burned or excavated. 'Shizz, what the hell happened down there?'

New termite-mound towers and lumpy structures had sprung up everywhere, and a large trapezoidal frame that must have been a newly built transportal stood out in the open. The Klikiss ruins were no longer ruins, but a full-fledged metropolis five times the size of the old towers she had seen on her first visit here. Dark forms like gigantic bugs moved about on the landscape. Some of the creatures climbed down from the alien towers; others took wing and flew.

Tasia suddenly remembered a bizarre piece of news that the Mage-Imperator had sent via green priest to King Peter. 'By the Guiding Star, those are the *Klikiss*! They came back to Llaro. They—'

'They demolished the whole damn colony,' Robb cried. 'That explains why nobody's answering.'

465

'I'd rather be facing the Eddy watchdogs.'

Nikko gripped the back of the copilot's chair to keep his balance. 'We can't assume everybody's dead. We don't know what happened. Maybe there are survivors. We have to check!'

'Take a look and draw your own conclusions.'

'No! We don't know enough! Some people might have gotten away. A lot of them. We can't just give up.'

'I wasn't giving up,' Tasia said. 'Not yet. But I don't think it's a good idea to go ask those bugs what happened. They look too damned much like the black robots. And I've got *issues* with those things.'

Robb leaned forward. 'What's that? Something shooting into the air.'

Dozens of small boxy ships launched from the burned fields, heading toward the *Osquivel*. The ground was covered with the angular craft, and they took flight like wasps from a rattled nest. 'Aw, hell, now they're after us.'

Robb was already turning them in a high-G loop. Tasia threw herself in front of the weapons controls.

'We can't just run away.' Nikko looked very pale. 'We don't know . . . we don't know for sure—'

Seeing how the creatures had wiped out the settlement, she decided there was no point in negotiating. She started taking potshots and blasted a pair of individual craft into debris. Another wave of the component craft streaked after them like bees.

The individual Klikiss units returned fire, shooting a high-intensity plasma burst unlike anything Tasia had ever seen. By making an extreme course correction that threw Nikko against the wall, Robb avoided the blast. He accelerated and dodged, scanning the wrinkled landscape, but saw no good place to hide among the arroyos and rock outcroppings.

'You've got no reason to complain about not having enough targets, Tamblyn. Stop gawking and keep firing.'

Tasia responded with a vengeance, three shots and three more destroyed Klikiss ships. 'Hey, our new weapons work like a charm.' The alien vessels closed in, and four of them opened fire at once. A powerful bolt scored the underside of the *Osquivel*'s hull; another grazed their engines, making Robb's cockpit instruments jump wildly.

Pulling himself forward against the heavy acceleration, Nikko slapped the comm system, activating their emergency signal and locator beacon. 'Mayday, mayday! We're under attack by the Klikiss.'

'Who do you expect is going to hear us, Nikko?' Tasia asked.

'Anyone who's still alive down there. There must be somebody.'

'There's a difference between being optimistic and being clueless. If they had any way of fighting the bugs, wouldn't they have done it already?'

Robb scolded her. 'Don't yell at the kid. What have you got against positive thinking?'

The *Osquivel* gained altitude, and Tasia saw two more vessels coming down toward them from orbit. How many more were up there in space? 'They're blocking us in.'

She shot at the two overhead ships, ruining one, and focused on four more that came at them from the sides. The alien craft were like oversized angry gnats in the air. Robb was hell-bent, diving toward the ground, streaking eastward. The sun had already set, and they would be in full night before long. Fortunately, they were far enough from the ruined settlement that no more alien ships joined the pursuers. The insect hive city down there had been chaotic and incomprehensible, and she wondered if the Klikiss had suffered some sort of recent turmoil.

The alien ships still after them were relentless, firing again and again. A solid shot struck the already damaged engine, and the *Osquivel* lurched downward. 'That isn't good,' Robb said.

Tasia concentrated her fire on the remaining attackers. 'Only five left. I can probably take them out.' As if to belie her assertion, another shot struck the *Osquivel* and damaged the good engine.

'We're not going to make it much farther,' Robb said. Around them, the sky had grown dim with twilight. They raced onward.

Tasia saw this as target practice, barely bothering to breathe. She wrecked two more Klikiss ships – three left. But Robb was unable to manoeuvre. He could barely control their descent. 'We're going down!'

Their albatross flightpath lured the Klikiss ships closer, ready for the kill. Tasia could have taken a shot, but first she let them come nearer. The Klikiss, seeing that they had mortally damaged the *Osquivel*, swept in, driving them downward.

'Come on, you bastards, just a little bit closer.' The component ships obliged. With a yelp of triumph, she hit the weapons controls and fired as many blasts as she could, as fast as the *Osquivel* could generate the pulses. All three enemy ships exploded in the air. 'Gotcha!'

'If you're going to do a victory dance, do it quick,' Robb said. 'Ten seconds until we hit – and don't expect it to be a soft landing.' The night-shadowed terrain rose up toward them, and Robb tried to head for a wide canyon. 'But don't worry. I practised this in the simulator.'

'Five years ago.' Tasia braced herself. 'Shizz, hang on!'

The *Osquivel* scoured the bottom of the canyon with its belly, scraping rocks, spewing dirt, slewing right and left. An avalanche of sound reverberated through the hull. Anti-flame foam sprayed around the engines. Crash webbing locked down around Tasia like a hunter's net.

When the ship came to a grinding rest, Tasia shook her head, trying to focus her eyes and clear the ringing from her ears. As Robb shut down the systems and assessed the major damage (one engine off-line, the other ruined, and most of their fuel spilled all over the landscape), Tasia quickly disembarked, and circled the ship to see how bad everything looked.

The *Osquivel* had come to rest near a lonely distant canyon, far from the obliterated colony settlement. 'What a mess.'

Nikko dug out the medkit and came out to stand beside her, looking forlorn. 'I've crashed too many times for someone my age.'

'Most people don't get a chance to crash more than once.'

The *Osquivel* still made groaning and clicking noises as it cooled and settled. The fire-suppressant foam fizzed as it soaked into the dry landscape. Otherwise, the Llaro night was very quiet and ominous.

'Some rescue.' Tasia looked around in the gathering dark.

'We wiped out all the ships chasing us,' Nikko pointed out, 'so maybe none of the bugs will know where to find us.'

Robb's face was drawn. 'We need to keep watch around the perimeter.'

'I'll rig weapons for personal defence. I think I can still fire some of the ship's guns. Let's hope we managed to, uh, crash unobtrusively.' Tasia suddenly bolted back into the ship, realizing that the emergency locator beacon was still pinging. She disconnected it swiftly, came out, and stood next to Robb. She put her arms around him and hugged him as they stared off into the night.

ONE HUNDRED AND TWO

JESS TAMBLYN

Their wental ship flew away from the scarred ice and tragic memories of Jonah 12, leaving behind a glimmering presence on the empty planetoid. The water beings guided them to a colourful, swirling soup of ionized gases and dissociated molecules, a nebula lit by the fires of newborn nearby stars. Jess now knew it was the site of an ancient battlefield where wentals had been torn apart by hydrogues and faeros, their molecules spattered like blood across the emptiness.

'But what sort of war was it?' Cesca asked. 'Why were you fighting the faeros as well as the hydrogues?'

'I thought the faeros turned against the drogues,' Jess added.

The faeros are allies of no one. They cooperate when it suits them, but they mean only to destroy. Us. The hydrogues. Everything.

The water-bubble ship flitted into the densest knots of vapour, and molecules coalesced around it. Together, he and Cesca used their skills in controlling the wentals to reintegrate the scattered water that had once belonged to the elementals, and the globe began to expand. Individual entities formed a collective strength.

470

How many more of the water beings had been spread across the cold vacuum? The silvery ship drank tiny droplets, pulling out pools that would become more wentals. Healing, strengthening, growing, *living*. Those were concepts and motivations that neither the hydrogues nor the chaotic faeros embraced.

Jess felt a burgeoning satisfaction fill him. Cesca pressed her fingers to the flexible membrane, watching and touching the wentals as they were resurrected. Visiting Jonah 12 had been a vivid reminder of the robot attack, the deaths of all the Roamers there, and how she herself had nearly died. Now they both felt so alive.

As their ship continued to cruise through the nebula, it grew ever larger, absorbing a multitude of anxious voices. *We have been rejoined. Now we must be distributed again, disseminated widely.*

Jess wasn't sure if he could find Nikko Chan Tylar or the water-bearer volunteers who had previously helped him spread the wentals. But he had another idea. 'We could go to Plumas. My uncles can use the Tamblyn water tankers to distribute these new nebula wentals.'

'While we gather even more,' Cesca added.

When they returned to the ice moon, Cesca was surprised and delighted to find her father visiting. He and Caleb Tamblyn often worked together, planned oddball business schemes together, and got into trouble together. Denn Peroni had come back to see that the water mines were now back in business.

In the completely refashioned underground chambers, a smiling Caleb explained, 'With the new availability of ekti and plenty of Confederation planets to serve, trade ships are sure going to need the water, oxygen, and other by-products we provide.' Chill steam puffed from his mouth as he spoke. 'Each day, more and more ships dock at our wellheads to fill their reservoirs.'

After trading with the Ildiran Empire, Denn had returned successful – and somehow changed. Even Jess picked up on the difference, sensing an unexpected resonance with the wentals in his own bloodstream.

When Cesca asked her father about it, Denn brushed most questions aside, but he could not stop his eyes from sparkling. 'Everything's different now! That green priest on Ildira, the Hansa engineers, they all changed, like an evolution. They found a new way of *thinking* and showed it to me.' Though he wore only a light vest and shirt in the cold underground grotto, he did not appear cold. Though not infused with wental energy, Denn seemed able to sense the elemental beings, hear their thoughts in a way that surprised Jess.

'I don't know what's gotten into him.' Caleb shook his head. 'But then, he never made much sense to me anyway. Should I worry about it?'

'No, you shouldn't,' Cesca said. 'It's not ... threatening or dangerous.'

Denn smiled at his daughter. 'Before long, I might even figure out how I can touch you again. Everything used to be a mystery, but now it makes so much more sense.' He clapped a hand on Caleb's bony shoulder. 'We will be happy to distribute the new wentals while you continue your search. We'll take a Tamblyn tanker and do it ourselves.'

Caleb scowled. 'Who are you to offer—'

'I'm the one who lent you the workers and equipment from Osquivel to fix your water mines.'

'Well, that may be so, but we didn't end up needing them as much as we thought we would. Jess and Cesca did most of it.'

'Good. In that case, why not do them a small favour?' Denn's grin did not diminish; he seemed entirely at peace. 'Paying back a debt is never a waste of time.'

'Well, of course not.'

Later, out on the surface of the frozen moon, Jess directed the segregated nebula wentals to stream away from his bubble and pour into the landed tanker. The revitalized water flowed like a glistening caterpillar, alive as it moved into the hold and spread out to fill every empty space without losing a drop. When the tanker was filled with the energized fluid, Jess and Cesca said their farewells and thanks.

Cesca looked deeply into her father's eyes, trying to understand what had changed about him. The wentals picked up on a closeness similar to the mental bond she and Jess shared, but this ability was broader, more all-consuming, than the wental connection. Denn seemed happier, stronger, as if he could be closer to her than ever before. 'It's wonderful, Cesca. Don't ever worry about me.'

'Are you going to explain what happened to you?'

He gave her a strange smile. 'Someday. I'm sure the wentals will comprehend it. The worldtrees are starting to. Right now, I need to understand it better myself. When I'm ready, I'll share this with my daughter, or the Speaker – *former* Speaker – of the Roamers.'

'In the last year, I haven't been much of a Speaker or a daughter.'

'You have been everything to me, dear Cesca. By the Guiding Star, don't ever forget that.'

ONE HUNDRED AND THREE

SIRIX

Defeated but not destroyed, broken but still surviving, Sirix struggled to keep his dwindling forces going. The battle group was battered from the clash at Llaro. He had lost many of his ships, Soldier compies, and black robots. The heavy EDF vessels had very little fuel remaining and almost no weaponry.

For the first time, he considered the real possibility of simply hiding, hibernating, burying all of the black robots on some isolated asteroid or moon, and just waiting for a few thousand years. But by that time, Sirix was certain the Klikiss would have swarmed unchecked across the Spiral Arm. He could not abide that, and dogged determination kept him going. There had to be some way.

He stumbled upon an unexpected advantage.

In the vastness of empty space, the prowling robot battleships encountered a lone Roamer cargo escort heavily loaded with ekti tanks. Sirix focused his attention and locked on his enhanced sensors. All of his surviving ships came to full alert.

'We should attack,' Ilkot announced. 'Our battle group is desperately in need of stardrive fuel.'

'Our battle group is desperately in need of everything.' Sirix studied the results of their cursory scans, forcing himself to be logical and consider the broader implications. Their very survival was at stake. 'By itself, that cargo load is insufficient to fuel our battle group for long. Allow the ship to increase its distance, while we remain just within sensor range. Perhaps if we follow this Roamer craft, it will lead us to an even larger prize.'

'We dare not let it escape.'

'It will not escape.'

As soon as the cargo escort detected the battle group, it deviated from its course and accelerated, regarding them warily, like one animal approaching another at a watering hole. The pilot would have concluded that these ships belonged to the Earth Defence Forces, known rivals of the Roamers.

The robot ships moved along their previous course, letting the Roamer think he had slipped past their sensors. Sirix launched a tiny probe to streak off in the wake of the cargo escort and transmit a directional beacon back. The Roamer continued to fly away, clearly believing he had nothing to fear. The cargo escort's enhanced engines could apply higher-than-expected thrust, so he probably thought he could build extra distance for himself, but the black robots were not fragile humans and could endure even higher acceleration.

After waiting as long as he felt necessary, Sirix began cautiously stalking his quarry. The robot-controlled ships strung out in a long line, careful to maintain enough distance that the Roamer pilot would not detect them. The trailing probe sent a clear signal, and they easily followed.

Sirix summoned PD and QT to the bridge to watch. He predicted this would be interesting.

Eventually, the Roamer cargo escort approached a dim star system lit by a brown dwarf. 'Sensors indicate no planets in this system habitable for biological life,' Ilkot said. 'The star's thermal output is insufficient.'

'Scan closer. Look for industrial activity. Artificial bases, satellites, any other ship traffic.' Sirix could calculate few reasons why humans would come to a place so unwelcoming to biological life-forms, unless they intended to hide their facility. He felt confident that his earlier conjecture was correct: The cargo escort would lead them to greater stores of fuel. He signalled for his battleships to close up ranks, waiting outside the brown dwarf system as the Roamer slowed, drifted in, and pinpointed its safe haven.

Ilkot reported, 'We have found a small facility, mostly artificial, made of processed metal. It carries a high thermal signature. The parent asteroid is less than half a kilometre wide.'

'It is a fuel-transfer depot of some sort,' Sirix concluded. 'Roamers would not want others to know the location of this facility. Approach with caution, maintain communications silence, and minimize engine output.'

The cargo escort docked at the small asteroid depot and shut down its hot in-system thrusters, but Sirix ordered his robots to wait a full hour to allow the people at the depot enough time to grow complacent. The gathered robot ships cruised silently closer, poised to strike.

Sirix announced, 'Roamers generally have few defensive weapons. Their mode of protection is to hide rather than fight. We must encircle and trap them, complete containment, not only to maintain our secrecy, but to avoid the loss of valuable spacecraft or materials. Fire your weapons with precision. We do not wish to destroy, and therefore waste, the stardrive fuel.'

'Or waste our weapons,' PD said.

Engines fired again, pushing the stolen EDF ships like projectiles in a last high-speed race toward their target. Before the startled Roamers could do any more than transmit an indignant inquiry, the black robots had overwhelmed them. The humans didn't even try to run.

Sirix studied the outpost, which was not much more than a tumbling rock with domes and subsidiary tanks welded on. He saw docking cradles for six cargo escorts. The depot's large ekti reservoirs were nearly full, ready for widespread distribution among Roamer facilities and human colonies, perhaps even to the Ildiran Empire. Four small ships were also parked there.

'Eleven life-forms aboard,' Ilkot said. 'No significant defences.'

PD and QT diligently offered to help, but Sirix took control of the Juggernaut's weapons systems himself. Without making any unnecessary announcement or threat, he destroyed the depot's life-support generators. It took him only one medium-power jazer shot.

The explosion made a beautiful pattern of fire and light; hot debris sprayed upward and kept drifting out into space, slipping away from the asteroid's low gravity. Sirix considered blowing up the four small parked ships as well, just to cripple the humans, but he could not afford to waste any viable equipment.

The Roamers howled in an annoying cacophony across the communication bands. 'All right, you Eddy bastards, we surrender! Damned pirates! Barrymore's Rock may be a small facility, but we are a member of the Confederation. By the Guiding Star, we demand that you take us to King Peter. The Earth Defence Forces has no right—'

Three other Roamers crowded closer to the screen. 'You destroyed our life support. We won't survive long—'

Sirix opened the channel, allowing them to see his black geometrical head and his squat beetlelike body. 'No, you will not survive long. And we are not interested in your surrender.'

He closed the channel and dispatched crews of robots to the depot. They needed no atmosphere or docking bays. They simply dropped out of the open bays of the EDF ships and streamed over to the small rotating facility, manoeuvring under their own power. This was the way battle was supposed to be.

The humans had barricaded themselves inside, but the robots cut directly through the outer hull, releasing a blast of stale air in explosive decompression, spilling the atmosphere into space like blood. Some sections of the metal walls caved in, too thin to support themselves without air pressure. As the power generators died, lights inside Barrymore's Rock shut off, leaving only dim tell-tale emergency glows.

The robots entered in pitch darkness. Shifting their optical sensors to infra-red, they hunted down any humans who hadn't been killed by decompression.

The cleansing was methodical and merciless. It was also un-hurried. Sirix took part in the massacre himself. These helpless victims were surrogate targets for the black robots' anger, com-pensation for all the losses they had suffered in the recent failed battles against the Klikiss. To him, the screams of the last few humans barricaded in sealed compartments were the equivalent of the music the breedex so enjoyed. It could never be sufficient, Sirix thought, but it was a start.

Two hours later, no further life signs remained aboard Barrymore's Rock.

He marched through the habitation domes, cargo com-partments, and storage chambers, relishing every moment. Torn bodies were strewn about, leaving bloodstains on the decks and walls. He found a thin young man with a red scarf and a pilot's uniform near the docked cargo escort. The others, presumably a family, consisted of three children, four men, three women. Their private quarters were cluttered with useless keepsakes and extensive recorded journals of their daily lives. Sirix had no interest in such irrelevant information.

Working together, black robots drained the outpost's ekti tanks, obtaining much more stardrive fuel than the single cargo escort had carried. They remained in the vicinity of the outpost for several days, refuelling all of the battleships. Conscious of how many vessels he had already lost, Sirix ordered Soldier compies to seize the four small passenger ships and the spidery cargo escort docked outside of the depot. Those craft could be useful for subterfuge, if nothing else.

All the robots returned to their EDF ships, which then drifted away from the uninhabited outpost. Sirix, though ready to move onward, now feared that the infestation of the creator race had spread far beyond his small group's ability to stop.

When all viable equipment was secure, he brought his Juggernaut back around and allowed PD and QT more target practice. The pair of compies fired repeatedly upon the domes, empty stardrive fuel reservoirs, and core asteroid. Sirix instructed them to continue the high-energy bombardment until nothing but unrecognizable rubble remained of Barrymore's Rock.

Then he directed his ships to move out again in a strong battle group, pleased with their efforts. 'Now we continue . . . until the very end.'

ONE HUNDRED AND FOUR

MAGE-IMPERATOR JORA'H

Adar Zan'nh's ships returned from the Mage-Imperator's mission of mercy with the human refugees from Cjeldre. Followed closely by Nira and her children, as well as Prime Designate Daro'h, Jora'h went out to meet them, anxious to learn how far the Klikiss had spread and how much damage they had already done. He feared he would have to face another war. Was the Klikiss race an enemy of the Ildiran Empire?

With brisk steps, nearly tripping over the scurrying servant kithmen, the Mage-Imperator descended the path from the Prism Palace and waited in the plaza for Zan'nh's ornate battleship to land. Bureaucrats, courtesans, rememberers, and lens kithmen all marched in a procession after him to welcome the Solar Navy home.

Aboard the orbiting assembly platforms, Tabitha Huck and her crews celebrated the occasion by launching nine new warliners, which accompanied the descending flagship. Swift streamers circled the warliners, performing intricate manoeuvres

480

in the sky. The joyful Ildiran people needed to know no more than that the Adar had been successful in his mission.

The flagship settled onto the mosaic pavement, its solar sails extended along with rippling metal pennants. Jora'h drew strength from Nira close beside him. Osira'h held Prime Designate Daro'h's hand as if she had remembered how to be a little girl again. Nira's children, with their strange eyes and unexpected fascinations, had been occupying themselves with Kolker's new 'revelations'. They had offered to show her, and the other green priest had eagerly encouraged it, but Nira remained too focused on reconnecting with Jora'h and guiding him.

Debarkation ramps extended, and after an anticipatory silence, Adar Zan'nh stepped out, leading a group of sub-commanders, followed by uniformed Solar Navy soldiers, and finally a group of human evacuees from Cjeldre. Only about a hundred of them. Nira waited for more, caught her breath, and said, 'That's . . . all of them?'

Zan'nh pressed his fist to the centre of his chest. 'We went to several other known colonies, Liege. Some were uninhabited, others devastated. On Cjeldre, though, we found these humans still alive.'

'Did you encounter the Klikiss? How many of them?' Jora'h asked.

'They have indeed returned, in full force. On Cjeldre, these humans had already been taken prisoner. If we had not arrived when we did, they would have been killed.' He sounded shaken.

'He saved us!' cried one of the humans from behind.

Zan'nh glanced back at the haggard refugees, then at his father again. 'Yes, Liege, we saved them.' He seemed awkwardly pleased with himself. 'It was not . . . honourable, what the Klikiss did on planet after planet.'

Nira opened her arms wide to the refugees. 'We're glad you're alive. We're glad you came here.'

People staggered down the debarkation ramp, reeling with gratitude. Jora'h spoke to the servant kithmen, who seemed ecstatic to have something to do, orders to follow. 'See that these humans are given comfortable quarters, fresh garments, medical attention, and any food they desire.'

The Cjeldre colonists let out a chorus of thanks. Some of them were close to collapse, others wanted to rush forward and embrace the Mage-Imperator, but Yazra'h stood guard, and no one could get past her.

The Adar watched the amazed and relieved expressions on their faces. He said quietly, 'You were right to send me on this mission, Liege. Had I gone sooner, I might have saved even more people.'

Zan'nh had not meant to criticize, but Jora'h felt guilt nonetheless. He had hesitated when Nira made her plea for the Solar Navy's help. He had not wanted to waste time or resources looking into a problem that he felt was of the humans' own making. He should have listened to Nira immediately. She asked him for so little, and Jora'h felt he owed her so much. After what the Ildirans did to the human test subjects on Dobro, the crimes and secrets over the generations – now all exposed, much to his shame! – he should never have hesitated. The Mage-Imperator owed them a debt that he could never repay.

He spoke quietly to Nira. 'Tell me how best I can help them now. Should they stay on Ildira? Should I send them back to Earth? You know I will do anything you ask of me.'

Nira's face hardened. 'Not Earth, and not Ildira. Those people went to Cjeldre because they wished to make a new life for themselves. They wanted a home they could call their own, and risked everything to join the Hansa's Colonization Initiative.'

Young Osira'h nodded vigorously, grasping the Prime Designate's hand as seven fast streamers whistled past overhead, still performing. 'Send them to Dobro, Father. Let them join the other human settlers there. Isn't that right, Daro'h? Let them build their colony the way the *Burton* colonists were promised.'

He felt Nira's distinct shudder, but she nodded. 'Make them that offer. It will help to heal the wound and begin to change their perceptions of you, and all Ildirans.'

Jora'h drew a deep breath. 'Yes, the wound must be healed. Maybe Dobro can become a new beginning, a place where humans and Ildirans can live in harmony. These colonists can go there and be free, with all the support we can give them. That's the way it should have been all along.'

The smile that lit her face was genuine. 'That is a good start, Jora'h.'

'Unless the faeros come and destroy it,' Daro'h said. The scars on his face looked very red in the bright sunlight.

As the servant kithmen and bureaucrats guided the Cjeldre refugees away, Jora'h remained contemplative. He had been considering this move for a long time, and now could not ignore it any longer. He had to take control of the bad situation before the humans took matters into their own hands. In order to regain their trust, he would have to do more than just offer some land on Dobro for a few refugee colonists. The centuries of Ildiran deception would cost them much support, possibly even ruin any chance of a real alliance with the humans. He had to make amends, build bridges.

'Dobro is only a first step, yet it is not enough. You know it is not. A token gesture such as this cannot *make it right*.' He looked into Nira's eyes, then glanced at Osira'h. 'You already told the green priests about the breeding programme, Nira. You shared your story and part of your pain, but explanation is not atonement.

That is something I must do. We cannot ignore this and hope that humans will forget about it. They will not.'

He did not hesitate, knowing he was doing this for *her*. What surprised him, however, was the contradictory fact that it felt good in his heart. 'I must face their leadership and admit what the Ildirans did to your people over the generations. I will apologize – and only then will I hope we might find some sort of redemption. I will go to King Peter, or Chairman Wenceslas, whichever you think is more appropriate.'

The traders Rlinda Kett and Denn Peroni had already explained the confusing schism in the human government, the new Confederation, the old Terran Hanseatic League. Apparently, the Hansa had walled itself off, while the Confederation grew, accepting all the different 'kiths' of humanity, from the colonists to the Roamer clans to Nira's beloved Therons. Jora'h had met Chairman Wenceslas and had also spent time with King Peter and Queen Estarra.

Nira's expression lit up even before he finished speaking. The Mage-Imperator made his announcement. 'We will go to Theroc. That is the heart and soul of the human race.' He held Nira, sharing her joy simply through the physical contact. 'We will leave as soon as possible.'

ONE HUNDRED AND FIVE

KING PETER

Every day, King Peter's hours were filled with discussions among representatives from Hansa colonies and Roamer clans. But for a short while late in the day — and only a short while — he and Estarra relished their time alone. After so many banquets and parties and celebrations, it felt good to have just a light meal together, sitting on the open balcony and staring out at the canyons of the forest and the great gap that showed the sky.

Even when he took time for himself and for his wife, Peter could not stop worrying about the Confederation. The government weighed heavily upon him. The formation of an entirely new system required so much discussion, so many agreements, and so many decisions. OX stood attentively beside them. The compy was making progress and was beginning to serve as a political adviser again.

Peter considered the dramatically changed situation between the Hansa and the Confederation, the Therons and Roamers, even the Ildirans. Now they had learned that Mage-Imperator

485

Jora'h himself was on his way to Theroc on some sort of embassy.

News of the horrible Dobro breeding programme, delivered via the green priests, had rattled Peter. On their visit to Mijistra, he and Estarra had liked Mage-Imperator Jora'h, and had given him a treeling for his Prism Palace. Having heard Nira's story, though, what was Peter to think? Perhaps it would be a good thing for them to meet face to face after all. He had hoped the Ildirans might become the Confederation's allies.

The Mage-Imperator could have gone to Chairman Wenceslas, but he had chosen Theroc. That would send a clear signal to the Hansa. But what if the Ildiran leader was no more trustworthy than Basil? Peter refused to believe that.

'We didn't know the scope of what we were getting into when we started all this, Estarra.' He picked up a green seedpod that popped in his mouth when he bit down. 'Oh, I had my training, and years of experience as King – as much experience as Basil would let me have – but did we jump off a cliff? And did all those people just follow me blindly?'

'With enough people, we can manage to catch each other,' Estarra said. 'We knew we had to break from the Hansa, to get free from the Chairman. You have the best possible experts to help you.'

'Yes, King Peter,' OX said. 'You do. All of the details, consequences, and legal implications that decide the actions of a planet or planets – those are what leadership is about. You must answer many questions: How loose or tight should the Confederation be? Is it a mutual support society, or an actual union? Should the orphaned Hansa worlds be treated as a unit or as individuals? It seems logical that each colony send its own representative, since each one has its own needs.'

Estarra agreed. 'Starting a new government is like starting a new family, both as king and as a husband. You do things you never expected to do, but you step up anyway. The human race is counting on us.'

He stroked her arm. 'For now at least, everyone has the same ideal, and we can all agree on the broad points.' Peter stared at the afternoon sun reflecting shimmers of green as it cut through the canopy.

'Keep your focus on what matters.' Estarra winced as a twinge of pain crossed her abdomen.

'Is something wrong?'

'No, this is exactly how it should be – according to my mother, the green priests, and everyone else I've talked to.' She breathed quickly, concentrated, and calmed herself. 'I'm going to be having our baby in another couple of weeks, Peter. It's not supposed to be completely effortless.'

He held her. 'I wish I could do something.'

'You already did. I'll concentrate on having this baby. You concentrate on ironing out the wrinkles in the government.'

'It's not that simple, Estarra.'

'Neither is childbirth, but we get through it. Remember, if the leaders are good, and the people themselves are good, then it'll all work out.'

'Tell that to Basil.'

'He'll have to live with his own decisions. You and I, and the Confederation representatives, have to decide what to do now.'

'Having a choice is a lot better than having a decision handed to me.'

The Teacher compy poured from a carafe of epiphyte juices mixed according to a recipe that Estarra's grandmother had concocted. Peter proposed a toast. 'No matter what we choose, we're better off than we were under the thumb of the Hansa Chairman.'

They both drank to that.

ONE HUNDRED AND SIX

DEPUTY CHAIRMAN
ELDRED CAIN

Fear made the population of Earth easy to manipulate, and Chairman Wenceslas took advantage of every weak mind, swayed every conscience. The re-energized Archfather continued to fan the flames of religious fervour. Selling the Klikiss as demons was an easy feat – and once the reaction began, the public accepted the next conclusion and the next. Some of the more gullible ones even bought into the concept that *King Peter* was responsible for the return of the Klikiss, if not actually in league with them.

The patriotic vehemence of a certain segment of the citizenry served to justify Basil's firm belief that he was right. Since he listened only to those who cheered his actions, the Chairman no longer needed dissenting opinions, rational arguments, or alternative ideas. Cain, deeply disturbed by what he saw, felt unnecessary. Recently, the only thing Basil trusted his deputy to do was tailor press releases and crack down on any misrepresentations that were not *approved* misrepresentations.

Chairman Wenceslas summoned Cain, and together they

rode in a shuttle up to where Lanyan's restocked and refuelled Juggernaut waited, looming like a military monstrosity protecting Earth. 'It's time to put the genuine fear of God into everyone – not just the citizens of Earth, but also all the outlaw colonies that deserted the Hansa in its time of greatest need.'

'The fear of God? Isn't that what you're having the Archfather do with his speeches and rallies?'

'It's time for more than words. I've had scholars dig up scriptural bases for him to cite. We can twist the sacred words to our own needs, and the people will march blindly along while they rattle their swords.'

Cain felt a knot in his stomach, and it wasn't from the shuttle's artificial gravity generators adjusting as they reached the Juggernaut. He decided to try one last time. 'Mr Chairman, you've always been a *rational* man, but you're forcing the human race to take giant steps backward. Why would you encourage mere paranoia and superstition? This isn't what a true religion stands for.'

'The Archfather is fully behind this action.'

'Since when have you cared about what the Archfather thought, sir? He's just an actor.'

'Indeed, I don't care what he thinks. I care what he *says*, and he says what I tell him to.'

When they docked in the *Jupiter*'s yawning hangar deck, they were received by an EDF escort party led by a stiff-backed and haughty-looking Lieutenant Commander Shelia Andez. Cain remembered her as one of the POWs rescued from the Roamers at Osquivel. She had olive skin, cinnamon hair exactly at regulation length, and eyebrows like dark parabolas on her face. Andez had been quite outspoken against the Roamers, making public statements that the Chairman couldn't have scripted better himself.

'The General will see you, Mr Chairman. We're looking

forward to what you have to say.' When she marched off, her movements barely made a wrinkle in her crisp uniform. The two representatives were flanked by an honour guard.

Walking through the *Jupiter*, Cain looked around uneasily. This had been Admiral Willis's ship, but Lanyan seemed to have instituted tighter procedures, stricter formalities. His headlong collision with the Klikiss on Pym had shaken him badly.

The General gave a brisk salute when they appeared on the bridge. He seemed eager to shake off any lingering impression of failure after his recent retreat, but Cain could see Lanyan had a shadow of worry about where the Chairman might send him. 'The Archfather won't explain what you mean by a "righteous punishment action".'

Righteous punishment action? The Archfather stood like a lord on the Juggernaut's bridge, his voluminous robes making him take up twice the space of an ordinary man.

The Chairman said, 'Lieutenant Commander Andez, please call up standard library images of the Hansa colony Usk. Play them on the screen so that I can explain your mission.'

'We shall go to Usk,' the Archfather said, his voice ponderous and overly important. Cain wondered if the religious leader had been instructed to maintain his new persona even here on the Juggernaut's bridge.

Andez moved quickly, stabbing buttons on the control panel as if they were small creatures to crush. 'Here it is, sir.' Stock images of a Hansa colony world appeared on the main screen.

Cain vaguely knew about Usk, had read reports here and there. A pleasant and innocuous world. He saw images of green fields, orchards blossoming with pink and white flowers, flocks of sheep, rolling hills, homesteads that covered vast acreage.

The Chairman said in a deprecating tone, 'An agrarian economy, a bit more than self-sufficient. The people are comfortable and complacent and had no qualms about severing ties with the Hansa.' Cain didn't point out that Earth had severed ties first. 'They tore up the Hansa Charter, declared themselves independent, and joined the Confederation. After all that, they expected to go about their lives as before.'

'They seem harmless enough, Mr Chairman,' Cain said.

'They rebelled against their legitimate authority! They walked away from the Terran Hanseatic League, embarrassing us in front of the other colonies. If we ignore this, we only encourage others to follow them.'

Andez spoke up, without being asked. 'As the General himself said when so many pilots deserted the EDF, the only way to stop this haemorrhage is to set one or more prominent examples in a manner so dramatic and unforgettable that others will think twice before defying us. It is long past time that we should do something to the breakaway worlds. In my opinion.'

General Lanyan seemed relieved to have an assignment he could really do well. 'I'm ready to crack down on Usk, Mr Chairman. We'll show them the error of their ways.'

'You must do more than that, General. Make an impressive example of the people of Usk, though you may find it unpleasant. I'm counting on you to do what must be done. The Archfather will assist you.' He stared at the General, and Lanyan hesitated only a moment before briskly nodding.

Though Cain did not dare to say anything aloud, he was certain he had stepped into a madhouse.

The Archfather wore a distant smile on his face. His sapphire-blue eyes seemed to be lit from within. 'Ah. It will be a real pogrom.'

ANTON COLICOS

Anton had never seen Vao'sh so excited. The rememberer's facial lobes flushed bright colours as he related the news. 'The Mage-Imperator intends to go to Theroc! It is said that he means to ask forgiveness for what the Ildiran people did on Dobro.'

The trip itself was another sudden shift for the Ildirans. By tradition, supplicants came *to* the Mage-Imperator. Their ruler, whom they considered without equal in any civilization, did not travel elsewhere to see an inferior leader. And he most certainly did not apologize.

But times changed. 'A bold move,' Anton said. 'Maybe a foolish one. Only history will tell.'

They met in the Hall of Rememberers, where the new diamondfilm plates were being mounted in place. Scribes had been busy etching new words, revising stanza after stanza according to the new information that Vao'sh and Anton had provided. Though at first he had been relieved and excited to get back to his 'real' work of translating the *Saga of Seven Suns*, Anton's eyes were scratchy from the overwhelming amount of reading and writing he had done in the past several days. He remembered cramming for exams back at the university, rehearsing his oral defence, editing his thesis again and again before finally receiving his degree. This, though, was far more intense. He and Vao'sh were reinterpreting an entire chronicle.

The corrected replacement panels included uncensored excerpts from the epic, and deleted the intentionally false tales. The story of the firefever killing all the rememberer kith was replaced with the grim truth of their assassination, so that the Mage-Imperator could rewrite history. The Dobro breeding camps were there, the unsettling civil war with mad Designate Rusa'h, even Jora'h's near treachery with the hydrogues. Ildirans were still grappling with the idea that real history was not always pleasant and heroic.

Though Chief Scribe Ko'sh and some hardliners continued to quietly protest, a new generation of rememberers was already studying the revised *Saga*. Some older historians, who had also accepted the chore of relearning what they had previously memorized, purged the now-discredited stories from their retellings. The changes would sink in eventually, but it would take time.

And now the Mage-Imperator was leaving. 'I take it Prime Designate Daro'h will stay here, in his stead?' Anton said. 'Is there such a thing as an "acting Mage-Imperator"?'

Vao'sh shrugged, imitating a gesture he had often seen Anton use. 'Yes, Daro'h will stay, and Yazra'h will remain here to defend Ildira and protect the Prime Designate, should he need it. Meanwhile, Adar Zan'nh will deliver the Cjeldre refugees to Dobro, as the Mage-Imperator promised.' Vao'sh looked at his friend, his face filled with joy. 'And I have not told you the best part, Rememberer Anton. *We* will write the story, you and I!

Mage-Imperator Jora'h has asked us to accompany him and document exactly what we see and do.'

Anton took a step backward, his foot crunching on a small shard of diamondfilm from a broken panel. Vao'sh continued in a rush, 'In order to expedite the journey, the Mage-Imperator will take only a processional warliner with a hundred Ildiran guards and advisers – and the two of us. Nira has already sent a message to let Theroc know we are coming.'

Anton decided to gather his notes and bring them along in hopes that he could deliver a copy of his work thus far to a trader on Theroc. Someone should be able to take the draft translations back to Earth, where innumerable undergrads and research assistants would paw through the new and exciting information. So long as he received appropriate scholarly credit for his work, Anton didn't mind. His work with Ildirans was by no means finished, and he intended to stay with them.

He looked at the other rememberers in the Hall, some of whom frowned sceptically at the new diamondfilm chronicles. 'Then we'd better start packing.'

ONE HUNDRED AND EIGHT

TASIA TAMBLYN

Throughout the rest of the night, the blackness was broken by mysterious noises. The sounds might have been perfectly normal and innocuous on Llaro . . . or they could well indicate preparations for a Klikiss ambush. It seemed likely that the three of them were the only ones left alive on Llaro who needed a rescue, and nobody from the outside would come looking for them for quite a while yet.

Tasia felt their best chance was to patch up the *Osquivel* and fly the hell out of there. The transport ship was sprawled prow-first in the wide arroyo where it had ploughed into the ground. 'We're stuck for now, but if we put our heads together we can figure something out. Roamers can work wonders with fast adhesives and medical tape.'

Robb stared at the battered hull. Klikiss gunfire and flying rocks at impact had done equal amounts of damage. 'This job goes way beyond my repair-kit knowledge.' Trained in the standard methods found in EDF manuals, he usually followed approved procedures to the letter. He had tested on Remoras and larger ships, knew how the engines functioned, and knew how to fit the components together. That was all.

Robb and Tasia tinkered with the damaged hull in the thin light of sunrise, pulling and hammering bent metal plates back into place. Nikko climbed out of the engine compartment, using his forearm to rub grease from his face. 'So, do you want the good news or bad news?'

'You mean it's not *all* bad news?' Tasia asked. 'That's good to hear.'

'Plenty of good news, considering. Our ekti supply is intact, the stardrive engines function – maybe not at one hundred per cent, but good enough to get us out of the Llaro system.'

Robb showed his teeth in an unexpected smile. 'Then we'll be out of here as soon as we patch up the hull.' He kicked the side of the ship. 'Making these breaches spaceworthy isn't going to be simple, but we can do it with the materials on hand. It'll take maybe four hours.'

Tasia was almost afraid to ask. 'So what's the bad news?'

'Our in-system engines are damaged. One is completely shot.'

'Can we fix it?' Robb asked.

'Fixing it isn't the problem. The fuel tank's ruptured and empty. *Empty*. Forget the ekti – we don't have any *standard* fuel. Once we get out into space we can fire up the Ildiran stardrive and get out of here. But we can't lift this hulk off the ground without any standard fuel.'

Tasia groaned. 'We're not likely to find a friendly fuelling station in that Klikiss city.'

'One problem at a time,' Robb said with a resigned sigh. 'Let's do what we can to repair the engines and the hull, and we'll work on the fuel problem in parallel. I just wish I had some clue where to start.'

Tasia climbed back up into the *Osquivel*'s spacious cockpit. 'I'll deal with getting the weapons systems online. That's a problem I can tackle. No telling when we might have to blast some bugs.'

They barely slept during the next day and night, taking turns at watch. Nikko kept himself busy and quiet, weighed down by the conviction that his parents, along with the rest of the Roamer detainees, were dead.

As darkness fell again, Tasia sat on a rounded brown boulder near the fringe of emergency lights around the crash site. Deeper in the canyon the shadows were thick and black. Out there, she could hear a rattle of something slithering through the rocks. The darkness grew deeper, closing in around her, making her jumpy. Tasia had a wide-dispersal flare in one hand, a twitcher in the other, and a heavier projectile gun at her hip. She would rather have been inside the wrecked ship and comfortable on her bunk, preferably with Robb beside her. Yes, comfortable.

Often, though, the most uncomfortable thing was the right thing to do. She sat on the hard rock, guarding against any approach from out of the night. Even with the shipboard weapons partially repaired, the three of them could never have held off a full force of the bugs.

She heard continued noises, another skitter of pebbles. From far off came a strange warbling chirp and she looked up, then heard the definite approach of footfalls, something much larger than a rodent. A rock clattered against another. Loose dirt trickled down the steep side of the canyon wall.

She sat motionless, waiting until the last minute, her hand sweaty on the twitcher. If the Klikiss were coming, the little stun weapon wouldn't do much, but she would open fire as soon as she was sure of her target.

A dry piece of underbrush cracked, and she heard a whispery sound, much closer than she had expected. Tasia didn't wait any longer, knowing the three of them would have to be very lucky indeed to survive this. She covered her eyes and activated the wide-dispersal flare, hoping to dazzle them long enough so she could fire. 'Robb, Nikko – I could use some help over here!'

The flare's harsh light burst out. Though Tasia had shielded her dark-adapted eyes, she struggled to make out the shapes, expecting to see an army of hideous creatures swarming down upon them. Shouts seemed to come from all sides, and Robb and Nikko ran to join the fight. Too many shouts, too many voices.

Instead of monstrous bugs, though, she saw a dark-skinned man and a shaggy old hermit accompanied by two others. They wore standard-issue colony jumpsuits that were a bit worse for wear. The dark-skinned man covered his eyes. 'Don't shoot.'

'We're friendlies, dammit!' The older man cursed. 'I didn't expect anything so dramatic. Sheesh! We're escapees from the colony.'

Robb and Nikko came running from the wreck. The dark-skinned man's eyes adjusted quickly, and he stepped forward. 'I'm Davlin Lotze. We saw your ship crash, picked up your emergency signal, and pinpointed your beacon before somebody silenced it.'

Nikko stopped and stared at one of the other men. 'Dad? Dad!' He nearly tackled Crim Tylar.

'Nikko! What the hell are you doing here?'

'Rescuing you. We came to rescue all the Roamers on Llaro!'

'But it didn't turn out exactly the way we'd planned,' Tasia added.

Crim's face looked bleak. 'That's for sure.' Nikko hesitated, as if realizing that he didn't want to ask any more questions.

Davlin spoke in a clear, businesslike manner. 'I don't think the Klikiss know where you are yet, but it would be best if we got to safety before daylight.'

ONE HUNDRED AND NINE

ADMIRAL SHEILA WILLIS

Even if Chairman Wenceslas insisted there was a war going on, Rhejak was where Admiral Willis wanted to be. She had met her mission objectives here and established a firm military presence, and was pleased to have done it without dramatically affecting the lives of the locals. The EDF too often used a heavy hand when all the situation required was a bit of finesse.

Her corps of engineers had constructed a large floating island of interlocking honeycomb segments on multiple pontoons. The raft-base gave the EDF occupation forces ample space for barracks and operations. When they required more area, the soldiers installed additional segments to expand their artificial island.

Signing off on a daily status log (which she barely skimmed), Willis sat on the edge of the raft platform and watched the giant tentacled creatures being herded about. Tired of eating rationpacks, she had arranged an exchange of supplies with the fishermen homesteaders. She paid through the nose for their seafood, no doubt about that, but Willis loved medusa meat. It had a squeaky texture like roast mushrooms and a rich flavour that reminded her of lobster, especially when drenched in butter substitute.

She had sent a fast scout ship back to Earth, informing the Hansa that Rhejak was secure. She knew the Chairman was anxiously awaiting word about when shipments would resume – rare metals, exotic minerals, kelp extracts – but she was still busy nailing down the operations, and knew not to make any promises that she might have trouble keeping.

Willis encouraged her troops to be good neighbours. 'Tuck your oversized balls firmly in your pants, choke down a dose of humility, and treat the inhabitants with respect.' By sharing trinkets and keepsakes brought from Earth, some soldiers earned a modicum of friendship. Hakim Allahu, through regular visits to Willis aboard the floating raft-base, had come to grudgingly accept the EDF's presence as unavoidable.

Though she might be lenient, she wasn't stupid. Conrad Brindle remained in command of the ten patrol Mantas overhead, and she had installed watchdog teams at the Company Works extraction facility. Other soldiers monitored and took turns running the machinery at the coral-grinding quarries.

Her Mantas had already chased away several Roamer ships that came to Rhejak as part of their usual trade routes. The Roamer pilots had sounded alarms, transmitted curses, or taken a few potshots at a Manta before racing away. But it was mostly harmless. There was just no way to please everyone . . .

At night, with operations shut down and the Company Works illuminated only by a few blinking locators, the dark waters were calm. Rhejak's two small moons lit the sky with a silvery glow. Medusas never slept, but floated along, burbling and hooting as if to keep themselves company.

A small explosion in one of the Company extraction towers set all the alarms ringing on the raft-base. EDF soldiers raced onto the honeycombed deck, shouting into their short-range comms and looking around for the source of the disturbance. Willis sprang from her bunk and threw on the first uniform she could find, tugging on her boots as she raced out onto the deck.

'Something's happening at the extraction plant, Admiral!'

Already heading for the skimmers they kept tied up to the edge of the raft, Willis yelled for a few nearby soldiers to join her. She jumped in and caught her balance as one young ensign untied the docking rope and another fired up the engines. While the craft bumped and splashed across the shallow water, Willis fastened the last few buttons on her uniform.

All the lights had come on at the Company Works. Alarms ratcheted through the sinuous pipes and framework towers of the extraction facility. The EDF guards stationed there shouted to each other in a combination of bluster and sheepish confusion. When too many conflicting transmissions crackled across the comm, Willis barked for a succinct report. 'It's rebels, Admiral. We don't know who they were, just caught a glimpse.'

'They weren't wearing much,' another voice broke in. 'Loincloths or trunks. I think it was a couple of medusa herders.'

Willis clenched her jaw. 'A few rowdy young men with a point to make and too much time on their hands.' When her pursuit skimmer pulled up to the humming Company tower, she could smell smoke. She climbed out of the swaying boat and addressed the guards. 'Where did they come from? And how the hell did they get past you? What's been damaged? Why weren't you watching? Who was on patrol?'

The guards didn't know which question to answer first. The saboteurs had arrived at water-level and climbed the towers with their bare hands and feet. A small explosion had shut down one of the six pumping stations, but the damage wasn't severe. In fact, the guards believed the bomb had been a diversion. The patrol on duty, disarmed by the friendliness of the locals, had probably been too complacent.

'Sounds like a flaw in our security planning. We gave the people of Rhejak an inch, and they took a tower. Get this place cleaned up and repaired. Wake up the Company crews and any EDF engineers you need. The faster we get the facility up and running again, the less of an impact those yahoos will have made.'

One of the guards led a flushed Company man who was dripping perspiration from his forehead. Willis remembered him as Drew Vardian, the facility administrator. 'That isn't the worst part. They knew what they were doing. They took two recirc sorters.' He raised his hands. '*Recirc sorters!*'

'That means nothing to me, Mr Vardian. Explain yourself.'

'Vital components, absolutely vital – the computer sensors that control the extraction and filtering systems. They sort out the metals and chemicals we want from the rest of the garbage. We can't run the Works without them.'

'Now, that's a fine piece of news. How did these rabble-rousers know what to do?'

'The Company uses locals for part-time work, anyone who wants to earn extra money, especially medusa herders.'

'So, they just yanked these sorter gizmos and swam off into the night? Can't we track them down?'

'They had small putter-boats, Admiral – fast enough to get away, but relatively short-range.'

'Then contact Lieutenant Commander Brindle. I want high-res scans of the vicinity. Get me two Remoras equipped with spotlights. We're going fishing.' Willis put aside any sympathy she had for the people of Rhejak. They had abused her trust.

The culprits turned out to be three young men, the oldest no more than seventeen. They were racing through the reef channels in an unlit putter-boat, confident they could remain hidden. From high above, EDF scanners quickly picked up their body heat, the emissions from their small engine, and the metallic components of the stolen recirc sorters they had loaded aboard.

Two Remoras swooped overhead and hovered with a blast of engines, to shine a white spotlight down on the fleeing boat. The young men sat in the rocking boat, flicking rude gestures at the pair of fighter craft.

Meanwhile, on the water, Willis downloaded the coordinates from the Remoras into her guidance computer and chased after the rowdies in the raft-base's fastest skimmer. As her skimmer closed in on the bright spotlights, she watched the three young men through telescopic lenses. 'Oh, crap. They're even stupider than I thought – stop them!'

But the men in the hovering Remoras could do nothing, and Willis's skimmer couldn't close the distance quickly enough. Stuck in their putter-boat over a deep channel, the three young men wrestled with two heavy hunks of machinery, each larger than a fuel barrel. Knowing there was no escape, the defiant kids rocked the components over the edge and into the depths. A splash swallowed the second recirc sorter just as Willis's skimmer closed in.

She yelled across the water, her face stormy with rage. 'What the hell do you think you're doing? Do you know what that equipment cost?'

'Cost? Maybe it bought us a few days' freedom!'

'Why should we work, so you can send everything back to the dirty Hansa?' a second boy yelled.

She got on the comm and called her engineers. 'Get divers. We need to recover those pieces.'

The youngest of the three boys looked as if he was about to cry. The trapped putter-boat swayed and rocked. 'We were just going to hide the sorters until you learned a lesson. Now see what you made us do? You made us throw them overboard!'

'I didn't *make you* into a moron, and I don't think your parents did, either. It's going to take more than being grounded for a few days to make up for what you did. A court martial and a couple of weeks in the brig might teach you all some respect for authority.' She gestured to the guards. 'Take them into custody and let Lieutenant Commander Brindle deal with them in the lead Manta. While they cool their heels in an EDF cell, they can reflect on how kind and gentle my occupation's been – until now.' Willis growled at the three boys shivering in their boat. 'Thanks to you, I'm going to have to change my tactics.'

The next day the Admiral demanded to see Hakim Allahu, as well as the heads of the Company Works, the reef quarry, and several of the larger homesteads. She brought them all to stand before her command hut like scolded children.

'Let's cut through the bullshit. Maybe you don't like what the Chairman's doing, but *you* provoked him in the first place. What the hell did you expect to happen if you spit in his face? You're damned lucky he sent me instead of somebody a lot worse.' Willis had specifically staged it so that the men had to stare into the bright sun as they faced her. 'When my ships first arrived, I didn't expect you to welcome us with flowers, but I did expect you to be *sensible*. Have you any inkling how much slack I've cut you? If one of the other Grid Admirals had come here, Rhejak might well be a prison camp now. I thought we had an understanding. Now, would someone please explain the nonsense that happened last night?'

Drew Vardian, still florid, said, 'Nonsense? How can you not

504

understand what those young men did? It makes perfect sense to me, and *I'm* the one they hurt.'

'A lot of people on Rhejak will support them,' Allahu added. 'You can't expect us to like being invaded by EDF bullies. You've already hurt our economy. We know of at least nine legitimate trade ships that your Mantas scared away.'

'You're no better than pirates,' said one of the fishermen homesteaders. 'We produce valuable commodities, and you come here with your battleships to steal it all from us.'

Willis began to grow angry. 'You're making some awfully big assumptions there, Mister. We haven't sent a single shipment back to Earth. In fact, nobody has even attempted to discuss trade terms with me, yet you're ready to complain about it, even blow up one of your own factories. Does that make any sense?'

Allahu blinked in disbelief. 'Are you saying you actually intend to *pay* for the assets you seized?'

'And at a fair price?' the Company man added.

'I'm saying, gentlemen, that we're at a watershed here. You forced me into a choice. We can either reach an accommodation, or I can crack down on your asses and run this place like a military academy. You choose. Can you keep your own people under control?' She studied their faces. 'I have to tell you, I kind of like this place, and I'd just as soon keep its special flavour intact. I won't make drastic changes unless you force me to.'

Neither Allahu nor the other representatives knew how to react to her offer.

Willis sighed. 'I see the cat's got your tongue. Let me start off with a few points of discussion. I'll hear your grievances and do my damndest to administer a peace. To begin with, I'll allow the reopening of outside trade with Roamers or whomever you want – for non-vital items, only. You can sell your reef-pearls and seafood, a percentage of your kelp extracts, and non-essential metals. The Earth Defence Forces and the Terran Hanseatic League will, however, retain priority on materials we deem necessary. And the Hansa will pay you for whatever we take – at a wholesale rate, of course,' she quickly added. 'Are those terms you can accept?'

'We can accept them.' Allahu looked at his colleagues. 'Maybe not happily, but it's better than being run as a military state.'

She turned to the Company man. 'Our dive teams have re-covered the two recirc sorters, Mr Vardian. I'll need you to clean up, test, and reinstall the components.'

'Piece of cake. We didn't expect you to find them in deep water that fast.'

'I didn't expect to be doing any of this, but it seems we have to roll with it.'

'Admiral,' Allahu interrupted, 'how will you get the Hansa to pay us for what they could just take?'

'They put me in charge of Rhejak and told me to secure your cooperation. It's my decision. What choice does the Hansa have?'

GENERAL KURT LANYAN

Bucolic Usk was as pleasant, peaceful, and vulnerable as the Chairman had suggested. Thus, General Lanyan felt it his duty to be as ruthless as possible. No warnings, no mercy, just results. The scheduled pogrom would serve as a great motivator for smaller, weaker colonies to fall into line. Lanyan had to make this look as bad as possible. That meant it would *be* as bad as possible.

He was sure he'd have nightmares about it for a long time.

Though he had not objected, the General didn't like the mission one bit. Chairman Wenceslas was going ridiculously overboard, but this was the lesser of two evils, allowing Lanyan to recover his honour and whatever clout he had lost. Besides, this was preferable to going head-to-head against the Klikiss again.

As the *Jupiter* loomed over the defenceless colony world, the Archfather stood on the bridge, looking at the images on the screen. He was a man of few words, generally reluctant to speak unless his phrases had been carefully scripted; Lanyan had seen his note cards and tip sheets. 'The people of Usk have already transgressed beyond forgiveness. Their only redeeming purpose is to serve as an example.' He smiled behind his great white beard. 'And they can serve very well in that capacity.'

Hundreds of troop transports roared down, crammed with soldiers. Remora squadrons flew above the dispersed settlements, ready with cargo-loads of thermal bombs and concussion explosives. They circled the homesteads, peppering the sky with sonic booms. Troops dropped into the small trading villages, the peach and almond orchards, the potato fields.

At a more leisurely pace, Lanyan and the Archfather descended in a diplomatic shuttle while soldiers rounded up the colonists at a central gathering point. Tight-lipped, the General monitored the progress. He transmitted orders to all of the troops. 'Whatever you do, don't hurt the green priest. This colony must have one. The Chairman wants to make sure the message gets out to all breakaway worlds.'

Remoras strafed the fields, grain silos, and barns with thermal bombs. Fires spread quickly across the dry alfalfa meadows. Panicked livestock stampeded, and the soldiers had to mow down the animals to keep themselves from being trampled. People hid in root cellars or hay lofts. Soldiers used twitchers on anyone who looked as if he might resist. When capturing the colonists one by one proved too difficult, the soldiers simply stunned them all, dragged them aboard ships, and dumped the limp bodies unceremoniously in the main village.

Demolitions crews set fire to farmhouses, refusing to let the weeping people retrieve their possessions. They launched explosive grenades and blew up fence lines made of piled stones. Sharpshooters immolated entire orchards with laser cutting beams. The air was thick with smoke.

A nearly naked female green priest was dragged into the

open square. She sobbed to see all the destruction. 'Why? Why?' seemed to be the only words she could say.

'Let her keep her treeling,' Lanyan said. He stood in the town watching, deaf to the shouted accusations, pleas, anguished screams. All the chaos and mayhem was being carefully recorded for the Hansa's later use.

The Archfather boomed out his pronouncement in the centre of the farming town. Each sentence fell like a sharp axe. 'Unison condemns the people of Usk! Radicals like you are a rot within our society. By turning against Earth, by following your pride, you brought down a curse upon our entire race. You demonstrated our weaknesses and our moral flaws. You left us wide open for the demons to come.' He jabbed a many-ringed finger at the cowering crowd. EDF soldiers paced about, holding their weapons ready.

The people stared in utter disbelief. Pillars of smoke rose into the sky. Their farmhouses were in ruins, the orchards and gardens destroyed, their sheep and cattle massacred. The green priest huddled next to her tree, almost catatonic.

The Archfather continued, 'Even now, Klikiss are attacking our isolated colonies elsewhere in the Spiral Arm. First they unleashed their evil black robots, and now they themselves have come. And what is next? Do they intend to exterminate all of humanity?'

Lanyan squelched his shudder at the reminder of the voracious Klikiss. Though he didn't believe for a moment that the alien race was some sort of demonic manifestation, the terrified settlers of Usk were willing to accept anything amidst the fire and blood and smoke.

A soldier ran up to Lanyan. 'General, we just completed our inspection of the local government offices. We discovered this recording, which you may find of interest.'

He inserted the datapak into a player and watched the town's five elders sit at a table to make a statement, happily declaring their independence from the Terran Hanseatic League, scolding Earth for abandoning them during a time of crisis. Then they announced their intention to become part of the Confederation. As Lanyan watched, grinding his teeth together, the men each lifted a paper copy of the Hansa Charter and made a point of tearing it to shreds in front of the imagers. Then the elders applauded each other for their brave actions, shook hands, and offered a toast 'to the future of Usk'.

When the Archfather finished his vitriolic speech, Lanyan came forward. The soldiers rigged a large projection screen, and he played the defiant charade for everyone. 'Find these five men and bring them forward.'

Soldiers marched roughly through the people, grabbing anyone who looked remotely like one of the council members and throwing them together until the ringleaders were separated out. They stood together, shouting, 'You can't do this. We are a sovereign world – an independent colony!'

Lanyan scowled at them. 'You are rebels and criminals. And you will be treated as such.' He turned to the green priest. 'Make sure everyone else in the Confederation knows that, as well. King Peter can't protect you. None of you.'

'You are damned!' the Archfather yelled, his cheeks turning red. 'And you must suffer for your sins. By your suffering, by purging this colony, you may help others to find their way back to righteousness.'

The five council members, who were not heroes but farmers or tradesmen, were dragged away from their friends. Nearby, soldiers built five simple but ominous crossbar structures. The Archfather commanded a punishment that came from Chairman Wenceslas himself.

While the village and farmsteads continued burning, Lanyan's men crucified the elders and left them hanging there, bloody and dying. The survivors of Usk were only just beginning to grasp the horrors of what had happened to them. The green priest could barely convey what she saw.

When the EDF soldiers forced the rest of the numb villagers to line up and re-sign the Hansa Charter, no one protested. No one seemed to have a voice left. Their every move was recorded by the watchful eyes of cameras and imagers.

'Our work here is done,' Lanyan said, struggling not to feel anything. Last, he ordered the small worldtree burned, cutting off the green priest from all contact.

The people of Usk were totally broken, all naïve defiance crushed. They would present no further problems, which was good, since he didn't want to waste the personnel to leave behind a watchdog force.

With the Archfather in the lead, Lanyan and his triumphant soldiers departed.

ONE HUNDRED AND ELEVEN

ORLI COVITZ

Sheltered, though not exactly safe, among the other refugees in the sandstone caves, Orli played her music, finding melodies. The synthesizer strips were among the few personal items she still owned. After all she'd been through, Orli had learned not to get too attached to anything, not to put down roots. But she could always carry music with her, no matter what disasters happened around her. Even if she lost her synthesizer strips, she could hum. Or sing. Margaret Colicos had taught her the words to the old song 'Greensleeves'.

The older woman had said that Orli might be special, that her music might have impressed the breedex enough to ensure her safety. But during her escape with all the others, there had been so much panic, violence, confusion.

Once Davlin described his group's escape from the Klikiss, and Tasia Tamblyn explained what she had seen during the *Osquivel's* flyover of the city, it didn't sound as if anyone had been spared in the settlement. After the robot invaders' departure, the Klikiss had levelled the town, presumably killing all of the colonists who

512

hadn't gotten away. Orli didn't know if the Klikiss had kept even Margaret alive. 'Are we the last ones left alive on this whole planet, DD? Seventy-six people?'

'And me.' DD was definitely worried, too.

'Yes, and you.'

'And UR. She needs some repairs.'

'And UR.'

Roamer technicians had made basic fixes to the Governess compy's arm socket, but it would take a far more sophisticated mechanic to install a new cybernetic limb. In the meantime, DD assisted the other compy in watching the children and helping the refugees. Orli wondered if the breedex was done with them now, or if the Klikiss would still try to hunt them down. Davlin had managed to keep everyone alive this long.

Sitting by herself, her back resting against the rough sandstone wall, Orli explored new, mournful melodies that captured the feelings she held inside. Though she kept the volume low, the sound permeated the shelters, evoking a shared mood among the uneasy survivors huddled around Davlin Lotze.

'We're already past capacity here,' muttered Mayor Ruis. 'We need food, blankets – in fact, we need just about everything.'

'What we really need is to *leave here*,' Crim Tylar said. 'Most of us didn't want to come to Llaro in the first place. Damned Eddies!' Nikko sat close to him, oscillating between the joy of finding his father alive and the sadness of knowing that his mother had died fighting the Klikiss.

'We've got the *Osquivel*,' Davlin said with determination. 'It's fixable – *and* it'll hold all of us. So let's figure out how to get these people out of here alive.'

'We've got a few tools and weapons, a handful of fighters, and everybody's experience, right?' Tasia said. 'Once we get the hell off this planet, we can come back with a real military force and fall on those bug bastards like an asteroid out of the sky.'

Davlin looked down at the crude charts he had made. 'If you can repair your ship's standard engines, I'll get you the fuel you need. I have two barrels stashed away, but we'll have to retrieve them.'

Robb's expression brightened. 'I didn't think it was going to be that easy.'

'Easy?' Mr Steinman let out a disbelieving snort. 'Davlin's forgetting to mention that he hid the fuel smack in the middle of Klikiss territory.'

'That does indeed pose difficulties,' DD agreed.

Concentrating on her playing, Orli half listened. She closed her eyes and let the quiet music remind her of cloudy Dremen, her father's optimism in moving to Corribus, a new hope, followed by disaster . . . and another new chance here on Llaro – then another disaster. Her music grew more sombre, and she gradually increased the volume.

Orli opened her eyes when Nikko came to sit by her and listen to her play. She noticed his distant expression, his sad face as he said, 'My mother liked music. She played it in our greenhouses – said it made the plants grow better.'

'Did it?'

He shrugged. 'It doesn't matter. I wish she was here.'

'I knew her, you know. Your parents took me in when the Klikiss rounded us all up in the stockade. She was so kind – and a great shot with a rifle.'

Nikko gave her a wistful smile. 'That's Mom. It's been such a long time since I saw her.'

Orli continued to play, her fingers moving automatically across the keypad as she told what she remembered about Marla Chan. Nikko talked about his family's greenhouse asteroids and how his parents had made sure he got away when the Eddies took all the other Roamers prisoner.

'I like your music,' he said, 'but I wish you knew some happier songs.'

'So do I.'

PRIME DESIGNATE DARO'H

After his father left for Theroc in his ceremonial war-liner, the Prime Designate struggled to carry out the functions of the Mage-Imperator. While Jora'h and Nira were healing wounds with the human government, Daro'h would shoulder the rest of the Ildiran Empire. *Acting Mage-Imperator.*

He was just a figurehead. One day, however, he would become the real Mage-Imperator and draw all the *thism* to him, just as his father had. At the moment, Daro'h stood on the dais in the skysphere reception hall, feeling lost as he gazed up into the overarching prismatic domes. He could not bring himself to sit in the expansive chrysalis chair. He did not belong there.

Daro'h had just begun to fulfil his other responsibilities, mating with numerous approved females. It should have been a joyous duty for him, but the grave and indefinable danger he sensed throughout the Empire robbed him of nearly all pleasure. And the feeling must be far stronger in his father. Something was definitely wrong in the *thism*.

Adar Zan'nh had left for Dobro, taking the humans from

Cjeldre to join the *Burton* descendants in building a viable colony. A fresh start. In spite of its dark history, in spite of the threat from Designate Rusa'h and his faeros, Daro'h missed that bleak world.

Osira'h stayed with the Prime Designate in the intimidating chamber, adding to his confidence just by being there. His little half-sister had shocked him on Dobro by leading an uprising among the human breeding subjects and forcing him to see the error of what the Ildirans had done for so many generations. Now the girl sat on the polished dais steps, sensing his troubled thoughts. 'Don't let yourself feel so overburdened, Daro'h. I went down into a gas planet to see the hydrogues, and I helped defeat them.' She chuckled. 'If I can do that, *you* can handle the Mage-Imperator's duties for a few days.'

He sat down by his half-sister on the hard, cool stone and put his arm around her. 'When you put it that way, how can I disagree?'

As if she had finished what she wanted to say, Osira'h got up. 'I have to go back to my brothers and sisters. We've discovered a very interesting ability, and we get better every day. Even Kolker doesn't understand it all.'

'I certainly do not understand it,' Daro'h said. 'I'm surprised you did not wish to accompany your mother to Theroc.'

'My mother *and* my father. And, yes, I did want to go with them. We all did. But I needed to be here more. Important things are happening.' Practically skipping, she left the audience chamber by a small doorway behind the chrysalis chair. He would probably never understand his strange sister.

Outside the smoky-glass doorways of the main entrance, Daro'h saw pilgrims, courtiers, and bureaucrats lining up to pass before him, to seek an interview, or just gaze upon the Mage-Imperator. He could sense their unsettled confusion and worries, and he could not assuage them. If he had indeed been the centre of all the *thism*, their emotions would have seemed like shouts in his mind.

Ildirans were a historically stable people, but all the recent changes had resulted in confusion and fear. Every kith was troubled by the social upheaval Jora'h's changes had produced, and the *thism* magnified their uneasiness, creating an ever-worsening feedback cycle. Daro'h did not have the power to stop it; he could only try to show stability for the rest of the Empire.

Before allowing any pilgrims to enter Daro'h's presence, Yazra'h cautiously circled the broad chamber with her three cats, making sure that she and the threatening felines were prominently visible. She was there to protect the Prime Designate with her life, just as she would have guarded the Mage-Imperator himself. Tossing her long hair, she came back from her prowl. 'The Prism Palace is secure, Prime Designate.'

Daro'h nodded with stiff formality. 'Thank you.' He drew himself up and looked out at the waiting visitors. 'All right. Send the next group forward.'

At her brusque signal, a flood of visitors entered the audience chamber. He greeted them, but his thoughts remained far away. Daro'h recognized Chief Scribe Ko'sh as the stern-faced rememberer walked forward to the dais. Ko'sh was accompanied by a formally dressed lens kithmen with painted markings on his temples and brow and a glittering medallion clutched in his hand. Ko'sh spoke without introduction, 'Prime Designate, we will speak to you, though we had hoped to address the Mage-Imperator.'

Daro'h raised his hands. 'All of these people came to see the Mage-Imperator. He cannot be here.'

The lens kithman blurted out quickly, 'But perhaps this is a good thing. You can speak to your father on our behalf.'

Yazra'h drew back her lips, affronted by any implied criticism of their father. 'The Mage-Imperator makes his own decisions,' Daro'h said coldly. 'I do not influence him. I follow him.'

'Of course.' Ko'sh bowed. 'But many of his recent actions are strange and disturbing.'

The lens kithman placed his palms together and raised them in front of his heart, lifting the prismatic medallion between them. 'People are fearful and come to us for guidance. We need to know how to answer them.'

Distraught, the Chief Scribe said, 'He tore down walls in the Hall of Rememberers. He asked two men – one of them a human! – to rewrite the *Saga of Seven Suns*.'

'I know all this. All Ildirans know it.'

The lens kithman did not seem to recognize the Prime Designate's brittle mood. 'And now he has departed from Ildira. No Mage-Imperator has ever gone to visit a human world before. The female green priest caused him to change his mind.'

'She is the mother of Osira'h, who was key to saving us all from the hydrogues.'

Ko'sh looked angry. 'A Mage-Imperator should never ask forgiveness!'

'Who are you to say what a Mage-Imperator should do?' Yazra'h broke in.

Daro'h felt a knot in his chest as he considered these rude comments. He had to be strong. He heard mutters among the pilgrims in the background. In truth, the Prime Designate had thought exactly the same thing, but he could not publicly agree with these men. He was especially troubled that they voiced their objections so openly, so he cut them off. 'Before you speak further, ask yourselves one important question: Do you trust the Mage-Imperator, your leader?'

The two supplicants were taken aback. 'Of course we trust him. He is the Mage-Imperator.'

Daro'h regarded them for a long moment. 'Then trust him. Your doubts resonate through the *thism* and weaken all Ildirans. You are causing harm. You are making us vulnerable. Go now and speak of this no further.' His voice was sharp. When Yazra'h stepped forward and the Isix cats padded down the steps, the two men beat a hasty retreat.

As he stood looking at the bright sunlight and waiting for the supplicants, Prime Designate Daro'h wished he had heard some sort of news from Tal O'nh or young Designate Ridek'h, or even the scout ships that Jora'h had dispatched to investigate the cold, dark silence in the Horizon Cluster. They were overdue, and that was most unsettling.

Daro'h rubbed his temples and saw his sister regarding him with appreciation. Yazra'h spoke quietly before the next visitor stepped into hearing range. 'That was well-spoken, Prime Designate, though I am not convinced you believe it. Just remember, our father is making necessary changes. He broke tradition when he selected *me* for his personal guard – which I believe was a wise choice.'

'You are right. But I cannot help but be reminded that our father's abrupt changes were what sparked the rebellion of Designate Rusa'h in the first place.'

ONE HUNDRED AND THIRTEEN

HYRILLKA DESIGNATE RIDEK'H

Limping along, the six Solar Navy warliners painstakingly made their way home after their encounter with the faeros at Hyrillka. Ridek'h stared at the stars in front of them, bright sparks on an ebony background. Their processional septa was missing one warliner – just as Ildira was missing one of its seven suns.

All of the soldiers aboard still resonated with the sacrifice of Septar Jen'nh, who had bought the escape of the other warliners without hesitation. Jen'nh had done it *for Ridek'h*. And so far the young Designate did not know what he had done to deserve it.

Tal O'nh sensed the boy's inner turmoil. 'Our priorities have changed, but you remain the Designate. You are our connection to the Mage-Imperator. Hyrillka is yours, and these remaining ships are yours.'

'Hyrillka is nothing. Everyone there is dead.'

'That is why it is so important for us to get to Ildira – to tell the Mage-Imperator and Adar Zan'nh. They must prepare to fight the faeros.'

After their violent escape from Hyrillka, the six warliners had huddled in empty space, completing emergency repairs, and now they were finally returning to the Prism Palace. Ildira's six close suns were the brightest stars on their viewing screen. Ridek'h could not wait to be back home. Safe.

As the warliners moved forward, some of the stars grew brighter. The bright dots moved, swirling like glowgems in a wind-blown fire. They came closer, grew larger, expanded. They were not stars at all.

Tal O'nh immediately sounded the alarm, calling the Solar Navy to their battle stations. 'The faeros! The faeros are coming again.'

Ridek'h gasped. 'But we used our stardrive engines to escape them. How did they track us?'

The old tal's faceted blind eye gleamed in the ever-brightening glare from the viewscreens. 'They did not need to track us. Rusa'h would have known we intended to come here. To Ildira.'

'How can we fight them? Our weapons were not effective before.'

'We run. Full acceleration. All ships — race for home!'

The acceleration drove Ridek'h back against the command rail. But the gigantic fireballs closed in with remarkable speed from all directions, closing a trap around the warliners. The faeros *changed* something all around them. The boy Designate suddenly felt as if he had stepped into an abyss. The always-comforting security net of *thism* vanished as the fiery elementals cut him off; Rusa'h and the faeros had somehow isolated every Ildiran aboard the six ships. Every soldier in the command nucleus groaned in dismay. Even Tal O'nh reeled. Everyone felt lost and disoriented. They were completely isolated from the thought network that joined all Ildirans.

Without orders, one of the six warliners turned and plunged

headlong into the wall of faeros, trying to break away. But the ornate battleship could not survive the incredible heat. The warliner melted, broke apart, its hull sloughing off into droplets of molten metal moments before the ekti tanks exploded.

With the death of the warliner, the fireballs seemed to grow brighter, like a fire blazing after fresh wood was added. Ridek'h reeled at the thought of all the lost lives, but did not feel the expected stabbing pain in the *thism*. An entire crew dead – and he was cut off! The faeros had plucked the hapless Ildirans from the soul-threads and taken those lives for themselves.

'Hull temperature rising,' announced the sensor chief.

The flames roared closer, forcing the trapped ships to come to a halt. A blazing ellipsoid loomed in front of the warliner, as if it somehow knew the boy Designate was aboard.

O'nh faced the dimmed screen, as defiant as he could manage. All the filters had been raised, blocking out most of the intense light. Ridek'h forced himself not to act terrified.

The rippling, gaseous outer skin of the faeros ship shimmered and boiled like a cauldron. To his horror, Ridek'h saw that the discoloured blotches and convection cells were more than just differing temperatures. Each superheated bubble that rose to the surface wore a *face*, the screaming face of a lost and tortured soul that the faeros had consumed. Ridek'h bit back an outcry.

Here were the bright life sparks of the scientific team that had been killed on Hyrillka; here, too, must be former Designate Udru'h, whom the faeros had annihilated on Dobro. Had the fiery entities swallowed the soulfires of the Solar Navy crew they had just destroyed? The faeros must be ravenous.

Watching the boiling, screaming faces manifest themselves on the fireballs, Ridek'h knew there were more, many more Ildirans the faeros had already killed. How many planets had they scorched across the Horizon Cluster? If, each time, the fiery beings cut their victims off from the *thism*, then the Mage-Imperator would not realize the full extent of the spreading disaster.

Rusa'h's booming voice tore through the comm system. 'The faeros need your soulfires. I have dampened their hunger and helped their numbers to grow by first quenching many lives in my former *thism* web. Now I have grown strong enough to rip Ildiran soulfires free wherever I find them. Even yours.'

The soldiers in the command nucleus cried out, then yelled in pain. Their flesh glowed, their bones became incandescent, and with a final cry, the crew began to erupt into purifying flames.

But Ridek'h and the old tal remained untouched. 'Stop! Stop this!' the boy shouted. But the fire kept growing. More crewmen vanished in a flash of heat, but the young Designate remained unharmed, as if Rusa'h did not intend to touch him. He turned to see crewmembers ignite at every station. The same thing must be happening on every warliner. 'Why are you doing this?'

'Because I need to,' Rusa'h's voice boomed back. The surrounding fireballs throbbed, drinking in the liberated soulfires.

Tal O'nh stood enraged but helpless at the command rail as all of his soldiers spontaneously burst into flame. The control panels melted and became inoperable. With final screams, the last crewmen disappeared into foul-smelling smoke.

And when he seemed sated, the faeros incarnate spoke again, pounding his words in the boy's head and sizzling across the now-unmonitored communications systems. 'You, Ridek'h – *you* I will leave untouched. I want you to tell my corrupt brother Jora'h. I want him to know exactly what he will soon face. Not even the Ildiran Empire can stop me. I will come back for you, when you are ready.'

Furious yet impotent, Tal O'nh railed at the screen, barely discerning the face of the mad Designate from the dazzling fire.

'The Solar Navy will destroy you! We defeated the hydrogues, and we will do the same to the faeros.'

Rusa'h was unimpressed. 'Let the sight of us be your last and brightest memory.'

A flare of light erupted directly in front of O'nh's face, a searing blast that took his remaining eye, reflected and flared inside the crystalline prosthetic in his other socket. O'nh reeled backward, his face blistered and burned. A low moan emerged from his throat.

Alone in the command nucleus, Ridek'h screamed. Each of the warliners had burned out, and the crews on all of the ships were dead. Only his mentor remained, and now O'nh was blinded.

At last, the faeros fireballs spread apart, turned, and streaked away. Ridek'h and O'nh were left to drift, sightless and helpless in the emptiness.

ONE HUNDRED AND FOURTEEN

NIRA

Theroc was as wonderful as she remembered, the world-trees as glorious, the forest as mysterious and remarkable. The nine verdani battleships in orbit were breathtaking as they parted to allow the Mage-Imperator's ceremonial warliner to pass through. Jora'h had brought her home at last!

The warliner occupied the entire meadow the Roamer engineers had cleared as a landing area for large ships. When she stepped out onto the familiar ground again, Nira felt reborn. The moment Theron sunlight touched her green skin, the troubles in the Spiral Arm vanished from her mind. The trees! The verdant smell in the air! She wept.

She looked up to see boughs overhead and jewel-winged condorflies buzzing about. 'Oh, I should have brought Osira'h,' she said longingly, wiping tears from her cheeks. 'All of my children.'

Jora'h took her hand. 'You will. This place is part of them as well. They deserve to see it for themselves.'

Nira had offered to be his spokesperson, an ambassador of

sorts, but the Mage-Imperator had decided to make his own peace with the King. She hoped the two leaders could build bridges between their races again, in spite of what had happened on Dobro.

Servant kithmen rushed out of the warliner to prepare the way as Confederation delegates – colourfully dressed Roamers, near-naked green priests, and ornately garbed Theron officials – arrived to greet them. Ildiran bureaucrats and protocol officers with the Mage-Imperator were uneasy with the alien surroundings, yet obviously impressed by the dramatic trees.

Without any particular fanfare, King Peter and a very pregnant Queen Estarra emerged from their group of officials to stand before the Ildiran leader. 'Estarra and I will never forget our visit to your Prism Palace. Thank you for returning the honour – though our tree city cannot compare with Mijistra.'

Jora'h extended his hand in the human gesture of greeting that he had practised. 'It does not need to compare. It has a grandeur all its own.'

By the warliner, Anton Colicos and Rememberer Vao'sh stood amazed among the other Ildirans. Nira envied the two men, imagining the thrill of seeing the gigantic trees for the very first time.

Theroc held all the best parts of her past. So much to see, so many memories to refresh, so many foods to eat ... Virtually everything had changed after two hydrogue attacks and an explosive wental regrowth. In all that time, Nira had gone from being a wide-eyed dreamer who loved to learn and tell stories, to a damaged woman who had been held hostage and brutally abused. But here, all in a rush, her youth and sense of wonder came back to her.

A group of green priests gave her their own warm welcome, surrounding her, touching her, accepting her. They all knew, in general, what she had endured on Dobro, and through telink she had asked them not to hate all Ildirans for it. She looked at Jora'h, her face full of questions, and he smiled back with an expression so warm and compassionate that she loved him all the more for it. 'Go. You should be with green priests now. Do not worry about me.'

Nira wrapped her arms around a towering worldtree, touching the golden bark and letting her thoughts flow into the verdani mind. Technically, this was no different from when she used the small treeling back in the Prism Palace, but the full intimate contact against her skin and the synergistic force of so many giant trunks around her made the profound experience more intense than she had remembered.

A skinny young woman of about twenty approached Nira, her forehead marked with an acolyte's tattoo. Her features were elfin, her hair tied back in neat bunches of braids. The girl reminded Nira of young Queen Estarra, and she realized who it was. 'Are you little Celli?'

'Not so little anymore! Would you like to climb with me to the canopy? Many of the green priests have already gathered there, and the acolytes would love to see you. We've all heard so much. Everyone knows your tale.'

'I told you only part of the story, I'm afraid. I wasn't sure how much you could take.'

'The worldtrees want to know everything. And so do we! I'll be a green priest soon.'

Nira remembered how enthusiastic she herself had been as an acolyte. 'I hope to bring other green priests and more trees back to Ildira with me, so I will no longer be alone there.'

Nira gazed at the high fronds and the inviting open sky above. Energy flooded through her muscles, and the trees seemed to offer hand and footholds she had not noticed were there. She scrambled up as if she were a young girl again. Laughing, Celli climbed up beside her.

When Nira poked her head above the topmost fronds, she drew a deep breath. Years of pain and sadness seemed to wash away from her. 'I had forgotten how wonderful it is.'

After being reunited with Jora'h, the man she loved, Nira had thought she would never consider leaving Ildira. She wanted to stay at the Mage-Imperator's side until she died. But she had forgotten the tempting song of the worldforest. Through telink, the flood of thoughts and knowledge and personalities created a comforting white noise. Every nerve in her skin tingled with reawakened energy.

One group of green priests, including Yarrod, sat high in the canopy apart from the others, not quite aloof, but absorbed in another part of their minds. She wondered if they were communing through telink, until she recognized that these must be Kolker's converts, here on Theroc.

Celli led her to a cluster of acolytes who looked at Nira with awe. Some of the green priests stepped across the tangled branches to greet her. 'We were terrified for you and angry at what you suffered, Nira, then uplifted by how you had survived. We must know all of the details. The worldforest must hear everything. The tale should be told well, and never forgotten.'

Nira's throat was dry. 'I know. I must tell it all, the bad parts and the good. Every detail. And you have to hear it and share it amongst yourselves.' She stared out at the trees and let a faint smile curl her lips. 'I know an accomplished storyteller who can help me.'

Late that evening, after the first banquet in the fungus-reef city, Anton Colicos sat dazed and enthralled, with Vao'sh beside him in the same mentally saturated state. While Jora'h attended intense, and practical, discussions with the King and Queen, Nira joined the two rememberers.

'I'll need a year to process everything,' Anton said. 'I'm over-loaded.'

The historians had spent the day with Jora'h and his entourage, touring some of the most impressive sights of Theroc, after which they enjoyed extravagant welcoming celebrations, not only from the royal couple but from Roamer traders and representatives of former Hansa colonies that had joined the Confederation. Insect songs and perfumed breezes drifted through the open decks of the high city, mingling with the loud conversation and laughter of Roamers and the singing and stringed instruments of Theron performers.

Nira said, 'I can explain whatever you don't understand, show you things that you never dreamed of. But I need you to do something for me, something important to the worldforest, and to history.'

Anton looked surprised. 'What's that?'

'I need someone who understands both humans and Ildirans – someone who was there. The two of you can work together. And I promise this won't be as difficult as correcting the *Saga of Seven Suns*.' Anton and Rememberer Vao'sh looked at each other. 'Anton Colicos . . . will you tell my story?'

She could see that the question startled him, then choked him up. The manner in which this story was told would influence how future generations viewed what had happened to her in the breeding camps on Dobro. It would have consequences for human and Ildiran relations for many years to come.

'I would be honoured. Absolutely honoured.'

ONE HUNDRED AND FIFTEEN

TASIA TAMBLYN

Their timing had to be precise or none of them would ever escape from Llaro. Absolute coordination was crucial. *Perfect timing.* No margin for error.

Right.

Under the late afternoon sun, Tasia monitored her chronometer, checked their location, and picked up the pace. She and Nikko had to be in position before deep twilight fell, and it would take both of them to do the digging and heavy lifting – after they actually found the buried fuel barrels. Davlin, meanwhile, had his own task. Then Robb would retrieve them ... *if* all the timing worked.

Meanwhile, several Roamer engineers from among the Llaro survivors had returned to the wreck of the *Osquivel* and set about completing the major repairs that would make the ship flightworthy again. Forget the manuals; this was all strictly seat-of-the-pants work. And Davlin Lotze claimed he could do the rest. His words were not mere bravado, either. Tasia believed him.

So she, Davlin, and Nikko had crossed the grasslands in broad daylight, screened by clumps of tan rocks or spiky pampas grass, and approached the ever-expanding perimeter of the insect colony.

'I doubt the bugs are looking for us anymore,' Davlin said in a hushed voice. 'By devouring the captive colonists, the breedex probably got what it needed, and the Klikiss seem to ignore anything they don't consider relevant.'

'Unless we poke a pointed stick in their eyes,' Tasia said.

'Let's try not to do that,' Nikko said quickly.

She peered over a low mound covered with dry thistleweeds to get her bearings. In the nearby insect city, armies of multi-legged workers excavated the dry dirt, built more towers, and dug tunnels to house their suddenly increased numbers. She saw more of them than she had ever imagined. 'Sooner or later, they're going to overrun the whole damned planet.'

'The breedex may just abandon Llaro and launch out to conquer other subhives,' Davlin said. 'We can always hope.'

'Then I wish the bugs would hurry up about it and leave.'

The three of them moved through gullies, around clumps of upthrust rock, and through patches of dry grain stalks until Davlin called a halt just beyond the perimeter the insect creatures patrolled. He sent a tight-channel signal to Robb almost below the horizon far behind them, and they all coordinated their movements. 'Time to split up. Good luck.'

'Follow your Guiding Star,' Tasia said to Davlin.

'We certainly plan to,' Nikko added.

Without further discussion, Davlin darted off. Tasia quickly lost sight of him as he picked his way toward the scar of the former colony settlement and the giant frame of the large new transportal standing just outside the main towers. Despite his stealthy moves, she couldn't imagine how Davlin intended to slip in among the alien structures with his heavy backpack, but that was his problem. She and Nikko had memorized the detailed topographical projections DD had made.

'If the fuel is where Davlin says it is, I'll need about ten minutes to find it,' she said. 'Starting now.'

'And another fifteen for us to uncover it.'

They found the cleverly made pile of rocks and the camouflaged marker. The pair nodded to each other, and began lifting the boulders, rolling them away, and digging into the loose dirt. Tasia's fingernails were torn and her palms raw, but she ignored the pain. She and Nikko continued to dig, keeping a lookout for Klikiss scouts and monitoring the ever-ticking chronometer, until they finally uncovered the tops of the sealed polymer barrels. 'Well, well, looks like we found us some buried treasure.' Enough standard fuel to take them far from here – if the Roamer engineers could make the *Osquivel* space-worthy again.

Only thirty seconds behind schedule. Davlin should be finishing his task, planting the last of his explosives, setting the timers.

'I'll clear it. You attach the anti-grav lifters.' Nikko threw himself into the work, wobbling the barrels back and forth in the dirt to loosen them. He wiped perspiration from his forehead with a grimy hand. 'Sure glad we don't have to carry these things.'

'Shizz, I'd roll them across the ground for kilometres if it was the only way to get them back to the ship.' She and Nikko wrenched the first fuel barrel free from the rocks and dirt, heaved it up out of the hole, then stood it on the clear ground. Without catching her breath, Tasia gestured toward the second buried container. 'Come on. Not much time.'

The darkness was getting thicker by the moment. Robb's voice came over the fine-channel comm. 'On my way. ETA twelve minutes – and on schedule, ladies and gentlemen.' Tasia had never heard anything so wonderful in her life.

Nikko looked up into the sky, searching. 'That's good news.'

'Only if Davlin does his part. Otherwise we're screwed.'

In the distance Tasia could see the tiny black shapes of scuttling aliens continuing their work even in the gathering dark. She checked the chronometer again. 'What's taking Davlin so damned long? How hard can it be?' They should hear the Remora's engines in another few seconds, and the bugs would surely notice them.

Suddenly, like the cadence of a drum corps, a succession of explosions rocked the Klikiss city. Small bombs went off with bursts of orange light and white smoke. 'There's the fireworks,' Nikko said.

'But where's Davlin?' Tasia fidgeted, wondering how fast the man could run. If he didn't get here in time, did he expect them to wait for him? She leaned against the two recovered fuel barrels and scoped out a good landing spot for Robb. 'Okay, we're rapidly wasting the effectiveness of our diversion here. Come on, Davlin! And Brindle!'

As if Robb had heard her, the EDF Remora roared in, flying so low to the ground that he practically scraped the rocks and grasses. Tasia had already provided a homing signal, and now she tossed two bright flaresticks into the flat area she had chosen for him. He could land safely here, but if the bugs were watching, they would detect the EDF ship. She had to hope they were too busy with Davlin's diversion.

Perfectly timed, a second flurry of explosions went off, burying the Klikiss warriors that had come to investigate the first round of sabotage.

Robb's Remora used back-thrusters to hover above the flattened grasses, spraying pebbles as it settled to the ground next to where Tasia and Nikko stood waving. He sprang out of the cockpit and opened the underbelly hatch. 'Here I am, ready or not. Got the fuel?'

Tasia and Nikko used the anti-grav lifters to wrestle the unwieldy barrels forward. 'Come on, come on!' she called.

Robb helped them heft the barrels into the cargo bay. 'Where's Davlin?'

As soon as they stowed the fuel containers inside the Remora, Nikko pulled himself into the stripped-down interior. Tasia looked over her shoulder, trying to guess how many seconds they could afford to wait. It would soon reach a crisis point. They all looked nervously out into the twilight.

Davlin jogged up, not even out of breath. He wore a barely disguised grin. 'The Klikiss are busy enough now. We can fly out of here at our leisure.'

Tasia said, 'Thanks, but I'll take my leisure back at the caves.'

When they were aboard the Remora with the fuel barrels securely lashed down, Robb fired up the engines again, raised the ship into the air, and streaked back toward the sandstone bluffs. As far as Tasia could tell, the Klikiss hadn't noticed a thing.

Behind them, the insects crawled over the collapsing towers and began to rebuild like ants after a downpour.

ONE HUNDRED AND SIXTEEN

DENN PERONI

They were cramped together in the cockpit for days, flying a tanker full of nebula wentals, and not once did Denn let Caleb Tamblyn get on his nerves. The grizzled old man had never seen Denn look so contented, happy, or excited about anything abstract – especially not a philosophy.

'I always had you pegged for a no-nonsense businessman, Denn. You look at the bottom line, add up profits and losses, determine efficient trade routes. By the Guiding Star, isn't that why Del Kellum asked you to run his shipyards?'

'None of that has changed, but I understand so much more now, things I never saw before.' Denn smiled, mainly for himself. 'And if I play my cards right, I can make even greater profits and manage my shipyard workers, my captains, and my facilities at higher efficiency. You should have seen how Tabitha Huck turned the Ildirans into a well-oiled machine. It was nothing short of a revelation. The Guiding Star is like a candle flame compared to this.'

'Whatever you say. Just as long as you don't start quoting poetry to me.'

'I doubt I could convert you if I wanted to, Caleb Tamblyn. Your skull's too thick for the *thism* to penetrate. But if you're interested, I could find someone to try it on you.' He looked hopefully at his friend.

'No thanks. Don't need it.'

Inside the cruising tanker, the energized wentals fused and flowed into one life force, restored from their long nebular exile. The water beings were connected as part of a common entity, yet they also had subgroupings, like families. The wentals in this ship, now alive, intact, and resynthesized, were eager to begin propagating, to share their energy and knowledge. Jess and Cesca had been right to give Denn this task. He felt honoured.

His daughter had suggested, and the Roamers heartily agreed, that the new wentals be taken to Jonah 12 with the other wentals they had recently deposited there. Denn had cheerfully volunteered to go with Caleb, claiming he intrinsically understood so much more about the wentals now. Caleb did not realize how greatly changed his long-time friend was, and now Denn had a captive audience.

'The wentals are part of the whole fabric of the universe, you know,' he continued, as if their conversation had never stopped, and indeed it hadn't. He never ceased looking for excuses to bring their talk around to the subject that fascinated him. 'The wentals and the verdani are different sides of the same coin. The green priests' telink is like Jess and Cesca's ability to communicate with the wentals. Now with this union of telink and *thism*, even our own human abilities – whatever they are ... oh, Caleb, you just can't understand.'

The old man gave him a wry frown. 'I'm not convinced you're feeling all right, Denn. You keep jabbering.'

Denn decided that a pragmatic argument might work on Caleb. 'Just think about the commercial possibilities. If all Roamers could connect with each other like green priests, imagine how much more efficient our traders could be. We could discover untapped markets, cooperate in ways we never imagined.'

'Oh? And how do you negotiate if you can't bluff?'

'We wouldn't need to rely on that. We could understand fluctuations, supply and demand. We could cooperate with unprecedented efficiency, form a large and powerful trading company.'

'Large and powerful,' Caleb said. 'Two words guaranteed to get my interest. Throw in "lucrative", and you've got my undying devotion.' Nevertheless, he remained sceptical as they entered the Jonah system. 'Next you're going to try to sell me an ice mine on a lava planet. We clans have been doing well enough for ourselves over the years by following the Guiding Star.'

Denn grinned. 'The Guiding Star is part of it, too.' Caleb rolled his eyes.

Moments later, the faeros attack cut off all further discussion.

Fifteen blazing fireballs streaked in around them like crashing meteors. In his heart and mind, connected peripherally to the sentience of the wentals in the cargo hold, Denn experienced a sudden wash of panic.

'What the hell?' Caleb said.

Filters cut across the viewing screens as the fiery ships hovered in front of the cumbersome tanker. Sweat burst out on Denn's forehead, as if the temperature inside the cockpit had soared, though the ship's systems fought against the thermal flux. Even so, Denn felt wonder as well as a fear. If the wentals and worldtrees were connected with the *thism*, then the faeros must be part of it as well.

Denn sensed danger, chaos. Something terrible. 'Caleb ...
I think we're in trouble.'

In the tanker's hold, the wentals swelled and throbbed. The
frenzied elemental creatures pounded on Denn's mind. He could
sense them, but not understand them through the new threads that
connected him with everything.

'What the hell do they want?' Caleb bent forward and shouted
into the comm system, 'Hello, faeros – whatever you are. We
mean you no harm. Please leave us alone.' He looked stupidly at
Denn, not sure what else to say.

The wentals became turbulent, agitated, knowing they were
too few to stand against these fiery entities. The faeros had come
for them, for the tanker, and – because he was connected to them
in a way that Caleb couldn't understand – Denn knew that he,
too, was vulnerable.

'Caleb, get to the evacuation pod.'

'Shizz, what's that going to do? They could melt the pod like
an ice chip in a furnace!'

'They don't want you. They want the wentals.'

'What did the wentals do to them? We're just minding our own
business here.'

Denn rose to his feet, grabbed the other man with unexpected
force, and dragged him out of his seat. He sent Caleb stumbling
toward the small evacuation pod, and the old man caught his
balance at the hatch. 'All right, all right! Come on, then!'

'I can't go. They'd follow, somehow.'

'I'm not flying alone out here in the middle of nowhere!'

'Go to Jonah 12. It's your only chance.'

'Jonah 12? There's nothing left—'

'If I survive, I'll come back and rescue you. If I don't survive,
then you would have been killed anyway.'

'What a wonderful choice.' Though he remained confused and

distressed, Caleb didn't argue further. He sealed the hatch and cycled the evacuation pod.

The faeros circled, targeting the wentals in the water tanker's hold. Denn could feel it. He barely noticed when the pod launched. Caleb tumbled out into empty space at the far edge of the solar system.

Alone inside the tanker, Denn tried to contact the roiling wentals, but his throat felt seared. The threads that he had recently recognized as *thism*, as echoes of telink, suddenly grew hot. The faeros pressed against the trapped water tanker, so bright that even the filters couldn't block it all out.

At least Caleb had gotten away.

Denn could sense something stronger, something ominous, like a flame rushing along a fuse. His new connections had opened a back door for the faeros to enter. His body grew hot, his skin started to sizzle, his eyes watered – and his tears turned to steam. He lifted his hands and saw his skin glowing with an inner fire, as if his very blood were boiling. Then he burst into impossibly hot flame, his whole body consumed from the inside out.

Fireballs engulfed the water tanker. The structural plates softened to dripping, vaporized metal. As the wentals began to boil, the hull split open and the released water gushed like a geyser.

The remnants of the Tamblyn tanker exploded, leaving nothing but gas and shrapnel. The vaporous wentals spread out, but arcing plumes of faeros corralled the water beings. The pulsing fireballs dragged the living wental water into the nearby sun.

MAGE-IMPERATOR JORA'H

L ong ago, Jora'h had visited the magnificent worldforest, leaving Nira and Ambassador Otema behind, foolishly believing them safe from his father's treachery. He had been so innocent then, never guessing the terrible things Mage-Imperator Cyroc'h had been doing right under his nose. When he returned to Ildira, his father had told him Nira was dead. A lie.

In private meetings, the royal couple and the Mage-Imperator discussed many matters of importance to them all. King Peter and Queen Estarra, who had also been tricked by political machinations, shared much about the dark dealings of Basil Wenceslas. Some of the Chairman's actions reminded Jora'h uncomfortably of what his own father had done. And the news grew worse.

The green priests were abuzz with horror over messages they had just received from a green priest on Usk, a small colony that had dared to declare its independence. Nira wept as she described to Jora'h what she had seen through the trees, the appalling bloodshed, the brutality of the EDF troops, the crucifixion of the town's elders. Jora'h was relieved that he had not mistakenly

541

travelled to Earth, expecting the Chairman to speak for all humans, as he himself spoke for all Ildirans.

The King and Queen had internal struggles to face, much as he had faced the mad Designate's rebellion in the Horizon Cluster. And the Mage-Imperator could help them. They could help each other.

On the day after all the formalities and receptions and feasts, Jora'h stood with his beloved green priest out under the sheltering canopy. The Theron people, Roamer traders, visitors from Confederation colonies, and more green priests gathered around to hear the Mage-Imperator make his announcement of contrition – the very reason he had left his Empire and come to the heart of the new Confederation. This was what he had needed to do all along, before the anger festered. Build bridges instead of burn them.

King Peter wore a formal but comfortable suit that struck a balance between uniform and royal raiment. Estarra looked beautiful in traditional Theron cocoon-weave garments that revealed the rounded swell of her belly, and reminded him with a pang that he had not been with Nira when Osira'h was born . . .

He faced an audience hushed with anticipation. It was time to make things right. Nira leaned toward him to whisper, 'I love you.' It was all the encouragement he needed.

Jora'h told them all about the Dobro breeding programme, without pause, without excuses. Then he did a thing that no Mage-Imperator had ever done: he asked *forgiveness* for his actions, and the actions of his misguided predecessors. Green priests repeated his words through telink so that every orphaned colony would know what the Ildiran leader said. No rumours, just facts.

Holding Nira's hand in his, Jora'h raised it in a gesture of strength and solidarity. 'The Ildiran Empire no longer hides secrets

– from you or from our own people. I can only hope to dispel these painful shadows by offering light and truth.'

King Peter surprised the Mage-Imperator by clasping his other hand. 'We have all been weakened by this past war and by past mistakes. We were trapped in bad situations because of the unwise actions of our predecessors.'

The Queen joined them. 'I want our own child to grow up in a different Spiral Arm, one of mutual strength and cooperation. Our peoples still face many enemies – terrible enemies.'

Jora'h knew the Queen was thinking of Chairman Wenceslas and the remnants of the Terran Hanseatic League, while he himself could not stop thinking about the faeros. How could his depleted Solar Navy possibly fight them? And both humans and Ildirans might need to worry about the ravenous Klikiss.

'Then do we agree to an alliance? Humans and Ildirans, your Confederation and my Empire, for mutual support?'

'Absolutely,' King Peter said. 'We need each other.'

DEPUTY CHAIRMAN
ELDRED CAIN

The massacre on Usk had been as awful as the Chairman promised, and he seemed quite pleased about it. Cain and Sarein sat in the headquarters offices watching the debrief summary General Lanyan had brought back with him, though Basil had specifically asked the General not to join them. Outside the slanted windows, bright zeppelins and slow airbarges drifted across the Palace District, as if nothing could disturb their leisurely routine.

Cain felt sick. He and Sarein were unable to tear their eyes away from the images of the crucified town elders, the burned farmhouses, the slaughtered herds, one man wailing about his destroyed orchards. Sarein seemed to be crying.

As he waited for the vidloop to finish playing, Chairman Wenceslas impatiently stared through the armoured glass of the office window and frowned at the skyline. If he had expected cheers or applause, he was disappointed. Finally he turned back, apparently oblivious to their aghast expressions. 'It's a sad state of affairs that forced me into taking such an unpleasant action, but at least we accomplished our aims. The Hansa and the EDF are strengthened, and the mission was a success – for once!'

Cain finally said in a raspy voice, 'Mr Chairman, do not show these images to the public. They will riot.'

'They will fall into line! We have laid the groundwork and issued clear pronouncements, and this will seal the last of it. No more ambiguities.' He reached forward to switch off the images. Sarein stared at the blank space on his projection desk as if expecting something else to jump out at her. 'Besides, I've already released the raw footage to the newsnets.'

Raw footage? Cain sat up so quickly he nearly tipped his chair over. 'Sir, that is unwise! You said you wanted me to work it into a special release as part of an announcement.'

Basil shrugged. 'I'm satisfied with it as is. The images speak for themselves, a clear indication that things are turning around for us. We've got the colony back.'

'By killing everything?' Sarein was quite distraught. 'That's what you think happened there, Basil? You didn't get Usk back, and you'll earn no loyalty when people see it here! Those were unarmed farmers.'

'We regained a crucial level of *respect*,' he said, unperturbed. 'I'm sorry you can't see that. More important than the colony itself, we demonstrated the Hansa's strength, which some of our colonies seem to have forgotten. We showed them that there are consequences to breaking agreements. This isn't a game. Once I release that report in all its gruesome glory to every breakaway colony, they'll fall like dominoes. Who will protect them? Peter and his trees?'

Out in the Palace District, the Archfather was leading another huge rally, and Cain could hear the restless murmuring, the fear-driven shouts as the citizens reacted to – and believed – the man's outrageous claims. Cain had read a draft of the speech and cringed all the way through it.

Basil straightened his suit jacket, studied his face in a small mirror mounted on the wall. He was not vain; he simply demanded perfection in everything, including himself. 'As Chairman, I regret many decisions. I can see and admit some of my mistakes. My most unforgivable error was in being too lenient. I waited too long before I was willing to show our strength. If I had not hesitated – if I had struck swiftly at the beginning of these little insurrections – I could have kept the Hansa strong.' He nodded, like a little boy who had been severely scolded. 'Yes, that is the only decision I truly regret.'

Sarein was doing her best to mask her expression, but the shock and horror still showed. Cain would never get the massacre out of his mind – a stark contrast to the earlier beautiful images of Usk with peaceful shepherds, blossoming orchards, prosperous farms.

Chairman Wenceslas gazed down at his blank deskscreen, as if still seeing things that he had long-since deleted. 'My own people never cease to surprise me. Success, then failure. They switch back and forth like a magician's hands. Sometimes it's so absurd I just want to laugh.' New screens popped up at his touch, and he stared down at them, nodding grimly, absorbed in his own work, as if Cain and Sarein weren't even there.

'I sent Admiral Willis with ten Manta cruisers to reassert our authority on Rhejak – and I've just received a "bill" from her! She expects the Hansa to *pay* for supplies and materials from our own colony. Willis made concessions to the locals, letting them push her around, and now she expects us to reimburse them for what the Hansa already owns.' He rolled his grey eyes as if to emphasize the sheer absurdity of the request.

'Do you want me to help you with the portrayal of the Rhejak situation?' Cain nervously cleared his throat. 'Should I release a carefully prepared statement to the newsnets?' Perhaps he could salvage this, somehow, and not let it turn into a horrific disaster like Usk.

'What more do we need to know? It's another rebellious Hansa colony. We are entitled to anything they produce. I knew I should have relieved Willis of command, but I gave her a second chance, against my better judgment. Another sad mistake on my part.'

'And how will you respond, Mr Chairman?' Cain looked at the dapper man, not flicking his gaze to the blank screen that had recently projected the images of the Usk massacre.

'Not to worry. I've already dispatched General Lanyan to deal with the matter. On Usk, we set a new tone for these unruly bastards who are intent on bringing down the Hansa. Once the General confronts Admiral Willis, he'll do what's required to make Rhejak – and the Admiral – fall into line.' He folded his hands. 'Afterward we'll have even more powerful images to disseminate via the newsnets.' Basil looked pointedly at Sarein, then at his deputy, slicing them with the scalpel of his gaze. 'Any other questions?'

Cain spoke before Sarein could say something she might regret. 'None, sir.'

Back in his own quarters, Cain sat in blissful silence, appreciating the perfect illumination on the painting. The masterpiece gave him solace when the universe seemed too insane for him to comprehend.

He drew a long, calming breath, tried to imagine himself falling into the painting – and away from the Hansa. Velasquez was a genius, unquestionably Spain's greatest master. Cain never tired of staring at the composition, the colours, the nuanced brushstrokes.

But he could not stop thinking of Chairman Wenceslas. The images of Usk haunted him more than the most violent and disturbing paintings of Goya. The Titan Saturn devouring his children. Worse, Cain knew that more incidents of such violence were surely to come.

He lost track of time, saw that he had passed more than an hour in the troubled waters of his mind, and stood, stretching to relieve the ache in his back from sitting on the viewing bench. He had already swept his apartment and assured himself that not even the Chairman had managed to slip in any surreptitious eavesdropping devices. Basil Wenceslas did not quite suspect his deputy of outright treason. Not yet.

On a secure channel, he contacted Captain McCammon, whom he knew to be off duty. 'Did you establish the repeater stations, Captain?'

'Yes, Mr Deputy. Several members of the royal guard assisted me.'

'And you are certain of their loyalty?'

'As certain as I can be. They are aware of certain details concerning the escape of King Peter and Queen Estarra. It's already enough to hang me,' McCammon said with a hint of black humour. 'If there is a weak link, I would know it by now.'

'Good. It's time to circulate the message as widely as possible. The Chairman keeps trying to stop it, and we will keep distributing it. King Peter will have his say, and the people will believe it.'

'I have no doubt of that, sir. But what will they do? Do you really expect a spontaneous uprising?'

'No. We may have to help them along.'

ONE HUNDRED AND NINETEEN

ADMIRAL SHEILA WILLIS

True to her word, Willis kept the EDF soldiers out of everyone's hair. She allowed Hakim Allahu to broker deals with Roamers for certain non-essential materials, while the EDF prepared a valuable shipment to send to Earth as soon as they received the Chairman's authorization for payment.

She stood at the edge of the floating raft-base, watching the colourful fish below dart in and out of the honeycombed segments, build nests, and nibble at algae that grew on the pontoons. Willis had caught many of her people surreptitiously dropping food into the water to watch the marine life eat.

No further incidents of sabotage occurred; Rhejak's authorities watched over their citizens with sharp eyes. Willis had made them understand that cooperation was best for everyone. The three young vandals had spent a week in the brig of a Manta, where Conrad Brindle had evidently scared the boys out of further mischief for the rest of their lives. 'I hate it when normally good kids put themselves on the wrong side of an issue,' he practically growled. The Admiral wondered what sort of concrete experience he had in the matter. She had served with his son Robb, and he'd always seemed a good kid.

When a gaunt young Roamer named Jym Dooley arrived with unexpected news, Allahu brought the trader to see Willis on her raft-base and announced, 'Admiral, the conflict is almost over! If your Chairman knows what's good for his people, he'll have to reach an accommodation with the rest of us.'

'That's a bold statement, Mr Allahu. Our guest hasn't even given me his message yet.'

Dooley had rumpled hair and a perpetual look of panic on his face. He was a thin, sallow-faced man of about twenty-four with a wispy, light-brown beard that did little more than make his cheeks look dirty. 'Ma'am, the Mage-Imperator has formally recognized the Confederation by going to Theroc and meeting with the King. He and Peter have formed an alliance.'

Willis let out a long breath. The lion's share of the abandoned Hansa colonies had already joined the Confederation, as had the Roamer clans, along with all of Theroc – and now the Ildirans. She nodded to Allahu. 'You're right. It sounds like the Chairman should cut his losses.'

'Do you think he'll do it?' Allahu asked.

'Not a chance.'

'Have you heard yet what the Eddies did on Usk? That news should turn any stragglers against the Hansa.'

Willis frowned. 'We haven't received any official communication in some time. What happened on Usk?'

Dooley was breathless. 'Eddy ships wiped out the colony town because the people tore up the Charter. Crucified the town elders, just to flex their muscles. Bastards!'

'You've got to be exaggerating. General Lanyan would never condone such an action.'

'Condone it? He was there. He *did* it.'

Willis rolled her eyes, tired of all the ridiculous rumours and exaggerations. 'I don't believe this for a minute.'

'Believe what you like. What do I care?'

Dooley headed back to his ship, which looked like a fat fuel tank with fins and several cargo pods welded to the sides. The affronted Roamer quickly loaded it with non-essential trade items – seafood and concentrated kelp extracts – and took off.

Before the first batch of new traders had departed less than a week ago, Willis had done a random inspection, just to make sure that no weapons or explosives were being smuggled in or out. The Roamer pilot looked agitated during the impromptu check, and the EDF searchers had uncovered a small valuable stash of reef-pearls that weren't on the manifest. Willis had let the embarrassed pilot go with a stern warning. As far as she was concerned, reef-pearls didn't have any more strategic importance than a bunch of fish steaks, and her leniency had earned her goodwill with the Rhejak natives. Since then, a few ballsy traders had cautiously ventured back, despite the Manta cruisers standing guard overhead.

Willis was sitting back in a deck chair, watching Dooley's overloaded ship lumber into the sky when Conrad Brindle contacted her on the command channel, interrupting her peaceful state of mind. 'Admiral, I have welcome news. General Lanyan just arrived – with your Juggernaut.'

'The *Jupiter*? Here?' She sat up straight, and the chair creaked a complaint. 'What does the General want? Why weren't we informed he was coming?'

'He wants to speak with you, but he doesn't sound too pleased.'

'He can tell me what's chafing his crotch when he gets here.' She went into the raft-base's communications shack. A bank of monitor screens displayed transmissions from surveillance satellites in orbit. The ten Mantas continued to patrol around Rhejak, primarily for show. On the screens she saw the Juggernaut cruise in at top speed, like a whale being chased by harpooners. 'Yes, indeed, something *is* chafing the General,' she muttered to herself.

The trajectory of Dooley's cargo ship changed as it reached the edge of the atmosphere. The Roamer pilot transmitted wildly. 'What's that Juggernaut doing here? Did you Eddy bastards trick me?'

'It's a new arrival, son. He's my commanding officer.'

'Roamer vessel, stand down and prepare to be boarded,' came a curt transmission. 'Your cargo is forfeit, and you'll be placed in custody.'

'What the hell?' Willis turned to her fresh-faced comm officer. 'Get me Lanyan on the horn right now.'

Gaunt Dooley, already frightened, changed course erratically and accelerated in the opposite direction from the ten Mantas on-station. Already at full speed, the *Jupiter* streaked right past the Mantas toward the small Roamer ship. 'Leave me alone!' Dooley transmitted, his voice cracking. 'By the Guiding Star, I've got authorization. I—'

Without any warning, the *Jupiter* opened fire. Willis watched the blip on the trajectory screen wink out as multiple jazers vaporized the cargo ship. For a full five seconds, she couldn't find words. Finally she hammered the transmit button and yelled into the pickup. 'General, what the hell are you doing? That was a civilian operating with my explicit permission!'

Lanyan's smug face crystallized on the screen. 'Good thing I was here to intercept. That man was clearly a Roamer agent – an enemy combatant.'

'Enemy combatant? He was a trader carrying a load of cargo! I watched the kid load the damn thing myself.' She felt sick.

'Did it slip your mind that we're at war with the Roamers?

My orders come directly from Chairman Wenceslas – as do yours. I'm transmitting a vidloop summary of my recent mission to a rebel colony world named Usk. The Hansa's position has changed from one of leniency to one of unification, which will be rigorously enforced if necessary.'

'I don't recall the Chairman ever *having* a policy of leniency,' Willis said.

But Lanyan had already begun broadcasting images from the Usk pogrom, which conveyed far more threat than any lecture could. She saw the EDF soldiers, the swooping Remoras, the burning fields and orchards, slaughtered sheep and cattle, colonist families murdered as they tried to flee their homes. The young comm officer beside her turned greenish and vomited on the floor.

'Amen to that,' Willis said. 'But please clean it up.'

Lanyan's face returned to the screen, smiling now. 'We sent that on an open channel, Admiral. Make sure that everyone has an opportunity to view it before I arrive. The Chairman believes we may be required to make a similar example of Rhejak. He was not amused by the bill you sent for materials you were ordered to acquire on behalf of the Earth Defence Forces. I could cite numerous irregularities sufficiently serious to relieve you of command.'

'The hell you could,' she said under her breath, but maintained a stony expression.

Lanyan continued, 'I'm on my way down there right now. Round up any ringleaders on Rhejak. Let me see the head of the Company Works, the planetary spokesman, if they have one, and anyone else you feel is important enough to take responsibility.'

She couldn't contain her objections any longer. 'General Lanyan, this is not proper. These people legitimately formed a new government. You have no authority here.'

'Ten Mantas and one Juggernaut give us all the authority we

need. Begin making your contacts, Admiral. When I arrive, we'll have ourselves a town meeting.'

Terminating the transmission, Willis shouted aloud, not caring who might hear. 'This is bullshit!' She turned to the sick-looking ensign. 'Transmit on a tight channel to my Mantas. Tell Lieutenant Commander Brindle to run a battle stations drill. Let him think we're just keeping things snappy for the General.'

'What are you going to do, Admiral?'

'I haven't a clue, but I want to be ready for anything. Escort Hakim Allahu and Drew Vardian over here as the General requested — then bring out all of our soldiers so we can form a welcoming committee.' Still weaving, the young ensign turned to rush off, but Willis called him back. 'Clean up that puke first.'

ONE HUNDRED AND TWENTY

TASIA TAMBLYN

They had retrieved enough standard fuel from Davlin's cache, and the desperate Roamer refugees had salvaged the *Osquivel*, declaring it ready for take-off. There was no reason to wait. No long goodbyes. No sentimental send-offs. Just leave. Now.

Over the past two days, Tasia had worked with Robb, Nikko, and Davlin to seal the ruptured fuel tank, using brute force to hammer and patch it into spaceworthy condition. They had to get the hell off of Llaro before Klikiss from the newly expanded subhive tracked down their crash site.

The refugees back at the bluffs were anxious to go. They knew their supplies could not last long, and with over seventy of them crowded in the primitive caves and overhangs, conditions were deteriorating rapidly. Tasia was sure that somebody would make a mistake soon, and the Klikiss patrols would spot them.

Out at the isolated arroyo, Davlin Lotze used a makeshift hand-pump to transfer the fuel from the barrels into the engine reservoirs; he even siphoned off the last fumes that remained in the lone EDF Remora. Altogether, they had enough to take off and get the refugees away from Llaro.

Nikko ran around the outside hull to check the *Osquivel's* numerous seals one last time, while Robb climbed into the cockpit to do his final diagnostics. DD and Orli, who rarely left the Friendly compy's side, followed him in. Tasia sat in the seat beside Robb as he sent a test burst through the engines; they responded with an extremely loud and gratifying roar. Pebbles and dust sprayed from the exhaust cylinders, and the ship lurched and jerked, like an impatient animal, anxious to bound away.

Covered with dust, Nikko dived inside, grinning. 'It works! It works!'

'Seal the damn hatch so we can test the pressurization,' Tasia said. 'Once we hit orbit, you don't want to be using tape and putty to fill pinholes.'

'I can help run diagnostics,' DD said. 'Please tell me how I can be of assistance.' The Friendly compy had been invaluable in reprogramming the engine control systems.

'I'll just stay here out of the way.' Orli's bright eyes watched everything.

The readings spun upward and held. Hull sensors verified that the seal integrity remained uncompromised. Tasia clapped her hand on Nikko's shoulder, then threw her arms around Robb. 'Bull's-eye!'

'Are we ready to go?' Orli asked, sitting up straight. 'Davlin told the people it would be another day, or probably two.'

Davlin gave her a calm smile. 'I didn't want to give them false hope. This way they won't be disappointed.'

Robb shut down the systems, not wanting to waste fuel. 'I'm convinced. Let's get back to the caves and tell everyone to head out.'

'We could just fly there,' Nikko said.

Tasia frowned at him. 'It'll be quite a trick to land a ship this big anywhere near the bluffs – not that we couldn't do it, mind you – but the *Osquivel* is barely holding together as it is. Take-offs and landings can be rough on a ship. How much do you want to increase our risk factor?'

'Not by much.' Nikko sounded concerned.

'It'll only take us half an hour to jog back to camp,' Orli said.

'Or run,' Davlin said. 'Let's go.'

They travelled under the cover of night, their eyes adjusted to the stars and shadows. DD marched ahead, leading the way, and Orli, who already carried her meagre possessions with her in a backpack, trotted after him.

'I do not wish to leave Margaret Colicos behind.' DD sounded forlorn. 'She is with the Klikiss.'

'We don't even know if she's still alive, DD.'

'Perhaps one day we can come back and check.'

'Sure,' Tasia said from behind them. 'One day. We'll bring along a whole friggin' military assault force.'

'That might work,' Nikko said.

Before they could reach the sandstone bluffs, Tasia thought she heard a flutter and hum, followed by a clicking sound in the darkness ahead. She didn't like it.

DD paused. 'Excuse me, but I detect movement ahead of us. Large shapes are approaching. Many life forms. Perhaps they are indigenous animals.'

'Not very likely.' Tasia instinctively moved closer to Robb.

Davlin's face seemed to be a mask made of carved wood. They all heard thrumming and buzzing too distinct to be ignored. In his hand he produced a flare grenade; Tasia didn't ask where he had gotten it. 'Let's see what we've got. Stand ready.' He looked around, assessing all the worried expressions.

'Stand ready with *what?*' Tasia asked. Nikko picked up two sharp rocks, and Orli did the same. Robb balled his fists.

Davlin tossed the grenade, counted out loud to five. Tasia flinched as a cascade of brilliant light gushed into the air. Blinking in the glare, she saw a dozen Klikiss scouts and warriors, along with some oddly pale humanlike hybrids. New hybrids.

Undeterred by the flare grenade, the Klikiss surged forward. Davlin, who had one of the few EDF weapons, shot until the charge pack was empty, blasting bugs, splattering gore. Their squeals were deafening. The attacking insects ignored their fallen comrades and closed in, driven by the intent mind of the subhive's new-generation breedex.

Robb stood back to back with Tasia. 'I'm ready to fight with bare hands and fingernails if I have to.'

'My brave hero. I'd rather go with a happily-ever-after scenario, though.'

DD remained beside Orli as if he meant to protect her. Remembering how she had stopped the Klikiss scout that had attacked their small party of escapees, she swung the pack off her back. If she could only get her synthesizer strips.

One of the Klikiss warriors extended a tube weapon and sprayed a stream of greyish-white fluid, splattering Orli before she could free her small keyboard. It targeted her on purpose, as if the breedex remembered exactly who she was. A cascade of hardening resin crusted her hands and arms. She squirmed, and another spurt from the web guns covered her mouth and neck.

The Klikiss shot their web guns to entangle and capture, rather than kill the small group. Within minutes the creatures had rounded up the humans, immobilizing them with the constraining resin. Tasia couldn't move against the gobs of hardening slime, could barely breathe. Armoured limbs grasped her, dragged her

away from Robb. She hated the fact that she wouldn't have a
chance to go down fighting – or tell the other refugees how close
they were to being home free. So close.

ONE HUNDRED AND TWENTY-ONE

CHAIRMAN BASIL WENCESLAS

No matter how meticulous he was, Basil never succeeded in predicting all the ways that people would rebuff him. In cracking down on the illegal disseminators of Peter's stupid condemnation, he had arrested seventeen ringleaders already. He issued statements along with manufactured proof to refute the childish lies and accusations. But soon another group picked up and distributed the declaration and Patrick Fitzpatrick's confession. The malcontents began to add horrific images from Usk and – more maddening than anything else! – they doctored and falsified the files so that Basil's actions seemed like a *bad thing*. He didn't find that amusing whatsoever.

Now Basil had heard – from an independent trader proudly crowing news as he rushed to Earth – the dramatic announcement of an alliance between Mage-Imperator Jora'h and King Peter. With that single statement, the Ildiran leader had made the abortive Confederation seem more legitimate than ever. Basil saw red for five full minutes and was not sure what he did or said during that time. He knew only that when he came back to himself, his temples were throbbing, and his skull felt as if it might split.

He blinked his eyes and saw Deputy Cain sitting across from him in his office, wisely saying nothing. Basil waited for the deputy to say something about his shocking outburst. He almost wanted the pale man to question him or make a comment, just so he could explode again. But Cain remained silent and patient, as if Basil had merely sneezed and needed a moment to recover himself.

The Chairman took a deep breath and realized that his throat felt raw. He wondered what he had shouted. He honestly couldn't remember. Now his voice rasped as he spoke. 'Send in Admiral—' He paused, his brow furrowed. 'Which admirals can I still rely on?'

'Admirals Pike and San Luis were dispatched to two more breakaway colonies. Admiral Willis is on Rhejak. Admiral Diente, however, is easily recalled from the asteroid-belt shipyards.'

'Bring him back then, without any fanfare.'

Cain was obviously struggling to react normally after the outburst he must have witnessed. 'What do you have in mind, sir?'

Basil listened carefully, trying to find any implied criticism in the deputy's voice. He trusted Eldred Cain less and less. So few people he could rely upon! Not even Sarein, though he had done his best to maintain a hold on her. He couldn't imagine how he had ever found the skinny Theron woman attractive. Now she seemed clingy, frightened, even shrill. The last time they had made love, he had lain awake afterward, worried that she might slip a dagger into his back during the night.

'Mr Chairman?'

Basil's nostrils flared as he came back to the important matter at hand. 'It's the Mage-Imperator, Mr Cain. Instead of coming to me, *the Chairman of the Terran Hanseatic League,* he went to Peter on his "embassy to humanity". He chose Theroc, not Earth. That is an insult we cannot ignore. We must demonstrate to the Ildiran Empire that we are the true government. With the Mage-Imperator's support we can consolidate the Hansa again and make it strong.'

'Mr Chairman, Ildirans don't understand human politics. The Mage-Imperator probably isn't aware of how our circles of power have changed, and was simply misinformed. I doubt he meant any slight.'

'Then we shall inform him properly. We'll give him a chance to apologize for his lack of foresight. I intend to make him our guest here on Earth. We'll find special quarters for him.'

Cain began to rise from his chair, but seemed to think better of it. 'What are you saying? How will you get the Mage-Imperator to come here?'

'We will invite him – by military force if necessary. According to reports, he is travelling with only a single warliner. As soon as he leaves Theroc, we can escort his ship to Earth. That is why I need Admiral Diente.'

Now Cain looked appalled. 'You're talking about kidnapping the Mage-Imperator? Are you trying to start a war with the Ildiran Empire?'

'Don't be so melodramatic.'

'Honestly, Mr Chairman, I am not. I'm absolutely certain that—'

Basil cut him off. He was getting tired of Cain's disapproving looks and comments. 'I have considered the consequences and made my decision. The Solar Navy was severely damaged – probably more so than our Earth Defence Forces – and you know how the Ildirans are. Once we have the Mage-Imperator, they won't be able to function for themselves. A bunch of sheep without a shepherd. We have the military strength, and we'll soon have the bargaining chip we need.'

Cain stared bleakly out the window, as if imagining the whole

Palace District in flames. 'I would beg you to reconsider, sir, but it wouldn't do any good. Would it?'

Basil gave him an icy glare. 'My primary grudge is not with Jora'h, but with Peter – constantly provoking me, trying to make me look like a fool. But I'll be happy to deal with the Mage-Imperator as well, if he forces me to do so.'

The deputy stood. 'You are stepping off a cliff, Mr Chairman. I hope you understand that.'

'We'll see who's right, Mr Cain.'

'Alas, sir, we will.' He turned to go. 'Now if you'll excuse me, I have preparations to make.' Cain was sweating. Basil didn't know what sort of preparations the man was talking about, nor did he care. He began to formulate the exact orders he would give Admiral Diente, and how he could make sure the man would not disappoint him, as so many others had.

He touched his deskscreen, called up Diente's file, and tracked down the location of all of his family members. Two daughters, a son, five grandchildren. That should be sufficient collateral. Yes, Diente would do as he was told.

ONE HUNDRED AND TWENTY-TWO

CESCA PERONI

Inside the water-bubble ship, she and Jess communed with another pool of wentals they had scooped up from a diffuse nebula. Cesca still couldn't grasp the scope of how many of the water elementals had been ripped apart in the ancient war, but her senses were becoming attuned, strengthened, extended.

Suddenly she felt shock and turmoil among the wentals, as if someone had struck a loud gong. An agonized cry resonated through the fabric of the universe.

Jess grabbed her as they drifted in the contained water of their ship. 'I don't know what it is. The other nebula wentals ... something awful, flames—' They both experienced a horrific mental scream. Wentals, *murdered*! And they knew it was the faeros.

Cesca could see it, feel it. 'They were dragged into a sun.' A cluster of the fiery beings had struck a Plumas tanker in the Jonah system – with her father and Caleb Tamblyn aboard!

More ripples, more elemental tremors. Worse, a much larger group of faeros was attacking elsewhere, a breathtaking force of thousands upon thousands of fireballs.

'Charybdis!' Jess shouted, his voice torn. Inside their shimmering ship, the newly retrieved nebula wentals swirled around them.
Cesca tried to bite back a moan, but the furious pain seemed to be
everywhere. Her father, Charybdis, so many wentals—

As if her eyes had opened onto a distant, foreign place,
she saw more than the energized water in which they drifted: a
churning alien oceanscape studded with a few lifeless black rocks
that poked above the water. She recognized the primary world
where Jess had re-established the wentals, where she herself had
been healed and changed. Where she and Jess had gotten married.

All the seas on Charybdis were alive, impregnated with wental
power. Now, as cluster after cluster of faeros swooped above the
vast ocean, the sentient waves rose up in defensive formations.
The very clouds themselves pulled together for battle.

Angry faeros appeared – first dozens, then hundreds, then
thousands – all of them miniature suns, blazing bright. Like stars
going nova, they scorched away the churning clouds, sent steam
gushing in all directions.

As the fireballs descended into the seas, the wental oceans
backed away, then surged forward to block them. The incandescent creatures fought. Energized water quenched innumerable
fiery entities, but still more came. The faeros began their
bombardment, flame upon flame, like lava scorching the black
rocks, the deep seas. The wentals on Charybdis could not stand
against such an overwhelming force. It seemed as if all the faeros
in the universe had converged here in an impossible, sterilizing
attack.

Agony ripped Cesca's heart. This couldn't be happening!
The faeros scorched the wental reservoir, incinerated the oceans.
Although the watery elementals lashed out with extensions of
themselves and extinguished numerous faeros ships, the rain of fire
continued. No matter how many fireballs fell smoking into the

dwindling bodies of water, a seemingly inexhaustible supply of faeros kept coming.

Inside their distant, protected bubble she blindly reached out to clutch Jess's hand. She welcomed his tight grip on hers, welcomed that small physical pain that was nothing compared to the horror and loss she was seeing on Charybdis. She screamed.

Their ship raced toward Charybdis, but they were much too far away to help. It would take them days to get there. They could bring no other wentals to add their strength. As the blazing destruction continued, Cesca and Jess struggled to understand why the fireballs had turned their vengeance against the wentals. Even the wentals did not comprehend the sheer fury.

Cesca's tears flowed, dissipating into the living liquid. As they continued to observe the last moments of the attack, the nebula water inside their own vessel grew hot – and began to boil.

ONE HUNDRED AND TWENTY-THREE

ADAR ZAN'NH

On their return from dropping the human colonists at Dobro, the Adar's septa encountered five burned warliners drifting in space. The crew was gone, thousands of Ildiran soldiers incinerated where they stood, now nothing but dark stains on the decks, at their damaged stations, sealed in their quarters. Each deck resounded with *aloneness*.

Aboard the processional flagship, Zan'nh found only Hyrillka Designate Ridek'h alive along with old Tal O'nh, blind and driven nearly mad by the darkness and sheer isolation.

Terrified to be on a ghost ship that reeked of cremated flesh, the boy had withdrawn into himself. Ridek'h lay curled on the deck, trembling with horror, when an anxious boarding party made its way into the warliner's command nucleus. 'Faeros! The faeros came. Rusa'h ...' His words rasped out like ashes.

Zan'nh had found no further sign of the fiery creatures on Dobro, and knew of no reported incidents at other splinter colonies. The Mage-Imperator, however, had sensed something more and more wrong in the *thism* and sent scouts out to investigate. Apparently none of them had returned.

And now this! Such an inferno taking the lives of thousands of Ildiran soldiers should have resonated like an agonizing scream through the *thism* – yet he himself had felt nothing. Was it possible that even the Mage-Imperator did not know?

Tal O'nh, his face burned, stared forward with two blackened and scabbed eye sockets. 'They cut us off. Burned the soul-threads and consumed our crew. All those people . . . Rusa'h said they would replenish the faeros.'

'How long ago?' Only by coincidence had Zan'nh detected the darkened ships on his trip back to the Prism Palace.

'Two days . . . maybe more,' Ridek'h said. 'Forever. Alone. Hard to tell.'

If they had been stranded any longer, Zan'nh realized, these two would have gone completely insane.

In a ragged voice, O'nh added, 'The faeros were heading to Ildira.'

ONE HUNDRED AND TWENTY-FOUR

KOLKER

Now that Kolker saw and knew far more than ever before, it did not matter to him where his body was. Standing placidly in a park not far from the Prism Palace, he felt he could be everywhere. He no longer even needed the treeling.

With his eyes half closed, Kolker sensed at least five of his converts nearby, humans who had stayed in Mijistra to work. He knew they would all spread the word. By now, even some Ildirans were listening; he had finally gotten the attention of the lens kithmen. Kolker began to feel very confident and satisfied.

Though this square had been rebuilt by unlimited Ildiran labourers, the place held sad memories for him. Here, hydrogue warglobes had crashed down into the city, maiming and killing thousands, including old Tery'l. Gazing into the light that flashed from his prismatic medallion, Kolker sensed that his philosopher friend was still there somewhere, linked by soul-threads, existing on the plane of the Lightsource. Tery'l would be proud of him now.

The green priest shifted his thoughts in another direction until he seemed to be standing beside Tabitha Huck aboard one of the new warliners. She and her mentally linked engineers and work crews had by now assembled twenty-one of the giant vessels, an unparalleled accomplishment in so short a time.

In the park, Kolker closed his eyes completely, feeling the warmth of the suns on his skin. He concentrated on watching Tabitha, vicariously joining her skeleton crew of human engineers and Solar Navy soldiers as they took the vessel on its first shakedown cruise.

Tabitha tested the in-system engines and the Solar Navy weapons. She primed their ekti tank and engaged the stardrive, and took the new warliner out on a circuit of the nearby solar systems. She strutted about on the bridge, issuing orders. The Ildiran crewmen followed her every suggestion as if she were the Adar himself.

'Approaching Durris-B, Captain Huck,' said one of the Ildiran station managers. She had assigned the title to herself and was quite pleased by it.

'Plot a tight orbit and swing close.' She wanted to see the dead sun for herself, a dark scar in the Ildiran psyche. Astronomer kithmen had continued to monitor the stellar cinder, hoping for signs of rekindled nuclear fires. Tabitha thought it a perfect war memorial.

'Let's check out our systems. Run full tests with our analytical panels and calibrate them according to previous baselines.' Even though Durris-B was a cooling ember that no longer shone of its own accord, the star retained all of its mass and gravity. Tabitha had the warliner approach with caution, constantly monitoring their engines to be sure they could pull away if necessary.

'Calibrations are off, Captain Huck. Durris-B exhibits far more thermal output than anticipated.'

'Remove some of the filters. Let me see for myself.' As she

watched, the burned-out lump began *sparking*. Light glimmered through from deep layers as if something had reignited within its core, like an ember fanned into flame. Durris-B began to brighten.

'We're seeing an energy spike.'

She did not want to take any chances with her new warliner. 'Increase our distance.' She turned to her Hansa engineers, not trusting the Ildirans to have sufficient imagination to figure out what was going on. 'How do you reignite a star – start its nuclear reactions again?'

'Not by any natural means.' One of her engineers frowned down at the bridge console. He shrugged. 'But remember, I used to design skymine pumps. What the heck do I know about stellar mechanics?'

Standing out in the open square of Mijistra, Kolker lifted his head to gaze with closed eyes into the cloudless sky. Around him, his other converts paused in their activities, also sensing something unusual taking place. The rest of the Ildirans in the city had not yet noticed any change.

'I don't like this,' Tabitha said in the warliner's command nucleus. 'Not one bit.'

Through her new connection with the *thism*, she could sense the Ildirans aboard growing uneasy. Finally picking up on that distant connection, the people in Mijistra became unsettled. Now everyone could feel the stirring sun. But the Mage-Imperator could not offer his strength or guidance; from far-off Theroc, he did not have the mental power to soothe them all, and the Prime Designate was not capable of doing it from the Prism Palace.

In the warliner's command nucleus, Tabitha shielded her eyes and cried out. Faster than automatic filters could cover the viewing screen, Durris-B brightened with a blinding flare as lightning bolts of power criss-crossed its uncertain surface. Tiny specks appeared

– huge balls of fire, great ellipsoids that streamed from the lower layers of the sun, like spores puffing out of an overripe mushroom.

'Faeros ships! The faeros have returned,' shouted one of the Ildirans.

'Turn about and get us back to Ildira,' Tabitha said.

Her crew challenged the new warliner's engines, accelerating as much as the untested systems could bear. One of the control boards burned out and another reacted sluggishly, but the huge ship began to pick up speed and pull away from the suddenly flaring star. Faeros boiled out of the cooling stellar depths by the thousands, flew into space like sparks from a cosmic grinding wheel, and disappeared from the Ildiran system.

Ten of the ellipsoids closed around Tabitha's warliner, like a flock of birds going after the same slow-moving insect.

Down in Mijistra's sunlit square, Kolker bit back a cry. He could feel Tabitha's fear reverberate inside him, inside all of them. Ten huge comets of flame loomed up, their surfaces a tapestry of ghostly, screaming faces.

A booming voice echoed in Tabitha's mind and across the warliner's comm systems. 'What is this *thism*? I have found your soul-threads – but who are you?'

'Kiss off!'

The faeros voice sounded intrigued. 'You are human, yet you have a conduit into the *thism*, like that human we consumed with the wentals . . . You also have a conduit that extends to . . . ah, the worldforest! The verdani mind.'

As more and more faeros streamed out of the reawakened sun, the ten fireballs tightened their circle around the warliner until the hull began to melt. Alarms shrieked from every main system. In the command nucleus, the consoles slumped into molten metal. The front section of the bridge exploded, but even the vacuum of space could not extinguish this kind of fire.

Kolker lost contact with Tabitha aboard the ship, feeling the pain like a sword thrust into his chest.

But it wasn't over. The dominating presence of the former Hyrillka Designate roared along the new soul-threads that Kolker himself had so carefully laid down. The voice hammered into his mind. 'I demand your soulfires to strengthen the faeros. You have given me the way.'

While thousands of fireballs raced out into space, ten of them led by Rusa'h moved implacably toward Ildira. Kolker could not block the faeros incarnate from his mind, from his *thism* or telink. Without opening his eyes he could see his other converts staggering. Two of them fell to their knees as they spontaneously caught fire.

Kolker struggled to block the searing lines and cut his converts off from the revelations – the *vulnerability* – that he had shared with them. But he could not save them, could not save himself. The faeros fire streamed like acid through his mind and through his body. Then, with a last flash and a spark, he became one of many dissipating curls of smoke in the air.

ONE HUNDRED AND TWENTY-FIVE

ORLI COVITZ

The Klikiss held Orli and her companions inside the old city. Though she had struggled against the hardening goo, the insect warriors had torn her backpack away from her. The breedex seemed to recognize what the synthesizer strips were and intentionally deprived the girl of them.

In addition, Orli was kept separate from Tasia, Robb, Davlin, and Nikko – because of her music, like Margaret Colicos? – and she felt very alone. DD had also been led away, and she had no idea what had become of the little compy. After removing her resin restraints and throwing her into a dusty, hard-walled cell, the Klikiss had stretched resinous excretions like prison bars across the chamber opening. The others were kept in a larger chamber down the tunnel, all of them without food or water.

At least Orli was close enough to shout to her companions and hear what they were doing; she could even see them if she pushed her head partway through the gummy barricade. The resin had an oily feel and smelled like burned plastic.

'We could work together, rip loose some of these web bars,' Nikko said. He threw his shoulder against the rubbery barricade, to little effect. Nikko tried to tug and pull at the strands. Even if they broke away the web barricade, however, Orli didn't know what they would do afterward. They were in the middle of a huge nest, with no way out.

Tasia yelled into the echoing corridor, as if the Klikiss could understand her. 'Hey! Would it help if I told you we hate the black robots, too? I could tell you stories that would make your exoskeletons crawl. We should be allies in a common cause!' The bugs patrolling the passageways did not pause, apparently ignoring Tasia's statement.

Robb said, 'You know, I've actually been in worse situations. And gotten out of them.'

'Me too. But getting *into* deep shizz isn't a habit I'd like to continue.'

Orli peered out into the interconnecting hallway. By now only a few traces of the old EDF base remained on the curved stone walls: pipes, electrical conduits, intercoms, and lighting systems that had been rigged up by the original colonists.

Two strange newbreeds walked into view with a stuttering gait. Briefly, before the pale creatures were gone, Orli glimpsed fleshy faces and shifting features that had a bizarre, indefinably human quality. None of the other Klikiss even had a hint of a *face*. The newbreeds seemed curious about the prisoners, and also somehow sad. A Klikiss warrior marched along behind them and, with a staccato hissing and clicking, chased the newbreeds away.

As if visiting a relative in a hospital wing, Margaret Colicos arrived with her compy beside her. 'DD! Margaret!' Orli reached her hand through a gap in the web-barrier.

The Friendly compy stopped at her small cell, his optical

sensors gleaming. 'I am pleased to see you alive and well, Orli Covitz.'

'Alive and well? The Klikiss are going to kill us all.' Orli doggedly clung to a spark of hope. 'Do you know where my synthesizer strips are?'

'I do,' DD volunteered brightly.

Margaret stopped in the corridor. 'Since the recent fissioning, there's a new breedex. It still knows who you are, Orli, but it also understands more about humans, now that it has incorporated so many attributes of the colonists.'

Davlin was listening at the second cell down the tunnel. 'That's a good thing, isn't it? If the Klikiss understand us—'

'Not good enough.' Margaret kept her attention on Orli. 'That means the breedex is less susceptible to previous distractions. I am afraid the music you play on your synthesizer strips won't be enough to eliminate you from ... consideration, after all. It still has great power, but the breedex has heard it before, and humans are no longer as special to it as I once was. We are all in danger.'

Farther down the tunnel, Davlin pressed up against the sticky bars. 'Margaret, you can help us get out of here. Bring us tools, Klikiss weapons – something to give us a fighting chance, at least.'

'What do the bugs want from us, anyway?' Nikko said. 'They already killed my mother, killed all the colonists! Isn't that enough?'

'How long are they going to hold us?'

'Can you find some food? Water?'

As everyone began to shout at once, Davlin raised his voice, cutting through the noise. 'If the hive has already fissioned, aren't we safe for now?'

Margaret said, 'The expansion phase has accelerated, and the new-generation breedex will fission yet again, as soon as possible.

The subhive continue to grow. These Klikiss intend to destroy all rival breedexes in the coming hive wars. Therefore, it must reproduce again, and it wants to incorporate you, your memories and knowledge, to give it an unexpected advantage over the other subhives – a weapon they won't suspect. The domates will come to gather us for the next round. Soon.'

Orli reached through the rubbery barricade toward the compy. 'DD, help me – convince her to help all of us.'

'You don't need to convince me,' Margaret said. 'Even if I could get you out of those cells, we wouldn't get far with so many Klikiss around. We'd certainly never get out of the hive city.'

'Listen to me,' Davlin said. 'If we escape, we can take you and DD away from here. We can take you *home*. Our escape ship is prepared and fully fuelled. We're ready to fly away – if we can just get out of here.'

DD seemed excited, turning to his master. 'Yes, the ship is ready, and I would very much like to leave here, Margaret.' Obviously, the older woman hadn't considered a real possibility for escape in a long, long time.

Orli stretched her other hand through the gap. 'Please, Margaret?'

Before she could answer, groups of Klikiss raced up and down the tunnels in a fury, apparently summoned by an urgent call. The older woman cocked her ear as if hearing something that no one else understood.

DD swivelled his head. 'I have detected an ultrasonic signal from the breedex.'

'Something's happening.' Even deep in the tunnels of the ancient city, they could hear whistling and clicking, great clashes, weapons detonating.

'Is it the EDF?' Nikko called from the cell. 'Does that mean we're rescued?'

'I doubt the Eddies would get off their butts and do anything,' Tasia said. 'But maybe the Roamers came. They might've gotten tired of waiting to hear back from us.'

Margaret's face showed real alarm now. 'No, it's not the human military. I think we've been attacked by another subhive.'

'You mean other *Klikiss* are attacking?' Robb said. 'Attacking us?'

'Attacking the breedex. The rival subhives have already begun to stake out their territory and destroy each other. Now we'll see if the Llaro subhive acquired enough unique knowledge to guarantee a victory over these rivals.'

'Don't expect me to lead the cheering section,' Tasia said.

Klikiss raced through the corridors, preoccupied with the crisis and ignoring the prisoners. Margaret and DD got out of the way. An explosion cracked the roof of Orli's cell, and a curtain of dust sifted into her hair. Several more pale humanlike hybrids lurched past with an awkward gait, followed by a towering domate, a *new* domate. It, too, had a hint of oddly human features.

When the creatures had scuttled past, Davlin took advantage of the disturbance and began to hurl himself at the stiff web strands that formed the bars. 'This is our chance – your chance, too, Margaret! While they fight the other bugs, they won't care about a few humans. We can run right past them.' With a full body blow he smashed into the barricade, and some of the resin broke away from its anchor point on the stone wall.

'He's right,' Margaret said, hurrying over to help him from the outside. 'Yes, I can go. I can be . . . free.'

DD strutted to Orli's cell, fixed his compy hands on one of the strands, strained, and broke it free. The girl squirmed through the sticky bars as DD moved to the larger cell, uprooted more of the webbing, and peeled the bars away enough that the other four prisoners could break free.

With Klikiss fighting Klikiss, the small group left the chambers behind and began to run.

One Hundred and Twenty-Six

Admiral Sheila Willis

General Lanyan's troop transport set down with an unnecessary flourish of landing jets in a cordoned-off space on the pontoon base. As ordered, Willis had dispatched skimmers to the Company Works and brought in Drew Vardian; transported Allahu from his home made of giant, empty medusa shells; and fetched five token homesteaders from outlying islands, as well as two prominent medusa herders. For good measure, she even brought in the three rowdy teenagers who had stolen the recirc-sorters from the mineral-extraction towers.

Willis asked every one of her troops stationed on Rhejak to put on their dress blacks, despite the tropical heat, and had them line up for inspection. Uniforms neat, hair combed, and boots polished. She pursed her lips. It wouldn't do to make a bad impression for the General. Her expression quickly degenerated into a scowl.

For the past several hours, the *Jupiter* had broadcast incessant images of the massacre on Usk. Willis couldn't imagine what the General thought he'd accomplish by that, except to bring out the worst in the Rhejak colonists. It seemed he wanted their fear more than their cooperation. So she obliged him, letting the man dig his own grave.

Willis set up large thinfilm projection screens on the raft-base to show the Usk disaster in gigantic format. Amidst the appalling destruction, the face of one particular young farmer – his blond hair unruly, his wide eyes reddened – seemed to symbolize the entire crime. He wept unabashedly as he watched his orchards levelled. 'My apples,' he kept wailing. 'My beautiful apples!' After ten minutes Willis had told the technicians to mute the sound. Enough was enough.

Willis inspected her troops who stood in parade formation, filling most of the raft deck. She had dressed in her formal service uniform (though the thing was ungodly hot) with all the frou-frou trappings. She had pinned on her medals, strapped on her ceremonial sabre and her sidearm. With her grey hair neatly clipped back, she wore her Admiral's cap, though she didn't waste time with make-up. General Lanyan didn't deserve it.

When the hatch hissed open on the General's troop transport, she whistled for her soldiers to stand straight in ranks. The representatives of Rhejak looked sick, unable to tear their eyes from the repeating images on the giant thinscreens.

'Damned Eddies always stick together.'

'—knew we shouldn't have trusted her.'

'—could have taken out this whole raft with five or six medusas.'

Willis turned a deaf ear to their comments.

Lanyan blinked in the sunlight and stepped forward. Fifteen hand-picked EDF soldiers followed him, all wearing *Jupiter* uniforms. Willis recognized some of them and fought back another scowl. The General had found the hardest of the hard-liners. He seemed to have a knack for that.

Lanyan seemed satisfied with her crisp salute. 'Admiral Willis, this looks like an acceptable reception.'

Willis was all business. 'I took my oath of service a long time ago, General. I know what the Earth Defence Forces and the Terran Hanseatic League stand for, and I pledged my life to serve those ideals.'

'You've had an odd way of showing it lately. I wish to address the troops and the locals. Did you gather representatives of the Rhejak dissidents, as I instructed?'

'They're here, General.' The natives were not difficult to spot, since they were the only ones not in uniform. Several wore little more than loincloths, showing off bronzed skin and muscular bodies, but Lanyan didn't bother to look. 'I prepared a podium for you, sir.' A small speaking stand with automatic microphone pick-ups stood under the blistering sun on the honeycombed deck. She lowered her voice, 'I can also bring you a parasol, if you like.'

He scowled as if she had just insulted him. 'That will not be necessary.'

Lanyan stepped up to the podium and glared at Rhejak's representatives like an angry parent. 'You have brought this punitive action upon yourselves.' He fiddled with the side of the podium, disappointed that his voice wasn't booming from the speakers. He looked at Willis. 'Is this broadcasting? I want everyone on this planet to hear me, as well as your ten Mantas in orbit.'

She gave him an innocent look. 'I'm sorry, General, but we aren't set up for full planetary and orbital broadcasting. My tech team can record your speech for later playback, and we'll distribute it as widely as you like. Or, if you really prefer to address everyone realtime, we can have components flown down from one of my Mantas – or the *Jupiter*. Would you like my comm officers to set that up? It'll only take a few hours.'

Lanyan was flustered. Obviously, he didn't want to look weak or incompetent. Neither did he want to wait. 'No. Record it and rebroadcast as soon as I'm finished.'

He turned back to the podium and tried to regain his momentum. 'As I said, you have brought this upon yourselves. The Hansa is rebuilding after the greatest war humanity has ever faced. We suffered great damage from the hydrogues, and we must not suffer further damage from our own people. Rhejak's intransigence will no longer be tolerated. The people of Usk learned this lesson at great cost.' He pointed to the thinscreens. 'The rest of the prodigal colonies must now learn the lesson as well.'

Willis stood at his side like a faithful supporter, though her hands were clenched at her hips. Behind the General, her ranks of soldiers were clearly upset, barely able to keep themselves from expressing their disquiet. Allahu tried to argue with Lanyan, but the hardline EDF honour guards drew their sidearms and aimed, ready to shoot him down.

The General raised his hands to stay them, then turned his needle gaze toward Allahu. 'You people had your chance to speak over the past few weeks, and we've heard more than enough. We don't want to hear any more.' Gathering steam, the General went on for another ten minutes without saying anything new.

Willis let him finish his blowhard statement, and when he paused, as if preparing some other harangue, she commandeered the podium, and addressed the uniformed ranks, whose faces seemed pale and uncertain. 'You are the best soldiers we have. You all remember why you joined the Earth Defence Forces. As soldiers, you've always known you would have to follow difficult orders. Our military has endured plenty of turmoil in recent years, not just from Soldier compies and hydrogues, but from embargoes and trade shutdowns that caused severe shortages. We had to abandon plenty of Hansa colonies because we just plain didn't have enough stardrive fuel to power our ships.'

'Damned right,' Lanyan put in. 'The Roamers and their embargo brought us to these straits.'

Now she smiled sweetly at him. 'Sir, we all just watched you destroy a civilian Roamer trader departing from Rhejak. Everyone here has heard King Peter's condemnation of your actions and those of Chairman Wenceslas. We've all listened to Patrick Fitzpatrick's confession. My troops are eager to hear your side of the story.'

Lanyan's face turned stormy. 'Admiral, you received strict orders to purge all traces of that message.'

Willis feigned a shocked expression. 'General! You don't have authority to censor the words of the *King*. So tell us, once and for all, *did* you give the order to destroy Raven Kamarov's ship after seizing its cargo of ekti?'

Lanyan rounded on her. 'I don't see what that has to do with our current mission.' It was not a very inspiring answer, and everyone understood his meaning. More of her soldiers muttered uneasily.

'I take that as a yes, then?' Willis swept her gaze over the Company boss, the medusa herders, the fishermen, and Allahu. The three teenage boys had looks of abject fear on their faces. None of these people deserved to be crucified, like those poor elders on Usk. 'General Lanyan, I won't force my soldiers to do anything I wouldn't do myself. And I won't ask them to follow orders that *I* wouldn't follow.'

'Exactly as it should be, Admiral. And now I will issue instructions—'

Willis slipped the twitcher from its ceremonial holster at her side. Before a look of befuddlement could settle completely onto Lanyan's face, she felled him with a burst of nerve-scrambling energy. He lost control of his muscles and collapsed into a shuddering puddle of arms and legs next to the podium.

The fifteen members of his hardline escort guard grabbed for their weapons, but Willis shouted, using the podium's microphone to boom out. 'You men, stand down! My troops, arrest these soldiers. As a command officer of the Earth Defence Forces, I hereby relieve General Lanyan of his rank and charge him – and all those men – with war crimes.' She glanced at the thinscreens and their images of Usk. 'I'd say the evidence is overwhelming, and it's about time we did something right for a change.'

She stood tall as the uproar built around her. Her soldiers, clearly delighted with the unexpected orders, ran forward to overwhelm the fifteen appalled hardliners.

PRIME DESIGNATE DARO'H

Durris-B had exploded into heat and light, reigniting, shining forth again into the Ildiran sky. The seventh sun was no longer dark and dead. But this was not cause for immediate joy.

Ten vengeful fireballs filled the Ildiran sky like suns. The air smelled of smoke and burned blood. Inside the Prism Palace, looking through the curved panes of the skysphere dome, Prime Designate Daro'h shouted for emergency action, but none of his advisers knew what to do.

Only an hour before, the first scout ship had finally returned from the Horizon Cluster, its crew horrified. They brought far worse news than even the Mage-Imperator had feared. Dzelluria was burned and destroyed, as were three other splinter colonies. No survivors. Needing to send a message directly to their father, the Prime Designate had sent Yazra'h to find Kolker. The green priest could use telink and the lone treeling in the rooftop greenhouses to contact Theroc and call the Mage-Imperator back to Ildira.

But out in the metropolis, Kolker and all of his known followers had gone up in flames. Ildirans panicked in the streets, and their terror echoed through the *thism* web, but Daro'h forced it away, doing what he could to quell the panic. With his father gone, he was in charge. The Ildiran Empire relied upon him.

'What do they want, Prime Designate?' cried one of the administrators. He stared up at the dazzling light that focused like lasers through the skysphere. Courtiers huddled inside the Prism Palace as if it could protect them, but Daro'h knew better than that. He had already seen what the faeros and the mad Designate could do.

Guard kithmen rushed into the chamber, holding their crystal katanas ready, prepared to die to protect the Prime Designate. But they could not save him by simply throwing their bodies in the way of the firestorm.

Yazra'h ran to Daro'h as the lights in the sky grew more intense. Her face was flushed, her hair damp with perspiration, her eyes shining. Her three agitated cats loped along beside her. Under one arm she carried a bolt of the dark material the Roamer trader had brought from Constantine III. 'If the human claims are true, this fabric will protect you against heat. Wear it.'

'I cannot hide from the faeros under a blanket.'

'You will wear it!' Yazra'h's voice cut off any further argument.

The ten grouped fireballs unleashed a bright flare like the after-effect of a solar storm, and one of the Prism Palace's towers cracked and shattered. Guards yelled, and people fled while shards of smouldering crystal tumbled down in a musical rain. Daro'h could feel a thrum through the *thism* as nearly a hundred Ildirans died in the single blast.

'Where are Osira'h and the other children? We must keep them safe.'

'We must keep you *all* safe,' Yazra'h said. 'I have already called for them.'

Daro'h assessed his options. The Mage-Imperator was gone, and Adar Zan'nh had not yet returned from Dobro, though he doubted even the Solar Navy could fight against these flaming vessels. 'I cannot leave the Prism Palace. I cannot abandon my people.'

'The faeros are not here to parlay with you, brother. They mean only to destroy. You can see that.'

Outside, a fireball landed in the square immediately in front of the Prism Palace, its intense heat melting a mirrorlike crater out of the stone, metal, and glass. From the rippling flames of its hull a man emerged, whose robes were made entirely of fire, whose blood was lava. His hair curled in wisps of dark smoke, and his flesh itself burned. He strode forward, leaving smoking footprints on the ground. Rusa'h, a faeros incarnate. He marched directly toward the front of the Palace as if he already owned it.

Smaller fireballs flurried around him like attenders, and fiery ships orbited the crystalline domes. Rusa'h blasted the doors aside and walked into the Palace's main reflecting corridor. His personal heat baked the smooth walls. Some of the thin panels shattered. Stone bubbled and buckled. He spread his hands, and so much heat rippled from him that even the ceiling sagged. His feet sank into the floor as he took another step.

Osira'h and her siblings ran into the audience chamber. 'He is coming! The mad Designate is already in the Prism Palace. Can't you feel what he is doing through the *thism*?'

Rod'h added, his face distraught, 'We already had to cut ourselves off from the entire network wall off the *thism* and form a sort of shield.'

Yazra'h threw the inflammable cloth around the Prime Designate and dragged him away from the chrysalis chair. There is no way you can fight it, Prime Designate!' She made a motion to her cats, which bounded out of the chamber and rushed down the hall, instinctively leading the way to safety. Osira'h and the other children ran after them.

Foolishly trying to intercept the faeros incarnate on his way to the skysphere, fifty guard kithmen charged into the hall and formed a living barricade, holding their weapons against the searing flames. Rusa'h simply raised his hands, and a wall of fire rolled toward them, roasting the Ildirans inside their armour, before an intense flash consumed them all. Their soulfires vanished into the widespread network of the faeros.

In a misguided gesture of loyalty, dozens of chittering servant kithmen threw themselves upon the fiery Designate, doing anything to delay Rusa'h's progress. They, too, perished.

Two more faeros appeared in the sky and closed in on the Prism Palace. The mad Designate strode through the mirrored corridors. Each footprint burned, then hardened behind him, leaving a clear trail of his progress.

Daro'h felt echoes of all the deaths as he ran. The *thism* seemed to be stretched to its breaking point. He knew that the Mage-Imperator would feel that agony from Theroc, but he was much too far away to be of any help.

MAGE-IMPERATOR JORA'H

After having formed his long-sought alliance and cleared his burden of guilt, the Mage-Imperator departed from Theroc. Now at last he could move forward; he and Nira could go home.

Jora'h felt a great sense of satisfaction. Nira had acquired several new treelings, as well as promises from five green priests who had agreed to come to Mijistra. He stood with her in the command nucleus as his ceremonial warliner headed away from the thorny verdani battleships guarding Theroc and outward into space beyond the green-and-blue planet. It had been a long time since he had felt so hopeful, so content. The Empire was, once again, on the right track.

Suddenly through the *thism* he felt a resounding call of alarm and pain. He stiffened, shuddered, and nearly fell backward as he cried out from the clamour in his mind. 'The fire! The pain. I can feel it across all of Mijistra!'

His connection with Prime Designate Daro'h was so clear, and the same echoing turmoil came through Yazra'h, through Osira'h, and many other Ildirans. Something truly apocalyptic was taking place – and he was far away from his people!

Nira sensed the shift as well. She touched one of the new treelings she had carried into the command nucleus. 'Kolker isn't there. No one else can use the treeling. I don't know what's happening.'

'It is Rusa'h. He has returned with his faeros. Daro'h warned us. I've got to get to Ildira immediately!' The warliner's stardrive engines were already building up energy. The *thism* resounded with tremor after tremor of chaos, destruction, and bright, bright fire. 'Faster,' Jora'h cried to the warliner's captain. Confident in his victory, Rusa'h no longer bothered to hide himself in the *thism*.

The ship's sensor operators, already feeling the emergency, scrambled at the controls. The tactical officer shouted an unexpected warning. 'Liege – large ships coming in! Right now, closing on us! Many of them. They belong to the Earth Defence Forces.'

As the warliner headed home at full speed, the EDF ships – a fully armed Juggernaut and four Manta cruisers – careened directly into its path.

'Why are they here? Take evasive action! I do not have time to deal with human politics. We must leave, now.'

'Shall I open fire, Liege?'

Jora'h was suddenly at a loss. The Solar Navy opening fire against the Earth Defence Forces? That made no sense. He had just entered into an alliance with King Peter.

Nira's face was drawn in anguish. 'Those ships may well be our enemies, Jora'h. Don't count on the EDF to be reasonable—' She touched her treeling again and let out a sharp cry. 'The treeling in the Prism Palace! It's just been destroyed. I'm cut off. The tree just . . . burned.'

Jora'h stared at the Earth military ships blocking his way. 'Yes.

If they will not move, we have no choice but to strike at them. Prepare to fire—'

The EDF Juggernaut took the decision out of his hands. The big battleship shot without warning, dealing the warliner's engines a crippling blow.

In the command nucleus, Solar Navy officers backed away from their sparking panels. The warliner lurched as more impacts resounded through the hull. Nira clutched her potted treeling to keep it from shattering on the deck. Jora'h stumbled into the command rail as the deck tilted beneath his feet. 'Why are they firing on us?' Feeling the faeros fire through the *thism*, he could barely think straight. Ildira itself was in terrible trouble. 'Get us out of here!'

'Our engines don't respond, Liege.'

'Open fire! Target their Juggernaut. Do whatever it takes to break us free.' His mind continued to spin. On this mission of peace and contrition to Theroc, he had not imagined he might find himself engaged in a war.

'Our engineer kithmen are already on the main decks, Liege. They do not know if they can effect repairs in time.'

Despite the thrumming heat and pain coming from her treeling after the faeros had struck Kolker, Nira needed to dispatch a report of what was occurring here. The Mage-Imperator was being attacked. Perhaps King Peter or some of the Roamer ships, even a verdani battleship, could rush from Theroc and offer assistance.

The image of an EDF admiral appeared on their screen. 'I'm Admiral Esteban Diente, and I extend an invitation to the Mage-Imperator. We'd like to have him join us.'

'An invitation? You have fired upon my flagship. That is an act of war against the Ildiran Empire.'

Diente's face was stony. 'Chairman Wenceslas wishes to

discuss matters of mutual interest with you, sir. I have instructions to escort you with all due honours to Earth.'

'I refuse! I have just learned of a crisis on Ildira. I must return to the Prism Palace without delay.'

'That is not an option, sir. Since your engines are damaged, we will tow your vessel.' Heavy-duty tractor beams had already attached themselves to the warliner's hull. Jora'h felt a jolt as the EDF ships tightened their grip.

'We're being kidnapped,' Nira said.

'And Mijistra is in flames!' Jora'h turned to face Diente on the screen. 'My need is urgent. You must let me return to Ildira. Now!'

Diente sounded so reasonable, he must have rehearsed his words many times. 'You have already spoken with the leader of an outlaw government. The Chairman, Earth's authorized representative, simply wishes equal time to confer with you.' Without letting the Mage-Imperator respond, Diente closed the channel and refused further requests for communication.

Jora'h was trapped, and his warliner could go nowhere. His beloved Palace was becoming an inferno of Rusa'h's revenge!

With a lurch, the warliner began moving. The Hansa battle group dragged them off toward Earth, and Jora'h could do nothing about it.

MARGARET COLICOS

Amidst the clash of the subhives on Llaro, the escaping humans were noticed no more than dust motes in a whirlwind. Insect warriors ripped apart their rivals, and the Llaro Klikiss pitted their strange weapons against equally odd destructive devices created by the invading subhive.

The escapees followed corridors, trying to circle around the loud and violent fighting zones. When they dodged two colliding Klikiss warriors, one of the spines nearly skewered Robb. Tasia managed to yank him away before the spine could do more than gash his back.

'Some would find the thought of humans being squashed by insects ironic,' DD observed.

'Not now, DD,' Margaret said.

More spiny attackers from the rival hive poured in, taking advantage of the new transportal frame, while smaller groups marched through the old trapezoidal wall in the ancient Klikiss city. Margaret noted a definite difference in the two opposing groups. The invaders had an older body design with blue and red

594

blazes across their carapaces. The fighters in the Llaro subhive were clearly superior, spawned after the domates had incorporated the colonists' DNA. Evolution, improvement. Though the invaders were causing substantial damage, they were being systematically slaughtered.

Margaret knew they had to escape before the end of the battle. Whichever Klikiss survived would turn their attentions to recapturing or killing all of the humans. She found it hard to believe they actually had a chance of getting away, but she helped guide them. 'I didn't think I would ever leave the Klikiss, DD.'

'Did you wish to stay here, Margaret Colicos?'

'Definitely not – but I'm not sure I belong in the outside world either. It's been years since I last saw Anton, and I don't know very much about the Spiral Arm anymore.'

'I can give you news summaries.' The Friendly compy was happy to help. 'However, my own information is somewhat out of date. Sirix did not grant me access to unfiltered information when I was his captive.'

Davlin urged them through the tunnels, moving from one connecting passage to another. Wincing from his injury, Robb called back over his shoulder, 'The Klikiss wrestling match here is the only current event that matters.'

Margaret pushed aside any lingering reticence by remembering who she had once been. 'DD, when you served us on Rheindic Co, I was an organized manager of an archaeological site, a determined leader, and a talented scientist.'

'I can replay many of our old conversations verbatim if you like. It may help remind you. Those were some of the most satisfying times in my entire existence.'

Orli ran ahead, her face flushed. At her insistence, they paused at a small pile of discarded items thrown into a noisome alcove. DD had located the girl's pack there in his brief explorations of the insect city, and Orli retrieved her synthesizer strips, teary-eyed. 'My father gave these to me.'

With frequent guidance from Margaret and DD, Davlin led the group up through one of the darkened structures until a wide opening of daylight showed their escape route. They all put on an extra burst of speed.

Outside, hundreds of next-generation Klikiss warriors ripped apart the rival insects emerging through the giant outside transportal. Bugs tore into bugs, smashing each other's carapaces, ripping segmented limbs out of sockets. Scouts and attackers flew about in makeshift aircraft, dive-bombing with resinous weapons to gum up and then kill rival Klikiss. The bedlam was incredible.

A crowd of pale humanoid Klikiss warriors faced off against one of the rival breedex's domates. Margaret watched the hybrid Klikiss strike down the enemy domate and pummel it into sticky shards of smashed armour.

The long drop-off beneath the window opening at which the prisoners stood was nearly twenty metres. 'We don't have enough rope,' Nikko said.

'Then we'll have to get to the surface in another way.' Davlin turned around.

Margaret anxiously assessed what was happening outside. The invading Klikiss would soon be defeated. 'We don't have much time.'

ONE HUNDRED AND THIRTY

ADMIRAL SHEILA WILLIS

While the Admiral kept the raft-base under a communications blackout, neither her Mantas nor the *Jupiter* knew what was happening. Willis turned her efforts to damage control.

Lanyan's fifteen hardliners shouted at her uneasy troops, calling them mutineers. 'We're your fellow soldiers! Your Admiral just shot the commander of the Earth Defence Forces. You'll be court-martialled and executed for—' The guard's words cut off as Willis zapped the loudest complainer with the twitcher as well.

She waved the weapon. 'If that's the only way to keep the rest of you cooperative, I'll use it again.' Sullen but infuriated, the guards shut up.

Willis raised her voice, so that the rest of her soldiers could listen as she paced in front of the captives. 'I prefer to think that any EDF soldier has a brain as well as a heart, and General Lanyan hasn't used either. He's broken so many laws and protocols that I don't have enough time left before retirement to list them all. Look at you, bragging about your massacre on Usk. And now you're threatening to do the same to Rhejak! Your Juggernaut shot down an innocent Roamer trader carrying a load of *seafood*, for heaven's sake! If anybody here thinks that was a good idea, then you're welcome to lodge a formal protest. In fact, you can sit in the brig and write me an essay on civic responsibility.'

She waited for a long moment, but no one accepted her offer. Her own crew began cheering. Hakim Allahu and his fellow Rhejak leaders clapped each other on the back.

'I don't see any fat lady around, but it's time for her to start singing.' Willis chose twenty-five of her own soldiers she was sure she could count on. 'Let's take that troop transport before the General's men aboard my *Jupiter* get too suspicious. We already know they've got itchy trigger fingers.'

Willis herded her special squad aboard the General's ship, knowing she didn't have enough firepower for a stand-up fight against an EDF Juggernaut. She had to take control before it could come to that.

Aboard the lead Manta's bridge, Lieutenant Commander Brindle was surprised to see her. 'Admiral! We've been trying to reach you. After the General began his speech to the troops, we lost all contact with the surface.'

'Yes, quite a communications breakdown.' She had insisted on running the troop transport in radio silence, transmitting no more than her classified ID beacon to get aboard the Manta.

Brindle was full of questions. 'But where is the General? This is not at all according to procedure.'

'I'll explain everything in a minute.' She strode to the command chair, and Brindle quickly relinquished it. 'Let me send a transmission to the *Jupiter*'s bridge.'

'I will contact their acting captain immediate—'

'No need.' Watching the *Jupiter* cruise behind them like a great armoured whale in space, she keyed in the coded sequence directly from her chair. A Christmas tree of lights twinkled, marking deck after deck. 'Send this. Don't bother waiting for an acknowledgement.'

'What is it, Admiral? Where is General Lanyan? Has something happened? The *Jupiter*'s acting captain has been sending constant inquiries—'

She regarded him with a cool glare. 'Do I look like I'm participating in a celebrity interview, Mr Brindle?'

The comm officer quickly said, 'Sending now, Admiral.'

The coded burst went out. Willis had never actually forgiven General Lanyan for commandeering her *Jupiter*. Now her lips curled in a satisfied smile as she watched the lights wink out, deck after deck. The *Jupiter*'s weapons ports dimmed, the engines died, leaving the Juggernaut dead in space.

'Admiral, something just happened to the *Jupiter*!'

Brindle took a step closer to the viewscreen. 'Are they under attack?'

'Don't worry. That ship won't cause us any more problems.' Willis shook her head in wonderment. 'I can't believe the General thought I'd forget my own guillotine code.' More likely, he hadn't dreamed she would use it.

Brindle rounded on her, his face full of anger. 'Admiral, this is uncalled for!'

'Expressly according to procedure, I have relieved General Lanyan of his command, citing numerous breaches of military protocol.'

'Breaches of protocol?'

'For starters, firing upon a Roamer noncombatant, murdering innocent civilians, maliciously destroying private property, and attempting a military coup of a lawful government.' Her smile was grim. 'I can come up with more, if you'd like.'

Before Brindle could say anything, several of the bridge crew cheered. 'It's about damn time, Admiral!' She had not under-estimated the effect the worsening news had had on her soldiers.

But she kept watching her second-in-command, marking him as a potential trouble spot. 'Do you have a problem with that, Mr Brindle?'

His jaw worked, and finally he said, 'Yes, Admiral – yes, I do. You have usurped the authority of your superior officer. You are required to follow the General's orders, whether or not you agree with them.'

'Study your history, Lieutenant Commander, and see how often "I was only following orders" holds up as a defence when crimes against humanity are committed. Have you reviewed the Usk images the General is so proud of? He meant to do the same here, without a trial, and without evidence! I'd never be able to sleep at night if I let him get away with that.'

She didn't have the time for a protracted debate, though. Since her exec was still wrestling with his doubts, she reached a quick decision. 'I don't want anyone on my bridge who's having second thoughts about what I intend to do. Confine yourself to quarters and think about it, Mr Brindle. Run this decision through your moral compass. If things go badly, I personally guarantee that you will not be implicated in anything that happens next.'

Without a word or even a salute, Brindle left the bridge. Willis sat rigid in her command chair and nodded to herself. 'General Lanyan said the Chairman only sent him with a skeleton crew because he wanted to show off his big guns. I need to round up a full-blown boarding party to go mop up on the *Jupiter*.'

She got up from her chair and paced around the bridge. 'I want to talk to each of my Manta captains. Now. I don't know how many will need extra persuasion, but I'd like to do this smoothly and cleanly. These ten cruisers are carrying enough weapons that we sure don't want them getting mad at us.' She got an idea. 'Oh, and cue up that message we received from King Peter – the one calling for sanctions against the Hansa. Replay it for everyone. After the Usk massacre, we've got a whole new perspective on what he's saying.'

She tapped her fingers on the armrest. Since they had all sworn their allegiance to King Peter in the first place, she assumed she'd be able to sweet-talk most of them. Even Lanyan's hardliners aboard the powerless *Jupiter* might be 'reasonable', if she had enough time to work on them.

ONE HUNDRED AND THIRTY-ONE

DAVLIN LOTZE

Klikiss battles continued to rage into the afternoon, and Davlin doubted their small group could remain success-fully hidden until darkness, when the cover of night would help them get away. He broke the problem into its component challenges and solved one piece at a time.

Though shaking and exhausted, all six of them were ready to go. Davlin could see that none of them had any intention of surrendering, even Margaret Colicos. The wound on Robb Brindle's back obviously pained him but did not seem to be life-threatening.

'This place is a maze,' said Nikko. 'And I get lost in the best of times. How are we supposed to find the old buildings, then find a way out and sneak past all those fighting Klikiss?'

'I could project a likely path,' DD said. 'Once we re-enter the original ruins, I can find a more appropriate exit for us.'

Orli put a reassuring arm around the little compy, but didn't say anything.

DD guided them back to the old city. However, by the time

they reached the weathered passageways, complete with bare-bones EDF conduits, electrical wiring, and intercom system, Davlin thought he detected a change in the Klikiss hive. Workers scuttled past, pausing only briefly to study the humans before shouldering them aside. Something was changing.

Listening to the clicking sounds, Margaret said, 'We have to get out of here. Soon. The breedex is about to finish destroying the other subhive.'

'Time to haul ass, then,' Robb said.

Davlin reached a decision. 'I know how to stall them – but I estimate there's only about a ten per cent chance this will work.'

'Ten per cent?' Nikko seemed disappointed in him.

'Better than zero per cent,' Tasia pointed out. She scratched her head and found a hard lump of leftover web material, which she discarded. 'What do we do?'

'*You* have to get outside, somehow. Make your way to the *Osquivel* and rescue the rest of the people at the bluffs. Tamblyn, Brindle, steal a Klikiss ground craft if you have to – you're smart enough to figure out the controls.' Davlin felt confident in turning over the responsibility to these two. They were certainly qualified to become 'specialists in obscure details', like himself.

'Sounds like you don't plan on meeting up with us again,' Robb said.

Margaret paused. 'I have no intention of abandoning you, Davlin, after all you've done.'

'I'll figure something out. I alter my plans as necessary. Don't wait for me. If everything goes smoothly, I'll be right on your heels.'

'If everything goes smoothly?' Nikko said with a groan. 'When has that ever happened?'

Davlin turned to Orli. 'I need your backpack.'

She reluctantly shrugged the straps off her shoulders. 'My synthesizer strips?'

'I need them to save us all. Now the rest of you, go!' Davlin didn't stay to talk. Grabbing Orli's pack, he ran along the tunnels, following electrical conduits toward the central systems that had been installed more than a year ago by the EDF watchdogs. According to the tiny monitor lights and sub-station boxes, the power was still running, at least intermittently. The bugs had cannibalized some components from the barracks, and disregarded other pieces.

More Klikiss scuttled through the corridors, some of them had missing limbs or cracked shells from the battles outside. The air smelled of dust and bitter insect juices. If the main clash was indeed over, the victorious Llaro breedex would hunt down the last of the invaders, and eventually Davlin's presence would intrude upon the hive mind's awareness.

Then the bugs would intercept him.

Through a small window opening, he glanced outside. At the trapezoidal frame of the new transportal, the Llaro hive's strongest warriors tore apart four of the invading domates. The tiger-striped monsters squirmed and struggled, but were utterly overwhelmed. They fought, and they died.

Davlin didn't care which side won. Either way, he had very little time.

The EDF's old control and communications centre was a small alcove closed off with a chain-link gate. Davlin easily cut through the links and was relieved to see that the Klikiss had ignored this small intrusion into their ancient city. It simply hadn't mattered to them.

He dropped Orli's ragged pack on the hard, stone floor. By now the others should have gotten outside. He counted on that. If they didn't make it away swiftly, the Klikiss would turn on them.

Davlin pulled out Orli's synthesizer strips and unrolled them on the stone floor. Still functional.

He activated the tiny power source, hooked up the leads, and ripped open a cover plate on the intercom system to attach the wires. A few random notes whistled into the air, but none of the Klikiss seemed to notice. He worked by instinct. During his many missions as a Hansa spy, he'd been forced to learn how every common system worked. If Margaret Colicos's tiny music box had made enough of an impact to disturb the breedex, then Orli's much-more-sophisticated music should have a similar effect. Davlin would give the bugs their fill of it. He prayed it would be enough.

He called up the library of tunes the girl had stored in the strips' memory and set it to continuous repeat. Adjusting the volume to its maximum level, he began the Play cycle.

Startling melodies emerged from the intercom speakers mounted at intervals throughout the ancient alien tunnels. A Klikiss worker scuttled down the passageway toward him, but as soon as the music began, the creature turned, as if stunned and disoriented.

The synthesizer continued to play, the melody building, the notes captivating the Klikiss. Listening via all its minions throughout the subhive, the breedex should be reeling.

Davlin slipped back out through the chain-link gate, closed it, and sprinted away. It was time to find another way out of here.

ADAR ZAN'NH

Zan'nh left behind emergency crews on each of Tal O'nh's five empty ships to effect necessary repairs and fly the much-needed battleships back to Ildira. In the meantime, the Adar needed to leave immediately. While Ridek'h and the blinded tal were taken to medical kithmen aboard his flagship, Zan'nh gave instructions for his warliners to fly to Ildira at maximum speed.

When they arrived, they found the faeros already there.

A dozen fireballs crowded the sky above the Prism Palace, swirling over the crystalline towers, setting the fountains and mirrors alight. One of the Palace's minarets had collapsed into a glassy, melted blob. Orange flares shining through the faceted walls suggested that a desperate battle was going on inside.

On the elliptical hill at the centre of the seven converging streams, pilgrims scrambled to find shelter from the firestorm. Unable to escape, each one turned into a living torch.

Zan'nh and everyone aboard the warliners could feel the resonating horror. Previously, when the mad Designate had taken his victims, he had excised them from the *thism* web before destroying them. Now, though, he let his conquest of Ildira pound through the *thism* like loud drumbeats, so that every person in the Empire was aware of what he was doing. Somewhere, Mage-Imperator Jora'h must feel the unbearable agony.

The Adar did not know how to fight an enemy like this. Tal O'nh's warliners must have used whatever weapons they had available. When he went to consult the blind tal in the ship's medical centre, O'nh said in a haunted voice, 'Our projectiles and explosives did nothing against them. Our warliner's armour could not withstand the heat. They are *flames*. How do you hurt a flame?'

Zan'nh stretched his mind, searched his imagination, wishing that Adar Kori'nh – even Sullivan Gold or Tabitha Huck – could have been there to guide him and offer advice. But he realized that was merely an excuse. The faeros were attacking the Prism Palace! He could not spend days gathering ideas to devise a solution. He had to think of something himself.

'Prepare the water reservoirs. We may be able to quench the fire by using everything we have.'

His warliners flew at full speed toward the blazing ellipsoids, and sprayed jets onto the faeros from their onboard water cisterns. Only a small retinue of the fireballs had come here to Ildira. Perhaps he could have some effect after all . . .

Like a boiler explosion, great clouds of steam roiled into the air, the superheated mist curling in all directions. The faeros continued to dip and bob, torching people in the city, circling around the Prism Palace. Now that the Adar's warliners had caught their attention, the flames grew brighter.

With a second run, Adar Zan'nh spilled water in the plaza in front of the Palace. When the cold water struck the superheated crystalline panels, they shattered. Hot flowing glass and metal congealed in odd shapes.

Two warliners concentrated their streams onto a single fireball, draining their tanks into the incandescent flames until the faeros dimmed and blackened, extinguished by the water.

Retaliating elementals surged up to collide with the Ildiran battleships. Zan'nh felt a resounding sympathetic pain as all of the crewmembers in the two warliners were incinerated, their soulfires absorbed into the faeros. Suddenly empty, without anyone manning the controls, the large Solar Navy vessels began a downward spiral, their engines on fire, their systems damaged. Both hulks crashed into the city.

The sky all around was pregnant with steam. A hot fog bank swathed the Adar's warliner and the Prism Palace in a thick cloud, temporarily hiding them. The faeros would find them soon enough.

'Adar! I am receiving an urgent transmission from somewhere within the Prism Palace.'

'What is it?'

'Prime Designate Daro'h and several others. They are trying to escape. They need our help.'

ONE HUNDRED AND THIRTY-THREE

NIKKO CHAN TYLAR

The area around the Klikiss city was strewn with giant insect carcasses. The buzzing and clacking sounds of the wild battles had now been subsumed by an eerie silence as the scouts and warriors dispatched the remaining members of the rival subhive. The smell nauseated Nikko.

As they ran past piles of the dead creatures, he pointed toward the giant new transportal. 'Look, something else is coming through!'

Victorious Llaro Klikiss returned through the shimmering gateway, carrying their greatest prize – the captive breedex of the rival subhive. Nikko gaped at the horrific monstrosity, instinctively knowing what it was. He had never imagined something so disgusting. Orli shuddered. Margaret put a hand on her shoulder and pulled the girl along, leading them all. 'Come! That will be our last big distraction!'

The eight Llaro domates, replenished in the recent fissioning, marched toward the captive breedex, ringed the enemy hive mind, and began devouring it. The air itself seemed to thrum with unimaginable screams.

And music began to play over the old EDF loudspeakers.

The startling melody made all of the Klikiss reel in their tracks. Orli stopped, apparently as startled as the insect creatures. Tears sprang to her eyes. 'That means Davlin made it!'

The effect was dramatic and instantaneous. Even the Klikiss on the battlefield wavered, though many were too far away to hear the notes. But what one Klikiss heard, the breedex heard, and disorientation spread among the rest of the subhive.

'That's a hell of a diversion,' Tasia said. 'And you can hum along with it, too.' She began to run toward the outskirts where the Klikiss had left their alien ground vehicles.

Nikko didn't think he'd ever been so utterly exhausted in his life. The ground vehicle, basically a framework with rolling mesh wheels and an engine, would let them cover ground much faster than they could travel on foot.

Robb and Tasia bolted directly past six warriors who stood clicking in confusion and waving their claws in the air. Some of the insect creatures blundered into each other, as if drowning in the melody, while others searched for the source of the broadcast. 'They don't see us. Take advantage of it!'

Nikko followed the others toward the vehicles. The Klikiss had no security systems and would not have made starting or piloting the contraption difficult. The bugs did, however, have multiple limbs, and he wasn't sure if one human with a single pair of hands could manipulate the controls.

Klikiss warriors lurched in front of them, caught up in the eerie melodies. Suddenly the music cut off. The loudspeakers inside the old city went dead.

'That means they killed Davlin!' Orli cried.

'Well, we know they killed the broadcast.' Tasia made a dash toward the nearest vehicle. 'Now we're in hard vacuum without a helmet.'

Like laser targeting systems, the Klikiss warriors swivelled their heads toward the escapees. The breedex looked directly through their eyes, seeing them. Seeing Margaret.

The old woman stepped forward defiantly, holding up the music box in her hand. A rush of unnatural clicking sounds came from Margaret's throat as she tried to communicate. Then she wound up the metal device, and the familiar melody began tinkling out. 'Run, all of you! Get to one of the vehicles.'

'Margaret, come with us,' DD wailed. Orli tugged on the little compy's arm.

'You heard the lady!' Tasia shouted. 'Run! I sure hope someone knows how to drive this Klikiss buggy.'

Margaret thrust the music box forward, letting the tune play for the monstrous creatures, for the breedex. The nearest warrior reached out a segmented forelimb and delicately, implacably, plucked the music box from Margaret's hand. Two scouts came at her from either side and grasped her. She tried to struggle, but they picked her up. Without harming her, they carried her off as Klikiss warriors closed in on the rest of the escapees.

'Margaret!' Orli shouted. Nikko pulled her onward, stumbling toward the wheeled contraptions.

Three Klikiss warriors marched toward the alien vehicles as well, accompanied by a taller creature – one of the strange human-influenced hybrids. This one was the size of a domate. Its exoskeleton was pale, and its elongated body had powerful arms and ripping pincers.

Nikko hesitated, but Robb gave him a push from behind. 'Quick, while they're still disoriented.'

Tasia jumped into the open-framed vehicle, studied the controls and experimentally pulled levers to test their functions.

Nothing seemed to work. 'This could be the shortest escape ever.'

The three Klikiss warriors and the pale halfbreed turned to focus on the intruders. Robb threw himself into the carriage beside Tasia, and he too began slapping at controls, trying to get the machine to move.

The warriors ringed them in, raising their sharp limbs. Nikko looked directly into the face of the whitish hybrid. The monster's features were awful, yet eerily familiar. The plastic, changing expression behind the stiff face plates seemed to mimic old memories, struggling to reconstruct the echo of a past existence.

With a jolt, Nikko saw in the creature's visage a hint of his mother. It flickered through a sequence of unfamiliar faces, other Roamers and colonists. Then, as if the newbreed recognized him, the ghostly face of Marla Chan Tylar snapped back.

Orli jumped down beside Nikko, trying to pull him to the vehicle, and also noticed what looked like Marla Chan Tylar, the woman who had taken her in. Frozen, Nikko faced the creature, waiting for it to strike both of them down.

Instead, the grotesque hybrid turned on one of the Klikiss warriors, grabbed its horned crest, and twisted the carapace hard, uprooting the creature's whole head. The startled warrior clicked and fluttered its wing casings, then slumped twitching to the ground.

The other two warriors, guided by a shocked breedex, turned from the escapees and fell viciously upon the newbreed that had turned against them. The pale hybrid fought back, thrashing and chopping.

'Let's go, dammit!' Tasia called.

Nikko stumbled backward and bumped into the vehicle but was unable to look away from the battle. Robb grabbed his arm and yelled in his ear. 'We're *leaving*.'

But the Klikiss ground vehicle wasn't going anywhere. A grinding sound came from the gears. The car lurched, and shuddered to a halt again.

The Marla-newbreed succeeded in killing a second warrior, while the third slashed at the pale flesh. Nikko couldn't understand what was happening. When the domates 'incorporated' genetic information from humans they devoured, did they retain some of the memories? Was an echo of his mother actually inside there?

Three more warriors arrived, driven by the breedex, and urgently joined the attack on the treacherous newbreed. The angry Klikiss surrounded the newbreed and tore it apart. Nikko groaned.

The engine began to make sounds, but Tasia still didn't know how to drive the thing. The Klikiss warriors advanced, covered with spatters of slime. Orli stepped away from the vehicle, to stand alone in front of them.

'What is she doing?' Robb shouted. 'Get aboard, kid!'

Orli began to sing a lilting melody in a clear but unpractised soprano. The melody was familiar to the Klikiss ... but different. With all her heart, Orli sang 'Greensleeves'. The breedex had never heard the music like this before. The warriors froze, raising their jagged limbs, cocking their heads. Orli kept singing.

It was all the time Tasia needed. At last she got the strange vehicle moving.

Shaken by what he had seen, Nikko grabbed Orli's hand and yanked her into the open-framed vehicle as it started to roll away. As soon as the girl's singing stopped, the Klikiss lurched forward again, but by now the groundcar was jouncing swiftly across the terrain.

Nikko and Orli sat next to each other, both stunned in their own way. DD was silent, and Nikko wondered if a compy could be disturbed.

'Whatever we just saw – I don't ever want to see it again,' Nikko said.

ONE HUNDRED AND THIRTY-FOUR

DAVLIN LOTZE

When the music cut off far sooner than he had expected, Davlin knew he was in trouble. A burst of static gushed like blood before the loudspeakers fell completely silent. The disoriented bugs must have found the synthesizer strips and torn them apart.

He had hoped to make his way out of the alien city before that happened.

Davlin tried to slink along the darkened corridors, keeping to the walls to remain unobtrusive in the shadows, but he couldn't possibly hide. With their feelers the Klikiss could detect vibrations in the air, and might even be able to smell or taste his presence as if he'd left a painted line behind him. Once the breedex started looking for him he couldn't hide.

He began to run.

He had secretly kept one emergency flare grenade and a metal pipe from the small EDF equipment shack. Minimal weapons, but he didn't feel comfortable without having something.

Reaching a small ventilation window a few inches wide, he

scanned the grounds. Out on the battlefield, the Llaro domates were feeding on the carcasses of more dead Klikiss, incorporating genetics, acquiring the DNA songs of the defeated subhive for the next fissioning. The breedex would reproduce again, to expand its numbers and replace the warriors fallen in the recent battle.

Well beyond the domates, he saw a group of humans rolling away in a Klikiss groundcar. Davlin let out a held breath, feeling tension drain from his shoulders. Now he knew the others had escaped, and was confident they could get to the *Osquivel* and fly away immediately after rescuing the rest of the survivors in the sandstone caves.

Seeing the others depart, Davlin also understood that he would never catch up with them. It was liberating, in a sense. That gave him the freedom to find his own way off of Llaro. He was, after all, a specialist in these sorts of things.

He decided that the transportal in the ancient hive city would be his ticket offworld. Any place had to be better than Llaro – provided he could find a planet that wasn't already infested with Klikiss.

He made his way deeper into the old hive city. He knew where the transportal chamber was, since he had come through it with the Crenna colonists when they first arrived. But when he sprinted into the central cluster of the ruins, he saw an alarming number of insect workers and scouts in the tunnels. The transportal wall must be close, but he might have to fight his way through.

Two spiny warriors waved their segmented forelimbs, turning armoured heads in his direction. Davlin immediately saw that the breedex would no longer ignore his presence.

He didn't hesitate. He sprang forward, aiming perfectly, and thrust his metal pipe into the thorax of the nearest warrior. It clacked its pincers, hissed, and whistled as it fell over. The creature's bulk was enough to wrench the pipe from Davlin's grip. The second warrior slashed at him, and the serrated limb ripped across his shoulders and down his back. He felt the insect claw grate on bone.

Stunned, he staggered away and past the remaining Klikiss warrior. Even bleeding profusely, he put on a burst of speed. The insect raced after him into the tight passage, its horned carapace scraping the rough walls. Davlin's legs felt cold and leaden, and he could hear the monstrous beetlelike creature right behind him. Fumbling, he withdrew the flare grenade but held off for just a moment. He turned a corner and staggered through an arched opening, at last finding the grotto where the trapezoidal stone window filled one wall.

Ten more Klikiss waited for him in the room, ready to fight. Several dead minions of the rival breedex lay on the floor, and workers were busy dismantling and carting the butchered bodies away. From behind, the warrior came hissing and clacking in pursuit. When the insect guards inside the chamber also began to move toward him, he flipped the activation switch, set the timer to three seconds, and tossed the flare grenade into the room.

He memorized his path ahead, and squeezed his eyes shut. He just had to get to the transportal wall. Bleeding, he staggered forward, counting to three, not even waiting for the flash. The intense burst of light drove the creatures back, and when he opened his eyes again, Davlin saw flaring spots. An alarming black static filled the corners of his vision. The pain from the open wound across his shoulders was incredible. Did the Klikiss exude some sort of poison? He could feel blood streaming down his back, down his legs.

At last he reached the stone window. The smooth trapezoid seemed to beckon him. He slapped his hand on it, but the portal remained solid. Reaching up to pick a coordinate tile – *any* tile –

he heard the Klikiss hiss, stir, and clatter forward. The grenade hadn't stunned them for as long as he'd hoped.

Davlin depressed a tile, and the transportal shimmered. He had no way of knowing which world it was, nor did he care. He tried to throw his body into what had been flat stone.

One of the Klikiss grabbed his leg. Sharp claws dug into his thigh muscle, setting hooks and yanking him backward. Davlin thrust his hands through the transportal in a desperate attempt to grab the frame. Another insect warrior fell upon him, seizing his arm, tearing him away from the stone gateway.

Davlin shouted and fought fiercely, but it was futile. Klikiss claws sliced the flesh of his arms; another sharp leg punctured his left side between the ribs. He was bleeding badly, too wounded to hurt them anymore.

The Klikiss warriors turned him around and pulled him back, leaving a long, broad smear of blood on the stone floor. Davlin looked up to see two domates arrive in the chamber. They blocked off the room, and he had nowhere to go.

ONE HUNDRED AND THIRTY-FIVE

YAZRA'H

The Prism Palace began to glow like a sun. Some of its grand domes had already melted. The faeros seemed to be everywhere.

The Ildirans needed their leader, even if the Mage-Imperator was not there. Prime Designate Daro'h understood his obligation – to find an effective way to fight against the unquenchable flames. And Yazra'h's job was to keep him alive.

She had dragged the Prime Designate from the skysphere chamber along with anyone else she could save. Even as they fled the throne room, the terrarium dome had turned into a giant magnifying glass. All of the plants and flying creatures blackened, withered, and burst into flames. The lone treeling atop the palace had been incinerated in the first pass of the fireballs.

When Adar Zan'nh's warliners struck back with water blasts from overhead, Yazra'h urged her companions to greater speed. The air itself scalded their throats and lungs. They ran through the shimmering passages, down stairs, across impossibly exposed halls, all in an effort to reach the outside. The three Isix cats bounded along.

Daro'h, still draped in heat-resistant cloth, asked, 'Can we get to the Adar's warliner?'

'I do not know – but we must leave the Prism Palace!'

Osira'h and her younger siblings had bright feverish eyes, though they said they had blocked off the new *thism*/telink they had learned, they seemed to be united in a way even Yazra'h had not seen before. Focused.

'We should go to where the seven rivers converge,' Osira'h said. 'We might be safe in the water underground – at least long enough to get to the Adar.'

Yazra'h grabbed the Prime Designate's shoulder and turned him down another passageway. 'Yes, we will do that. Out here!' She led the way until they emerged through a vaulted side entrance into stifling air that smelled of burnt meat. Each breath scalded their lungs with hot steam from the Solar Navy bombardment. Broken panes of crimson and yellow glass left colourful, dangerous debris all around.

Faeros danced across the sky, arcing plumes of flame like solar flares. The Adar's warliners continued emptying their water reservoirs in their struggle to extinguish the fireballs. Another blackened faeros ship dropped like a dying ember into the city. Yazra'h's eyes burned every time she tried to look at the spectacle.

Hundreds of guard kithmen had already died, unable to stand against the heat. Now Yazra'h saw a squadron of mirror-armoured jousters – champions – rushing together to face the elemental enemies. The burly athletes had thrown on their full mirrored armour, adjusted helmets, and grabbed their prismatic laser staves. She had fought alongside these men, trained with them, pitted her skills against theirs, and she considered them her friends. Yazra'h knew their exceptional abilities. Perhaps their weapons would work where others had failed.

When a faeros ellipsoid swooped down at them, she shouted to her Isix cats, and they ran back into the meagre shelter of the vaulted overhang. Daro'h flung his flame-resistant cloth like a blanket around himself, Osira'h, and the other children, pulling them all down together as the flames approached.

The jousters raised their laser lances, sent out a flurry of razor-sharp beams, then ducked behind their mirrored shields. Some of the men screamed as gushing fire penetrated cracks and joints. Others stood firm, reflecting the flame and light with their mirror shields. While the bright ricochets did no damage to the ellipsoid, the shields deflected the worst of the thermal attack.

By the time the fireball had passed, leaving heat ripples and a snapping sound in the air, more than half of the jousters had succumbed and lay in a pile of gleaming, shattered armour. One of the survivors rasped with a damaged voice, 'Go, Yazra'h! Take the Prime Designate away!'

Her group finally reached the spectacular inverse fountain where the seven raised streams intersected and poured down a gullet to where canals redistributed the water. Osira'h leaned over the open hole. 'We've been down there. We can make it if we jump.'

'Do as Osira'h says.' Yazra'h did not have time to question. Her cats leapt out of the overhang, fur bristling, lips curled back. Dropping his protective cloth, Daro'h stepped forward to help the children.

A fiery avatar of the fallen Hyrillka Designate emerged from an arched doorway, light flaring all around him. His blaze scintillated against the crystalline panes of the Palace. His expression was calm and satisfied, but his voice boomed. 'Where is Jora'h?'

'My father is safe from you!' Daro'h shouted back.

In a misguided protective gesture, one of Yazra'h's Isix cats sprang straight at the flaming man's throat. Rusa'h made a mere gesture, and the intensity of the flames around him brightened into a flash. Yazra'h screamed as her cat disappeared in a burst of smoke. The other two animals yowled, but Yazra'h shoved her cats behind her as a jagged sadness cut at her heart. Her face twisted in a snarl, but she would not throw her life away uselessly.

'Osira'h, get into the water. Now!' The girl grabbed her brother Rod'h, and they leapt together over the edge of the foaming water-fall into the pool below. Gale'nh, Tamo'l, and Muree'n followed quickly.

Rusa'h launched gouts of fire from his hands. Just in time, Yazra'h snatched up the flame-proof cloth and held on, protecting Daro'h, herself, and her two cats. She felt the buffeting waves hammer them, the furnace-blast of air too hot to inhale. Her fingers were singed and blistering.

The last few jousters locked their mirror shields, roared in defiance at the mad Designate, and pushed their lances forward to fire more laser bolts. One man actually thrust his crystal spear into the flaming body. The faeros incarnate writhed, cried out, and shattered the crystal lance before a wave of rolling fire cascaded around the mirrored jousters. They all dropped. Even their armour was insufficient against such a powerful attack.

'Must I stand and watch them all die for me?' Daro'h cried.

Yazra'h pushed him toward the waterfall. 'No! You must let them buy your escape.' She was not gentle as she shoved him into the cascading flow, then bodily knocked her reluctant cats in after him. Just as Rusa'h spewed more fire at her, she threw herself over the edge and fell down into the misty roar. Narrowly missing her, the shock front rippled over the top of the converging streams, creating a geyser of concealing steam.

She dropped at least ten metres, buffeted by pouring water, and plunged into a deep and blessedly cool pool where tangles of people and animals were struggling to swim. Her skin was burned and blistered. Much of her hair was singed, and she could barely see. Her two drenched cats paddled to keep themselves afloat.

'This way,' Osira'h called out. They followed the current along a channel, passed through a catacomb, buffeting each other, and were finally swept out into one of the canals emerging from beneath the elliptical hill. Far from Rusa'h.

The water was choked with the blackened bodies of pilgrims killed by the overflying fireballs. When the canal widened, Yazra'h pulled a bedraggled Osira'h and Gale'nh to the shore, splashing through mud that caked their reddened skin. After helping Rod'h with his younger sisters, Prime Designate Daro'h got out the communicator he had brought with him, and called for Adar Zan'nh. The response was immediate and gratifying.

'We have pinpointed you. I will send a fast cutter to pick you up. We cannot keep fighting these fireballs.'

Overhead, even as the faeros in the sky grew brighter, the Adar's warliner swooped, and Yazra'h spotted a tiny craft descending toward them. By the time the cutter landed, she had gotten everyone out of the water and through the reeds on the bank. She and Prime Designate Daro'h, Osira'h and her four siblings, and the two surviving Isix cats scrambled into the rescue craft, frightened, exhausted, and burned. But alive – all of them were alive.

The Solar Navy cutter remained on the ground for less than two minutes before racing back to the flagship, leaving the fires of Ildira behind.

ONE HUNDRED AND THIRTY-SIX

TASIA TAMBLYN

Even battered, patched, and covered with dirt from the crash, the *Osquivel* was the most beautiful thing Tasia had ever seen.

After escaping from the Klikiss city, they had raced, bounced, swerved and lurched across the uneven landscape, navigating by starlight, instinct, and nerve. DD had done his best to guide them, while Robb and Tasia struggled with the bizarre controls. Although some Klikiss had given chase, the escapees had gotten some distance ahead.

Robb pulled the groundcar to a stop in the isolated canyon when they saw the ship ahead. With a groan, Tasia climbed out of the utilitarian Klikiss vehicle. Though swift, it was anything but comfortable. 'Everybody, get aboard as fast as you can. We'll have to fly to the caves. I don't look forward to landing there, but I'm not wasting any more time.'

Orli pointed ahead of them. 'Someone's already there. It's Mr Steinman!'

Steinman, Crim Tylar, and three other Roamers stood by the

transport ship, holding weapons and shining lights at the vehicle. 'About damned time you got here!' Steinman said. 'What took you so long?'

'A little run-in with the Klikiss,' Robb said. 'We lost Davlin.'

'And Margaret Colicos,' DD added.

'Dead?'

'Who knows?'

The Roamers looked deflated. Nikko's father shook his head. 'Then we have to go back for them.'

'We've got orders not to,' Tasia said, her voice curt. 'Davlin would kill us himself if he thought we would risk all those people to save him. And to tell you the truth, I'm sure it's too late.'

Robb said, 'We've got to get out of here now. The Klikiss are hunting for us.'

Tasia cocked an ear and thought she heard clicking, skittering. But the insects couldn't have tracked them yet. 'Stay alert, DD. Use your sensors. See if you can give us fair warning.'

'I will do that, Tasia Tamblyn.' She shuddered, reminded of her own compy EA, who had been torn apart by Klikiss robots. She hated the whole damned lot of them – the original race *and* their robots.

Crim Tylar hugged his son. Nikko's breath hitched. He didn't mention what he thought he had seen in the pale Klikiss hybrid. Nikko could barely deal with the knowledge, and obviously didn't want his father to know. Not yet.

Steinman said, 'When you didn't come back yesterday, we packed up. When we still hadn't heard anything by this afternoon, we decided to come here and wait, in case you needed some rescuing.' He hefted one of the energy-discharge weapons he carried. 'We were ready.'

'In the meantime, I ran a systems check and prepped the engines,' Tylar said. 'I was going to give you another hour before we flew the ship to the caves.' He looked at Nikko. 'I'm glad you came back.'

DD turned his polymer face toward the starlit sky, his optical sensors glowing. He swivelled his head back toward Tasia. 'I am afraid a great many Klikiss are coming – low-flying ships and some solo flyers.'

Tasia didn't waste time. 'Everyone in. Now!' She rushed the Friendly compy aboard, waited for the others to race up the ramp, and shut the hatch. 'Company's on its way! Get flying – how fast can we load the refugees aboard?'

'A swarm of Klikiss adds considerable incentive.'

Before the bugs could appear, Robb lifted the transport above the lip of the arroyo, and with the running lights off, skimmed along only a few metres above the grasses and rocks, hoping they wouldn't be seen. 'Tamblyn, do you remember anything tall that might get in our way?'

'I walked it half a dozen times, but I'm not sure.'

'I knew we should have taken the time to fix our local sensors.' He overcompensated, jumping upward when he saw a cluster of boulders. Crim Tylar sprawled on the deck, but quickly picked himself up again.

In less than ten minutes, they spotted the silhouettes of the sandstone bluffs pocked with caves and overhangs. 'I don't know if there's a good place to land, Brindle. Set down anywhere you can and we'll start cramming people in.' She turned to Crim Tylar. 'What's our total, if everybody makes it?'

'You think somebody might want to stay behind?'

'I think we might need to rush things.'

'Seventy-eight, I think. Some of them kids.'

'And UR,' DD said.

'That's well within our capacity,' Robb said. 'Don't worry about a thing.'

'Who's worried?'

He chose a bumpy patch of rocks and dirt in front of the main bluff and brought the *Osquivel* down with a blast of exhaust and thrown dust. Tasia was the first out of the hatch, and the others followed as Robb locked the struts down to temporarily stabilize the ship. He kept the engines rumbling.

'All aboard!' Tasia bellowed, already seeing people running toward the ship. 'This is the last transport off Llaro, and the bugs are right on our tails! We'll have to use express boarding procedures!'

'That means everybody *run!*' Steinman yelled. He and Tasia sprinted to meet them.

Figures scrambled forward, some carrying packs and satchels, others just running as fast as they could. Mayor Ruis was in the middle of the group, shouting encouragement, nudging everyone along to the *Osquivel*. 'Where's Davlin? He should be helping us.'

'Sorry,' Tasia said. Ruis's face fell and he shook his head in disbelief. Feeling a need to explain, Tasia added, 'He bought us the time we needed to escape. He promised to find his own way off Llaro.'

Ruis seemed to grasp at that faint hope. 'Well, then, who am I to doubt him? He always manages to come out on top.'

Though she had only one arm, the Governess compy shepherded the children under her care. UR cajoled them to move as fast as they could. Though several children were crying, they had all lived in fear for a long time. DD hurried out to help the other compy. Orli took two of the younger children by the hands and rushed them up the ramp.

'No assigned seats,' Nikko said, standing next to his father. 'In fact, not enough seats at all. Just pile yourselves in and we'll sort it out once we get airborne.'

As the last ten people jostled toward the bottleneck of the

hatch, DD stared out at the sky. 'Tasia Tamblyn, many more Klikiss are approaching. They must have followed us.'

'Didn't think we'd outrun them for long.' She shouted to the stragglers. 'Move it! Fifteen seconds and I'm closing the hatch. Anybody not aboard gets left behind. Dive headfirst if you have to.' Panicked, the remaining survivors dropped their packs and possessions, and thrust each other forward, frantic to get in. Everyone made it, and Tasia had to elbow two colonists aside so she could seal the hatch.

Climbing back into the pilot seat, Robb coaxed the repaired engines, watching the gauges, adjusting the controls. Tasia made her way to the cockpit, nearly deafened by the din of frightened passengers. Robb looked up at her with genuine concern. 'If we blow out something, we'll be stuck here forever. We never had time to do a real test flight, not even a full-fledged engine check.'

On the cockpit status screens, Tasia adjusted the sensor band to scan the sky overhead. Numerous blips circled closer. 'Sure, Robb. Take all the time you want. Five, ten seconds – whatever you need.'

Without waiting for a go-ahead, Nikko reached between them and punched the vertical take-off jets on the co-pilot's controls, and the *Osquivel* shuddered off the ground. The ship rose higher into the air just as the low-flying Klikiss ships swooped after them like stinging wasps. Three buzzing solo warriors crashed into the hull, scratching at the hatch and windowports, but the injured creatures fell off and dropped to the far-distant ground.

Higher up, Klikiss ships closed in from several directions. Robb and Nikko jointly worked the piloting controls, taking the ship on a steep ascent. 'Everybody strap in!' Tasia shouted as she crawled into position at the repaired weapons controls. She took a scattershot approach, figuring that anything her beams hit would be a target. On the screens, four fluttering machines vanished in small explosions.

'Let's see how much acceleration we can take,' Robb called.

Orli and Steinman held onto a bench in the back passenger compartment. DD and UR somehow maintained their balance, as if their feet were fastened to the deck.

Overhead, the scanners showed a group of interlocking Klikiss spacecraft descending from orbit. 'That could be a problem,' Tasia said.

'Then start shooting!'

With another flurry of blasts, she cleared a hole in the formation. Flaming Klikiss wrecks tumbled through the air around them. The *Osquivel* continued its steep ascent as they pulled away from the atmosphere. They tore through the massed alien vessels, scattering some, outdistancing the rest.

With a sigh of relief, Tasia nudged Robb aside and took the piloting controls. 'Let me drive.' She didn't allow herself to breathe normally again until she had engaged the stardrive and left Llaro far behind.

PATRICK FITZPATRICK III

I f anything, Patrick's feelings for Zhett were stronger than ever. 'I come from a very rich family, but I don't have much to offer you. Not anymore.'

'You've already given me the best gift, Fitzie, one I'll always treasure.' From one of the many pockets in her jumpsuit, she withdrew a folded piece of paper and opened it to display the colourful (if somewhat crude) drawing of a bouquet of flowers he had left at her quarters, when trying to get her attention.

He saw it and chuckled. 'You kept that?'

'Of course I did. I could tell how much heart you put into it. Not much *skill*, but definitely a lot of work.'

'I wasn't even sure you'd gotten it. You never answered me.'

'I didn't think you deserved an answer. You hadn't apologized yet.'

'You never gave me a chance! You wouldn't let me talk to you.'

She shrugged as if that were somehow an irrelevant detail.

'Well, at least I came clean. I tried to atone for everything

I did. I confessed all of my terrible actions that hurt the Roamers.'

Zhett sighed with exasperation. 'But you never apologized to *me*.'

He blinked at her and couldn't find any words. Finally he said, 'What do you mean? I spoke in front of all the skymine chiefs. I told all the Roamers and the whole confederation what I had done. I faced your board of punishment. I even walked the plank for you!'

Zhett raised her dark eyebrows. 'You're not listening, Fitzie. You didn't apologize *to me*.'

Despite the grand scale and far-reaching consequences of all the terrible mistakes he had made, he realized what Zhett had needed to hear. 'I'm sorry I tricked you. I'm sorry I locked you in that asteroid chamber and led you on so that I could help the others escape. I used you, and you never deserved to be treated like that. I'm sorry I hurt your feelings.'

'That's a step in the right direction, but we'll keep working on it.' She kissed him again. 'And I'll reward you every time you get it right.'

When Zhett presented him with a satiny ribbon embroidered with intricate clan symbols, Patrick didn't understand the significance. Del Kellum, though, looked extremely proud. 'You've been working on that betrothal band for years, now, my sweet.'

'I have not,' she quickly responded. But she flushed when her father gave her an entirely sceptical smile.

'Hold out your wrists,' Kellum boomed to the pair. Zhett raised her hand. Patrick started to raise his left one, but Zhett picked up his right hand and placed it next to her own. They faced each other.

Kellum looked at him. 'This *is* what you want, isn't it – to marry Zhett, I mean?'

Patrick glanced from the young woman to her father, not

hesitating for a moment. 'Of course it is. I . . . just don't know your ceremonies.'

'That's all right, by damn. We make them up as we go along.'

Zhett chuckled. 'Right! You're the most hidebound Roamer traditionalist I've ever met, Dad.'

'Shhh. Don't give away my secrets. This young man's not part of the clan yet.'

They stood on a small private balcony of the Golgen skymine, rather than a large receiving deck or launching bay. Kellum might have forgiven Patrick for some of his transgressions, but the clan leader wasn't ready to make a complete show of acceptance just yet. The thin force-field barrier kept cold chemical breezes out, but Patrick still felt a rush of goose bumps tingle down his back as he touched Zhett.

'Thank you for accepting me among you, sir. And thank you for not making me walk the plank.'

'And you'd better not make me regret that decision, by damn.'

'I won't. I promise.' He couldn't take his eyes from Zhett, and he didn't think that his sense of wonder at finally being with her would ever wear off. 'I wish my grandmother could be here to see this. Your father and the old Battleaxe have a lot in common.'

Patrick could only imagine what Maureen Fitzpatrick's reaction would be when she learned that her blueblood grandson, with all his good breeding and family obligations, had chosen to marry a *Roamer girl*. His grandmother would be beside herself, but she had no say in the matter – which would probably bother the old woman more than anything else.

Kellum took the strip of fabric, lashed their wrists together, and cinched it into a knot. Patrick found it more comfortable to turn his hand palm-to-palm with Zhett's and intertwine his fingers with hers.

'Now you are bound together by the threads of your lives and the threads of your love. The knot is always there, no matter what others see.' He stepped back and propped his hands on his hips. He seemed to be expecting something.

'Now what am I supposed to do?' Patrick whispered.

Zhett leaned forward and kissed him long and deeply. When they finally ended their embrace, he said, 'Oh, I like that part.'

ONE HUNDRED AND THIRTY-EIGHT

SIRIX

Since first awakening from hibernation centuries ago, Sirix knew that the surviving black robots could trust no one. He had loathed the original Klikiss, he had known the Ildirans must eventually be destroyed, and he had learned to hate the newcomers – the humans.

He refused to believe his once-great metal swarm was defeated.

Out of his fleet of stolen EDF warships, only twenty vessels remained, one of them a Juggernaut. A few independent groups of black robots had rejoined his ships, returning from various enclaves. But Sirix and his companions were still not safe. They had been hounded by the Klikiss, harried at battleground after battleground, driven onward.

His ever-shrinking core of loyal followers retreated from system to system. Over two-thirds of the Soldier compies had already been destroyed. Far more painful was the loss of thousands of unique black robots, powerful machines with long memories. All those comrades . . .

Sirix had planned to dominate the Spiral Arm by now, reacquire all of the Klikiss worlds, and annihilate the humans. Instead, on planet after planet, the returned Klikiss seemed invincible, their numbers inexhaustible. Though the robots had had EDF weapons and a strategic advantage, the Klikiss overwhelmed them repeatedly, destroying more of their battleships, and pursuing them with swarmships.

He would go to ground, for now. The ragtag vessels returned to what Sirix considered his place of origin, at least during this round of existence. The twenty warships arrived in the Hyrillka system and closed in on the far-flung ice moon where the first group of robots had been frozen for thousands of years. In their long-standing bargain – and deception – with the Ildirans, the robots had waited here, hidden in hibernation, until a Mage-Imperator had directed his workers to go to the Hyrillka ice moon and 'accidentally' reawaken them, five hundred years ago.

The same moon seemed a good place to recover and make plans. Was the wisest course of action simply to hide for another thousand years? He and the other black robots would decide. With the EDF ships circling low over the dark moon, Sirix and his fellow robots descended to the lumpy ice surface.

As always, PD and QT accompanied him. 'We are interested to see this historically relevant site,' PD said.

'The Hyrillka moon is now our sanctuary. Our projected plan has significantly altered.'

Scuttling across the icy terrain on fingerlike legs, Sirix easily found the remnants of their old hibernation hive. Some of the tunnels excavated by Ildiran miners had collapsed over the past five centuries. Ilkot and two other black robots tore away the blockage. Some brought EDF thermal cutters and melted new access passages into their base within the ice.

Once he was deep inside with his companions, where the light was dim and the temperature incredibly cold, Sirix finally felt somewhat safe.

'Attrition is our prime vulnerability,' he said to the gathered black robots. 'We have slain hundreds of thousands, perhaps millions of the Klikiss, and yet the breedexes produce more and more warriors, builders, every sub-breed they have.'

Ilkot swivelled his head; his red optical sensors shining a faint bloody light on the icy walls. 'When any one of our robots falls, it is an incalculable loss. Unrecoverable.' By Ilkot's accounting, seven thousand, eight hundred ninety-four of their number had already perished.

Sirix doubted the robots could ever rebound from such a devastating blow. Since they had failed to conquer Earth, and since the humans had ordered the destruction of the major compy-manufacturing facility, Sirix didn't even have the option of replenishing his Soldier compies.

'We will be happy to offer any advice we may have,' QT said.

The accumulated knowledge of thousands of black robots had been unable to offer a viable solution, nor had the tactical programming of huge groups of Soldier compies. Sirix doubted the two Friendly compies could say anything significant.

'The solution to our crisis is clear,' PD piped up. 'We need more Klikiss robots.'

That much was painfully obvious, but Sirix had known the compies would suggest nothing useful. 'There are no more Klikiss robots. We have restored all that were placed in hibernation.'

'That is not what PD suggests.' QT seemed to have come to the same conclusion. 'You must build more Klikiss robots. New robots. Find someone who will manufacture them for you.'

Sirix paused. He heard the other robots thrumming. Such a preposterous idea had never occurred to them. The black robots had been created millennia ago by the Klikiss, programmed by them. Each robot was an individual with a long-scarred history and a hatred for the insect creators. Klikiss robots had never before built copies of themselves, as if they were mere *machines*.

But there was no fundamental reason why not . . .

'An excellent suggestion, PD and QT. Thank you for your insight.' He surveyed the other black robots. 'We must acquire a manufacturing and industrial facility and force the inhabitants to do what we need.'

ONE HUNDRED AND THIRTY-NINE

ADMIRAL SHEILA WILLIS

Willis was damned glad to be at the helm of a Juggernaut again, where a real Grid Admiral belonged. She had left two guardian Mantas at Rhejak, and for the first time, Hakim Allahu considered their presence reassuring rather than threatening.

The *Jupiter* was headed for Earth. Of all the crewmen aboard the Juggernaut and the ten Mantas, only one hundred sixty-three refused to cast their lot with her. Rather than pressuring them, Admiral Willis had told them each to follow their own conscience. They knew the Chairman's orders, had seen the images of Usk (some of them had been there themselves), and had listened to King Peter's condemnation.

Very few who had served under her at Rhejak failed to support her choice. During their time on the ocean world, the soldiers had seen how the 'heinous rebels' were just trying to make a life for themselves. They observed firsthand how distorted and inaccurate the Hansa's blatant accusations had been.

Those who insisted on toeing the EDF line were mostly

General Lanyan's cronies, and the brig levels were filled with malcontents. Willis treated them as well as she could and promised to drop them off at Earth, but only under certain conditions. It was the right thing to do, the honourable thing to do (although the decision might come back to bite her in the ass one of these days). But they were still members of the Earth Defence Forces, even if they were confused about the legitimacy of their leaders.

'Approaching the outskirts of the Earth system, Admiral. How close do you want us to get?'

'Just close enough to drop a baby on the doorstep. Round up a guard party and start escorting our prisoners to the launching decks.' She had arranged for a troop transport to carry the soldiers who wanted no part of her 'mutiny'. Her engineers had tinkered with the ship's systems, deactivated the weapons, and installed governors in the engines to limit the speed. It would take half a day for the transport to limp to the asteroid-belt shipyards.

Stretching extravagantly, she walked to the lift doors. 'I'm going down to the brig myself to see the General off.'

She dropped down to the launching bay where her security troops watched over a florid General Lanyan. The after-effects of the twitcher had left him with a splitting headache for a couple of days, but that was gone now. He glared, outraged at what she had done. 'You have made an enemy for life, Willis.' She knew he had intentionally left off her rank.

'Maybe, but I'll rest easier knowing that I saved the population of a whole world from your bad decisions – or should I say the Chairman's bad decisions?'

'You should say, "Yes, sir, General," and then follow orders.'

She rolled her eyes. 'I'd love to talk more, but I can always argue with a blank bulkhead if I want to have a similarly productive discussion. You should be thankful we're bringing you home rather than taking you to the Confederation where you would stand trial.'

'You wouldn't dare. Even you know better than that.'

'I know a lot more than I used to, General. If it's any consolation, until recently it was a pleasure and an honour to serve under you. Maybe someday you'll come around.'

He had looked at the single ship with a mixture of surprise, anger, and pride as he watched his troops march aboard. 'One troop transport? It's only designed to carry a hundred men.'

'A hundred men *comfortably*,' she corrected. 'You have a hundred and sixty-three. You'll have to crowd together, but your loyal EDF soldiers will make the best of it.'

He glowered. 'This is a big mistake, Willis.'

'Oh, mistakes were definitely made. We just differ on the interpretation.'

She had considered carrying Lanyan with her as a prisoner, to present him to the Confederation as a war criminal, but she didn't even know where she herself stood. Willis wasn't sure which of them was more likely to stand trial.

The defection that bothered her the most was that of her own exec, Conrad Brindle. He had changed into his formal uniform after being confined to his quarters; she hadn't chosen to throw him into the brig with the others. She felt very awkward when he marched into the launching bay to join Lanyan in front of the troop transport. When Brindle looked at her, his expression was unreadable. 'Sure you won't reconsider, Lieutenant Commander?'

His voice was chill. 'I cannot in good conscience become part of a mutiny against my commanding officer or the government of Earth. My own son has already chosen to be a deserter. That's enough disgrace for our family, thank you.' He turned his back on her and followed Lanyan aboard. Brindle himself would be the pilot.

She stepped back behind the atmosphere field as the bay doors opened and the troop transport dropped out. The single ship drifted away from the group of Mantas, powered up its limited engines, and headed toward the distant asteroid-belt shipyards, where the soldiers would be taken back in among the Earth Defence Forces.

'Troop transport successfully away, Admiral.'

Willis felt a pang, wishing that things had gone differently, but tough decisions rarely came out cleanly. 'And the engines and life-support are functioning properly?'

'Yes, Admiral. It will reach its destination, but we'll be long gone before the EDF can bring out any guard dogs.'

She made her way back to the bridge. Now she had a real battle group under her control, and Chairman Wenceslas could ill afford to lose so much of his remaining fleet. Ten Mantas and a Juggernaut.

When she sat in the command chair again, she said, 'Set a course for Theroc. Let's see if King Peter can use a few battleships.'

ONE HUNDRED AND FORTY

CELLI

'You are ready, child, and the worldforest is ready for you,' Yarrod said to Celli. He placed another smear of dye juice on her cheek. 'I have never seen the trees accept an acolyte so swiftly.' Even though he spent much of his time in a rush of joy and sharpened perceptions since joining Kolker's 'group', her uncle still performed all of his other duties, and he was still clearly proud of her.

She felt warm inside. As an acolyte, she had *known* when she was ready. The worldforest wanted her, and now Celli understood that it had always wanted her. But the patient worldforest had waited for her to come to the same conclusion. 'I've been practising for a long time, even if I wasn't officially an acolyte.'

Solimar and the green priests had applauded the fact that she would soon join them. When he hugged her, Celli knew this was one of the last times they would have that silent barrier between them. Soon, she and Solimar would understand each other completely. Their communication would be total.

At last, Celli felt as if she belonged. For most of her life, she'd had no real guidance, no expectations placed upon her. Reynald, Beneto, Sarein, Estarra . . . they had all been given a clear path. But not Celli, the youngest daughter. Now she knew that the trees had intended her to be a green priest like Beneto, and that was what she herself wanted.

After marking each of her cheeks with the new stain, Yarrod explained little about what would happen to her. 'It is what all acolytes must pass through before they become green priests. You will do it, as I did, as did all of us.'

When she had pestered Solimar for more details, even he had been coy. 'I don't want to spoil the surprise.'

And so, Celli sprinted off alone into the densest, most mysterious part of the forest. She wanted Solimar to come with her, but that was not allowed. This had to be her own journey. With a spring in her step, she covered kilometres, running to places she had never before seen, verdant meadows and thickets even more surprising than the place where she had discovered the wooden golem of Beneto growing.

When Celli came upon a quietly welcoming glen, her instincts told her that she had to walk inside. She was being guided by the trees, the first whispers of telink. Branches, vines, and fronds parted, as if every bit of plant life were sentient. She felt no fear at all as the foliage wrapped her like a cocoon, pressing close in a strange embrace – until she became one with the worldforest . . .

KING PETER

Peter was convinced that Celli's exciting news had triggered the Queen's labour. Very shortly after her little sister bounded off into the deep woods to become a green priest, Estarra's water broke.

Theron doctors and midwives were called. Roamer women rushed to offer far more assistance than was necessary for a simple birth. King Peter stayed by Estarra's side in their quarters as the contractions came. This was their first child, and no one could guess whether the delivery would be fast and easy, or long and difficult. For Peter, every moment seemed to last forever.

Estarra's brow was beaded with perspiration, but she seemed more concerned about his obvious anxiety than her own pain. 'Don't worry about me – women have been doing this for millennia.'

'But *you* haven't, and you don't get a practise run.' He squeezed her hand more tightly than he had intended. He couldn't stop thinking of how Basil had done everything in his power to kill this baby, and he feared the Chairman wouldn't stop even after the child was born. But he and Estarra had beaten Basil before, and they would do it again.

'This might take a while,' she said during a lull between contractions. 'If you have important work to do, you know where to find me.'

'My important work is right here. Not even one of those blustery Roamers could pull me away.' He looked quickly to the doorway. 'Besides, I've got OX to intercept any so-called emergencies.' The Teacher compy was becoming so proficient at his work that Peter temporarily delegated all business to go through OX, so he could concentrate on Estarra and their baby. The Teacher compy dutifully brought him hourly summaries, which had been vetted and analysed.

Not surprisingly, Idriss and Alexa were worried parents. Though Estarra was their fourth child, this was their first grand-child. The two hovered about, looking more flustered than when they had been faced with political challenges as leaders. 'Oh, I wish Reynald and Beneto could be here to see this,' Alexa said, stroking her daughter's brow.

'And I wish Sarein would come home,' Idriss added. 'It doesn't seem likely that she'll ever become a mother.'

When Peter saw Mother Alexa's obvious love and worry, he was reminded with a pang of his own mother, Rita Aguerra. In his old life, before he was forcibly made King, Rita had come home bone-weary after long shifts but still found ways to spend time with him and his three brothers. Now, as King, Peter could have done so much for her. But that family was gone – not only his mother, but Rory, and Carlos, and little Michael, as well. The impending birth of his own child made the pain of losing them fresh again. He missed them so badly that he had to close his eyes and take a deep breath. They were all dead . . . thanks to Basil.

Despite the initial excitement and panicked reaction, Estarra's labour lasted for more than a day. A Roamer midwife looked bored after the first seven hours. 'She's certainly not in a hurry, is she?'

'Is that good or bad?' Peter asked. 'Is something wrong?'

'It's perfectly normal for a first pregnancy,' said a Theron doctor with a scolding glance at the Roamer woman.

Estarra drank some juice and sat up, already looking drained. 'It seems like it's been forever.' She gritted her teeth and sucked in deep gasps as another set of contractions hit her. She forced a smile at Peter. 'But I can manage. This can't be any harder than sitting through endless political banquets and Hansa committee meetings, can it?'

Meanwhile, the green priests and the worldtrees grew uneasy and agitated, as if something strange were happening out in the Spiral Arm. Yarrod and the other green priests had gone out into the forests to have private councils. The converts to Kolker's new *thism*-telink connection and the original green priests worked together, sharing their concern. Even in orbit, the huge verdani treeships clustered warily together.

Finally, the next morning, Estarra went into hard labour. The contractions increased in intensity and frequency, and the Roamer midwife no longer suggested performing a Caesarean just to 'get it over with'. Watching Estarra's obvious discomfort, her determination, and her unflagging spirit, Peter felt helpless. But when he tried to pull away and pace the room, she grabbed his arm and kept him at her side.

After the long wait, the birth itself came swiftly. Estarra looked exhausted, bedraggled, and completely full of joy. Wrung out, Peter sat at her bedside, and the two of them held their newborn son. The little boy was perfectly healthy, and cried with enough gusto to ensure that everyone in the worldforest heard him. Filled with wonder, Peter touched the tiny nose. Mother Alexa seemed to be walking on air, while Father Idriss stood with tears streaming down his cheeks into his black beard.

Peter gazed at his wife and infant son with a new depth of immeasurable love he had never known existed. Again, he wished his mother could have been beside him. This would have been her first grandchild, too. Rory, Carlos, and Michael would all have been uncles . . .

Even that bittersweet memory could not overpower his happiness. The baby boy had Estarra's eyes, and wispy dark hair like Peter's had been, before the Hansa reprofiling had changed him to blond. He bent and kissed his son's forehead, more proud of this than anything else he had ever done.

'We'll name him Reynald, after your brother,' he whispered to Estarra. 'If that's all right with you?'

'Yes, I'd like that very much.'

ONE HUNDRED AND FORTY-TWO

CHAIRMAN BASIL WENCESLAS

As Basil had instructed, the Mage-Imperator's captured warliner was brought to Earth without any fanfare. Held in place by powerful tractor beams, the ornate ship was hauled to the EDF base on the Moon and held where it would not be visible to casual observers. Jora'h would need thorough debriefing and instructions before the Chairman could allow him to be seen in public.

Basil shook his head. Another supposed ally who had turned against the Hansa, another disappointment, another betrayal . . .

Admiral Diente deserved a commendation for his efficient handling of the operation, and the Chairman would make sure he got it. Willis, on the other hand, should be executed for treason. General Lanyan along with his beaten and embarrassed (but demonstrably loyal) soldiers had returned home in disgrace. Basil was so furious he had refused to speak with Lanyan, though the man had issued several increasingly desperate-sounding reports. Maybe Admiral Diente should be put in charge of the Earth

Defence Forces; so far he was the only man who had actually done what he was ordered to do . . .

As a formality, Basil took Deputy Cain with him to the Moon. Since the Mage-Imperator had at least one green priest aboard, he also considered bringing Sarein, the ostensible ambassador from Theroc, but she had criticized and questioned far too much recently. He decided to keep her out of this. Despite his efforts to keep her firmly under his thumb, he was no longer sure he completely trusted her.

And then there was Cain. The deputy was clearly troubled as they travelled to the EDF base. 'I doubt the Ildiran Empire will ever forgive you for this.'

Basil sighed. 'I know you don't approve, but I assure you this is the right decision. I can see the light at the end of the tunnel. Everything will fall into place as soon as I make the Mage-Imperator see reason.'

The lunar base was not designed for comfort. It was a stripped-down, no-nonsense facility where military trainees learned to cope with minimal amenities. The floors and walls were sealed stone, the furnishings made of metal and glass manufactured from the regolith. Jora'h had probably never lived under such austere conditions in his hedonistic life. Basil didn't feel sorry for him.

Though the Mage-Imperator waited, Basil was in no hurry to see him. Upon arriving at the Moon, he changed into a fresh business suit, freshened up, and checked his appearance before walking to the holding area with his deputy. EDF soldiers guarded the door to the tunnel barracks that had been set aside for the Ildiran leader and his entourage. The hostages had to share sanitation facilities, and they ate standard EDF ration packs in a communal mess. Basil was sure they would get used to the conditions.

Inside the common area, Jora'h looked agitated and cold.

Unlike his fat old predecessor, this Mage-Imperator had been willing to venture forth from his Prism Palace. He probably regretted that now. If only he hadn't gone to Theroc first . . .

'Welcome to the Hansa, Mage-Imperator,' Basil said. 'I apologize for these accommodations. In time, we may arrange to provide additional comforts.'

'In time?' Jora'h strode to Basil. 'You cannot keep me here. I am the Mage-Imperator of the Ildiran Empire, not a pawn or hostage to be dealt with at your whim.'

'You are here as my guest. Considering our times of political change, the Terran Hanseatic League and the Ildiran Empire have much to discuss. Once we have concluded our business satisfactorily, I will be happy to let you go back home.'

'I must return to Ildira immediately!' Anger crossed Jora'h's face, and his braid writhed like a snake on hot pavement. Basil flinched, surprised to see it move of its own accord.

A female green priest walked up beside Jora'h. 'Ildira is under attack by the faeros! Mijistra is on fire. The Mage-Imperator must be there to lead his people. The Solar Navy is being pummelled.'

Basil received this unexpected news with great interest. What in the world had the Ildirans done to anger the faeros? And if the already weakened Solar Navy was preoccupied with a new enemy, then so much the better. The Earth Defence Forces would not need to worry about retaliation from them. 'Then I am pleased to offer you a place of safety here with us. We will protect you.'

The green priest spoke up again. 'I already sent messages through the worldforest as soon as we were captured. King Peter and Queen Estarra know that you've taken the Mage-Imperator hostage.'

'Peter is welcome to come here himself and make a pathetic attempt to rescue him.' Basil was glad he had taken the treeling away from this woman; she would neither be sending nor receiving new messages. Cut off, these people were completely under his control.

A human scholar was also in their party. Anton Colicos looked somewhat familiar to Basil, and then he vaguely remembered the young man. Anton had called attention to the disappearance of his parents, Margaret and Louis Colicos, and asked for the Hansa's help to find them. During his time among the Ildirans, Basil wondered if Anton had learned anything of value about them. He would direct that the scholar be interrogated.

Deputy Cain touched Basil's elbow. 'Sir, perhaps we should continue our discussion at a later time when emotions have settled down somewhat.'

'My people are under attack,' Jora'h said. 'I will only grow *more* agitated, not less.'

'Nevertheless, my deputy makes a good suggestion, and I have an important meeting with the Archfather back at Hansa headquarters. I just came to greet you and to initiate our conversation.' He flashed a friendly smile, the kind he had almost forgotten how to make. 'You and your party can sit tight here. No need to worry about a thing.'

Basil turned, and the EDF guards sealed the barracks tunnels behind him, cutting off the angry outcries. The Chairman was genuinely smiling as he and Cain returned to their shuttle.

The Archfather arrived in the highest levels of the Hansa pyramid. He was another person who knew his proper place and followed instructions. Given time, the Chairman hoped to put together an appropriate team of people who believed in his personal vision. Only then would the Hansa be strong again.

The leader of Unison held daily rallies to foster the atmosphere of fear and paranoia caused by the returning Klikiss 'demons'. Basil doubted the insect race cared one whit about human civilization; the known colonist victims had simply been in the wrong place at the wrong time. If the Klikiss had been nearly extinct, they couldn't be much of a military threat, despite General Lanyan's wild report about Pym.

Cain sat with him in the office as the Archfather read over the new speech Basil had written. The Chairman mused, 'Rational and political control will not work on the people anymore. I gave them the benefit of the doubt, hoping they would put aside their petty bickerings for the good of all humanity. To my chagrin, that strategy has not been successful.'

'What other tactic will you use, Mr Chairman?' Cain seemed reluctant to hear the answer.

'Laws can help control a rational pool of citizens, but they are also open to endless debate and reinterpretation. *Religious* law, on the other hand, is much more clear-cut. It allows no compromise and gives us the wedge we need.'

'They will see through such a ploy, Mr Chairman. People are more intelligent than that.'

Basil chuckled. 'History proves otherwise, time and again.'

The Archfather set aside the new speech with a furrowed brow. 'This is highly inflammatory.' When Basil shot him a look, the bearded man quickly amended, 'And excellent in its composition. You are right to rile up the people.'

'Practise it well before you deliver it. It's an important address.'

'Aren't they all important, Mr Chairman?'

'Of course they are.'

Muttering to himself, the Archfather retreated from Basil's offices, leaving him alone with the deputy. 'I understand these things, Mr Cain. In order to generate truly significant religious fervour – which is what I need – the Hansa requires a charismatic religious leader. Our well-heeled Archfather simply cannot fill that role. He is too tame. We need a new King to lead under the aegis of Unison. You see, the people are directionless, hungry for a real monarch again. He will be our saviour.' He pressed a button to summon the candidate he had kept in isolation for so long. 'I've been planning this for quite some time.'

Basil had interviewed the young man extensively, gone over his training scores, and finally determined that he was ready and fully cooperative. It was time.

Captain McCammon marched in, leading a dark-haired Prince with brown eyes and a facial structure that looked hauntingly familiar – an echo of King Peter's features, the same chin, the same brow. Basil had intentionally requested that the hair not be doctored, the eyes not be recoloured. The Chairman wanted their Prince, their new King, to look exactly as Peter would expect him to.

Deputy Cain stood up, trying to place the young man in his proper context.

'This is our new Prince, whom the Archfather will crown as soon as possible. We'll introduce him to the population of Earth and send messages far and wide, even to representatives of the Confederation on Theroc.'

The young man properly extended a hand to shake Cain's.

'I want you to meet King Rory.' Basil allowed himself a smile. 'Peter will know exactly who he is.'

ONE HUNDRED AND FORTY-THREE

DAVLIN LOTZE

He was still bleeding – and still breathing – as the Klikiss warriors dragged him to the hall of the new breedex. Davlin continued to struggle, because he did not know how to give up. He felt a sense of resignation rather than despair. Giddy from the loss of blood, he realized dully that his left leg was broken, along with a few ribs. The sharp pain that came with every deep breath told him that something was hurt very badly inside him.

The Klikiss pulled Davlin into the dim and vaulted room. The breedex's chamber reminded him of the stinking lair of a dragon. But he was no knight in shining armour. He could barely crawl. Davlin thrashed again, tried to pull himself free. The blood on his arms and back made him slippery, and the warriors had to clamp down harder with the claws on their jagged forelimbs.

One of the huge new domates loomed beside the entrance. Though the creature still had prominent tiger stripes, its body was different from the previous generation, subtly altered to be more human, though no more sympathetic. When another swollen domate lumbered into the chamber, then two more, Davlin realized what was about to occur.

The Llaro breedex had won the recent clash, and the victorious domates had spent hours gorging themselves, walking the battlefield and acquiring genetic material from the rival breedex's soldiers. Now, all eight domates were splattered with ichor, their jaws, carapaces, and limbs crusted with dried fluids.

To win the ongoing hive wars, the Llaro breedex needed to vastly increase its numbers – again. Though the last fissioning had occurred only recently, after the previous domates consumed the Llaro colonists, the next wave of Klikiss matured rapidly, devouring every available scrap of food in the ever-expanding hive complex. The new breedex had bloated and expanded at an extraordinary rate, and now needed to continue its geometric expansion.

And Davlin would be part of it. The warriors dumped him unceremoniously just inside the chamber. The striped domates dragged him across the rough floor, leaving a fresh trail of blood.

Then he saw the breedex.

The hive mind was a loathsome, roiling mound of individual components, like clumps of maggots crawling over a rotting corpse. A huge mass of smaller grubs comprised a single body that filled the centre of the chamber, an abstract sculpture. It shifted, and something akin to a head rose up, turning to Davlin. He could sense a terrible yet incomprehensible intelligence somewhere inside that movable mass.

The breedex regarded him as if it knew exactly who Davlin Lotze was, knew everything about his past and his secrets. Could it have residual memory echoes from the Llaro colonists? Even if it did, he expected no mercy. He tried to push himself up, but could not balance on his broken leg. 'What do you want with me – with any of us?'

The chamber filled with a buzzing, chittering din, as if he were in the middle of a cloud of locusts. He received no answer – at least nothing he could understand. The background buzz grew louder. His blood continued running onto the stone floor, and he nearly passed out as black curtains of weakness fluttered around him. Davlin remained conscious only by sheer force of will. 'What do you *want?*' he shouted again.

The thoughts of the breedex mind pounded against him like a physical wind. His skull ached. Behind him, workers scritched and scrabbled, slathering resinous concrete material across the doorway, walling him into the breedex's chamber with the domates. The domates stood at attention, waiting, willing.

Davlin tried to crawl away, but he had nowhere to go. He refused to accept that it was futile. 'Humans don't deserve this. We were never your enemies. *Understand* us before you try to destroy us, because we will fight back.'

The plural mass that formed the bulky hive mind began to dissociate. Hundreds of thousands of the grubs – larvae of various sub-breeds – sloughed down. The breedex lost its shape, becoming a ravenous myriad. The hungry pieces squirmed and writhed toward Davlin.

But first they encountered the passively accepting domates. By consuming the striped domates, the grubs would mature into large monsters, subtly different from the previous generation, stronger and more aggressive. At the moment they were small and individually weak.

Davlin used his balled fists to smash the grubs as they came at him, crushing one after another into the floor. But it was like trying to stop a downpour by catching individual raindrops.

In the middle of what had been the shifting body of the

breedex, he saw a larva that was shaped differently. It rose like a miniature king cobra, and Davlin understood intrinsically that this was the seed of the next generation's breedex. It turned its glinting eyes toward him, fixing on his face. The breedex wanted to acquire *him* personally.

More grubs crawled forward. The domates waited, their segmented limbs spread wide, their hard shell casings cracked open to provide access to the tender flesh inside.

Unexpectedly, Davlin spotted a glint of metal, a square box no larger than the palm of his hand. Margaret's wind-up music box. Knowing the music's strange power over the Klikiss, he rolled away from the grubs, ignoring the pain in his back, ribs, and leg. He tried to grab the device, but one of the domates snatched Margaret's keepsake – and smashed it into little metal pieces. The last tinkle of sound was not at all musical.

Now Davlin did feel despair. He collapsed backward, looking up just in time to see waves of hungry larvae sweeping across the striped bodies of the domates. They began to tunnel in, burrowing, chewing, digesting. The myriad little creatures made swift work of all eight domates, and the large carcasses toppled into sticky, dripping debris like driftwood floating on the tide.

When the breedex larva approached him, Davlin did not recoil. Instead, he threw himself forward, ignoring the pain. He had been trained to fight, to kill, not to surrender. His hands wrapped around the writhing creature, but it was slick and tingly, as if covered with liquid electricity, tangible *thoughts*. Davlin grasped it, and instead of struggling away, the breedex larva wrapped around him in a contest of wills, as much as a battle of physical strength.

Davlin did not let go, and the immature breedex began to falter. Never in its experience had it encountered such mental intensity and determination instead of fear. The malleable hive mind was forced to change. Davlin knew he could not survive, but that didn't mean he would accept defeat.

The grubs swarmed over him.

ONE HUNDRED AND FORTY-FOUR

JESS TAMBLYN

When they finally reached isolated Charybdis, he and Cesca found only a smoking ruin. The primordial atmosphere was thick and poisoned with sour, sulphurous clouds. The rocks, once submerged, were now baked and blackened. Whole oceans had been boiled away. These wentals had been eradicated.

'It looks like hell came here.' Jess's words were little more than a haunted whisper. He didn't need to speak. Cesca was as horrified as he was.

'We can't leave them like this. We have to do something.'

'We will, Cesca. Oh, we will.'

Yes, we must set things right, the wentals said in their minds. *Through you, we will become strong. Perhaps we will be strong enough.*

They already knew what had happened here from receiving the thoughts of the distant, devastated beings. Jess had needed all of the elemental strength in his body to drive back the fury and stop the boiling backlash in their bubble ship. They were alive, but he didn't think they would ever be safe again.

Before, he and Cesca had felt the wondrous strength of the water entities swirling through them; now, they experienced ripple after ripple of pain and loss, just by standing in the ruins of Charybdis. This must be how the wentals felt when they were torn apart in space, their molecules strewn across a cosmic expanse. And this must be how the water elementals felt when they were dragged silently screaming into the hot atmosphere of a sun.

Jess and Cesca emerged trembling from their bubble ship, the only living things on the scalded planet. The water they had retrieved from the nebula clouds remained protected within the energy membrane. Some craters held sterile, bubbling pools, but the water here was dead. The life force of the wentals had been purged from the water on Charybdis. The clouds were heavy and suffocating, the corpses of wentals thrown into a sky battlefield.

The energy that the faeros had unleashed was unimaginable. Jess could not comprehend the anger of the fiery beings.

'Why would the faeros do this?' Cesca was weeping, and Jess held her. Even the energized water seeping from her tear ducts would not be potent enough to reawaken the water here. Would Charybdis be forever tainted? 'Why do they want to destroy the wentals?'

Because they are chaos. They are fire.

Fury began to build in his very core. 'That's not a good enough explanation. Not for me.' Jess remembered the esoteric balance between order and chaos, entropy and construction, life and un-life. But it wasn't a *reason*.

He walked barefoot on the smoking black stones. 'There is no reason for it, but it *is*. We must stand against it. We will!' He inhaled, purposely filling his chest with the weak steam, the last gasps of a few now-dead wentals. Somehow, he felt the strength increase within him. 'I don't care how devastated this planet is, we will bring wentals back to Charybdis. We'll gather more and more

660

of them out in the Spiral Arm. And I swear that never again will the faeros take us by surprise.'

A swell of hope and determination filled them, husband and wife. Even the wentals inside Jess and Cesca and in the bubble ship took heart and rallied their energies. Jess understood that they were not facing the end. Not at all.

'This is war,' he said.

ONE HUNDRED AND FORTY-FIVE

FAEROS INCARNATE RUSA'H

Ensconced in the Prism Palace where he belonged, Rusa'h glowed and shimmered, shedding animated fire and light at the heart of an immense magnifying prism. The bright reflections passed through the crystal walls and blazed outward in a beacon. The light on Ildira was bright, very bright indeed.

Now that the fiery elementals had reignited the darkened sun of Durris-B, the glory of the Empire would be greater than before. The faeros over Mijistra were gorged with more than ten thousand soulfires they had consumed from helpless, short-sighted Ildirans. *His* people. Now each one of them understood the truth of the Lightsource, the purifying flame. If only they had listened before. Finally, he had the strength to *compel* them to listen.

He did not mean to destroy this great city, but to save it. Cleanse it.

Sadly, the chrysalis chair, his rightful throne, had been unable to endure the magnificence of his presence. It lay scattered about him in remnants of ash and pooled precious metals that flowed across the floor. Everything inside the Palace was dead and burned.

He felt sated – temporarily. He had lost two of the great fireballs because of Adar Zan'nh's attack, but high above the Prism Palace, the pulsing fireballs expanded, throbbing. Reproducing, at last. They began to split apart – doubling, then tripling their numbers as they spread across the Ildiran sky.

Meanwhile, the rest of the faeros had embarked on great battles against the wentals. The final conflict was just beginning.

Thanks to the green priest he had found here, the one who began his own *thism*-telink network, Rusa'h had access to a new conduit – directly into the vulnerable worldforest. The faeros incarnate sent out his thoughts like a flaming javelin. Sparking and rushing, the fiery elementals followed him along the soul-threads until he encountered the exotic, oddly familiar network of green priests and their telink.

In the past, humans had been disconnected from Ildiran *thism*, but now Rusa'h plunged irresistibly toward the waiting green priest minds, through open connections that Kolker and his followers had unwittingly created. He found one, then another, and another. The fire raced invisibly toward the heart of the worldforest.

ONE HUNDRED AND FORTY-SIX

CELLI

When the worldtrees enfolded her in a verdant embrace, Celli felt as if she were being surrounded by leaves and fronds, vines and roots. A brief sensation of fear, of smothering – and then the whole forest, the whole world, the whole *universe* opened up for her.

During the metamorphosis, she drifted far from her body, her mind racing through the infinite pathways of interconnected trees and green priests around the Spiral Arm. During that brief time within the verdani mind, she saw and experienced more than she had absorbed in the nineteen previous years of her life. Celli plunged into millennia of history, of towering battles, destruction and defeat, the wars with the hydrogues and the faeros. She also saw hundreds of worlds through the eyes of the green priests who lived there.

The Spiral Arm was more wonderful than anything she had imagined. Finally, after years of missing Beneto, her mind rushed outward, and she was able to directly contact her brother in his immense verdani battleship guarding Theroc from space. She could feel herself as part of him, sense his enormous thorned branches as extensions of her arms and legs. It was wonderful! In her own mind Celli could feel Beneto laughing with her.

After an unknown time that might have been days or mere minutes, she emerged from the thicket. Celli felt the feathery strands of her hair falling out. Her skin had shifted from a coppery tan to a smooth emerald green, and now it tingled at the touch of sunlight. She flexed her fingers, looked at her forearms, touched her face. She had never thought the colour green could be so beautiful. Celli was the same as always, but better, enhanced, and filled with greater understanding.

Exhilarated, she sprinted back to the fungus-reef city. Kilometres passed in a breeze, and she barely felt her feet touching the forest floor. Then with a new energy, she sprang to one of the lower fronds, pulled herself up. Like an arboreal creature, she bounded from one branch to another, spinning, flying, leaping, landing. Treedancing had never been like this before! She seemed to be in the embrace of the whole forest, and she could never fall. Was this what Solimar felt all the time? Now, Celli could enjoy – and share – her gymnastic moves in a way she had never imagined.

And she could never get lost. Every piece of the worldforest was a piece of *her*. Through telink, she learned many other things, news from around the Spiral Arm and close to home. Ah, Estarra had given birth to her baby! Celli felt a stab of disappointment because she hadn't been there, but she would spend much of her time with the little boy, helping where she could. She knew that King Peter and her sister were going to name the child Reynald. Celli felt a lump in her throat. Of course they would name him Reynald!

When she reached the clearing beneath the fungus reef, several green priests were gathered, including Yarrod and his followers. The King and Queen were high above, gazing down from a balcony; Estarra held her baby in her arms, and, oh, the way she smiled!

Solimar came toward her, and they embraced, connecting in a way that they had never done before. While she was still cocooned within the worldforest thicket, she had contacted him through telink, and they had excitedly spoken with each other. But now that she saw him in the flesh, the connection seemed even stronger.

Now that she was familiar with telink, she sensed that Yarrod and his followers were distant, separated from the rest of the network. As the wonder began to fade away, she realized what had been a thrumming undertone in the back of her mind. The verdani were indeed restless, disturbed ... angry – or was that *fear*? Something dark and dangerous was abroad in the Spiral Arm. Yarrod and his converted green priests seemed the most susceptible.

'What is it, Solimar? Do you understand it?'

He shook his head. 'No more than anyone does. Yarrod won't tell us. It's something his converts know—'

Then Yarrod's body went rigid, his arms thrust straight out at his sides, his fingers splayed. His green skin shimmered with an inner energy. With a rush of combusted air, he became a pillar of fire. His fellow converts likewise ignited, standing together like human torches in the meadow. Something was rushing along their mental strands – something against which they could not defend. Yarrod and his companions fell to the ground as silhouettes painted in ash.

High up in orbit, the looming verdani battleships began to spin about. She could feel Beneto there, feel him fighting, cutting himself and his gigantic thorny form off from the rest of the worldforest. Then she felt one of the treeships catch fire, even in the vacuum of space, like a fever in the blood.

The trembling pain built and intensified. Celli staggered backward, and Solimar was with her. Both of them touched the overlapping gold-scale bark of the immense trees, desperately seeking an anchor. Trying to help the trees fight.

The worldtrees could not escape the horrific fire coursing invisibly toward them through their own network. All around the clearing, six of the largest trees physically trembled, then began to steam and smoke. The faeros had found their way inside the verdani network, like a spark to tinder. From its core outward, the largest tree exploded into a column of fire. The other giant trees began to blaze from the roots upward, but they were not consumed. Instead, the incandescent worldtrees shone with waves of heat, fire coursing through the heartwood, heating but not destroying. Flametrees.

The faeros had seized them, possessed them, and would not let the worldforest mind be burned. Like frozen torches towering over the canopy, the six trees blazed hotter and hotter, and the rest of the forest seemed to shrink away.

As Celli and Solimar ran away from the flames, the unquenchable fire spread.

GLOSSARY

ADAM, PRINCE – predecessor to Peter, considered unacceptable candidate.

ADAR – highest military rank in Ildiran Solar Navy.

AGUERRA, CARLOS – Raymond's younger brother.

AGUERRA, MICHAEL – Raymond's youngest brother.

AGUERRA, RAYMOND – streetwise young man from Earth, former identity of King Peter.

AGUERRA, RITA – Raymond's mother.

AGUERRA, RORY – Raymond's younger brother.

ALEXA, MOTHER – former ruler of Theroc, wife of Father Idriss and mother of Reynald, Beneto, Sarein, Estarra, and Celli.

ALINTAN – former Klikiss world.

ALLAHU, HAKIM – main representative of Rhejak.

ALTURAS – Ildiran world in the Horizon Cluster, formerly conquered in Imperator Rusa'h's rebellion.

ANDEZ, SHELIA – EDF soldier, former captive of Roamers at Osquivel shipyards, now serves with General Lanyan.

AQUARIUS – wental-distribution ship flown by Nikko Chan Tylar.

ARCHFATHER – symbolic head of Unison religion on Earth.

BARRYMORE'S ROCK – isolated Roamer fuel depot.

BARTHOLOMEW – Great King of Earth, predecessor to Frederick.

BATTLEAXE – nickname for former Hansa Chairman Maureen Fitzpatrick.

BEBOB – Rlinda Kett's pet name for Branson Roberts.

BEN – third Great King of the Terran Hanseatic League.

BENETO – green priest, second son of Father Idriss and Mother Alexa, killed by hydrogues on Corvus Landing, returned in a wooden body as an avatar of the worldforest, then later joined with verdani battleship.

BIG GOOSE – Roamer derogative term for Terran Hanseatic League.

BLAZER – Ildiran illumination source.

BLIND FAITH – Branson Roberts's ship, destroyed during an escape from Earth.

BREEDEX – the hive mind of the Klikiss, which controls and creates all the breeds in a subhive.

BRINDLE, CONRAD – Robb Brindle's father, former military officer, returned to active duty; assisted Jess Tamblyn in rescuing prisoners held by hydrogues deep within a gas giant.

BRINDLE, NATALIE – Robb Brindle's mother, former military officer returned to active duty.

BRINDLE, ROBB – young EDF recruit, comrade of Tasia Tamblyn, captured and held prisoner by hydrogues after trying to contact them at Osquivel, rescued by Jess Tamblyn.

BURTON – One of the eleven generation ships from Earth, seized by Ildirans at Dobro and its passengers used for breeding experiments.

CAIN, ELDRED – deputy and heir-apparent of Basil Wenceslas, pale-skinned and hairless, an art collector.

CARGO ESCORT – Roamer vessel used to deliver ekti shipments from skymines.

CELLI – youngest daughter of Father Idriss and Mother Alexa.

CHAN – Roamer clan.

CHAN, MARLA – Roamer greenhouse expert, captured by the EDF and held on Llaro; mother of Nikko Chan Tylar, wife of Crim Tylar.

CHARYBDIS – primordial water planet, site of Jess Tamblyn's original dispersal of wentals.

CHRISTOPHER – fourth Great King of the Terran Hanseatic League.

CHRYSALIS CHAIR – reclining throne of the Mage-Imperator.

CJELDRE – former Klikiss world, settled by human colonists.

CLARIN, ROBERTO – former administrator of Hurricane Depot, captured by EDF and taken to Llaro, where he is the ostensible leader of the Roamer detainees.

CLOUD HARVESTER – ekti-gathering facility designed by Hansa; also called a cloud mine.

COHORT – battle group of Ildiran Solar Navy consisting of seven Maniples, or 343 ships.

COLICOS, ANTON – the son of Margaret and Louis Colicos, translator of epic stories, sent to Ildiran Empire to study the *Saga of Seven Suns*. Anton was nearly killed on Maratha when Klikiss robots attacked; only he and Rememberer Vao'sh survived.

COLICOS, LOUIS – xeno-archaeologist, husband of Margaret and father of Anton, killed by Klikiss robots at Rheindic Co.

COLICOS, MARGARET – xeno-archaeologist, wife of Louis Colicos and mother of Anton, vanished through transportal during Klikiss robot attack on Rheindic Co and lived among Klikiss.

COMPANY WORKS – extraction facility on Rhejak.

COMPETENT COMPUTERIZED COMPANION – intelligent

servant robot, called compy, available in Friendly, Teacher, Governess, Listener, and other models.

COMPY – shortened term for 'Competent Computerized Companion'.

CONDORFLY – colourful flying insect on Theroc like a giant butterfly, sometimes kept as pets.

CONSTANTINE III – stormy, primordial planet, site of Roamer facility to extract polymers and raw materials from its thick atmosphere; known for exotic flame-proof materials.

CORRIBUS – ancient Klikiss world where Margaret and Louis Colicos discovered the Klikiss Torch technology, site of one of the first new Hansa colonies.

COVITZ, JAN – Dremen mushroom farmer, father of Orli, moved to Corribus in transportal colonization initiative, where he was killed in Klikiss robot attack.

COVITZ, ORLI – Dremen colonist, moved to Corribus with her father Jan, where she was one of two survivors of the Klikiss robot attack. Later, she moved to Llaro to join the Crenna refugees.

CRENNA – former Ildiran splinter colony, evacuated due to plague, and resettled by humans, then later frozen when its sun died in hydrogue-faeros battles.

CUTTER – small ship in Ildiran Solar Navy.

CYROC'H – former Mage-Imperator, father of Jora'h.

CZIR'H – Dzelluria Designate, the first leader to fall to Designate Rusa'h's rebellion.

DANIEL – Prince candidate selected as a replacement for Peter, left stranded on neo-Amish world of Happiness.

DARO'H – the Dobro Designate-in-waiting after the death of Mage-Imperator Cyroc'h.

DD – Friendly compy owned by Margaret Colicos, seized by Klikiss robot Sirix, then escaped through a transportal to rejoin Margaret.

DESIGNATE – any purebred noble son of the Mage-Imperator, ruler of an Ildiran world.

DIAMONDFILM – crystalline parchment used for Ildiran documents.

DIENTE, ESTEBAN – one of the four surviving Grid admirals after the hydrogue war.

DIO'SH – Ildiran Rememberer, murdered by Mage-Imperator after he discovered the truth about the former hydrogue war.

DOBRO – Ildiran colony world, site of human-Ildiran breeding camps.

DOMATE – largest sub-breed of Klikiss, silver carapace with black tiger stripes. The domates acquire and provide genetic material to the breedex during reproductive fissioning.

DOOLEY, JYM – Roamer trader at Rhejak.

DREMEN – Terran colony world, dim and cloudy; chief products are saltpond caviar and genetically enhanced mushrooms.

DROGUE – Deprecatory term for hydrogues.

DROPSHIP – fast-delivery vessel used by EDF.

DUBOV, YURI – colonist farmer on Llaro.

DURRIS – trinary star system, close white and orange stars orbited by a red dwarf; three of the Ildiran 'seven suns'. Durris-B was extinguished in hydrogue-faeros war.

DZELLURIA – Ildiran world in the Horizon Cluster, first world to be conquered in Rusa'h's rebellion, ruled by Designate Czir'h.

EA – Tasia Tamblyn's personal compy, destroyed by hydrogues and Klikiss robots.

EARTH DEFENCE FORCES (EDF) – Terran space military, led by General Kurt Lanyan.

EDDIES – slang term for soldiers in EDF.

EKTI – exotic allotrope of hydrogen used to fuel Ildiran star-drives.

ESTARRA – second daughter, fourth child of Father Idriss and

Mother Alexa. Current Queen of Terran Hanseatic League, married to King Peter.

FAEROS – sentient fire entities dwelling within stars.

FIREFEVER – ancient Ildiran plague.

FITZPATRICK, MAUREEN – former Chairman of the Terran Hanseatic League, grandmother of Patrick Fitzpatrick III, nicknamed 'Battleaxe'.

FITZPATRICK, PATRICK, III – General Lanyan's protégé in the Earth Defence Forces, presumed dead after battle of Osquivel but captured by Roamers in Del Kellum's shipyards. Later, in love with Zhett Kellum, he abandoned the EDF, stole his grandmother's space yacht, and went in search of the Roamers.

FRACTURE-PULSE DRONE – new-design EDF weapon, also called a 'frak'.

FREDERICK – previous Great King of the Hansa, Peter's predecessor, assassinated by hydrogue emissary.

FUNGUS REEF – giant worldtree growth on Theroc, carved into a habitation by the Therons.

FURRY CRICKET – innocuous furry rodent found on Corribus.

GALE'NH – experimental halfbreed son of Nira and Adar Kori'nh, third oldest of her children.

GAROA – Ildiran world in the Horizon Cluster, formerly conquered in Imperator Rusa'h's rebellion.

GEORGE – second Great King of the Terran Hanseatic League.

GLIDERBIKE – flying contraption assembled from scavenged engines and framework materials, augmented by colourful condorfly wings.

GOLD, SULLIVAN – administrator of the Hansa's modular cloud harvester at Qronha 3, held captive by Ildirans.

GOLGEN – gas giant where Ross Tamblyn's Blue Sky Mine was destroyed, now site of renewed Roamer skymining, particularly by clan Kellum.

GREAT KING – figurehead leader of Terran Hanseatic League.

GREEN PRIEST – servant of the worldforest, able to use worldtrees for instantaneous communication.

GUIDING STAR – Roamer philosophy and religion, a guiding force in a person's life.

GYPSY – space yacht flown by Patrick Fitzpatrick III, renamed after he stole it from his grandmother to search for Zhett Kellum.

HANSA – Terran Hanseatic League.

HANSA HEADQUARTERS – pyramidal building near the Whisper Palace on Earth.

HAPHINE – gas giant planet formerly infested with hydrogues.

HHRENNI – Star system, site of Chan greenhouse asteroids.

HIFUR – abandoned Klikiss world, recaptured by robots.

HORIZON CLUSTER – large star cluster near Ildira, location of Hyrillka and many other splinter colonies. Most of Rusa'h's rebellion took place in the Horizon Cluster.

HREL-ORO – arid Ildiran mining colony, devastated in a hydrogue attack.

HUCK, TABITHA – engineer aboard Sullivan Gold's cloud harvester, held captive by Ildirans, and turned her talents to helping in the war against the hydrogues.

HURRICANE DEPOT – Roamer commercial centre and fuel-transfer station, destroyed by EDF.

HYDROGUES – alien race living at cores of gas-giant planets.

HYRILLKA – Ildiran colony in Horizon Cluster, from which Designate Rusa'h began his rebellion; the Klikiss robots were rediscovered frozen on one of the outlying moons.

IDRISS, FATHER – former ruler of Theroc, husband of Mother Alexa and father of Reynald, Beneto, Sarein, Estarra, and Celli.

ILDIRA – home planet of the Ildiran Empire.

ILDIRAN EMPIRE – large alien empire, the only other major civilization in the Spiral Arm.

ILDIRAN SOLAR NAVY – space military of the Ildiran Empire.

ILDIRANS – humanoid alien race with many different breeds, or kiths.

ILKOT – Klikiss robot, companion to Sirix.

ISIX CATS – sleek feline predators native to Ildira; Jora'h's daughter Yazra'h keeps three of them.

JACK – first Great King of the Terran Hanseatic League.

JAZER – energy weapon used by Earth Defence Forces.

JEN'NH – septar of Tal O'nh's processional group of warliners.

JONAH 12 – icy planetoid, site of Kotto Okiah's hydrogen-extraction facility, destroyed by Klikiss robots.

JORA'H – Mage-Imperator of the Ildiran Empire.

JUGGERNAUT – large battleship class in Earth Defence Forces.

JUPITER – enhanced Juggernaut battleship in EDF, flagship of Admiral Willis's Grid 7 battle group.

KAMAROV, RAVEN – Roamer captain, destroyed with his cargo ship on secret EDF raid.

KELLUM, DEL – Roamer clan leader, in charge of Osquivel shipyards and a Golgen skymine.

KELLUM, ZHETT – daughter of Del Kellum, in love with Patrick Fitzpatrick.

KETT, RLINDA – heavyset merchant woman, captain of the *Voracious Curiosity*.

KITH – a breed of Ildiran.

KLIKISS – ancient insect-like race, long vanished from the Spiral Arm, leaving only their empty cities.

KLIKISS ROBOTS – intelligent beetle-like robots built by the Klikiss race.

KLIKISS TORCH – a weapon developed by the ancient Klikiss race to implode gas-giant planets and create new stars.

KOLKER – green priest, friend of Yarrod, stationed on Sullivan Gold's cloud harvester at Qronha 3, held captive by Ildirans.

KORI'NH, ADAR – leader of the Ildiran Solar Navy, killed in suicidal assault against hydrogues on Qronha 3.

KO'SH – chief scribe of the Ildiran rememberer kith.

LANYAN, GENERAL KURT – commander of Earth Defence Forces.

LENS KITHMEN – philosopher priests who help to guide troubled Ildirans, interpreting faint guidance from the *thism.*

LIGHTSOURCE – the Ildiran version of Heaven, a realm on a higher plane composed entirely of light. Ildirans believe that faint trickles of this light break through into our universe and are channelled through the Mage-Imperator and distributed across their race through the *thism.*

LIONA – green priest assigned to Del Kellum's skymine on Golgen then the Osquivel shipyards.

LLARO – abandoned Klikiss world where Roamer detainees are kept after being captured by EDF; also, new home of Orli Covitz and the survivors from Crenna.

LOST TIMES – forgotten historical period, events supposedly recounted in a missing section of the *Saga of Seven Suns.*

LOTZE, DAVLIN – Hansa exosociologist and spy, sent to Rheindic Co where he and Rlinda Kett discovered how to use the Klikiss Transportal system. Later, he left Hansa service and went in hiding to live on Llaro with other Crenna refugees.

MAGE-IMPERATOR – the god-emperor of the Ildiran Empire.

MANTA – mid-sized cruiser class in EDF.

MARATHA – Ildiran resort world with extremely long day and night cycle.

MARATHA PRIME – primary domed city on one continent of Maratha, destroyed by Klikiss robots.

MARATHA SECDA – sister-city on opposite side of Maratha from Prime, destroyed by Klikiss robots.

MEDUSA – giant tentacled creature herded on Rhejak. Its

shell is large enough to be used as a dwelling, and its meat is prized.

MIJISTRA – glorious capital city of the Ildiran Empire, site of the Prism Palace.

MOON STATUE GARDEN – sculpture exhibit and topiary at Whisper Palace.

MUREE'N – experimental halfbreed daughter of Nira Khali and a guard kithman, youngest of her children.

NAHTON – court green priest on Earth.

NEBULA SKIMMERS – giant sails used to scoop hydrogen from nebula clouds.

NIRA – green priest female, Jora'h's lover and mother of his halfbreed daughter, Osira'h. Held captive in breeding camps on Dobro, then freed.

OKIAH, JHY – former Speaker of the clans, died on Jonah 12.

OKIAH, KOTTO – Jhy Okiah's youngest son, a brash and eccentric inventor.

O'NH, TAL – second highest-ranking officer in Ildiran Solar Navy, one-eyed veteran with an inset jewel in his empty socket.

OSIRA'H – daughter of Nira and Jora'h, bred to have unusual telepathic abilities.

OSQUIVEL – ringed gas planet, site of secret Roamer shipyards.

OSQUIVEL – new personnel transport built to retrieve Roamer detainees on Llaro.

OTEMA – former ambassador from Theroc, green priest sent to Ildira where she was murdered by Mage-Imperator Cyroc'h.

OX – Teacher compy, one of the oldest Earth robots, instructor and adviser to King Peter; his memories were mostly wiped during Peter and Estarra's escape from Earth.

PALACE DISTRICT – governmental zone around Whisper Palace on Earth.

PALAWU, HOWARD – Hansa Chief Science Adviser, vanished while investigating Klikiss transportal technology.

PD – one of two Friendly compies, formerly belonging to Admiral Crestone Wu-Lin, taken as 'students' of Sirix.

PERONI, CESCA – Roamer Speaker of all clans, trained by Jhy Okiah. Cesca was betrothed to Ross Tamblyn, then Reynald of Theroc, but has always loved Ross's brother Jess. Now infused with wental power, she joined Jess in his work for the wentals.

PERONI, DENN – Cesca's father, a Roamer merchant.

PETER, KING – King of the Hansa, married to Estarra; he escaped Earth and established a new Confederation on Theroc.

PIKE, ZEBULON CHARLES – one of the four surviving Grid admirals after the hydrogue war.

PLUMAS – frozen moon with deep liquid oceans, site of the Tamblyn clan water industry, nearly destroyed by tainted wental inhabiting Karla Tamblyn's body.

PRIME DESIGNATE – eldest son and heir-apparent of Ildiran Mage-Imperator.

PRISM PALACE – dwelling of the Ildiran Mage-Imperator.

PUTTER-BOAT – small, low-powered craft used on Rhejak.

PYM – abandoned Klikiss world resettled during Klikiss Colonization Initiative.

QRONHA – a close binary system, two of the Ildiran 'seven suns'. Contains two habitable planets and one gas giant, Qronha 3, where skymining was destroyed by hydrogue attacks.

QT – one of two Friendly compies, formerly belonging to Admiral Crestone Wu-Lin, taken as 'students' of Sirix.

RAJANI – Roamer clan, one of the investors on Constantine III.

RAJAPAR – former Klikiss world.

RECIRC SORTER – recirculation sorter, vital filtering component of the Company Works extraction facility on Rhejak.

RELLEKER – Terran colony world, popular as a resort, destroyed by hydrogues.

REMEMBERER – member of the Ildiran storyteller kith.

REMORA – small attack ship in Earth Defence Forces.

RENDEZVOUS – inhabited asteroid cluster, centre of Roamer government, destroyed by the EDF.

REYNALD – eldest son of Father Idriss and Mother Alexa, killed in hydrogue attack on Theroc.

RHEINDIC CO – abandoned Klikiss world, now central transfer point for the transportal network.

RHEJAK – former Hansa colony, an ocean world of reefs, medusa herders, and fishermen. Main products include kelp extracts, reef-pearls, rare metals and chemical compounds.

ROAMERS – loose confederation of independent humans, primary producers of ekti stardrive fuel.

ROBERTS, BRANSON – former husband and business partner of Rlinda Kett, also called BeBob.

ROD'H – experimental halfbreed son of Nira and the Dobro Designate, second oldest of her children.

RUIS, LUPE – mayor of Crenna colony settlement.

RUSA'H – former Hyrillka Designate, degenerated into madness after a head injury, and began a revolt against the Mage-Imperator. Rather than allow himself to be captured, he flew his ship into Hyrillka's sun.

RUVI, RICO – administrator of Rheindic Co transportal facility.

SACHS, ANDRINA – facility manager of Constantine III.

SAGA OF SEVEN SUNS – historical and legendary epic of the Ildiran civilization, considered to be infallible.

SAN LUIS, ZIA – one of the four surviving Grid admirals after the hydrogue war.

SAREIN – eldest daughter of Father Idriss and Mother Alexa, Theron ambassador to Earth, also Basil Wenceslas's lover.

SCHOLLD – former Klikiss world.

SEPTA – small battle group of seven ships in the Ildiran Solar Navy.

SEPTAR – commander of a septa.

SHANA REI – legendary 'creatures of darkness' in *Saga of Seven Suns*.

SHIZZ – Roamer expletive.

SHONOR – Ildiran world in the Horizon Cluster, formerly conquered in Imperator Rusa'h's rebellion.

SILVER BERET – sophisticated special forces trained by EDF.

SIRIX – Klikiss robot, leader of robotic revolt against humans, captor of DD.

SKYMINE – ekti-harvesting facility in gas giant clouds, usually operated by Roamers.

SKYSPHERE – main dome of the Ildiran Prism Palace. The skysphere holds exotic plants, insects, and birds, all suspended over the Mage-Imperator's throne room.

SOLIMAR – young green priest, treedancer and mechanic. Celli's boyfriend.

SOUL-THREADS – connections of *thism* that trickle through from the Lightsource. Mage-Imperator and lens kithmen are able to see them.

SPEAKER – political leader of the Roamers.

SPIRAL ARM – the section of the Milky Way Galaxy settled by the Ildiran Empire and Terran colonies.

SPLINTER COLONY – an Ildiran colony that meets minimum population requirements.

STEINMAN, HUD – old transportal explorer, discovered Corribus on transportal network and decided to settle there. He and Orli Covitz were the only two survivors of the black robot attack on Corribus; they joined Crenna refugees on Llaro.

STREAMER – fast single ship in Ildiran Solar Navy.

STROMO, ADMIRAL LEV – Admiral in Earth Defence Forces, General Lanyan's second in command, killed during Soldier compy revolt.

SWEENEY, DAHLIA – DD's first owner, as a young girl.

TAL – military rank in Ildiran Solar Navy, cohort commander.

TAMBLYN, CALEB – one of Jess and Tasia's uncles, currently running the Plumas water mines.

TAMBLYN, JESS – Roamer in love with Cesca Peroni, infused with wental energy.

TAMBLYN, KARLA – Jess's mother, frozen to death in ice accident on Plumas, revived by tainted wentals.

TAMBLYN, ROSS – Jess's brother, betrothed to Cesca Peroni, killed in the first hydrogue attack on Golgen.

TAMBLYN, TASIA – Jess's sister, currently serving in the EDF, captured by hydrogues at Qronha 3, and freed by Jess.

TAMBLYN, TORIN – one of Jess's uncles, twin to Wynn.

TAMBLYN, WYNN – one of Jess's uncles, twin to Torin.

TAMO'L – experimental halfbreed daughter of Nira and a lens kithman, second youngest of her children.

TELINK – instantaneous communication used by green priests.

TERRAN HANSEATIC LEAGUE – commerce-based government of Earth and Terran colonies, also called the Hansa.

THEROC – forested planet, home of the sentient worldtrees.

THERON – a native of Theroc.

THISM – faint racial telepathic link from Mage-Imperator to the Ildiran people.

THOR'H – eldest noble-born son of Mage-Imperator Jora'h, former Prime Designate who joined Rusa'h's rebellion; he died on Dobro.

TOKAI – Roamer clan, one of the investors on Constantine III.

TRANSGATE – hydrogue point-to-point transportation system.

TRANSPORTAL – Klikiss instantaneous transportation system.

TREEDANCERS – acrobatic performers in the Theron forests.

TREELING – a small worldtree sapling, often transported in an ornate pot.

TROOP CARRIER – personnel transport ship in Ildiran Solar Navy.

TWITCHER – EDF stun weapon.

TYLAR, CRIM – Roamer detainee on Llaro, father of Nikko.

TYLAR, NIKKO CHAN – young Roamer pilot, son of Crim and Marla.

UDRU'H – former Dobro Designate in charge of breeding programme, killed by faeros and Rusa'h.

UNISON – standardized government-sponsored religion for official activities on Earth.

UR – Governess-model Roamer compy, held at Llaro with other Roamer detainees.

USK – breakaway Hansa colony, populated mainly by farmers.

VAO'SH – Ildiran rememberer, patron and friend of Anton Colicos, survivor of the robot attacks on Maratha.

VARDIAN, DREW – chief of the Company Works extraction facility on Rhejak.

VERDANI – organic-based sentience, manifested as the Theron worldforest.

VORACIOUS CURIOSITY – Rlinda Kett's merchant ship.

WARGLOBE – hydrogue spherical attack vessel.

WARLINER – largest class of Ildiran battleship.

WENCESLAS, BASIL – Chairman of the Terran Hanseatic League.

WENTALS – sentient water-based creatures.

WHISPER PALACE – magnificent seat of the Hansa government.

WILLIS, SHEILA, ADMIRAL – commander of Grid 7 EDF battle group, one of only four remaining Grid admirals to survive the battle of Earth.

WOLLAMOR – former Klikiss world, resettled by humans in the Klikiss Colonization Initiative.

WORLDFOREST – the interconnected, semi-sentient forest based on Theroc.

WORLDTREE – a separate tree in the interconnected, semi-sentient forest based on Theroc.

WYVERN – large flying predator on Theroc.

XALEZAR – former Klikiss world, resettled by humans in the Klikiss Colonization Initiative.

XIBA'H – legendary Mage-Imperator who enlisted the aid of the faeros against the Shana Rei.

YARROD – green priest, younger brother of Mother Alexa.

YAZRA'H – oldest daughter of Jora'h, his official guard; she keeps three well-trained Isix cats.

YREKA – former Hansa colony world, now a major trading centre for Roamers and breakaway colonists.

ZAN'NH – Adar of the Ildiran Solar Navy, eldest son of Mage-Imperator Jora'h.

ZED KHELL – former Klikiss world.

POCKET
BOOKS

HIDDEN EMPIRE

The Saga of Seven Suns – Book One

KEVIN J. ANDERSON

In the far future, humanity began to search the stars, sending out vast spaceships that would take generations to reach their goals. In the depths of space they encountered the Ildiran empire – apparently the galaxy's only other intelligent civilisation. The Ildirans came to Earth and passed on the knowledge of their stardrive, allowing humanity to expand to the stars.

Almost two hundred years after that first contact, there are human colonies proliferating through the galaxy. As Mankind seizes the future, danger comes from the past, for two human archaeologists glean forbidden knowledge from the ruins of a dead world . . .

ISBN 978-0-7434-3065-4
PRICE £7.99

POCKET
BOOKS

A FOREST OF STARS
The Saga of Seven Suns – Book Two
KEVIN J. ANDERSON

It has been five years since humanity's heady expansion among the stars came to an abrupt, and violent, halt. With space travel heavily curtailed, and supplies of fuel dwindling, young King Peter has no choice but to impose strict rationing.

But the Hydrogues are not the only enemies of humanity. The Leader of the Ildiran Empire forges tangled alliances among all the combatants in order to protect his failing civilisation. The mysterious Klikiss robots continue to work their sinister plans. And archaeologists Margaret and Louis Colicos vanish. Rlinda Ketta and Davlin Lotze are sent to investigate and soon realise that the Colicos's discoveries may lead to an incredible new way to travel between worlds . . . or to the awakening of enemies even more fearsome than the Hydrogues.

ISBN 978-0-7434-3066-1
PRICE £7.99

POCKET
BOOKS

HORIZON STORMS

The Saga of Seven Suns – Book Three

KEVIN J. ANDERSON

The titanic war between the elemental alien hydrogues
and faeros continues to sweep across the Spiral Arm,
extinguishing suns and destroying planets. Chairman
Wenceslas and King Peter must now unify the human
race with iron-fisted policies in a final bid to stand
together – or face total annihilation.

But disparate civilizations are forging new alliances
that threaten the old order. The Roamer and Theron
clans will not yield their independence, and the new
Mage-Imperator Jora'h now faces a threat that no other
Ildiran leader has ever seen – a civil war that could
break apart the entire Empire.

ISBN 978-0-7434-3067-8
PRICE £7.99

POCKET
BOOKS

SCATTERED SUNS

The Saga of Seven Suns – Book Four

KEVIN J. ANDERSON

The destructive hydrogues continue their war against humans and the fiery entities, the faeros – a struggle that kills planets and extinguishes whole stars. Newly crowned Mage-Imperator Jora'h, the leader of the ancient and vast Ildiran Empire, struggles with new knowledge he has learned: an ancient bargain and long-standing treachery that may finally bring peace with the hydrogues . . . though it could mean the extermination of the human race. But Jora'h's empire is destroying itself from within, when his mad brother launches a bloody rebellion across the Ildiran planets, appointing Jora'h's own first-born son as its leader.

In a galaxy torn by war, treachery, and shifting alliances, no one can know the truth about their friends or enemies.

ISBN 978-1-4165-0290-6
PRICE £7.99